W9-BWB-291

TALES
of the
PRIMAL LAND

Tales *of the* Primal Land

BRIAN LUMLEY

SUBTERRANEAN PRESS 2015

Deluxe Hardcover Edition

ISBN
978-1-59606-689-2

Subterranean Press
PO Box 190106
Burton, MI 48519

subterraneanpress.com

THE HOUSE of CTHULHU

FOR MALYGRIS

Contents

Introduction

Of Teh Atht, White Sorcerer of the
Great Primal Continent of Theem'hdra,
and of Sundry Matters Concerning an
Age Forgotten Except in his Prehistoric
Document, *Legends of the Olden Runes*.

by Brian Lumley [based on the original notes of Thelred
Gustau, whose introduction follows]:

Long before Atlantis, before Uthmal and Mu, so distant in time
past that a very great majority of today's scientists might never be
persuaded of its existence, there *was* in primal Theem'hdra an hitherto
unknown, unguessed Age of Man. How long ago exactly? I could say
that this mighty continent existed twenty millions of years ago, but that
would be pure guesswork. Perhaps it was forty millions, a hundred...
I do not know.

I only know that in 1963, while observing at comparatively close
range the fantastic eruptions of Surtsey as that island rose up from
the sea off Iceland, I fished aboard my boat a massive piece of volcanic flotsam whose fortunate recovery seemed destined to reshape the
thinking of the entire anthropological world!

The thing was both astonishing and awesome. Astonishing in that, embedded in the mass of grey-white, foamlike rock, a ball of blue glass like an eye clearly showed through the wash of waves. Awesome in that this mass (whose glassy passenger was, even at first glance, quite obviously an artifact of some sort) had recently been ejected from the heart of a newborn volcano.

Once they had the thing on board, my men were quick to break away the still warm lava crusts about its large glass core, then to carefully carry that nucleus to my cabin. Grey droplets of sea water still clung to its surface, and the soapy scum of lava and volcanic dust obscured its true colour and…contents. But when I had cleaned it with a towel, then those of my crew with me gaped and gasped and for a moment the magic of Surtsey's fiery birth was almost entirely forgotten.

For here was something that surely could not be! Locked in the bluish glass was a box of dull yellow metal in the shape of a nine inch cube. It had hasps and hinges and was covered with mystic symbols and the grimacing faces of krakens and dragons, hybrid dwarves and giants, serpents and demons and other night-things from all four corners of myth and legend. Without opening that box—indeed, before ever I stole my first glance at its interior and contents—I knew that it was ancient…but I could never have guessed that it *predated the very dinosaurs*, at least those sorrily defunct creatures whose bones decorate today's museums. "But," you are thinking, "the very earliest of men had not yet evolved, would not for ten millions of years after the dinosaurs had disappeared…" Oh? Well, I once thought so, too.

We put into port in Reykjavik and I took the glass ball with me to an hotel. It was solid, this sphere, and yet curiously light, made of glass unknown to modern science. After I had taken many photographs and shown the thing to a number of friends and colleagues—all evidence to support any claims I might later wish to make—then I sat down to determine a way to get at the golden box within.

Had the sphere been hollow, then a simple shattering of the glass might suffice, but it was not, and I had no wish to damage the box. In the end, nine frustrated days later in London, I procured a jeweller's diamond-tipped drill and commenced what I thought must prove an almost intolerably long process of drilling. In this I was mistaken.

I had drilled no more than two holes into the sphere, each to within an inch or so of its box nucleus, when there began to flow from the second hole an oily blue substance that smoked on contact with the air. Patently in drilling the second hole fractionally deeper than the first, I had broken through to this previously invisible agent which must surround the golden box. It must, too, be under some pressure, for it bubbled up the drilled hole and bled thinly down the outside of the sphere—and wherever it flowed the glass melted away like butter!

So acrid were the fumes that rose up ever thicker, I was soon driven to desert the house and had to abide in ignorance the passing of whatever catalytic reaction was taking place within. When the smoke had cleared some minutes later, on rushing to my work table, there I saw the golden box lying in a few slivers of evaporating glass. Even these rounded ice-like chips I tried to save, washing them under cold water; but to no avail, the catalyst had an unbreakable hold on them. And so finally I turned my attention to the box...

How my fingers trembled when, having wiped down the workbench top and removed the box to my study proper, I eased back the hasps and lifted the lid on hinges which were as well oiled as if attended to only yesterday! For a long moment I could only stand and stare, all atremble and breaking out in a sweat of fevered anticipation, but then I forced myself to a semblance of calmness and set about to take more photographs...and more yet as I lifted each item from the box to spread across the table.

There was a tiny silver whistle whose mouth was sealed with hardened wax; several small dark bottles of thick liquid, each marked in redly glowing hieroglyphs on a sort of leathery label; a magnifying glass in a square golden frame delicately filigreed with intriguing arabesques and inlaid at the corners with iridescent mother-of-pearl; a tiny skull, as of a monkey, but with only one eyesocket central in the forehead, all covered in gold leaf except for the eye, which was a ruby big as my small fingernail; a folded map of sorts on a type of parchment which began to disintegrate as soon as I attempted to spread it (mercifully, I was able to get a photograph, though not a good one, before the thing had completely crumbled away to a fine dust, and merciful too that this was the only item in the box to be wasted in this manner); a set of silver dividers in perfect working condition; a beautiful bamboo flute of exquisite workmanship, carved with miniature mountains and forests, and with seascapes where boats bore curiously rigged sails whose like are elsewhere unknown in all Man's history; a lead pendant in the shape of a lizard devouring its own tail; the great, needle-sharp, curved ivory tooth of some beast of prey, with a hardwood handle set into its root end making of it a deadly dagger; and finally, beneath all of these lesser treasures, runebooks and scrolls and documents, all of fine skins no thicker than paper but lubricated in a way which left them supple after God-only-knows how vast a stretch of time.

Several loose leaves there were, too, finely hieroglyphed in figures completely new to me and almost certainly beyond the talents of any of today's cryptographers or runic interpreters; and as I laid these carefully on my table a draught disturbed them, threatening to blow them onto the floor. I used the first thing to hand—the ancient glass in its square frame—to pin them down, and so accidentally stumbled across a most fantastic revelation.

Whoever had stocked this golden box and sealed it within its now completely disappeared shell, had not only wisely and deliberately protected it against its journey into future aeons but had also forseen certain of the difficulties its discoverer must eventually face. Beyond doubt he had been a scientist of sorts, this man, but this was surely much more than mere science!

My head swam dizzily and I clutched at the table's edge, steadying myself. I blinked my eyes and looked again...then stared... And finally, rubbing furiously at my eyes, I shakily pulled up a chair and sat down to peer yet again, unbelievingly (or at least believing myself to be suffering the most astonishing delusions) at the hieroglyphs that now swam up large through the blue-tinged glass of the magnifier.

They were hieroglyphs no longer!

Now I could read those immemorial minuscules as easily as if I had written them myself, for now—or so it appeared through the impossible lens of the magnifier—they were in German, the language of my youth! Eagerly I read a page, two, three, unbelievingly copying the words down in scratchy English as I scanned them through that incredible glass, watching the blurred, alien and unknown characters and symbols writhing into clearly discernible words, phrases, sentences and paragraphs as I slowly slid the magnifier over them where they lay.

Then a tragedy. My hand was so a-shake, my eyes watering with the strain of staring at this continual, mesmerising metamorphosis, that I dropped the glass and gasped horrified as it cracked sharply against a corner of the golden box. Instantly a thin trickle of oily blue liquid seeped out from the interior of the lens—and need I relate what next took place? Less than twenty seconds later no trace remained of that miraculous lens, only its square golden frame and a rapidly dispersing mist of acrid smoke...

For a moment I despaired, cursing myself for a clumsy fool and almost crying out loud in my frustration; but then I snatched up my scribbled notes, three pages of them, and realised that all was not lost! In these few scraps of paper I had a key, one which would unlock the secrets of the manuscripts just as surely as any magical magnifier—but much more slowly. Oh, so very slowly.

For nine long years I have laboured—not only over my translations but also to gain recognition of an Age of Man predating prehistory!—but while I have successfully translated a good third of Teh Atht's runebooks and manuscripts, I have failed dismally to impress any real authority with the enormity of the treasure I found in a lava bomb hurled from the throat of a volcano.

Perhaps if my find had been less spectacular...if I had told no one of the disappearing sphere and lens of glass...and certainly had I made no mention of the magnifier's wondrous powers of translation, things might have been different. As it is: still I am irked considerably to be looked upon as "somewhat peculiar," or as "quaintly eccentric," and this despite my previous reputation and the fact that I have photographic evidence and friends who will vouchsafe the truth of what I say. My photographs must of course be "fakes," and all of my good friends mere "dupes."

And so what more can I say or do? Well, if I cannot tell the world of Theem'hdra, the Primal Continent at Earth's Dawn, in the way it should be told—as by a scientist above the lowly japes and deceptions of which I stand accused—then I am obliged to tell of it in some other manner. If I cannot present Teh Atht's words as statements of fact or at very least fragments of myth or fable from a time beyond time, then I must present them as modern fiction.

In this my good friend and collaborator Brian Lumley has been of tremendous assistance, colouring the legends as I unfold them and preparing them one by one for popular publication. If this was not Teh Atht's purpose, that this tomorrow-world of ours know of his own dimly fabulous time, then I am at a loss to say what his purpose was. Surely he had some such in mind when, placing his treasures in the golden box, he sealed it in its glassy sphere, and taking whatever other precautions were necessary for its aeon-lasting protection he sent it winging down all the ages of time from dim and distant but no longer forgotten Theem'hdra!

Thelred Gustau

What shall we say of that continent at the dawn of time, in the first "civilised" Age of Man? Its inhabitants called it Theem'hdra, which is a name beyond translation; but how may we, looking back into the bottomless abyss of the past, name or classify a landmass which must, by now, have been above and below great oceans many times, returning in the main to its individual rocks and pebbles, and those in their cycle to finely sifted sands? Atlantis by comparison was yesterday...

We might perhaps think of Theem'hdra as Pangaea, but *not* the Pangaea visualised by today's experts. And that is not to castigate or belittle in any way those authorities whose choice it has been to turn blind eyes upon Thelred Gustau's work. No, I merely point out that their Pangaea, the "popular" Pangaea, was, in the grand scale of things, last week. In the same scale Theem'hdra was probably months ago.

And yet for me, as for Gustau, the Primal Continent no longer lies in the dim and fabulous past. Working as I have upon my colleague's translations, preparing them for publication as modern "fictions," I have grown to know Theem'hdra as I know my own England. It is a place to which I might journey simply by closing my eyes and sending my thoughts winging out on a mission of...race memory? I know the mammoth plains as well as I know the woods of my own childhood, the twisty alleys of Klühn as thoroughly as the steep streets of Durham City.

...Theem'hdra is of volcanic origin. Two volcanoes are mentioned in Teh Atht's manuscripts, both active in his time, but we base our claim in respect of the continent's origin mainly on what Thelred Gustau remembers of the map from his golden box; in that and in the photographs, however poor, which he managed to obtain before the parchment map disintegrated.

From Gustau's reproduction it can be seen that central Theem'hdra is a vast inland sea, almost circular, of about five hundred miles in diameter and ringed by the Great Circle Mountains. South-west of this inner ocean and within the surrounding range lies a mighty volcano which is in fact a secondary cone, still quietly active and now and then disturbingly grumbly. Surely the throat of the *original* volcano is now the mighty inner sea itself, and the crater walls, eroded by the winds, rains and tremors of a young planet, are now those same Great Circle Mountains?

But what a volcano that must have been! A fire-spewing cauldron five hundred miles across: Krakatoa itself would be the merest squib by comparison! Thus, in what was probably the most violent of all primal convulsions, Theem'hdra was born. And as the ages ticked by there were men...

On a line due west of the inner sea's centre lies the continent's second active volcano, an island cone standing off in the Unknown Ocean. This volcano, in its birthing, brought down and destroyed and buried beneath a lava plain the city of Bhur-Esh, which knew its heyday when Klühn, the modern capital on the eastern coast almost three thousand miles away, was merely a fishing village. Nevertheless, and while Bhur-Esh is to Klühn what Ur is to, say, modern Cairo, legends of Bhur-Esh came down to Teh Atht in his wizardly apartments overlooking Klühn's great bay, and he dutifully recorded them in his runebooks. And so we know the story of Kank Thad the barbarian, who departed slowly from and returned quickly to Bhur-Esh all in the same day, and thereafter wandered no more...

To return to the eastern coast:

Almost eight hundred miles south of Klühn—across the Lohr and several smaller rivers, surrounded by dense coastal forests—lies the city of Yhemnis. It is a splendidly barbaric city of gold, ivory and ironwood, home and citadel of swart Yhemni slavers and pirates. East again, across the stormy Straits of Yhem and eighty sea-miles distant, the jungle-island Shadarabar (with Shad, its capital, squarely facing

Yhemnis on the mainland) is also home to Yhemni tribes. Mercifully these dark brown peoples are as often at each other's throats as at war with the rest of the Primal Continent's more civilised people. But from this it must not be reckoned that the Yhemni are Theem'hdra's only barbarians—no!

For diagonally across the continent, at its north-westerly extreme, is a land of fjords and lochs and chilly waters. Nomadic wooly mammoths wander the great plains to the west of this region, hunted by towering white savages who—while there are many individual tribes and families—generally go under the group name of Northmen. More commonly, however, they are known simply as Barbarians!

The true Northern Barbarian is easily recognised: by his massive strength, his lightly browned skin, his love of soft women and hard drink, his rapidly alternating moods (between soaring high spirits and deepest, darkest depressions), his dread of sorcery, and by the distinctive mane of hair he wears, short and bristly, from nape of neck to base of spine.

Fishermen famed for their hunting of the great whales, sailors crafted in boat-building, warriors dreaded for the sheer madness of their berserker rages—yes, and traders, too, whose pelts and ivory are valued highly in Khrissa and Thandopolis—the Northmen are colourful, heroic characters, with a whole-hearted love of piratical adventurings and tall-tale telling and song-singing. They are also wanderers who may be found far from their chill homeland, in almost every part of Theem'hdra.

Of Khrissa (mentioned above, a cold and lonely city of basalt slabs at the mouth of the Greater Marl River four hundred miles east of the Mammoth Plains): its gaunt, sparsley-clad priest-inhabitants are a race aside from the majority of Theem'hdra's peoples. Tall and thin they are, bald-pated and shaven of all bodily hair; and equally austere their lives. Aye, for their sole task in life would seem to be the sending of prayers to their many gods that the ice barrier to the north might encroach no closer to the northern shores of Theem'hdra.

In the Year of the White Whales—when the ice only stopped after mounting the thousand mile reef, while to the east it even cast its creeping frosty-silver cloak about the feet of Tharamoon—Khrissa's priests sacrificed no less than three hundred of their women in order to still the deadly white advance. Woe betide any stranger in Khrissa when the ice crackles out of the north and the winter snows drift deep and ominous!

North-east of Khrissa, indeed, at the most northerly point of the mainland, there, ten miles out in the Chill Sea, Tharamoon the Mountain Island rises silent, forbidding and forbidden. Atop the highest needle peak a massive castle of grey stone glooms against greyer skies, and even though its one-time wizard inhabitant, Mylakhrion the Elder, is long dead and blown as dust in the wind, still the island lies vacant; for no man would tempt the monstrous magicks and curses Mylakhrion doubtless called down upon that blasted rock in his last days. No, not for all the wizard's treasures, fabled to rest with his bones, broken at the base of the castle's walls...

But while Mylakhrion, ancestor of Teh Atht himself, was old in Theem'hdra's youth (he had been dead eleven hundred years when Teh Atht dreamed his dreams of the BEGINNING and the END), nevertheless other, darker magicks had survived the centuries, creeping down the years to modern Theem'hdra.

Until recently the most hideous of all of these dark forces was chained, by rune and spell of Elder God, in a bottomless crypt upon Arlyeh, island of nameless ruins mid-ocean between the Frostlands and Klühn. And it was the reaver Zar-Thule who, together with the men of his dragonships, sailed in unto and landed upon the island, seeking out the priceless treasures of the House of Cthulhu... But that is another story.

Of the Frostlands, bitter regions to the east of the Great Ice Barrier:

Yaht Haal was the only city beyond the confines of the Primal Continent proper known to Theem'hdra's peoples: Yaht Haal, the Silver City at the edge of the Frostlands, which Zar-Thule sacked before his ill-omened landing upon Arlyeh. He sacked Yaht Haal and burned it down, torturing and killing all of the city's priests and doing worse things to its gentle, fur-clad snow-folk. And following the rape of the Silver City, the very next winter, the Great Ice Barrier came down and buried its desecrated temples and houses deep beneath crystal glaciers; for there were no longer priests and wizardlings to keep the ice away with their chants and spell-spinnings.

Now, I may seem to be making a lot of Theem'hdra's magicians and wizards and sorcerers, and I know that in our 20th Century such are frowned upon as the stuff of fairy tales and fables. But I repeat that Theem'hdra was *millions* of years ago, when this world of ours was still a very young one, whereon Nature experimented and created and did myriads of strange and nightmarish things. After all, Nature herself was in her youth, and she had not yet decided which talents men should have and which should be forbidden, discontinued.

In some men, in certain women, too, the wild workings of capricious Nature wrought weird wonders, giving them senses and powers additional to the usual five. Often these powers were carried down through many generations; aye, and occasionally such a man would mate with just such a woman, and then, eventually, through genealogical patterns and permutations long forgotten to 20th-Century scientists, along would come the seventh son of a seventh son, or the ninth daughter of a ninth daughter...and then?

Oh, yes, there was certainly magick in those times, though perhaps today, in our "enlightened" age, we would find different names for such as wizards, lamias, weirdlings and warlocks. For Nature has never truly ceased her dabbling, and now we casually acknowledge such words as telepathy, telekinesis, teleportation, and so on. And was not Einstein himself a magician, whose runes were just as powerful as any wizard's in old Theem'hdra?

But that is to labour a point... And so let us now return to the topography and anthropology of Theem'hdra:

North of the Bay of Monsters, between the mighty River Luhr and the Great Eastern Peaks, lie the Steppes of Hrossa where dwell the fierce Hrossaks. Tremendously skilled riders of fearsome lizard mounts, warriors almost without peer, the Hrossaks feud intermittently with the armies of massive-walled Grypha at the mouth of the Luhr, and with the Yhemni in their coastal forests. Other than the occasional raid or skirmish, however, the bronze Hrossaks are content to live at peace in their steppes where they farm and pride themselves in practicing the arts of war, and where they breed their lizard herds, providing leather and meat and sport a-plenty. The River Luhr is sacred to them and they will not cross it, and the peaks of the eastern range are much too high for them; generally, they are not good climbers.

Across the Luhr to the west, two hundred and fifty miles away rise the foothills of the Great Circle Mountains, within which, to the east of the inner sea, oozes the slimy Marsh of Slugs. Even the wildest, loudest adventurers dare only mention this vast and boggy nightmare of a region in the merest whispers, for that's the sort of place the Marsh of Slugs is—all forty thousand square miles of it! And so we'll linger there no longer but move on west across the great crater sea to the Inner Isles.

Central in that enclosed sea which was once the throat of a vast volcano, like green jewels strewn on a mantle of beautiful blue, the Inner Isles reach up their lava mountains to touch the sky. Here, rumour has it, dwells a tall, slender, comb-headed race of silver-grey beings who are not entirely human. Their houses are wooden and nestle on the slopes of their mountains; their needs are simple and are all supplied by the islands themselves and the teeming sea; their ways are gentle, even though they have strengths not immediately apparent, and their lives are ones of quiet and peaceful contemplation.

Yes, and their minds are the finest in all Theem'hdra, with senses that reach beyond the normal range of those we know. They are called the Suhm-yi, which means "the Rarely Seen," and it is because they are so rarely seen that we can offer no real proof of their existence, only the tales of wandering barbarians whose travels have taken them over the high northern rim of the Great Circle Mountains and across the deep blue inner sea.

Thus the area enclosed by these volcanic mountains holds both terror and beauty...but it also holds mystery. Mystery in the shape of massive stone cubes, featureless blocks with sides hundreds of feet long, which stand amidst the inner foothills all along the western range and are fabled to be the long-vacated houses of the world's first race, which was not human but came down to Earth from the stars in Theem'hdra's prehistory. Great mystery there, aye, and mystery too in the Black Isle, standing dark and still in a subsidiary lake of the inner sea to the north-east; but of that place, so far, we know nothing except that it is there...

And that in the main is Theem'hdra. From the bay of Klühn in the north-east to the Paps of Mam, Mother of Gods, at the continent's south-westerly extreme, and from the grim Teeth of Yib and the fjords of the north-west to Shadarabar off the south-east coast. In all, the continent is about 2400 miles east to west and 2000 miles north to south, with a total land area of about 3,750,000 square miles.

Including the peoples of Yaht Haal (if any remain alive) Theem'hdra houses six distinct races: the Northern Barbarians, the scattered white settlers of the coastal cities, the fabled Suhm-yi of the Inner Isles, the Hrossaks of the steppes, the swart and fiery Yhemni, and a pigmy race fabled to dwell in the Marsh of Slugs. Its gods are many, and some of them are in no way gods for prayers, rather for cursing by. Gleeth, blind Moon God, is believed to be benevolent, as is Shoosh, Goddess of the Still Slumbers, and Mam, Mother of Gods; but Ghatanothoa is a dark and doomful god—and even more so Cthulhu, though His worship is mercifully restricted to small, secret sects—Yib-Tstll, too. Then there are the Ice-Gods, whose names are kept secret by the priests of cold Khrissa, except for Baroom, God of the Avalanche, whose name is often invoked at the great drinking festivals of the Northmen.

And so little more remains to be told of Theem'hdra. Oh, there are rivers and lakes, towns and cities and other places that I have not mentioned; yes, and others I myself do not yet know, will not until Thelred Gustau translates more of Teh Atht's runebooks—but that lies in the future.

Thus I welcome you to the fables and legends of a time long dead and hitherto forgotten. If you choose to think of them as "fictions" in the modern vein, well, that is your choice. For myself: I have come to know Theem'hdra quite intimately and can go there simply by closing my eyes and sending my mind winging back across the aeons. Why not join me there, now, in that raw adventurous world in an age before all other ages of man, in the Primal Continent at the dawn of time?

POSTSCRIPT

...Since penning the above, for use as an introduction to an original book of Thelred Gustau's translations, the fantastic, the inexplicable has occurred. No, on second thought perhaps the occurrence was not entirely inexplicable; but if my guess is correct, certainly it was fantastic.

I had known for weeks that Thelred was excited about something, and, in respect of his age, I had warned him against the excessive amount of work he was putting in on Teh Atht's *Legends of the Olden Runes*. It had seemed to me that he was neither eating nor sleeping normally and that something—some aspect of his work of which he had made no mention—had become an obsession with him.

On the day in question his housekeeper, Mrs. Petersen, prepared a breakfast which he no more than glanced at before hurrying to his study. There, as the morning grew towards noon, he sat at his desk with scratchily moving pen in hand and all the paraphernalia of his golden box within easy reach.

All through the forenoon he sat, disposing of a continuous supply of coffee, climbing from one level of high excitement to the next, until noon when he left the study and retired to his bedroom. The look on his face as he passed by Mrs. Petersen was: "wild, flushed, exultant!—but he was also plainly very tired." He asked that she rouse him at 7 P.M. and place coffee and sandwiches in his study before going home.

She followed his instructions to a point, but was so concerned by her employer's behaviour that she did not immediately go home. Instead she sat in her little kitchen and listened to the muffled sounds of the professor stirring in his study...to those, and to his frequent, excited exclamations.

She must have drowsed, for her next memory is of a terrific blast of sound, of a triumphant cry in the professor's voice, of a deeper, bass booming which could only barely be described as a voice, and finally of a splintering, crashing impact that shook the very house.

Rushing to his study she threw open the door on a scene of chaotic disorder. In the ceiling the chandelier swung on its chain and cast flickering shadows from light-bulbs made faulty by whatever blast had wrecked the room. Books and documents lay scattered all about; loose leaves still fluttered to the carpeted floor; the great bay window had been forced outwards from its frame into the garden, where even now a great shadow stirred black against the night.

Mrs. Petersen staggered to that unnaturally shattered window in time to see...a shape! A shape like that of a monstrous bird or bat that loomed up massive before rising into darkness to the whirring thrum of great wings, a black silhouette bearing upon its back the lesser shape of…a man!

I was among the few, called upon by the police early the next day, to go along and make what I could of Mrs. Petersen's story. Did I have any idea exactly what the professor was working on?—they wanted to know—and had I known that he was experimenting with explosives? And what *sort* of explosives might they have been? These and many other questions, all of which I could only answer by shaking my head in utter bafflement. Plainly it had been an explosion of some sort that caused the damage to the professor's study, particularly the window, but that did not explain his total absence.

Surely there should be a body, or at least—traces of one! But no, there was nothing like that, no sign of any harm done to his person. What then had happened? And if he lived, where was Thelred Gustau now?

Later I was allowed to gather all of his scattered notes, documents, books and miscellaneous curiosa together, examining each item for damage…and then the puzzle began to piece itself into a pattern. Some weeks were to pass, however, before my conclusions were concrete, and even then they were not such as I might pass on to the police.

The clues were in Thelred's notes, in those copious if disjointed scribblings formed partly of translated fragments from Teh Atht, mainly of his own excitement at some tremendous breakthrough which he was sure was coming. And of course that breakthrough had come, on the night of the blasted study, the bass alien "voice," and the bat-bird shape that bore a triumphant manlike figure away into unknown dimensions.

For Thelred had written of the strange properties he believed to lie hidden in the stopped-up silver whistle, and of the potent energies locked in a tiny bottle of golden-yellow liquid from Teh Atht's box. He had likened these items to certain things hinted at in the peculiar, almost esoteric works of Dr. Laban Schrewsbury, and at the

same time had jotted down notes concerning gigantic flying crea
tures called "Byakhee" and a tentacled, immemorially worshipped
God-thing named Hastur.

Tenuous clues, all of them; and yet had he not recently complained
bitterly of the ever-increasing scorn with which erstwhile colleagues
now greeted his work? And had he not often stated his desire to be
"away from all this...?" Never at peace with the hustle and bustle of
our 20th Century, always seeking the solitude of vast ocean vistas and
the lure of distant desert places, what was there to hold him here? And
by "here" I mean in this world of men, at least in the present-day world
of here and now.

Often he had declared his admiration for those tales of olden
Arabia, where djinni might be found in magic lamps and brave men
sought adventure high above the world on arabesqued, gravity-
defying carpets. And now...has he discovered a magic carpet of his
own, astride the back of a transdimensional Byakhee, which might
fly him to those worlds of wonder he so admired?

Deny me if you will, but in my mind's eye I see him working at
his desk, see him leap to his feet with an astounded exclamation to
tremulously sip of the golden mead. I hear him hoarsely chant the
invocation to Hastur and blow on the whistle so recently unstop-
pered. Aye, and then the blast of energy that heralds the coming of
the Byakhee, tumbling the contents of the study and blowing out the
windows while yet the summoner stands unharmed.

I see it all and know that it must have been so, for of all the incunabula of the golden box only the silver whistle—that and one of the
tiny bottles—were absent upon my investigation...

And now I alone am executor to the estate, and I know that soon I shall
have mastered the legends writ so many aeons ago in alien cyphers
upon the fine skins of Tch Atht's runebooks. What Thelred Gustau
started I shall finish, but until then there are those fables already
translated which, as I have said before, you may accept for what they
are or, if you so desire, name "fictions" in the modern vein. The choice
is yours.

How Kank Thad
Returned to Bhur-Esh

FOREWORD

W hen Thelred Gustau originally invited me to read what was
then his latest translation from Teh Atht's *Legends of the
Olden Runes*, with an eye to my preparation of the work for publication, he also placed in my hands some associational information
about the locale of the story and certain of its participants. This
information follows:

Long before Klühn ever became the capital city of Theem'hdra—
indeed, at a time when Klühn was little more than a fishing
village—then, to the extreme west of the continent at the edge of the
vast Unknown Ocean, in a valley girt round by the Ghost Cliffs of
Shildakor, lay the city of Bhur-Esh. Two thousand years later when
Klühn had grown up, Bhur-Esh, its valley, and the Ghost Cliffs too
were long gone, buried beneath a lava desert, and out in the Unknown
Ocean a new volcanic island stood grey, forbidding and still silently
smoking... But we are only interested in Bhur-Esh in its heyday.

For then the streets of the city were crowded and narrow and
crooked so as to be almost labyrinthine. They were lined with shops

and bazaars and brothels where merchants from all over the known world thronged to barter, buy and vend any and everything that could possibly be vended, bought or bartered. And in Bhur-Esh such merchants could carry on their businesses in almost perfect safety; because of its topography the city had very few thieves—it will be seen that they had nowhere to run!

As a self-supporting seaport and city (the inhabitants considered themselves collectively as a "nation" in their own right), Bhur-Esh was and had ever been neutral, neither attacking its neighbours nor being attacked. The pincerlike arms of the bay reaching out to the Unknown Ocean were high and sheer oceanward and well fortified within, with turrets, ramparts, arrowslits, and quarters for hundreds of soldiers; a regiment was kept there permanently. Too, in strategic places, ballistae loomed in impregnable rock-cut bastions on top of those arms, with hundreds of heavy boulders ready for the hurling.

That was one of the reasons why Bhur-Esh was neutral; the other, apparently, was the Ghost Cliffs of Shildakor. As Teh Atht himself has written: "What army except an army of wizards might broach such insurmountable barriers?" But these same barriers also worked in another way, explaining Bhur-Esh's deficiency of criminals and why, once discovered, there was no sanctuary to which they could flee. The cliffs were unscalable, the narrow mouth of the bay constantly guarded and equipped with a toll bridge.

The bay was wide at the landside and the cliff-enclosed valley was by no account small, so that while Bhur-Esh itself was a sizeable city with suburbs sprawling eastward almost to the very feet of the sheltering Ghost Cliffs themselves, nevertheless it occupied only a twentieth part of the "kingdom."

Between the calm waters of the bay and the city's west wall, fields stretched in green expanse, with farmhouses and barns scattered here and there and cattle enclosures and patchworks of growing crops; and lining these fertile fields at north and south hard-packed roads lay beneath the beetling rocks. These roads led from the barracks and quarters of King Vilthod's soldiers, on the outskirts of Bhur-Esh, to the battlements of the rocky bay arms.

The King's palace stood magnificent and serene, "a pinnacled splendour to the eye of the beholder," at the city's hub. Its walls were surrounded by cropped, luscious-green grass imported from the bar barous North, and archers sat atop the walls with crossbows of eastern design to ensure that no man walked, sat or stood upon King Vilthod's grass. For the King's grass was his pride and joy—its seed paid for grain by precious grain, nurtured to lush life and maintained by a bevy of gardeners—and the like of its northern green was unheard of elsewhere on the shores of the Unknown Ocean. Teh Atht tells us that: "Many an unwary stranger, perhaps fancying a juicy blade of grass to chew, had discovered a flighted bolt growing in his chest or throat before the grass could dangle from his lips..."

Likewise prized by the King, for its architecture and yellow-walled beauty (not to mention the money it doubtless provided his coffers, which was probably why he had built it directly behind the palace), was the High-Court of Bhur-Esh. The High-Court stood tall and golden, but not nearly so splendid as the palace, in a plaza of white-walled gardens and winding pebble paths, "between delicate fountains and airy marble statues of gods and heroes long gone." Within its spacious halls the worst members of Bhur-Esh's criminal element—few, as explained—were tried by Thamiel, Chief Seeker of Truth to the King.

Normally the main courtroom was sparsely attended; a few chroniclers with their styli and tablets; a bard or two to sing Woes or Delights after the passing of sentence or declaration of innocence; the provost guard; a smattering of out-of-work city types, and the family and friends of the sinned-against and sometimes of the transgressor. On the day of which Teh Atht tells in the following legend, however, things were very different...

I

Never before had a man the like of Kank Thad the barbarian been brought to trial at the High-Court. His crimes had been many and varied and all sorts of imputations had been brought against him in the hour or so during which his case had been heard. In fact, no case *had* been heard, merely the basic facts: that Kank Thad was accused of Murder most foul and that, among other sundry offences, he had spat and done worse things on the palace-encircling grass of King Vilthod.

At the time of the latter blasphemies, some days earlier, the archer who had seen these acts had been nonplussed as to what action to take. There were edicts for sitters on the grass, and for standers or walkers upon it, but Kank Thad had done none of these things—he had merely extruded a gob of saliva grassward from the road where he stood admiring the palace. A passer-by, shocked and thinking to see the barabarian cut down at any instant, had whispered to him from a safe distance of what he did, advising him to move quickly along; whereupon Kank Thad had hailed the archer who still pondered his course of action atop the wall:

"Hey, archer on the wall!"

"Move on...get on with you!" the flabbergasted archer had returned.

"Archer," cried Kank Thad unperturbed. "I am told that one may neither sit nor stand nor walk on the grass. Is this true?"

"Aye."

"And spitting?"

"There are no orders. No one has—spat—before, on the grass!"

"And being a good archer of the King," the Northman grinned evilly up at the flustered man above, "you may only act on written or spoken instructions?"

"That...is true. Now move on!"

"Not yet, my friend archer," answered the barbarian, whipping up his clout and wetting with a loud guffaw on Vilthod's beloved grass.

Then, before the mortified archer had time to aim his crossbow, the hairy great white savage had turned to stride drunkenly off down a winding street in whose tortuous coils he was soon lost to sight. That archer, a dull fellow as witness the tale, was employed atop the palace walls no longer; for having reported the occurrence to his commander he had been stripped of rank and sent to the High-Court wherein slavish, menial tasks might be found more suited to his talents. There this day he had spotted Kank Thad and brought his charge against him—one of many.

The barbarian's debts were legion. He owed taverners for ale by the gallon and meat by the platter, and a hosteler two weeks' rent for the kennel wherein he'd slept. These were among his heavier debts; his lesser ones were far more numerous.

Having at length been kicked out by the irate hosteler, he was charged with vagrancy too, and finally he was accused of murder. This being the most heinous of his deeds—barely, remembering the episode of the grass-wetting—it was the murder for which he found himself eventually called to answer.

"You have heard all against you. How say you then, barbarian? Are you innocent—or guilty of vile murder?" Thamiel asked his all-important question of the huge, chained savage before him.

Kank Thad, scarred horribly from cheek- to chin-bone down one side of his face, his left eye forever half-closed in a scar-tissue grimace, leaned against one of the carven basalt pillars to which he was manacled and grinned. His grin was evil as his aspect, square yellow teeth leering from behind hard, thin lips. A towering hulk of a man, he spat on the mosaic floor of the courtroom, tossing back his mane of jet hair—which grew, like that of all his race, in a narrow band right down to the base of his spine—before answering.

"Murder?" he scoffed. "That's a word I didn't know before I was washed up on your piddling beach when my good ship sank in the bay. And I'd never have come here if that storm hadn't forced me to seek safe harbour. Listen: in my homeland to the north, when two men fight and one wins, the victor is no murderer! Aboard my ship, if a man got spitted in a fair fight, his body went to feed the fishes and the one who lived was left to tend his scars! Murder? Of what do you speak, baggy one?"

Thamiel winced at the barbarian's words. The heavily-jowled, flabbily-bodied Seeker of Truth had put up with the iron-thewed Northman's insults all through his trial, and Thamiel's patience was running low. Still, he was a man renowned for the Perfection of his Justice, and he could be just even now—before this sea-rat died!

"You will say nothing in your defence, then?"

"I wanted a woman," the scarface answered with a shrug of his powerful shoulders, "and that one—" he pointed a shackled hand across the courtroom at a brightly daubed slut in the stalls, "was the one I wanted. I'd had her before when my money was good, and what's wrong with a bit on account, I ask you? She makes a good cushion for a boozed-up body. And I'll tell you something, you pallid sack of a man: a night with that one—why!—it would add ten years to your miserable life!" He grinned again, reconsidering that last. "—or finish you off for good!"

Fatty folds of flesh trembling in rage, Thamiel gawped and spluttered, then remembered the Faultlessness of his Justice and brought himself under control. "Wench," he spoke to the girl, "you have heard all that has gone…have you any last words for or against Kank Thad the Northman?"

Here the barbarian believed himself to be on firm ground. Had he not praised the girl, in his way, and had he not also given her a good night that time?—and paid for it too, by Yib! He had not taken into account the fact that he was now destitute, with only a battle-notched blade to his name; and of what use to a tavern-whore is an ugly barbarian with an insatiable lust, an empty pocket and a too-ready sword?

"That I have!" Lila the whore shrilled, her hair hanging down over her more than ample, passionately heaving bosom. "I was bought and paid for by Theen of King Vilthod's Guard, aye, and on our way upstairs in the tavern of Hethica Nid, when this—this latrine slime—took me from him!"

"*Took* you from him?" Sitting at Thamiel's right hand, Veth Nuss the Mousey spoke up in his squeaky, tremulous voice. "Took you from an Officer of the King's Guard! Didn't Theen have his sword?"

"He did, Lord," Lila answered, "but the barbarian came up behind us and plucked it from his side!"

"This was not told before," Thamiel frowned, interested despite himself and his desire to get the thing over with.

"The questions were not asked, Lord," Lila protested. "I was asked only if Kank Thad *killed* Theen—and he did!"

"Well, go on…go on, girl, tell it now," Thamiel urged.

"Well, the barbarian took Theen's sword and flipped it point up into the ceiling of the tavern. Theen attacked him, but—" she glanced grudgingly at Kank Thad, "the northman is—*big*, Lord. He shrugged Theen off and laughed at him. And then—"

"So it is true then," Thamiel broke in, "that Theen was weaponless when the barbarian struck him down?"

"Aye!" Kank Thad suddenly shouted from between his pillars, "that's true enough. Tell them, Lila, you ungrateful ratbag—tell them just how 'weaponless' the guardsman was—and may your paps rot in the telling!" He hung in his chains and roared with berserk laughter.

"As Theen—" Lila hesitantly continued when finally the giant's laughter subsided, "—as he leapt to try to regain his blade stuck high in the ceiling, Kank Thad, he—he..."

"Yes, girl, what did the barbarian do?" Thamiel impatiently pressed.

"He—he struck Theen a very low blow."

"Eh?" Veth Nuss the Mousey frowned and shook his head. "Can you not be plainer, wench?" he squeaked.

"I lopped away his manhood with Gutrip, my once-true sword!" Kank Thad screamed in hellish derision. "Ripped it away and flipped it to the tavern dogs from Gutrip's tip. Murder, you say? Why!—I did the man a favour in putting him out of his misery. What good's a man who can't—"

"*Silence!*" Thamiel thundered, hoisting himself pudding-like to his feet. Even the low muttering and chattering from the galleries had stopped, and white faces peered in awe and horror at the hulking, manacled barbarian in his chains. Thamiel, shaken to his soul at the loathsomeness conjured by the Northman's admission, his composure utterly shattered now, stood with his finger pointing, trembling. "By your own words—" he finally managed, "you are *guilty!*—and now I pass sentence..." He drew himself up to his full height of five feet three inches and, barely remembering the Unimpeachability of his Justice, said: "Let thy sword be sundered!"

II

"Let the sword Gutrip be sundered!" The words of the Seeker of Truth were echoed to a hall outside the courtroom proper and a man, a minor court attendant but once an archer of the palace walls, clad now in a shift of mean cloth, laboured in under Gutrip's weight. He was grimly smiling for all his workworn appearance. He placed the weapon on tall marble blocks, its plain-guarded pommel on one, its point on another, its chipped middle suspended. The ex-archer raised a great iron hammer, at which Kank Thad—perhaps remembering better days before swinish habits sank him low—hauled on his chains and roared in an agony as if he himself were being tortured.

"By Yib, *no*, the blade is not to blame! Gutrip—" His anguished cry tapered off as the grinning court attendant, also remembering better days, brought down his hammer and shivered the scarred sword into a dozen flying shards.

"Gutrip—" the great prisoner groaned low in his throat. "Oh, Gutrip…"

"Let the spinning of the Silver Decider commence!" cried Thamiel.

Again the fallen archer moved, climbing the steps of a dais in the centre of the courtroom where, on a block of faceted crystal, a silver arrow balanced within a ring of rune-inscribed iron.

"Know you, Kank Thad, of the choice to be made?" Veth Nuss squeaked in his mouse-voice.

"I have a choice of punishments?" the barbarian brightened. "Yib—but this sounds better! What choice do I have? Is one of them banishment? If so, then ban—"

"*Silence!*" Thamiel of the Meritorious Justice thundered again. "The choice is not yours but that of the Silver Decider. If, when the arrow stops its spinning, the point faces into the north…then you go north, to the Ghost Cliffs of Shildakor. If the point faces to the south—then you go south, to the Square of the Sundering!"

"Ghost Cliffs?" The barbarian shuddered ever so slightly and his mane bristled all down his back at this hint of thaumaturgy. "Sundering? I like the sound of neither. Explain, O bulging bilge-barrel."

"Gladly," Thamiel whispered, actually smiling through the barbarian's irreverence as he thought on the Transcendence of his Justice. "The Ghost Cliffs of Shildakor stand a mile high, sheer and stark, often overhanging and reaching in certain seasons into the very clouds. On a clear day a man might see the top through a good glass, and some day a man might even climb to the top—but this has not happened yet. The bones and tatters of a thousand fallen climbers litter the lower slopes. You, too, Kank Thad, might try the climb, depending upon which way the Silver Decider points."

"And the Square of the Sundering?" Little of the Northman's hairy spirit remained, but he managed to retain an almost theatrical bluster even yet.

"Why, is it not obvious? The dust in the Square of the Sundering is brown with dried blood, barbarian, and yellow and white with the pounded bones of men quartered there between four great horses bred for the task..."

"Hah!" the prisoner snorted. "I've yet to see the horses that might rip a son of Kulik Thad in pieces." He flexed his mighty muscles and the heavy chains and thick manacles groaned.

"Aye," Thamiel nodded his head, "we have had such before. We don't like to see our horses tired, though, by powerful muscles. And why should such be allowed when a couple of sword thrusts in the right places can help the job along a bit? A hack at a tendon here, a thrust at a stubborn joint there—"

"Ahem..." Veth Nuss ahemmed, reminding Thamiel of the Utter Insurmountability of his Justice, telling him not to elaborate. The punishments were surely enough in themselves without graphic descriptions. Thamiel smiled fatly at the barbarian's new expression—then gave the man atop the dais a signal. With a metallic whisper the Silver Decider began to spin, and eventually its pointer slowed...and stopped!

The arrow balanced delicately, stationary on its pivot—pointing north. Kank Thad was for the cliffs!

"Away with him!" At Thamiel's command ten powerful blacks seated on a stone bench rose, split into two parties, released the chains from the pillars and dragged the struggling, cursing Northman out of the courtroom and down a passage from which his fading blasphemies echoed for a goodly while. Away they took him, away to the deepest cells in the deepest dungeons under the white walls, pebble paths, airy statues and delicate fountains of the surroundings of the High-Court of Bhur-Esh.

Thus came Kank Thad to the city's dungeons, and in particular to that deepest of deep cells wherein only death-sentenced criminals wait—or prowl, or howl, or pray to heathen gods or whatever—during the short, short hours of their last night on Earth. Kank Thad, however, was no howler but a son of Kulik Thad; nor was he a prowler, for he saw little sense in wearing himself out wandering to and fro in the confines of his cell when tomorrow he had a great cliff to climb; and the only god he knew was one Yib-Tstll, who is no god to pray to but whose name may fairly be used in cursing; and so, because there seemed little else to do, the barbarian simply lay down in his cell and slept—he slept the sleep of a babe in arms until the night guard came on duty.

As fortune would have it his watchman was a Northman like himself, who first came to Bhur-Esh as a stripling stolen by swart slavers from Shadarabar in the east. Thasik Haag was a slave and a youth no longer but a greybeard now, and trusted as one whose duty is his all and holy above all other things. Thus Kank Thad's pleas (he was never one to miss out on any kind of chance, no matter how slim, in a tight spot) for the sake of the memory of northern lands with barbarous names fell on stony ground, and while he did at least wrench a tear or two from Thasik Haag's one good eye with his tales of the Mammoth Plains and the great hunts of home, he could in no way conjure a desire in the heart of that worthy ancient to assist him.

Instead, and in return for the barbarian's tales of dim-remembered northern territories, his jailer told him all he knew of the Ghost Cliffs of Shildakor: how Shildakor had been a wizard in immemorial times whose adventurous son had attempted to climb the great walls surrounding Bhur-Esh and the valley—and of how the boy fell and died! The wizard had straightway ensorcelled the cliffs, laying down a curse upon them, that henceforward ghosts would ever inhabit their crevices and niches.

Too, Thasik Haag was willing to share his supper and a skin of sour wine, and later he brought out a trothyboard and counters that they might play a game or two through the bars. In this he made a fatal mistake for he was a good player, and the sons of Kulik Thad—Kank especially—were not known for sporting natures but rather for short and fiery tempers.

Towards morning, when the first light was creeping in wispy mists over the eastern cliffs of the valley, down in that deep cell the loser of many trothy games, holding to a mere snarl the bull yell of anger that had grown in his chest all night, reached through the bars and grasped his keeper's windpipe in both of his hands. This had been the barbarian's plan all along, but damn it—he had first wanted to win at least one game!

Hauling hard, Kank Thad flattened his victim to the bars so that the astonished watchman was unable to draw his shortsword;

and then, so as to make a quick dispatch and offer the greybeard no opportunity to cry out, he dug his fingers in and hauled even harder until skin, flesh, cartilage, windpipe and all parted from the writhing neck of Thasik Haag in a crimson welter of blood and sinew. The watchman hardly knew what had happened, for he was well dead before his murderer let his corpse sink down to the floor to rest. Then Kank Thad set about to make a systematic search of the old man's body.

It was all of an hour later when the captain of the dungeon guard descended the nitre-sweating stone stairway down to that deepest cell...there to find the shattered shell of the good and faithful Thasik Haag, and, crouching behind the bars in a corner of his cell in a black and murderous rage of hate and frustration, the great scarfaced Northman. Even with the watchman's shortsword the barbarian had been unable to force an escape. At first sight of this horror-fraught scene the captain's hand went straight to his belt—where dangled the great key Kank Thad had thought to find in Thasik Haag's pockets...

Half the city of Bhur-Esh, it is told, turned out to watch Kank Thad take his departure of this world, gathering in select groups according to status at the feet of the Ghost Cliffs of Shildakor. Thamiel was there, of course, ringed around by a dozen guardsmen with loaded crossbows. He had gained an odd respect for the barbarian since learning of the additional murder of Thasik Haag: the Northman was definitely a berserker and even more dangerous than first believed! But safe in his impregnable circle Thamiel was, as ever, puffed up in the contemplation of the Indefectibility of his Justice.

Kank Thad's thoughts were for once chaotic as his bonds were released and, at half-a-dozen spearpoints, he was forced to mount first the piled bones and stinking shreds of corpses long fallen from the Ghost Cliffs of Shildakor. Noisome and slimy to his sandaled feet were those carrion remains, and given to crumbling and pitching him down into their vileness. Nonetheless he made his way for some fifteen feet over this debris of malefactors gone and finally turned with his back to the bare rock face.

"Climb, barbarian," Veth Nuss squeaked from Thamiel's flabby side.

"Climb, O minuscule? And what if I choose simply to sit here on a comfortable skull and drink in this marvellously ripe air?" Kank Thad hated to be ordered to do anything, and especially by one tiny as Veth Nuss. At a sign from Thamiel there came the whistle of cleft air as a bolt buried itself deep in the sandy rock through the Northman's free-hanging hair between his left cheek and shoulder.

"Look a little to your right, savage—and be warned!" Thamiel hissed as the huge murderer threw up an arm in anticipation of further missiles. When he saw that no more bolts were forthcoming, Kank Thad lowered his arm and did as directed, staring along the cliff to his right—and then he swore.

"*Yib!*" His curse was a mere whisper. At a distance of no more than a few paces a grisly skeleton sat, skewered through the eyesocket to the cliff.

"Aye," Thamiel offered, just loud enough to be heard, "he was one, just like you, who thought not to climb but sit on a skull and drink in the ripeness of the air." His voice changed abruptly. "*Now get on— My nostrils rot with the stink!*"

So the climb commenced and at first the going was relatively easy, with plenty of protruberant stones and knobs of rock, gaping fissures, and ledges, so that soon Kank Thad was quite high above the breathless crowd gathered there expressly to watch him fall. He did not intend to fall, however, for back home as a youth he had used to climb the sea-cliffs for gull eggs with the best of them; and now, when he'd reached what he thought a sufficient elevation, he paused on a wide ledge and turned to peer down at the multitude of tiny, tiny faces beneath him. The Seeker of Truth in his scarlet turban stood out plainly, with Veth Nuss at his side in the now slowly scattering circle of guards.

"O landwhale," the barbarian called down. "Hey Thamiel. You—woman-bosom!"

"I hear you," Thamiel called back, his voice trembling with rage at the new insults and the disturbing and embarrassing titters of the thronging assembly. "I hear—but will not listen. Go on climbing, or..."

"Or what, spherical Lord? I'm already out of range of your weapons. Iron bolts are far too heavy to ever reach me up here."

For the next few minutes Kank Thad sat back on his wide ledge and roared with laughter as bolts clattered against and bounced from the face of the cliff below his position. The closest shot fell short by at least the length of his body. On his ledge, wide enough to walk two horses, a great boulder lay half embedded in the weathered sand. The Northman went to this rock and, out of sight of the crowd below, prised it loose and hoisted it slowly, muscles straining, to his chest. Then he carefully put the boulder down again and stepped back to the ledge's rim.

When Thamiel saw him come back into view he called out: "We'll wait until you either resume climbing or attempt to come down, barbarian. The latter action, I may point out, will only hasten your inevitable death…"

Looking down, Kank Thad positioned the "landwhale" in his memory's eye, stepped quickly back and again hoisted the boulder, rushed forward and tossed it from him, barely maintaining his balance as the well aimed projectile sped out and down as truly as a shot from a hurling-engine handled by an officer of Vilthod's artillery.

Thamiel was quick for one his size, and well he needed to be, flinging himself like a mobile mountain to one side and taking two of his guards with him. Veth Nuss, however, had not been looking (he was prone enough to attacks of vertigo on the thick Tzulingen carpets of his chambers in the High-Court without peering at the fly-like human way up on the Ghost Cliff walls), and the boulder all but drove him into the earth. He emitted not a single squeak but crumpled like a wafer beneath the boulder and spread out in a scarlet stain on the stony ground. One uncrushed arm and hand protruded from the now shattered boulder's perimeter, and, as irony would have it, the hand was clenched and balanced on the thumb, which pointed down…

III

For a few seconds there was a silence broken only by Kank Thad's uproarious laughter from on high—and then a multitude of hushed "Oohs" and "Ahhs" of horror went up from the crowd and a scream of rage from Thamiel the Seeker of Truth. A few seconds more and bolts were whizzing, sent more zestfully than before and decidedly, Kank Thad thought, more dangerously.

Earlier, when first he'd paused upon this ledge, the barbarian had seen a runner dispatched in the direction of the palace guard's quarters. He knew that some of Vilthod's guardsmen were longbowmen, and that their flight arrows might easily end his sojourn in this lofty aerie forever; and so he decided it was time to move on, and there was only one way to go—

When the longbowmen arrived at the base of the cliffs a short while later, the barbarian was already out of range and climbing steadily. Nonetheless, at Thamiel's command and strictly to hasten the Northman on his way, an experimental arrow was loosed, fell short, and just missed cutting down a cotter on its return.

In another quarter-hour, when Kank Thad next thought to look down, the people were less than ants and the spread city was but a toy. Away to the south lay the Unknown Ocean—placid in the bay like a pond, tossed and wild without—sparkling in the sun and with gulls wheeling about like white midges on the horizon.

Again the barbarian found himself a ledge on which to rest, amusing himself by flinging great boulders from it and picturing in the eye of his imagination the chaos these missiles would create below. They did indeed cause chaos—and death—and soon the crowd, all bar Thamiel and his guards (and some few others who were there now to stay) went home. Thamiel was determined to remain till the very end, observing the spiderlike antics of the sentenced man through his powerful glass.

By now Kank Thad was almost half-way to the top, taking his time, making frequent pauses—though his muscles were far from tired—systematically checking and observing the cliffs above so that he might always choose the best route. In two shallow niches he had passed crouching skeletons, doubtless remains of bygone climbers who had found themselves too tired or frightened to carry on or turn back. There they had starved and died, shivering in fear of their terrible predicament—and perhaps of something else...

For a while now, as he climbed, Kank Thad had been pondering the tale told him by Thasik Haag, of Shildakor and the legendary curse he'd brought down on these cliffs following the fall of his son from their heights. A mist had started to weave up from the rock-walled valley below, and the vertical slabs had quickly dampened and turned cold to his touch.

Now oddly enough (or remembering Shildakor's curse, naturally) this mist went unobserved by Thamiel, still watching through his glass, but it was very real to the Northman and it cut his climbing speed by half. For this was a ghost-mist, raised up by the ancient sorcery of Shildakor, to worry and dismay would-be climbers…and Kank Thad was suitably worried and dismayed!

Still, he had carried out observations of the not quite sheer face up to a point some eighty feet or so immediately above him, and mist or none there had seemed plenty of good hand and footholds over that distance. He decided to push on—it would be bad should he find himself stuck here for the night—perhaps the mist would clear as quickly as it had come. But Kank Thad's previous visual reconnaissance proved of little use in the rising banks of fog now surrounding him and cutting down his field of vision to a few scant feet, and soon he found himself for the first time in trouble.

Below, through his glass, Thamiel could see how slow and tortured the barbarian's movements had become, and he chuckled to himself as he watched. Spreadeagled, the big man was, on the awful face, moving upwards inches at a time, and the Seeker of Truth expected to see him fall at any moment. No man—certainly none in Thamiel's time—had ever gone so high before, and the gross, red-turbaned judge did not want to miss this insolent murderer's inevitable slip. One slip was all it would take now.

Yet even as these exceedingly pleasant thoughts were passing through Thamiel's mind, Kank Thad had spotted a reprieve of sorts. Just when it seemed his hand and footholds had run out—when nothing but a flat, smooth surface loomed in front and an abyssal emptiness behind—he saw, just a little to his left, a concavity in the face of the cliff from which long ago a great stone must have fallen. A gentle slide, letting his body fall sideways and to the left, would allow him to put his head and shoulder over the lip of the hole before gravity claimed him completely. Kank Thad looked once at his sandaled feet, to make sure they were firmly seated, pushed himself to the left with his hands, and then, as his motion picked up speed, he saw the—*thing*—that awaited him in the misted darkness of the concavity!

The barbarian's first impulse was to fling himself away, which would of course prove fatal, but his horror of the thing in the hole froze him rigid—and it saved his life! It was Thasik Haag sat there—legs adangle from the hole, the pipes of his throat hanging out in threads of gristly red and yellow, his good eye bulging and his black tongue lolling—Thasik Haag, or rather his shade. But even as the barbarian's rigid fingers struck the corpse-thing it disappeared, vanishing into mist and leaving the hole empty and once more friendly.

Kank Thad unfroze in the very last instant of time, his hands shooting forward into the small cave and his shoulders hunching to take the strain as his arms spread wide and wedged. For a second the lower half of his body hung in space, and then he hauled himself up and into the hole.

"Ye Gods!" he whispered to himself, the short hairs of his mane rising on his spine as he thought of the thing he had seen. "Ye Gods—but they named these cliffs aright and no mistake!"

By the time the barbarian was over his initial terror the mist had cleared somewhat, and he could see what looked like a good wide ledge some three man-lengths higher. He levered himself from the hole backwards and began to traverse the next section of his climb. It was not easy: projections were slight and toeholds shallow, and for the first time he felt the strain on his powerful muscles. Eventually he was only an arm's length below the ledge, which was when he gave a huge thrust with his legs and threw his arms up and over—*and into a gory mess*!

With one leg cocked on the ledge he reared instinctively back… and barely managed to hang by his fingertips as his leg slipped and the full weight of his huge frame fell on his hands. A ghost, of course, he knew that even hanging there—a mass of blood and squashed guts and brain—and an arm, and a clenched hand with the thumb pointing down… There had been a flattened grin on the face of the lich, and for an instant Kank Thad had thought to hear a mouse-like squeak of disapproval. Veth Nuss!

Slowly, a monstrous fear clutching his heart, the great Northman pulled himself up and peeped over the lip of the ledge. Nothing! Just a hard shelf of rock with a few pebbles. Wearily the barbarian hauled himself up and lay full-length where the lich of Veth Nuss had stretched in ruptured loathsomeness only a few heartbeats earlier.

Now Kank Thad had had two warnings, and he knew what to expect of the rest of his climb.

Ghosts?... Damn them all, for no lifeless ghost could ever harm a man of warm flesh and hot blood! What he must do was simply...*ignore* the things, should any more of them appear. If only they wouldn't come at such inopportune moments!

But try as he might the barbarian could not ignore them, and toward the end of his tremendous climb he came across at least a dozen more. Swart Yhemni slavers from the distant East; grisly, bearded Northmen, fathers of buxom daughters lost to Kank Thad's wiles and lusts; taverners who'd called time far too early for a barbarian's thirst, or denied him credit in the first place—many of them. And so there should be, for the scarfaced Northman was an old hand at murder and all of these ghosts had been his victims...

Far below, Thamiel's suspense was almost too great to bear. The afternoon was drawing out and his flabby neck ached with the strain of peering upwards through his glass. Even to that instrument the climbing savage was now only a fly, and Thamiel gave a shrill cry of disbelief and frustrated rage as he saw that fly suddenly merge with the high horizon of the Ghost Cliffs of Shildakor. Kank Thad had done it!—the barbarian had climbed the mile-high cliffs!

He had indeed, and his great lungs banged away in his chest and his great muscles throbbed and ached as he rested his elbows atop the nightmare abyss. His eyes swam and the sweat stood hot on his forehead; but not for long, for here a cool wind constantly blew from the east, blowing sand and grit in his eyes and bringing a final curtain of fog from the unseen valleys and unknown places beyond.

"I, Kank Thad, have done it!" the savage roared to the world. "What no man ever did before, that I—" He opened and closed his mouth, hanging on his elbows, peering into the mist. Then he shook his head and with a worried grin recommenced his broken cries of victory and self-esteem. "That I have—"

His boasting finally gurgled into a choked silence and the wind keened into his bared teeth...

Eyes bugging, the barbarian saw the horror lurch from out of the mist, saw the thing that had been a man crumple to its knees while still advancing, saw it reach out for him with jerking, crooked fingers and heard the agonised, rasping rattle of its throat. Clad in a bronze and leather breastplate, in thonged sandals and a leaden kirtle, it came—and its green features were twisted in eternal agony and its eyes blazed with the red light of revenge.

"Yib!" the barbarian croaked, and then: "Get you gone, Theen of Vilthod's Guard! I know you, lich—and you're impotent to harm me in death even as you were in life. Aye, and for that matter impotent of all else!"

Yet still the shade came on, shuffling on its knees before the Northman who fell back until once again he was hanging by his fingertips only. Blood flowed freely from between the horror's thighs, ghost-blood that yet splashed Kank Thad's face and ran scarlet down his straining arms, lich-blood that yet wetted the smooth rock of the cliff and made it slippery to the barbarian's fingers. In his mind's eye the terrified Northman saw himself once more in the tavern of Hethica Nid, and for the first time he recognised the monstrousness of the drunken atrocity he had perpetrated there. More freely yet ran the blood from the apparition's violated loins, wetter the rocks and slimier still.

"Oh, Gutrip!" the barbarian moaned once. "Why did you let me use you so?"—with which his fingers slipped in the blood and his great back arched in a death-embracing rigor and his eyes closed to shut out forever that ancient world.

And his body fell with the speed of one of those stars that slide down the heavens at night...

A mile below, Thamiel broke into a little dance and chortled and slapped his fat thighs, flinging his glass away in his complete exuberance and finally giggling hysterically. It had looked like the barbarian had won, and then, for no reason apparent in his glass, the great savage had fallen. Oh, how he laughed and stamped his feet.

Then, remembering his Imperishable and Immaculate Justice, he puffed himself up, set his scarlet turban a trifle more correctly upon his head—and quickly got out of the way.

And a few seconds later Kank Thad returned to Bhur-Esh.

The Sorcerer's Book

I, Teh Atht of Klühn, having ofttimes conversed with my wizard ancestor, Mylakhrion of Tharamoon (dead these eleven hundred years), now tell the tale of how that mighty mage was usurped by his apprentice, Exior K'mool. At least, history has always supposed that he was usurped.

The story begins some fifty-three years before Mylakhrion's demise, at the fortress city Humquass on Theem'hdra's eastern strand, where that oldest and craftiest of sorcerers was the then resident mage, answerable only to the King himself. Humquass is no more, swept away by tides of time and war and Nature, but the legends live on.

I

Now in that day Humquass was a warrior city and its King, Morgath, was a warrior King; and the walls of the city were high and wide, with great towers where the soldiers were garrisoned; and the King's territories extended to the south, even to the Hrossak border which Morgath would push back if he had his way. For the King hungered for those southern lands and his warrior's heart ached for a kingdom which would enclose not only Hrossa to the River Luhr, but Yhemnis too. And Morgath would send ships across the Straits of Yhem to annex even Shadarabar, the island stronghold of savage black pirates.

As for Mylakhrion: he had served the King for fifteen years, since that time when first he came out of the west and across the mountains into Morgath's fierce kingdom. Aye, and in his way Mylakhrion had been a faithful servant, though truth to tell there were those who wondered who served whom.

For Mylakhrion's palace was greater than the King's—though far less opulent—and where Morgath received common men, Mylakhrion would receive none at all. The mage's familiars gave audience in his stead, speaking with Mylakhrion's voice and in his manner, but any emergence of the sorcerer himself was a singularly rare thing. Indeed, the very sight of Mylakhrion abroad and active in the topmost turrets of his palace tower—no less than the passing of comets across the sky or eclipses of the sun and moon—was almost invariably taken as portent of great wonders...and sometimes of dooms and disasters. And lesser mages seized upon such sightings, reading strange weirds into the wizard's ways, what little was known of them.

One thing which was known for a certainty was Mylakhrion's great age; not his actual age in years, but the fact that he was far older than any other living man. So thin as to be skeletal—with wrinkles to number against his years upon a skin of veined parchment pale as moonbeams—and with a long, tapering beard almost uniformly white, the wizard *was* ancient. Grandfathers could remember their grandfathers whispering of sorcerous deeds ascribed to his hand or wand when they themselves were mere children; and it was known for a fact that a previous apprentice of Mylakhrion's, one Azatta Leet, had recently died in Chlangi at an estimated age of one hundred and eleven years!

But in general the sorcerer's astonishing longevity was not much mentioned. People were mindful of his magnitude—and of Morgath's dependence upon him—and it was deemed neither moot nor even wise to probe too deeply into the hows, whys and wherefores of his attainment to so great an age. For all that he was ancient, still the mage's mind was brilliantly clear, his eyes undimmed and his sorceries (benevolent or otherwise) marvellous and utterly unfathomable to adepts of lesser learning. Moreover, he might not take kindly to allegations of vampirism and the like, practised to extend to eternity his existence in the world of men.

And in their thinking and their muted whisperings, the wizard's would-be compeers came close to the truth; for in his long search for immortality Mylakhrion had indeed performed many morbid magicks, though mercifully vampirism was not numbered amongst them. That is not to say he would *not* be a vampire if in that way he might prolong his life or regain his lost youth, but he knew better than that. No, for vampires were far too restricted and their lives in constant danger from attendant perils. Besides which, they were not truly immortal, not as Mylakhrion desired to be. He wanted to live forever, not to be eternally undead—or if not eternally, at least until the stake should find his heart.

On many occasions that master of magick had believed himself close to hitting upon the correct formula for immortality, that at last his feet were set upon the right path, but in the hour of his supposed triumph always he had been frustrated. He had prolonged his life far beyond the normal span, most certainly, but still he had grown old and must eventually die. And in any case, who would wish to live forever in a defunct body?

Now, knowing that his years were narrowing down, his search was more desperate and his disappointments deeper as days passed into years and the solution drew no closer. Now, too, he saw his coming to Humquass as an error; for while Morgath protected him and provided for his purely physical needs, his demands upon him grew more and more tiresome and consumed far too much of his time. Of which he might not have a great deal left.

For being a warrior King and going often to war, Morgath was constantly in need of favourable forecasts for his battle plans. Too, he sought for dark omens against his enemies, and he was no less interested in their stars than in his own. What with prognostications and astrological readings, auguries and auspices, personal weirds and bodements in general, Mylakhrion had not the time he required for his own all-important interests and darkling devotions.

Nor could the King's business be kept waiting, for the Hrossaks and Yhemnis had their wizards too, and Mylakhrion was required to turn aside the monstrous maledictions and outrageous runes which these enemy mages were wont to cast against Humquass and its King. Black Yoppaloth of the Yhemnis, a sorcerer of no mean prowess, was particularly pernicious; likewise Loxzor of the Hrossaks; and so it can be seen that Mylakhrion was hard put to attend his many duties, let alone pursue his own ambitions. And perhaps that would explain, too, Mylakhrion's reasons for sticking so close to his apartments. Why, his duties were such as to make him virtually a prisoner there!

And yet Mylakhrion had prospered under Morgath and so felt a certain gratitude toward him. Moreover, he liked the King for his intelligence. Aye, for intelligent kings were singularly rare in that day, particularly warrior-kings. And so the sorcerer felt he must not simply desert Morgath and leave him to the mercies of his equally warlike neighbours, and his frustration continued to grow within him.

Until the dawning of a certain idea…

Now among the city's common wizards—real and assumed—there dwelled one Exior K'mool, a talented apprentice of Phaithor Ull before that mage rendered himself as green dust in an ill-conceived thaumaturgical experiment. A seer whose betokenings showed promise despite the fact that as yet they remained undeveloped, essentially Exior was oneiromantic. His dreams were prophetic and generally accurate.

And it came to pass that Exior dreamed a dream in which Mylakhrion took an apprentice to assist him in his sorceries, and Exior himself was the chosen one and rose to great power in Theem'hdra in the service of Morgath, King of Humquass. Upon awakening he remembered the dream and smiled wryly to himself, for he believed his vision had been born of wishful thinking and was in no way a portent of any real or foreseeable future. But then, a day or two later, Mylakhrion made it known that indeed he sought a young assistant…

Exior's heart soared like a bird when first he heard this news; alas, for a little while only. For how could Exior—a ragged street-magician who sold charms and love potions for a living and divined the futile dreams of his penniless patrons for mere crusts of bread—possibly apply for a position as apprentice to Mylakhrion the Mighty? The idea was preposterous! And so, however reluctantly, he put aside the notion and forced himself to consider his vision as purely coincidental to Mylakhrion's requirement.

And as days passed into weeks so Mylakhrion gave audience to many young men who presented themselves as prospective employees. As usual, the interviews were carried out through his familiars (though many applicants got no farther than Mylakhrion's gate) while the wizard, unseen by those aspirants who were actually allowed to pass into his palace, busied himself with more pressing matters in hidden rooms. In this way, many who might have impressed quite favourably confronted by a merely human interviewer—even by so awe-inspiring a man as Mylakhrion—found themselves completely overwhelmed in the presence of his familiar creatures; for these were three great bats whose faces were those of men!

Indeed, they had once been men, those fearsome familiars; wizards who had formed a sorcerous triad to crush Mylakhrion when he refused to join them. Unfortunately for them, his talents had been greater than all of theirs combined, hence their hybridisation. That had been many years ago, however, before ever he came to Humquass, and Mylakhrion had all but forgotten the details of the thing. He trusted his familiars implicitly; and besides, they had only the faces of his old enemies. Their minds were their own, or Mylakhrion's when he chose to use them as he now used them.

Finally, when even the older, failed magicians of Morgath's lands began to present themselves at Mylakhrion's gate, Exior K'mool dreamed again; and in his dream he saw the man-faced bats nodding to him in unison before bidding him enter Mylakhrion's inner sanctum, where that Master of Mages was waiting to hand him his robe of apprenticeship. That was enough.

At dawn of the next day Exior dressed himself in his finest jacket and breeches—the ones with only a few minor repairs—and made his way tortuously through the mazy streets of Humquass to the walls of Mylakhrion's palace. There, at the great gate, he timorously took his place behind three others and waited...but not for long. A small barred window opened in a door in the gate and each of the other aspirants was cursorily dismissed in his turn. Seeing this, Exior began to turn away, at which point a voice stopped him. It was the voice of the man whose face peered through the barred window, and it said:

"Young man, what is your name?"

"K'mool," said Exior stepping warily forward. "Exior K'mool."

"And do you seek employment with Mylakhrion?"

"I do," he answered, wondering at the echoing and sepulchral quality of the man's voice. "I desire to be...to be the mage's apprentice."

"You seem uncertain."

"I am certain enough," said Exior, "but I wonder—"

"If you are worthy?"

"Perhaps." He nodded nervously.

"My master likes humility in men," said the face at the window. "Aye, and honesty, too. Enter, Exior K'mool."

The door in the gate opened soundlessly and Exior took a deep breath as he stepped over its sill. He expelled the air in a loud gasp as the door closed behind him, and glancing about wide-eyed he was almost startled into flight at sight of the things he now saw. But where to flee? Where a moment before the sky had been blue and the sun warm, now, seen from this grey courtyard, the heavens were dark with racing clouds and a chill wind ruffled the fur-covered body of...of the bat-thing whose man's face had spoken from the window in the gate!

"Do you fear Mylakhrion's familiar, Exior K'mool?" asked the great bat-thing. "Or are you alarmed at the season here, which is ever different to that outside."

"A little of both, sir, I fancy," Exior finally managed.

The bat-thing laughed a loud, baying laugh and flapped aloft. "Fear not," it boomed, hovering in the air, "but follow behind me and you shall see what you shall see."

Exior gritted his teeth, put his fear behind him and strode after the creature across the windswept courtyard to enter into the palace proper: a stark and massive building of huge basaltic blocks with openings like black mouths which seemed to grimace hideously. Following the flap of membranous wings, he mounted corkscrew stairs of stone within a tower whose base must surely be big as the tavern where Exior lodged; and soon, arriving at a landing, he found the freakish familiar waiting for him before an entrance whose arch was carved with all the signs of the zodiac. Now, as the creature hopped across the threshold, he followed into a vast room whose contents held him spellbound in a single instant of time.

Mylakhrion's familiar settled itself upon a high perch, where it hung upside down the better to observe Exior's astonished reactions. After a little while it said: "And are my master's possessions of interest to you, young man?"

"Indeed they are!" the youth gasped, his jaw ajar and his eyes gazing in ghastly fascination all about the room. Why, if the contents of this single room were his, even Exior K'mool could be a mighty magician!

For here were scattered all the appurtenances of Mylakhrion's art, every sort and description of occult apparatus. There were acromegalic skulls of monstrous men and shocking skeletons of things which never had been men; strangely shaped phials and bottles filled with quiescent or bubbling liquids of golden, green or dark hues, all of a usage utterly unknown to Exior; bagpipes made of ebony and ivory and the cured intestinal sacks of dragons, whose music was doubtless used in the propitiation of certain demons; shelf upon shelf of books bound in brown leathers and yellow skins, and at least one whose umber bindings bore—Exior would swear to it—the purplish mottlings of tattoos!

Here too were miniature spheres of alien worlds and moons, mapped out and inlaid with cryptic runes of gold and silver; and all slowly turning where they hung from the fretted ceiling on ropes of tiny cowries. And here pentacles of power adorning the mosaic walls and floor, glowing with the inner fire of the gem-chips from which they were constructed. And sigil-inscribed scrolls of vellum upon a marble table, together with a silver-framed magnifier, an astrolabe, calipers and tiny bronze weights. And central in the room and resting alone upon a small stand of carved chrysolite, a great ball of clouded crystal.

The workshop of Theem'hdra's greatest wizard, thought Exior— his entire library too—and all in this one room! But as if divining his very thoughts, the perch-hung chiropteran shook its head. "Nay, lad," the creature said, "for this is only one tenth of a tenth part of all my master's mysteries. I am his most trusted familiar, and yet there are rooms here which I have never entered, and others I would not even dare to seek out! Nay, this is merely his room of repose."

"And am I...am I to see...*him*?" Exior asked.

"If you are so fortunate to be chosen as his apprentice, certainly you shall see him. Daily. Perhaps too often! He shall instruct you thus and thus, and you shall do so and so. And if you are quick to learn, one day you may even grow mighty as Mylakhrion himself."

"I meant," said Exior, "am I to see him...now?"

"That depends..." the creature answered, and went on: "But now there are things I must ask you, Exior K'mool, and you shall answer truthfully to each and every question."

Exior nodded and Mylakhrion's familiar demon continued: "Good! Then answer me this: why do you seek this position?"

"I would study under the greatest mage in all the land," Exior answered at once. "Also my master would know how best to employ my own minor talents."

"And what are those talents?"

"I scry the future in dreams," said Exior. "Aye, and my dreams have never lied to me."

"Never?" The sepulchral tones of the bat-thing seemed honed with a certain scepticism.

"I have common dreams like any man; but there are special dreams, too, and when they come to me I can usually recognise them."

"And is that all you are, a dreamer?"

The blood began to burn in Exior's face, but he felt less humbled than angry. "I also translate tongues, read runes and fathom cyphers," he snapped. "My seer's eyes scry the meanings of even the most obscure languages, glyphs and cryptograms."

"Is that all?" The creature's voice was cold as deep, dark oceans of ice, drawing all of the heat out of Exior in a moment.

"I...I mix potent potions, and—"

"Love potions?" The bat-thing seemed almost to sneer.

Exior knew when he was beaten. Furious, he turned on his heel to leave the room, the tower, Mylakhrion's palace, the whole ridiculous idea behind him—and found his way blocked by two more giant chiropters. They did not speak but merely stood as statues in the arched entrance, their men's faces observing through speculative eyes Exior where he paused in confusion.

Finally, from behind the youth, the inverted one spoke again: "He who acts in haste often acts foolishly—and regrets at leisure. How do you answer that?"

Exior turned sharply upon his examiner. "He who accepts insults and taunts from his inferiors is an even bigger fool!" he hotly retorted.

The bat-thing righted itself upon its perch. "And do you consider Mylakhrion's favourite familiar your...inferior?" Its voice was the merest whisper now—the *hiss* of a dry leaf blown across a graveyard slab—but its human eyes were bright, hard and unblinking.

"That face you wear," said Exior K'mool, his words coming cracked from a throat suddenly dry as dust, "once sat upon a man's shoulders. Fool I may be, but my life and limbs are my own and I speak with my own voice. In short, I am still a man—and better a foolish man than some hybrid horror spawned of a wizard's—" And there he broke off, for the three were laughing at him, baying dinningly where they faced him, their booming laughter echoing loudly in the great room.

Astonished, and because there seemed little else to do, Exior waited until they were done and the one on the perch once more addressed him. "Mylakhrion," the creature finally informed him with a strange smile, "likes humility and honesty in a man, as I believe I have mentioned aforetime. He also likes a little spunkiness, on occasion—but not too much, for that might be mistaken for audacity. Forwardness and fools he will not suffer, but cowardice he abhors! You have done well, Exior K'mool—and now my master will see you."

And all three familiars nodded as one creature, just as Exior had seen it in his dream.

"Seer, be seated," said Mylakhrion, and the youth at once recognised his voice as being one and the same with that of the bat-thing.

Mylakhrion sat upon his night-black throne and studied Exior minutely, coldly, with no emotion whatever visible in his straight-backed mien. His silver eyebrows were thin and turned sharply upward at the temples, and beneath them his eyes were of that same palest blue as the Outer Immensities glimpsed ofttimes by Exior in his dreams. Strange those eyes and almost vacuous, but at the same time filled with terrible lore and a knowledge forbidden to common men and middling mages alike.

His hands, where they protruded from the bell-like cuffs of his robe and rested upon the arms of his throne, were long and thin and their nails sharply pointed; their colour, as that of his much wrinkled face and sandaled feet, was a pale umber like unto certain parchments. A cold old man, Mylakhrion, and his gaze even colder. He trained that gaze upon Exior as the youth sat down upon a tiny stool close to the somewhat raised dais where sat the sorcerer himself.

The apartment was starkly bare in comparison with that "room of repose" wherefrom Exior had been guided to this even loftier chamber. It had a balcony with a balustrade of marble gargoyles, opening upon a frightfully vertiginous view (a wintry vista, despite the true season) of some drear and windswept desert where mounds of rubble hinted of extensive ruins. Exior did not recognise the scene, and he was sure that it lay not anywhere in the vicinity of Humquass.

Now there was no king in all Theem'hdra who would normally allow the house of a common man to overshadow his own; but Mylakhrion was distinctly uncommon, and besides, he required a place higher than any other to facilitate his far-seeing, and for the propitiation of elementals of the air; and so Morgath had never voiced complaint. But the plain fact of the matter was that the sorcerer liked to be remote from mundane men; and where better than high in this forbidding and precipitous palace tower, this veritable aerie of a room?

Exior had been brought here by the three familiars, and their spokesman had accompanied him into the room through great brazen doors. Once Exior was safe inside, however, the bat-thing had quickly departed; whereupon Mylakhrion had appeared from the balcony to climb the three small steps of the dais to his throne of polished jet.

Now in that dim and sparsely furnished place, with only the light from the balcony to relieve the gloom—and that a dim and dingy light—Exior K'mool and Mylakhrion the Mighty gazed each upon the other, would-be wizard and Supreme Sorcerer alike. And whatever the thoughts of the youth in the presence of this legended enchanter, they were soon cut short as Mylakhrion commenced his own examination.

"So, young man, and you would be my apprentice, would you? Well, then, there is more I must know about you; what suffices for my familiars may not satisfy me. First let me tell you of the work, and then you must say if you are still interested; after which and depending upon your decision, I may ask you to perform a small task for me. If you perform well—and *only* if the task is completed to my satisfaction—then you shall be my apprentice. That may be to look too far ahead, however, for you might not care much for the work."

Mylakhrion paused for long moments and turned his strange eyes to the grey, racing clouds beyond the gargoyle balusters. The sharp nail of one of his fingers tapped for a little while, thoughtfully, upon the hard arm of his throne. Then, without returning his gaze to Exior, finally the wizard said:

"The hours will be long, and when there are not enough of them for any one day I shall make more. Never have nothing to do. And you must put aside fear; I have no room for it. There will be liches here to take horrid advantage of one who is afraid, for I am a necromancer. But as well as the dead, I call up spirits black and white, demons and devils and saints alike. I hold intercourse with ghouls, gaunts and wraiths, with werewolves, gnomes and jinnees; aye, for there is much to be learned from them. And remember: just as idle hands wither, so slothful minds mortify. I converse at length with Demogorgon; from time to time I sleep with succubus and have fathered lamia, harpy, vampire and elf. And all of them—my wives, children and changelings—they occasionally visit me. They call me master, and so shall you, and I am a *hard* taskmaster. Tasks are not allowed to remain unperformed; nothing which may be done today is ever done tomorrow. And for all that I have done; still I am unchanged. Aged, yes, but a man still—and mortal! And I seek immortality, Exior K'mool, which is why you are here: to lessen the burden and save time for me. For once time is fled, who may recall it? And again I say to you, remember: stitches in time save myriads! You will assist me not alone in many small tasks—be my messenger, potwatcher, my sweeper, linguist, my rune-reader, seer—but in great works and experiments also. And of all my knowledge shall you partake, learning and growing wise in the ways of magick. BUT—" (and abruptly the wizard paused, leaving Exior breathless as if he himself had spoken all of these words) "a warning! Never *never* seek to subvert my cause, change my course or deliberately and maliciously do anything to cause me discomfort, neither of mind nor of body! And if you are a good apprentice, then, when I am no more—" And again he paused.

In a little while, as Exior sat and fought to still his trembling, Mylakhrion turned his eyes back to the youth. "And are you still interested?"

Unable to find words, Exior merely nodded.

II

As **night drew** on and the sun sank down behind the mountains, Exior smelled a great storm blowing up and hurriedly sought shelter. He tethered his yak just within the mouth of a small cave hidden in the lee of wind-carved crags, then carefully checked to ensure that this was not the lair of some wild beast. Grumbling as he worked and occasionally cursing, he lighted a fire in a hollow place and brewed himself a pot of tea.

Six months ago he had looked back from his tail-end position in an escorted caravan leaving Humquass and smiled as he watched the walls of the city slowly merging into the southern horizon; since when he had not smiled a great deal, had faced dangers galore and covered thousands of miles in the performance of Mylakhrion's "small task"— which still remained unperformed. Now Exior had reached the end of his ability to endure any more hardship, the end of his tether, and he ought also to have reached the end of his journey. But...

"Go west," Mylakhrion had instructed him. "Cross the Eastern Peaks, pass between the Nameless Desert and the Mountains of Lohmi, follow the sun over wide and rolling plains to the foothills of the Great Circle Mountains, and there turn your feet northward. Keeping the foothills on your left hand, follow the edge of the plain and in the space of two days you will find a city lost in the desert sands.

"At the edge of the city's ruins lying closest to the foothills, there you will spy the broken fang of a once great tower, and in its base a door. Now listen carefully, Exior K'mool, for this is most important. Deep beneath the tumbled tower, hidden in a catacomb of caves, there within a secret chamber you will find a Great Book. It is locked and lies upon a pedestal of onyx. Bring me that book, Exior K'mool, and thereafter be known as Mylakhrion's apprentice!

"But know too, young man, that the dangers will be many and the way long and hard... Now, how do you say?"

Once more, like a fool, Exior had agreed; and shortly thereafter he joined a caravan heading north. After eight days he left the caravan and struck out over the eastern range, crossing in a week. Another month took him to the Nameless Desert, and another saw him in the long grasses of the central plains. There his horse was bitten by an adder and he was obliged to proceed on foot. Two more months and autumn was drawing to a close; and now along with winter the Great Circle Mountains loomed, in whose foothills Exior met with friendly nomads and bought from them his yak. Five more weeks took him to the borders of the Desert of Ell, and for three days now he had been wandering north-west between desert and foothills.

By now he should have sighted Mylakhrion's lost city, but so far it remained lost. Lost, too, Exior K'mool, if he continued for very much longer with his quest. His water was low, food down to crusts; there was little or no grass for his beast—which in any case was old and tired—and worst of all the days were growing shorter and the skies darker with the rapid approach of winter. Indeed, before finding his refuge for the night, Exior had recognised the bleak and wintry landscape as that seen from Mylakhrion's tower room, and the clouds which fled ever south were those same clouds he had thought peculiar to the sky over the sorcerer's palace. Obviously Mylakhrion had spied out the way for him; why, then, had he failed to find the lost city?

That night, dreaming, the youth saw a great fang of stone rising from drifted sand and tumbled blocks. His dream was recurrent, but each time his slumbering spirit approached the visioned pile so the howling gale would startle him to wakefulness in his blanket, that or the cry of his frightened beast where it stood trembling in the lightning-illumined door of the cave. Mercifully the storm's direction was away from Exior's refuge, for its fury was such that it moved a vast amount of sand and both man and beast might easily have been entombed.

As it was, rising cold, tired and hungry from his troubled and fitful slumbers, Exior saw that the storm had blown itself out; also that he had been presumptuous to doubt those directions given him by Mylakhrion. For now, where great waves of sand had stretched to the horizon, the scattered remnants of a once mighty city lay uncovered to his bleary gaze. And not far off, within a stone's throw, a certain shattered spire drew his eyes as a northstone draws a nail. Without doubt this was that tower of which Mylakhrion had foretold, beneath which Exior would find the maze of caves and eventually the secret chamber and volume of ancient magick!

The youth fed himself and his beast as best he could, drank a little from his leather bottle and dampened the yak's nose and mouth, then walked the animal beneath wintry morning skies to the base of the crumbling but still massive monument. Alas, in the sand drifted against its base he could find no door; but above, almost within reach, fallen blocks revealed a dark hole somewhat wider than his shoulders.

Now before proceeding any farther, Exior made a pause and gave some thought to one other thing Mylakhrion had told him. There might well be a "guard," the ancient magician had warned, a spirit or demon set to watch over the secret room and its book; for the book contained such powerful magick that whosoever possessed it could make himself mighty above all men. It had belonged to a great sorcerer and necromancer, that book, but in a war of wizardry he had been obliged to flee the city in the desert and the book had been left behind. Even as he fled, the city was brought to a great ruin by his enemies, and thus it had remained to this day.

That had all been more than five hundred years ago, however, and only recently, through his own thaumaturgies, had Mylakhrion discovered again the lost city and fathomed its ancient secrets. And by now the "guard," if indeed such existed, must be much diminished through time and disuse; and surely Exior should have no trouble with a magick grown so small and centuries-shrivelled...

Well, perhaps not; but nevertheless Exior frowned worriedly as he made torches, piled stones and finally climbed until he could squeeze in through the hole in the wall of the tower. Cobwebby gloom met his eyes, and dusty, spiralling steps that wound down into darkness.

He took one last look out through the hole at the drear landscape of tumbled blocks and fallen, shattered pillars—a landscape which now seemed much more friendly than the gloomy bowels of this ages-old tower—lighted a torch and commenced his descent.

Round and down he went, brushing aside or burning cobwebs out of his way; and tiny scurrying things moved aside for him, and dust trickled from ledges where the centuries had piled it; and only the gloom and the winding steps descending ever deeper into bowels of fetid earth…

After what seemed an inordinately long time, Exior reached the bottom and found himself in a great cavern whose walls were honeycombed with tunnels and caves. On guard against whatever might be lurking down here, he was making to explore the largest of these passages when a great rumbling roar froze him in his tracks. A belch of animal fury, the warning had issued from that very tunnel he had been on the point of entering. Trembling in every limb, Exior lighted a second torch and stuck it in the sandy floor, then drew his sword and waited for whatever it was that prowled these eerie excavations: doubtless that "guard" of which Mylakhrion had forewarned.

In a little while the demon appeared and jerked forward on spindly legs into the central hall. Half-spider, half-bat that being, and twice as big as a man to boot. With curving fangs like white scythes, and eyes big as saucers, the thing loomed over Exior and glared down at him; and finally, with a voice that rumbled volcanically and brimstony breath, it spoke:

"What do ye here, little man? This is a forbidden place. Begone!"

Exior shook his head in dumb defiance and held out his torch and sword before him. And finding his voice, he said: "I run an errand for my master, and you shall not stop me."

"And what is the nature of your errand?" questioned the demon.

"To find a room and a runebook," said Exior with many a gulp. "Also, to take that book back to my master."

"I know room and book both!" the creature answered. "Aye, and I guard them well. Wherefore it is plainly my duty to eat ye…or would ye care to play a game with me?"

"A game?" replied Exior, who vastly preferred any alternative to being eaten.

"Ye shall have a choice," the demon explained. "Go now and I shall do ye no harm, but if ye stay ye must play my game. If ye win the game ye may take the book and I at last may rest—but if ye lose..."

"Then?" Exior prompted, his heart in his mouth.

"Why, then I shall eat ye!" answered the monster with a great coughing laugh.

"And what is the nature of this game?" asked Exior, wondering where best to strike the beast to bring it down, and whether he had the strength for such a stroke.

"I shall say ye a riddle," the demon replied, "and ye must tell me its meaning."

Now Exior's mind grew alert as he readied it for the trial; for there never had been a riddle or rune whose meaning eluded him for long, and despite his great fear he could not refuse the demon's challenge. "So be it," he said, "let's hear your riddle."

The spider-bat laughed again, then very rapidly and in a loud, clear monotone said:

"TI DNAMMOC I...MOOR TERCES EHT OT EM DAEL DNA, ERA YLLAER UOY SA UOY EES EM TEL WON, EMAG EHT NOW GNIVAH...EM MRAH TON YAM DNA NOISULLI ERA UOY... SESSENKAEW RUOY DNA, NOMED UOY WONK I!"

To which Exior at once and excitedly replied, "My answer is: *'I know you demon, and your weaknesses. You are illusion and may not harm me. Having won the game, now let me see you as you really are, and lead me to the secret room. I command it!'*"

The demon gave a great cry (of relief, Exior suspected) and immediately shrank down into the shape of a tiny lizard which wriggled away into the mouth of one of the tunnels. It paused to look back, whereupon Exior lighted a third torch and followed on behind. In a little while the lizard led the way to a door of brass and squeezed beneath it. When Exior shoved the door open on squeaking hinges, the tiny creature had disappeared.

The room was circular, domed and starkly bare; except for its pedestal of onyx and the Great Book which lay upon it, thick with the dust of five long centuries and more. Quickly Exior crossed to the pedestal and laid his trembling hands upon the great, jewel-crusted cover. He blew away the dust and gazed awestruck at old leather inlaid with ivory, jade, gold and fabulous gems; and at the hasps and lock, green with age and neglect; and last but not least at the weirdly-wrought key where it lay beside the priceless volume.

And he remembered what Mylakhrion had told him: that in this book were writ the secrets of suns and moons, times past and times as yet unborn, and all the wonders of wizards dead and gone and the lore of darkling dimensions beyond the familiar three. Knowledge enough to make a man mighty above all other men. And Exior picked up the key and turned it protestingly in the ancient lock.

Then, as he began to lift the heavy cover—

Runes graven in the onyx pedestal caught his eye, and he let the cover fall back upon pages unseen. The glyphs were rare, obscure as the ages, and writ in a cypher to bedazzle the mind of any but a master cryptographer born. Such was Exior K'mool.

Brows drawn together in concentration, lips moving silently as they traced strange words, by the light of his fitful torch he read the runes. Then, lighting yet another torch the better to see, he read them again—and snatched back his hand from where it rested upon the sorcerer's book. For the message was very clear: that without a certain protection, the essence of any man brash or foolish enough to read the book would be torn from him, leaving him empty and foolish and bereft of mind, will and soul!

The protection, however, was comparatively simple: it was a moon-rune, rare but well enough known to Exior, designed to propitiate the protective power of Mnomquah, God of the Moon and of Madness, known commonly as Gleeth. And now the youth knew that indeed the book's secrets were marvellous and monstrous, for Gleeth is a god who from his celestial seat sees and therefore knows all; and his moon-runes are correspondingly powerful.

Without hesitation Exior said the rune out loud, and when the echoes of his voice had died away he opened the forbidden volume to the first page. There, in rubric pigments which yet glowed despite the inexorable trickle of time's sands, the warning was repeated: that Gleeth's protection be sought before reading. Since he had already availed himself of the necessary precaution, Exior turned the next page, which bore no signature but commenced straightway with words of baleful might, and with bated breath he began to read...

For long and long Exior read the book, and when his torches were finished he carried it up to the light; and for two days he read on and for two nights he sat and considered and did not sleep. He gave the patient yak his last crust, the last of his water, and on the morning of the third day closed the book and locked it. Then he stood up beside the ruined tower and looked all about at the drear desert and the sand-sundered city.

His eyes were pale now and chill, with shadows beneath, which were dark above the parchment of his cheeks. And his hair, no longer jet but grey; and his entire mien that of an old man heavy-burdened with wisdom and knowledge and sin, while yet his back was straight and his limbs young.

For an hour he stood thus, then turned to his yak. Alas, the poor beast lay dead and a vulture picked at its eye, which was torn by the bird's beak. Angered, Exior said a word—a single *word*—and the vulture gave a startled cry and sprang aloft, falling lifeless in the next instant. And the yak shook its head, got to its feet and gazed upon its master. It gazed with one dim old yak's eye, and one which was sharp and bright and that of a vulture.

Then Exior tied the book to his saddle and mounted himself upon his beast's back, and so he left the Desert of Ell and made for home...

III

Three months and three weeks later, a stranger in a cowled cloak and riding upon a blinkered yak arrived at the gates of Humquass beneath its beetling walls. Without any of the usual formalities (for which gross inefficiency he must later make blustered and only half-believed excuses) the Commander of the Guard raised the gate and let the stranger in; and Exior—for such it was, as well you know—went straight to the palace of Mylakhrion.

There the gate in the wall opened at his approach and he passed through without hindrance, tethering his beast in the wizard's courtyard. And where beyond the city's walls all was early spring and the trees budding and flowers burgeoning into bloom, here a midsummer sun blazed down and the heat was stifling where lizards lazed atop white walled gardens of gardenias.

Exior paused not before this wonder nor even considered it, but entered the main tower where waited Mylakhrion's familiars. They gazed upon them, and he upon them; and then they bowed down low before him and let him pass. And so he mounted the stone-hewn stairs to seek out Mylakhrion in his lofty lair.

On this occasion, however, he had no need of ascending to so great a height, for Mylakhrion pottered in his room of repose. There Exior found him, and there the mage gave him greeting of a sort.

"Ho, Exior K'mool! So, you are returned to me at last, and just as I began to suspect that some ill had befallen you. And do you bring me the fruits of your quest?"

Exior said nothing but merely stared at the master mage, observing him curiously and with mixed emotions through his changed eyes. He threw back his cowl to show locks grey as Arctic oceans above a face almost pale as that of Mylakhrion himself. Then he approached a table and brushed its surface free from clutter, placing his linen-wrapped parcel centrally and untying its fastenings. And laying back the coverings he displayed the Great Book, and as Mylakhrion drew nigh he gave him the key.

Now the sorcerer's silver eyebrows rose a little; and without questioning Exior's silence or his strangely altered appearance, he took the key, opened the book and turned back its jewel-crusted cover. Then—

Mylakhrion frowned and his briefly risen eyebrows fell down low again over suddenly narrowed eyes. He turned his gaze to Exior and gloomed upon him, saying: "Youth, the first page is torn out! Do you see the broken edge, the riven vellum?"

And now, in a voice fully frosty as that of his master, Exior answered, "Aye, I have noted it."

"Hmph!" The enchanter seemed disgruntled and a little disappointed, but in another moment his curiosity returned. "So be it," he said, "for what is one leaf on the tree of all dark knowledge?"

Now during his journey home Exior had made a diabolic decision. As can be seen, he had determined to be done with Mylakhrion
and so had torn out from the book the opening admonition. He
reasoned thus: that having read the book he now had power to
become mighty above all men, even above Mylakhrion himself.
There would be no room for two such sorcerers in Humquass,
wherefore the greybeard must go. And what better instrument of
an abrupt assassination than this fearful, ruin-recovered volume of
morbid magicks?

Unsuspecting and unprotected, Mylakhrion would read, and the
book would bind him in its spell, crush him, destroy him utterly. For
if the power of the thing were such as to seize upon Exior's spirit, sap
the colour from his hair and flesh and sear his very soul—and him
protected!—how then would the venerable Mylakhrion fare, all frail
with age and weighted down with the burden of his unguessed years?

Well, he had lived long enough, and his release would be a kindness of a sort. And anyway, the awakened Exior would make a poor
apprentice, who possessed power at least the equal of his supposed
master. So let Mylakhrion read and bid him farewell, and then
announce to the city the presence of a new and still more powerful
mage in the palace of the sorcerer.

Thus had Exior plotted and now he stood upon the threshold of
his destiny; and the book was open and Mylakhrion sat before it at
the table; and as that self-confessed necromancer began to read out
loud, so Exior shuddered as were he dead and felt the furtive tread
of ghouls on the soft earth above. An icy fist seemed closed around
his heart and a question burned in his brain. How then was he
brought to this? A murderer most foul, Exior K'mool, who once was
a dreamer and mixed love potions for pennies? Even as Mylakhrion's
voice made its sepulchral booming and rolled the work's rare words,
so Exior gave a little cry and started forward; at which the sorcerer
looked up.

"Is aught amiss, Exior?" There seemed a certain slyness in his
question. "Do you fear to hear these marvels and monstrosities? Shall
I read them to myself then, in silence?"

Exior shook his head. Was he afraid? Nay, for he had said again
Gleeth's moon-rune and feared not. Not for himself. "Read on,

master," he answered; but there was a catch in his voice which he had believed extinct.

Mylakhrion nodded. "So be it," he said, his voice fallen to the merest whisper. For a little while, in silence, the two gazed into each other's eyes; and those of the elder were narrowed now and very bright. Finally they fell once more to the written page.

And so that master of mages read on until he reached the bottom of a certain leaf, and as his fingers went to turn the page Exior once more gave a start. He knew the revelations overleaf were such as must surely sear any mere mortal, which Mylakhrion was of his own admittance. And again that fist tightened upon Exior's heart as he knew himself for a traitor.

"Stop!" he cried as the page began to turn. "Look no more, Mylakhrion! If you would save your sight, your mind, your very soul, *be still*!... For I have deceived you—"

Slowly Mylakhrion looked up and smiled. Even Mylakhrion, he smiled! And it was a real smile, banishing much of his customary coldness as the morning sun lifts rime from spring flowers. Exior saw that smile but did not understand; and Mylakhrion asked, "Do you fear for me, Exior K'mool, or for yourself? For your conscience, perhaps?"

"For both of us, if you will," answered the other harshly. "Whichever way you would have it—only read no more. There is a protection, lacking which the book's blasphemies will blast you! The warning was writ on the first page, which I tore out..."

"Oh?" Mylakhrion's smile diminished somewhat. Deliberately he turned the page, and when Exior made to snatch the book from him he held up a hand of caution. "Peace, young man. Watch—and learn!" And without further pause he read the page to its end.

During the reading Exior saw shadows gather in the room as with the approach of night. There commenced a strange tremor and a muted thunder which had their sources in the air of the room itself. Crystals splintered and phials flew into fragments; finely wrought mirrors shivered into shards and liquids boiled up and overflowed their crucibles; aye, and cracks appeared in the very walls while dust and debris rained down from the ceiling, ere Mylakhrion was done. Then he closed the book and looked up, and still he smiled. Nor was his mien changed at all, and the reading had done him no ill whatever.

"I... I—"

"Be silent and listen," Mylakhrion commanded. "You have done well, Exior K'mool, as I suspected you would. And you will make a fitting mage for Morgath, given time. As for me: now I up and get me gone to Tharamoon. And on that bleak and northern isle I shall build me a tower, as is my wont, and there seek that immortality which ever confounds me. This palace here in Humquass: it is yours. You have earned it, every last stone."

"I have earned it?" Exior was amazed. "But I am a traitor, and—"

"You were *almost* a traitor," Mylakhrion answered, "and that is the difference. You could not know that I am ever protected against dark forces, and that the book would not harm me. Therefore, when you would have stopped me from reading, you showed mercy. I like that quality in a man, Exior K'mool! And you have many qualities. Some humility, a deal of honesty, a little daring—and now, too, wisdom and mercy! All to the good, young man, for without them you could never succeed.

"Moreover, your talents are of the sort Morgath needs above all others. Myself, I was never much of a one for such minor magicks and studied them not extensively. But you? You are a seer and read runes and portents. You reckon well the auspices and faithfully foretell the future. Aye, and the King will be well pleased with you."

Mylakhrion stood up and took hold of Exior's shoulders. "Tomorrow you meet him, Morgath the King, and the day after that I leave for Tharamoon. How do you say to that?"

"But—" Exior began. And again: "How...why—?"

"Enough!" Mylakhrion lifted his hand. "It is finished."

"But all of this," and Exior gazed all about, "mine? I cannot believe it! Will you take nothing with you?"

Mylakhrion shook his head. "All is yours—except I shall take my wand with me, and my familiars three. And the book..."

"The book, of course!" Exior nodded. "And with it make yourself mighty above all men. Yes, naturally."

"No," Mylakhrion smiled again, "for I am that already. I will tell you why I take these things. My wand because it suits my hand, and my familiars because I am grown used to them. Their faces remind me of my youth, when I defeated them in a wizardly war. As for what I leave behind: these things were never really mine. They were gifted to me, or I purchased them, or won them by use of my magick. They are as nothing. But the book—that is mine." His eyes gazed searchingly into the other's face.

And now Exior gasped and his own changeling eyes went wide.

"Ah! I see the truth dawns on you at last," said Mylakhrion. "Your face grows gaunt with a great wonder and your jaw falls open. Rightly so—" and he nodded. "You are of course correct, Exior K'mool, and now you know all. The rune book is an old friend of mine and I would never leave without it. Not unless my leaving was enforced, as happened to me once long ago in the Desert of Ell...

"No, the book goes with me. For who can say when I shall have the time to write another?"

The House of Cthulhu

Where weirdly angled ramparts loom,
Gaunt sentinels whose shadows gloom
Upon an undead hell-beast's tomb—
And gods and mortals fear to tread.
Where gateways to forbidden spheres
And times are closed, but monstrous fears
Await the passing of strange years—
When that will wake which is not dead...

"Arlyeh"—a fragment from Teh Atht's *Legends of the Olden Runes*. As translated by Thelred Gustau from the Theem'hdra manuscripts.

Now it happened aforetime that Zar-thule the Conqueror, who is called Reaver of Reavers, Seeker of Treasures and Sacker of Cities, swam out of the East with his dragonships; aye, even beneath the snapping sails of his dragonships. The wind was but lately turned favorable, and now the weary rowers nodded over their shipped oars while sleepy steersmen held the course. And there Zar-thule descried him in the sea the island Arlyeh, whereon loomed tall towers builded of black stone whose tortuous twinings were of angles unknown and utterly beyond the ken of men; and this island was redly lit by the sun sinking down over its awesome black crags and burning behind the aeries and spires carved therefrom by other than human hands.

And though Zar-thule felt a great hunger and stood sore weary of the wide sea's expanse behind the lolling dragon's tail of his ship Redfire, and even though he gazed with red and rapacious eyes upon the black island, still he held off his reavers, bidding them that they ride at anchor well out to sea until the sun was deeply down and gone unto the Realm of Cthon; even unto Cthon, who sits in silence to snare the sun in his net beyond the edge of the world. Indeed, such were Zar-thule's raiders as their deeds were best done by night, for then Gleeth the blind Moon God saw them not, nor heard in his celestial deafness the horrible cries which ever attended unto such deeds.

For notwithstanding his cruelty, which was beyond words, Zar-thule was no fool. He knew him that his wolves must rest before a whelming, that if the treasures of the House of Cthulhu were truly such as he imagined them—then that they must likewise be well guarded by fighting men who would not give them up easily. And his reavers were fatigued even as Zar-thule himself, so that he rested them all down behind the painted bucklers lining the decks, and furled him up the great dragon-dyed sails. And he set a watch that in the middle of the night he might be roused, when, rousing in turn the men of his twenty ships, he would sail in unto and sack the island of Arlyeh.

Far had Zar-thule's reavers rowed before the fair winds found them, far from the rape of the Yaht Haal, the Silver City at the edge of the frostlands. Their provisions were all but eaten, their swords all ocean rot in rusting sheaths; but now they ate all of their remaining regimen and drank of the liquors thereof, and they cleansed and sharpened their dire blades before taking themselves into the arms of Shoosh, Goddess of the Still Slumbers. They well knew them, one and all, that soon they would be at the sack, each for himself and loot to that sword's wielder whose blade drank long and deep.

And Zar-thule had promised them great treasures from the House of Cthulhu; for back there in the sacked and seared city at the edge of the frostlands, he had heard from the bubbling, anguished lips of Voth Vehm the name of the so-called "forbidden" isle of Arlyeh. Voth Vehm, in the throes of terrible tortures, had called out the name of his brother-priest, Hath Vehm, who guarded the House of Cthulhu in Arlyeh. And even in the hour of his dying Voth Vehm had answered to Zar-thule's additional tortures, crying out that Arlyeh was indeed forbidden and held in thrall by the sleeping but yet dark and terrible god Cthulhu, the gate to whose House his brother-priest guarded.

Then had Zar-thule reasoned that Arlyeh must contain riches indeed, for he knew it was not meet that brother-priests betray one another; and aye, surely had Voth Vehm spoken exceedingly fearfully of this dark and terrible god Cthulhu only that he might thus divert Zar-thule's avarice from the ocean sanctuary of his brother-priest, Hath Vehm. Thus reckoned Zar-thule, even brooding on the dead and disfigured hierophant's words, until he bethought him to leave the sacked city. Then, with the flames leaping brightly and reflected in his red wake, Zar-thule put to sea in his dragonships. All loaded down with silver booty he put to sea, in search of Arlyeh and the treasures of the House of Cthulhu. And thus came he to this place.

———

Shortly before the midnight hour the watch roused Zar-thule up from the arms of Shoosh, aye, and all the freshened men of the dragonships; and then beneath Gleeth the blind Moon God's pitted silver face, seeing that the wind had fallen, they muffled their oars and dipped them deep and so closed in with the shoreline. A dozen fathoms from beaching, out rang Zar-thule's plunder cry, and his drummers took up a stern and steady beat by which the trained but yet rampageous reavers might advance to the sack.

Came the scrape of keel on grit, and down from his dragon's head leapt Zar-thule to the sullen shallow waters, and with him his captains and men, to wade ashore and stride the night-black strand and wave their swords...and all for naught! Lo, the island stood quiet and still and seemingly untended...

Only now did the Sacker of Cities take note of this isle's truly awesome aspect. Black piles of tumbled masonry festooned with weeds from the tides rose up from the dark wet sand, and there seemed inherent in these gaunt and immemorial relics a foreboding not alone of bygone times; great crabs scuttled in and about the archaic ruins and gazed with stalked ruby eyes upon the intruders; even the small waves broke with an eery *hush, hush, hush* upon the sand and pebbles and primordial exuviae of crumbled yet seemingly sentient towers and tabernacles. The drummers faltered, paused and finally silence reigned.

Now many of them among these reavers recognised rare gods and supported strange superstitions, and Zar-thule knew this and had no liking for their silence. It was a silence that might yet yield to mutiny!

"Hah!" quoth he, who worshipped neither god nor demon nor yet lent ear to the gaunts of night. "See—the guards knew of our coming and are all fled to the far side of the island—or perhaps they gather ranks at the House of Cthulhu." So saying, he formed him up his men into a body and advanced into the island.

And as they marched they passed them by other prehuman piles not yet ocean-sundered, striding through silent streets whose fantastic façades gave back the beat of the drummers in a strangely muted monotone.

And lo, mummied faces of coeval antiquity seemed to leer from the empty and oddly-angled towers and craggy spires, fleet ghouls that flitted from shadow to shadow apace with the marching men, until some of those hardened reavers grew sore afraid and begged them of Zar-thule, "Master, let us get us gone from here, for it appears that there is no treasure, and this place is like unto no other. It stinks of death—even of death and of them that walk the shadow-lands."

But Zar-thule rounded on one who stood close to him muttering thus, crying, "Coward!—Out on you!" Whereupon he lifted up his sword and hacked the trembling reaver in two parts, so that the sundered man screamed once before falling with twin thuds to the black earth. But now Zar-thule perceived that indeed many of his men were sore afraid, and so he had him torches lighted and brought up, and they pressed on quickly into the island.

There, beyond low dark hills, they came to a great gathering of queerly carved and monolithic edifices, all of the same confused angles and surfaces and all with the stench of the pit, even the fetor of the *very* pit about them. And in the centre of these malodorous megaliths there stood the greatest tower of them all, a massive menhir that loomed and leaned windowless to a great height, about which at its base squat pedestals bore likenesses of blackly carven krakens of terrifying aspect.

"Hah!" quoth Zar-thule. "Plainly is this the House of Cthulhu, and see—Its guards and priests have fled them all before us to escape the reaving!"

But a tremulous voice, old and mazed, answered from the shadows at the base of one great pedestal, saying, "No one has fled, O reaver, for there are none here to flee, save me—and I cannot flee for I guard the gate against those who may utter The Words."

At the sound of this old voice in the stillness the reavers started and peered nervously about at the leaping torch-cast shadows, but one stout captain stepped forward to drag from out of the dark an old, old man. And lo, seeing the mien of this mage, all the reavers fell back at once. For he bore upon his face and hands, aye, and upon all visible parts of him, a grey and furry lichen that seemed to crawl upon him even as he stood crooked and trembling in his great age!

"Who are you?" demanded Zar-thule, aghast at the sight of so hideous a spectacle of afflicted infirmity; even Zar-thule, aghast!

"I am Hath Vehm, brother-priest of Voth Vehm who serves the gods in the temples of Yaht Haal; I am Hath Vehm, Keeper of the Gate at the House of Cthulhu, and I warn you that it is forbidden to touch me." And he gloomed with rheumy eyes at the captain who held him, until that raider took away his hands.

"And I am Zar-thule the Conqueror," quoth Zar-thule, less in awe now. "Reaver of Reavers, Seeker of Treasures and Sacker of Cities. I have plundered Yaht Haal, aye, plundered the Silver City and burned it low. And I have tortured Voth Vehm unto death. But in his dying, even with hot coals eating at his belly, he cried out a name. And it was *your* name! And he was truly a brother unto you, Hath Vehm, for he warned me of the terrible god Cthulhu and of this 'forbidden' isle of Arlyeh. But I knew he lied, that he sought him only to protect a great and holy treasure and the brother-priest who guards it, doubtless with strange runes to frighten away the superstitious reavers! But Zar-thule is neither afraid nor credulous, old one. Here I stand, and I say to you on your life that I'll know the way into this treasure house within the hour!"

And now, hearing their chief speak thus to the ancient priest of the island, and noting the old man's trembling infirmity and hideous disfigurement, Zar-thule's captains and men had taken heart. Some of them had gone about and about the beetling tower of obscure angles until they found a door. Now this door was great, tall, solid and in no way hidden from view; and yet at times it seemed very indistinct, as though misted and distant. It stood straight up in the wall of the House of Cthulhu, and yet looked as if to lean to one side...and then in one and the same moment to lean to the other! It bore leering, inhuman faces and horrid hieroglyphs, all carved into its surface, and these unknown characters seemed to writhe about the gorgon faces; and aye, those faces too moved and grimaced in the light of the flickering torches.

The ancient Hath Vehm came to them where they gathered in wonder of the great door, saying: "That is the gate of the House of Cthulhu, and I am its guardian."

"So," spake Zar-thule, who was also come there, "and is there a key to this gate? I see no means of entry."

"Aye, there is a key, but none such as you might readily imagine. It is not a key of metal, but of words..."

"Magic?" asked Zar-thule, undaunted. He had heard aforetime of similar thaumaturgies.

Zar-thule put the point of his sword to the old man's throat, observing as he did so the furry grey growth moving upon the elder's face and scrawny neck, saying: "Then say those words now and let's have done!"

"Nay, I cannot say The Words—I am sworn to guard the gate that The Words are *never* spoken, neither by myself nor by any other who would foolishly or mistakenly open the House of Cthulhu. You may kill me—even take my life with that very blade you now hold to my throat—but I will not utter The Words..."

"And I say that you will—eventually!" quoth Zar-thule in an exceedingly cold voice, in a voice even as cold as the northern sleet. Whereupon he put down his sword and ordered two of his men to come forward, commanding that they take the ancient and tie him down to thronged pegs made fast in the ground. And they tied him down until he was spread out flat upon his back, not far from the great and oddly fashioned door in the wall of the House of Cthulhu.

Then a fire was lighted of dry shrubs and of driftwood fetched from the shore; and others of Zar-thule's reavers went out and trapped certain great nocturnal birds that knew not the power of flight; and yet others found a spring of brackish water and filled them up the waterskins. And soon tasteless but satisfying meat turned on the spits above a fire; and in the same fire sword-points glowed red, then white. And after Zar-thule and his captains and men had eaten their fill, then the Reaver of Reavers motioned to his torturers that they should attend to their task. These torturers had been trained by Zar-thule himself, so that they excelled in the arts of pincer and hot iron.

But then there came a diversion. For some little time a certain captain—his name was Cush-had, the man who first found the old priest in the shadow of the great pedestal and dragged him forth—had been peering most strangely at his hands in the firelight and rubbing them upon the hide of his jacket. Of a sudden he cursed and leapt to his feet, springing up from the remnants of his meal. He danced about in a frightened manner, beating wildly at the tumbled flat stones about with his hands.

Then of a sudden he stopped and cast sharp glances at his naked forearms. In the same second his eyes stood out in his face and he screamed as were he pierced through and through with a keen blade; and he rushed to the fire and thrust his hands into its heart, even to his elbows. Then he drew his arms from the flames, staggering and moaning and calling upon certain trusted gods. And he tottered away into the night, his ruined arms steaming and dripping redly upon the ground.

Amazed, Zar-thule sent a man after Cush-had with a torch, and this man soon returned trembling and with a very pale face in the firelight to tell how the madman had fallen or leapt to his death in a deep crevice. But before he fell there had been visible upon his face a creeping, furry greyness; and as he had fallen, aye, even as he crashed down to his death, he had screamed: "Unclean...unclean...unclean!"

Then, all and all when they heard this, they remembered the old priest's words of warning when Cush-had dragged him out of hiding, and the way he had gloomed upon the unfortunate captain, and they looked at the ancient where he lay held fast to the earth. The two reavers whose task it had been to tie him down looked them one to the other with very wide eyes, their faces whitening perceptibly in the firelight, and they took up a quiet and secret examination of their persons; even a *minute* examination...

Zar-thule felt fear rising in his reavers like the east wind when it rises up fast and wild in the Desert of Sheb. He spat at the ground and lifted up his sword, crying: "Listen to me! You are all superstitious cowards, all and all of you, with your old wives' tales and fears and mumbo-jumbo. What's there to be frightened of? An old man, alone, on a black rock in the sea?"

"But I saw Cush-had's face—" began the man who had followed the demented captain.

"You only *thought* you saw something," Zar-thule cut him off. "It was only the flickering of your torch-fire and nothing more. Cush-had was a madman!"

"But—"

"Cush-had was a madman!" Zar-thule said again, and his voice turned very cold. "Are you, too, insane? Is there room for you, too, at the bottom of that crevice?" But the man shrank back and said no more, and yet again Zar-thule called his torturers forward that they should be about their work.

The hours passed...

Blind and coldly deaf Gleeth the old Moon God surely was, and yet perhaps he had sensed something of the agonised screams and the stench of roasting human flesh drifting up from Arlyeh that night. Certainly he seemed to sink down in the sky very quickly.

Now, however, the tattered and blackened figure stretched out upon the ground before the door in the wall of the House of Cthulhu was no longer strong enough to cry out loudly, and Zar-thule despaired for he saw that soon the priest of the island would sink into the last and longest of slumbers. And still The Words were not spoken. Too, the reaver king was perplexed by the ancient's stubborn refusal to admit that the door in the looming menhir concealed treasure; but in the end he put this down to the effect of certain vows Hath Vehm had no doubt taken in his inauguration to priesthood.

The torturers had not done their work well. They had been loth to touch the elder with anything but their hot swords; they *would not*— not even when threatened most direly—lay their hands upon him, or approach him more closely than absolutely necessary to the application of their agonising art. The two reavers responsible for tying the ancient down were dead, slain by former comrades upon whom they had inadvertently lain hands of friendship; and those they had touched, their slayers, they too were shunned by their companions and stood apart from the other reavers.

As the first grey light of dawn began to show beyond the eastern sea, Zar-thule finally lost all patience and turned upon the dying priest in a veritable fury. He took up his sword, raising it over his head in two hands...and then Hath Vehm spoke:

"Wait!" he whispered, his voice a low, tortured croak, "wait, O reaver—I will say The Words."

"What?" cried Zar-thule, lowering his blade. "You will open the door?"

"Aye," the cracked whisper came, "I will open the Gate. But first, tell me; did you truly sack Yaht Haal, the Silver City? Did you truly raze it down with fire, and torture my brother-priest to death?"

"I did all that," Zar-thule callously nodded.

"Then come you close," Hath Vehm's voice sank low. "Closer, O reaver king, that you may hear me in my final hour."

Eagerly the Seeker of Treasures bent him down his ear to the lips of the ancient, kneeling down beside him where he lay—and Hath Vehm immediately lifted up his head from the earth and spat upon Zar-thule!

Then, before the Sacker of Cities could think or make a move to wipe the slimy spittle from his brow, Hath Vehm said The Words. Aye, even in a loud and clear voice he said them—words of terrible import and alien cadence that only an adept might repeat—and at once there came a great rumble from the door in the beetling wall of weird angles.

Forgetting for the moment the tainted insult of the ancient priest, Zar-thule turned to see the huge and evilly carven door tremble and waver and then, by some unknown power, move or slide away until only a great black hole yawned where it had been. And lo, in the early dawn light, the reaver horde pressed forward to seek them out the treasure with their eyes; even to seek out the treasure beyond the open door. Likewise Zar-thule made to enter the House of Cthulhu, but again the dying heirophant cried out to him:

"Hold! There are more words, O reaver king!"

"More words?" Zar-thule turned with a frown. The old priest, his life quickly ebbing, grinned mirthlessly at the sight of the furry grey blemish that crawled upon the barbarian's forehead over his left eye.

"Aye, more words. Listen: long and long ago, when the world was very young, before Arlyeh and the House of Cthulhu were first sunken into the sea, wise elder gods devised a rune that should Cthulhu's House ever rise and be opened by foolish men, it might be sent down again—even Arlyeh itself, sunken deep once more beneath the salt waters. *Now I say those other words!*"

Swiftly the king reaver leapt, his sword lifting, but ere that blade could fall Hath Vehm cried out those other strange and dreadful words; and lo, the whole island shook in the grip of a great earthquake. Now in awful anger Zar-thule's sword fell and hacked off the ancient's whistling and spurting head from his ravened body; but even as the head rolled free, so the island shook itself again, and the ground rumbled and began to break open.

From the open door in the House of Cthulhu, whereinto the host of greedy reavers had rushed to discover the treasure, there now came loud and singularly hideous cries of fear and torment, and of a sudden an even more hideous stench. And now Zar-thule knew truly indeed that there was no treasure.

Great ebony clouds gathered swiftly and livid lightning crashed; winds rose up that blew Zar-thule's long black hair over his face as he crouched in horror before the open door of the House of Cthulhu. Wide and wide were his eyes as he tried to peer beyond the reeking blackness of that nameless, ancient aperture—but a moment later he dropped his great sword to the ground and screamed; even the Reaver of Reavers, screamed most terribly.

For two of his wolves had appeared from out the darkness, more in the manner of whipped puppies than true wolves, shrieking and babbling and scrambling frantically over the queer angles of the orifice's mouth...but they had emerged only to be snatched up and squashed like grapes by titanic tentacles that lashed after them from the dark depths beyond! And these rubbery appendages drew the crushed bodies back into the inky blackness, from which there instantly issued forth the most monstrously nauseating· slobberings and suckings before the writhing members once more snaked forth into the dawn light. This time they caught at the edges of the opening, and from behind them pushed forward—*a face!*

Zar-thule gazed upon the enormously bloated visage of Cthulhu, and he screamed again as that terrible Being's awful eyes found him where he crouched—found him and lit with an hideous light!

The reaver king paused, frozen, petrified, for but a moment, and yet long enough that the ultimate horror of the thing framed in the titan threshold seared itself upon his brain forever. Then his legs found their strength. He turned and fled, speeding away and over the low black hills, and down to the shore and into his ship, which he somehow managed, even single-handed and in his frantic terror, to cast off. And all the time in his mind's eye there burned that fearful sight— the awful *Visage* and *Being* of Lord Cthulhu.

There had been the tentacles, springing from a greenly pulpy head about which they sprouted like lethiferous petals about the heart of an obscenely hybrid orchid, a scaled and amorphously elastic body of immense proportions, with clawed feet fore and hind; long, narrow wings ill-fitting the horror that bore them in that it seemed patently impossible for *any* wings to lift so fantastic a bulk—and then there had been the eyes! Never before had Zar-thule seen such evil, rampant and expressed, as in the ultimately leering malignancy of Cthulhu's eyes!

And Cthulhu was not finished with Zar-thule, for even as the king reaver struggled madly with his sail the monster came across the low hills in the dawn light, slobbering and groping down to the very water's edge. Then, when Zar-thule saw against the morning the mountain that was Cthulhu, he went mad for a period; flinging himself from side to side of his ship so that he was like to fall into the sea, frothing at the mouth and babbling horribly in pitiful prayer—aye, even Zar-thule, whose lips never before uttered prayers—to certain benevolent gods of which he had heard. And it seems that these kind gods, if indeed they exist, must have heard him.

With a roar and a blast greater than any before, there came the final shattering that saved Zar-thule for a cruel future, and the entire island split asunder; even the bulk of Arlyeh breaking into many parts and settling into the sea. And with a piercing scream of frustrated rage and lust—a scream which Zar-thule heard with his mind as well as his ears—the monster Cthulhu sank Him down also with the island and His House beneath the frothing waves.

A great storm raged then such as might attend the end of the world. Banshee winds howled and demon waves crashed over and about Zar-thule's dragonship, and for two days he gibbered and moaned in the rolling, shuddering scuppers of crippled Redfire before the mighty storm wore itself out.

Eventually, close to starvation, the one-time Reaver of Reavers was discovered becalmed upon a flat sea not far from the fair strands of bright Theem'hdra; and then, in the spicy hold of a rich merchant's ship, he was borne in unto the wharves of the city of Klühn, Theem'hdra's capital.

With long oars he was prodded ashore, stumbling and weak and crying out in his horror of living—for he had gazed upon Cthulhu! The use of the oars had much to do with his appearance, for now Zar-thule was changed indeed, into something which in less tolerant parts of that primal land might certainly have expected to be burned. But the people of Klühn were kindly folk; they burned him not but lowered him in a basket into a deep dungeon cell with torches to light the place, and daily bread and water that he might live until his life was rightly done. And when he was recovered to partial health and sanity, learned men and physicians went to talk with him from above and ask him of his strange affliction, of which all and all stood in awe.

I, Teh Atht, was one of them that went to him, and that was how I came to hear this tale. And I know it to be true, for oft and again over the years I have heard of this Loathly Lord Cthulhu that seeped down from the stars when the world was an inchoate infant. There are legends and there are legends, and one of them is that when times have passed and the stars are right Cthulhu shall slobber forth from His House in Arlyeh again, and the world shall tremble to His tread and erupt in madness at His touch.

I leave this record for men as yet unborn, a record and a warning; leave well enough alone, for that is not dead which deeply dreams, and while perhaps the submarine tides have removed forever the alien taint which touched Arlyeh—that symptom of Cthulhu, which loathsome familiar grew upon Hath Vehm and transferred itself upon certain of Zar-thule's reavers—Cthulhu Himself yet lives on and waits upon those who would set Him free. I know it is so. In dreams...I myself have heard His call!

And when dreams such as these come in the night to sour the sweet embrace of Shoosh, I wake and tremble and pace the crystal-paved floors of my rooms above the Bay of Klühn, until Cthon releases the sun from his net to rise again, and ever and ever I recall the aspect of Zar-thule as last I saw him in the flickering torchlight of his deep dungeon cell:

A fumbling grey mushroom thing that moved not of its own volition but by reason of the parasite growth which lived upon and within it...

THARQUEST AND THE
LAMIA ORBIQUITA

From Teh Atht's *Legends of the Olden Runes*, as translated by
Thelred Gustau from the Theem'hdra Manuscripts.

I

Now Tharquest the wandering Klühnite, riding hard from Eyphra
in the West where he had angered the High Priest of the Dark
Temple of Ghatanothoa by getting his lately-virgin daughter with
child, came over the Mountains of Lohmi and spied the once-gilded
spires and great walls of Chlangi. Even crumbling Chlangi, which is
called the Shunned City.

Not unfairly is Chlangi named, for indeed her approaches—aye,
and her walls, streets and deserted houses—they are shunned. Even
now, though many years are fled since the olden runes were writ, still
they are shunned...

In Chlangi a robber-king ruled over a rabble of yeggs and sharpers, exacting taxation from the scabby whores and unscrupulous
taverners in his protection and allowing such to vend in peace those
poisons peculiar to their trades. And Tharquest frowned when he saw

the city; for some twenty years gone when scarce a child he had visited the place, which was then wondrous in its opulence and splendid in the colour and variety of visitors come to admire its wonders.

Then the city had been abustle with honest, thronging merchants, and the wineshops and taverns had sold vintages renowned throughout the known world—especially the pure clear wine pressed with skill from Chlangi's own glass-grapes. The domes and spires had been gilded over; the high walls white with fresh paint: the roofs red with tiles baked in the ovens of busy builders, and all in all Chlangi had been the jewel of Theem'hdra's cities.

But now the city was shunned by all good and honest men, had been so for ten years, since first the lamia Orbiquita built her castle nine miles to the north on the fringe of the Desert of Sheb. In that time the gold had been stripped from all the rich roofs and the vines of the glass-grapes beyond the north wall had grown wild and barren and gross so as to flatten their rotting trellises. Arches and walls had fallen into disrepair, and the waters of the aquaducts were long grown stagnant and green with slime. Only the rabble horde and their robber-king now occupied the city within its great walls, and without those walls the ravenous beggars prowled and scavenged for whatever meager pickings there might be.

And yet Tharquest feared not as he rode his black mare down from the Mountains of Lohmi, for his departure from Eyphra had been of necessity swift and he carried little of value. Even his mare—which he had stolen—wore no saddle upon her back, and her rein was of rope and the bit in her mouth of hard wood.

Most disreputable, Tharquest looked, with his robes torn and dishevelled in the flight from Zothada's father, and his eyes all baggy from many a sleepless night's riding. Still, he had a friend in Chlangi: Dilquay Noth, once an adventurer like himself and now a pimp for the city's less loathsome whores. At Dilquay's place he knew he would find food and shelter for the night. Then, in the morning, he would press on for Klühn on the coast, where a rich widow-wife awaited his caresses. In any case, he doubted if the High Priest of Dark Ghatanothoa would follow him here—not into the supposed sphere of ensorcellment of the lamia Orbiquita.

Himself, Tharquest had small faith in spells and enchantments—what little he had seen of such had been the quackery of village tricksters and stage magicians and yet indeed in those days such things were. As in all inchoate worlds, Nature had not yet decided which gifts and talents she should let her creatures keep. Or rather, she had experimented and decided that there were lines better not continued. Slowly these discarded strains were disappearing, but every now and then one would be born seventh son of a seventh son of a wizard. And he too, if he remembered the keys, might inherit in addition to the usual five Nature's tossed-aside talents. Aye, and there were strangely endowed women, too.

So Tharquest came to Chlangi, and seeing the encampments of beggars without the walls and the way their narrow, hungry eyes gleamed as they fastened on the black flanks of his mount, he quickened the mare's step until his torn cloak belled in the sun and dust behind him. But the beggars made no move to molest him and he passed them through.

Into the evening city rode Tharquest, through the rotting wooden remnant of what had once been the mighty West Gate. Then, passing carelessly under a crumbling arch, he was knocked from the back of his mount by a robber who clung spiderlike to the high stonework. Down he went and into the dust, to be hauled dazedly to his feet and disarmed by two more brigands before being dragged before robber-king Fregg.

When Fregg heard Tharquest's tale of his escape from the raging Priest of Ghatanothoa he laughed, and his cutthroat courtiers with him. Why! This Klühnite was obviously a brigand no less then they! They liked him for it and directed him out of Fregg's sagging pile—which was once a most magnificent palace—and on his way to find his friend Dilquay Noth the pimp.

Dilquay, he soon discovered, was doing well, living in a house not far from the palace wherein he kept his girls. Well-fortified the place and seated atop a small hill, like a castle in its own right and necessarily so; for pimping is a dodgy business in any city, and surely more so in Chlangi the Shunned...

Tharquest approached the great stone house—once the High Court of the long fled King Terrathagon, now the brothel of Dilquay Noth—up a flight of winding, basalt steps, arriving at a great iron-studded door with a little gated window. A rap or two at the oaken panels with the pommel of his simple sword brought bright blue eyes that peered from within. A gasp of recognition…and the door was at once thrown open. There in the spacious doorway, the burly, bearded Dilquay Noth.

"Tharquest the Wanderer, by my beard!—and bruised and banged about to boot! By all the Dark Gods, but you look beaten, my friend. In and sit you down—and tell me how come your clothes are torn and your face unshaven, you who live by your pretty looks!"

But for all his words Dilquay was not overly surprised by Tharquest's sudden appearance in Chlangi. Some nine months gone, when he had heard from a wandering beggar how Tharquest had taken the Sacred Oath of Ghatanothoa to be admitted as a novice to the priesthood in Eyphra, he had straightway sent the same beggar with a note to the adventurer telling of his whereabouts and demanding an explanation. What on Earth was Tharquest—the hero of many a grand defloration—thinking of, Dilquay had wanted to know, binding himself to a Dark God and swearing continence for ever?

Thus, when Tharquest's troubles came to a head in Eyphra—or when they came to a belly, as it were—and when the Priestess Zothada's size had finally given way the Klühnite's real reasons for desiring a bed within the Temple of Ghatanothoa, then the wanderer had stolen a mare and made for Chlangi, to a friend who would succor him and see him on his way to Klühn and the bright blue sea…

Now, seated in Dilquay's spacious apartment—better appointed, Tharquest noted, than even Fregg's hall in the fast-falling palace—they swapped memories of olden adventures. Finally the bearded pimp told of how, after leaving Tharquest's side to settle with Titi the Whore, he had talked her into giving up her trade and opening a brothel of her own with Dilquay himself to protect her rights. That had been four years earlier, at a time when Chlangi's streets had still been fairly well filled, but now Dilquay was thinking of leaving the city. This was not, as he explained, for fear of the lamia Orbiquita, but simply for scarcity of trade.

It was at this juncture that Titi the ample entered; aye, even legendary Titi of a Thousand Delights. Straightway she fell on Tharquest and gave his neck a hug, crying: "Ah!—but I knew that our wanderer, who can sell his services to any hot-blooded woman in all the known

world, could never settle to the servicing of a mere God! Why!—
I've girls here would pay you, if they knew what I know—except you
wouldn't look at them twice, not even for money!" She laughed.

"Titi," cried Tharquest, struggling from her grasp. "By
Ghatanothoa's defiled temple, but you're more beautiful than ever!"
He was lying, for Titi had never been beautiful, but there was a cama-
raderie between them and it was good to see the face—even the
slightly pockmarked face—of so old a friend.

And so, after much drinking and chewing and chatting, came
the night. Dilquay and Titi went off to organise their ladies and
Tharquest, well feasted of meat and drunk of not unreasonable wine,
found himself tucked up in a clean bed in a room of his own. In his
reeling, boozy head before he slept, he kept hearing Dilquay's tales of
the lamia Orbiquita, and in his lecherous soul there burned a drunken
plan for yet another amorous adventure...

Dilquay had pointed out to Tharquest the fact that none of
Chlangi's robber-men were handsome, and few of them young, and
had then gone on to explain why. The lamia Orbiquita had taken
all of the strong, young, good-looking men for herself and had left
the city to the battle-scarred brigands and whore-poxed pirates who
now inhabited her. This was why, Dilquay said, Tharquest himself
must soon move on or attract Orbiquita's attention. For the lamia
lusted like a succubus after handsome, strong-limbed men, and was
not above stealing into Chlangi in the dead of night on bat wings
to lure off the occasional handsome wanderer she might hear was
staying there.

She was said, too, to be beautiful, this lamia—but evil as the pit
itself. And it was known that the beauty men saw in her was only
an illusion, that the real Orbiquita was a well-poxed horror saved
from the rot of centuries only by her own magical machinations.
Furthermore, it was told that should any man have strength of will
enough to resist the lamia once she had set her black heart upon him,
then he could carry off with him all of the hoarded treasures hidden
away within her castle.

...Now *that* would be a real adventure!

II

In the morning, lying abed while he properly thought the thing out, finally Tharquest made his decision. He would visit this lamia and stay the night, and the following morn would leave her unsated taking her treasures with him. Dilquay and Titi paled on hearing of this brash scheme, but they could not deter Tharquest with even the direst tales.

When later that same day the robber-king also heard of the Klühnite's plans, he laughed and wished him luck and gave him back his twice-stolen mare. Thus, following a midday meal at Dilquay's, Tharquest set off through the fallen North Gate and pointed his mount's nose toward the Desert of Sheb. And in their encampments the beggars who saw him take his departure tittered and slapped lean thighs, debating upon how soon the wanderer's mare would come galloping back alone, lathered and red-eyed, and how then there would be meat again in the camps of the ragged starvelings...

After eight miles, by which time the castle of Orbiquita was a dark-spired outline against the early horizon—an outline reflecting neither beam of sunlight nor, indeed, any light at all, standing magically shaded even in the hot sun—Tharquest came to a shepherd's cot. He was thirsty by then and so tethered his mare and knocked upon the door of the rude dwelling. Pleasantly surprised was he when the door was opened by a young and gorgeous girl of long limbs, raven hair and great green eyes that looked upon him coyly as their owner bade him enter.

So Tharquest entered and seated himself and was given water. Then, his thirst quenched, he asked of the girl her man's whereabouts. His question came of sheer habit, for in Tharquest's life men—particularly husbands—were hazards to be avoided wherever possible. But she only laughed (showing teeth like pearls) and twirled girlishly about (showing limbs like marble cut by a master sculptor) and told him that she had no man. She lived with her father who was out after strayed sheep and not expected back for two days at least.

Now any man would have been tempted, and Tharquest sorely so, but he wanted to get on and reach Orbiquita's castle and earn his fortune. Remembering this through the flesh-lust that suddenly gripped him, he stood up and begged the lady's pardon but he must be gone, at which she bowed low (displaying breasts curved and golden as the full moon) and inquired of his destination. On discovering Tharquest's intentions her great green eyes opened very wide and she all but burst into tears, deploring his plans for wealth and greatness and pleading with him thus:

"Oh, wanderer, you are surely handsome and strong and brave—but yet more surely are you mad! Know you not the *power* of this lamia?"

"I have heard," Tharquest answered, "how Orbiquita has the means to show herself as a great and ravishing beauty, when in truth she is ugly and ancient and loathsome. But I have also heard how, if a man resist her enticements—presented succubus-like in the night—he might walk off unscathed in the light of day with all the treasures he can carry, even with the wonderful treasures of her grim castle. This I intend to do, for the lamia can only take her victims during those hours when the sun is down, and I do not intend to sleep. I shall stay awake and keenly attentive, wary of all things within yon castle's walls."

"Oh, Tharquest, Tharquest," she pleaded, "I have seen so many such as you pass by here, though none so godly of form, and have given them water to succor them on their way. But—"

"Aye, go on, lass."

"Always it is the same. They go to the castle full of high inspiration and bravado, but only their horses—flanks lathered, eyes burning red in awful fear—ever return! For the lamia is never satisfied with a *piece* of a man but takes all of him, fuel for her fires of lust and horror. No, you must not go to the castle, fair Tharquest, but stay here with me and share my bed this night. I'm so lonely here and often afraid. And in the morning, then return you whole and happy to the Shunned City; and perhaps, if I who have little experience of men please you, take me with you?..."

And again Tharquest was warmed and felt a great temptation. But here he had a novel thought: was he not yet to be tempted by the lamia Orbiquita herself? And must he not resist such temptation for his life? Why!—if a mere shepherd girl might so readily set his senses spinning, what chance would he have against the succubus-like creature of the castle? No, let the girl be criterion for his intended night's continence; and Tharquest, swinging himself athwart the black flanks of his mare, laughed as he offered up a blasphemous blessing to Dark Ghatanothoa.

"May your gods protect you then, Tharquest," the girl called after his belling, tattered cloak.

"I have no gods," he called back, "save perhaps Shub-Niggurath, black ram with a thousand ewes." And he laughed.

"I'll wait for you," she cried. "Then, should you win your riches, your continence need not be extended beyond endurance…"

A short while later Tharquest came to the lamia's castle. The brooding, shrouded pile was girt around with strangely motionless trees, and as the wanderer had noted from afar, even standing in the sun it was oddly shaded. Beneath the trees by a narrow, silent streamlet he tethered his mare, proceeding on foot across the moat to the massive door. With the castle's turreted spires looming darkly above, he felt more than a little afraid, and he peered cautiously in at the open door. All was gloom and cobwebby dimness within, but the thought of the great reward soon to be his and the knowledge that the lamia only took her lusty nourishment at night bore up the wandering Klühnite's spirits.

Slowly he explored each room of the place, cellars to lofty spires, and as he did so his eyes grew more accustomed to the dimness and showed him a weird and singular thing. Each of the castle's rooms contained a bed of the finest cushions and silks, and at the foot of each bed great piles of clothing lay. There were boots and sandals and buskins, cloaks and capes, jackets and jerkins; trews, kilts and breeches; turbans, hoods and fancy titfers; shirts and kerchiefs and gauntlets and every thinkable item of manly attire—but nothing suitable for a woman. Why!—here were wardrobes for a hundred, nay, two hundred men… But where were those men? Who had they been?

Again Tharquest became sore afraid, glancing nervously about him, holding tight to the pommel of his simple sword and thinking on what he knew of the queen of this shadowed and unpeopled pile, the lamia Orbiquita. Dilquay had told him how, though she only took her prey at night, she would often assume human form in the hours of daylight to forage about and spy out the land for suitable victims. Possibly that was what she was even now about, and, heartened by the thought that he was at least alone in the castle, Tharquest engaged upon a systematic search of the place for the treasure fabled to lie hidden therein.

...Long into the afternoon he searched, finding neither jewels, gold nor wealth of any sort; neither priceless miniatures nor gilt-framed masterpieces. Not a single solitary coin did he find, but he did come across a room in which a great table stood fresh prepared and laden as for a banquet. There were great platters of meat and smaller dishes containing toothsome morsels and sweetmeats; flagons of white, red and green wine, and one as pure and clear (or so the wanderer thought) as the glass-grape wine of olden Chlangi; exotic fruits of every size and shape and colour; oysters, shrimps, lobsters and crabs; cocktails of flowers served with the black honey of ocean-girt Ardlanthys—the sort of banquet a man might order prepared for his guests on the day of his wedding...

...Aye, and in certain parts, the night of his funeral!

And feeling hungry, Tharquest tasted of the foods and sipped of the wines, finding all delightful to the palate and very satisfying. Then, uplifted physically and relaxed mentally, he set to and bound him up some torches from turbans in the piles at the feet of the beds in the various rooms. These he dipped in tureens of scented oil at the banquet table, and for torch handles he used wooden legs broken from chairs in that same room. Night was coming on apace now, and the Klühnite, without having noticed how weary he had gradually grown since sipping of the various wines, suddenly found himself tired.

III

Soon the sun sank down into the realm of Cthon and Tharquest, for the nonce, gave up his torchlit searching and wandering through the castle's rooms. He found himself a high room with only one door and one slitlike window. The door he braced against opening with a rough wedge of wood at its bottom before lying back on his bed of cushions and silks, his simple sword within easy reach of his right hand. Thus, in the flickering light of a scented turban-torch, the adventurer closed his heavy eyes in reluctant sleep.

And a strange dream came to him, wherein Tharquest wandered amidst green forests and swam in blue and sparkling pools of winelike water. A nymph there was, too—of silken tresses, with eyes deeper than the unplumbed Pool of Xthyll, slim and with flesh of living marble—who led him to her orchid bower and held out her arms to him.

Dying, the torch sputtered and gave off oily fumes as the dreamer turned in his bed and reached out avid, hungry hands over the ruffled silks—

—Tharquest coughed as the fumes reached him, coughed and choked and his mind began to rise up from abysses of sleep. Desperately he stretched out his arms and his body to the fading, wavering nymph within her evaporating bower—*and contacted horror*!

Horned and warty skin, rough as bark to his touch! Protruding nodules and suppurating sores! Breasts flabby, slimy and writhing! Hands with nails like claws of great crabs, and panting breath in his face smelling worse than the effluvia of the Burial Catacombs of Hroon! This, then, was the lamia Orbiquita!

Tharquest leapt shrieking awake, simple sword in trembling right hand, his left hand thrusting out a fresh torch to catch the embers of its dying brother. Flaring light—and a *Thing* that grew bat-wings even as he gazed in morbid fascination, launching itself from the bed to the window, pausing there for a moment in the slitlike opening to glare lustfully at him, then sliding off into the night with a hideous cackle and rustle of leathern membranes!

For an hour then Tharquest busied himself, hanging drapes of cloaks and capes at the window and strengthening the fortification of the door by forcing a second wedge in at its top. Eventually, satisfied that he had done all he could to ward off any further attempts at his seduction and destruction by the lamia, the Klühnite sat back upon his bed and surveyed the results of his work in the flickering torch-light. Now that the job was done, he gave thought to what had passed and how close he had been to unutterable horror.

But eventually Tharquest's trembling limbs and quaking soul calmed, until, as his heart slowed its wild beating and his eyes began to ache with the strain of glaring about the room at the leaping shadows, the drugged wine of the lamia again brought down the ramparts of his awareness. The lids of his eyes slowly lowered, his terror-taut muscles slackened and his breathing slowed, his head fell to his chest and his body toppled gently over backward until he lay flat on the bed with his simple sword close beside him.

Some time passed while Tharquest sank deeper into sleep, and the second coming of the lamia Orbiquita went completely unbeknown to the slumbering Klühnite. She came as a twist of smoke, issuing in at the crack of the door, forming…forming…

Again in his dream the wanderer chased his laughing nymph through exotic forests ribboned with sparkling winestreams and pools, and again she led him to her bower of orchids, reaching out to him and pouting prettily and moving her body most seductively.

Tossing and turning in his bed, moaning in his sleep and whispering words of love remembered of many an adventure of old, Tharquest reached out his hands and found the beautiful body of the nymph. And at this the lamia rejoiced greatly, for she had altered her form (an art at which she was greatly adept) to that of a young girl, that she might better fool the handsome young wanderer. Violently he pulled her toward him—and in so doing caused his sword to fall with a clatter from the bed to the floor.

Tharquest heard the sword fall—even through his dreaming flesh-lust he heard it—and his sleeping mind was distracted from its course. Too, in the semi-awareness of his disturbed dream, he now discovered peculiarities: that the flesh his hands had found was cold as the spaces between the stars, and that the breath issuing into his face carried the same carrion stench he had known before! And abruptly he remembered where he was and what he was about.

Again the Klühnite came awake, leaping from his suddenly repellent bed. In mid-leap he plucked up his fallen sword in barely articulate hand, snatching at the low-burning torch on the wall. There upon the bed as he held the torch out at trembling arm's length, lay the perfect form of the nymph of his dreams! One shaky yet resolute step took him to the bedside, but even as he gritted his teeth to thrust his sword into the girl's side her body turned to smoke, streaming swiftly out under the door and leaving only the echo of an awful chuckle behind—that and the memory of a horror that had seemed to rot even as its substance became smoke!

More weary than ever but determined now to fortify the room as fully as possible, Tharquest lit a third torch, then stumbled about stuffing linings torn from capes and jackets into the cracks of the door and blocking the window slit completely with other articles of clothing. By the time he had finished the drug in his blood had reached its peak of potency and it was as much as he could do to keep his eyes open. The room swam and seemed to blur before him as he mazedly sought his bed of silks and cushions…

As the adventurer fell once more asleep, the lamia was already on her way back to her castle. She had flown into the Desert of Sheb to certain caves she knew—caves that went down to the very pits at Earth's core, where red imps leap from one lava pool to the next—and there she had warmed her chill and loathly flesh by hell's own fires that the imitation of life thus imbibed might better fool the man come to seek her treasures.

Still hot from hell she burned when she flapped down atop her pile. Aye, even so hot as to leave cloven prints burning in the stones of those ramparts—but much of her heat was lost as she formed herself into a pool of water to seep into the cracks of the stone and down, down toward Tharquest's room.

Again he was oblivious of her coming, slumbering on as tiny droplets of lamia-formed moisture gathered on the ceiling and ran down the walls.

…Yet even sleeping and dreaming, the Klühnite was now cautious. Without truly remembering the reasons for his reticence, nevertheless he followed his laughing nymph carefully. Such caution could not last, however, for was he not Tharquest the Rake, known in seventeen cities for his audacity and impudence and banned forever from fourteen of them through those same improprieties? When the nymph held out her arms to him he went to her, whispering false words of love to a yet more faithless lover, courting her as the tiny male courts the bloated black widow spider, reaching out his hands for her…

Fortunately for Tharquest, the drug was now past its greatest strength and fast waning in potency, and the warnings of past, sleep-fogged encounters with this nymph lingered yet in the eye of his inner memory. Her flesh was warm, true, and her body smooth and having none of rough lumps or pustules—but as he moved his body towards her and made to kiss her lips...

That horrendous smell!

In the nick of time, with no instant to spare, again the adventurer leapt from the arms of that poisonous princess of passion, leapt from her to catch up his sword and smite again and again at the bed... which was suddenly wet with liquid so that his blade came away dripping. And the droplets from his sword mixed with the moisture soaked through the now empty bed to the stone floor beneath, and the entire living pool swiftly flowed away down a narrow crack in the stonework and was gone. Again an eerie chuckle floated back to the shuddering Klühnite.

Very frightened but clearer in his mind now that the drug was dead and absorbed into his system, Tharquest saw that while the torch in the wall burned so low as to give very little light, yet there was a secondary light in the room. Its source was the windowslit where his raiment barricade had started to settle and slip. He tore the piled garments away, and there in the east a golden glowing haze already showed on the horizon. The sun was not yet up, but it would not be long.

Only thinking to be out of the place, Tharquest ripped away the silken wadding and wooden wedges from the door. He passed with a shaky laugh out into the castle's corridors, showing a flash of his former impudence as he sought himself the most magnificent cloak and boots he could find in exchange for his own tatters. Down the stone steps he went, simple sword secure in its scabbard, and as he reached the great outer door—then came his reward!

IV

Even as he made to leave the pile, a stone flag in the wall near the door pivoted outward revealing an inner cavity, and out from the hole cascaded the most fantasic treasure the wanderer could ever have dreamed of.

Tourmaline, turquoise and topaz; onyx, opal and pearl; garnet, jade and emerald; rose quartz, zircon and lapis lazuli; ruby, sapphire and bloodstone; diamond, aquamarine and amethyst—jewels and precious stones of every sort and size! And gold! And silver! Coins of every realm on Earth, and some, Tharquest fancied—because of their shapes and the images graven upon them—from yet more distant places. Strings of black pearls big as marbles; crowns and tiaras and diadems of alien design; jeweled daggers and golden effigies of strange gods—an endless stream of untold wealth, all flowing out upon the floor!

And so Tharquest knew he had won, and it was a matter of only a few seconds to fill his pockets with some of the choicest pieces, a continent's ransom. Thus, well weighted down with fantastic jewels and priceless bric-a-brac, the wanderer passed from the castle of Orbiquita, and as the golden glow grew yet brighter beyond the far horizon he made his way quickly to his tethered mare. Freeing the animal's rope rein, he was about to mount when he heard his name called. Glancing about, he soon saw the shepherd girl approaching in a hooded cloak through the silent trees.

"Tharquest!" she gasped, peering fearfully about. "Oh, Tharquest, I feared you would be lost—that the lamia would devour you—and so I had to come here to know for certain. I thought never to see you again!"

He smiled his audacious smile and bowed low, doffing his hat and flicking his luxurious cloak. "The lamia is defeated," he cried, "and was there ever any doubt but that this was the way it must be? Did you truly believe that I might fail? And riches—" He dipped into a pocket and tossed the girl a glowing green gem even as green as her eyes and of a like size. "Why!—what could that bauble alone not buy?"

"Oh, Tharquest, Tharquest!" She clapped her hands in delight and glowed with pleasure, holding her prize up to the far dim light beyond the trees, and peering into its green-fire depths. Then, as she bowed low in acceptance of the gift, the Klühnite glimpsed once more those soft delights first viewed in her father's cot, and he remembered her parting words of the previous afternoon.

Aye, and she must have recognised that look in his eyes, for she laughed and twirled about, her hands to the fastenings of her cloak. And lo!—when next she faced him that cloak lay at her feet and she stood naked and coyly blushing there in the silent glade.

Yet ready as he ever was, the wanderer had learned things that night, and as he leaned forward as if to kiss her his hand secretly fondled the hilt of his simple sword. But no, her breath was sweet as honey, her lips warm with life, her flesh smooth and delightful to the wanderer's touch. And so Tharquest quickly threw off his robes and they fell together to the green grass in the glade of stirless trees—

—And the sun not yet up above the horizon!

And her breath (sweetened by an elixer of Djinni brewed deep in the Desert of Sheb) was sugar as her lips fastened upon him. And her flesh (again warmed by hell's own fires while red imps skipped across the lava pools) quivered warmly under him. And her body (shaped by that art of which she was adept) opened up beneath him and sucked him in, skin and blood and bone and all, fuel for her fires of lust and horror. And Tharquest gave but a single shriek as he went, hearing in his passing the shrill screaming of his suddenly terrified mare...

Later, glutted the nonce and needful of rest, the lamia Orbiquita flapped off on leathern wings in the direction of her shepherd's cot, there to sleep through the morning and lie in waiting for the next adventurer to happen that way.

And later still there was tumult in the camps of the starvelings beneath Chlangi's walls—tumult and the preparation of cooking pots and pans—as a black mare, lathered about her flanks and red-eyed in a fearful and nameless dread, came galloping to her doom.

To Kill a Wizard!

"They come and they go, these wizard-slayers," whispered Mylakhrion to his currently favourite familiar, a one-legged jackdaw of spiteful mien. "Some creep in the night like thieves—" (the ancient mage stifled a yawn, of boredom perhaps) "—others bound boldly over the drawbridge, eyes flashing fire and swords aglint; and there are those who disguise themselves as simple men seeking an old, fatherly magician's advice." He chucked the bird gently under its curving beak. "But then, I don't need to tell you these things, do I? You yourself have slain a wizard or two, in your time."

"I have, I have," croaked the bird, his bright button eyes unblinking, his head cocked to catch his master's words. "You also, Mylakhrion, I would have slain, were your protections less potent that time." And there was bitterness in the jackdaw's croaky voice.

"Come now, Gyriss," Mylakhrion softly chastened, his voice like a fall of autumn leaves. "After all this time—how many years?—is there still enmity between us? *You* came to Tharamoon seeking to slay me, remember? And I wonder, were our roles reversed, would I still live to talk to you? I doubt it. As to your welfare: who else in all Theem'hdra would procure these good nuts, at today's prices, in order to pamper a balding, one-legged jackdaw?" He dangled his long fingers in a bowl of almonds.

"But once I had *two* good legs," croaked Gyriss. "And as for nuts—which you magick out of thin air, at no cost at all—why, I ate only the rarest viands and drank only the finest wines!"

"Wines!" the wizard chuckled. "Choice meats. Whoever heard of a jackdaw eating rare viands? You're an ingrate, Gyriss, and in a mood tonight, that's all. Was I ever unkind to you?"

"Only the once," came the answer, as sour a croak as ever Mylakhrion heard.

"Ah! But then it was you or me," he answered, adjusting the wide sleeves of his rune-embroidered robe. And his voice was colder now. "Anyway, it bores me to review all that. What use to open up old wounds, eh? Now let it be, Gyriss, and come tell me what you make of this." He nodded toward his great blue-green shewstone of crystal where it was set central at the flat apex of a tripod table all carved of black wood and inlaid with gold and ivory arabesques.

The jackdaw hopped from its perch to Mylakhrion's shoulder with scarce a flutter, peered with him at the shewstone which, as the wizard drew an intricate figure in the air with his forefinger, at once grew cloudy as from some eruption of internal aethers.

"See! See?" said Mylakhrion, as the mists in the crystal ball opened like ethereal curtains upon a bleak and wintry scene. "I've been watching him approach for days now, and at last he has reached Tharamoon itself. How say you? Is this not just such a wizard-slayer, come to try his luck?"

Gyriss craned his feathery neck and looked closer, his beady eyes agleam. He saw a man in a boat, sailing stormy waters on the approach to Tharamoon's crescent bay. "Aye," he croaked, "but no ordinary slayer by a mile. I know this one. He is Humbuss Ank, a Northman—and quite recklessly mad!"

"A Northman!" Mylakhrion narrowed his silver eyebrows, drew them close together over his sharp nose. "Mad, you say? *Hah!* But they are berserkers all, these men of the fjords! You, too, were a wild one, if memory serves..." And to himself he remarked the bird's keen eyesight, for he himself had discerned no clear detail of the figure in the boat except that it was a man.

The jackdaw's feathers stood up along his spine. He shook himself, sprang aloft, flew round the rim of the high tower room crying:

"Berserkers all, berserkers all!" and alighted again on Mylakhrion's hunched shoulder. "True, true," he croaked, "but even more so in the case of Humbuss Ank. And with good reason."

"Say on," commanded Mylakhrion, keenly interested. He had somehow guessed that Gyriss might be knowledgeable in the subject of wizard-slayers.

"This one's father, mother, and elder brother," the jackdaw explained, "were slain all three by the cold magicks of Khrissan ice-priests. It happened at a fording- and trading-place on the Great Marl River, and this is how it was:

"It was in the late autumn of the year and the coming winter would be a bad one; already the ice crept over the Reef of Great Whales, and the skies were ominously heavy with more than their fair share of snow and blizzard. Thull Ank and his strapping wife Gubba had trapped well; their haul that year was of the highest quality. The trading went well—for a while, anyway. But Humbuss' brother, Guz, drank too much of the bitter wine of the ice-priests, and when he was drunk made much sport of their ice-gods and -goddesses.

"So they slew Guz and his father both with their magicks, and took Gubba back with them to Khrissa as a sacrifice to the very gods her son had scorned. Aye, and they stole all their pelts and goods, too—word of which eventually got back to Humbuss, a mere lad then in Hjarpon Settlement. Since when he is grown to a man and lives only to kill wizards and priests and all such purveyors of magick wherever he may find them. And now at last it seems he's come for you, Mylakhrion of Tharamoon..."

"My thanks, Gyriss," said Mylakhrion archly. "Though why I should detect accusation in your tone I cannot say! Towards myself? Because I, too, am a wizard? That is as it may be; but I am not one of Khrissa's cruel mages, nor indeed do I make human or any other sac-rifice to strange gods. As for women, I respect them—the human sort, anyway. I forced myself upon a lamia or two in my youth, but only as ritual ingredients in my spells. So do not glare your beady accusations at me! Now then, let me look more closely at this berserker come to kill me..."

He narrowed his eyes at the bird, but deliberately refrained from asking how Gyriss knew so much about Humbuss Ank. Then without further pause he drew another figure with his finger, a shape which seemed to fall slowly from fingertip to shewstone and be absorbed by it. And lo!—the picture in the crystal ball swam up large as life, larger than the very crystal itself, until wizard and familiar both might fancy they were themselves integral in the frore and windswept scene.

And Mylakhrion seemed to stand upon Tharamoon's pebbly strand within the bay, with Gyriss flapping upon his shoulder; and they watched as the lone boat battled the breakers to finally shoot through the sharp volcanic rocks of the reef and into calmer water unscathed. The ragged sail was lowered as the boat swept on ashore, and down from his reeling craft sprang a man into the frothing surf even as the keel of his boat bit sand and grit; so that in a trice this northern adventurer was dragging his vessel ashore, hauling it up the beach with arms that looked utterly tireless.

Fingering his beard, Mylakhrion nodded thoughtfully. "A strong man, this one, Gyriss."

And his familiar—perhaps too eagerly, too gladly—agreed saying: "That he is, that he is! No wily warrior this, Mylakhrion, but merely strong. Brainy?—never! But brawny? As an ox, brawny! A man to laugh in the face of your magicks, this Humbuss—aye, even in the face of hell itself! He'll storm on through all your mirages and illusions, no matter how monstrous, and damn any demons you may conjure back to the dark where they're spawned. It is not so much that he is invincible, rather that he thinks he is. Mind over matter, O master—which is a sort of magick in itself!"

"Hmm!" mused the wizard darkly, a trifle surly now. "Let me look closer. I wish to see his face."

Meanwhile: the Northman had made his boat secure in the lee of the cliffs, which now he set about to scale. And Mylakhrion floated up light as a feather to where the invader swarmed up those sheer crags like a monkey. He looked into Humbuss' face, even into his blackly glittering eyes, and Humbuss saw him not. For of course this was only a picture in a shewstone, however real it might seem.

And Mylakhrion saw a man whose soul was empty, bereft of any last vestige of honour or decency. His black eyes were narrow, cruel and full of lust; his hard mouth was twisted in a sneer; his blunt nose and hollow left cheek were grimly scarred, and his squat nostrils sniffed the chill night air like those of a great bloodhound. His narrow black mane stood up stiffly down his back, like the risen hackles of a dog; and diagonally across that broad, muscled back he bore a mighty broadsword, strapped there in its leather scabbard, its blade notched from many a fierce affray.

Then Mylakhrion drew back and away into his tower retreat, and Gyriss flapping still where he clung to his shoulder. And the wizard snapped his fingers, at which the shewstone cleared and became simply a blue-green ball of crystal, quiescent and opaque.

"Gyriss," said Mylakhrion then, "this man is a brutal slayer, and yet I relish not the thought of killing him. Indeed killing is not my way at all, for it lacks sensitivity. So tell me, how may I stop this thing before it goes any further?"

Gyriss flew to his perch and sat preening, saying nothing.

"Well? Have you no ideas?"

"What can I say?" the jackdaw finally croaked. "He's a brute and a berserker on a lifelong quest for revenge."

"Revenge? I think not," said Mylakhrion. "No, there's more than that brings him here." At which the jackdaw gave a small start, glad that his master was looking the other way. "He may have *started* this life work of his out of some perverted sense of duty to his priest-slain kith and kin," Mylakhrion continued, "but since then it has got quite out of hand. Now I think he kills because he likes it, or for profit. So much I divined when I looked into his face. If it is the former, mayhap I'm in trouble. If the latter—"

"Then you can buy him off with a pouch of priceless gems," croaked Gyriss.

"Why not?" said Mylakhrion, bringing his pacing to an abrupt halt. "Indeed, why not? I have a vault full of jewels, and what use are they to me?"

"No use at all," said Gyriss, "when you can simply conjure them out of the air—as you conjure my nuts!"

"But that must be a last resort." Mylakhrion paced some more, holding up a finger. "For if I'm to give gems to this one, next year there'll be a dozen like him. First I shall attempt to deter him with magick!"

"But he scorns magick," answered Gyriss. "Many another mage has tried to frighten him off. And where are they now?"

"I do believe you're enjoying this!" said Mylakhrion with a glare. "Nathless, what you say is probably true. Still I shall *try* to frighten him away. It's that or kill him out of hand, and I won't spill blood if it can be avoided—as you are well aware." And he glowered pointedly at Gyriss, who for his part croaked:

"You could always transport him back whence he came..."

"In the last year or two I've transported—how many wizard-slayers?"

"Four, by my count," answered the bird at once, "plus a pirate ship and its motley crew."

"Correct!" snapped Mylakhrion. "A pair of dull brigands back to Klühn; a black pirate princeling back to his jungled island, him and his ship and all his crew with him; and a deranged Hrossak hunter back to the steppes. I weary of transporting! Also, word may soon get out that transportation is my sole defence! What's more, if it's true that this Humbuss Ank has killed so many sorcerers, by now he may well have some small understanding of magick himself. The cancellation of the rune of transportation is easily achieved, if a man knows the words. And once one spell is broken, then other enchantments are checked that much easier. Spells are like building blocks which interlock: remove one and the entire wall is weakened. No, I'd not risk that with this one—except if I fail first to scare him off."

"So," said Gyriss, summing up, "you'll scare him, or transport him if he won't scare, or buy him off as a last resort. And is that the sum total of the measures you'll take against him?"

"It is!" snapped Mylakhrion. "And it must suffice, else I'll be left with no choice but to kill him."

"*If* you can," croaked Gyriss quietly, wickedly.

"What?" cried the wizard. "If I can? And how, pray, may he prevail, against a fortress of magicks and machineries such as this tower of mine? You try my patience, Gyriss!" And he stamped his foot on stone flags. "Perhaps you'd welcome my demise? And would you remain a jackdaw forever? For you surely will if some barbaric doom befalls me. Who then to open my runebook and read the words which alone may unspell you, ungrateful bird?"

And Gyriss was rightly cowed, and hunched down into himself upon his perch. "I meant only to say," he croaked, "that if you're to set

guards and traps and such you'd best be about it. By now Humbuss
Ank has scaled the cliffs and strides this way. Some twenty miles, as I
gauge it. Rough country, but still he'll be here before morning."

"Hmph!" grunted Mylakhrion. And, "Calm yourself, Gyriss.
There's time enough and more. As for his chances: a snowflake would
stand more chance in hell! Methinks you make too much of him.
Myself: I shall be fast asleep when—if—he gets here. I would not
soil my hands on him but leave such servile chores to others far less
sensitive. Attend me if you will, I go now to make the arrangements..."

Mylakhrion's tower was reached via a drawbridge across a chasm
too wide for jumping, whose sheer sides went down endlessly into
darkness. Beneath the tower itself were many mazy vaults whose contents were conjectural and at best dubious; above the ground stood six
floors serving various purposes. Topmost consisted of a storeroom,
pantry and kitchen, bath- and steam-room, small study, and observatory for astrological readings. Gyriss had never seen those rooms: they
were forbidden to him, as was the wizard's bedchamber and orchid-
decked conservatory on the penultimate level.

That left four floors with which the jackdaw was familiar. The
great room with the shewstone was one of three interconnected rooms
on the fourth level, beneath Mylakhrion's bedchamber, which also
contained the vast majority and endless variety of his thaumaturgical books and experimental apparatus. The next floor down was a
maze of storerooms, usually all but empty, for Mylakhrion conjured
most of his supplies as required. But beneath that the two lower floors
were dangerous places indeed for would-be intruders. For built into
the rooms therein were certain mechanical devices so designed as to
utterly incapacitate all unwary thieves and the like. They were veritable mantraps, which now Mylakhrion would bait. But first he'd set
his guards on the narrow and stony path beyond the drawbridge, by
which route Humbuss Ank must needs approach.

So down he went to the vaults with Gyriss (who didn't much care
for the dark) where he animated three stone statues and led them stiffly
up out of darkness and across the drawbridge. On the far side he turned
and faced them, and scowled his disgust at them. For they were—
had been—favored familiars in their time, and he had placed some
small trust in them. But many years agone they'd turned on him and

deliberately lured a wizard-slayer here, for which Mylakhrion had punished them by turning them to stone. He'd punished the wizard-slayer, too—one Gyriss Kag—replacing them with him. But once in a while he'd bring them up and let them ease their joints, and at times he even had work for them. Now was such a time.

The three were chiropterans, great bats who wore the faces of men they'd once been. Now as they stumbled in Mylakhrion's wake he spoke to them, saying: "A man is coming who would kill me. You—" he pointed to the first man-bat, "—will remain here, at the drawbridge. If he comes this far you will offer him this for his trouble and tell him to turn aside." And he gave the chiropteran a fat pouch of gems. "Fail to turn him back," he answered, "and I'll stand you forever on the balcony of my tower observatory to weather in the wind and the rain."

Then he walked half a mile with the other two and paused again, speaking to the second of them: "You will remain here. If my would-be slayer comes this far, you will utter the rune of transportation and hurl him back whence he came. Failure to do so will see you broken in two halves upon this very spot, where time and nature will mold your pieces into small stones."

After a further half-mile he stopped again where the path wound down a steep cliff, and to the third bat-thing said: "You will astonish the man with illusions, and afraid for his life he'll flee. In the event he does *not* flee—you shall be dashed into small, small fragments. I, Mylakhrion, have spoken!"

And with Gyriss on his shoulder he returned to his tower, set his mechanical protections, proceeded up the winding central staircase to his bedchamber. At the door he took the jackdaw on his finger, saying: "There. And fear not for me, Gyriss. I shall sleep like a babe, and this Northman shall not disturb me. Begone!" At which the bird descended to the room of the shewstone, where for a while he sat in utter silence, waiting for his master to fall asleep…

Within the half-hour, unable to hold off any longer, Gyriss flapped silently to a balcony and across it into the fast approaching night, and flew up to peer into his master's bedchamber through the single great window there, which fortunately stood open. The room was all of mosaics, covering floor, walls and ceiling. Above flew ebony swallows in a lapis-lazuli sky; the walls were a jade forest with jewelled birds of paradise; and the floor was of chrysolite ferns, inlaid with an hundred marble monkeys.

There slept Mylakhrion, as his huddled form beneath the satin bedclothes testified. But to be absolutely certain, Gyriss passed through the window into the forbidden room and swooped once on silent wings around the bed to hear the wizard snoring. Satisfied then, he left the tower and sped across the drawbridge, following the path toward the distant Bay of Tharamoon. And beneath him he spied the three chiropteran guards where Mylakhrion had placed them. Eventually in the gloom he saw the Northman Humbuss Ank striding toward him and he descended, flying well over the other's head.

"Humbuss!" he croaked then. "Look up. It is I, Gyriss Kag."

The barbarian saw him, paused, guffawed and slapped his thigh. "What? And is it really you, Gyriss, who once swigged ale with me and slew the occasional wizard? Come down and speak to me, if you're one and the same, and explain why you've called me here to this cold and lonely crag."

Gyriss alighted on the other's mighty shoulder. "I'm him, all right!" he croaked. "Do you remember that ill-omened night each of us boasted how he'd be the first to breach Mylakhrion's protections and kill him? Drunk, we were, and me so drunk that I set out at once to be started on the quest. But you held back, saying you'd work your way up to him by degrees. Do you remember?"

"I do," said Humbuss, still mirthful. "And it seems I was right to be cautious. He was too much for you, eh?"

"Indeed he was, and too much for many another I've called here. But not, I pray, too much for you. For with my help, old friend, you'll surely slay him."

"Well, so far so good," growled Humbuss. "I followed the course you set me across the sea and through the ragged reef, and here I am. You mentioned a treasure, Gyriss, and I desire it. Also, I desire the great prestige of killing Mylakhrion the so-called 'immortal.' But what would you have out of this?"

"Only my human form once more returned to me," answered Gyriss. "And the satisfaction of seeing Mylakhrion die! For after you've killed him you'll read a certain rune of restoration from his great runebook and I'll be a man again. After which I'll show you his treasure house."

"Good enough!" Humbuss agreed. "And now: how may you help me, eh?"

And Gyriss told him all about the three guardians of the way, and something about the drawbridge, and more about Mylakhrion's tower itself. Following which he flapped aloft and returned the way he'd come, his heart filled with treacherous satisfaction...

Meanwhile, back at the tower: a tiny black spider surveyed her jack-daw-ruined web at Mylakhrion's window, and angered spun a silken thread and drifted on it to where the wizard slept. She alighted on his cheek and crept into his ear, and Mylakhrion awakened, listened, smiled and sat up. He waited for her to emerge, then carefully carried her back to her web, which he repaired at once with a word and a wave of his hand.

"My thanks, small friend," he whispered, and slowly descended to his room of many magicks—even to the room of the shewstone...

Humbuss Ank came upon the first man-bat and commanded him, "Stand aside!"

"Much as I would like to, I cannot," answered the chiropteran. And he conjured an illusion wherein he swelled up massive as a mountain. Humbuss laughed and pushed him off the cliff, and stiff from his stony sojourn in the vaults he could not fly but fell like an icicle in the melt—and like an icicle was dashed into small, small fragments, as Mylakhrion had decreed.

Half a mile later Humbuss came to the second guard and said, "Out of my way, bat-thing!"

To which the other answered: *"Sdrojf eht ot kcab—Kna Ssub-Muh, enogeb!"*—which was the rune of transportation.

But Gyriss had told him the rune's reversal, and before the spell could take effect Humbuss cried: *"Diputs, gnud lae!"*—and hacked the chiropteran in twain. Just as Mylakhrion had prescribed.

And finally, when he came to the drawbridge, Humbuss found the third guard waiting, who offered him the jewels and bade him turn aside. But the Northman merely snatched the jewels from him and scornfully shouldered him out of the way, then ignored him utterly and turned to face the drawbridge. And scattering small handfuls of jewels into the abyss as Gyriss had instructed, he commanded: "Drawbridge, show me where you really are!" And the jewels passed through the illusory drawbridge and into the abyss; but to one side they fell not, and Humbuss stepped out across what seemed thin air, letting jewels drop in front to guide him safely across. And so at last he entered in through the door in the tower's base.

Now Gyriss had warned him about the two lower levels, and so Humbuss was wary. But even as he glanced in through the main door of the lower level's complex, so the jackdaw came fluttering down from above to remind him of the dangers:

"'Ware, Humbuss! These are not treasures you spy but illusions!"

Humbuss looked again. The floor of the room behind the open door was tiled with small hexagonal mirrors, so that all in the room seemed duplicated. What he saw, therefore, seemed doubly awesome. For in that room were heaped treasures beyond all human dreams of avarice, where every known gem—and many unknown—spilled from piles upon the mirror floor! And even as he stood there with the juices of greed making his mouth moist, so a mouse scampered across the threshold and ran in amazement, ogling his mouse-reflection, to and fro amidst the glitter and the wealth. But no harm befell the mouse.

"It is the floor!" cried Gyriss. "The mouse has no weight, but only place the tip of your great sword upon the floor beyond that door—"

Humbuss did so—and scarce had time to withdraw his blade before the scintillant illusion vanished! And in its place a brilliant flashing of silent, silver blades, a sieve of shimmering motion, a mesh of metallic teeth and shining scalpels. And all so silent! So that in a moment the room breathed out a fine damp mist of mouse-essence and closed its door gently in Humbuss' face.

And even Humbuss Ank was a little awed by the room's deadly efficiency, so that he needed no urging to climb the stone stairs to the next level. Gyriss flapped along behind him, but the bird seemed more anxious now. "'Ware, Humbuss, 'ware! When I came to kill Mylakhrion, I stepped upon a floor of fine mosaics, all shaped like a flight of jackdaws—and see what became of me!"

Already the Northman had reached the next level and would not have paused a moment—had not his narrowed eyes glimpsed beyond a second open door such a harem as to send even a eunuch into a frenzy of passion! And no eunuch Humbuss Ank but hot-blooded Northman.

"*Stars!*" he gasped. And the ladies where they feasted at a circular table all glanced his way, and smiled, and wriggled, and beckoned him to come in.

"No!" cried Gyriss. "This, too, is a machine, and that door is a door to another place, not of this world. It is a place Mylakhrion knows. Look again: these are not women but succubi and lamias. And see what they're eating, Humbuss. *Only look at their repast!*"

Humbuss looked. Beneath the circular table, visible now that the mist of lust was off his eyes, the great fat body of a man writhed and twitched where it was bound to the table's central leg. But his head went up through the table, and was open at the top like an egg—into which the ladies dipped their silver spoons...

Shuddering, even Humbuss Ank, he drew back from the door and climbed again; and up past the third and fourth floors went barbarian and bird together, to the very door of Mylakhrion's bedchamber—which also stood open.

Now Gyriss grew excited indeed. "Only once have I been within," he croaked as quietly as possible, "and so cannot help you here. The chamber seems innocent enough, but from here you're on your own. I will not watch, for I admit to feeling faint from my own treachery."

"What?" hissed Humbuss in amazement. "He's a foul magician, is he not?"

"The mightiest," Gyriss agreed. "But his magicks are more nearly white than black. I will not watch."

"Faintheart!" said Humbuss. "He made of you a crippled bird!"

"Because I came to kill him," squawked Gyriss, but not loudly "Since when...he has not been unkind to me. You still have time to go back, Humbuss..."

"Bah!" thundered the barbarian. And, "Have done!" And he strode across the mosaic floor to where the wizard's figure stirred as he came sluggishly awake beneath satin bedclothes. And as if mysteriously guided, Humbuss' booted feet stepped not once upon a capering marble monkey, but always on the spaces between. Up went his sword as the bedclothes were thrown back, and down in an arc of tarnished, notched steel—

—To strike in halves a squawking, treacherous jackdaw!

And from behind, where Gyriss had fluttered at the door, now came a low sad sigh, and a sombrous voice saying: "Welcome, Humbuss Ank, to the house of Mylakhrion!"

Humbuss whirled, saw the magician materialise there, whose night-black wings grew into a cloak of glowing runes; and gawping his astonishment he stepped forward. Alas, his left foot came down upon a scampering monkey.

Then, in an instant, the mosaics parted and up from below hissed an hundred silver scythes, striking once and returning below before the mosaics could close again. And all so quick that Humbuss did not see, or even feel, the blade which sheared his trunk-like left leg cleanly above the knee...

In the morning Mylakhrion buried Gyriss in a tiny grave in his garden behind the tower. And watching from the high balcony of his observatory, a lone chiropteran of stone stared blindly down and prayed only for good weather. And chained to the neck of the stony man-bat a tiny one-legged monkey gibbered and complained bitterly.

Mylakhrion heard his cries, looked up and smiled. "No, no," he cried, shaking his head. "There you stay for now, my friend. At least until your temper's improved. And even then you must be house-trained.

"Indeed, for the personal habits of Northmen are utterly notorious..."

CRYPTICALLY YOURS

THE FOLLOWING LETTERS, NUMBERED ONE TO
EIGHT, ARE IN THE MAIN SELF-EXPLANATORY.
THEY WILL SERVE ADMIRABLY TO ILLUSTRATE
SOME OF THE MANY PERILS FACING PROFESSIONAL
WIZARDS IN THAT BYGONE AGE WHEN THE
WORLD WAS VERY YOUNG AND MAGIC WAS
NOT MERELY A WORD IN BOOKS FOR SMALL
CHILDREN...

I

Domed Turret of Hreen Castle,
Eleventh Day of the Season of Mists,
Hour of the First Fluttering of Bats.

Esteemed Teh Atht—

You will doubtless recall that we were apprenticed together
(along with Dhor Nen, Tarth Soquallin, Ye-namat and Druth of
Thandopolis) under Imhlat the Great; also how we vied, each against
the others, in aspiring to greatness in our chosen profession. Though
we were mere lads then (how many, many years ago?), still I remember being impressed by your own industry. Aye, even I, Hatr-ad of

Thinhla, whose peer is not known east of the Inner isles, was *most* impressed by the sorcerous industry of Teh Atht. You were a likeable lad—friendly despite the ceaseless competition and bantering and occasional bickering—for which reason I now call upon you, in the name of the comradeship we shared in Imhlat's tutelage, for assistance in a matter of extreme urgency.

Mayhap it has come to your attention that of the six apprentices mentioned above only we two and one other, Tarth Soquallin, remain alive? The others are recently fallen foul of ill-omened, indeed *evil* fates, for all three have met with strange and terrible deaths! Not only Dhor, Ye-namat and Druth, but Imhlat the Teacher, too! Even Imhlat the Great—whose gnarled old hands instructed us in our first passes, weaving weird designs of power in the air—he, too, is gone, wasted away in a grey rot that descended upon him from the moon (they say) and took him all in the space of a single night.

Now I know not your thoughts in this matter, or even if you've considered it at all, but it seems to me that certain dark forces roam free and rapacious in Theem'hdra, and that their fell purpose is the destruction of her wizards one by one, thus plunging the entire continent into an age of darkness, when the light of sorcery will be extinguished forever! If I am correct then our lives, too, are in peril... for which reason I have set up every possible magickal barrier against these unknown agents of evil. This of course is the reason for my letter: to beg of you a certain rune (which I am given to believe may recently have come down to you from your long dead ancestor, Mylakhrion of Tharamoon?), that I might finalise the security of Hreen Castle.

I refer specifically to the Ninth Sathlatta, which—or so I am informed—is a protective device efficacious over all other magicks in the whole of Theem'hdra. Were it indeed your good fortune to be in possession of this spell, I would count myself ever in your debt upon safely receiving a copy of the same.

Take care, Teh Atht, and beware the nameless terror that surely lurks in Theem'hdra's shadows, threatening us all—

Yours for the Numberless Rites of Lythatroll—

Hatr-ad the Adept.

In addition—

Perhaps you know the whereabouts of that inveterate wanderer, Tarth Soquallin? If so, be so good as to advise me of the same that I may also warn him of the hovering horror...

Hatr-ad.

II

Topmost Tower of Klühn,
Eighteenth Night,
Hour of Clouds Wisping across the
Full Moon...

High-born Hierophant, O Hatr-ad!—

Honoured was I, Teh Atht, to receive your correspondence, even though it cost me the services of a most faithful retainer—and him his life! As to how this came about: I am myself at a loss to explain it.

I can only assume that those same dark forces of which your note so eloquently warns entrapped the bat to which you doubtless entrusted the missive, replacing that messenger with the great and winged Gaunt which assaulted my apartments over Klühn in the hour before dawn of the 12th day. Mercifully I myself was not to house, and so the monster took a manservant in my stead, almost obscuring with his blood the words you so carefully inscribed in cypher upon the parchment which I later found clenched in his lifeless fingers.

Thus it would seem that your warning was indeed most timely, and I thank you for it. As to your request for a copy of the 9th S., please find the same enclosed. Note that, remembering well your penchant for cyphers, I have couched the rune in just such a frame—albeit a simple one—the better to amuse and entertain you, however briefly, during your leisure hours.

Alas, I have no knowledge of Tarth Soquallin's whereabouts, but be sure I myself shall now take all precautions to avoid whichever evils befell our former colleagues, and that I remain, in eager anticipation of your next—

Yours for the Exorcism of Org the Awful,

Teh Atht of Klühn.

III

Hidden Vault beneath Hreen Castle;
Twenty-first Night;
Hour of the Tittering Without the Pentagram.

Brother in Blessed Sorceries, O Teh Atht—

A thousand thanks for your letter—and for the cypher-inscribed 9th S., which I shall duly translate as soon as I get five minutes to spare—both safely arrived yester-evening in their silver cylinder affixed to the leg of a great eagle. The bird itself, alas, fell prey to an over-zealous archer in my employ, whom I shall punish fittingly. Still and all, it were not entirely the man's fault, for he had strict instructions with regard to any alien invader of my keep, and was not to know that the bird was but a messenger of your esteemed self.

It was indeed a mercy, brother, that you were away upon the advent of the Gaunt which killed your retainer, and I shudder in contemplation of what might have taken place had you been present to receive so monstrous a visitor! My condolences at the loss of a faithful servant, and my joy that you yourself were spared so terrible an ordeal. Indeed you were correct in assuming that my messenger was but a bat, and I am filled with rage at the vileness of that agency which could so readily turn dumb, harmless minion into ravenous beast!

Now to a matter of even darker import: for we two are now the sole survivors of Imhlat's school for sorcerers, Tarth Soquallin having recently succumbed to the unknown doom! Aye, even Tarth the Hermit, gone forever from the world of men, for I have it on good authority that he is, alas, no more. It would seem that in the midst of magickal meditations he vanished from a cave—a hole in the face of a granite cliff, with no windows and only one stout door—after uttering but a single piercing scream. When finally his disciples broke down the door, they found only his wand and seven rings of gold and silver...those things, and a number of tiny golden nuggets which may once have filled certain of his teeth...

Oh, my brother, what is to be done? The very thought of the evils that surround us and the perils which daily press closer fills me with a nameless dread—or would, if I did not know that my old friend, Teh Atht, is at hand to assist me and offer his sound and unimpeachable advice in these darkest hours—

Yours for the Moaning Menhir,
Hatr-ad.

On afterthought—

Since I really have very little time to waste on riddles—however entertaining they may be—would you be so good as to forward with your next the key to the encyphered 9th S.?

Gratefully—
Hatr-ad.

IV

Sepulcher of Syphtar VI;
Thirty-eighth Evening;
Hour of the Unseen Howler.

Master of Mysteries, O Hatr-ad—

Confirmation of Tarth Soquallin's demise reached me almost simultaneous with your own doom-fraught epistle (I envy you your informants!), and not only his demise but those of several other sorcerers, too, though lesser known and further flung. Ikrish Sarn of Hubriss was one such, and Khrissa's Lord-High Ice-Priest another. Thus have I come down into the tomb of Syphtar VI to seek out his spirit and inquire of it, but lo—Syphtar answers not my call!

Indeed strangeness is abroad, Hatr-ad, even *great* strangeness! It would seem that some dark spell of thaumaturgic impotence is upon me, so that my sorceries are utterly without effect. Can I doubt but that the source of this new infamy is that same secret centre of evil whence ooze the poisonous spells which, one by one, drag down our fellow sorcerers to dreadful doom and death? Nay, I cannot doubt it; it must surely be so.

But with regard to these measures of yours for the protection of Hreen Castle against whichever evils theaten: I may be able to offer the very ultimate in protections, beside which even the ninth Sathlatta pales to insignificance! You were indeed correct in deducing that my ancestor Mylakhrion bequeathed to me certain of his secrets, and that these have recently come down to me across the centuries. Aye, and one of them is a rune of the greatest power, of which I would freely advise you if only I could be sure that my letter would not be intercepted!

Obviously a spell of this magnitude must never fall into the wrong hands, for…

My friend—*I have it*!

Upon a skin which I shall enclose, please peruse the characters of an unbreakable cypher to which I alone possess the key. When next you write, enclose some proof positive by which I may know that our correspondence is completely confidential and secure, and by return I shall forward the key to the cypher, thus placing the greatest of all protective runes in your hands.

Rest assured that I have already used the spell in my own defence—indeed, this very morning—wherefore I fear no evil in the length and breadth of Theem'hdra. (It dawns on me that this near-stultification of my other magicks, of which I have already made mention, must be a side-effect of the greater power, whose task is after all to dampen dangerous sorceries! This is a mere inconvenience as compared with my very life's safety, and doubtless the effect will soon wear off.)

But a warning: the only man who may break down the wall of this protection is one who understands its construction; and once this is done even the smallest spell will work against the one thus betrayed. Naturally I fear no such betrayal from my brother Hatr-ad the Illustrious, else I should not offer this information in the first instance. Be certain, too, that I have not studied the rune sufficiently to understand its reversal; and I trust you will likewise refrain from deliberately discovering the means by which the protection may be cancelled?

In all such matters I have the greatest faith in my brother-sorcerer, Hatr-ad, and thus, in eager anticipation of your next letter, I remain—

Yours for Enduring Enchantments,

Teh Atht of Klühn.

On Afterthought—

With regard to the encyphered 9th S.: It seems I've lost the key! I wrote the thing down on a scrap of parchment which I've since mislaid. There are several such cyphers I use but I have neither the time nor the inclination to divulge all of them. However, this should no longer present a problem, since the new rune supercedes and is far more powerful than the 9th S.. In any case, your own devices have been adequately efficacious to date, as witness (happily) your continued existence!

Sorcerously—

Teh Atht.

One other matter—

My fears over the confidentiality of our correspondence are not unfounded, I assure you, and I warn you to examine such carriers as we use most carefully. The pigeon that brought me your last missive had no sooner delivered up its cylinder than it flew asunder in a thousand searing fragments! I conjecture that it had been fed pellets of some agent, which, reacting with the bird's inner juices, produced this monstrous effect. Certainly the body fluids of the poor creature were become so mordant that the walls of the tower in which it exploded are now pitted and blackened most severely! Mercifully, I was not harmed, nor any retainer of mine.

Will this vileness never end?

Yours—

Teh Atht.

V

Aeries of Hreen Castle;
Nest of the Fanged Hawk;
First Day of the Season of the Sun;
Dawn—

Illustrious Engineer of Illusions,

Most happily I report my continued good health, despite all the spells doubtless cast against me by those unknown agencies of which every sorcerer in all Theem'hdra now goes in dread fear and loathing. Without a shadow of a doubt I owe my well-being in great part to you…for which reason I trust that you, too, are well and that no evil has befallen you?

Your tomb-bat messenger from Syphtar's sepulcher reached me safely, carrying its precious rune, and in the tenth day following my receipt of the same I at last translated the thing from the glyphs in which you had so cleverly enciphered it. Aye, for I am now familiar with your system, Teh Atht, and I marvel at the magnitude of a mind that could devise so mazy a cryptogram! It was not so very difficult, however, once I had broken the code that hid from my eager eyes the 9th S., for it would appear that all your codes are cast in pretty much the same mold. You may now rest easy in the knowledge that your spell shall not fall into alien hands, and that the need to supply me with a key to the code no longer exists…

Moreover, before I commenced the inscribing of this letter here in this high place, I made the necessary signs as the sun came up and I said the words of the rune, and lo!—now I am protected against all evils. All thanks to you, Teh Atht, who succored me in my hour of greatest need.

Yours in the Discovery of Mysteries—
Hatr-ad.

VI

Chamber of Infirmity—
Third Day of the Sun—
Hour of the Tide's Turning.

Honourable Hatr-ad,

Overjoyed as I am to hear of your own continuing good health, alas, I cannot report a similar condition in myself. Indeed no, for I am the victim of several severe disorders—which by their very nature I know to be most unnatural! Unnecessary to go into details, but suffi-cient to say that I am unwell. Even unto death am I, Teh Atht, unwell...

Only the most powerful of unguents and nostrums keep me alive (for my spells no longer work and I am obliged to rely upon merely common cures) so that even the writing of this letter is an ordeal to one whose hands tremble and jerk in unendurable agony as his body festers and rots! If you could see me, Hatr-ad, I believe you would shriek and run from the horror I am become—and I am completely at a loss to remedy the matter of my own free will.

Thus my letter is a plea, that you put aside whatever else engag-es you at this time and weave your most beneficent sorceries on my behalf—else I am done for! For without a shadow of a doubt those same fell forces of which you forewarned are upon me, and lo—I am at their mercy!

My decline commenced almost immediately upon receipt of your last—which, bat-borne and innocent in itself, was nevertheless like some harbinger of doom—and as it progresses so it accelerates. It would seem as though a combination of plagues, cankers and con-tagions are upon me, and without outside help I am doomed to an hideous death even within the space of ten days, possibly less. How this can possibly be when I am protected by the Rune of Power I am again at a loss to say. The evil which is abroad in Theem'hdra is powerful indeed!

I can write no longer. The pus that seeps from my body's pores threatens to foul the vellum upon which I scrawl this final plea: that you spare no single second but come immediately to the assistance of—

Thine in Ultimate Torment,
Teh Atht...

VII

Hreen Castle—Imperial Residence of:
Hatr-ad. Mightiest Magician in all Theem 'hdra—
First Night of the Full Moon;
Hour of Gleeth's Blind Smiling on the Eastern Range.

Doom-Destined Teh Atht—

Not without a modicum of remorse do I, Highborn Hatr-ad, inscribe this final epistle—the last you shall ever read! Indeed, of all other sorcerers in Theem'hdra, you were the one I most respected: for if ever a man were sufficiently gifted to oppose me in my great ambition—of which I was often wont to boast during our apprenticeship in old Imhlat the Idiot's tutelage—then you were that man. Or so I thought...

Perhaps my words recall to your obviously age-enfeebled mind that ambition of mine? Aye, I'm sure they do, for oft and again I swore that one day I would make of myself the most powerful sorcerer in all the land. That day is now at hand, Teh Atht, and you above all other men have assisted me in the realization of my dream.

Now, too, it is plain to me that I ranked you o'er high among magicians, for who but a fool would give away a spell of ultimate protection?—and in so doing *rob himself of that very protection*! Aye, Teh Atht, for surely you have guessed by now that I am the origin and the source of the terror over Theem'hdra? Surely you are now aware whose spells they are that bring down the land's sorcerers in their prime, that rot you yourself in your bed, where even now you lie impotently awaiting death? Nor can that death be so very far away now; indeed, it amazes me that you survive, if you survive, to read this letter!

Even now I would not openly betray myself thus had not word reached me of your confinement, and of the fact that your throat has rotted so that you speak not, and that your body is so wasted that you are barely capable of the feeblest stirrings. Yet, if your very eyes are not utterly dissolved away, you will be able to read this, for I have written it in one of your own codes that no other may know of my triumph.

But what pleasure is there in an empty victory, Teh Atht? For surely my triumph would be empty if in the end none remained to know of it? Thus I now reveal all to you, that before you die you may know of Hatr-ad's victory, of his ambition fulfilled. For surely now I am indeed the greatest sorcerer in all Theem'hdra!

My thanks, Teh Atht, for your inestimable aid in this matter, without which I might yet be sorely pressed to bring about the desired result. Now you may rest your festering eyes, my old and foolish friend, in the final sleep. Go, and find peace in the arms of Shoosh, Goddess of the Still Slumbers...

Yours for the Dream of a New Age of Magickal Empire,

Hatr-ad the Mighty.

VIII

Room of Red Revenge;
Apartments over Klühn;
Day of Recovering,
Hour of Truth!

O Most Misguided, Miserable Hatr-ad—

Heartless one, I fear that your odious ambitions are come to an end—and better for Theem'hdra and all her more worthy wizards were that ending not protracted. Therefore let me linger not over the matter but get to its root with all dispatch.

For you were unmasked, o murderer, long before you chose to show your true face. Nathless it was deemed only fair and just that the truth be heard from your own lips before sentence was passed. The truth is now known...and I have been chosen to pass sentence.

Even now I can hardly ponder the enormity of your crimes without feeling within myself a gnawing nausea, that so vile and monstrous a man could guise himself as "friend" in order to go about his death-dealing devilments!

Murderer! I say it again, and the punishment shall fit the crime...

As to why I bother to write this when your fate will speak volumes of its own, there are reasons. Mayhap amongst your retainers, cronies and familiars there are those who, lusting after similar lordly stations, would carry on your fiendish business in your wake? To them, I, Teh Atht, address this warning—mazed in no cypher but writ in the clear, clean glyphs of Theem'hdra—that it suffice to set their feet upon more enlightened paths.

As for enlightenment: allow me now to unravel for you the more tangled threads of this skein, that you may see yourself as do we, whose sorceries are deemed white (or at worst grey) against your black!

To begin:

Throughout all Theem'hdra I have my informants, who work under no duress but are all beholden to me in one way or another. From them, barely in advance of your first letter, I learned of the dissolution of Druth, the demise of devil-diseased Dhor, the eerie exanimation of Ye-namat, and even the terrible termination of old Imhlat the Teacher.

Now, it were perhaps no surprise had but one or even two of these old comrades gone the way of all flesh; it is not uncommon for sorcerous experiments to go sadly amiss, and the dead men were crafty sorcerers all. But *four* of them?

Moreover I found it a singularly suspicious circumstance that Hatr-ad—who never found reason to communicate with me before, and of whom I had heard precious little of merit in the long years since our mutual apprenticeship—should be so quick off the mark to recognise the advent of malevolent powers and warn me of them.

Then when I gave thought to all you had written, it dawned on me that indeed I had suffered certain discomforts of late; nothing serious but...headaches and creaking joints and bouts of dizziness now and then. Could they have been the residue of malicious spells sent against me and deflected by the protections which are ever present about my apartments?

If so, who had sent these spells and why? To my knowledge I had no dire enemies, though certain acquaintances might be trifling jealous of me. Indeed, such was my mode of life, and my days so free of troubles, that I had often thought me to relax the magickal barriers that surrounded me—it were such a bother to keep them renewed. Now I was glad I had not done so!

Then my thoughts returned to you, Hatr-ad; even to Hatr-ad, whose boasting in the Halls of Nirhath, where Imhlat the Teacher instructed us, was not forgotten but sounded suddenly loud and ominous in the ears of memory. Your boasting, and your off-stated ambition...

Years by the score had gone by since then, but do ambitions such as yours ever really die?

Now Tarth Soquallin, even Tarth the Hermit, wandering wizard of the deserts and mountains, had always been a great and true friend of mine, and if it were true that some nameless terror was bent upon the destruction of Theem'hdra's sorcerers—particularly those who had studied under Imhlat— how then had Tarth fared in this monstrous coup?

Well, he and I had long since devised a means by which I might know of his approximate whereabouts at any given moment. In a cupboard unopened for seven years, after much searching, I found the device: a pebble, not unlike a northstone which, when dangled at the end of a thread, would always point out Tarth's direction. Discovering him to be in the west, and by the agitation of the pebble knowing him to be not too far removed, I reasoned he must be upon the Mount of the Ancients and to that region sent one of my eagles with a hastily inscribed message. (It seemed to me both easier and speedier to contact him directly than to inform you of his location that you yourself might then "warn" him of the so-called "nameless terror.")

Lo, the answer came back within a day and a night, saying that indeed he, too, had suffered minor pains and irritations, but pointing out that while he was not properly protected, as I was, nathless an evil agency would find it hard going to do him lasting harm, since he was so constantly on the move. A spell let loose to find its own way is far less potent than one directed to the known haunts of its recipient!

Furthermore, Tarth agreed to a little necessary deception. This was simply to let it be known that he was dead of strange sorceries, and to assist me in the speedy dissemination of this information by use of his disciples. Ah!—and how swiftly indeed word of Tarth's "demise" reached you, Hatr-ad (whose agents were doubtless on the lookout for just such news?), and how graphic the details of his disappearance, all bar his wand and rings and his teeth of gold!

Aye, and that was the end of Tarth's aches and pains—though this was not to be discovered for awhile—for what use to send out death-dealing spells against a man already dead? Eh, Hatr-ad?—

In the meantime I did several things. I worked swiftly, for I did not wish to delay o'erlong in answering your letter, but in the end my plan worked well enow. First, I sent off a request to an informant of mine in Thinhla, that he employ a certain system (in the use of which I also instructed him) to detect any hurtful magickal emanations from Hreen Castle. Second, I sent further messages of warning to Ikrish Sarn of Hubriss, to Khrissa's nameless Lord-High Ice-Priest, and to many another sorcerer, advising all to disengage quietly from their normal affairs and "disappear," and also to put about soft-muted tales of doom, disease and death. Third, I answered your letter, sending you an addled version of the Ninth Sathlatta and couching it in cyphers which I knew you would eventually break—but not too soon...

Still and all, my suspicions were as yet unfounded, the evidence against you all circumstantial—though I did deem it strange that the unknown Agency of Doom had not yet taken you yourself, when it had already accounted for men who were by far your sorcerous superiors!—and so I refrained from taking any premature action against you. After all, why should you write to me in the first place—and possibly alert me to your own dark hand in the horror—if indeed you yourself were not in mortal fear of the nameless thing?... Unless you were simply seeking some other way to do away with me, since patently the initial attack had done nothing more than discomfort me. Aye, and word had come to me by then that there were certain strangers in Klühn who daily made discreet inquiries in respect of my health. (Men of Thinhla, as it later became known!)

But then, simultaneous with your second letter, word arrived from Thinhla in respect of Hreen Castle, your own abode, and the *veritable miasma of morbid magicks emanating from it*! No protective thaumaturgies these, Hatr-ad, but lethal spells of the very blackest natures, and so at last I recognised beyond any further doubt that direful agency whose hand was set against Theem'hdra's wizards...

Had any such doubt remained in my mind, however, then were it most certainly removed by the mode of messenger you employed: the great Gaunt, the pyrotechnic pigeon and, with your third, my own bat whose wings I now found dusted with potent poisons. You may well have written the last in the aeries of your castle, but surely was it sent to me from some foul crypt beneath Thinhla's deepest foundations.

By then though I had already supplied you with Mylakhrion's most powerful protective spell and a means by which its code might be decyphered and its reversal discovered. Just so, Hatr-ad—and lo, you sent just such a vilely reversed spell against me, thus to weaken me and leave me defenceless in the face of your sly sorceries.

Well, evil one, the spell could not work against me, for contrary to what you were made to believe, I myself had not used Mylakhrion's magick! Thus your casting was most easily deflected and *turned back upon its very author*!

...Aye, and you are utterly defenceless, Hatr-ad, while even now those sorcerers whose doom you plotted conjure spells to send against you; and no use to try Mylakhrion's rune a second time, for it will only work once for any single person. So you see, o wretch, that there is no avenue of escape from the sentence I now pass—which is: that you shall suffer, even unto death, all of the black magicks you yourself have used or attempted to use in your hideous reign of terror! The list is long:

From Tarth Soquallin and myself: The Skin-Cracks, Temple-Throbs and Multiple Joint Seizures; from Ikrish Sarn and Khrissa's Ice-Priest: the Inverted Eyes and the dreaded Bone-Dissolve; and from many another wizard various castings of greater or lesser measure. Moreover we have not forgotten the dead. On behalf of Imhlat, Dhor Nen, Ye-namat and Druth of Thandopolis, we send you the Green Growths, the Evaporating Membranes and, last but not least, the Grey Rot!

Sentence is passed. You are granted one full day upon receipt of this in which to put your affairs in order, but thereafter until you are no more you shall suffer, in ever-increasing doses, the forementioned afflictions. Waste not your remaining hours in further fruitless malevolencies; spells from all quarters have been cast about you that any such emanations shall only rebound upon you.

However, I am authorised to remind you that there is one way in which you may yet cheat us all, Hatr-ad; but if you do, at least do it gloriously! The towers of Hreen Castle are high, I am told—indeed, they are almost as high as your frustrated, evil aspirations—and gravity is swifter and surer than the knife or pellet of poison...

The choice is yours.

Cryptically—

Teh Atht.

MYLAKHRION THE IMMORTAL

There was a time in my youth when I, Teh Atht, marvelling at certain thaumaturgical devices handed down to me from the days of my wizard ancestor, Mylakhrion of Tharamoon (dead these eleven hundred years), thought to question him with regard to the nature of his demise; with that, and with the reason for it. For Mylakhrion had been, according to all manner of myths and legends, the greatest wizard in all Theem'hdra, and it concerned me that he had not been immortal. Like many another wizard before me I, too, had long sought immortality, but if the great Mylakhrion himself had been merely mortal…surely my own chance for self-perpetuity must be slim indeed.

Thus I went up once more into the Mount of the Ancients, even to the very summit, and there smoked the Zha-weed and repeated rare words by use of which I might seek Mylakhrion in dreams. And lo!— he came to me. Hidden in a grey mist so that only the conical outline of his sorcerer's cap and the slow billowing of his dimly rune-inscribed gown were visible, he came, and in his doomful voice demanded to know why I had called him up from the land of shades, disturbing his centuried sleep.

"Faceless one, ancestor mine, o mighty and most omniscient sorcerer," I answered, mindful of Mylakhrion's magnitude. "I call you up that you may answer for me a question of ultimate importance. A question, aye, and a riddle."

"There is but one question of ultimate importance to men," gloomed Mylakhrion, "and its nature is such that they usually do not think to ask it until they draw close to the end of their days. For in their youth men cannot foresee the end, and in their middle span they dwell too much upon their lost youth; ah, but in their final days, when there is no future, then they give mind to this great question. And by then it is usually too late. For the question is one of life and death, and the answer is this: yes, Teh Atht, by great and sorcerous endeavour, a man might truly make himself immortal...

"As to your riddle, that is easy. The answer is that *I am indeed immortal*! Even as the Great Ones, as the mighty furnace stars, as Time itself, am I immortal. For ever and ever. Here you have called me up to answer your questions and riddles, knowing full well that I am eleven hundred years dead. But do I not take on the aspect of life? Do my lips not speak? And is this not immortality? Dead I am, but I say to you that I can never truly die."

Then Mylakhrion spread his arms wide, saying; "All is answered. Farewell..." And his outline, already misted and dim, began to recede deeper still into Zha-weed distances, departing from me. Then, greatly daring, I called out:

"Wait, Mylakhrion my ancestor, for our business is not yet done."

Slowly he came back, reluctantly, until his silhouette was firm once more; but still, as always, his visage was hidden by the swirling mists, and only his dark figure and the gold-glowing runes woven into his robes were visible. Silently he waited, as silently as the tomb of the universe at the end of time, until I spoke yet again:

"This immortality of yours is not the sort I seek, Mylakhrion, which I believe you know well enow. Fleshless, bodiless, except for that shape given you by my incantations and the smoke of the Zha-weed, voiceless other than when called up from the land of shades to answer my questions...what is that for immortality? No, ancestor mine, I desire much more from the future than that. I want my body and all of its sensations. I want volition and sensibility, and all normal lusts and passions. In short, I want to be eternal, remaining as I am now but incorruptible, indestructable! That is immortality!"

"There is no such future for you, Teh Atht!" he immediately gloomed, voice deeply sunken and ominous. "You expect too much. Even I, Mylakhrion of Tharamoon, could not—achieve—" And here he faltered and fell silent.

I perceived then a seeming agitation in the mist-wreathed phantom; he appeared to tremble, however slightly, and I sensed his eagerness to be gone. Thus I pressed him:

"Oh? And how much *did* you achieve, Mylakhrion? Is there more I should know? What were your experiments and how much did you discover in your great search for immortality? I believe you are hiding something from me, o mighty one, and if I must I'll smoke the Zha-weed again!—aye, and yet again—leaving you no rest or peace until you have answered me as I would be answered!"

Hearing me speak thus, Mylakhrion's figure stiffened and swelled momentarily massive, but then his shoulders drooped and he nodded slowly, saying: "Have I come to this? That the most meagre talents have power to command me? A sad day indeed for Mylakhrion of Tharamoon, when his own descendant uses him so sorely. What is it you wish to know, Teh Atht of Klühn?"

"While you were unable to achieve immortality in your lifetime, ancestor mine," I answered, "mayhap nathless you can assist me in the discovery of the secret in mine. Describe to me the magicks you used and discarded in your search, the runes you unravelled and put aside, the potions imbibed and unctions applied to no avail, and these I shall take note of that no further time be wasted with them. Then advise me of the paths which you might have explored had time and circumstances permitted. For I *will* be immortal, and no power shall stay me from it."

"Ah, youth, it is folly," quoth he, "but if you so command—"

"I do so command."

"Then hear me out and I will tell all, and perhaps you will understand when I tell you that you cannot have immortality...not of the sort you so fervently desire."

And so Mylakhrion told me of his search for immortality. He described for me the great journeys he undertook—leaving Tharamoon, his island-mountain aerie, in the care of watchdog familiars—to visit and confer with other sorcerers and wizards; even journeys across the entire length and breadth of Theem'hdra. Alone he went out into the deserts and plains, the hills and icy wastes in pursuit of this most elusive of mysteries. He visited and talked with Black Yoppaloth of Yhemnis, with the ghost of Shildakor in lava-buried Bhur-Esh, with Ardatha Ell, a traveller in space and time who lived for a while in the Great Circle Mountains and studied the featureless, vastly cubical houses of the long-gone Ancients, and with Mellatiquel Thom, a cousin-wizard fled to Yaht Haal when certain magicks turned against him.

And always during these great wanderings he collected runes and cantrips, spells and philtres, powders and potions and other devices necessary to his thaumaturgical experiments. But never a one to set his feet on the road to immortality. Aye, and using vile necromancy he called up the dead from their ashes, even the dead, for his purposes. And this is something I, Teh Atht, have never done, deeming it too loathsome and danger-fraught a deed. For to talk to a dream-phantom is one matter, but to hold intercourse with long-rotted liches…that is a vile, vile thing.

But for all his industry Mylakhrion found only frustration. He conversed with demons and lamias, hunted the legendary phoenix in burning deserts, near-poisoned himself with strange drugs and nameless potions and worried his throat raw with the chanting of oddly cacophonic invocations. And only then did he think to ask himself this question:

If a man desired immortality, what better way than to ask the secret of one *already* immortal? Aye, and there was just such a one…

Then, when Mylakhrion spoke the name of Cthulhu—the tentacled Great One who seeped down from the stars with his spawn in aeons past to build his cities in the steaming fens of a young and inchoate Earth—I shuddered and made a certain sign over my heart. For while I had not yet had to do with this Cthulhu, his legend was awful and I had heard much of him. And I marvelled that Mylakhrion had dared seek out this Great One, even Mylakhrion, for above all other evils Cthulhu was legended to tower like a menhir above mere gravestones.

And having marvelled I listened most attentively to all that my ancestor had to say of Cthulhu and the other Great Ones, for since their nature was in the main obscure, and being myself a sorcerer with a sorcerer's appetite for mysteries, I was most desirous of learning more of them.

"Aye, Teh Atht," Mylakhrion continued, "Cthulhu and his brethren: they must surely know the answer, for they are—"

"Immortal?"

For answer he shrugged, then said: "Their genesis lies in unthinkable abysses of the past, their end nowhere in sight. Like the cockroach they were here before man, and they will supersede man. Why, they were oozing like vile ichor between the stars before the sun spewed out her molten children, of which this world is one; and they will live on when Sol is the merest cinder. Do not attempt to measure their lifespans in terms of human life, nor even geologically. Measure them rather in the births and deaths of planets, which to them are like the tickings of vast clocks. Immortal? As near immortal as matters not. From them I could either beg, borrow or steal the secret—but how to go about approaching them?"

I waited for the ghost of my dead ancestor to proceed, and when he did not immediately do so cried out: "Say on then, forebear mine! Say on and be done with beguiling me!"

He sighed for reply and answered very low: "As you command...

"At length I sought me out a man rumoured to be well versed in the ways of the Great Ones; a hermit, dwelling in the peaks of the Eastern Range, whose visions and dreams were such as were best dreamed far removed from his fellow men. For he was wont to run amok in the passion of his nightmares, and was reckoned by many to have bathed in the blood of numerous innocents, 'to the greater glory of Loathly Lord Cthulhu!'

"I sought him out and questioned him in his high cave, and he showed me the herbs I must eat and whispered the words I must howl from the peaks into the storm. And he told me when I must do these things, that I might then sleep and meet with Cthulhu in my dreams. Thus he instructed me...

"But as night drew nigh in this lonely place my host became drowsy and fell into a fitful sleep. Aye, and his ravings soon became such, and his strugglings so wild, that I stayed not but ventured back out into the steep slopes and thus made away from him. Descending those perilous crags only by the silvery light of the Moon, I spied the madman above me, asleep yet rushing to and fro, howling like a dog and slashing with a great knife in the darkness of the shadows. And I was glad I had not stayed!

"Thus I returned to Tharamoon, taking a winding route and gathering of the herbs whereof the hermit had spoken, until upon my arrival I had with me all the elements required for the invocation, while locked in my mind I carried the Words of Power. And lo!—I called up a great storm and went out onto the balcony of my highest tower, and there I howled into the wind the Words, and I ate of the herbs mixed so and so, and a swoon came upon me so that I fell as though dead into a sleep deeper by far than the arms of Shoosh, Goddess of the Still Slumbers. Ah, but deep though this sleep was, it was by no means still!

"No, that sleep was—*unquiet!* I saw the sepulcher of Cthulhu in the Isle of Arlyeh, and I passed through the massive and oddly-angled walls of that alien stronghold into the presence of the Great One Himself!"

Here the outlines of my ancestor's ghost became strangely agitated, as if its owner trembled uncontrollably, and even the voice of Mylakhrion wavered and lost much of its doomful portent. I waited for a moment before crying: "Yes, go on—what did the awful Lord of Arlyeh tell you?"

"...Many things, Teh Atht. He told me the secrets of space and time, the legends of lost universes out beyond the limits of man's imagination; he outlined the hideous truths behind the N'tang Tapestries, the lore of dimensions other than the familiar three. And at last he told me the secret of immortality!

"But the latter he would not reveal until I had made a pact with him. And this pact was that I would be his priest for ever and ever, even until his coming. And believing that I might later break free of any strictures Cthulhu could place upon me, I agreed to the pact and swore upon it. In this my fate was sealed, my doom ordained, for no man may escape the curse of Cthulhu once its seal is upon him...

"And lo, when I wakened I did all as I had been instructed to attain the promised immortality; and on the third night Cthulhu visited me in dreams, for he knew me now and how to find me, and commanded me as his servant and priest to set about certain tasks. Ah, but these were tasks which would assist the Great One and his prisoned brethren in breaking free of the chains placed upon them in aeons past by the wondrous Gods of Eld, and what use to be immortal forever more in the unholy service of Cthulhu?

"Thus, on the fourth day, instead of doing as bidden, I set about protecting myself as best I could from Cthulhu's wrath, working a veritable frenzy of magicks to keep him from me...to no avail! In the middle of the fifth night, wearied nigh unto death by my thaumaturgical labours, I slept, and again Cthulhu came to me. And he came in great anger—even *great* anger!

"For he had broken down all of my sorcerous barriers, destroying all spells and protective runes, discovering me for a traitor to his cause. And as I slept he drew me up from my couch and led me through the labryinth of my castle, even to the feet of those steps which climbed up to the topmost tower. He placed my feet upon those stone stairs and commanded me to climb, and when I would have fought him he applied monstrous pressures to my mind that numbed me and left me bereft of will. And so I climbed, slowly and like unto one of the risen dead, up to that high tower, where without pause I went out onto the balcony and threw myself down upon the needle rocks a thousand feet below...

"Thus was my body broken, Teh Atht, and thus Mylakhrion died."

As he finished speaking I stepped closer to the swirling wall of mist where Mylakhrion stood, black-robed and enigmatic in mystery. He did not seem so tall now, no taller than I myself, and for all the power he had wielded in life he no longer awed me. Should I, Teh Atht, fear a ghost? Even the ghost of the world's greatest sorcerer?

"Still you have not told me that which I most desire to know," I accused.

"Ah, you grow impatient," he answered. "Even as the smoke of the Zha-weed loses its potency and the waking world beckons to you, so your impatience grows. Very well, let me now repeat what Cthulhu told me of immortality:

"He told me that the only way a mere man, even the mightiest wizard among wizards, might perpetuate himself down all the ages was by means of reincarnation! But alas, such as my return would be it would not be complete; for I must needs inhabit another's body, another's mind, and unless I desired a weak body and mind I should certainly find resistance in the person of that as yet unborn other. In other words I must *share* that body, that mind! But surely, I reasoned, even partial immortality would be better than none at all. Would you not agree, descendant mine?...

"Of course, I would want a body—or part of one—close in appearance to my own, and a mind to suit. Aye, and it must be a keen mind and curious of mysteries great and small: that of a sorcerer! And indeed it were better if my own blood should flow in the veins of—"

"Wait!" I then cried, searching the mist with suddenly fearful eyes, seeking to penetrate its greyness that I might gaze upon Mylakhrion's unknown face. "I...I find your story most...disturbing...my ancestor, and—"

"—and yet you must surely hear it out, Teh Atht," he interrupted, doom once more echoing in his voice. And as he spoke he moved flowingly forward until at last I could see the death-lights in his shadowy eyes. Closer still he came, saying:

"To ensure that this as yet unborn one would be all the things I desired of him, I set a covenant upon my resurrection in him. And this condition was that his curiosity and sorcerous skill must be such that he would first call me up from the Land of Shades ten times, and that only then would I make myself manifest in his person... *And how many times have you called me up, Teh Atht?*"

"Ten times—fiend!" I choked. And feeling the chill of subterranean pools flowing in my bones, I rushed upon him to seize his shoulders in palsied hands, staring into a face now visible as a reflection in the clear glass of a mirror. A mirror? Aye! For though the face was that of an old, old man—*it was nonetheless my own*!

And without more ado I fled, waking to a cold, cold morn atop the Mount of the Ancients, where my tethered yak watched me with worried eyes and snorted a nervous greeting...

——————

But that was long ago and in my youth, and now I no longer fear Mylakhrion, though I did fear him greatly for many a year. For in the end I was stronger than him, aye, and he got but a small part of me. In return I got all of his magicks, the lore of a lifetime spent in the discovery of dark secrets.

All of this and immortality, too, of a sort; and yet even now Mylakhrion is not beaten. For surely I will carry something of him with me down the ages. Occasionally I smile at the thought and feel laughter rising in me like a wind over the desert…but rarely. The laughter hardly sounds like mine at all and its echoes seem to linger o'erlong.

Lords of the Morass

No greater goldsmith in all Theem'hdra than Eythor Dreen, whose works in that wondrous metal, particularly his sculptures, were admired by all and sundry but only ever commissioned by kings, who alone could afford them. Kings, aye...and the occasional sorcerer.

Since I myself have always found transmutation tedious (while the alchemy is simplicity itself, the consumption of time and energy is enormous!), and because Eythor had guaranteed me a massive discount on his gold, I commissioned him to amass and fashion the required amount in a likeness of myself.

This was no act of vanity, but in those days I was often the target of lesser magicians whose malicious sorceries were ever disturbing my experiments and studies; and so I required an effigy of myself upon which all such injurious spells and curses might

SPEND THEMSELVES IN MY STEAD. THE SCARRED
AND PITTED CONDITION OF THAT SCULPTURE
NOW—AS IF WORKED UPON BY MORDANT LIQUIDS
AND SEARED BY WEIRD ENERGIES—SURELY
STANDS MUTE WITNESS TO MY WISDOM IN THIS
MATTER...BUT THAT IS ALL ASIDE.

IN ORDER TO DO THE JOB JUSTICE, DREEN CAME
TO STAY WITH ME FOR SOME LITTLE TIME IN MY
APARTMENTS OVER THE BAY OF KLÜHN; WHICH
WAS WHERE HE TOLD ME THE FOLLOWING TALE.
I HAVE NO REASON TO DOUBT A SINGLE WORD OF
IT, BUT THE READER MAY JUDGE FOR HIMSELF.

TEH ATHT...

I

We were on the central plain, Phata Um and I, following a streamlet towards its source somewhere in the Great Circle Mountains. Far to the north lay the Desert of Ell, and to the south, not too far away, the Nameless Desert of dark repute. We panned for gold in the silty basins below gentle falls, wherever bends occurred in the stream, and whenever the surrounding formations looked auriferous to our prospectors' eyes.

Initially we had worked a middling vein in the Mountains of Lohmi, fleeing south empty-handed when a band of robbers out of Chlangi discovered our diggings, stole our gold and ran us out of camp. All was not lost, however, for we managed to retain a camel, two yaks and most of our equipment—not to mention our lives! And so we decided to wend our way to the Great Circle Mountains, follow them north to the River Marl and so up into Khrissa. From there a boat would take us home to Eyphra...if we could afford our passage on such a vessel.

Setting out across the plain, we prospected as we went and eventually came upon the streamlet, there finding a few small nuggets. Now gold has been, is now and always will be a curse upon mankind.

Men will kill for it; women sell themselves for it; its lure is irresistible. It brings dreams sweeter than opium and its colour has trapped the warmth and lustre of the very sun. It has a marvellous malleability all its own, and its great *weight* is that of the pendulum of the world! What could we do, Phata Um and I? We followed the stream, of course, and we found more nuggets. And the farther west we proceeded, the more and bigger nuggets we found.

Now for certain the stream flowed down out of the Great Circle Range, and equally obvious the fact that it passed through a vein rich beyond precedence. The nuggets and dust we had taken from the stream already were sufficient to set us up comfortably, but the *source* of this wealth, the mother lode—ah!—that would make us rich beyond all dreams of avarice; aye, and all our descendants after us. So it pleased us to fancy.

But here let me tell you about Phata Um, my partner. He was younger than me by ten years, Phata: big, blond, slow moving, with the frame and supple limbs of a young god—but quiet and generally resentful of people. They made fun of his slow, easy-going ways—of his slow smile and his shyness. But they made it behind his back. He could pull the head off an ox, that one, and a single blow from his mighty fist would surely crush and kill any lesser man.

That was why he was a prospector. There is no one to laugh and poke fun at you in the mountains or along the great rivers. Only other prospectors. And because I myself am not much for company—a bit of a loner, you might say—why we got along splendidly, Phata Um and I. I suppose I might put it in a nutshell by stating quite simply that if I was the brain of our partnership, then Phata was the brawn; but at the same time I hasten to impress that I was *not* his master but a true partner, and the split was always right down the middle. Phata was like a little brother to me and loved me dearly, and for my part I guarded his interests as were they my own.

Indeed, in country wild and uncharted as this, my partner's interests *were* my own; his senses of direction and survival were unexcelled, and I swear he was as great an outdoors man as any long-maned barbarian from the north-west. Where I could get lost and starve in a back-street in my own town (I exaggerate a little, you understand) Phata Um could happily navigate the stormy Teeth of Yib or dwell for a six-month in the heights of the Great Circle Mountains themselves; and all without the least discomfort!

Even before we met Phata had been a great traveller; he knew the mountains, plains and deserts, the rivers and the lochs—all of the places where a man would go to commune with himself, to find peace in utter loneliness. Which was why I listened to him whenever he had something to say about the dangers of the regions in which we travelled; and usually I would follow to the letter his advice in such matters—except where gold was concerned. Nor was I alone in my avarice, for Phata too would seek far beyond all wise or commonsense boundaries for sight of that heavy, yellow, precious stuff of dreams.

Such was now the case as, still following the stream, we entered the foothills of the Great Circle Mountains. As we went we still collected the occasional nugget and continued to fill our tiny leather sacks with dust; and the fact that already we were wealthy men served only to spur us on, despite Phata's warning that we rapidly approached a region of extreme hazard. For as my partner began to read signs in the sudden luxuriousness of vegetation and the steamy breezes blowing from the distance-misted peaks, so he remembered things heard from other adventurers who perhaps trod this road before us. Phata himself had never wandered this way, and now he told me the reason:

Rumour had it, he said, that at the foot of the mountains where they climbed sheer to the sky, in a place where volcanic vents drove jets of steam and boiling mud high into the air, there one could find a marsh and a jungle of tropical aspect. More green and luxuriant than the coastal forests of the south, that region, whose fringes housed a pigmy race of men at once curious and terrible. Their weapons were blowpipes whose darts were dipped in orchid-extracted poisons, and their gods—

Their gods were monsters of the marsh, great slugs as big as mammoths, whose nocturnal habits had awed the pigmies since time immemorial, elevating the monstrosities to the plane of deity. Of the worshippers of these loathsome beasts, Phata had also heard it said that they were shy. Normally they would keep their distance and only intervene when strangers pressed too closely upon their preserves: their settlements and the marshes where dwelled their slug-gods, which were *taboo*, forbidden to any outsider.

A little more than this my partner knew, but not much. The pigmies respected strength, but if a man was a coward...then let him not go into their jungles or anywhere near their marshes. Their darts were swift and certain and their cruelties toward their enemies enormous. They had filed teeth and they ate the flesh of any that wronged them; either that, or they fed them to their slug-gods.

And so Phata's warnings should have been deterrent enough, and perhaps would have been but for his final word: that he had also heard it said of these little men that they all wore great bangles and necklets and earrings—aye, and massive noserings, too—and all of purest shining gold! Which seemed to me to hint that the mother lode might well lie central within their domain. So be it; we would befriend them, if indeed they existed at all...

Well, they did exist and we found them—or rather they found us—but not for a good many days.

In between we panned and pocketed, and ever the fruits of our labours were richer, until our yaks were heavy burdened with the weight of our wealth. And the forest grew up around us as we followed the stream toward its source, so that we walked in rich leaf-mold through sun-dappled groves of exotic blooms; and ever the way became more lush and steamy. The foliage grew more tropical in appearance, and the raucous cries of beasts and birds more frequent and more clamorous, until it became hard to believe that we were on the mainland at all but must surely, miraculously have been transported to orchid-wreathed Shadarabar across the Straits of Yhem.

By now our beasts had had enough. Their hooves were not made for this sort of terrain and they grew more rebellious by the hour. We put them on long tethers in an open if somewhat bushy pasture close to the stream and left them there, at the same time relieving the yaks of their golden burden, which we buried in an unmarked cache pending our return. Then we pressed on.

Now it was not our intention to avail ourselves of more gold, not at this time, but simply to see if Phata's myths and legends had any truth in them. In any case, we had neither the strength nor the facilities for handling more of that weighty stuff; but our curiosity was aroused in respect of the pigmies and we wanted to know more about them, to see them for ourselves and perhaps strike up a trading relationship with them. Of course, being prospectors, we still greatly desired to know the *location* of the mother lode—that mighty deposit whose merest traces had been washed downstream over long centuries—but only as a prelude to future and better equipped expeditions.

After three more days of penetration into the now dense jungle, always following the stream—though this was now much more difficult due to the generally swampy nature of the region—Phata Um and I arrived at a blue lake whose central island seemed feathered with a village of tiny houses on shivery stilts, above which drifted the blue and grey smoke of cooking fires. Small brown men in hollow-log canoes fished in the lake with nets weighted with nuggets of gold, and their appearance was in accordance with Phata Um's earlier description. His informants had not lied.

At this point we might have turned back, or perhaps negotiated the lake until we discovered once more the course of the stream on its farther shore, except that any such decision was taken completely out of our hands. For two days and nights now we had suspected that we were observed, that secret watchers lurked behind the hanging vines, in the thickly clustered ferns and wide-leaved foliage, and on several occasions slight movements had been noted on our flanks which had a stealth not normally apparent in common animals. We had felt intelligent eyes upon us where we walked the stream's bank, and there had been whistled calls which had not the ring of ordinary birds but hinted of the conveyance of certain secret messages.

Nevertheless, and for all that we were prepared for the confrontation and had indeed expected it sooner or later, we started horribly when the flared snouts of long blowpipes emerged suddenly from the lakeside's fringing foliage; and without conscious volition both Phata and I reached for our knives. With ferocious warning hisses—filling their cheeks with air as they came into view and gripping the stems of their deadly weapons with their teeth—the pigmy party emerged from hiding and we saw that we were surrounded.

"Well," said I, placing hands on hips and smiling, however nervously, "this is what we expected, Phata…but what do we do now?"

II

My partner said nothing but having recovered from his initial shock he merely held out his great hands before him at arm's length, his fists open and palms uppermost. Lying in the cup of his left palm, in clear view, was a tiny golden whistle with which I had heard him imitate certain birdcalls. Deliberately and very slowly he placed the whistle in his mouth and blew a mellow, throaty warble, somehow managing to smile the while. The pigmies immediately lowered their weapons and clustered to him, their brown eyes aboggle, their mouths brimming with a strange and primitive language beyond our ken. Encouraged, Phata broke into a piercing trill which trailed off into a series of sharp, piping chirrups of inquiry.

The pigmies were enthralled. One of them, stepping forward, pointed excitedly at his own mouth and said something utterly unintelligible. When Phata frowned and shook his head, the little man looked momentarily frustrated and began to hop up and down; but then he grinned, stopped dancing and handed Phata his blowpipe. This was done with a spontaneous naivete which could in no way be construed as acknowledgement of subservience; but it did have the effect of leaving the pigmy's hands free. The smallest fingers of these he now placed in the corners of his wide mouth, and using fingers and mouth together he delivered a sustained blast of a whistle which was very nearly deafening. Phata and I made loud noises of approval and I ventured so far as to pat the performer upon his brown back.

It was now my turn to show my talents, and being something of a sharp (that is to say, I have a certain knack at sleight of hand), I confounded the small folk by pulling nuggets of gold from their ears and noses, by making my thumbs disappear and reappear momently, and by use of my speciality, which was to toss a nugget into the air—only to have it fall back to earth as a shower of fragrant flower petals. Child's play for sure, but effective beyond all expectations. We had mighty *juju* indeed, Phata and I, and the N'dola—for so they called themselves—made us most welcome from that time forward. Alas, this happy state of affairs was not to last; but of course we were not to know that.

In no time at all we found ourselves seated in a hollowed-out log canoe and paddled out to the isle of the N'dolas, where immediately we were taken to see the chief, An'noona. An'noona's hut was taller and bigger than any other, and its stilts correspondingly stronger; but they nevertheless trembled and swayed a little as the chief himself—a tiny, ancient, wizened pigmy—descended fragile looking ladders to meet us.

Close by was a large open space with a dais and throne, upon which the chief seated himself with a pair of pigmy councillors standing behind him. Phata and I were led to the space in front of the dais, where once again we performed our repertoire of tricks. Thankfully, An'noona was no less appreciative than his subjects, and each phase of our performance was greeted with hand-clapping and a great deal of chatter and grinning. And my partner and I kept smiling, but we exchanged meaningful glances at sight of all the sharply pointed teeth which the concerted grinning so amply displayed.

Just as we were reaching the end of our show, a disturbance at the rear of the pigmy crowd (for by this time the entire village had turned out to see us) drew our eyes. And now, as the milling ranks of tiny people grew silent and shrank back from the place of the disturbance, so for the first time we saw the tribal witch-doctor, Ow-n-ow. At first glance we knew we had an enemy in this evil looking midget; the way his hooded eyes met ours, the way he pointed with his feathered wand and shook his bone rattle in imitation of a deadly snake told us so.

And now he approached, with many a leap and bound, gyrating wildly as the crowd gave him room and his naked feet sent the dust flying. Right up to us he came, leaping high in the air to point his gold-tipped wand first at me, then at Phata Um. And now he paused before us, arms akimbo, his wicked monkey face contemptuous as he silently defied us to do our worst.

"What now?" asked Phata Um from the side of his mouth. "They hate cowards."

"Then we must show them what we're made of," I countered. "Now is not the time for faint hearts. Let's see if we can deflate this little dung-beetle." So saying, I stooped and pretended to snatch up a handful of sand, which I hurled straight into the witch-doctor's face!

Instinctively, he threw up his hands before his eyes—but instead of stinging dust and grit he found himself surrounded by a settling shower of tiny, rose-tinted petals. Before he could recover, Phata Um took hold of his shoulders and lifted him up bodily until he stared directly into his startled, frightened eyes. The little man knew that my partner could crush him there and then, if he so desired. Phata did no such thing but merely blew a deafening blast on his whistle, already secreted in his mouth. Then he put the shrieking, wildly kicking little man back down on his feet again.

Backing off in confusion, Ow-n-ow tripped and sat down hard in the dust, and the momentarily silent crowd at once burst out afresh with hoots of derision and raucous catcalls, until the witch-doctor scrambled to his feet and fled. Then for some little time the clearing was full of tiny mimics who replayed over and over Ow-n-ow's downfall and less than graceful exit, until the chief clapped his hands sharply and brought the assemblage back under control.

Briefly, in a voice wizened as its owner, which yet carried across the clearing, An'noona then spoke to his subjects, the while pointing at Phata and me where we patiently stood; and in the next instant the entire crowd prostrated itself before us, then quickly jumped up and danced all about us. We had been accepted—which did not say a lot for Ow-n-ow's popularity!

After a moment or two An'noona stood up and came forward on the log dais until his eyes met ours on a level. He lifted a heavy golden chain from his neck and placed it over Phata's head, unclasped from his own krinkly hair a massive brooch of gold crusted with gems and pinned it to my jacket, then stood back and admired us. Not to be outdone, Phata handed the chief his golden whistle, and for my part I gave to him a jewelled northstone set on a pivot in a little silver box. Delighted with this exchange of gifts, An'noona went back to his hut and Phata and I were left in the care of his councillors.

One of the latter pair—little more than a youth but with a great head of almost acromegalic proportions, which bore a livid scar running from his left temple to his chin—astounded us by speaking to us in our own tongue, however distorted by a twanging barbarian influence and accent. His name was Atmaas (the Knowing One) and he stumblingly explained his familiarity with our language by telling us the following story:

As a boy Atmaas had been constantly mocked by the other children of the tribe because of his cranial deformity. Eventually, unable to bear any more of these jibes and taunts and general cruelties, one day the dam broke within Atmaas and he fled the village into the Great Circle Mountains. There he was befriended (in however harsh and brusque a manner) by a dozen wandering, outcast barbarians from the north-west. They took from him his golden bangles, nose-ring and other trinkets, but in return gave him food and taught him their tongue.

Atmaas was quick to learn—which argued for a sound brain in that large, ugly skull of his—and soon his proficiency was such that he was able to converse freely with the longmaned outcasts from the north. Now they were able to question him about his golden ornaments, which had been divided between them, and they asked him to lead them to his homeland where they might find more of the precious yellow metal. At first he attempted to dissuade them, and such were his warnings that three of the barbarians did in fact split off from the main body; but the rest were not cowed by the lad's tales of great slug-gods and poisoned darts, and they pressed him to show them the way to his swampy homeland.

Fearing for what they might do to him if he refused them (and perhaps relishing a little the thought of sweet revenge for miseries his tribe had heaped upon him in the past), Atmaas at last agreed and brought the barbarians down out of the mountains, through treacherous swamps and reptile-infested forests to the lake of the N'dolas.

They arrived by night, and silently the barbarians paddled out to the island and stole into the village. Their intention was to fire the village and raze it down, killing any pigmies who might escape the holocaust; and perhaps they might have succeeded, for certainly the village was at that time tinder dry and the element of surprise was on the side of the northmen.

But by now Atmaas was beginning to feel pangs of guilt and remorse; and so, as the barbarians ran silently here and there in the night, setting fire to stilts, ladders, animal pens and the logs of the perimeter walls, so he stole away to the great golden gong whose voice was only ever heard in times of danger. As the fires began to take hold, he beat upon the gong and cried out in a loud voice to tell the men of the tribe to bring out their weapons and defend themselves and their families.

One of the startled barbarians came upon him as he thus thundered, and in a berserker rage sought to cut him down The single blow from the northman's sword caused the hideous gash to Atmaas' face and hurled him down half-dead; and thus he remained while the tribes-men in their high windows picked off the barbarians one by one with their poisoned darts. And at last, when the fires were under control, then the villagers discovered Atmaas where his crumpled body lay; and now they knew of his bravery—knew Atmaas of the Ugly Head as a hero—and now too they set about nursing him back to health.

Indeed, the chief's wives were given that responsibility, so that during Atmaas' convalescence old An'noona spoke often with him and soon came to know of the pigmy lad's intelligence. And so impressed was the chief that he made an order that henceforth any child of particular brilliance or talent should be named Atmaas after the hero; and thus Atmaas himself became first among An'noona's advisors. This was the youth's story...

III

By now night was drawing in, and soon a waxing moon was riding high above a mist that seemed to settle from the sky. Lanterns were lighted and Atmaas led us to a small hut on short stilts, which he indicated was ours for as long as we cared to stay. Now was not a time for sleeping, however, but for rejoicing; and when Phata and I would have gladly climbed the short ladder to bed, Atmaas stopped us and pointed through tendrils of thin mist and wisps of fragrant fire smoke to where numerous lanterns were bobbing and gathering at a central place. There was to be a feast, Atmaas informed—a celebration, a gorging of choice gobbets, a great guzzling of mildly opiate and heav-ily intoxicant beverages—and all for us! For An'noona had found us pleasing and desired to honour us.

Already the night was a muted hubbub, the air filled with enticing, exotic smells and the sounds of strange instruments; so that Phata and I felt a rising excitement as we tossed our necessaries in through our hut's high doorway and followed Atmaas to the feast. And as we seated ourselves cross-legged before a vast, low log table, of which there were a dozen, so an endless stream of laden platters of gold began to appear. There were more than two hundred of them, all of thick, beaten gold, all heaped with every sort of meat and fish and fruit and nut, until the tables were a-groan with their weight. Finally, by the time it had grown totally dark beyond the circle of lantern light, when it seemed that the entire tribe must be seated in the central clearing, only then did An'noona appear, taking his place at the head of our table.

The chief smiled a toothy smile at us and made a sign with his hand; and the horde at the tables immediately began chattering and chewing, and the babble grew deafening as a pigmy band struck up on tomtoms, wind and string instruments. We too would have eaten, for the sight of all this food had made us hungry and it was impossible to stop our mouths from watering; but we held back, however reluctantly, until Atmaas who sat with us saw our hesitation and knew the source of our discomfort.

No, no, he informed us: there were no enemies of the N'dolas on the menu tonight. There were ribs of wild pig and steaks of water buffalo, moorhens and jungle quails, river oysters and rainbow trout and smoked eels of a rare and delicate texture—but no man-flesh, no. Of course, there was one who would dearly love to see *us* trussed up and simmering in the cooking pots, who even now stood to one side in the shadows and kept his evil eyes glued upon us where we sat. And Atmaas, inclining his great and misshapen head, indicated where we should look to see this would-be malefactor.

Even before we turned our heads that way, Phata and I knew who the silent watcher would be. None other but Ow-n-ow, the witch-doctor himself. We would be well advised, Atmaas needlessly informed, to keep out of the way of the *nganga*, lest he find a way to pay us back for the humiliations we had heaped upon him. And all through the celebrations which followed, from time to time as the night wore on, we would feel Ow-n-ow's gaze burning upon us, Phata Um and I, and so knew beyond any slightest doubt that Atmaas' advice was well founded.

What with the gorging on marvellous gobbets, however, and gulping down great two-handed jars of beer—and the pigmies doing their intricate tribal dances, and the music which grew, as the night progressed, more wild and rhythmic and repetitive, so as to become almost hypnotic—Ow-n-ow gradually slipped to the back of our reeling minds, becoming less a threat than an annoyance. Until eventually, drunk as lords, stepping carefully over the still forms of little men where they had fallen in their excesses, as the sky to the east began to lighten a little, we wove our weary way to our hut and climbed, however teeteringly, to bed.

And even here the pigmies were not remiss in their hospitality; for giggling coyly in the darkness of our tiny rooms were a pair of pigmy girls, black as the night but not nearly so secretive, who had doubtless waited for us through all the long hours of revelry and who now set about to put the finishing touches to our welcome. Through the thin, woven wall of my room I heard Phata's puzzled, boozy query: "Well, little one, and just what am I supposed to do with you?" And I smiled at the silence which then ensued, being certain that just like her sister who now pleasured me, Phata's visitor had doubtless taken the initiative...

For the next three days and nights we did very little. Indeed, two whole days were required merely to recover from the festive excesses of our welcoming celebration, so that our condition was only very shaky as we went about the village and took note of the tribe's way of life, its customs, habits, its social structure in general, and particularly its utensils, even the commonest or most mundane of which were of gold. It was a source of constant astonishment to us to see boys fishing in the lake with hooks of pure gold, and gardeners at work with forks and hoes of that same precious metal, and girls washing their scraps of clothing in great basins of the stuff!

Then, on the fourth day, Atmaas came to us and told us that An'noona had decided to honour us above all others. For no other outsiders had ever entered the fane of the slug-gods or seen the treasures therein, and this was the invitation which the chief now extended to us. Moreover, we were also to be his guests at the quarterly propitiation of the gods themselves; when with our own eyes we might gaze upon those monsters as Ow-n-ow called them out of their deep swamps to accept burnt sacrifices of buffaloes and pigs. For in two more days the moon would be at its full, and then it was that the ceremony must take place; and for a further three-month the slug-gods would be appeased and the village would prosper. First, however, we were to visit the fane of the gods and offer up our prayers to those gigantic gastropod deities; for it was only right that we who had found favour in the eyes of An'noona should now ask it of his gods.

That same afternoon, as Phata and I finished a simple meal prepared and served by our pigmy paramours, An'noona and his councillors, accompanied by the *nganga* Ow-n-ow, came to where we sat in the shade of our hut. Atmaas explained that we were to go with them to the fane of the slug-gods, and so we followed the party to the lake's edge where the chief's royal barge—a trimaran built of terrific tree trunks—lay waiting with its crew of smooth-muscled paddlers. With the chief seated centrally and in the prow, his retinue close behind him, and with Phata and me each in an outrigger, we soon were on our way.

Long that journey and tiring, so that the team of twenty paddlers was obliged to work in shifts of ten; but soon our craft had entered the wide body of the river where it came down from the central mountains and then, against the steady but gentle flow of water, we made good headway between banks strewn with orchids and overgrown with dense foliage and huge trees whose vines hung down to the river itself. And again we felt ourselves transported as if by magick to jungled Shadarabar.

As the hours passed so the night drew in, and great moths came to investigate the lanterns with which the trimaran's crew lighted its watery way; and as the full moon rose up into the sky, so we were able to discern ahead the rising cliffs of a great canyon. Only then did Phata and I know the real source of the river, which could be nowhere else but the mighty Inner Sea itself. For this was one of those outlets by which that imposing inland ocean emptied itself through the Great Circle Mountains.

And so, by light of moon and lantern, we proceeded until, deep within the defile, the canyon opened out to form a sort of small valley within the range. Here, on the nothern bank of the river, the land was a rank swamp a-crawl with lizards, crocodiles and great frogs which ran, slithered or hopped through rotting foliage and creeping vines of an unnatural, venomous black and green. And away in the dark distance, where the great cliffs rose up once more against the starry night, there we could see the glowing, smoky red fires of volcanic blowholes, which we knew for such by a sulphurous taint in the warm, clinging air of the place.

To the south there was neither bank nor marsh, only great cliffs rising into darkness, whose feet the river followed from that mighty Inner Ocean of legend. Here the current was a little stronger, the water deeper, and our craft hugged the sheer rock as it moved slowly forward.

Now Atmaas called to us from his position to the rear of the chief, pointing to the sprawling swamps of the northern aspect. That was forbidden territory, he told us, *taboo*, the domain of the slug-gods, where two nights from now we would see them called forth by Ow-n-ow to accept the tribe's tribute. But no sooner had he finished speaking than Ow-n-ow himself, whose seat was in the stern of the central hull, gave a great howling laugh that echoed back from the rock walls like the lunatic chorus of a pack of hyenas!

White in the near-darkness, I saw Phata's face as he turned it to stare at the *nganga* where he sat in the rear, rocking in crazed glee, his glowing eyes first on me, then on Phata, as if he knew some marvellously malicious joke about us and would love to tell it. But at that very moment, taking our minds off the evil witch-doctor, there came the cry of a pigmy who stood and leaned forward in the prow of the larboard outrigger, drawing all eyes to where he swung his lantern in darkness. For here the cliffs had been washed away to form a vast cave like the yawning mouth of some monster, into whose inky shadow our craft now slid as we stared about in lantern-flickered gloom.

Here the water was calm and still, and as torches were lit to augment the light of the lanterns, so we found ourselves in a high-domed natural cavern whose branching throat went back into untold labyrinths of rock. Huge stalactites hung from the bat-clustered ceiling. Between those needle points the paddlers now guided the royal vessel unerringly toward one dark canal whose walls seemed all agleam with winking, luminous green eyes. Since the channel was narrow, however, and since Phata and I occupied the outriggers, we were soon able to discern that these winking points were not eyes but the facets of fabulous emeralds in their natural state, imbedded in the glassy walls and polished by untold centuries of flooding waters! Moreover, the walls themselves were yellow with thick branching veins of raw gold! The place was nothing less than a vast, natural treasure cave; and I admit that my throat grew dry, as Phata's must have done, at the thought of the untold wealth mere inches from our itching fingers.

In a few moments more the channel widened out and we saw to our left a wide shelf of rock which reached back toward the cave's shadow-hidden wall. And I knew at once that this was the fane of the slug-gods, for the sight that greeted my unbelieving eyes in that secret place was of such magnitude that it utterly dwarfed all which had gone before.

Can you picture endless ranks of great gastropods—giant slugs fashioned in precious yellow metal, with stalked eyes of uncut emeralds big as a man's fists—marching away into the gloom of the place; and the flames of the torches and lanterns reflected into our eyes from the nearest sculptures, until it seemed that the whole cavern flowed with molten gold, through which auric effulgence the emerald-eyed monsters seemed silently to glide on carpets of golden nuggets, imbued with an awe-inspiring sentience all their own? You cannot, nor could any man who has not seen it with his own eyes!

IV

As our eyes grew accustomed to the yellow dazzle, so we noted that upon rock-cut ledges to the rear of the temple stood dozens of smaller slug replicas, some large as dogs and others no bigger than small rats— but all of solid gold. We were given no great time to consider the vastness of the wealth here amassed, however, for no sooner had we disembarked to stand upon the great shelf than the members of An'noona's party prostrated themselves and Atmaas indicated that we should do likewise.

All of us, with the sole exception of Ow-n-ow, went down on our knees, heads bowed; and now, without more ado, the tiny *nganga* began his dance of propitiation. As he danced—a weird, gliding dance, hands held at the sides of his head, index fingers extended in imitation of horns—so one by one, beginning with the chief himself, each member of An'noona's party stood up, took out from his ceremonial robes a miniature golden slug and went to place it in its chosen niche, returning immediately and once more prostrating himself.

Even with bowed heads Phata and I managed to keep track of all this, until we were the only ones who had not paid tribute to the gods of this grotto fane. We need not have felt dismayed, however, for

Atmaas had not forgotten us. Where he kneeled beside us, he produced two tiny miniatures from his red robe, giving one each to my colleague and me. Phata rose first, went to the wall and found a tiny niche for his effigy. As he returned so I rose up and did likewise—at which the chief and his retinue stood up as a man and solemnly applauded.

And all of this time Ow-n-ow kept up his eerie, gliding dance in imitation of the great slugs. Then, of a sudden, the witch-doctor hurled himself down amidst ankle-deep golden nuggets, wriggled on his belly to the base of the largest effigy and kissed its yellow bulk in a sort of frenzied fervor; following which he slowly stood up. Again the chief's party applauded, we two outsiders also, and with that the ritual was over.

We all returned to the trimaran, Ow-n-ow bringing up the rear, and in a solemn silence broken only by the dip of paddles and the grunts of the paddlers, we returned through the great cave to the river. Thus, in the dead of night, Phata Um and I were brought weary but full of wonder back to the pigmy village; and thus, all unbeknown to us, Ow-n-ow had set in motion that monstrous plot with which he intended to destroy us...

The following morning I sought out Atmaas and took him to one side. If tomorrow night, at the full of the moon, Phata and I were to witness the calling forth of the actual slug-gods to accept burnt offerings, we would not want to be caught short (as might well have happened in the cavern fane) by being unprepared. Thus I begged Atmaas that he tell me whatever he could of the great creatures and explain the nature of the imminent ceremony. Would it be in any way similar to the proceedings of the previous night?

No, the pigmy youth informed, last night had merely been preparatory to the main event. What we had done last night was a prayer for the increase of the giant gastropods by increasing the number of their effigies. What we would do tomorrow would be an appeasement, that the slug-gods might look favourably upon the N'dolas and the tribe itself prosper. And in answer to my further questions he told me more about the "gods" themselves, though I suspected he was clever enough to realise that I had little or no faith in the creatures as true gods; in which deduction he would have been absolutely correct.

Why (I wanted to know) did the pigmies sacrifice cooked flesh to their gods, when it seemed to me that in the wild the diet of the creatures must surely be raw, be it flora, fauna or whatever? In answer to which Atmaas told me a very strange tale indeed.

The slug-gods (he said) were of a most capricious nature, with moods often as transient as the phases of the moon. Normally they fed on the vegetation of their swamps, though certainly they were omnivorous and could happily consume whatever presented itself. Indeed, it had more than once been apparent that their moods went hand in hand with their diet, which was the main reason that the sacrifice would be of sweet, cooked meats: to sweeten their tempers, as it were, and guide them to beneficent thoughts in respect of their worshippers.

But what in the world did Atmaas mean (I pressed) by his statement about the moods of the gastropods? In what way might their diet possibly determine their actions, beneficent or otherwise? Here the great-headed youth was at a loss. He did not know *how* it could be so, he said, only that it *was* so. Three years ago, for instance, there had been a plague of crocodiles. The rivers, swamps and forests had been alive with them. In the swamps particularly, the creatures were so numerous that the morass heaved with their movements. And so of course a great many were eaten by the slug-gods, being simply ingested before they could get out of the way.

This precipitated a period of nightmarish activity in the gastropods, which only ended when the crocodiles themselves died from lack of food or were killed off by the pigmies, who organised massive hunts specifically for that purpose; to decimate the reptiles and thus deny them as food for the slugs, which in turn should curb the wholly unprecedented—*activities* of those deities.

When I further pressed Atmaas in respect of these activities he was at first loth to answer. But eventually he told me that I must try to understand: the actions of gods were invariably hard for mere mortals to fathom. Who, for instance, might follow the whims of the moon-god in his continuous waxing and waning? Who could say when it would or would not rain? Or when the sun-god would choose to dry up the river? Or why the gods did these things at all? And if the great elemental gods were hard to understand, how then these purely mundane but utterly strange gods of the swamp?

As to what the slug-gods had done to terrorize the pigmy tribe: that was simple. They had adopted the sly, voracious, murderous ways of the crocodiles themselves. That is to say they had become *like* the unfortunate reptiles upon which they had fed, developing despicable habits and growing vile in their attitudes even toward the N'dolas. Aye, and some of them had even made their way through the canyon to the pigmy village; and that had been a very terrible time indeed!

But a slug big as a mammoth is not a crocodile, for all that it adopts the other's ways; and however sly it may be, still it may not come upon a man unobserved. As soon as the villagers knew their danger they called on Ow-n-ow to do something about it; and he, using knowledge passed down from past generations of *ngangas* before him, knew exactly what he must do. Having crocodile appetites without crocodile stealth—which with their bulk would be quite impossible—those few gastropods which made the journey to the village were quite ravenous. They no longer required vegetation but flesh, which for the most part their great size denied them. Ow-n-ow's answer to the problem was therefore simplicity itself. He merely *fed* the great beasts—on rabbits.

At this point I might have fancied that the pigmy youth was pulling my leg, but Atmaas assured me it was so and that he told only the truth. Following the destruction of part of the village wall by the slug-gods as they foraged for meat, on the very next night Ow-n-ow put out a great number of live rabbits tethered to small shrubs. The gastropods, when with the fall of night they returned, immediately took the bait and retreated into the forest shade to digest their victims—and they never returned.

In the early hours of the next morning they were seen making their way back along the river toward the canyon, all atremble and furtive—if that may be imagined—as if anxious now to be gone from the tribe's territory back to their own domain. And it was noted that they were now as timid as—as rabbits! And when Atmaas told me this last, finally I began to understand.

Over all the long, dim centuries since the Beginning, Nature had endowed the gastropods with a unique talent: the short-term ability to assume certain of the characteristics of whichever species they chanced to feed upon in their browsing. How or why this was so was a mystery, but so are so many things in Nature. Perhaps the talent had been a guard against great predators, when by eating the flesh of one such—perhaps accidentally fallen—the slugs would "inherit" its knowledge and so be able to combat or at least avoid the unwanted attentions of others of its sort. Whichever, the puzzle was too great for my fathoming.

Having talked with Atmaas for well over an hour, I wandered freely through the village, amused myself for a little while watching the pigmy children at play, and was thus engaged when Phata found me. He had borrowed a large canoe, he said, and a fishing net. Having watched the village fishermen, he now wished to try their methods for himself. Would I care to join him? Having little else to do, I agreed.

But down at the lakeside, as I dragged Phata's borrowed craft into the water and while he was busy folding his net thus and so, I noticed in the tall reeds close by a grinning, evil face which gazed intently upon our activities. Then the face was gone, but not before I had recognised it as the poisonous visage of Ow-n-ow. He was not done with us, that little man, not by a long shot. And all through the rest of the day that fleeting glimpse of his face, framed by reeds, kept returning to the eye of my memory, so that on several occasions Phata was moved to inquire if aught were amiss...

That afternoon it was very hot and so we slept in hammocks slung in the shade of our hut; but as evening came on we were up and about to greet our pigmy paramours as they came, all giggles and flashing white pointed teeth, to serve our evening meal. They ate with us, as usual, but no sooner had we begun to eat than there came a surprising diversion. Ow-n-ow, coming upon us from somewhere close at hand, clapped first myself then Phata Um upon our shoulders where we sat, chucked our concubines under their chins, and chuckling (benevolently?) went on his way.

"What in the name of Great Black Yib—?" I began.

"Perhaps the *nganga*'s mother-in-law died!" Phata grinned. "Or maybe he's just unwell, eh?"

"Let's hope so!" I answered. And laughing, however wonderingly, we finished our meal—which act, apart from climbing in a sort of drunken and totally inexplicable stupor to our beds, was all that we were ever able to remember of that entire evening and night!

V

That we had been drugged—the girls, too—did not become apparent until late the next morning, when rising haggard and in great misery from our beds we discovered An'noona, his councillors, a triumphant Ow-n-ow, and several other tribal dignitaries waiting for us to put in an appearance. And once Atmaas had made clear just what was going on—why, then we also knew just whose hand had done the deed! For now we found ourselves accused of an infamy far and away above all others; and of course it was Ow-n-ow who brought the charge against us, and his glib tongue which condemned us as Atmaas stumblingly did his best to translate the *nganga*'s accusations.

Oh!—and how that little monster had excelled himself in his deviltry!

He had noticed (as he now explained to a rapidly growing crowd of silent pigmies) a certain furtiveness about us in the fane of the slug-gods; and he had also observed the way our fingers lingered over the golden nuggets and effigies in that holy place. Then, because he had not wished to believe that we were capable of such evil thoughts and unnatural avaricious urges, he had put the matter to the back of his mind, telling himself that he—even Ow-n-ow, a *nganga* of the greatest power and perception—must be mistaken.

But then, later, he had seen us with a canoe out on the lake. What had we been doing, he had wondered? We had seemed to be fishing, and yet...could we have been practising the art of canoeing? If so, why?

Finally, last night, we had retired early, very early indeed, and this too had puzzled the witch-doctor (or so he said). Indeed his suspicions were such that he waited until dusk to see us stealing through the quiet village to the lakeside, where we boarded our canoe and paddled away up river into the evening mist. He had then returned to our hut, intending to waken our sleeping-partners and question them as to our mysterious activities. He was unable to waken them, however, for they were in a deep, drugged sleep and would remain so until the drug had burned itself out of their systems. We (quite obviously) had drugged them in order to hide our absence from them.

Thoroughly alarmed now, Ow-n-ow had waited all through the night; and finally we had returned through the early morning mists, mooring our canoe and stealing back to our hut in a most suspicous and secretive manner. Then the *nganga* went to our canoe and discovered, within its hollowed interior where doubtless it had fallen from one of our pockets, a golden, thumb-sized miniature of a slug-god! So saying, and as Atmaas continued to translate, Ow-n-ow held up the alleged proof of our guilt for all to see.

And now the pigmies had drawn back from us, their mouths open in shock; even Atmaas (though I could see he was torn two ways) staring up at us in a sort of astonished disbelief; aye, and our pigmy paramours too. Frankly, I was too stunned to make a move, but Phata Um suffered no such restriction. He strode forward, his great hands reaching down and toward Ow-n-ow's scrawny neck. And certainly he would have killed the treacherous, lying little dog there and then—had he not found himself staring down the flaring snouts of half-a-dozen blowpipes, appearing almost magically in the hands of pigmies whose services had doubtless been acquired by the *nganga* against just such an eventuality.

Now we were ringed about by the tiny warriors, and quick as a flash our accuser had climbed like a monkey to our hut and disappeared within. A moment passed and we could hear the witch-doctor rummaging about—then another moment in complete silence—and finally, dramatically, the small fiend reappeared at the top of the ladder, his hands weighted with a pair of golden miniatures large as babies' skulls.

That was enough, the dog had done for us!

Oh, I suppose we might have argued, but I doubt that we could have won. The "evidence" against us was far too strong. We were haggard-looking, as well we would be after a night of furtive canoeing and temple desecrating; the girls we slept with could neither confirm nor deny our presence through the night, for of course "we" had drugged them; and most damning of all, Ow-n-ow had produced those golden miniatures, proof positive that we had indeed robbed the fane of the slug-gods.

And in our favour—nothing! We had no proof at all of our innocence, not a shred of it, and any denials or counter-accusations we might make must be through Atmaas, who would surely be seen as biased in our favour. And so, unprotesting, still a little dumb-founded by it all, we were taken away, bound hand and foot and locked in a tiny bamboo stockade or cage; and there we spent the day, working at the thongs that bound us and dreaming of sweet revenge against the little black devil whose evil wiles had brought us to this pass.

Toward late afternoon Atmaas came to see us, and just a single glance at the long and doleful face beneath that heavy, bulbous head of his was sufficient to tell us the worst. The pigmy council had met; we were guilty; our punishment would be...would be—

But he did not need to say any more; even a blind man could have seen our futures...

How would it be done? I asked the youth. When? But before he could answer I went on to tell him of our innocence, of Ow-n-ow's treachery. I may even have started to babble a little (for certainly I was afraid for my life) but Phata Um's elbow in my ribs warned me to be quiet. And of course he was right for the N'dolas despised cowards, and Atmaas was a N'dola after all.

Finally, after sitting in a sort of sad silence for many minutes, at last the lad told us the worst, the how and the when of it. Which did nothing at all to calm us or allay our burgeoning fears.

It would be tonight! Oh, and there would be sweeter meat than pig and buffalo on the menu of the slug-gods this night. As to how: we would be staked out at the edge of the swamp, amidst the slaughtered, roasted beast carcasses; and when the great gastropods came in answer to Ow-n-ow's calling, then we would be put quickly out of our misery by a fusillade of poisoned darts. We would see the slug-gods, aye—and at very close quarters indeed—but mercifully we would never know the slow, deadly burn of their digestive juices.

Only one more thing I asked of Atmaas before he left us: that he ensure the poisons would be quick. In answer he told me that I need have no fear. One or two darts would merely paralyse, but five or six would certainly kill. Since we would be feathered by at least a dozen darts each...and he shrugged, however sadly, and left us to the speeding hours.

When the river mists were beginning to curl and the sun was sinking toward the high horizon of stirless trees, then they came for us. We were bundled without ceremony into a log canoe which took the tail position in a large procession of these crude craft, being paddled round the island and along the tree-shaded river toward the great canyon. And if our single previous trip along that way had seemed a long one, this present journey passed in a flash.

For to my mind it was only a very short time indeed before our craft beached on a loamy, swampy shore; and there we were lifted from the canoe and carried to an area of comparatively dry ground, and propped with our backs to the boles of trees so rotten that they were close to falling. Now that we could gaze all about, we saw that this was none other than that great swamp where the canyon widened into a sunken valley; and that apart from this small clearing at the edge of the river, the swamp pressed close, dark and ominous on all sides.

Never in my life had I looked upon a region of grimmer aspect than the one which presented itself in that swamp. Huge humps of nameless, rotting vegetable debris rose everywhere, between which the mud bubbled up with a yellow froth of sulphur. Massy leaves, green and black and glossy, lay low to the surface, cloaking the movements of things which wriggled, crawled or swam through the quaggy morass beneath. And occasionally there would come a commotion of foliage and flesh, a thrashing of leathery limbs and clashing of jaws as battle was joined or prey snapped up; and in a little while the eerie silence would once again descend, only to be broken by the distant screams of predators or the noisy emission of pockets of gas bursting in great bubbles which oozed up from the depths of the bog.

"A great place for gods!" said Phata, his voice full of a doleful sarcasm. "But better by far for demons..."

By now the pigmies had built fires in the clearing close to the water's edge, where they proceeded to roast the many carcasses which they had brought with them from the village. And as the light quickly faded so the aroma of cooked flesh began to mingle with the fetors of the marsh, and the figures of the pigmies where they worked and moved became as grey ghosts in that awful twilight.

"Phata," I said, my voice a whisper, "this looks like the end. Man, I'm frightened!"

"Aye, me too," growled my friend, "but the end is not yet—not quite. I've been working on these bonds of mine, and I believe—*uh!*" And for a moment he fell silent and peered about with lowered brows, making sure that his actions went unobserved. "My hands," he finally continued, "are free—but I'll keep them behind my back a while longer. What of the thongs that bind you?"

"No good," I shook my head. "I haven't your strength, Phata. But listen, if you can move your feet a little, get them tucked in behind my back—"

Gloomier still the glade as I got my stiff fingers to work on the knots which bound Phata's feet, and as the fires burned lower so the golden edge of the moon appeared above the forest and distant cliffs. When Ow-n-ow saw that first moonbeam come stealing into the darkening clearing, then he laughed hysterically—like a maniac where he stood at the water's edge—and in another moment he laid back his head and gave a great baying howl which echoed all through the horror-laden swamp.

VI

Frantically now I worked on Phata's knots, for the fires were turned to embers, the sacrifices all prepared and the night closing in like a great black fist. And away in the swamp there were flickering blue ghosts, faint as foxfire but mobile and monstrous. The pigmies had seen these lights too, and the bulk of them soon retreated to their canoes. Some were left, however, who beat around the edge of the clearing with clubs and long, sharp knives, keeping away the crocodiles and other creatures attracted by the far-drifted aroma of cooked flesh.

Aye, and others of the pigmies there were too, who simply stood in a group with their blowpipes and waited. And then there was An'noona, seated in a sort of open, bamboo sedan, with his bearers close to hand; and finally Ow-n-ow, the grinning black devil, who now commenced that gliding, twin-horned dance of his, that impersonation of a slug as he moved about the clearing. Every few minutes he would pause, cup his hands to his mouth and utter a strange, coughing bark, the snort of a wild, alien thing. And in answer to this calling—

The blue fires came closer, glowing through the rotting, creeper-festooned swamp, moving less aimlessly now and with a sort of terrible purpose. And suddenly it dawned on me that this must be the sign of the slug-gods; that they glowed with that same luminosity as their lesser, aquatic cousins cast up on Theem'hdra's shores. In the instant of realisation, the last knot binding Phata's feet came loose in my fumbling fingers—and in that self-same moment the blowpipe marksmen formed themselves into a line.

Ow-n-ow's dance was no longer a dance so much as a darting here and there in the darkness and a crazed snuffling and snorting; but worse by far were the answering calls which now issued from out the swamp itself! The slug-gods were closing with the clearing; it would not be very long before Ow-n-ow ordered that we be killed, following which the rest of the pigmies would flee the clearing and doubtless watch the spectacle of their deities feasting from the safety of the river.

No sooner had this last thought come to me than An'noona's bearers picked up his litter and bore the chief swiftly away toward the river. The beaters at the edge of the clearing likewise took their departure, their actions made hurried and clumsy through a shivery terror which was now clearly apparent in their every move. Until only Ow-n-ow and the marksmen remained, and they too fearsomely a-tremble as they cast all about in the night with bulging, staring eyes.

By now the bluely luminescent slug-gods were close indeed and their coughing calls loud in the darkness; and lesser predators must surely have left the immediate vicinity as they sensed the approach of those Lords of the Morass, for apart from the aforementioned calls and the continual bursting of gassy bubbles, all was now silent. Even Ow-n-ow had ceased his dancing and calling, and he stood with the marksmen where they awaited his command. Then—

Suddenly, with a great rupturing of squelchy, rotten toadstools, one of the towering vegetable humps at the far side of the clearing was shoved aside; and in the next instant a great shape moved slowly into the glade. We saw it—outlined in its own blue glow, silhouetted against the night—that vast slug-shape whose eyestalks stood out like horns from its head, whose *motion* was a slow contraction and expansion which was yet sufficient to glide the thing along at a not inconsiderable speed.

Even as the great gastropod appeared, a second creature's head and waving eyestalks slid into view at the edge of the clearing close by; and now Ow-n-ow gave his near-hysterical word of command, and at once the pigmy marksmen lifted their blowpipes to their lips. This was what Phata had waited for. As the pigmies moved, so he moved.

In one motion he turned to me, ripped away the thongs that bound me to my tree and scooped me to his shoulder. No time to work on my actual bonds, however, those bindings which yet held my feet and hands fast; for even now a great head swayed out of the darkness, bluely-illumined eyestalks turning this way and that, and a corrugated grey-blue bulk loomed close.

Then I heard Phata's grunt as a dart struck him, and almost simultaneously I felt a swift stab at my own shoulder where another poisoned missile found its mark. In another moment we were away, Phata plunging into the swamp, wading chest-deep through slime and weed and vilely smelling rot, and me over his shoulder, head down, my face brushing the very skin of that quaggy, scummy surface.

Screams of fury behind us and harshly gabbled orders—and the *hiss* of darts cleaving the noxious air—and a second sharp pain in my back—and Phata grunting three, four times in rapid succession as his broad back and shoulder took the brunt of the fusillade. But then the clearing was behind us, lost in a boggy mist, through which the many blue-glowing forms of the slug-gods were seen faint as ghost-lights receding in our fetid wake.

For a little while longer Phata ploughed through nameless mire, where at any moment we may well have disappeared for ever beneath its surface, but then at last he stumbled up on to a sort of island and dumped me against the broad bole of a squat, stunted tree. It was the work of mere seconds then for my mighty friend to tear away my bonds, and at last I was free—but free to face what fearsome future?

For already I could feel the poison from the darts working in my system, numbing my mind and body and blurring my vision, though the darts themselves had been shaken loose during our flight through the swamp. Phata, having taken perhaps half-a-dozen darts—a lethal dose according to Atmaas—must have been in an even worse condition, but so far his enormous vitality was buoying him up. Even he was beginning to succumb, however, and as he swayed before me where I sat with my back to the tree I could see that it would soon be all up with him.

"Well, old friend," I said in a gasping voice which surprised me with its faintness. "Is this the end for us, then?"

"For me, most likely," he answered, "for I took too many of their damned darts. And you?"

"Just two—but enough to stretch me out for a while, I fancy. The swamp will do the rest."

"At least you have a chance—" Phata began, but I angrily cut him off with:

"You would have had a far better chance, great fool—all the chance in the world—if you'd just looked after yourself! A man like you, why!—it would take more than this measly swamp to stop you!"

"I've no regrets, my friend," he grunted, "except perhaps I would dearly have loved to snap Ow-n-ow's twiggy neck! Also, it's a bit of a disappointment to die rich…"

I tried to stand, to embrace him, to weep in my frustration, but no longer had the strength for any of these things. Instead I merely collapsed against my tree, shivering in a poison-induced fever, barely aware that Phata had broken off a stout branch for a weapon and now stood over me, legs spread, club dangling from his great hand.

When he spoke again his voice seemed to come to me from a thousand miles away, but even so it carried hope. He was never one to give in easily, Phata Um.

"If you can make it through the night, perhaps you'll get out of here yet. And if I can stay active long enough—who knows? Maybe the poison is less potent than Atmaas believes. I may yet work it out of my system."

"Phata," I managed to mumble, "you could be right. I pray that you are…" And after that, all else was a drugged nightmare.

A nightmare, yes, for the things I seem to remember of that night were never meant to be in any ordered, sane or waking world. How best to describe it?

I became for the most part unconscious, but every now and then I would stir up from the grip of the drug, usually to discover that I had been awakened by the sounds or commotions of combat! Combat, aye, for Phata had not succumbed (though I shall never be able to comprehend the sheer, raw power of will and physical energy which kept him on his feet) and now he had the swamp's predators to deal with.

Up they came out of that near-luminous murk; the sliding things, the snapping things, and always Phata there to greet them with his club. And oh the snarls of crocodiles with broken jaws and shattered skulls, the hissing of snakes split asunder, the squelching of crushed leech-things fat as a man's thigh, and the squeal of great bats knocked clean out of the misty, reeking air before they could make clear their intent! And never a one of them allowed to touch me, not while Phata Um retained what little must now remain of his strength and senses.

But in the end he was done, even Phata, and I felt his hands on my numb face and heard his whisper in my weirdly singing ears:

"Eythor," he said, kneeling beside me, his huge shoulder to the bole of the squat tree, his arms hanging limp. "The night is near spent and a dull glow lights the eastern sky. I too am spent, however, and I know it. It is the heart, the lungs, the organs which the pigmy poisons attack, and I have not worked them out of my system but into it..." And he paused for long moments, his breathing ragged where he slumped against me.

"I have noted," he finally continued, "how in this last hour the swamp's lesser monsters have moved away—and I know why. The great slugs, in their nocturnal foraging, are headed this way. The sacrifices were doubtless succulent and welcome, but not enough. The slugs are night-feeders, Eythor, and as dawn approaches they feed all the more rapidly, taking their fill before returning to some secret place to sleep out the day.

"Now, I am finished and I know it—but you can survive. You may live—but not if the slugs find you. So I have split my club to give it a sharp point, and now I go to do what I can to keep the great beasts at bay. I think they are simple creatures, like their lesser cousins, and if so they may fear me and my stick more than I fear them.

"You may not see me again, Eythor, for which reason I now say farewell!" Then I felt his cold lips on my brow, and somehow I forced open my eyes to see him lurch to his feet and stagger away into swirling, misty mire. I would have called him back, but my paralysis was now almost complete, my fever at its peak.

The last I saw of him, his silhouette was limned against an oh so faint, uncertain light—that of the coming dawn. But there were other lights, and far less friendly: gliding blue ghosts that told of the rapid encroachment of the swamp's giant gastropods. Then, for what seemed a very long time, I knew no more...

VII

...**When next I** recovered consciousness I was very weak, but I knew that I had survived the ordeal. The dullness had passed from my senses and though my body and limbs felt like lead, still they were mine once more—and at least they *had* feelings! So it may be imagined the degree of my shock and horror when, upon opening my eyes, I found myself staring up into the brown orbs of a grimacing pigmy face!

For a single instant my heart almost stopped—but in the next moment I knew that this was Atmaas, that the grimace was no more than a concerned, questioning smile distorted in my eyes by the abnormal bulge of his head, and that somehow Lady Fortune once more beamed upon me. I tried to smile in return—and immediately remembered Phata Um.

The joy occasioned by my awakening passed from Atmaas' face as a cloud passing over the face of the sun, and so I knew the worst. After that I quickly grew very tired—indeed, I believe a great deal of my spirit passed out of me—and I desired to know no more. Before I slept a pigmy girl, my own sweet concubine, fed me a warming broth (for certainly I could not feed myself), following which exhaustion overtook me...

My recovery from that time forward was slow but sure, and as time passed so I pieced together the story of what had happened—at least from Atmaas' point of view—during my long period of unconsciousness. Which leads me to the final and strangest part of my story.

All through that first long night, while I lay in a drugged coma at the foot of a tree on that small island in the mud, and while Phata Um stood over and protected me, the pigmies had waited to see what they might see. When we escaped and ran (rather, when Phata ran with me draped over his shoulder), Ow-n-ow had described our flight as a declaration of guilt, for rather than stay and face the justice of the slug-gods we had chosen the unknown terrors of the swamp. It would avail us naught; the pigmies would wait until morning and if we had not returned by then they would know for certain that we were finished.

Then they had sat in the safety of their canoes and watched the glowing gastropods as they glided through the glade of the sacrifice and took their burnt offerings. And the hours had slipped by and Gleeth the smiling moon-god walked the night sky of Theem'hdra, so that when the first glow of dawn was glimpsed down the river, then Ow-n-ow declared that we must be dead and the slug-gods appeased. With the departure of the great gastropods from the island, the chief and his councillors, the *nganga* too and certain of the tribal elders, returned to make sure that indeed the sacrifice had been received.

And it was seen that all the offerings had been taken, to the very last pig, and so for a further quarter the N'dolas would surely prosper. Then, after clearing away the gory debris of that vast repast, lesser dishes were prepared and the pigmies broke their fast and conjectured amongst themselves upon the fate of the two who had dared profane the temple of the slug-gods.

Most certainly we were dead and gone, they were all agreed, devoured by the swamp's predators or sunken in its quicksand coils; for the marksmen with their blowpipes were certain that their fusil-lade had been utterly lethal. And so the sun rose up higher in the sky and steamed away the mists, and the N'dolas prepared to take their leave of the place. Which was when, in broad daylight, the incredible and completely unbelievable took place before their very eyes.

Out from the swamp (where by now it should be resting in some deep, shaded and secret grove), up on to the island of the sacrifice, glided the lone shape of a great gastropod. And beneath its waving eyestalks, held loosely in a mouth of rough plates like giant rasps, the figure of a man was clearly discernible, head down and limbs limply dangling. My figure, as Atmaas was later to discover. As the pigmies on the island fled before the gliding shape of this mighty Lord of the Morass, so the creature proceeded to the centre of the clearing where I was deposited gently upon the sun-dried sward.

Safely out on the river once more and anchored to its bed, the log craft of the pigmies bobbed gently as their boggling crews followed in astonishment the actions of the slug-god where its slate-grey bulk stood over my crumpled form. And there they stayed as the day drew on and the sun rose to its highest, hottest point. And all the while they whispered about what it all meant, that this great slug-god should thus jeopardise its own life by standing out in the searing rays of the sun and giving shade to one who had robbed its temple.

Or could it perhaps be, the whisper began to be heard, that the outsiders had not been guilty after all?

Ow-n-ow heard the whisper, too, and grew wrathful. No, he protested, the man had been brought back by the great gastropod as a punishment. Plainly the man was not yet dead, for every now and then he would give a twitch, or move however fitfully. Patently the slug-god waited for him to awaken, when without a doubt it would straightway devour him—but not before he was made to see the end to which his iniquities had brought him.

But An'noona, who was growing more doubtful by the hour, could find little of any merit in Ow-n-ow's assessment of the situation; moreover, Atmaas was openly critical of the evil *nganga's* explanation of this hitherto unheard of occurrence. Why, it could plainly be seen (Atmaas declared) that the slug-god *stood guard* over the outsider! It suffered the very rays of the sun upon its hide, which must in the end destroy it, simply to give him shade!

So the day wore on, and the sun beamed down as its orb moved across the sky, and the corrugated hide of the slug-god dried out and lost its greyish sheen. Occasionally a great croc would slide out of the swamp on its belly and make its way to where I lay—only to have the vast gastropod block its path with great grey body and cavernous grinding jaws...

By the time the shadows of afternoon began to lengthen the slug-god was plainly suffering. Its hide, completely dry now and beginning to turn a dull, sickly purple, had developed sores and cracks, and its movements had lost all of their previous co-ordination and rhythmic sinuosity. The creature was dying, which anyone but a fool must surely see.

And that could only mean that Ow-n-ow was a fool, for still he insisted—however blusteringly—that he was correct. A fool, aye...or a damned liar!

Finally An'noona lost his temper and put it to the *nganga* that if he was so well versed in the ways of the gods, perhaps he should go ashore on to the island and ask the great creature what it was about. Ow-n-ow, to give him his due, turned on the chief and demanded to know if An'noona had lost faith in his *nganga*? At which Atmaas had leaped to his feet in the chief's trimaran to confront the furious witch-doctor and curse him roundly for a liar and a blackguard.

And Ow-n-ow had no other choice but to do as the chief had suggested, for as a man the N'dolas were on their feet behind An'noona and his chief councillor, and the *nganga* could see that to refuse the challenge would be to lose face irretrievably and relinquish forever his power in the tribe of the N'dolas.

Nor was he given the chance to wriggle out of it; for while no order had been given, still the crew of the chief's craft brought the trimaran around until the tip of its larboard outrigger was touching the island, and all eyes were on the *nganga* when at last he stepped ashore. For a moment he stood there, seemingly undecided, with his back to the river and its flotilla of canoes; but then he squared up, stood erect, and finally he stepped forward. Right up to the rear of the slug-god he went, where its hide was cracked now like old leather, with some vile ichor oozing out of the cracks, and reaching out his hand he touched the purplish bulk of the thing.

At this a low, awed murmur went up from the pigmies in their massed canoes; but the gastropod moved not at all, though its great body pulsed as it had pulsed for many a long hour, listlessly and with no sign of cognition. Only the mighty head showed life, and even there the eyestalks drooped and were visibly a-tremble; and occasionally the great mouth would grind on nothing, in a sort of dumb agony.

Taking heart, Ow-n-ow moved slowly along the length of the slug's body until he approached its head. There he paused, and the eyes at the end of their rubbery stalks gazed dully upon him where he stood. At that very moment, even as the tiny witch-doctor and the massive gastropod came face to face, so I had chosen to move. With spastic jerks and twitches I changed my position on the ground where I lay; whereupon Ow-n-ow gave a cry of rage, snatched a long, curving knife from his belt and hurled himself upon me—or would have done but for the intervention of the mighty slug.

As if seeing Ow-n-ow for the first time—even as the *nganga* flew at me where I lay in a helpless heap—the slug-god was suddenly galvanised into action. The massive head swung down, the great jaws opened and snapped shut on Ow-n-ow's small black body, and the grinding plates moved with the inexorable, utterly undeniable motion of glaciers. The *nganga* screamed—once—and then was still; and with a toss of its slaty head the huge beast hurled his mutilated doll corpse into the swamp.

Then the body of the beast stiffened and in another moment it rolled slowly over on to its side. But even dying it was careful that I was not crushed. And finally all was still, and the gastropod lay beside me, its monstrous head close to my own.

For a long, long time then there were only the lapping of the river and the sounds of the swamp, and even these seemed muted. Then An'noona commanded that I be lifted up and taken aboard his trimaran; and finally, silently, overawed by all they had seen and with low-mouthed prayers on their lips, the pigmies departed from the swamp of the slug-gods and returned to their island village.

———

When I was well again I went back to the swamp with Atmaas and together we ventured into the glade of the sacrifice. There the remains of the slug-god—its tremendous, cartilaginous skeleton and huge rough plates of vestigial shell—lay where the beast had fallen, picked clean by lesser monsters. There, too, was that which explained everything, at least to me.

Amidst shreds of corrugated hide and fragments of chalky bone I found a smaller skeleton, that of a man. The rings on its fingers were Phata's, and round the bony neck was the heavy golden chain given him in friendship by An'noona.

THE WINE OF THE WIZARD

Editorial Note:

Patently this penultimate tale *is* a fiction; but knowing what I do of Thelred Gustau's own disappearance, and something of the circumstances surrounding the disappearance of his nephew at that earlier time, I like to conjecture that its words fly perhaps not too wildly astray of the mark. As for the actual meat of the story, which commences proper with Chapter III: that is a direct translation from Teh Atht's writings.

> MYLAKHRION'S POWDER, CONCOCTED AT GREAT EXPENSE FROM HIS OWN FORMULA & WITH *EXACT* REGARD TO MEASURES & INGREDIENTS, MUST I FEAR REMAIN AN UNKNOWN QUANTITY. THE MEREST PINCH, TAKEN AS SNUFF, PRODUCES MARVELS GALORE, WHOSE EFFECTS ARE SO WONDERFUL THAT THE POWDER COULD WELL PROVE ADDICTIVE. WHAT, THEN, ITS POTENCY WHEN BREWED UP IN A MEASURE OF WINE SUCH AS MY AWFUL ANCESTOR WAS WONT TO IMBIBE?
>
> ...TEH ATHT.

I

Do not drink it!" Thelred Gustau warned his nephew, Erik, as he passed him a tiny phial of greenish powder. "Merely prepare the wine—a sort of sherry, you say—and let me have it when the stuff is properly mature. I require it for certain tests, and of course I don't know exactly what this powder is or what it can do. Its mildest effect, I suspect, is to produce grotesque hallucinations. We shall see. But since Teh Atht specifies that it might be used in this wine of his 'awful ancestor,' and since you have a talent for producing these home-brewed concoctions—"

"Sherry," said Gustau's young visitor. "Quite definitely. But uncle, how old did you say this recipe is?" And he smiled, however wanly.

His uncle glanced up from his work-bench, where already he was absorbed once more in his work, and said, "Hmm?—its age?" The scientist frowned. "Why, no," he answered, "I can't really tell you how old it is—not with any measure of certainty—but I believe it predates the dinosaurs."

"That's what I thought you said." Erik managed another smile. "Very well, I'll brew your wine for you. Perhaps it will help take my mind off things."

Now his uncle suddenly grew concerned. He stood up and came round his oddly littered bench to lay a solicitous hand on the younger man's shoulder. "Listen, Erik. I know how bad things have been for you, and I don't want to sound cruel or uncaring, but you're not the first man who has had to face up to such a thing. Give yourself time. I know she meant everything to you and there's a place inside you that feels empty and dead, but it will pass. Believe your old uncle, it's not the end of the world."

Erik Gustau nodded. "I know, I know. But it feels like the end of my world. Uncle, she was so young! How do such things happen? If there's a God, how can He let such things happen?"

The older man could only shake his head.

Erik Gustau was only twenty three years of age. Tall, blond, hand some as all the Gustaus were, he was a young man in his physical prime. And yet now there was this air of total dejection about him. A great light had gone out of his life; out of his eyes, too, which had once been bright and piercing blue. Now they were dull, disinterested, only very rarely given to smiling. What good the money his grandfather had willed him, when the one he had built his world around was no more? Shoulders which had been strong and square drooped a little, and a walk once bounding and full of life seemed now the measured tread of an old man...

II

And now, with the tiny phial of greenish powder in his pocket, Erik Gustau made his way across the heart of London from his uncle's Woolwich address, and as he went he almost forgot the reason for his visit. Ever uppermost in his mind there loomed his lost love's face, and again and again he would find himself cursing the name of that incurable disease whose insidious tentacles had taken her from him and into an early tomb.

He knew of course that his uncle had only set him the task in hand to free him from the dreadful lassitude which sorrow had seemed to stamp into him; he knew also that there were greater talents to whom the task would have been better entrusted. Nevertheless he had decided to undertake its completion, if only to satisfy the other's curiosity and let the older man believe that in his way he had helped him recover from his bereavement.

Thus when he returned to the beautiful home he had readied for his lost love, and to the anxious servants who waited there, he set to work at once and brewed up a gallon of Mylakhrion's wine, applying himself diligently to the notes his uncle had prepared for him and adhering as best he could to the incredibly ancient formula or recipe. And so, some seven weeks later, the wine came into being...

It came with a warning from Benson, Erik's gentleman's gentleman, who awakened him one morning from miserable, repetitious dreams with the ominous statement that something had "exploded" in the cellar! He at once remembered the wine, stored away in bottles for almost two months, and clad only in dressing-gown and slippers rushed downstairs.

In the cellar he found seven of his eight carefully labelled bottles shattered, their heady contents hurled to oblivion, and the eighth with its cork still bounding about the floor while a red fountain splashed the whitewashed ceiling. When at last he managed to ram the cork home again in the neck of the bottle, all that remained of a gallon of Mylakhrion's wine was an amount somewhat greater than a large glassful. This sole remaining bottle he carefully wiped down and reverently carried with him to his study on the ground floor.

There, sitting in an easy chair with the bottle on an occasional table before him, he dimly remembered something of his uncle's warning not to drink it, and something else of the tale accompanying it: of a time lost to man in the mists of predawn, where the first great civilisations of man were raised in a primal continent. And with the morning sun striking through his window and setting the wine to glowing a dull red, it suddenly seemed to him that he could smell the warm winds of that time-lost land and taste the salt of the mighty Unknown Ocean which washed its golden strand.

But then he shook his head. No, it was only the fumes from the escaped wine in the cellar that he could smell; his imagination had done the rest. Still, the red-glowing stuff looked remarkably palatable through the clear glass of the bottle. Almost unconsciously he removed the cork, poured a small glass half full, and set it upon the table close to the window. As he did so a heady fragrance rose from the bottle and seemed to hang round his head in an almost tangible cloud.

Now the sun caught the rim of the fine wineglass and set it a-sparkle, and mirrored through the wine Erik could see his garden, all umber-tinted and reversed by the wine and the curve of the glass. Reversed as he wished he might reverse his life—or end it altogether.

Almost without noticing it, he took the glass in his hand, raised it to his lips, and sipped a half-mouthful, washing his palate and allowing that nectar of primal origins first to cool, then to sear his astonished throat! Unsteadily he replaced the glass by the window, half-rose to his feet, and fell back in his chair as a wave of dizziness passed over him. And again his eyes went to the glass.

Ah! But this time he saw no umber garden reflected in its bowl. Instead he saw—or read, or heard, it really does not matter—the beginnings of a strange story from a world far distant and lost in the dim mists of time...

III

There had been a time when the sheer cliffs of Shildakor were a mile high, utterly impregnable and cursed by the long-dead wizard for whom they were named, so that no man might ever climb them. But that had been more than five hundred years ago in Theem'hdra's youth, when the Primal Land knew a strange era of half-barbaric civilisation and of sorcery, and when Bhur-Esh was a mighty city-state between the Unknown Ocean and Shildakor's sheltering cliffs.

Now those cliffs were great rounded nodding heads of pumice and volcanic rock, riddled with caves which stared blindly out over the Unknown Ocean, where the unruly waves were calmed even to this day by the olden, stony promontories whose twin arms once guarded the bay of Bhur-Esh. For spells and enchantments grow old even as continents and worlds, and Nature's own forces are at times more powerful than the builded walls of men or the mumbled runes of wizards.

Out in the Unknown Ocean, Ashtah the volcano isle still rumbled; but never so loudly as on that day, when rising up from the deeps, it had hurled molten death into the Vale of Bhur-Esh, forming a great roaring ramp between boiling sea and cliffs and removing forever the city and its rulers and the farmers who tended their beasts and crops outside the city's walls and beneath the sheer and mighty Ghost Cliffs. All of them gone, all but a handful of survivors, swept away by rivers of rock from Earth's heart; a proud people no more but a paragraph written upon a single scorched page of a planet's history. And in this Bhur-Esh was little different from other cities and civilisations which would follow down the aeons, though geologic ages would pass before Atlantis and Mu, and a handful of years more before Pompeii...

But after a time, when wind and weather began to work their ways—when the lava slopes grew green again and the great fishes came back to the warm seas, and when Ashtah settled down quietly to smoke and smoulder far out in the Unknown Ocean beyond the bay—then the descendants of the holocaust's survivors returned and made their homes in the lava caves, and they built stout doors and windows to guard against the inclement seasons. They floored their dwellings with planks cut from trees felled atop the now gentle cliffs, and the skins of animals were the rugs on their floors. They built garden walls, and brick chimneys for their fires, and fishing boats to go out in the bay for food; and as the years passed so the people prospered and grew in number. They became skilled at hollowing out or discovering new dwellings in the lava, and used the debris of their work as soil; and their terraces went down from the cliffs to the sea, laden with trellis-grown grapes rich and red from the fertile pumice.

So the people of New Bhur-Esh flourished, and where the former city and citizens had been utterly self-contained and -sufficient, they traded their wines with the wild, dark-haired Northmen and the merchants of Thandopolis, who came in their dragonships and merchantmen; and all in all they were a happy people, even living in the constant shade of Ashtah, which sometimes rumbled mightily or vented great columns of smoke into the clear blue skies of Theem'hdra. Aye, even in the shade of the volcano—and of the greater evil it housed—they did their best to be happy.

As for that greater evil: it was a shadow fallen on New Bhur-Esh out of the East, the necromantic shadow of a black sorcerer from the coastal forests beyond the nameless river. For even as the population of the lava valley grew and prospered, so rumours came from the East of a Yhemni Magus whose ebon skin was never so black as his heart, which was so steeped in sin as to be putrid.

Hurled forth from outraged Grypha of the Hrossaks, spurned by the inhabitants of the jungle-hidden cities of his native coastal forests, driven from beneath the walls of Thinhla under threat of death by fire, the necromancer Arborass sought new lodgings—and rumour had it that he sought them in New Bhur-Esh. Now when they heard this whispered abroad, the elders of the valley tribe (for they were considered and thought of themselves as a tribe as opposed to a nation) came together in meeting to decide what was to be done about this Arborass, and this was their decision:

Just as Grypha and the Black Cities and Thinhla had turned him and his acolytes back from their borders, so must they; for it was of old renown that if ever a wizard made unopposed camp within a town, then that town was doomed by its own slothfulness, and must soon dance to the wizard's tune. Thus when the black, skull-prowed ship of Arborass sailed out of the West to cleave the calm waters of the bay with night-black oars, and when the necromancer himself stood up in the prow and gazed upon the valley's strand, he saw only the sharp weapons and fires of them that waited on his landing, and the sharper eyes of wise men who would not suffer a wizard to set foot upon their land.

And the necromancer Arborass swelled up in his rage, and his head was a great black shaven skull with eyes of fire, which towered above a billowing cloak of black velvet embroidered with silver runes. He stood in the prow of his devil's boat and raised his taloned arms as if to administer a great curse—then calmed himself and said:

"So, I am threatened with knives and fires, who have come these long sea-miles only to be your friend and protector. So be it...but before ten days are done, and before the setting of the tenth sun, you shall welcome me ashore. Even with open arms shall I be welcomed. Aye, and my weary rowers also, who tire of the sea's toil." And as the oars dipped and turned his ship seaward once more, so the people of New Bhur-Esh saw the necromancer's jest—for his rowers were sere mummies whose semblance of life was a blasphemy commanded by the necromancer himself!

IV

Now among them that gathered on the beach and saw this thing, and watched Arborass rowed out to sea once more by his mummied crew, was a lad of some thirteen years called Ayrish: which meant foundling. Learning the fisherman's trade, Ayrish lived with the poorest family of the cave-dwellers, for they had found him on their doorstep as a babe and had grudgingly taken him in. What were his origins no man could say, but it was thought a village girl had been his mother, and that in her shame she had lain him on a doorstep to be found.

Ayrish was big for his age and handsome, but ever he wore the marks of much toiling and the black bruises of beatings. The master of his house was a drunkard and bully; his three true sons were older than Ayrish, sullen and full of spite; so that in a word, his lot was not a happy one. Nevertheless he worked harder than the others for his keep and grew stronger each day, and without a mother's care waxed supple of limb and hard of will. And the three he called brothers, though they were not his brothers and dealt sorely with him, were a little afraid of him; for where they were dull and ran to idle fatness, the wit of Ayrish was sharp and his muscles firm, so that they thought one day he might turn on them.

Now, watching the necromancer Arborass rowing out to sea, and seeing that his course lay straight for the volcano isle Ashtah, Ayrish spoke up, saying: "You should have killed him, you men!"

"What do you know, boy?" an Elder at once rounded on him. "And who are you, a motherless chick not long hatched, to talk of killing? Arborass is a necromancer and wizard; aye, and a hard one to kill, be sure!"

"Nevertheless, you should have tried," answered the lad, undaunted. "The rumours say he is a fire-wizard. He commands the fires that rage."

Now another Elder grabbed Ayrish and shook him. "Boy, we did not let him land, you saw that. Why then should we fear him? And what fires may he command out on the bosom of the sea?"

All of them laughed then, and none louder than the louts Ayrish called brothers, until he said: "And what of Ashtah? Is not the volcano a raging fire, however much he seems to sleep? And what if Arborass wakes him? See, the wizard steers a steady course!" And all of them saw that the lad was right.

"He would not dare return," the Elders blustered. Ayrish, struggling free of them, said nothing. But to himself he said, *We shall see, in ten more days!*

Three nights and two days passed with never sight nor sound of Arborass and his magics; but on the third day, at noon, a mighty column of steam shot up from Ashtah and formed a leaden blanket in the sky. All through the afternoon the boiling continued, and an early, unseasonal night settled over New Bhur-Esh, and lightnings flashed and rumbled in the grey, rolling sky.

In the morning the Elders said that was that, and they brushed their hands together to dismiss Arborass, for surely he was boiled alive. But the next evening, at dusk, a great voice was heard echoing over the sea, and the ground trembled and shook, and rings of smoke went up from Ashtah as from some strange and sinister engine. On this occasion no one spoke of Arborass, for the great voice that had thundered was his, but magnified a thousand times.

In the afternoon of the eighth day a chanting was heard, rolling in on a breeze off the sea, and the voices were of those long dead, which had the reedy quality of flutes. And when the chanting was done, there came once more a great booming of laughter; and all the people of the lava valley knew that indeed Arborass lived and worked strange wonders.

On the ninth day Ashtah hurled a mighty cluster of lava-bombs aloft, which hissed down into the sea between the volcano and the bay, causing clouds of steam and waves which washed up fishes roasted in their thousands. This was early in the morning; but midway to noon a second eruption rained glowing rocks within the bay itself. At noon a third peppered the shallowest waters of the bay and sank a number of anchored craft; and three hours later a fourth devastated the beach. And the people of New Bhur-Esh saw that this regular vomiting of the volcano had clear design, for always the fires fell closer and closer to the vines and gardens and yards of the boat-builders; aye, and closer to their homes in the face of the old cliffs. And the stench of sulphur was everywhere, and the people cowered in their cavern houses.

Now, as the afternoon passed in troubled silence and night grew on, when it seemed that Ashtah's fearful game was at an end, there sounded again over the sea the chanting of Arborass' mummy acolytes, and the necromancer's mad laughter; so that all of the people feared what the morning would bring. For the next morning would be the tenth, when Arborass had prophesied his return…

V

The strange visions receded in Erik Gustau's mind like a frost steamed away by the morning sun, and his astonishment at finding himself awake and seated in his chair close to the window of his study knew no ends; for the thing had been so real that he had thought to find himself in his bed and dreaming. Especially since the boy Ayrish (had that been his name?) had seemed so very familiar to him. But then, tasting a lingering fragrance in his mouth and seeing the small wineglass glowing in the sunlight, he remembered; and filled with an almost mesmeric amazement, he tilted the glass tremblingly to his lips once more...

Ten years were passed away now, since the coming of Arborass the necromancer and wizard to New Bhur-Esh, and Ayrish was grown to a young man. None remembered the youth's remark, uttered on that day when the wizard was turned away from the strand and his tomb-looted rowers bore him out to sea—that the men of the lava valley should have killed Arborass—but all remembered the tenth day and the wizard's return.

All the night before the ground had shivered while Ashtah rumbled, and the dawn was a scarlet thing splashed by the sun on volcanic clouds, and the beach afloat with rotting fish and squids. Mist lapped thick and scummy on the dawn ocean like curdled milk, through which—on oars which plied with a soundless and soulless mechanism—Arborass' black ship, sails furled up, came gliding in to beach with a hiss of crushed gravel.

All the Elders were there together with the men of the valley tribe, holding a line as the wizard stood up in the skull-carved prow. "And would you resist me?" he asked in a soft voice as fires smoked behind his baleful eyes. "And who then says me nay? Which is the spokesman, and what message has he for me?"

At this the wisest and oldest of all the Elders came slowly forward, frail in his years but with a strength of mind and will which all knew and respected. "Turn back, Arborass," he warned in quavery voice. "We valley people would have naught of fire-wizards and necromancers. Aye, and if you step down from your ship, then be certain we shall kill you!"

And Arborass turned his back on the shore and them that stood there, raising his arms on high and calling on Ashtah which smoked in the sea. "Oh, do you hear this mischief, Ashtah?" his voice rolled on the undulant mist. "And what is your answer, Mighty One, to this threat against your true and faithful priest and servant?"

At that the volcano roared and hurled aloft a ball of fiery rock, which sped across the sky and rushed down upon the strand. All the Elders and men cowered back, except the old one whose age—and whose horror—bound him to the spot as were he chained there. And the rock fell on him and drove him into the sand and shingle of the beach, hissing and steaming and filled with the stench of roasted flesh. Aghast, the men were frozen for long seconds and held their eyes averted; and when they would have rushed upon the wizard in his ship, Arborass faced them once more and eyed them through heavy-lidded orbs. And in a very low voice he spoke again to the volcano, but every man of them heard his whispered words:

"Ashtah," he said. "O Mighty One, hear me. If I am harmed by these sinners who own you not—if a single stone be hurled or spear cast, if a tiny bruise or cut be made in me—then crush them to a man, and all that is theirs with them, and level this valley with the hot outpourings of thy inmost being! Do you hear me, Ashtah?" And the ground rumbled and shook until all of them that stood there were hurled down upon the wave-washed sands.

Then said Arborass, "It is good that you prostrate your miserable selves; Ashtah will preserve them that worship him and heed the words of his priest." And when the men of the valley looked up, they saw that the necromancer had stepped down from his ship, his ravaged rowers with him, and that indeed the wizard was come amongst them…

VI

But that was all of ten years ago, and much had come to pass in the years flown between. Of the wizard: at first his demands were not excessive, and his comings to New Bhur-Esh were never more than one in any month. Then, on the occasion of the twelfth visit—when the people had begun to grumble of this wizard-priest no one wanted, who must be kept in bread, meat, fish and wine—suddenly his needs were seen to be far more than the mere necessities of life.

For Arborass now demanded a girl, who must be of eighteen or nineteen summers but no more, and she was to be made ready for him to take back to Ashtah when next he came. The volcano-God demanded sacrifice, he said, to appease him in his merciful but ever restive slumbers; and to prove a point he asked Ashtah if he were satisfied with the worship of his people, to which the volcano answered in a rumbling and a spouting of fire, and a hail of blazing boulders which sank half of the fishing fleet at anchor in the bay. So that at last the valley-dwellers knew the price of the wizard, and perhaps a few of them remembered the words of a small boy who had said they should kill this curse come upon them from the sea.

On the day before Arborass was due, the Elders gathered in their meeting place to decide what might be done; but ere they could talk Ashtah belched a cloud of steam, which drifted in off the sea. And when it hung low in the sky over New Bhur-Esh, then lightning came out of it and wrote in molten fire on the ground, DOOM.

And so each girl of eighteen and nineteen summers was given a number, and a pebble marked with that number was placed in a leather sack, and each of the girls was made to put in a hand and draw out a pebble until only one remained. The number of the final stone would mark the identity of the unfortunate maid; and so was Ashtah's first sacrifice chosen from the girls of the valley tribe. And this was the awful custom which prevailed from that time on, twice in every year, so that Ashtah would be appeased and leave the people of New Bhur-Esh in peace...

VII

And so things had stood for ten long years while Ayrish grew to a man, and for the last three years he had given court to a girl of one of the valley's richest families; and this kept secret from her father, who wanted nothing of paupers and foundlings. Meanwhile the family Ayrish lodged with had prospered, mainly due to his prowess as a sailor and fisherman, but the youth had been kept in poverty while his so-called brothers grew more sluggish yet and their manners more swinish.

And Leela, the girl he loved, was past eighteen and already had stood once with the other maidens to draw pebbles from the leather sack, on which occasion she had been spared. Now, in some four months' time, she must undergo the ordeal once more, and if she again survived twice more, before her age took her beyond the limits set by the volcano-god's wizard priest. Except that each time there would be fewer girls, for many families with daughters had fled New Bhur-Esh forever and taken their girls with them.

Soon, too, it would be the day of the games, which took place only once in every three years, when the young men of the tribe sported for the hands of its maidens. Ayrish had already asked Leela to be his wife, and she had been pleased to answer yes. It was, however, the custom to sport for a girl; and so, as the day grew closer, Leela prayed to all the beneficent gods of Theem'hdra that Ayrish would do well. The day came and the three Ayrish called brothers were also at the games, mocking the foundling as usual and poking fun at his rags. Moreover, all three had set their hearts on Leela, who was the loveliest girl in all the lava valley.

Ayrish did well with the spear, average good at the lifting, and was fastest of all at the running; and so his points were better than average. Then came the wrestling. Now his brothers, being heavy and brutish, were good wrestlers. Also, because they were used to giving Ayrish the occasional clout, they did not worry that he would be in the circle with themselves and the best of the other young men. They were sure that they could beat him and all the others together, and so take their pick of the village girls. Aye, and the brother who was champion wrestler, he would then lay claim to Leela. So they thought...

The pebble circle was prepared and the contestants stepped within, and when the Elders clapped their hands, then the youths were at it. And in a very little while, only four remained within the circle: Ayrish and his brothers.

Now they banded together and circled about Ayrish, intending to have done with him before fighting among themselves; but where they were now weary, he was fresh and fast as ever. As they came at him he tripped one and winded another, then went to throw the weakest from the ring. But this one threw sand in his eyes and near-blinded him, which was a foul. Maddened, Ayrish lashed out and broke the other's jaw, so that now only two brothers faced him.

Of this pair the winded one tried to get behind him while the other came in like a bull, and the first grabbed him round the neck to choke him while the other butted him; and this too was foul fighting. Angered again, Ayrish kicked one in the crotch and booted him from the circle, then turned on the largest of the three who clung to his neck. Aye, and he thrashed him soundly; but in the fighting, blind with blood and passion, both men reeled from the ring together.

Now the points were counted and a draw declared, and Ayrish was asked which maid he would claim. He claimed Leela—but so did his brutish brother!

A tie-breaker was organised (spear-casting, at which Ayrish was reckoned the inferior of the two) and targets were placed upright in the ground. But then, before the contest could begin, the brutish one spoke up:

"Away with the targets! I have my target: it is the ill-mannered, ill-clad ingrate who presumes to call me brother! When I make my cast, it shall be directly at him—if he has the stomach for it..."

"That will suit me very well," answered Ayrish.

Seeing the bad blood between them—and because they had chosen the same maid, which could only lead to later troubles; also because several of the Elders were the friends of Ayrish's foster-father, and knew that he favoured his true son—all were agreed that the twain should cast to the death: and this was the way of it. They would toss a coin, and the winner would make first cast from a distance of fifty yards while the loser stood blindfolded and motionless. If the cast missed its mark, then the other should throw, and so on, until such time as one was struck dead.

The swinish one won the toss and hurled his spear at Ayrish across the paced-out distance. Perhaps his aim was off, or perhaps Leela's prayers were answered, for the spear passed between the left arm and body of Ayrish, harming him not. Then it was his cast.

The other was blindfolded, the distance once more paced out and a marker set, and Ayrish began his run; but hearing the thudding of his feet, the brutish brother cried out in terror, snatched off his bandage and ran away. At the appointed mark, Ayrish let fly his shaft—which cut the other down in mid-flight and pinned him dead to the earth. Thus ended the games.

Now the victor turned to the two remaining brothers, one holding his jaw and the other holding his groin, and said: "So be it. Now are you satisfied, brothers mine? Or would you, too, challenge me?" Which offer both declined.

Then Ayrish went to Leela's father and asked for her, but her father said: "Not so fast, young man! Can you provide a house for her?"

"I shall make a home for her," Ayrish answered.

"Good!" said the other. "When you have done that, then we shall talk again." And he laughed, for there was no cave left in all the valley, so that he was sure Ayrish would fail to make a home for Leela.

"Will you give me one year?" asked Ayrish.

"I will not!" replied the other. "Must my daughter wait a year for a man to provide a house for her? I will give you a six-month, and not a day more."

And Ayrish had to be satisfied with that...

VIII

The youth told Leela what he was about, said his farewells to the tearful girl and straightway went to his boat. Now the boat in fact belonged to his foster-father, a small vessel with oars and a sail; but the owner, tearing his hair and grieving the loss of a son, made no protest and let him take it; and the two remaining sons were likewise glad to be shot of him. All except Leela, who waved farewell to her man as he set sail out of the bay.

And for many days Ayrish sailed south, hugging the coast and searching for a likely spot whereon to build a house for Leela. At last he came upon a place much like the valley of New Bhur-Esh but smaller, where green-clad cliffs guarded a calm bay whose waters were shielded from the ocean's tumult by a low-lying reef; and at length he found a passage and sailed his fragile craft in to a safe harbour.

Now Ayrish walked upon a golden beach and stepped beneath the shade of cool trees where parrots perched amid clusters of great nuts, and he saw that the earth was fertile and its fruits plentiful. Wild pigs rooted in the bushes, curious of Ayrish and unafraid, and pigeons nested in the forest bowers and made soft song. The air was sweet here, with nothing of the stink of volcanoes, and a stream of fresh water sparkled and ran down from the cliffs to a pool, and from there to the sea. And Ayrish explored the forest and stream and entire valley, even to the foot of the tall, unscalable cliffs, and found no other person dwelling there; whereupon he knew that this was where he must build Leela's house.

He found a cave in the white cliffs where they were draped with ivy, and a series of caves within, all hollowed out long ages gone when the pounding ocean was deeper; and many of these lesser caves were like windows which gazed out upon the shore and the valley and forest. So Ayrish found his house, and now he set about to put it in order. He paved the floors with rose-tinted, curiously veined stones from the beach, and he built steps and stairs of felled trees and tough creepers. He painted many of the white walls with the delicate blue dye of seasnails, which were plentiful on the shore, and he planted orchids from the forest in the cliff ledges about the ivy-hung windows. And all in all his house was finer than any house in all the wizard-haunted valley of the volcano.

Then, when all was done, he set sail for New Bhur-Esh; but not with so light a heart as might be reckoned. No, for he was troubled by recurring thoughts of the necromancer Arborass, and of the time of the sacrifice, which again approached. Aye, and he was anxious; for Leela must once more draw a numbered stone from the sack, and yet another maiden must go with Arborass to the isle of the volcano-god, rowed out to sea by his worm-ravaged crew and never seen again. These were the thoughts which troubled Ayrish as he set his sails north, but in his wily mind he had a plan.

Quite simply, he would return to New Bhur-Esh, speak to Leela's father, and before the day of the choosing of the sacrificial maid he would steal Leela away and return with her to their new home. Aye, and if her father and family had any sense at all, then would they give up their riches and belongings—which could provide little of pleasure in a place such as the lava-valley—and leave the tribe to its lot, returning with the lovers to a new and happier life and clime. So thought Ayrish...

Alas, a storm blew up one day that wrecked him on a wild shore of barren scrubland; and because his boat was broken, now Ayrish must journey on foot. Day after day he ran and rested, ran and rested, eating what he could find and drinking wherever he found fresh water. And when he slept, which was rarely, still it seemed that he was running; and in his nightmares a hissing river of smoky lava surged ever nearer.

Until at length he was come to New Bhur-Esh, and clambering and sliding down the lava crags went straight to Leela's house, even bearded and in his tatters, and there presented himself—at a door freshly painted with the thick black pitch of sorrow! And even thundering at the door, Ayrish knew what this foretokened.

His Leela was gone, taken that very hour and rowed out to Ashtah by Arborass' sere mummy servitors!

Now Ayrish waxed wroth, and taking Leela's father by the neck he shook him and cursed his name, saying: "Oh, you, who promised her to me: what madness is this, that you have let the necromancer take her? Why is Arborass not dead first—or you, dead?—but not her, taken!" And such was his grief and rage that he was like to throttle the man and murder all his household.

Then Leela's mother spoke up, crying, "It was not all his fault, Ayrish—though as much his as anyone's. He thought your brothers might save her."

"Them?" cried the agonised youth. "Why them?"

"When you were gone they paid her court, but she would have none of them. And they swore that if her number was on the last pebble in the sack, then that they would protect her with their own lives. And still she would have nothing of them. And the last pebble did have her number, and when the wizard came for her, because your brothers feared the wrath of the volcano-God, they did nothing!"

"They are not my brothers but men of this accursed valley!" cried Ayrish. "And you lava-lovers *never* do anything!" And he hurled the near-throttled master of the house aside like a rag doll.

Next he ran to the cave of his foster-father and battered down the door, and striding in he sought out that pair he once had called brothers. Drunk they were and swinish, but he rattled their heads together and tossed them forth, and dragged them down to the beach and doused them in the sea. And when they were sober he said to them:

"So, and would you steal my woman away in my absence? Aye, and then let Arborass take her without ever lifting a finger? Very well, *now* you shall lift a finger, and more than that if you value your lives. For if Leela dies, be sure your own lives are forfeit!"

Now the rest of that day Ayrish ate good meat and red, and he drank sweet water and a little wine; and all who saw him as he racked his desperate brain and stamped to and fro on the beach—bearded, ragged, wild and red-eyed—thought he must be mad. His once-called brothers thought so too, and grovelling in the sand as he cursed them, they made plans of their own.

Then, as the smoky sun sank down into the Unknown Ocean, limning Ashtah a black silhouette, and as the sea grew darkly green, Ayrish dragged the cowards aboard a boat and set sail for the volcano isle; and all who saw them go knew that they would never see them again…

IX

Now when their boat was out beyond the bay and half-way sailed toward its doleful destiny, then Ayrish and the brothers felt an unaccustomed swirl to the waters and a current which tugged them ever faster toward fire-crested Ashtah. There was only a crescent moon, and this half-hidden by sulphurous clouds, and something of a murky mist lay on the sea which gave them good cover. But the current which drew them unerringly toward the volcano isle was strange, and with all of his sailor's craft Ayrish had no knowledge of it. He suspected, though, that it was more than merely the race of an ebbing tide.

As for the brothers: they sat sullen and silent while Ayrish handled the tiller; and the closer they got to Ashtah, the more sallow their faces and nervous their shifty eyes. And as they went so Ayrish whispered his plan to them, which was this: that they would seek out Arborass in the night and kill him, drive a stake through his heart, cut off his head and burn him; which is the proper way to deal with wizards. The brothers heard him and grew more afraid of Ayrish than of the isle now looming from the mist, for surely was he mad.

And as they ran on that strange and silent water, Ayrish lowered the sail and bade them take up the oars; and they closed with the black and craggy rocks of the place, and Ayrish jumped ashore and tied up the boat to a spur of lava. Then, while he was about this task, the brothers came up behind him and smote him with an oar, saying:

"*This* for our brother, whom you slew! And farewell to you, madman, who would kill a wizard! What? A wizard? A man with the power to command volcanoes and the art to raise up the very dead? Aye, and if we see you again, foundling, surely it were pulling on Arborass' oars with the rest of his tomb-risen crew!"

And they left him there on the rocks, and manning the oars drew away into the night. And only then did they learn of the watchdog Arborass had set over the nighted island, which was the sea itself! For row as they might and however zestfully, still they could not pull free of the place, and dawn found them exhausted and adrift a stone's throw from the lava crags of Ashtah's shore.

High in his eyrie—a corpse-constructed tower of black lava blocks and narrow windows, perched on the very rim of Ashtah's throat—Arborass saw them there in the sea and sent his minion mummies to deal with them. Down went the soulless ones and into the necromancer's boat, and out to sea where the brothers hauled on their oars once more in a useless frenzy. And the mummies cast spears through them where they sweated and toiled, and they fell into the sea.

"So perish all who would sail too close in the night!" cried Arborass from on high, and laughing he returned to his diversions.

Now Ayrish, who had awakened with the dawn and climbed to the foot of Arborass' pile, heard the wizard's words and saw the death of the brothers in their boat; and so he knew that the necromancer's mummies were at sea and their master unprotected. Then he quickly found the tower's door and passed through into the wizard's lair; and he heard Arborass' laughter echoing up from unseen vaults beneath.

Following winding lava steps into the heart of the rock, Ayrish soundlessly descended and came upon the wizard in his inner sanctum. Now keeping silent and watching the doings of the man, he saw Arborass pass through a secret door, and in his turn he followed him. And in that innermost place, finally he saw Leela, all naked and lovely and a-swoon. She lay upon an altar-like slab which could be tilted by means of a lever, and the slab stood before a fiery blowhole whose rim was red with heat from Ashtah's heart. And Ayrish saw that when the slab was tilted, then would Leela plunge to her doom in the liquid rock of Ashtah's loins.

Now on that selfsame slab, close to Leela's head, were censers of smouldering opiates whose fumes subdued the girl; and as Arborass disrobed Ayrish saw that the necromancer would take first-fruits before feeding his god. And a red rage rose up in Ayrish as he thought of the misery of so many girls gone this way before. And such was his fury that he no longer owned his senses.

As Arborass went to the girl, so Ayrish leaped out upon him, a great knife uplifted in his hand. Arborass heard!—saw!—grasped the lever!—screamed as Ayrish's knife pierced him!

Now the youth swept the girl from the slowly tilting slab and made to carry her from the place; but the necromancer, dying, called upon his mummies to kill them. Down into that secret place the returning dead ones shuffled, and two of them snatched Leela from Ayrish's arms while the others sought to stab him with their spears. And he was struck, and the spear tore a wound in his side.

Then, in his pain and horror, Ayrish became filled with the strength of ten. Before the mummies could pierce him again, he snatched up two of their number like bales of straw and hurled them at the staggering necromancer. Now mummies, wizard and all fell atop the tilting slab, and all slid therefrom into Ashtah's fiery maw. In the next moment, even in the blinking of an eye, the rest of Arborass' tomb-spawn crumbled and fell to dust where they stood, and all the volcano isle shook itself as a man starting from evil dreams.

Then Ayrish took up the girl from where she had fallen, and he tottered from Arborass' tower even as it slid into ruins and toppled into Ashtah's furnace throat. And down the shuddery carven steps went Ayrish, and deliriously into his boat where it bumped against the rocky wharf and rolled on the choppy waters; and as Leela began to come awake he placed her in the middle of the boat, took up the oars and plied madly for the open sea.

Now, with Arborass dead, the island no longer exerted its magnet pull, and soon Ayrish was well clear of the volcano. But the sea grew rougher yet as Ashtah thundered, great waves rising and frothing in all directions; and the youth, weak from his scarlet wound, rose up from where he sat to attend to the sail. And at that very moment the boat tilting like a cockleshell, Ayrish was tossed overboard and dragged down in the wrack of ocean!

Up Leela sprang, recovered from her drug-induced swoon, and clinging to the boat's side she scanned the frothy deep and flying spume. And "Ayrish" she cried uselessly against the storm. "Ayrish! *Ayrish!*"

But only the volcano answered, with roar of steam and spouting lava flood. And splitting his sides in fissures of fire, Ashtah hurled his molten might aloft. God no more, he vented his fury upon the sky— and all the steamy bile of his belly fell in the valley of New Bhur-Esh.

"Ayrish! Ayrish!" the maid screamed again through the maelstrom of wind and water—and miracle of miracles, from somewhere close at hand, suddenly she thought to hear her lover's answer!

X

"Ayrish!" the maid's cry receded along with the rush and roar of the storm. *"Ayrish—"* it became the merest whisper. But to Erik Gustau, lolling in his chair, it seemed the name she cried was now his own! And her voice...*that* voice! The sweet, anguished voice he had thought never to hear again except in memory or later, God willing, in heaven. Could it be? A faint, far echo in a sounding shell: "Erik! Erik!"

Snatched awake, startled from his dream by hope and horror combined, the young man sprang up from his chair and reeled with a feverish vertigo. Rivered in sweat he clung to his table, glared at the spinning room, cursed the fickle god of fever-dreams whose spiteful hand had snatched him back.

Then he remembered the wine!

His glass stood empty, but wine enough in the bottle. "Lilly!" he cried after his dream, which suddenly he knew was more than any mere dream. "Lilly!" And tilting the bottle to his lips he drank it dry...

The post-mortem verdict was death by misadventure. But in fact Erik Gustau's lungs were found full of salt water. Indeed, upon hearing his master's cry and bursting in the door, Benson found him lying in a pool of water.

As for the deep gash in his side...

A mystery, the entire thing, which must forever go unexplained. And then there was that which even Benson dared not tell. For he must now seek a new master, and things were bad enough without making them worse. Who would employ a proven liar or madman?

Who would believe that upon entering his master's study and finding him stretched upon the floor, drenched and dead, Benson had thought to hear, as from a great distance in space and time, the glad, wondering cries of lovers reunited, the snap of sails filling in the wind, and the hiss and crash of a sundered island sinking in a primal sea?...

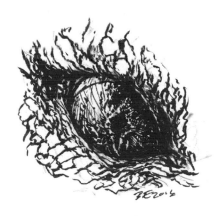

The Sorcerer's Dream

As translated by Thelred Gustau, from
Teh Atht's *Legends of the Olden Runes*

I, Teh Atht, have dreamed a dream; and now, before dawn's light
may steal it from my old mind—while yet Gleeth the blind God
of the Moon rides the skies over Klühn and the stars of night peep
and leer hideously—I write it down in the pages of my rune-book,
wherein all the olden runes are as legends unfolded. For I have pondered the great mysteries of time and space, have solved certain of the
riddles of the Ancients themselves, and all such knowledge is writ in
my rune-book for the fathoming of sorcerers as yet unborn.

As to why I dreamed this dream, plumbing the Great Abyss
of future time to the very END itself, where only the gaunt black
Tomb of the Universe gapes wide and empty, my reasons were many.
They were born in mummy-dust sifting down to me through the
centuries; in the writings of mages ancient when the world was
still young; in cipherless hieroglyphs graven in the stone of Geph's
broken columns; aye, and in the vilest nightmares of shrieking
madmen, whose visions had driven them mad. And such as these
reasons were they drew me as the morning sun draws up the ocean
mists on Theem'hdra's bright strand, for I cannot suffer a mystery to
go undiscovered.

The mystery was this: that oft and again over the years I had heard whispers of a monstrous alien God who seeped down from the stars when the world was an inchoate infant—whose name, Cthulhu, was clouded with timeless legends and obscured in half-forgotten myths and nameless lore—and such whispers as I had heard troubled me greatly...

Concerning this Cthulhu a colleague in olden Chlangi, the warlock Nathor Tarqu, had been to the temple of the Elder Ones in Ulthar in the land of Earth's dreams to consult the Pnakotic Manuscript; and following that visit to Ulthar he had practiced exceedingly strange magicks before vanishing forever from the known world of men. Since that time Chlangi has become a fallen city, and close by in the Desert of Sheb the Lamia Orbiquita has builded her castle, so that now all men fear the region and call Chlangi the Shunned City.

I, too, have been to Ulthar, and I count it a blessing that on waking I could not recall what I read in the Pnakotic Manuscript—only such awful names as were writ therein, such as Cthulhu, Tsathoggua, and Ubbo-Sathla. And there was also mention of one Ghatanothoa, a son of Cthulhu to whom a dark temple even now towers in Theem'hdra, in a place that I shall not name. For I know the place is doomed, that there is a curse upon the temple and its priests, and that when they are no more their names shall be stricken from all records...

Even so, and for all this, I would never have entertained so long and unhealthy an interest in Loathly Lord Cthulhu had I not myself heard His call in uneasy slumbers; that call which turns men's minds, beckoning them on to vile worship and viler deeds. Such dreams visited themselves upon me after I had spoken with Zar-thule, a barbarian reaver—or rather, with the fumbling mushroom *thing* that had once been a reaver—locked away in Klühn's deepest dungeon to rot and gibber hideously of unearthly horrors. For Zar-thule had thought to rob the House of Cthulhu on Arlyeh the forbidden isle, as a result of which Arlyeh had gone down under the waves in a great storm... but not before Zar-thule gazed upon Cthulhu, whose treasures were garnets of green slime, red rubies of blood and moonstones of malignancy and madness!

And when dreams such as those conjured by Zar-thule's story came to sour the sweet embrace of Shoosh, Goddess of the Still Slumbers, I would rise from my couch and tremble, and pace the crystal floors of my rooms above the Bay of Klühn. For I was sorely troubled by this mystery; even I, Teh Atht, whose peer in the occult arts exists not in Theem'hdra, troubled most sorely.

So I went up into the Mount of the Ancients where I smoked the Zha-weed and sought the advice of my wizard ancestor Mylakhrion of Tharamoon—dead eleven hundred years—who told me to look to the ORIGIN and the AFTERMATH, the BEGINNING and the END, that I might know. And that same night, in my secret vault, I sipped a rare and bitter distillation of mandrake and descended again into deepest dreams, even into dreams long dead and forgotten before ever human dreamers existed. Thus in my search for the ORIGIN I dreamed myself into the dim and fabulous past.

And I saw that the Earth was hot and in places molten, and Gleeth was not yet born to sail the volcanic clouds of pre-dawn nights. Then, drawn by a force beyond my ken, I went out into the empty spaces of the primal void, where I saw, winging down through the vasty dark, shapes of uttermost lunacy. And first among them all was Cthulhu of the tentacled face, and among His followers came Yogg-Sothoth, Tsathoggua, and many others which were like unto Cthulhu but less than Him; and lo!—Cthulhu spoke the Name of Azathoth, whereupon stars blazed forth as He passed and all space gloried in His coming.

Down through the outer immensities they winged, alighting upon the steaming Earth and building great cities of a rare architecture, wherein singular angles confused the eye and mind until towers were as precipices and solid walls gateways! And there they dwelt for aeons, in their awful cities under leaden skies and strange stars. Aye, and they were mighty sorcerers, Cthulhu and His spawn, who plotted great evil against Others who were once their brethren. For they had not come to Earth of their own will but had fled from Elder Gods whose codes they had abused most terribly.

And such were their thaumaturgies in the great grey cities that those Elder Gods felt tremors in the very stuff of Existence itself, and they came in haste and great anger to set seals on the houses of

Cthulhu, wherein He and many of His kin were prisoned for their sins. But others of these great old sorcerers, such as Yogg-Sothoth and Yib-Tstll, fled again into the stars, where they were followed by the Elder Gods who prisoned them wherever they were found. Then, when all was done, the great and just Gods of Eld returned whence they had come; and aeon upon aeon passed and the stars revolved through strange configurations, moving inexorably toward a time when Cthulhu would be set free...

So it was that I saw the ORIGIN whereof my ancestor Mylakhrion of Tharamoon had advised me, and awakening in my secret vault I shuddered and marvelled that this Loathly Lord Cthulhu had come down all the ages unaltered. For I knew that indeed He lived still in His city sunken under the sea, and I was mazed by His immortality. Then it came to me to dwell at length upon the latter, on Cthulhu's immortality, and to wonder if He was truly immortal... And of this also had Mylakhrion advised, saying, "Look to the ORIGIN and the AFTERMATH, the BEGINNING and the END."

Thus it was that last night I sipped again of mandrake fluid and went out in a dream to seek the END. And indeed I found it...

There at the end of time all was night, where all the universe was a great empty tomb and nothing stirred. And I stood upon a dead sea bottom and looked up to where Gleeth had once graced the skies; old Gleeth, long sundered now and drifted down to Earth as dust. And I turned my saddened eyes down again to gaze upon a gaunt, solitary spire of rock that rose and twisted and towered up from the bottom of the dusty ocean.

And because curiosity was ever the curse of sorcerers, it came to me to wonder why, since this was the END, time itself continued to exist. And it further came to me that time existed only because space, time's brother, had *not quite* ended, life was *not quite* extinct. With this thought, as if born of the thought itself, there came a mighty rumbling and the ground trembled and shook. All the world shuddered and the dead sea bottom split open in many places, creating chasms from which there at once rose up the awful spawn of Cthulhu!

And lo!—I knew now that Indeed Cthulhu was immortal, for in Earth's final death spasm He was reborn! The great twisted spire of rock—all that was left of Arlyeh, Cthulhu's house—shattered and fell in ruins, laying open to my staggering gaze His sepulcher. And shortly thereafter, preceded by a nameless stench, He squeezed Himself out from the awful tomb into the gloom of the dead universe...

Then, when they saw Cthulhu, all of them that were risen up from their immemorial prisons rushed and flopped and floundered to His feet, making obeisance to Him. And He blinked great evil octopus eyes and gazed all about in wonderment, for His final sleep had endured for aeon upon aeon, and he had not known that the universe was now totally dead and time itself at an end.

And Cthulhu's anger was great! He cast His mind out into the void and gazed upon cinders that had been stars; He looked for light and warmth in the farthest corners of the universe and found only darkness and decay; He searched for life in the great seas of space and found only the tombs at time's end. And His anger waxed *awesome*!

Then He threw back His tentacled head and bellowed out the Name of Azathoth in a voice that sent all of the lesser Beings at His feet scurrying back to their chasm sepulchers, and lo!...nothing happened! The sands of time were run out, and even the greatest magicks had lost their potency.

And so Cthulhu raged and stormed and blasphemed as only He might until, at the height of His anger, *suddenly He knew me!*

Dreaming as I was and far, far removed from my own age, nevertheless He sensed me and in an instant turned upon me, face tentacles writhing and reaching out for my dreaming spirit. And then, to my eternal damnation, before I fled shrieking back down the corridors of time to leap awake drenched in a chill perspiration in my secret vault, I gazed deep into the demon eyes of Cthulhu...

Now it is dawn and I am almost done with the writing of this, and soon I will lay down my rune-book and set myself certain tasks for the days ahead. First I will see to it that the crystal dome of my workshop tower is covered with black lacquer, for I fear I can no longer bear to look out upon the stars… Where once they twinkled afar in chill but friendly fashion, now I know that they leer down in celestial horror as they move inexorably toward Cthulhu's next awakening. For surely He will rise up many times before that final awakening at the very END.

Aye, and if I had thought to escape the Lord of Arlyeh when I fled from him in my dream, then I was mistaken. Cthulhu was, He is, and He will always be; and I know now that this is the essence of that great mystery which so long perplexed me. For Cthulhu is a Master of Dreams, and now He knows me. And He will follow me through my slumbers all the days of my life, and evermore I shall hear His call… Even unto the END.

TARRA KHASH: HROSSAK!

FOR ANYONE WHO EVER DWELLED
IN AN IMAGINARY LAND

Contents

ACKNOWLEDGMENTS

My thanks to Francesco Cova, and especially to Paul Ganley of Weirdbook Press. With the exception of "Told in the Desert," which first appeared in the Italian magazine, *Kadath*, all of the stories in this volume were first published in *Weirdbook* and one other Weirdbook Press publication.

TREASURE OF THE SCARLET SCORPION

I

In the coastal, tropical forests east of Thinhla, lost amid creeper-cursed and vine-entwined ruins of an ancient city—where orchids took root in crumbling courtyards and shifty-eyed chameleons swayed atop the slumping piles of primal ziggurats—there lay the toppled temple of Ahorra Izz, the scorpion-god, whose stone steps went down to caverns of forbidden treasure beyond all dreams of human avarice. Guarded to east and west by twin rivers no man had ever named, whose steamy banks crept with crocodiles and whose waters teemed with tiny, terrible flesh-eating fishes—and by jungles of hybrid vegetation voracious beyond any appeasement, whose spines and suckers were armed with potent poisons—the place would seem unassailable and the treasure of Ahorra Izz entirely safe from all outsiders... And yet—

At least one man had been there, had filled his pockets to brimming with brilliant red gems, and had survived to tell of that hellish hothouse of rotting ruins and vampire vegetation—but only at the expense of his freedom...

It was four long years now since Tarra Khash the Hrossak had stumbled half-dead into Thinhla. So thin as to be almost fleshless, full of a delirious fever, in his semiconscious nightmare he had gibbered and moaned of the treasure of the scarlet scorpion. And yet he was lucky, for if the scum of the city had found him in that condition—if his staggering feet had taken him into the city's stews or fleabitten flophouses—then Tarra Khash would certainly have vanished; swiftly and silently removed, food for the great fishes that follow the galleys and split the water dorsally in Thinhla's harbour. As it was, he collapsed outside the walled courtyard of a convent, where dwelled seventeen sweet sisters of mercy whose devotions were to Theem'hdra's benevolent gods and goddesses. And there they found him in the dawn: life all but ebbed from him, a scarlet fortune bursting from his pockets like clots of blood frozen in some cold and alien hell.

For three months they tended and nursed him, returning him to life and flushing from his system poisons which would surely have killed a lesser man; and as the fever went out of him so his strength flowed back, and soon he was able to frown and question and ask for his treasure, that scarlet wealth of rubies wherewith his pockets had been stuffed. And all of this time his presence in the convent remained a secret; because the sisters were what they were, no one questioned the fact that they now paid for certain of their provisions with tiny red rubies. No one, that is, except Nud Annoxin, Thinhla's fattest, richest and most loathsome jewel-merchant.

Such was Nud Annoxin's interest that he set a spy to watch over the convent day and night; and when at long last Tarra Khash took his leave of the place and found himself a proper lodge in the city, then the secret watcher reported that occurrence to his fat and offensive master. Also the fact that Tarra Khash appeared to pay his way with rubies of a rare and flawless beauty...

Now the Hrossak was not a subtle man; little more than a barbarian, as were all the men of the steppes beyond the River Luhr, he was big, blunt, occasionally brutal, but above all, open as a book with its covers laid back. Another man endowed with Tarra's wealth might have tried to keep his secret hid, might have purchased a large property and employed hirelings to guard him and hoard both. But Hrossaks believed in living and few men of the steppes would willingly pen themselves, to which general rule Tarra was no exception. Now that his health was returned to him he began to live as he had lived before, and life to Tarra Khash could only be poured from a bottle, gnawed from a juicy bone, or found in the purple-sheeted bed of a bawdy-house belle. Which was why he was the perfect subject for the wiles of one such as Nud Annoxin...

Waking up late one hot morning, in his tavern bed above the waterfront, Tarra stuck his tousled head out of his high, small-paned window, smelled nets drying in the sun and the salt breeze off the Southern Ocean, and licked lips dehydrated by yestereve's alcoholic excesses. He remembered entertaining thoughts of a woman, and then of drinking to the idea until it became untenable, and finally of staggering back here under a reeling moon to climb corkscrew stairs to his horribly revolving bed. Now he laughed at such memories, then quickly groaned at the dull ache his laughter conjured up from the ghosts of his boozing.

Food, that was the answer! The Hrossak cursed himself for a fool. All of that drinking on an empty stomach. Well, he could remedy that: not the hangover but the emptiness, at least. A hearty breakfast would do the trick, washed down with a draught or three of good ale. Tarra grinned as he dressed and thought back on his life; but as his thoughts took form so his grin faded, and he grew remarkably philosophical for a Hrossak. There once was a time when he would drink for the hell of it, but since leaving the convent he seemed to drink only to forget...to forget the horrors he had known in the temple of Ahorra Izz!

And yet even now he could not be sure whether it had been real, or whether he had dreamed it all. He had certainly *not* dreamed the treasure of the nether-caverns; no, for the pockets of his wide belt were even now full of perfect rubies large and small; but what of the rest of it? Tarra Khash shuddered as he sat down on his bed to roll up the sleeves of his shirt and the wide-cuffed bell-bottoms of his trousers, to peer yet again at the dozens of tiny white scars which marred the bronze tan of his calves and forearms… And suddenly his hunger abated somewhat as a renewed desire for strong liquor rose up in him like a tide.

Now naive as the Hrossak was, he was not so dumb as to dwell on the seamy side of Thinhla without taking certain precautions—not while he was master of so much wealth. Eventually he intended to board a ship bound for Grypha, make his way up the Luhr and so back to the steppes; but for now he was satisfied to recuperate in his own way, to convalesce in a manner befitting his near-barbarian status, and Thinhla had more than enough amusements and diversions for a man of the Steppes of Hrossa.

As for his precautions: they were simple enough. This garret room, for instance: unassailable from the outside, it looked down precipitously upon the wharves. And its stout oaken door, double-barred and bolted—with a padlock whose single heavy key Tarra wore around his neck—would admit no one he wanted kept out. And so, no matter how drunk, he felt perfectly safe to sleep here; and awake—why!— who in his right mind would tackle a grinning Hrossak with arms like a bear and a wicked sabre sharp as a well-honed scythe?

As he left the tavern and made his way into the backstreet away from the wharves, Tarra came around a corner and bumped (by accident, apparently) into a fat, jolly-looking man who caught hold of his brawny arms to steady himself. This was Nud Annoxin—wearing a very false aspect—who had made a covert study of Tarra's habits and quite deliberately chosen this morning to place himself in the Hrossak's way. Now the fat man unhanded Tarra and bowed, as best his belly would allow, before introducing himself.

"Nud Annoxin," he informed, holding out a pudgy hand. "My pardon, sir, for almost tripping you; but dreaming of a hearty breakfast and a gallon of ale, I was not watching my way. I've just returned from a profitable business trip in the hinterland—but a dry affair and almost completely void of victuals—and now I hie me to my favourite eatery. You're a steppeman, I see. Perhaps you have an appetite?"

"Aye," Tarra grunted, "I'm a Hrossak—and a hunger on me, certainly—and something of a thirst to boot!"

"Then say no more," said Nud with a nudge and a wink. "Come, be my guest. I dwell not far from here; and no finer wine cellar in all Thinhla." And he took Tarra Khash by the elbow.

The Hrossak shook himself free and looked momentarily suspicious. "Your favourite eatery, you said."

"Most certainly!" cried Nud, standing back. "My own house, I meant, whose kitchen is that of a veritable king of gourmets!" He patted his stomach. "Can't you tell? But come, will you be my guest? And after we've eaten, perhaps my dancing girls may entertain…?"

That last did the trick, for now the jewel-merchant had offered all three ingredients in the Hrossak's ideal brew of life. Tarra grinned and slapped Nud's meaty back, which made all of his flesh tremble like so much jelly, then bade him lead the way and gladly followed on behind.

Four long years gone by, but the Hrossak remembered every detail of that first meeting as if it were yesterday. More clearly, in fact, for there had been precious little in between to dilute or dim the memory. Only this deep damp well of a cell and his nightly, self-imposed task of cutting hand- and footholds in its walls, which were too far round in the circle to climb as a chimney.

And yet Nud Annoxin had delivered all he promised—much more, to tell the truth. There had been food all through the fore and afternoon, and drink by the flagon—a deluge of drink—until Tarra's head swam in it like a fish in blinding, bubbly, sparkling shallows. And dancing girls (Annoxin's "daughters," the fat liar said, though Tarra had doubted it) and more food and wine. And Nud had grown merrier (or had seemed to), telling the story of his life to Tarra Khash; and oh!—they had become fast friends.

Until Tarra too told his tale: the story of how, wandering east of Grypha, he had paused to cast a line in the Bay of Monsters; and of the large fish he caught, and the greater Roc-bird that caught him and fish both; of the journey westward clutched in terrible, rib-cracking talons, until the Roc's nest of five hunger-crazed chicks big as lions was sighted atop a jungle-girt crag; then of stabbing his feathered captor, and of falling to the jungle's verdant floor cushioned by the carnivore's carcass; and finally of stumbling upon the lost city and the discovery of the temple of Ahorra Izz, its stone steps descending, the caverns of rubric-glowing riches…and—

And there the Hrossak came to his senses—or what was left of them—but far too late. Drugged, he lay supine upon Nud Annoxin's couch; and the fat merchant, sober as a judge, dragged from him the whole story in most minute detail; all the while forcing resistless potions down his throat, until the words poured from him and left him empty, unconscious, and doomed to dwell for the rest of his life in the deep, well-like dungeon wherein Nud's eunuchs then tossed him.

II

As to why Nud had not simply killed him: he was not happy that Tarra had told all. If the jungles were so dire and desperate, the swamps so full of foot-long leeches and the rivers a-leap with needle-tooth fishes, how then was the Hrossak come all these leagues to Thinhla? And all alone and unaided. Better to keep him in a deep dungeon and milk the whole truth from him bit by bit. For Nud was not satisfied with the rubies stolen from Tarra's belt; he wanted more—he wanted the entire treasure of the scarlet scorpion!

And so time passed, months growing into years, and Nud Annoxin going often to peer into the well-cell's deep throat, to coax and cajole Tarra Khash and drag from him bits of information, some of which even Tarra thought he had forgotten. But in the stillness of long nights, when only the cheeping of rats disturbed the silence, then the Hrossak chipped at the rotten mortar of his circular cell wall and slowly formed his life-ladder; and he swore a grim vengeance on the fat jewel-merchant, when at last his fingers should reach the rim and haul him up from hell…

"Tarra?" came Nud's greasy voice one late afternoon, echoing in his captive's subterranean sinkhole and sending the rats scurrying. "Tarra, are you listening?"

"What else have I to do, fat dog?" And Tarra looked up to see Nud's rim-peering face high overhead.

"My friend, I have a flagon of fine wine, a fresh loaf of bread and a wedge of cheese. Aye, and a question, too."

"First the wine, the bread and the cheese," answered Tarra. "Then the question."

"And you'll answer truthfully?"

"As best I can, though for a fact I know that when you've done with me you'll simply let me rot down here."

A bucket was lowered with the aforementioned fare, while Nud tut-tutted and denied Tarra's charge, saying, "Come, come, old friend, let's not speak of tomorrow. Have I not promised that when my hirelings return with treasure and a well-marked map, that then I'll set you free? But until one or two such really do return, and until I have the map to hand and a portion of the treasure to prove it—"

"I stay where I am, eh?" said Tarra softly. "Well, it's my belief that when you have the route and a small sack of ruby-shards, then you'll send me down a flagon floating with poison. Either that or you'll block up this hole entirely." And then he gave himself up to the food and drink, for Nud had not fed him for a day or two.

Finally, when the chomping and swilling ceased and Nud heard only the Hrossak's low breathing, he called down: "Listen, and I shall tell you of my progress, which previously was far too slow..."

Now Tarra Khash had heard most of this before. He knew that Nud liked the sound of his own oily voice, and that he reiterated mainly for his own benefit, and so sighed as he resigned himself to the jewel-merchant's monologue. Anyway, he had nothing better to do, and it amused him in a grim sort of way (as much as he might be amused in this rat-infested hole) to learn of Annoxin's many trials and not so many tribulations.

"More than three years agone," the fat man began, resting elbows on rim and many chins in cup of flabby palms, "you told me your tale of the rogue Roc, of its death under your knife, of your fall to forest floor and subsequent discovery of ruins, temple and treasure. Since when, little by little, by one persuasion or another, you've remembered your route out of that place and other things important to my plan; and I, by use of certain hirelings—*many* hirelings, in fact, and well paid to boot—have attempted to retrace your steps.

"I asked you, you'll recall, how you crossed the nameless river and where. And you replied near its mouth, where the water was salt from the Southern Ocean; for the terror-fish are of a fresh-water species and not much given to swimming in brine, likewise the crocodiles."

"All true," replied Tarra, stifling a sigh. "Including the curved, giant palm-leaf plank I used for boat."

"I was coming to that," said Nud, annoyed, "but let it pass." He paused for a moment before once more taking up the tale.

"Well, I sent out three men and they crossed the river at place and in manner prescribed—and one came back to tell of the death of his mates from fever, himself expiring within a day and a night. Now you, too, were taken by fever but survived. How? Your strong Hrossak blood, I supposed. Should I next employ Hrossaks? And where to find such, for you're a rare breed west of the steppes.

"What say Yhemnis? Ah! Now there was a thought. Yhemnis: black as pitch, born and bred in jungled Yhem, whose blood must taste singularly sour on the tongue of the fever-fly, for he rarely sips it. And so I found me four frizzies, bent them to my will, gave them directions and sent them forth. But what if they should fail to return? How should I know what became of them? And how might I follow their progress?"

"How indeed?" the sunken Hrossak sighed.

"Why!—by enlisting the aid of Thinhla's master-mage, Hatr-ad of Hreen Castle!" Nud enthused. "For in his shewstone he could surely see afar, through river mist and jungle leaf alike. Aye, and expensive the hire of his talents, I might add—but worth it, I expect, in the long run...

"Now then, it had also occurred to me to put it to you, you'll further recall, how come the vampire vines, noxious orchids and poisonous plants in general had failed to fetch you down. And after some small starvation you had answered that when you fell with Roc through jungle roof, your crash was brake by bush whose thickly clustered black berries besmeared you head to toe in their smelly juices—"

"—Whereafter none of the viler vegetation bothered me at all," Tarra quickly finished.

"Just so," Nud sniffed, a trifle miffed. "And so I instructed my blacks that when they came to the place of lethiferous leafage, there they must seep themselves in the fruit of the black berry bush before proceeding farther. Which they did, for Hatr-ad saw it in his sphere. After which he saw them no more..."

"The swamps," Tarra knowingly nodded.

"Indeed, the swamps," purred Nud, "whose sucking depths you'd omitted to mention, or mentioned merely in passing, placing more emphasis on their inhabitants—leeches who'd sluice a man dry in a trice. And so it went, the perils and protections, banes and balms; and all extracted most tortuously—and *expensively*—from caged and crafty Hrossak. Oh, you gave up the tale in outline most willingly—and at our very first meeting at that—since when, in respect of fine detail, a more reticent rascal I've yet to discover. But for all that, still your days are numbered, Tarra Khash."

Tarra's ears pricked up at that and his mind began to race. Nud's voice was far too soft and his threat had sounded imminent, and still a few handholds to scrape before rim be breached and vengeance wreaked. Tarra's mouth grew a little dry and he damped it from the flagon before carefully choosing his next words, which were these:

"So, my end draws nigh, hey? You sound most sure of yourself, Nud, who came with a question which yet remains unasked. And when you do ask it should I answer, whose fate would seem hung upon that very thread?"

"This time," answered Nud, "the answer is not imperative. Your words may save a future life or two, no more. And certainly not mine, for I shall never journey in yonder jungles, be sure."

"Then ask away," said Tarra, mind alert as he sought a way to extend his life, at least until he could snuff out Nud Annoxin's.

"Let me first tell you how far we have come," answered Nud. "Seven sorties now I have sent against the river, jungle, swamps and hideous herbage, and six of them disappeared forever from the world of men. Ah!—but of the seventh party—one survives! And he, too, has visited the temple of Ahorra Izz. Moreover, he went down into the subterranean sepulchre and returned therefrom to the upper world! Hatr-ad saw it in his shewstone, though some dire magic kept him from penetrating the caverns themselves. Four descended and one climbed back, pockets abrim with scarlet fire; and even now that one retraces his steps, returning to his grateful master with well-marked map and fortune in gems...

"Very well, my question is this: what of the other three? What is it lurks beneath the scorpion-god's shattered temple, which blots out three and allows a fourth to live?"

After a long moment, weighing his words most carefully, finally Tarra Khash answered, "Two things I experienced in those shadow-cursed caverns. One of which was real, for I shall carry the scars forever...the other of which—"

"Yes?" pressed Nud Annoxin.

"—Of which I will not speak. Not yet."

Now it was Nud's turn to sigh. "I can starve it out of you," he softly threatened.

"That will take some little time," Tarra answered, "for before ever I speak again—even of the first temple-hidden terror—I shall have from you a further flagon, loaf and cheese-wedge." And with that he fell silent.

Up above, Nud ranted and raved a while, threatened, pleaded in the end, then sent for the Hrossak's specified victuals. And only when he had those things in his great hands did Tarra tell of the first terror.

"Scorpions," he said.

"Scorpions?" (Suspicion and surprise, and the vision of a fat face frowning in confusion, causing Tarra to smile a very little).

"Certainly! In the treasure-caves of a scorpion-god, what else would you expect?"

"The scars you spoke of!" Nud now gasped. "I saw them on your calves and forearms when you were stretched helpless on my couch: white pinches against the tanned leather of your limbs!"

"Scorpions," confirmed Tarra Khash. "Scarlet scorpions, and lethally venomous. The caverns are acrawl with them!"

"Liar!" cried Nud in another moment. "A hundred stings you suffered, according to those scars, and yet you live? How so?"

"I am immune!" whispered the other. "The grey cousin of the scarlet scorpion is not unknown on the steppes, where as a child I was stung nigh to death. I was legend as a lad, renowned for the number of stings I'd taken, which should have killed but merely sickened; until in the end I took no ill at all but won many a bet by courting the scorpion's barb. Immune, Nud, aye—and the minions of Ahorra Izz killed me not, though for a fact my scars declare their determination! And there's this lad, you say, escaped arachnid's ire when three for sure succumbed? Perhaps he too is immune. Valuable, that one, Nud Annoxin."

"Immune!" and now Nud slapped fat thigh, "You think so? The dear lad!"

"Perhaps," Tarra grunted, "and perhaps not. For there was that other thing I saw—or think I saw—in the ruby caves...but of that I will not speak. Not now."

"Speak!" cried Nud in sudden rage. "Speak now, I command it!"

"No," the answer echoed from below, and in deep gloom the Hrossak shook his head. "Since your sole surviving hireling is three-quarters way home by now, you'd best ask it of him. *If* he makes it. But if you really cannot wait...why, then you must starve me!" And he chuckled, albeit grimly, as he hugged his wine, bread and cheese— small but precious provender—to his bosom...

III

That night (Tarra could tell it was night from the descent of darkness most utter; also from the silence which settled over and reigned in the vast and high-walled house of Nud Annoxin), the Hrossak climbed his prison's funnel to the topmost extent of his hand and footholds, and working longer and harder than ever before he probed and picked and gouged, with only his horny fingers as tools, until faint stirrings were heard overhead and the grey half-dark which was day seeped down once more into his cylinder dungeon. Then, fearing that Nud's eunuchs might find him where he clung like webless spider to wall and discover his four-year secret, he climbed down again to the bottom, curled up in nitrous damp and at once fell asleep.

Now Tarra Khash was not normally much of a one for dreaming (his sleep was usually much too shallow, from which he would rise up in a trice) but on this occasion he slept like a dead man. It was the sleep of exhaustion, of the culmination of four years of contained loathing and revenge lusted after, and it was a sleep well deserved. For Tarra knew that in the next night he would finally breach the wall, then that he would find the fat man in his bed and let out his life in a stream scarlet to match any flood of red-glowing jewels.

And so he dreamed, but not of escape, not of vengeance. No, he dreamed of his visit to that forbidden, jungle-drowned fane of Ahorra Izz, and of what had transpired—or what he had *thought* transpired—in those vasty vaults beneath. It could of course have been, probably had been, the fever. But—

There had been the stone steps leading down, festoons of smoky cobwebs like the ropes of some death-ship's reek-shrouded rigging, great piles of dust centuries sifted and vaulted ceilings furred over with the myriad clustered forms of *Cynonycteris*, the bat of the mastabas, whose glittering eyes were sinister scintillant. And at each landing stood a carven stone scorpion, once scarlet, whose ancient paint had fallen like flakes of rust; and each successive idol larger than last, until at lowest level the likeness of Ahorra Izz stood half as tall again as Tarra Khash, with massive rubies for eyes and a curved, high-swaying, scythe-like sting of a silver metal whose secret was surely lost to time immemorial.

In his dream Tarra paused and stared up at the ruby eyes of the idol, and at the great sting which formed, even as he watched, a pearly liquid globe, big as his fist, to fall with a splash from wicked tip to dusty, flagged floor. In the genuine arachnid this droplet would be venom, but in its massive likeness of hard stone and unknown metal... surely moisture seeped from the high ceiling? What else, possibly? Whichever, Tarra paused not but passed on; and with his head feverishly aswim, finally he came to red-glowing cavern. Almost volcanic, that inner glow; and now the Hrossak saw what appeared to be an actual crater brimming with fiery lava—and walls all aglow with a moving warmth as of coals under a bellows—and all without slightest trace of heat!

Only then, dreaming, did he know the source of the ruddy light—just as he once had known it in reality. For the crater-like depression of the floor was in fact a huge and sunken bowl—and the contents of the bowl were myriad rubies, ranging in size from pin-head to pigeon's eggs! And all around the walls dusty, inward leaning mirrors of bronze, reflecting and heightening that Tartarean rubescence.

At that point Tarra's sleeping figure moaned most piteously at the bottom of his prison pit. For even dreaming he knew what would next occur, as indeed it *had* occurred four years ago—with one

small difference. *This* time, alerted by a sudden and gigantic scut-
tling, knowing what he must see entering the treasure cave behind
him, Tarra lifted feverish eyes to that mirror which faced the cave's
entrance, and saw—

Yes, certainly, Ahorra Izz the scorpion-god!

But more, he saw himself—or should have. Except that the man
who gazed back from burning bronze was *not* Tarra Khash! Another,
this other—a stranger. And now the Hrossak remembered all of his
previous visit to that cursed cavern: how that great stone statue come
to life stood over him—scarlet and quivering with rage—its mighty
stinger poised, adrip with pearly poison. And how in that moment
he had felt upon his naked forearms, upon his legs from knees down
where breeches hung in tatters, a hundred tiny stabs from scarlet miniatures of monster, and knew the cavern crawled with scorpion horde.
Then—

"They harm ye not, my little ones," had come the clacking voice
from morbid, mandible mouth. "Your flesh puffs not, but merely
twitches at their barbs; your blood drinks their venom with a rare
thirst! Who be ye?" And the massive stinger had poised itself above
Tarra's broad back.

"Tarra Khash," answered the Hrossak, turning to face the monster-
god, Ahorra Izz himself, where he blocked the entrance. "A man of the
steppes, whose friends the grey scorpions are. And many the playful
sting I've known, which never harmed me, nor I your scorpion minions."

"Is it so?" had come the horridly clacked question.

"Indeed," Tarra had answered, deliriously snatching up a handful
of livid, living death. "See?" and he grinned as a half-dozen stingers stabbed and stabbed again. "It is our game, you see, in no degree
malicious."

"Who sent ye?" the demon then had clacked, his poised and
needlessly poisonous scythe visibly retracting somewhat, relaxing.

"No one but fate," cried Tarra, swaying with fever and unaccustomed dose of venom both. "Perhaps to let you know you still have
worshipper amongst men—one, at least!"

The monster had nodded once, slowly, and his faceted jewel eyes
had regarded the Hrossak strangely. Then: "Others have been here,
Tarra Khash. Once in a hundred years, perhaps, one such will come,

and sometimes two. Strayed wanderers and seekers after treasure, wizard-sent thieves, savages cast out from heathen tribes. But never a worshipper, until now. As for the others: their bones are dust. And now I am tired of visitors who wake me from my slumbers immemorial. Know ye this, Tarra Khash, that I may take whichever form I wish. E'en yours if I so desired. And from this day on if ever I be waked, then walk me forth for sure to seek him out who sent the wakener. As for ye—"

"Aye, kill me," the reeling Hrossak had then prompted. "For if you don't the fever surely will, or deadly jungle."

Ahorra Izz shook his jewelled head. "Not I. Lay ye down and sleep, Tarra Khash, and when ye rise up eat of the food which ye shall find and drink of the sweet water. Then take what ye will of this ruby hoard and get ye gone..."

Then the Hrossak, falling to his knees and sending rubies flying, had offered up a loud cry—of thanks perhaps, perhaps a fevered shriek—a prayer?—and toppled sideways cushioned by the gems. And knew no more.

This had happened, and now, dreaming, Tarra Khash *knew* it had happened. But in his dream he was someone else, some other. And now the conversation went like this:

"They harm ye not, my littles ones, whose stings pierce not the leather which ye wear. *My* sting, however, will pierce mail and split the wearer to the bone! What say ye?"

And Tarra, who was *not* Tarra, fell upon his padded knees and babbled and screamed.

"Cease now or die at once!" clacked Ahorra Izz, and the screaming turned to sobbing and fitful, spastic grovelling.

"Who sent ye?"

"Nud Annoxin," came the sobbing cry. "The fat jewel-merchant of Thinhla. He sent me. Spare me, spare me!"

"And did he also send the three whose unprotected ankles felt of my minions' stings?"

"Aye, aye, 'twas Nud. Nud Annoxin sent us!"

"Man," said the monster in another moment, "die!" And his stinger flashed forth and shattered skull through helmet, ripped breast through fine mail and leather, sliced trunk to groin through steely belt, leather breeks and all; and so Nud's hireling fell in two directions.

Then Ahorra Izz looked down on what had been a man and his arachnid form shimmered as if seen through smoke; his outline changed, shrank; he became—

—The selfsame man whose halves now lay on blood splashed hoard! And this the dreaming Tarra Khash saw from two different angles, through bulging, separated eyes which glazed even as he started awake with horrified cry upon his well-cell's slimy floor...

That had been at noon. At noon, too, had Hatr-ad espied in his shewstone the hooded hireling striding the plain at the edge of the coastal forest and heading straight for Thinhla. And Hatr-ad's beady eyes had brightened as he recognised the man's mode of dress and his shape, and he nodded eagerly and licked thin lips greedily at sight of the small but fat sacklet at the man's belt. But then, when Thinhla's mage (a mean magician, known better for dark than kinder magicks) might have winged a bat messenger on its way to the house of Nud Annoxin—just at that moment when he made as if to turn from his shewstone—something about the rapid approach of this lone survivor of all Nud's expeditions arrested his attention, striking him at odds.

High in his turreted tower at Hreen Castle, the pallid mage frowned and gazed again down hooked nose into the swirling depths of his sphere, causing with his concentration swiftly gathering mists to draw back again from the conjured scene. Indeed, there was something odd about this survivor of Nud's quest. Several things, most odd... His preternatural speed for one, who should by rights be exhausted from jungle-trekkings, river-crossings, avoidances of perilous plants and such. And yet he came on apace, his long, tireless, almost mechanical stridings most eerie to watch. Why, at this rate he would be here in Thinhla before the midnight hour!

Hatr-ad remembered Nud speaking of this one: who rubbed himself with ointments against insect bites and took with him upon the quest an assortment of protections against every possible eventuality lethal. Aye, a professional he, and rightful survivor. And the miles flying beneath ceaselessly striding legs, and noon sun striking hot on him; for which reason, doubtless, he had put up his hood against its furnace glare.

Hatr-ad frowned harder yet, his concentration growing as he drew the striding figure closer, closer, until the shewstone was filled with cowled head, until he could peer into the shadows beneath that cowl—at glowing ruby coals that burned for eyes in a face mottled grey and vacuous as that of a dead man! The strider *was* a dead man!

Then, before the mage could make another move, his ears seemed to ring to a clacking, imperious command, cold as northern snows. *"Begone, watcher! Get ye gone from me—lest I seek ye out also, e'en as I seek Nud Annoxin!"*

At which Hatr-ad shrank back at once from his sphere and let its misty drapes fall. And shaking in every limb he descended from his aerie and set about renewing the magickal protections about Hreen Castle. He put his familiar demons atop the battlements, and he locked himself in a deep and secret room for the remainder of that day and two more… None of which was ever brought to the attention of Nud Annoxin.

At the eleventh hour a striding stranger approached the east gate and entered into the torch-flickered shadow of its arch. The guard commander might normally have stopped him, and indeed had approached him so to do; but there was that about the cowled stranger which forbade any real interference, and in passing his cold hand pressed into that of the sergeant something hard and glittery in the dark, which later proved to be a priceless ruby; so that the question of the stranger's entry into Thinhla did not arise.

And at the gate of Nud Annoxin's high-walled house a similar scene, where eunuchs who had been ordered to keep watch for the lone quester's return now found themselves recipients of riches. And into Nud's house the stranger strode, all unannounced, to the very door of the jewel-merchant's private chamber…where he rapped with deathly knuckles upon heavy oaken panels.

Ever since the first hour of utter dark, Tarra Khash had worked on the high walls of his prison. Stuck like a fly to curving surface, he frantically clawed at crumbling mortar; a nameless urgency drove him constantly to take risks. Such was the violence of his attack upon the wall that on several occasions he nearly shook himself loose from his precarious position, which would almost certainly be a fatal occurrence. But finally, somewhere between the eleventh and twelfth hour, he was able to thrust an arm upward until bloodied fingers found the rim.

After that—

A matter of moments to haul himself to freedom, seconds to let his senses soak up the faint feelings of the night, minutes to discover a room with jewelled ceremonial swords upon its walls and to take one...and at last, silent as a shadow, he crouched with murderous intent before the door of Nud's own room—which stood open! Even as he paused in momentary indecision, Tarra's foot touched something fallen to the floor. A pouch or sacklet, of the sort used for jewels or nuggets—except that the contents of this one were already fleeing its loosened neck: scarlet scorpions, their stingers rampant and deadly!

The scorpions alone would not have sufficed to stop Tarra, but there was more. A dim light within the room threw shadows into the corridor. The Hrossak saw the shadows and in the next moment heard voices, one being Nud's—babbling, disbelieving, gasping for breath— the other...

Oh, Tarra Khash recognised the other! Its clacking notes were unmistakable; and the Hrossak's scalp crawled as he drew back with silent snarl from the open door. Then: one shadow expanding, elongating, changing; and the other, fat and human still, falling into a kneeling position, hands raised in supplication. The Hrossak paused no longer but turned to flee. He went, knowing now the source of that earlier urgency, knowing also that he was too late, that Ahorra Izz himself had beaten him to the prey.

Confirming his thoughts, as he vaulted a low balcony out into the spacious gardens, he heard a mighty swish as of a giant's scythe and a great tearing of flesh—and Nud's rising scream cut gurglingly off at zenith. Then, horror riding upon his ragged back, Tarra was climbing the wall. No thoughts of gems or thievery this night. Only of flight. He had the jewelled sword and that was enough. He wanted nothing more. Not from this house.

Not from the cursed and fear-crazed house of Nud Annoxin...

Isles of the Suhm-yi

I

Astonished, the bronze-skinned man in leather breach-clout and sandals, with jewelled ceremonial sword in its long curved sheath strapped to his broad, well-muscled back, kneeled beside the dead but still-warm corpse of Lula Arn. The steppeman knew her not, this daughter of the Inner Isles, knew nothing at all of the Suhm-yi other than vaguely-remembered campfire whispers, myths and legends. The Suhm-yi, aye, "the Rarely Seen"—but now the Hrossak saw that indeed the myths did not lie, that the Inner Isles of the crater sea were in fact peopled by a race of...well, by beings other than men. Indeed, by beings *un*human, for the dead body, whose golden eyes he now closed against the sun's glare, was not—despite its obvious femininity, its beauty—a human corpse. She was, or had been, Suhm-yi, and this tiny jewel of an island must have been her home.

A great anger stirred in the bronzed breast of Tarra Khash. His nostrils flared. And men called his brothers of the steppes savages! But the black-hearted band responsible for this...they were the real barbarians. Northmen, and their stink lingering yet over this lovely, alien body they'd ravaged and robbed of life.

The girl had been tall, fine-limbed and comb-headed; though her silver-grey, brutalized flesh was dull now in death, in life its sheen must have been quite wonderful. There was an elfin, ethereal something about her hard to define. It made Tarra Khash sorry he had never spoken to her; he felt sure her tongue would have been music to his ears, whose usual fare was the guttural oaths of polyglot taverns, or the hot, sultry whispers of the whorehouse. Well, he couldn't speak to her, not now—odds were they wouldn't have had anything to talk about anyway—but he knew who to speak to *about* her.

A certain long-maned, boastful brute of a Northman, Kon Athar, born of the cold fjords and lochs far north of the River Thand. Oh, yes, Kon and his gang of wandering cutthroats were responsible for this. One more reason why Tarra Khash would take the greatest possible pleasure in slitting that bull barbarian's throat ear to ear. One reason among several. Tarra knew of two others at least…

***

It was six months now since the Hrossak had fled Thinhla on the Southern Ocean, heading north-west with a caravan bound for Thandopolis. Or perhaps "fled" is too strong a word; instead let's say "removed himself from," for in fact Tarra Khash had rarely fled anything in all his young life. But his adventures before, and in Thinhla, had been terrific, and their culmination had been one from which most men might reasonably flee. Tarra's long years in that seaport city, prisoned at the bottom of a deep, dried-out well, had been literally years of living death. Except he had not died.

And since then—certainly since reaching Thandopolis—Tarra Khash had lived as only a true Hrossak can. His years of deprivation had neither reduced him in spirit nor detracted from his zest for life; rather had they sharpened his appetite for all the good things so long denied him.

Rich when first he'd made his ill-omened entry into Thinhla— loaded down with rubies from the jungle temple of Ahorra Izz, scarlet God of Scorpions—Tarra had been a ragged beggar when he left. All save his ceremonial sword, stolen from the house of the fat jeweller Nud Annoxin, who no longer had need of it…or of anything else for that matter. And a single fine stone, prised from the hilt of that wand of death, had paid the Hrossak's way in sophisticate city, so that his five-month stay in Thandopolis had been both curative and pleasurable. To eat red meat and drink good, sweet wine; to bathe in clean waters and breathe the balmy air of freedom; and above all to sleep in silken sheets (and rarely alone) and thus soften those calluses hard come-by in Nud Annoxin's deep well-cell: these things had returned him fully to health and former heartiness.

Alas, a hale and hearty Hrossak has ever been *genius loci* for all the demons of mischief, and Tarra Khash no exception.

An irate taverner, his plump daughter well seduced and by now doubtless plumper still, had sufficed to bring about Tarra's speedy departure. It had been that or kill the taverner (or worse still wed the girl, and three-quarters of Theem'hdra still unvisited, still unseen) which hadn't left horny Hrossak a deal of choice. And so, following the lonely Thand east toward its source, finally he'd met up with a pair of prospectors working the winding riverbanks.

Gold was a lure he couldn't resist, not after they'd shown him the prize nuggets already wrested from river's rush; and working with the pair, Ilke Phant and Bogga Tull of Thandopolis, Tarra had soon packed away a pouch or two of nuggets and dust of his own. And as the days stretched into weeks they'd all three panned their way through the foothills of the Great Circle Range, into the scarps and gulleys of the mountains themselves. Then—

—Enter Kon Athar and his bully-boys.

They came at night, and city lads and Hrossak alike fast asleep and dreaming of riches untold, exhausted from their hard day's work. And Kon and his five, coming out of the darkness and shadows, creeping like dogs, their white teeth aglint in guttering firelight, their swords upraised...

Bogga's death-scream had roused Tarra up, and Ilke's last throaty rattle had certified the danger. Then...the feel of his weapon's jewelled hilt in hard bronze fist, and the snickering of the steely blade as it cleared its sheath in a *hiss* of slicing motion—but too late! Tarra hadn't even glimpsed the hulking coward whose blow cracked his skull and buffeted him head over heels down the riverbank and into the darkly swirling Thand. But before the blackness closed over him he heard an oath and a hoarse laugh, and a voice that cried: "Missed that one, Kon Athar! But the river'll do for him, be sure…"

Thus it was the waters bore him away from scene of slaughter, casting him up at last—half-drowned, half-frozen—on a shingly shore where the river broadened out, a full mile from the erstwhile camp he'd made with two firm friends.

And what of Ilke and Bogga now…?

II

The morning sun had warmed him to life, soaked and stiff and fingering gently the gash beneath tangled brown locks and the chicken's egg fresh-laid on tender scalp. But no sooner on his feet, and a fish from the river raw in his belly for breakfast, than Tarra gritted his straight strong teeth and headed upstream once more, his aching head and body full of red revenge. He knew who'd struck him down, knew also that Kon Athar's name—and the names of those he ran with—were a curse on the lips of decent folk from Thinhla to Hjarpon Settlement. Aye, and the barbarians would know Tarra's name, too, before he was finished with them. This he had promised himself. ·

And so to last night's camp and the sad, sickening sight waiting there. A sight which brought up half-digested fish from Tarra's gut for all that his sort were not much known for puking at murder, mutilation and such; for it's a hard world in the steppes east of the Luhr. And no gold to be found, not even the twin gold teeth which used to flash in Bogga's laughing mouth. And the corpses stripped naked, for even their clothes had value. And Ilke's little finger missing from his left hand, where a wide golden ring had fitted too tight and glittered too bright.

As for Tarra's own gold: his pouches were lost in the river, the dust and nuggets returned whence they came.

And so he'd buried his friends there, beneath a jutting ledge, and blocked them in with boulders from the river's rim, and stood a while over them, head bowed, till certain they acknowledged his tribute. Then down to the river again, this time following the trail of last night's tumble; and sure enough his sword was there, half-buried in sliding grit and pebbles. In the dark the Northmen had not seen the jewelled hilt where it protruded close to river's edge. But they'd see it soon enough, that sword—by their own black god Yibb they would!

———

After a little while he picked up their trail. Following their tracks was no hard task; they'd little enough to fear, that band, or so they must have thought. And follow it Tarra did, all they way to the great waterfall where the Thand flowed out of the crater sea; and up the side of the falls, too, to stand in the spray-wreathed saddle and gaze inwards upon that vasty lake whose bed was once the throat of creation's mightiest volcano.

And with the melt of spring finished and the sun beating down upon him and making rainbows, the Hrossak had marvelled at Nature's rawness and felt the blood racing in his veins. And the beat of his heart had quickened as he saw, far out on the deep blue bosom of that mountain-girt sea, the single rude sail of a roughly fashioned raft, and the tiny figures of the six who plied oars and paddles to speed their vessel away from the suck of the great falls.

A burly raft at least, be sure, for six big lads like these...but none such required for one man alone. Then Tarra had clambered down from saddle to shore, finding him a tree washed up from which he stripped all but two strong branches, and to these lengthwise made fast a stouter branch, so building himself a catamaran such as used by fishers on the lakes of his steppes. And using his jacket and breeks for sail, and fashioning a paddle which would also serve for rudder, he soon set off in hot pursuit of the greater vessel and the six who sailed her. From which time on, for all of a dozen days and nights, the Hrossak had lived on fish; until at last he'd come upon the Inner Isles.

The first of these was so tiny as to be little more than a rock; but it had trees with great nuts and others with fruits, and from the crest of its single peak—

Open now to Tarra's gaze the Inner Isles in all their jewel-bright beauty, reaching away like a string of emeralds cast upon a blue, blue mirror. And somewhere out there a raft and six; and now the Hrossak believing he knew why they'd come this way, those reavers. For if they'd heard the same rumours he'd heard—why, it was obvious!

These were the isles of the Suhm-yi, a mysterious race legended to have gained unlimited access to a magnificent cache of rare gems, with which its members would deck themselves head to toe till they glowed with the sheen of rainbows. If that were true, then these islands were ripe for the sack. Indeed now that he thought of it, Tarra could hardly see why they hadn't been sacked before! Of course the rumours also had it that the crater sea was aswim with monsters (not that Tarra had seen a one), and wasn't there something else tickling the back of his mind? About the Suhm-yi themselves having weird powers, which made them favoured of the gods? Well, perhaps, but the Hrossak wasn't much for chasing misty memories.

And all through that long day Tarra had paddled and sailed between the islands, finding nothing at all upon the first three save trees and birds and dwarfy pigs. But on the fourth…

It had been bigger, that fourth isle, all of a mile or more long. Landing, the Hrossak had seen smoke rising thick and black from some spot beyond a spine of low hills. Though crater sea were mainly tideless, still he dragged his makeshift craft out of the water a little way before climbing the wooded, flower-decked slope at the trot; and having chosen what seemed the easiest route—a worn way, where often feet had passed before—he saw that indeed others had made the climb, and most recently. No more than three or four hours ago.

Cresting the spine of hills the Hrossak had moved more slowly, carefully, soon coming upon a wedge of rock like a lookout rising from a tangle of trees and flowering shrubs. And to its summit ladders of lashed bamboo, and at its base an oddly-structured house—or what remained of a house.

Half-lost in vines and orchids, that dwelling, but gutted now with fire and burning still. The place had loamy gardens and a deep well, low walls of cemented conches and verandas seemingly unsupported…all wreathed in smoke and asmoulder now. And the frame of its roof, collapsing in ruin even as Tarra Khash looked on, showed a strange but pleasing skill in design and structure unknown to human builders in all the length and breadth of Theem'hdra; so that he knew he watched the fall of a house of the Suhm-yi. And the smoke rising thick and black as the day wore to its close, and the island deserted and still. No bird sang; no wild piglet squealed, not now; even the gentle wash of waves seemed hushed where they foamed a little upon the isle's far shore.

Now Tarra's movements had grown more cautious yet, his eyes bleak as they reconstructed scenes unseen save in his imagination. He saw the Northmen climbing the path to the crest, coming across the house at base of lookout rock. He saw them close on the house, swords drawn. Then…a figure, fleeing, male or female he knew not. His eyes were on the path leading through shrubs and doubtless down to the beach below, just as the path behind had led him up from the shore where his boat was beached. And upon that path flying footprints, dainty and four-toed, almost obscured by more obvious scuffs. And while one had stayed to loot and fire the house, five others had followed their prey, just as Tarra Khash now followed.

And going with him as he descended through shrubs, the island's silence like a shroud, so that despite the glare of the late afternoon sun the way seemed full of shadows and gloom. But Tarra's eyes missing nothing, and his mind building upon what he saw. Here a scattering of shingle and sand, where a flying, frightened figure stumbled and sprawled, and a spot of blood upon a stone, where rested for a moment a grazed knee; then the leaping footprints once more, but not so widely spaced as those of a man. Female, this unseen, fleeing creature.

Now the beach where the footprints ran in sand—hither and thither and to and fro and back, frantic—and nowhere else to run. And the heavier prints of booted feet closing, and Hrossak's heart beating to a crescendo in his chest. Behind a low dune the prints converged, and there he had found the body of Lula Arn. Not decked with jewels, no, but he could well see how that silvery skin of hers must flash in life, like mother of pearl in the sea or gemstones under the sun, and he could well imagine the source of the legend. Here, now, the legend itself, brutalized and dead…

III

Tarra Khash stood up.

He had kneeled there for some little time beside the dune, unaware of the sun's slow sinking as his thoughts had wandered. But now, as shadows lengthened, he grew aware not only of evening's creep but also of a slender canoe, beached some small distance down the strand. The canoe had not been there before, of that he was sure. And yet… he had heard nothing.

He stood stock still, squinted his eyes, saw etched the small shadows cast by prints leading from craft to green cover of thickly grown shrubbery. And he felt eyes upon him where he stood, a perfect target. Did they have the use of weapons, the Suhm-yi? Tarra knew not; but if they did, and if this one wished him dead, then were he already dead. He let tense muscles relax, controlled the creep of gooseflesh, stooped and carefully, tenderly lifted up the corpse in his bronze Hrossak arms.

And up the path to gutted house he carried her, to the garden where he dug a narrow grave. Orchids to cover her, to keep the uncaring earth from her silvery flesh, and a cairn of stones above in the manner of the steppes, though Tarra was sure no wild beast here would trouble her grave. And always upon him in the twilight the weight of eyes, the knowledge that death lurked close as an arrow's *hiss*. For aye, the Suhm-yi knew the use of weapons.

Hearing nothing, still the Hrossak knew he was not alone, that another stood with him now in the quiet, shadowed garden. He raised up his bowed head, gazed steadily into eyes golden as his were brown…stared also at the slender arrow nocked, whose barbed head centered on his chest.

A movement in the surrounding shrubbery!

So swift the Hrossak's eye could barely follow, a flash of silver-grey as bowman fell into a crouch, pivoted, let fly his deadly shaft—and a piglet squealing once! The silent watcher (for surely this could be none other) seemed to melt into shadowy greenery, returning in but a moment with skewered piglet, handing meat and arrow both to Tarra Khash, then standing back from him.

Hungry? the Hrossak was that all right, and he'd had his fill of fish!

He set up a spit well away from the grave and cairn, brought driftwood up from the beach (for he would not use timbers from the house), kindled a small fire and hunkered down, his mouth watering as the pork began to roast. And later, having eaten, he returned to the grave where the Suhm-yi male sat; and there they sat apart and yet together, all through the night…

In the chill of morning Tarra woke with a start, jerking his head erect from where it had lolled. His limbs were stiff from sitting but the sun was already beginning to warm them, with golden disc fresh-risen from scarlet crater sea. The house white ashes now, bringing back memories to sleep-fuddled mind of all gone before. And no sign of the Suhm-yi male, but a small mound of fresh fruit close to hand, breakfast for a yawning Hrossak.

While Tarra ate, Amyr Arn came, standing before him with questioning look in his huge, golden eyes.

"Good morning," said the Hrossak, unsmiling. "And I thank you for the fruit." The Suhm-yi made no answer but stared intently.

Tarra cocked his tousled head. "Is there something? Can't you speak? Or is it that my tongue's so wildly different from yours?" He shrugged. "Ah, well—" and made to climb to his feet. But in a moment the Suhm-yi's hand lay four-fingered upon his shoulder, and in another Amyr Arn sat cross-legged, facing him.

Tarra waited, and in a while said, "There's much to be done. I have to be up and about. I follow the Northmen, who are in my debt just as they are in yours. I mustn't tarry here..." And again he made to rise. This time Amyr Arn offered no resistance but also came to his feet, saying:

"You follow them who did this?"

Tarra nodded. "For revenge!" almost before realising he'd been spoken to in his own tongue. "But...you know the language of the steppes! Who taught you?"

"You are my teacher, bronze one. As you speak, so I learn. The Suhm-yi have a way with tongues."

The Hrossak was astonished, then suspicious. "You'd make a fool of me? What creature is it, however strange, learns another's language so quickly—and so well?"

"It is an art of the Suhm-yi," the other seemed to shrug, his tone of voice silver as his skin. "Part is learned from the lips, the rest from the mind that works them."

"You read minds, too?" Tarra shook his head. "And you a naked savage!"

"I read feelings, emotions," the un-man did not appear insulted. "You felt right, bronze one, and your emotions were real and warm. Otherwise—" again the shrug, "—it would not have gone well for you last night. Not in that moment when you laid hands upon my Lula."

Tarra stared at his naked, comb-headed host and nodded. "I sorrowed, aye. They owe me a deal of sorrow, that half-dozen, and not a little gold to boot. But you have lost much more." He frowned. "So you would have killed me last night? And yet the Northmen are not dead."

"I was fishing," said the other, the silver notes of his voice a fraction tarnished now, "else were they surely dead—or I myself dead—even though our olden laws decry vengeance as a great evil. But...I was not here. I did not see them until they were well out to sea, and even then they did not see me. But when I returned here...then I found you. And I found Lula."

Tarra nodded again, sighed and sadly shook his head. But after a moment he ventured a smile. "How are you called, man of the Inner Isles?"

"My name is Amyr Arn. And yours?"

"Tarra Khash, a Hrossak. A man of the steppes, far from home."

"And I am Suhm-yi." Amyr turned to face the cairn, golden eyes unblinking, but clouding a little, Tarra thought. He bowed his combed head. "She was my mate."

After a while the Hrossak said, "But you're young, Amyr Arn. I know not your ways, but time is a great healer for all men and creatures. There'll be other maids of the Suhm-yi for you."

Amyr shook his crested head. "No, not even if I wished it. We were the last. I *am* the last."

"The last? Of your race? I don't understand."

"It was a plague, came from the south-east in a cloud of red dust, blown on winds which never blew before. And all the isles of the Suhm-yi east of here covered in a red ash, and all the Suhm-yi themselves dead in a day and a night—save Lula and I, who saw the cloud but suffered not its red rain of ashes. And now she too is no more."

"So you really are the last of your race!" Tarra said, adding, "And indeed your loss is greater than mine..."

Down on the beach Amyr Arn looked at Tarra's crude craft and shook his head. "You sailed the crater sea on that? But no, you can't hope to hunt them down with vessel such as this! And with this sail—why, they must surely see you coming! I endorse your enterprise—even though vengeance is not the way of the Suhm-yi—but I cannot give a deal of credit to your chances. You will expend all of your strength in paddling and sailing your craft. In my canoe, however..."

"You'll not go with me?" Tarra found himself constantly taken by surprise by the strange being. "But surely you'll want your share of—"

"No," the Suhm-yi shook his head. "Have I not made myself clear? Vengeance was never our way. Last night was different. Last night I might easily have killed even you, my friend. And if I had come upon them about their evil business..."

"I understand," said Tarra gruffly, but he really didn't. Was life really so cheap to Amyr Arn? And the life of his one love—*the* one love in all these Inner Isles, this entire world—at that? Well, so be it. Some men are lusty fighters born, and some are not. And anyway, Amyr Arn was not even a man. Not human, at any rate. Who was Tarra Khash to query the ways of strange, unhuman beings?

The other knew his thoughts. "There are...things I must do," he said. "Anyway, I shall be with you, in spirit at least. What will you take with you?"

Tarra shrugged. "Sweet water and a little meat. A couple of yellow fruits and a great nut." And he shrugged again.

"And in your memory a picture of me, Tarra Khash," implored the other, "last of the Suhm-yi. Remember me all your days, as I shall remember you. And who knows, perhaps we shall meet again, though I doubt it."

And one hour later, the Hrossak set out in Amyr's canoe...

IV

Now, with all the Inner Isles in sight, (at least the nearest of them, and the rest clustered close, so that from one island one could usually see the next) Tarra quickly learned the skills necessary to send Amyr's canoe skimming low over the calm waters of the crater sea; rapidly closing the gap, he suspected, between himself and the Northmen he pursued.

Two small islands he saw with smoke rising, and knew that this could only be the work of the six. And quickly ensuring that the reaver band had departed, he spent the night upon the second of these jew-elled islets, rising early with the dawn. But having breakfasted and climbed to the island's tallest place, there he stood at a loss and gazed out upon the crater sea. No fires or smoke to be seen, and nowhere in sight the crude craft of the Northmen or its sail. Then the thought came to him that, discovering the islands empty of human (or of Suhm-yi) life, perhaps the barbarians had given up their pointless arson. One sets fire to another's property to do him harm, cause him grief; but if he is already dead, what profit then in burning his house? And surely by now the Northmen had seen, as Tarra had seen them, Suhm-yi skeletons sprawled where the plague of red ash had taken them?

All very well, but those columns of black smoke rising to the blue skies had been as signal fires to Tarra Khash, leading him on in the wake of those reavers with whom his score lay still unsettled. He frowned and considered the problem. Now what would *he* do, and which route take through these Inner Isles, if *he* were reaver seeking gold and gemstones?

Away eastward, central in a scattering of smaller islets, stood per-haps the largest of all the isles of the Suhm-yi, whose mass must be almost as great as all the others put together. Surely the reasoning of the barbarians would not differ so widely from Tarra's own? Surely they, too, would now realize that if aught were here worth the pil-laging, then were that something most likely found upon the greatest landmass, doubtless the principal isle of the Suhm-yi?

Very well, there must he go, and hopefully collect a debt in his own and in Amyr Arn's account. Aye, and with luck and justice settle the business once and for all…

Meanwhile, Amyr Arn had not been idle.

In a second, older canoe dragged out from mossy berth in tangled undergrowth and bathed in crater sea's soft brine to swell dried-out hull and fill fine cracks, the last of the Suhm-yi had sculled tirelessly a day and a night. Now he prepared to beach his craft upon a strand forbidden of yore, where only the naked feet of High Priests of the Suhm-yi had previously trodden, and only then in great reverence.

For the isle was Holy of Holies, and in aspect alone would suffice to send away the merely curious. No jewel of the crater sea, Na-dom, but a gaunt crag whose single fang reared from the deeps like some sea-beast's talon, which beckoned not but forbade intrusion. And no green thing growing thereon, where neither lizard crawled nor bird nested; and the rock itself black as if painted over with pitch. And Na-dom stood well off from the other Inner Isles, for which reason the gods of the Suhm-yi had, since time immemorial, been given to visit there; or rather, they had allowed themselves to be called thereto.

And because of the spire's ominous aspect, and insomuch that Amyr stood in awe of the place, he had indeed approached most reverently, plying his paddle soft as the fall of feathers and bowing his head as he beached his canoe in the tiny bight where a huge and ocean-hollowed cave gloomed like some slumbering ogre's mouth in the base of the rock. There, after long moments, finally Amyr lifted his head and gazed with wide golden eyes upon the cave and crag. And where the first gaped like an untended wound, the second towered skyward, a bleak look-out whose sides seemed precipitous beneath summit unattainable.

But...Amyr was not entirely unfamiliar with Na-dom, Isle of the Gods. True, he had never before set foot thereon, and even now felt that his presence was probably an abomination in the eyes of the olden gods, but he was not totally ignorant. Long years gone, when Amyr was very, very young, his own father had been High Priest. And that wise and honorable elder of the Suhm-yi had been close indeed to his only son. Their minds had been almost as one, so that Amyr had gleaned from his father something of the nature of the ocean-girt rock.

And as the old one had grown older still and passed on the sigil of High Priesthood to a younger priest, so his tongue had loosened a little and occasionally he would whisper in his sleep of Na-dom's cave and the steps therein, which formed a narrow way to soaring summit. Amyr had paid little attention then, but now he remembered all.

Aye, but he knew that while the powers of the gods were strange and far-reaching, they were often loath to answer the invocations even of their most elderly and practised priests—and how then the pitiful pleadings of an uninitiated youth?

Weary from his paddling and fatigued from fasting—for he had not eaten nor even thought of food for himself since the murder of his mate—Amyr now sighed, dragged his canoe from the shallows, entered the yawning cave and sought the rock-hewn steps. And indeed he found the way narrow, the stone slippery and the chimney steep, so that he must needs sling his bow over one shoulder and so keep his hands for balancing and for grasping the rough walls.

And tall that crag, so that it seemed a half-hour at least that Amyr toiled upwards; and gloomy, for only a little light filtered down from above and hardly anything from below, except in his ears the sullen hush of wavelets in the shingle-strewn bight.

Now, about the gods:

As stated, Amyr knew that they did not dwell upon the roof of this rock, but might, in auspicious circumstances, be called down to light upon it—normally through the medium of a priest of the Suhm-yi. And he also knew that Gleeth, the blind God of the Moon, was high-ranking amongst the gods of the Suhm-yi. It might just be that he could call up Gleeth himself to his aid—or rather, to the aid of Tarra Khash—but he doubted it. Gleeth was after all very old and very nearly deaf; he heeded calls rarely; and blind, he could not see to perform any but perfunctory services. So Amyr had heard it whispered. But...Gleeth *was* advisor to the gods, and the Elder of their Council, and so would make a useful ally. *If* he could be roused up from his centuried slumbers. The occasion was auspicious, however, for tonight would be his night, when a full and golden moon would be riding the skies over the Inner Isles.

And at last Amyr Arn came to the roof of the rock, and there sat him down to rest a while from his labours. On his way he had passed many lesser caves leading off from the winding stairway, and had allowed his eyes briefly to gaze upon the contents thereof; so that now he knew the legended treasures of the Suhm-yi were on no account mere legend. For indeed Na-dom was a treasure-house, whose lesser caves were caches for rubies, opals, diamonds, gold, ivories and jade and pearls galore; and now the last of the Suhm-yi could see why men of the outer world—the world beyond the rim of the crater sea—might desire to come here. Especially such men as Kon Athar and his brutes.

But the thought of those murderers roused him up and strengthened his resolve, and he set about his supplications there and then, repeatedly beseeching Gleeth that he hear him and come in answer to his call. And so he kneeled and mumbled and muttered (if that term be at all applicable to the silver tones of the Suhm-yi) all the long day, directing his will upon the solitary spire of weather-fretted rock rising like a finger up from the flat summit's table, whose stem was pierced by a perfectly oval hole like the eye of some petrified Cyclops; and slowly the sun sank down over the sea and the shadows lengthened, at first imperceptibly, then ever more rapidly...

V

Weary as Amyr Arn himself, Tarra Khash had reached the shallows of the principal isle of the Suhm-yi in that hour immediately after noon when the sun stands seemingly immobile in the sky and the air shimmers with his burning rays; when the sea lies still and calm and blue, almost seeming to *hiss*, but silently; and small silver fishes leap from dazzling water to fly a little way, as if deliberately breaking the stillness and reminding the world of its vasty reel and rush through the cosmos of space and time.

The beach was broad and white, with little of cover for Tarra and his canoe, and the crater sea a great unblemished blue expanse upon which burly Hrossak and slender craft both must surely stand out sore as a gap in otherwise perfect teeth, or mote in a bright eye; but of options he had none. And surely were the six here, for their raft stood drawn up and beached above the narrow wash of wavelets, alerting the Hrossak to their prior advent. Aye, and if Kon Athar had set a lookout, then were Tarra Khash observed. Well, so be it...

But the northern reavers had set no lookout, and so Tarra's own coming had gone unobserved and his presence here unknown (for the nonce), while some way inland Kon Athar and his five made their hulking, shambling way down the main thoroughfare of a deserted Suhm-yi city.

It was a straight and dusty street of finely-fretted stone, where several of the principal buildings went even so high as four storeys, showing architectural skills prodigious and awesome in the eyes of any average, untutored Northman. Except that Kon Athar and company were never much awed by anything of skill or beauty, unless it were perhaps skill in fighting or beauty in a well-proportioned and comely woman. And even then, the first they would pervert with cowardice or cheating, and the second bring down to beastliness, so that all was destroyed by them.

And there, in a walled square of paths and trees, before the open portals of a large and impressively ornate stone edifice, the barbarians found a fountain where water spurted still, there pausing to slake their thirst and reckon their course from this point on. One of them, Kon's right-hand man—a bulky, black-maned brute named Bejam Thad, whose name alone was ill-omen and whose cowardly blow, on the night of the murder of Bogga Tull and Ilke Phant, had plunged Tarra Khash only half-conscious into nighted, swirly Thand waters—now spoke up:

"I'm thinking, Kon," he growled, "we've come far enough—and for little enough. Naught here worth the sweat of reavers born, in these isles of silence and dust and skeleton corpses. And for a fact no treasure such as lured us here in the first place!" His tone, while in no wise threatening, was sullen beyond a doubt... Perhaps too sullen.

Kon Athar glanced at Bejam Thad and the corner of his slack mouth twitched a little. Kon was gross even for one of his breeding. IIis eyes were black and his grimy, matted mane of hair yellow, which was a rare colour for Northmen and so set him apart. It swept wild down his back like the mane of a lion. But dull the yellow now as he stripped off his goatskin jacket and plunged it unceremoniously into the font's pool, instantly fouling the water with clouds of dirt and dust and pungent sweat. Naked from the waist up, Kon's muscles rippled like coiling serpents. And his eyes glinted narrowly as he answered:

"Is it so, Bejam?" From hot conduit throat and cavern lungs such soft and gently spoken words. But Bejam Thad no fool:

"Kon, we're like brothers, you and me. Brothers can talk—say what's in their minds..."

The other nodded. "And they can fight, too," he replied, dragging soaking jacket from font and wringing it in gnarly hands that squeezed out every last drop of water in a trice. "I *had* a brother, Bejam, remember? He was my twin—and I killed him."

Bejam Thad paled. "But we've been more than brothers. Why, I love you!"

"And I you," Kon slapped his back, grinning mirthlessly. "But 'ware—'twixt love and hate stretches a skin thin as fjord ice in the melt." He hung his jacket over his shoulder. "Tread wary, for the water's swift and cold beneath." Then his oh-so-soft voice took on more of its accustomed grittiness. "Any odds, why d'you say we're doing so badly? There've been wenches to stick, not so? And booze—though precious little since Thandopolis, I'll grant you that. And I admit that the Suhm-yi wine we found wasn't agreeable. But as for loot—we had rich pickings from those oafs on the Thand, didn't we? Why, you never saw so much gold in your life, not in one place! And what of the finger- and ear-rings lifted from those skinny, stinking Suhm-yi corpses? A small fortune there."

"Aye, not bad, I suppose," the other yielded with a shrug, "though a bit played out now. But...a queer gang, these Suhm-yi. Four-fingered, four-toed? How's *that* for queer? And their skins—" he wrinkled his nose.

One of the others, little more than a lad, spoke up: "You didn't complain so loud when you had that Suhm-yi bitch bucking under you like a wild pony! Though damn! you yelped a bit with her nails in your back!"

Bejam glared at him. "Wipe your snots, pup—while you've still a nose to wipe!"

"What killed 'em, you think?" asked a fourth reaver, his words cutting through Bejam's heat. This one was tall as a pole and twice as thin, but tough for all that; and he had the sword's-reach of a giant to boot. "The Suhm-yi, I mean..."

His question was directed at Kon Athar, who pursed his lips and considered it before answering: "I've thought about it. That island where we found the female, for instance. It was well away from the main group—which was why she lived while the rest died. At least, that's how I see it."

"Eh?" Bejam grunted. "How do you mean?"

Kon raised sun-bleached blond eyebrows. "This damned red dust," he said. "Did you notice any of it on the island of the female?"

"Why, no, come to think of it," Bejam frowned.

"Think?" Kon's eyebrows climbed higher. "You?" His tone was heavy with sarcasm. "Self-praise indeed!"

"Well what in the seven hells...?" Bejam burst out, tired now of game and thinking both, "Dust is dust!"

Kon grinned broadly. "Aye—but this dust was death! Volcanic, I'd guess, and poisonous." He laughed harshly as his men began hastily dusting themselves down. "Not now, you buffoons, but poisonous in its falling! Clogging the air and turning to red brick in Suhm-yi lungs—and stinking of sulphur and the reek of hell's own chimneys—which is all volcanoes are, of course."

"Poisoned, aye!" the smallest reaver whispered, scowling at the red dust where it lay thickly blown in gutters and corners. "Breath of devils, belched from inner earth!"

"But it did our work for us," Kon Athar reminded. "We'd be hard-put by now if these isles were a-crawl with Suhm-yi." He glanced about, scowling. "Where's young Bandr Toz?"

The reaver he referred to was that same youth who had lipped Bejam Thad. The latter now issued a scowl to match Kon's own, saying:

"A yappy, scampering pup, that one—forever sniffing where he shouldn't. I saw him a second ago on his way in through yon doorway. Perhaps he felt, and feared, my need to give him a good clout!"

"Bejam," said their leader, sighing mightily, "you're a big brave lad and no error—but you forget now and then that we've a clouter elect right here in our midst. Bandr's a pup, aye, and yappy as all pups are, but one day he'll make a very fine hound indeed. By which time you'll be old bones and good for nothing much except sitting by the fire and slurping soup. Now kill him if you must and be done with it, but don't clout him. Not so he'll remember, anyway."

"Kon!" came Bandr's cry from where he suddenly appeared in gloom of door, excitement shrilling his voice almost to cry of wench. "Their history, here—all here! Pictures on the walls, carvings—and they tell it all!"

"History? What's he gabbling?" Bejam scowled again.

"Tell all of what?" Kon Athar called back, stretching himself up from rim of font.

"Why, of the Suhm-yi!" the youth shrilled louder still. "Of them, of their gods...*and of their treasure!*"

VI

Tarra Khash, **when** he set his mind to it, was a man of reason. He had his rages, as most men do—his passions and his thunders—but never those blind passions and thunders renowned of the Northmen. Which possibly explained why, despite all his adventuring, he was still sound of mind and limb in a world where magic and monsters were frequent hazards, where life was cheap and swords kept ever sharp and ready.

In short he had a keen mind to match his brawny bronze back and arms, and at times when danger threatened—for instance, in the shape of a large fistful of coarse-maned reavers from the north—he was given to using that mind with a cold and calculating dexterity. How easy it would have been to let hot blood surge, to go roaring inland with flashing sword and foaming lips...and to die there in some dust-blown, alien street. And lie where he fell and rot under countless suns, until even his bones were dust in the wind, and never a grave or a marker to tell the world that this had been Tarra Khash, a Hrossak.

But why wear himself out in the seeking of enemies who, in the fullness of time, must surely return to this very spot, this pebbly strand where their raft lay beached just above the narrow tidemark? Let them be the tired ones when, returning to the beach, they would face the might of full-rested Hrossak. It was as simple as that...

No, not quite so simple.

Surprise, too, would be on Tarra's side. Aye, and what a hot, red and raw surprise it would be! Tarra smiled grimly, smacked his lips in anticipation, sharpened his wits. Time was now of the essence: time to work, time to rest, time to strike. First the work.

He carried his canoe up the beach, following the broad swath of scattered sand and pebbles tossed aside by booted reaver feet; but where the earth turned stony he veered off to find storage for his slender craft in a clump of boulders. Then, at a spot not far from Kon Athar's trail, he found himself shade from a sun already slipping fast from its zenith, ate of his provisions and made to rest himself; but before that, on impulse, he made one further excursion and climbed to the crest of the coastal ridge. Inland the terrain was mainly flat to the foot of a distant mountain range, but keen Hrossak eyes minutely scanned the land between.

There were cities out there, shining white in the sun—the strange cities and towns of the Suhm-yi, all ghostly and ashimmer now, and empty of life save somewhere the shambling shapes of barbarian intruders. And apart from them, and from Tarra himself, the entire island seemed a place of strangely dreaming ghosts, of moaning dust-devils and destinies unattained.

Tarra returned to his cover and stretched himself out. Never had he felt so alone, not in all his life, not even at the bottom of Nud Annoxin's well-cell, and for all that he was far from cold, still he shivered as the shadows slowly stretched themselves out, straight black fingers crawling on the rocks and shingle and stunted yellow grass.

It took some little time before Tarra slept, and when at last he did the sun was falling faster and the shadows creeping apace. And visible now, far out over the sea, a milk-misty hemisphere like the domed head of some aquatic behemoth rising from the deeps—the moon, eager to be up and abroad in the night skies of Theem'hdra…

For long hours Amyr Arn had crooned the moon-runes of Gleeth, blind God of the Moon, his supplications going up from the rock of Na-dom first into the evening, then the twilight, finally the night. And Gleeth had seemed lured by the Suhm-yi's summons, for slowly but surely his celestial course had crept him through the heavens until even now he began to pass behind that uppermost pinnacle of Na-dom, that pierced rock-finger whose empty socket was oval as an eye. And the moon itself the orb which would fit that socket perfectly, when at last the transit was at its full.

Never had Amyr Arn seen so full a moon, nor ever a moon so beautiful…unless it were when his and Lula's love was new, when all the world had seemed beautiful beyond compare.

Oh, Lulu! Lulu! Last maid of the Suhm-yi. Gone, gone now and all promise gone with you. A race no more. Perished the Suhm-yi…

Amyr got to his feet. Cramped and cold he shivered as he gazed at the golden orb in the sky, whose rim was even now obscured by flank of spindly needle rock. Ah, such a moon! For in those primal days the craters were not so many and the mountains of the moon less high, and its ball so perfectly a ball.

"Gleeth! Gleeth!" cried Amyr Arn, unmindful now of the proper conjurations. He threw up his arms to the dark sky, as if to fasten upon the golden orb itself, and cried of his grief, his rage, his love, his hate. He told all the tale: of the coming of the red dust, the death of the Suhm-yi, the tiny island paradise where only two had been saved, untouched by the terror-dust blown on strange winds from stranger lands. Cried of the rape and murder of Lula, of the blood-quest of a brawny, brassy Hrossak, whose fierce pride and lust for vengeance had taken him where Amyr himself was forbidden to go.

"Forbidden, aye!" he cried, striking at the needle rock with clenched fist. "Forbidden by god-given laws—which you know well enow, Old Gleeth, for you were the god who gave them. They came down from the moon, those laws, and by them since time immemorial have all the Suhm-yi faithfully abided. And so I am forbidden to strike mine enemy, who has so sorely stricken me. Which is why I am here now, to crave justice. If I may not smite him and them who worked this evil upon the last of the Suhm-yi, then give your aid, I beseech it, to one who may—to the Hrossak, Tarra Khash. Do you hear me, Gleeth? Ah, wake up, old God of the Moon!"

And now the golden disc of the moon showing a quarter-sphere through the oval orbit of the rock; and the rock itself like a thin, one-eyed menhir looking out the corner of its eye, but looking at nothing; and Amyr beginning to despair that all his prayers had gone unheard, would remain unanswered. "Gleeth! Ah, Gleeth!" he cried again. "Will you not at least answer me?—if only to deny me! I know you are blind, or very nearly so, and almost deaf from the unending songs of the stars, but are you also dumb?"

Half-way into the oval orbit now, and more like an eye than ever, finally the moon—or Gleeth, the soul and spirit of the moon—gave ear to Amyr's impassioned plea…and answered it! Thin and reedy that ghost-voice, that god-voice, wavering and indistinct in Amyr's ears or mind:

"Who...who calls me up from...from my centuried slumbers? And...and why?"

"What?" Amyr was astonished. "Have you not heard me? For hours I have called upon you! Have I not told you of the doom of the Suhm-yi, who were ever your most faithful worshippers? And did I not—"

"Yes, yes...all of that...I know, I know!" Gleeth was irritable now, not quite awake and sour in his drowsiness. *"But...who are you? A priestling?...A Suhm-yi priestling?"*

"No!" cried Amyr in his despair. "My father was a priest—a High Priest—but I have never held such office."

"Not...not a priest?" Gleeth began to lose interest. *"Ah!...Not...not a priest, after all..."* His voice, mental or physical, was fading.

"I am the last of the Suhm-yi!" Amyr howled. *"The last,* d'you hear? And before I hurl myself down from Na-dom's peak, I ask this one boon for all my race."

"...Last?...Na-dom?...Boon?..." The voice faded away, drowned out by the moaning of a small night-wind come to investigate the shouting.

Amyr threw himself down on Na'dom's dome and clawed at the rock until his four-fingered hands bled. A waste, all a waste. He had failed. Last of the Suhm-yi, and a failure. Better if he had gone with Tarra Khash; better to die in defiance of god-given laws than to die utterly ignored of the gods.

And the face of the moon, blandly golden, blindly serene, standing central in the eye of the needle rock...

VII

Tarra Khash had heard them coming a mile away. Awakened by voices blown to him on cool night breezes, he had kissed his curved ceremonial sword—sharp as a razor for all its fancy jewelled hilt—and moved lithely into the shadow of a boulder where the trail narrowed and the reavers could pass only one at a time. And as their coarse, hated northern accents grew louder, along with the scuff of booted feet and slither and clatter of pebbles, so he waited, ready to pounce upon the six.

Bejam Thad led the bunch, or rather strode at its head. Kon Athar never went first, not in the night, not even on this dead Suhm-yi island. He did not fear the night, Kon, but who could say what might or might not lie ahead? And anyway, it pleased Bejam Thad to play at being leader. Better to have him in front than behind on a night such as this, for surely the time would come when he would tire of playing and seek to lead in earnest. They were all the same, the Thads, Kon knew: treacherous! And so he brought up the rear.

Which meant that he did not even see Bejam's death but merely heard a double *hiss* in the moon-silvered darkness—the first being that of Tarra's scimitar cleaving the night in a bright, curving flash, the second the rush of air from Bejam's collapsing lungs, whistling from his severed neck.

Then Bejam's blocky headless body tumbling, and the second and third reavers in line crying out their astonishment and rage, colliding as they drew their own blades; and a figure in the full moonlight stepping forward over Bejam's body, grim and menacing as he sought to pick a target in the confusion.

The second barbarian fared no better than Bejam. He'd cleared his weapon sure enough, but stumbled as he moved forward over the body of his erstwhile comrade. Tarra had moved back a pace, but seeing the man trip he lunged forward with the point of his curved sword, which passed clean through the other's chest, ribs, spine and all.

Bandr Toz was next, whom Bejam Thad had thought a pup; but youth has its advantages, not the least being speed of thought and reflex.

Bandr snatched at the vibrating, transfixed frame of the man in front even as he died and would have fallen, hurling the upright corpse forward upon Tarra Khash. Tarra was unable to withdraw his blade, for his second victim seemed to follow him as he backed off. Indeed—despite the fact that it even now chattered a death-rattle direct into Tarra's face—the glaring, dead thing impaled upon his blade seemed intent upon knocking him from his feet! And fall Tarra did, thus losing his advantage but at least regaining command of his weapon as it jerked free of the rolling reaver's ribcage.

In the time it took Tarra to spring to his feet, however, the remaining four were through the gap. Bandr Toz, following up his ploy with a forward rush, was almost immediately upon the Hrossak, his sword splitting the air towards Tarra's head. Tarra ducked, felt steel tug at his hair, took both hands to scimitar's hilt and spun his body like a top in the manner of a steppe dervish. The first six inches of his weapon's blade entered Bandr's flesh at his side and left it at his navel, not killing him immediately but good as. Bandr went down coughing blood, cursing the Hrossak through scarlet-foaming lips.

"Three down and three to go!" roared Tarra. "And who's next of you craven dogs?"

The three closed in on him a little, while Bandr Toz writhed and cursed where he lay coiled in moonlight. "A murdering Hrossak!" Kon Athar panted, spitting his accusation as Bandr shuddered and moved no more. "But who...? Why...?"

Tarra knew there was little time left for lengthy words. They were still dazed, these Northmen, but that wouldn't last. He backed away a little, feigning a stumble and falling to a crouch, then coming upright with a fistful of sand and pebbles.

"A Hrossak, aye," he answered Kon, "but no murderer. I leave that to dogs such as you—night-crawlers who'd kill men in their sleep for a fistful of gold!"

The tallest of the three—that thin and gangling giant with arms long as an ape's—was closest to Tarra and inching closer. Now he gasped his recognition. "This must be the one Bejam knocked into the river!" And with those words he sprang.

His reach was amazing—and his aim deadly! Tarra turned and felt the other's blade like a fire where it singed his ribs—but at the same time he hurled his handful of dirt straight into the thin giant's snarling face. The other cried out, staggered—then shuddered mightily as Tarra's scarlet steel chopped him crosswise ear to breast. And as the thin man crumpled, so the Hrossak shouldered him to one side.

"And two to go!" he cried, still backing away. "Two more dogs, before Bogga Tull and Ilke Phant may rest in peace."

"Rush him!" cried Kon.

He and the smallest reaver sprang together, but Tarra had moved so that the fallen giant lay in the way. Kon saw his ploy and leaped over the corpse; the small reaver was not so wily. Tripping, he flew forward—full on to Tarra's point. The steel popped through his throat, punching out in a dark spray from the back of his neck—but in the next moment Kon's own blade, a massive straight-edged broadsword, came crashing down and shivered Tarra's scimitar into shards before he could draw it back from the choking reaver's throat. And as the small man died, so Tarra turned and ran for the beach, Kon Athar laughing as he stalked him down the sand and pebbles trail, under a full and apparently merciless moon.

Tarra still carried the jewelled hilt of his broken scimitar. At ocean's rim he hacked at the lashings of Kon's raft, kicked its members flying hither and thither. But the Hrossak was weakening and he knew it.

Blood seeped from the gash along his ribs, action and effort and flight had near-drained him; weaponless, he stood little or no chance against the brutish, hulking Northman. Oh, he could still stab him, but long before he got close enough for that, Kon Athar's mighty sword would have halved him.

Kon knew this too, and leaned upon his sword and grinned when he came upon Tarra and saw what he had done to the raft. "That can be mended," he rumbled low in his throat, "but you will be quite beyond repair."

Tarra stood panting, holding his wound, incapable of further effort and unwilling to flee. "Do your worst, baseborn scum of frozen fjords," he answered. "Woman-killer!"

That stung. "Woman-killer?" the reaver roared. "I've killed only men, Hrossak—a good fifty of them—in my time."

"And a woman," Tarra insisted, "whose body I found on a tiny jewel island, ravaged and murdered!"

Kon Athar started, frowned, then laughed. "A woman? Nay, lad, a creature! Suhm-yi, that one."

"A woman for all that, dog!" Tarra cursed.

Tired of talking, Kon scowled and shrugged. "Have it your own way. Me, I've a raft to repair, treasure to find and steal, and so can't linger here." Two-handed, he weighed his great sword, advancing upon the Hrossak.

"Treasure?" the other hastily questioned, clinging to life, hoping to hold his adversary back for a second or two. "What treasure? Where? Here?"

"No," Kon shook his head, sending matted mane flying. "Not on this island. But there's a holy place where their priests made offerings to the moon, to stupid old Gleeth. There go I."

"'Ware, barbarian," said Tarra Khash. "Gleeth may be a little deaf and somewhat blind, but he's in no wise stupid. Why, the Hrossaks themselves give praise to Gleeth!"

"Aye," Kon nodded, coming close (but not so close Tarra could stab him) and lifting his sword on high, "and look where it's got you, eh?"

Behind Kon the moon stood full and round in the sky, a golden halo around his dark, evil head—a halo split by the upraised blade of his sword. "If you're a true believer, Hrossak," he grunted, "then call on your gods now, for it's farewell to all this."

And Tarra really *did* believe: he believed he was about to die. But…not yet! Not without one last…

He hurled the hilt of his sword like a knife, saw Kon twist aside as the broken blade tangled in his jacket. And the barbarian laughed deep in his throat, lifting his sword higher yet as he stepped in for the kill…

VIII

Twice this night Old Gleeth had heard his name impugned, once by a worthy creature and once by a creature worthless, and now he was fully risen from a rarely-broken slumber of ages. And Gleeth remembered what Amyr Arn had told him, and his thoughts were now quicksilver, even as the moon is silver on wintry nights.

"Amyr Arn!" came that voice in the mind of the huddled Suhm-yi male, high on the rock of Na-dom. *"Quick, take up your bow, while still there's time!"* And no way infirm that voice now: neither infirm nor wandering but full of an awesome strength; the strength of the moon itself, which moves whole oceans on the merest whim, and balances the lunar orb above the world, bright beacon on the darkling land.

"What?" Amyr Arn came to his feet, took his bow and nocked an arrow. And eager now this revenant, last of the Suhm-yi. "Have you finally hearkened, Old Gleeth? Do you give me my boon?"

"Indeed! Be quick and take it. Draw back your bowstring, let fly your shaft!"

"But—" Amyr gazed all about into the empty night. "Where?"

"Through the hole in the rock, where else? Directly into mine eye. Sight as you understand it was never mine, Amyr Arn, and your arrow cannot harm me. But I am not so blind I can't see right from wrong. Aye, and deaf I am, but not so deaf I may ignore the outraged cries of the murdered dead!"

Amyr aimed, let fly his shaft—and through the hole in the rock sped that avenging arrow...and disappeared!

But before it passed from this place, this time, into some other—before Amyr saw its blurred form flicker from existence—he saw something else. A blink, yes! The blink of a great blind eye, into which, without pause, his arrow had sped upon an unthinkable journey...

Tarra Khash saw that same blink—that split-second opening and shutting of the moon's eye behind Kon Athar's head—but he did not see the arrow which, materializing out of the moon's face, sped to its mark in the barbarian's spine. He *did* see Kon's blade tremble on high, when by now it should be rushing down in a deadly arc, and he did see the barbarian's eyes flash open in astonishment and hear his breath rush out in a great gasp. Then it was as much as he could do to get out of the way as the Northman toppled.

After that—

Time only to find the feathered shaft buried in Kon's back, to staunch the flow of blood from his own ravaged ribs, and gather up the jewelled hilt of his scimitar. Time only to lift the small pouches of gold from Kon's pockets, and to drag his canoe painfully down to the sea. And only when he was well out on the moonlit bosom of the deep, time to begin breathing as normal and let his risen hackles settle down and his nerves stop jumping.

Then he was away as fast as his rapidly stiffening wound would let him paddle, and never a backward glance. For Tarra Khash had had his fill of these isles of the Suhm-yi. What were they, after all, but isles of shadows and ghosts...and magick?

Magick, aye, for how else might one explain Amyr Arn's arrow in Kon's back, and Amyr himself nowhere to be seen? Then Tarra remembered something he *thought* he had seen: the blink of the moon's great golden eye, which seemingly spat out an arrow to strike a man dead.

And lifting his face up to the night sky, the Hrossak yelled: "All praise to you, Old Gleeth! A steppeman gives his thanks..."

And as the gooseflesh crept again on his arms and back he paddled a little harder, following the moon's path across the silent crater sea...

TOLD IN THE DESERT

Footsore, weary, and black now, rather than his native bronze—
his hide crisped by the inescapable sun and corrugated by weeks
of wind-blown grit—a lean and ragged Hrossak staggered under a
waning moon across seemingly endless drifts of sand. Lost, hungry
and athirst, he knew the end was near. Dawn would bring the sun,
freed once more from Cthon's nets to rise above the rim of the world
and let down his golden, shimmering curtain of heat. The desert would
become a furnace, a sea of dunes to trap and reflect the heat inwards,
baking human flesh like that of a pig on a spit. After the many adventures Tarra Khash had known, it seemed somehow improper that he
should now die here in so mundane a fashion, but that appeared to be
the way of it.

Better, perhaps, to take the hilt of his jewelled ceremonial scimitar—only the hilt, with perhaps an inch or two of sharp blade
remaining, for the weapon had been shattered in a grim and grisly
fight—and slit his wrists and stretch out upon the sand, there to
sleep his last long sleep and dream his last short dream. But…hope
springs eternal.

Where he was, Tarra Khash knew not. Only that he headed
east, and that six months had passed since he crossed the crater sea
and climbed the Great Circle range of mountains which girt that

land-locked ocean about. Since when he had wandered, finding water where he might, until there was no more water left to find and Death stalked him over this wasteland of yellow sand and sun-bleached stone, white now in the crisp light of stars and moon.

And so blunted by privation his once-sharp mind, and so weary his bones, that it took long and long for the fact to dawn that while his bleeding feet ploughed in sand, nathless he wandered in the drift-drowned streets of some ruined, crumbling and forgotten metropolis, some city of sand—lost in the desert no less than Tarra Khash himself. And indeed, he thought himself delirious when, approaching what had been the city's heart along a once-great thoroughfare, he saw, where mighty avenues of sand cojoined, a single silken tent and the glow of some strange nomad's fire.

But mirages were ever attendant unto the blazing sun Tarra knew, and never spawned of the moon (though certainly odd things happened when the moon was full!), and fever dreams (to which he was no stranger) were rarely accompanied by aromatic wafts from roasting, richly-spiced meats. And staggering closer he rubbed at grit- and night-inflamed eyes, seeing beside the tent a carpet spread with cushions, upon which reclined two figures, one being clad in raiment of silver while the other wore cloth of gold. So that again the thought occurred: *perhaps it is only a dream...*

Overcome by a sudden bout of dizziness, he fell to his knees and felt sand sting where desiccated skin split open, and gave a little cry from lips parched and puffed...at which the figure in gold came upright in a trice. Tarra saw, reached out, shuffled forward on tortured knees, fell at last and rolled over on to his back. And there he lay, gazing up at a sea of stars bright as jewels, where a horned moon sailed low on the rim of his vision—to be eclipsed in a moment by a figure bending over him and a face which gazed into his face.

And a voice rich as deep red wine, saying: "Woman, bring a little water, and help me draw this stricken creature into the light from the fire." A strange voice, aye, deep and strong but somehow gentle; and yet one which Tarra guessed had been hard and cold as glacial ice in its time. But not tonight.

He felt hands tug at him and could do little to help; but in another moment sweet water touched his lips and the dried-up pores of his mouth cracked open in spontaneous rejoicing. He drank, coughed, drank again...and cool life began to course in veins quenched of Death's destroying flame. And now at last they could help him to his feet, and guide him stumbling to their fire...

———

For what seemed a very long time Tarra ate of smoking, tender meats and drank of light, refreshing wines, until he was almost ready to believe that he had in fact died and departed Theem'hdra for some Hrossak heaven of which steppe theology was totally and inexcusably ignorant. Or perhaps the gods of the desert, mistaking him for a nomad, had accepted him into a nomad heaven. Well, if so, it was taking them an inordinately long time to discover their error and cast him out.

Finally, with many an appreciative belch (a custom of theirs, he fancied or hoped) he fell back and rested himself from his feasting. And now, too, he offered his most heartfelt thanks for the life-saving repast and tossed down the jewelled hilt of his broken sword in payment. His golden-robed host—surely a lord of sorts, who sat cross-legged and watching Tarra, as he had watched since his arrival—took up the hilt and admired its gems, but shook his head and handed it back.

"No, my friend," he said in that curious voice of his, "you owe me nothing. Your company on this night of nights is more than ample repayment."

"Then," said Tarra, who had small sacks of gold tied about his waist, "at least let me pay for a little water—just a little—in which to bathe myself. Poor company I'll make, stinking of sweat and dirt and desert, and sitting here sore in my every quarter!"

"Man," said his host, smiling a strange smile, "I do not own the oasis yonder," and he nodded into the shadows beyond his tiny tasselled tent. "Its presence is providential, a boon to all travellers in this parched land."

"Oasis?" Tarra came creakingly to his feet, staring unbelieving into the dead city's central place. There beyond the tent, where certainly in the city's heyday a fountain might have spouted, tall palms made dark, stirless silhouettes against skies whose brilliant jewel stars were mirrored at their feet in deep dark waters. Tarra blinked fevered eyes and looked again. Why, now that he saw it, he could almost *smell* the water! Passing strange that he had not noticed the palms before. Or perhaps he really had stood upon Death's darkling threshold, his senses dull as the body that housed them.

But certainly the oasis was there, and so: "Will you excuse a Hrossak sore in need of bathing?" he mumbled, scarce glancing at his lordly host but gaping at the palm-fringed pool. And drawn more surely than moth to flame, he crossed to that blessed basin and gradually, gaspingly, stepped down deeper and deeper into cool depths of laving liquid; until he floated there as in the most delicious dream, his cracked skin soothed and anointed and soaking up water like a sponge. And like oiled hinges, Tarra's joints came unstuck and his coarse hide turned back to skin, however blackened, and at last he drifted to the bank where he sat and washed away all the aches and pains of his body and the sloth of his fatigued mind. So that while he cleansed himself he pondered something of the strangeness of his situation.

Clear-minded for the first time in—how long?—he considered all. This wasteland was doubtless the ill-omened and Nameless Desert, wherein legends whispered of just such a sundered, smothered city. Nothing strange in that...but an oasis? Now maps were scarce in Theem'hdra, but Tarra had always had an interest in such and had studied them minutely whenever the occasion arose. But no map he ever saw had shown a water-hole here. And the place in such utter abandon. Why, the pool was more a small lake, doubtless sprung from some deep well! Possibly the olden collapse of the city had been due to a gradual blockage or drying-up of ancient natural springs, which had now replenished or opened themselves up once more. In which case nomads would eventually find it, name it, and life would flourish here again.

But...the Nameless Desert? Hundreds of miles to Chlangi the Doomed across the Mountains of Lohmi, and farther yet to Eyphra on the River Marl. And so...whence came the lord and lady here?—how, and why? Where were their yaks, their beasts of burden? Nowhere in sight, at least. And where the servants of the pair, whose eminence was obvious? Perhaps camped elsewhere, thus ensuring the privacy of their master and mistress.

But...no footprints in the sand save Tarra's own, no distant glow of campfires, no evidence at all to support the theory that his benefactors were escorted and protected by a retinue of servitors. Most odd...

The Hrossak finished his ablutions and looked back beyond the tent to where the two sat together, silent in the guttering firelight and the gleam of stars and crescent moon. They leaned a little toward each other, and there was a sadness in the scene. Had they been young lovers, then even now were they safe in the tent, naked as babes and twining in silken sheets, hot in each other's arms. But they were in those years when lust has given way to a truer love, when the companionship and trust of years has blossomed into a greater understanding and a fondness beyond the youthful fascination of mere flesh. A oneness.

They were fortunate, Tarra thought, beyond measure fortunate. In that they had each other. And he felt the stirring of a certain loneliness deep inside, for he had no one...

What?—he checked himself, snorting. *What...?* He snorted again.

A man alone, aye, and better that way by far. What?—a wandering, unfettered Hrossak—lonely? Ridiculous the very thought! But he felt an ache in himself for all that. Funny to think that one who just an hour ago had stumbled doggedly from Death's relentless pursuit should now seemingly begin to despair the futility of living! And yet again Tarra Khash snorted. The futility of life? Hah! It was only the chill of the pool which caused him to shudder, nothing more, as he made to put on his ragged breech-clout.

"Hold," said that rich strong voice close at hand, breaking into his thoughts and causing Tarra to start under the palms. He had not heard the approach of his host—wondered, indeed, how anyone could have managed it in the mere moments elapsed since he had peered curiously across the sand-sunken thoroughfare, past the tent, to where the two had sat upon their fine carpet—but here he was, and handing the Hrossak garments of sheeny silk at that.

"Be at your ease in decent raiment, Tarra Khash, soft against your roughened skin. Keep them as long as you may."

Tarra was overawed. "But these clothes...I mean, I can't..."

"Not that there's aught amiss with a breech-clout—in the right place and at the right time. But not, I fear, in the Nameless Desert's sundered city; not at night, when the chill of the desert tends to bite. Now dress and join us at the fire and tell us your tale."

"My tale?" Tarra looked vacant; but with a smile the man had already turned away, a shadow beneath the palms. "My tale..." the Hrossak mumbled again, then called out loud, "Aye, why not? I've a tale to tell for sure! If it will...amuse..." But he was talking to himself. He shrugged, put on baggy silken breeks and shirt, and made for the low-guttering fire.

Now Tarra knew that by rights he should sleep. That way the good wine, the food, the water in which he'd swum and cleansed himself, would all work on him to their best effect and he'd rise up a new man, fit once more to face whatever lay ahead. But at the same time he knew he stood in the debt of the man in gold and the woman in silver: sore in debt. Without their intervention—had he not stumbled upon them in the night—then Tarra Khash had been one dead Hrossak for sure. Fit only for the morrow's vultures.

And sure enough he had a tale to tell. And who better to tell it to than a man who knew his name without ever being told it?

So...tell it he did, cross-legged in the glow of the fire, upon which his host tossed a knotted, sun-bleached tree root to bring it sparking and crackling awake. He told of all of his wanderings:

Of the tribal feud which had driven him from the steppes in the first place, swearing to return one day and right a great wrong—of his adventures in the coastal forests far to the south, and in the subterranean vaults of Ahorra Izz, the god of scarlet scorpions—of his sorry sojourn at the house of Nud Annoxin in Thinhla, and his feverish flight therefrom—of his doings in Thandopolis (but not all of them, for the gentle lady's sake) and his subsequent panning for gold in the foothills of the Great Circle Range—of the murder of two new-found friends at the hands of fjord-bred barbarians, and of the sudden demise of those same dogs at his own hands, with the help of Gleeth, blind old God of the Moon—and finally of his journey from the Inner Isles of the Suhm-yi to this place, this wilderness of sand with its lost city and life-giving oasis.

"And that," he finally concluded, "is that. Here I found the two of you, and was restored. There is no more, the tale is told."

His host nodded. "Indeed. A fine tale. And well told. It has given us pleasure." His lady agreed, saying:

"The gods favour you, Hrossak, for your goodness. They would not let a good man die but guided you here. And now you grow weary and would doubtless sleep. There is a blanket in the tent. Go there, cover yourself, sleep well. And please, no protestations. Tonight my husband and I sit beneath the stars. Tonight we have no need of sleep. Tomorrow, perhaps…"

Tarra looked at her for long moments, looked also at his host. He was tired, true, but…

"Hrossaks," he said at last, "are not generally known for their curiosity. By token of which I am unusual. In any case, it is an old custom in the steppes, about the campfires, to answer one tale with another. It could be said, I suppose, that I presume upon your already unrepayable generosity, and yet—"

"You would have a story?" his host smiled a slow sad smile, and nodded. "I know of that custom. Very well—but understand, it is merely a story, a fable, a trivial thing. Your tale was a chronicle of your life, your adventures. A tale of blood and swords, of monstrous men and beasts. A wild, surging, passionate thing. Mine will be a tale of lovers parted and sorrow turned to red revenge. By comparison, a sad thing."

"A tale is a tale," said Tarra Khash, "and I would hear it."

"So be it," said his host. And this is the tale he told.

***

Once upon a time, oh, many, many years ago, before even Mylakhrion, that mightiest of wizards, was grown to maturity—indeed in an age when Mylakhrion was the merest apprentice in the tutelage of Khrissa's ice-mages—there dwelled here in the Nameless Desert, which was then a fabled, far-flung forest, a magician of no mean prowess whom we shall call Dramah, because that was not his name. But he was a good man as wizards go, and none went in fear either of Dramah or of his sorceries, which were white magicks as opposed to black. Aye, and he had the girl of his young dreams for wife, and they had lived together long and long, and happy, in each other's arms.

Now in those days there was a king of these parts, a man of many great strengths and some great weaknesses, one of which being his gluttony. Gylrath was his name, Gylrath the Great; but a joke whispered among his people was that his name referred not alone to deeds but more properly to the size of his belly! Be that as it may—his gluttony and all—still he was king. And his wizard advised him, read runes and omens and auguries for him, cast protective spells about his palace and lands, and so on and so forth. So that the king, Gylrath, might be thought more than satisfied with the works of his wizard. And so he might have been, except...

The king had gout, and Dramah...well, he was a wizard, *not* a physician. And as the king's condition worsened, so that worthy mage found himself more and more the butt of his sire's bad temper. And particularly galling the fact that the cure was in the king's own hands. All Gylrath need do was control his eating and drinking, and his temperance would do the rest; his grossly swollen left foot would shrink commensurate with his diminished intake of rich, rare foods.

Unfortunately, for all that the wizard could do nothing about King Gylrath's condition, he had at one time in an unguarded moment mentioned to his monarch a certain legended panacea, all of whose exotic ingredients were in his possession save one. This one missing agent was the crushed root of the green and poisonous swamp orchid of Shadarabar across the Straits of Yhem, where seldom a white man, even a wizard, had ever dared set foot. Many Yhemni tribes were known as cannibals, their forests and swamps full of malignant monsters, hybrid beasts and carrion birds, where crept vile vegetation and injurious insects.

But it seemed the king had taken no note of his wizard's words on that subject...until a morning dawned when Gylrath's pain was very great, when finally recalling the slip of that good mage's tongue, he demanded that a quest for the green orchid of Shadarabar commence at once, and that once found the root of the flower be brought back with all dispatch to his palace, and that there the panacea be prepared and a cure affected.

Now the king's wizard was a learned astrologer, and he read in his own stars a terrible calamity should he undertake this quest on behalf of the king; and so he pleaded with Gylrath that the journey be postponed until the auspices stood more in favour. Gylrath would have none of it, ordering that the mage be on his way at once, lest his lands and lordly house be taken from him and he himself cast out to seek service with some other monarch. And the good mage read the king's signs, seeing that they, too, were less than favourable, and told this also to Gylrath. Whereupon the king waxed wroth indeed, stating that it seemed his magician sought only to deny him a cure for his ailing foot, and warning him that it were best he got about his wizardly duties without more ado.

And being good and loyal—even to a master such as Gylrath, and for all that the king himself was wrongheaded and wilful—Dramah sighed and said a fond farewell to his wife, took up his runebook and soared southward upon a carpet endowed by his magick with the power of flight. And thus his search commenced.

Alas, because of its poisonous qualities, the green orchid was much sought after by the blacks of Yhem for use upon the points of their blow-darts, spears and arrows; and even in jungled Shadarabar itself, that darkest of Yhemni strongholds, the species was fast nearing extinction.

And through six long fruitless months of searching, Dramah grew ever more dismayed. Because of the thickness of jungle growth, the density of swamp's lethiferous leafage, he was in the main at a loss with regard to using his flying carpet, and going afoot into these boggy, hothouse places was fraught with peril.

But go he must, and uncomplainingly, for other than Gylrath's disagreeable nature—which might well abate upon production of the sought for panacea—Dramah's life was good and he had all he could desire of splendid things. Aye, and the great forest a beautiful place to live, where nowhere were seen the blistering drifted dunes which today are all that remain of that forgotten demesne.

And so the months grew into a year, and Dramah longed for home and gradually sickened from the fevers of the swamps and the foulness of their vapours. The insects stung him and drank of his blood, likewise great leeches which inhabited the sullen waters; and on more than one occasion only his magick saved the sorcerer from certain death. But as the mage weakened so the efficacy of his spells suffered, and toward the end of his search he spent much of his time racked upon a Yhemni pallet in a smoky village of savages, who revered him because he was a wizard.

And tossing in just such a fever—one which lasted for twenty days and nights—Dramah did not see the visiting Yhemni chief who took a fancy to his carpet and bore it away with him, never knowing its thaumaturgical properties. So that when at last Dramah awakened and raised himself up from his fevers, it was only to be plunged into deepest despair by discovery of his great loss.

But at last he found the green orchid and procured its root, and tried to be firm in his conviction that the worst was behind him and that the disasters foreseen in his stars now lay in his wake, all overcome and receding. And so he prepared for his return to the Nameless Desert, which was in those bygone days a great and green forest.

Alas, the worst was not yet.

Because of the loss of his carpet, Dramah must now employ lesser marvels to speed him on his journey; and to this end he unwrapped from oiled skins that great runebook containing all of his spells and enchantments. There was a spell there for the conjuring of boots which walked with the speed of a running yak, and another to turn miles into half-miles and legs into stilts. And...

Worms had eaten of the oiled skins! Dramah could not believe his eyes, his ill-fortune. The skins were in holes and a rot born of the swamps had found its way into the bundle. Aye, and the illuminated pages of the runebook all in tatters, with neither sigil nor cypher visible in the mould, so that all fell into smoking dust from Dramah's trembling fingers!

And a year and a quarter elapsed since last he had seen his beloved wife, and still a journey of months ahead, of privations and agonies and fever dreams. But locked in Dramah's head countless smaller spells and thaumaturgies, protection against the perils of the way, which should at least give him advantage over any merely mundane traveller.

And so he set out.

Long the jungle trails to Shad, and wide the Straits of Yhem— where Dramah's chartered Yhemni ship was tossed by storm and whirled in resistless maelstrom—and dense the mainland's coastal forests before fever-weary eyes lighted upon the grass-lands and steppes of

Hrossa. And many the dark dream sent to torment the mage through endless nights of tossing and turning, while his skin burned and sweated and the poisons of the swamps coursed in his veins.

Dreams of dark omen, of nightmare portent. And Dramah, because his knowledge of oneiromancy was great, read in these dreams DOOMS and DAMNATIONS, so that he smoked of the Zha-weed and called upon the ghosts of his very ancestors for their aid and advice. And in this that long-suffering sorcerer knew he risked great disfavour, for ghosts are loth to be disturbed and Dramah's forebears had been mighty wizards all.

Nathless they heard his pleas, saw his plight, came to him one by one in the turmoil of his dreams.

And he said to the first of them: "I know you not, only that I am of your blood, your line. Grant me a boon."

"What is it?" asked the shade.

"Give me that which will speed me home."

"I cannot," the revenant shook its hooded head. "But I may tell you this..." And he told Dramah how armies might be whelmed at the utterance of a word, so that the dreaming mage knew that this one had been a great warrior wizard. And that thunderous Word of Power lodged itself firmly in the tortured mage's mind.

Then, upon another night, came a second spirit, and this one's voice was a whisper of reeds in the wind. "How may I help you, Dramah, son of the sons of my sons?"

"O ancestor mine," said Dramah, "I seek transportation to my house, which is far and far away, to the loving wife who awaits me there. Make the miles between dwindle; give me wings; speed my feet homeward."

"No," the spirit shook its mummied head, its worm-fretted lips quivering, "that is beyond me. But I do not come empty-handed." And from skeletal fingers Dramah accepted a vial of amber fluid, whose purpose his long-dead ancestor explained in whispered detail, so that Dramah knew him for a powerful alchemist.

And in time yet a third night visitor came, of whom Dramah implored the same boon, and who likewise denied him but offered instead a strange spell. "A whistle?" Dramah's perplexion was plain. "Of what use a whistle?"

"There are whistles and whistles, child of my children's children," said the mist-shrouded visitant, "and in my day I was acclaimed the greatest whistler of them all." And he whistled a weird tune which entered Dramah's mind and stayed there, so that he might never forget it.

Finally, upon a night when the mage had crossed the River Luhr and the Great Eastern Peaks lay upon his right hand—indeed when the mighty forested domain of Gylrath lay only weeks and days distant—there came a cereclothed ghost who gifted to him a rune awesome and awful; of which Dramah made careful note, then put at once to the back of his mind. For this latest lich had been a necromancer, knowing all the secrets of Death and the lands beyond; and Dramah considered it an event of great ill-omen that this had been his final visitor.

Now, as the footsore sorcerer covered the last of those miles of his journey, so the fevers left him and his strength returned. And though his mien was changed forever (grey now his hair and faded his once-bright eyes) in spirit he remained the same…at least until he came to the forest's edge.

Came there—and found the forest burning!

And all about in the fire and reek, the huts of woodsmen and the mean cottages of the king's gamekeepers in flames, and the men themselves slain and their women murdered or carried off. And in a daze Dramah came to his own house, whose great garden walls had kept the blaze at bay, and entering found an old and faithful retainer who told him all that had passed while he was away: how a barbarian warlord had arisen amongst the tribes of Lohmi, and how that warrior had banded all the tribes together and brought them down out of the mountains to war with Gylrath. How even now the king lay ensieged in his great walled city at forest's heart, while barbarians scoured the land about for women to ravage and goods to plunder.

But when Dramah asked for his wife, then his ancient servant bowed his head and fell silent and spake no more. And divining the truth, Dramah went to Gylrath's city; even to that besieged city whose name has never since been spoken, word and legend of which were long-since stricken from all books and charts. And there he saw the barbarian horde ringing the walls about, and when they would come upon him spoke that Word of Power given him by a certain dead ancestor.

And lo!—the army out of Lohmi was whelmed, turned to sere dust in a moment and blown away on the wings of a demon wind.

Now the city's defenders, all that were left of Gylrath's troops, looked down from the walls and saw Dramah alone where barbarian hordes had laid in siege. But they knew him not, this ragged wizard whose doomful mien could in no wise be that of the Dramah they had known, long gone upon a king's mission into the south. And when he called up to them to open the gates, then they took up their bows and would have slain him; except he whistled a peculiar note, then several more, weaving them into a tune. And lo!—the city's walls trembled and split assunder, and tumbled down as if riven by lightnings and earthquakes.

And the survivors of the crashing walls cowered back and offered no interference as Dramah went to the palace and came before his monarch where Gylrath lay sick abed. Sick, aye—sick with terrors and tremblings and fear for his own skin. And the king was surrounded by his ladies and courtiers, and by platters of succulent meats, dishes of fruit and flagons of wine, with which he comforted himself.

When Gylrath saw Dramah he rose up at first astonished, then outraged. And unmindful of the mage's strange air and the ominous alterations in his bearing and aspect, Gylrath blustered and roared until he foamed at the mouth, saying:

"Where have you been, dog of a wizard? Sent out upon a child's errand and only now returned, these many months later! Speak!" For as yet the king knew nothing of the whelming of the barbarian horde, nor of the sundering of the city's walls. And in his great fear of the mountain warriors he was nigh distraught, for at any moment his defences might be breached and the enemy loosed upon the palace and Gylrath himself.

"Good news, Gylrath," Dramah bowed low, his face unchanging. "For I have returned with the root of the green orchid."

"What?" the king's amaze was vast. "*What?* A flower's root? Man, mine enemies are upon me! What use such petty potions now?"

Still the wizard's visage remained calm and strange, and seeing this many courtiers and ladies gradually backed away and made quietly from the king's chambers. "The barbarians are no more, O King," said Dramah. "I blew them away, dust upon the wind."

Gylrath's mouth fell open. "Is it so?"

"It is so, sire," said the mage.

Now the king commanded a runner go see if it was so, and the man returned saying it was. But he also whispered to Gylrath of the matter of the utterly sundered walls. Enraged once more the king pointed an accusing finger at Dramah, saying: "And what of the city's walls and my defenders?"

"They would not let me in. Indeed, they would have slain me, who only desired to serve his king," said the mage. And still unchanged the sad, vacant expression upon his face, the monotony of his voice.

"Then I shall slay *them*!" cried Gylrath, "Those of them that remain—to a man."

"And yet you did not slay the barbarians who took my belongings for their own and ravaged my wife unto death," said Dramah; and now there was a strange yellow fire burning in his eyes.

"I had my lands to protect, my city, my palace!" the king protested. "How then might I be expected to protect the lodge of a wizard at the very edge of the forest?"

"How indeed?" Dramah nodded his understanding, his voice sinking to a whisper, the fires in his eyes blazing brighter.

"But I sent out my generals with all their troops, who fought bravely—or so I'm told."

Now Dramah lifted his eyebrows. "You were not with them, O King?"

"What? You would expect me to fight? With a foot like mine?"

Dramah smiled a mirthless smile—seeing which, several more courtiers and ladies left the king's chamber. "Well, my liege," the wizard finally answered, "at least the cure for that is at hand. Your great foot shall soon be shrunken down, highness, and all your miseries at an end."

"Then get about it at once!" Gylrath commanded, for he was the king and all his enemies destroyed, and so his fear was forgotten.

And Dramah prepared his potion thus and thus (which should be prepared so and so). And he made this sign high and wide (which should be low and narrow). And he spoke the right words in the wrong order, until at last an ointment steamed in a bowl, which with dispatch the mage applied to Gylrath's great blue and lobsterish foot.

At once—upon the instant—the king uttered an "Oh!" and an "Ah!" and settled back sighing upon his silken cushions, closing his eyes in the abrupt and delicious relaxation of his pain. And as his grotesquely distorted foot commenced to shrink, so Gylrath reached out his hand and took up a bunch of grapes, munching until their juices ran down his jowls; for a sudden thirst was on him. And after the grapes he quaffed down a great goblet of wine at a single draft.

And more courtiers and ladies fled the room, for the fires behind Dramah's eyes were grown fierce now and feral. Only the king himself seemed blind to the sorcerer's silent passion, for he had eyes only for the wonder of his rapidly shrinking foot—and for the platters of food surrounding him where he lay. And, "Look! Look!" he cried in his delight. "See what my most worthy mage has done!" And he reached for a slab of steaming meat; for now he felt of a great hunger, as if he had not eaten in days.

Down went the bloated member, its poisonous hues fading fast and all the puffiness going out of heel and toes; until in a trice the king's foot was returned to normal shape and size, and all pain vanished along with throbbing flesh.

But hand in hand with the rapid reduction of his foot came a sharp increase in Gylrath's already overactive appetite, so that he could scarce speak for the viands and fruits and wines with which he stuffed and swilled his mouth; and still no alarm in the king, merely delight at the cure Dramah had wrought upon his no longer distended member.

Ah!—but while Gylrath himself was blind to the strangeness here—to a sudden and dramatic change in the very atmosphere of the palace, which now seemed charged with an hideous expectation—not so his court flunkies. Only a handful of these remained now, and when Gylrath gave his first sharp cry of pain, they too departed in less than decorous haste.

And now Dramah's eyes were balefires and his face a skull fixed in what might have been a mirthless grin. And when the king cried out again Dramah's jaw fell open and he bayed and boomed and laughed a laugh harsh and throaty as the rattle of Yhemni crotala; and his back and sides jerked and heaved with his laughter, which was quite mad and loud so as to utterly drown out the king's shrieking.

For the shrinking of Gylrath's foot had not stopped upon its attaining the correct dimensions but continued without abate, and now the skin covering that offending member was white as driven snow and slack as a eunuch's foreskin. And not only the king's foot but all of his limbs, shrinking away and whitening while his skin lay in pallid folds about his once-great neck and arms and thighs. Indeed all of his person, shrinking away...with the exception of his belly.

Gylrath's belly, to the contrary, came rising up, splitting his satin breeks, shiny as a ripe apple and spherical as the full moon! And still he crammed his screaming mouth with food and slopped wine into his contorted, quivering jaws. Too late he saw how he had wronged his mage; too late he recognized the monstrous magick wrought upon him. And now Dramah stopped laughing, glared once upon the white and swollen spider-thing which gobbled and gibbered upon the bed, swelling huge amidst white and billowing expanses of defunct skin, then turned and with never a backward glance strode from the chamber, a man demented.

And a white foam flecked the corners of the sorcerer's mouth, and whoever saw it covered his eyes and fled him at once. So that he stalked through the palace like a spectre, and only Gylrath's choking, slobbering screams to accompany him.

And where Dramah walked, there he scattered amber droplets from a vial given him in a certain dream; and fine marble fell to sand all about him, and statues of onyx crumbled away, until the palace was a sagging ruin. And still the shrill, agonized wails of the ensorcelled Gylrath continued—but only for a little while.

For as Dramah made away from the palace of the king—now a tottering pile which spilled sand from its every portal—there came a final shriek which gibbered quickly into silence, preceding briefly the sound of a rending too terrible to describe...

Then Dramah left the city, scattering droplets along his way, and all who saw him knew the place was cursed, took up belongings and fled. And in a day and a night the entire area of the city was a desert; the sand rapidly spreading outward like a blight, consuming all that remained of what had been a great and wondrous forest. Aye, and even today the blight spreads, though much more slowly now.

Well, for many a weary day Dramah wandered and raved in his madness, until rising up one morning he knew what he had done and wept. And remembering his wife, dead now and gone forever from the world, he wept again long and loud and unashamed.

Gone forever, unless...

For at last Dramah had remembered the rune given him by the fourth dream-lich, and now he knew what he must do.

Putting aside all other things he made his preparations; and a joy was in him as the correct season approached, bringing with it an auspicious quarter of the moon; and the stars turned in their inalienable orbits and became positioned aright. Then, at the precise minute of the hour, he offered up a last prayer for all wizards past and wizards yet to be, and in no small trepidation said the words of the rune; upon which, in the merest blink of an eye, Dramah became one with the sands of this vast and Nameless Desert.

Gone—gone like the good wife of his young dreams—but not gone forever!

For the magic of the rune was this: that in giving up his own worldly life he had engineered the return of his dear wife from the world of shades; so that he might be with her again, full-bodied and -minded, but for only one night out of any year, which night would be upon the anniversary of the utterance of the rune. And this was the boon his necromantic ancestor, who had known all the secrets of life and death and the lands beyond, had given Dramah in a dream.

And now the tale is told...

The fire had guttered down to red embers and Tarra could no longer hold off his weariness. His eyelids drooped and his head nodded where he had slumped down upon the carpet in his fine silks; and Shoosh, Goddess of the Still Slumbers, called him gently to her arms and would not be denied. Nor was his fatigue entirely natural, for his limbs were leaden now and answered not at all the commands of his will. It was as if he were drugged, or perhaps hypnotized. Aye, and certainly his host's voice had been hypnotic in its timbre. But...still there was a question Tarra Khash would ask, if only his trembling lips would obey him.

They would not, but no matter: it seemed his host had read his mind.

Through shuttering eyes the Hrossak regarded the pair where they sat opposite, now in each other's arms, and they smiled at him. And the man in gold said:

"What? You think that I...?" And he gave a little chuckle. His voice was teasing when he continued: "No, no, Tarra Khash, not I. I merely came here to fathom the mystery of the tale, that is all. To discover if a myth might not in fact be reality. For indeed this is the night, and this is the place. But..." and he shrugged. "Dramah and his lady came not, only a Hrossak lost and athirst—and very, very weary. So sleep, Tarra Khash, and do not let the question trouble you. May your dreams be pleasant, and all the gods of the steppes be with you."

To which, by way of reply, Tarra sighed and began to snore...

***

Dawn's light and chill roused him up, before the sun was full-risen. He felt well and restored and good for a thousand miles. Which was as well, for he might have all of that and more to go.

Of the oasis, the tent, the carpet and his breeks and jacket of silk—nothing, no trace. But he found his breech-clout tossed down in the sand.

Aye, and something else:

Two low mounds of sand in human outline, flowing one into the other. One flecked with gold, the other with silver...

CURSE OF THE
GOLDEN GUARDIANS

I

Thin to the point of emaciation and burned almost black by a pitiless sun, Tarra Khash came out of the Nameless Desert into dawn-grey, forbidding foothills which, however inarticulate, nevertheless spoke jeeringly of a once exact sense of direction addled by privation and dune blindness. For those misted peaks beyond the foothills could only be the southern tip of the Mountains of Lohmi, which meant that the Hrossak had been travelling a little north of due east, and not as he had intended, south-east toward his beloved and long-forsaken steppes.

Another might have cursed at sight of those distantly looming spires of rock in the pale morning light, but Tarra Khash was a true Hrossak for all his wanderlust, and not much given to bemoaning his fate. Better to save his breath and use the time taking stock and planning afresh. Indeed, it could well prove providential that he had stumbled this way instead of that, for here at least there was water, and an abundance of it if his ears played him not false. Surely that was the thunder of a cataract he heard? Aye, and just as surely his desiccated nostrils seemed to suck at air suddenly moist and sweet as the breath of his own mother, as opposed to the desert's arid, acrid exhalations.

Water, yes!—and Tarra licked his parched lips.

Moreover, where there's water there are beasts to drink it, fish to swim in it, and frogs to croak in the rushes at its rim; and birds to prey upon frogs and fishes both. But even as thoughts such as these brought a grin to haggard Hrossak features, others, following hard and fast upon their heels, fetched on a frown. What he envisioned was nothing less than an oasis, and never a one-such without its lawful (or often as not *un*lawful) masters and protectors. Mountain men, perhaps, well known for their brute natures; or polyglot nomads from the desert, settled here in what to them must surely be a land of plenty.

Or...or perhaps he made too much of a mere sound, a touch of moisture in the morning air. For after all he *had* ventured here by chance; perchance he was the first such to venture here. Still, better safe than sorry.

Tarra had several small sacks of gold tethered to a thong about his waist. Other than these he wore a loincloth and carried a scabbard slung diagonally across his back, in which was fixed the jewelled hilt of a curved ceremonial sword; but just the hilt and a few inches of blade, for the rest had been shivered to shards in battle. Tarra kept the broken sword not for its value as a weapon but for the jewels in its hilt, which were worth a small fortune and therefore held high barter value. A man could buy his life many times over with those gemstones. Moreover, anyone seeing that hilt stuck in its scabbard would picture an entire sword there, and a Hrossak with a scimitar has always been a force to be reckoned with.

Jewels and gold both, however, might well prove too much of a temptation, for which reason Tarra now removed the sacklets from their thong and buried them beside an oddly carved rock. That was better; few men would risk their necks for a sweaty breech-clout, and scarcer still one who'd attempt the removal of a man's personal weapon!

And so Tarra climbed rocks and escarpments toward sound of rushing water and taste of spray, and along the way ate a lizard he killed with a rock, until after half a mile an oft-glimpsed glimmer and sparkle was grown to a shining spout of water descending from a high, sheer cliff. By then, too, the sun was up, and the way grown with grasses however coarse and bushes of thorn, then flowers and a scattering of trees with small fruits, and some with carobs and others with nuts. Here a small bird sang, and there the coarse grasses rustled, and somewhere a wild piglet squealed as it rooted in soil now loamy. A place of plenty indeed, and as yet no signs of Man or of his works, unless—

—Unless that was firesmoke Tarra's eager nostrils now suspicioned, and a moment later more than suspicioned: the tangy reek of a wood fire, and the mouthwatering aroma of pork with its juices dripping and sputtering on smoking, red-glowing embers.

By all that was good!—sweet pork for breakfast, and a pool of clear water to draw the sting from sandpapered skin and soothe the stiffness from creaking joints. Tarra went more swiftly now, lured on irresistibly; and yet he went with caution, until at last he reached the rim of a great bowl-like depression in a wide terrace of rock beneath beetling cliffs. And there, lying flat upon his belly, he slowly craned forth his neck until the cataract-carved pool below, and its sandy margins, lay visible in every aspect to his desert-weary eyes. And a sight for sore eyes it was:

The pool was round as a young girl's navel, and its waters clear and sparkly as her blue eyes. Fish there were in small shoals that Tarra could plainly see, and reeds along one curve of bank, giving way to a species of wide, low-hanging willow which grew in a clump where the rock was cleft. And there sat one who looked like an old man half-in, half-out of the sweet green shade, at his feet a fire whose smoke rose near-vertical to the sky, except where gusts of spume from the waterfall caused it to eddy.

Even as Tarra watched, the old man (if such he was) baited a hook and tossed it on a line into the pool, where fish at once came speeding to investigate. The Hrossak glanced back over one shoulder, then the other. Nothing back there: the foothills and mountains on one hand, the shimmering desert on the other. And between the two this hidden pool, or rather this lake, for certainly the basin was a big one. He relaxed; he scanned the scene again; his mouth watered at the delicious, drifting odour of roasting meat. Down below a fish took the hook, was hauled in a frenzy of flexing body and flash of scales dripping from the water. It joined several more where they glittered silver in a shallow hole close to where the old man sat. He baited his hook again, turned the spit, swigged from a wineskin. Tarra could stand no more.

Here the descent would be too steep; he would break a leg or even his neck; but over there, close to where the waterfall plunged and turned the lake to milk, were rounded terraces or ledges like steps cut in the rock, and projecting boulders for handholds. No problem...

He wriggled back from the rim, stood up, loped around the edge of the bowl toward the waterfall. Almost there he stopped, used his broken sword's scant inches of blade to cut a bow, strung it with the thong from his middle. Two straight, slender stems for flightless arrows—crude but effective at short range—and he was ready. Except...

It is never a wise move to come upon a man suddenly, when he may well be shocked into precipitious and possibly violent reaction. Tarra went to the head of the water-carved steps, leaned casually upon a great boulder and called down: "Halloo, there!"

The basin took up his call, adding it to the thunder of plummeting waters: "Halloo, there—*halloo, halloo, halloo—there, there, there!*"

Down below, the lone fisherman scrambled to his feet, saw Tarra Khash making his way down slippery terraces of stone toward him. Tarra waved and, however uncertainly, the man by the pool waved back. "Welcome!" he called up in a tremulous croak. "Welcome, stranger..."

Tarra was half-way down. He paused, yelled: "Be at your ease, friend. I smelled your meat and it aroused a small hunger in me, that's all. I'll not beg from you, though, but merely borrow your hook, if I may, and catch a bite of my own."

"No need, no need at all," the other croaked at once, seemingly reassured. "There's more than enough here for both of us. A suckling pig and a skin of wine...which way have you come? It's a strange place for wanderers, and that's no lie!"

Tarra was down. Stepping forward he said, "Across the Nameless Desert—which is just a smidgeon dusty this time of year!" He gave his head a shake and dust formed a drifting cloud about his shoulders. "See?"

"Sit, sit!" the other invited, fully at his ease now. "You'll be hungry as well as thirsty. Come, take a bite to eat and a swig of sweet wine."

"I say gladly to both!" answered Tarra Khash. "But right now, the sweetest thing I can imagine is a dip in these crystal waters. What? I could drink the lake dry! It'll take but a moment." He tossed his makeshift bow and arrows down, stepped to pool's rim. The scabbard and hilt of sword stayed where they were, strapped firmly to his back.

"Careful, son!" the oldster cautioned, his voice like dry dice rattling in a cup—but the Hrossak was already mid-dive, his body knifing deep in cool, cleansing waters. "Careful!" came the warning again as his head broke the surface. The old man fairly danced at the pool's rim. "Don't swim out too far. The water whirls toward the middle and will drag you down quick as that!" he snapped his fingers.

Tarra laughed, swilled out his gritty mouth, turned on his back and spouted like a whale. But the oldster was right: already he could feel the tug of a strong current. He headed for the shelf, called: "Peace! I've no lust for swimming, which seems to me a fruitless exercise at best. No, but the dust was so thick on me I grew weary from carrying it around—*Ho*!" And he hauled himself from the water.

A moment later, seated on opposite sides of the fire, each silently appraised the other. The old man—a civilized man by his looks, what Tarra could see of them; possibly out of Klühn, though what such as he could want here the Hrossak found hard to guess—was blocky turning stout, short of stature and broken of voice. He wore loose brown robes that flowed in the nomad fashion, cowled to keep the sun from his head. Beneath that cowl rheumy grey eyes gazed out from behind a veil of straggling white hair; they were deepset in a face much seamed and weathered. His hands were gnarled, too, and his calves and feet withered and grey where he shuffled his open leather sandals to scuff at the pebbles. Oh, he was a grandfather, little doubt, and yet—

Tarra found himself distracted as the other teased a smoking chunk of pork as big as his fist from the spit and passed it over the fire on a sharp stick. "Eat," he growled. "The Nameless Desert is no friend to an empty belly."

Feeling the sun steaming the water from his back, Tarra wolfed at the meat, gazed out over the lake, dangled a toe languidly in its waters. And while he munched on crisp crackling and tore at soft flesh, so the other studied him.

A Hrossak, plainly, who beneath his blisters and cracked skin would be bronze as the great gongs in the temples of Khrissa's ice-priests. Not much known for guile, these men of the steppes, which was to say that they were generally a trustworthy lot. Indeed, it was of olden repute in Klühn that if a Hrossak befriends you he's your friend for life. On the other hand, best not to cross one. Not unless you could be sure of getting away with it...

The old man checked Tarra over most minutely:

Standing, he'd be a tall one, this Hrossak, and despite his current leanness his muscles rippled beneath sun- and sand-tortured skin. Hair a shiny, tousled brown (now that dust and dirt were washed away) and eyes of a brown so deep that it was almost black; long arms and legs, and shoulders broad as those of any maned and murderous northern barbarian; strong white teeth set in a wide, ofttimes laughing mouth—aye, he was a handsome specimen, this steppeman—but doubtless as big a fool as any. Or if not yet a fool, then shortly.

"Hadj Dyzm," he informed now, "sole survivor of a caravan out of Eyphra. We had almost made it through a mountain pass and were headed for Chlangi—our planned watering place, you understand—on our way to Klühn. Mountain scum ambushed us in the eastern foothills. I played dead, as did two others..." (Tarra, still munching, glanced quickly about and to the rear, his keen eyes missing nothing.) Dyzm nodded: "Oh, yes, there *were* three of us, myself and two young bucks. But..." He paused, seemed to withdraw a little and catch at his breath. Tarra could almost taste him biting his lip. Well, he wouldn't pry. The old man could keep his secrets. Anyway, it was easier to change the subject:

"Khash," he said. "Tarra, to my friends. I'm heading for Hrossa— or should be! Now—I suppose I'll rest up here for a day or two, then get on my way again. Go with me if you will, or is your aim still set on Chlangi the Doomed?"

The other shrugged. "Undecided. Chlangi is a place of brigands, I'm told, and your Hrossa is likewise somewhat...wild?"

"You'd be safe enough with me, and there's sea trade with Klühn— though not much, I'll admit. Again, I've been away for many a year; relations may well have improved. One thing's certain: if a man can pay his way, then he's welcome in Hrossa."

"Pay my way!" the other laughed gratingly. "Oh, I can do that all right. I could even pay you—to be my protection on the way to Chlangi—if you were of a mind." He dipped into his robes and came out with several nuggets of gold, each big as a man's thumb.

Tarra blinked. "Then you're a rich merchant, Hadj Dyzm, or at any rate a man of means! Well, I wish I could be of assistance. But no, I believe it's Hrossa for me. I'll think it over, though."

Dyzm nodded. "Fair enough!" he barked in that strange rough voice. "And in my turn I shall give some thought to your own kind offer. But let me say this: of all my treasure—of the veritable *lumps* of gold which are mine—those nuggets I have shown you are the merest motes. For your help I would pay you ten, nay twenty times what you have seen!"

"'Ware, man!" Tarra cautioned. "Men have been killed for a toothful! Speak not of lumps—at least not so carelessly!" It was a true statement and a sobering thought.

They sat in silence then, eating their fill for a long while, until the pork was finished and the wineskin empty. By then, too, the sun was riding high in a sky so blue it hurt, and Tarra was weary nigh unto death.

"I'm for sleeping," he finally said. "I'll be happy to find you here when I awaken, Hadj Dyzm, and if you are gone I'll not forget you. Peace."

Then he climbed to a shady ledge almost certainly inaccessible to the oldster, and with a single half-speculative glance at Dyzm where he sat in the shade of the willows below, and another out across the glittery pool, he settled himself down to sleep...

II

Tarra Khash was not much given to dreaming, but now he dreamed. Nor was his dream typical, for he was not a greedy man; and yet he dreamed of gold.

Gold, and a great deal of it. Heaps of it, ruddily reflecting the flickering light of a torch held high in Tarra's trembling fist. Trembling, aye, for the dream was not a pleasurable thing but a nightmare, and the treasure cave where the dreaming Hrossak waded ankle deep in bright dust not merely a cave but—

—*A tomb!*

The tomb of Tarra Khash! And as behind him its great stone slab of a door pivoted, shutting him in forever—

—Tarra came awake in a moment, jerking bolt upright with hoarse cry and banging his head on jutting rim of rock whose bulk had kept the sun from him. But now…the sun already three parts down the sky and shadows stretching; and already the chill of evening in the air, where overhead kites wheeled against a blue degrees darker, their keen eyes alert for carrion; and the great pool grey now where it lay in the shade of the basin, and the spray from the cataract a veil of milk drifting above the fall.

Tarra lay down again, fingering his skull. He shivered, not so much from chilly flesh as a chill of the spirit. A dream such as *that* one were surely ill-omened, whose portent should not be ignored. Tarra touched his bump again and winced, then grinned however ruefully. What? A Hrossak full-grown and troubled by a dream? Terrors enough in this primal land without conjuring more from surfeit of swine-flesh!

"Ho!" came a gritty, coughing shout from below. "Did you call me? I was sleeping."

Tarra cloaked himself in his wits and sat up—this time more carefully. "I wondered if you were still there," he called down. "I couldn't see you in the shade of your tree, and the fire appears to be dead."

"What?" Hadj Dyzm came from cover, stretched and yawned. He poked for a moment at dull embers, then snorted a denial. "No, not dead but sleeping like us. There…" and he propped a dry branch over hot ashes. By the time Tarra had climbed stiffly down, smoke was already curling.

"Fish for supper," said Dyzm. "If I may depend on you to see to it, I'll go tend my beasts."

"Beasts?" Tarra was surprised. "Beasts of burden? Here?" He stared hard at the other in the dying light. "You said nothing of this before. Things take a turn for the better!"

"Listen," said Dyzm. "While you slept I thought things over. I've a tale to tell and a proposition to make. I'll do both when I get back. Now, will you see to the fish?"

"Certainly!" the Hrossak answered, kneeling to blow a tiny flame to life. "Beasts of burden, hey? And now maybe I'll reconsider your offer—my protection, I mean, en route for Chlangi—for it's a shorter way far to the so-called Doomed City by yak, than it is to the steppes on foot! And truth to tell, my feet are sore weary of—" But Hadj Dyzm was no longer there. Humped up a little and wheezing, he had made his way carefully upward, from one rock terrace to the next higher; and he needed his wind for breathing, not chatting to a suddenly gossipy Hrossak.

Tarra, however, chattered only for effect: chiefly to hide his hurried reappraisal of this "stranded merchant." Stranded, indeed! How so? With beasts of burden at his command? There were deep waters here for sure, and not alone in this crystal pool!

Using his broken blade the Hrossak quickly gutted the fishes, spitted them together on a green stick and set it over the stinging smoke, then checked on Dyzm's progress up the side of the bowl. And...he could climb surprisingly well, this old man! Already he was at the rim, just disappearing over the top. Tarra let him get right out of sight, then sprang to his feet and raced up the terraces. At the top he followed Dyzm's trail beneath the cliffs to where the water came down in a near-solid sheet from above, its shining tongue lunging sheer down the slippery face of the rock. No need for stealth here, where the thunder of the fall deadened all else to silence.

Then he spotted the oldster, but—

On the other side of the fall? Now how had he managed to get across? And so speedily! The old fellow was full of surprises, and doubtless there were more to come; Tarra must try to anticipate them.

He watched from the shelter of a leaning rock, his gaze half-obscured by rising spray from the lake. Dyzm's animals were not yaks but two pairs of small camels, which he now tended in the pale evening light. Tethered to a tree in the lee of the cliff, three of them had saddles and small bags, the other was decked more properly as a pack animal. Dyzm put down a large bundle of green branches and coarse grasses collected along the way and the camels at once commenced to feed. While they did so, the old man checked their saddle bags. And furtive, old Hadj Dyzm, as he went about his checking, with many a glance over his brown-robed shoulders, which seemed a little less humped now and, oddly, less venerable. But perhaps that was only an effect of the misty light…

Keeping low and melding with the lengthening shadows, Tarra retraced his steps to the bowl, down the terraces to the lake, and was just in time to keep the fishes from ruin as the fire's flames blazed higher. So that a short while later, when Dyzm returned, supper was ready and the fire crackled a bright yellow welcome, its light reflecting in the water along with night's first stars.

Seeing that all was well, Dyzm handed Tarra a blanket he'd brought back with him from his camel-tending; Tarra threw it gratefully across his shoulders, drawing it to him like a robe. Hunching down, they ate in silence; and then, with the last rays of the sun glancing off the western rim of the bowl, the old man shoved a little more wood on the fire and began to talk:

"Tarra Khash, I like you and believe that you're a trustworthy man. Most steppe men are, individually. Oh, it's true I know little enough about you, but we've eaten together and talked a little, and you've given me no cause to suspect that you're anything but a right-minded, fair-dealing, strong-limbed and hardy Hrossak. Which are all the qualifications you need to be my partner. Hear me out.

"If you hadn't come on the scene when you did—indeed, only half an hour later—then I'd have been long gone from here and even now on my way to Klühn via Chlangi, and to all the many hells with trail brigands and bandits! And fifty-fifty I would make it unscathed, for I'm a survivor, d'you see? Not that I'd normally complain, even if I didn't make it: a man has a life to live and when it's done it's done. Being a Hrossak, you'd agree with that, I know.

"Ah! But that's a poor man's philosophy, Tarra Khash—the philosophy of defeat. For a poor man has nothing to lose, and what's life itself but a burdensome, lingering thing? When a man becomes rich, however, his viewpoint changes. And the richer he becomes, the greater the change. Which tells you this: that since coming here I have grown rich. So rich that I am no longer willing to risk a fifty-fifty chance of hying myself to Chlangi all in one piece. Aye, for what's wealth if you're not alive to enjoy it?

"Wait!—let me say on. Now, I can see your first question writ clear across your face. It is this: how, by what means, have I, Hadj Dyzm, a poor man all my life, suddenly grown wealthy? Well, this much I'll tell you—" He brought out a weighty saddle bag from beneath his robe, spread the hem of Tarra's blanket over the smooth rock, tipped out contents of bag.

Tarra's jaw dropped and his eyes opened wide, reflecting the glow and glitter and gleam of the heap of gold and jade and jewels which now lay scintillant in the fire's flickering. And: "By all that's…!" he gasped, stretching forth a hand. But before his fingers could touch, Dyzm grasped them in his own wrinkled paw.

"Hold!" he cautioned again. "Wait! You have not heard all. This is but a twelfth part of it. Eleven more bags there are, where this one came from. Aye, and an hundred, a thousand times more where *they* came from!"

"Treasure trove!" Tarra hissed. "You've found a cache!"

"*Shh!*" said Dyzm sharply. "A cache? A hoard? Treasure long lost and buried in the desert's drifting sands?" Slowly he shook his head. "Nay, lad, more than that. I have discovered the tombs of a line of ancient kings, who in their time were wont to take with them to the grave all the treasures gathered up in all the days of their long, long lives!" And chuckling hoarsely, he patted Tarra's knee through the blanket.

The tombs of kings! Treasures beyond avarice! Tarra's head whirled with the sudden greed, the poisonous *lust* he felt pulsing in his veins—until a cooling breeze blew upon his brain from dark recesses of memory. In his mind's eye he saw a huge slab of stone pivoting to block a portal, heard the shuddering reverberations as that massive door slammed immovably into place, felt the weight of a million tons of rock and sand pressing down on him, keeping him from the blessed air and light.

He drew back his hand and stopped licking his lips. His eyes narrowed and he stared hard at Hadj Dyzm.

The oldster gave a harsh, hoarse chuckle. "That's a rare restraint you show, lad. Don't you want to touch it?"

"Aye," Tarra nodded. "Touch it? I'd like to wash my face in it!— but not until you've told me where it comes from."

"Ho-ho!" cried Dyzm. "What? But we haven't settled terms yet!"

Again Tarra nodded. "Well since you're so good at it, let's hear what you've to say. What are your terms?"

Dyzm stroked his gnarly chin. "The way I see it, with you along—especially in Chlangi—my chances for survival go up from fifty-fifty to, oh, say three out of four?"

"Go on."

"So let's settle for that. For your protection I'll pay you one fourth part of all I've got."

Tarra sat back, frowned. "That doesn't sound much of a partnership to me."

Dyzm chortled, low and throaty. "Lad, these are early days. After all, we can only take so much with us—*this* time!"

Tarra began to understand. "As I prove myself—that is, as you continue to survive, which with my protection you will—so my percentage will improve; is that it?"

"Exactly! We'll return—trip after trip until the vaults are emptied—by which time you'll be earning a full half-share and there'll be men enough in our employ to keep all the brigands in Theem'hdra at bay!"

"But where are these vaults you speak of?" Tarra asked, and got exactly the answer he'd expected:

"Man, if I told you that at this juncture...why, what need of me would you have then? Anyway, the vaults are impossible to find; I myself found them only by dint of sheerest accident. Aye, and I have sealed up the hole again, so that it's now doubly impossible."

Tarra grinned, however mirthlessly. "It would seem," he said, "for all your high opinion of Hrossaks, that this one is only trustworthy up to a point!"

"If there's one thing I've learned in life," Dyzm answered, "it's this: that *all* men are trustworthy—up to a point." He pointed at the fortune nestling in the corner of Tarra's blanket, tossed down the saddle bag. "But keep them," he said. "Why not? And take them up with you to your ledge to sleep the night, where a poor old lad with a pot belly and bandy legs can't reach you and choke your life out in the dark. But don't talk to me of trust and mistrust, Tarra Khash..."

Tarra reddened but said nothing. Truth to tell, old Dyzm's arrow had struck home: the Hrossak *had* taken his precautions before sleeping, and he'd done a fair bit of suspicioning, too. (Only thank goodness the old fox hadn't seen him following him, else were there a real tongue-lashing in the offing!)

At any rate Tarra said no more, nor old Dyzm, and after sitting awhile in silence they each began to make their arrangements for the night. The Hrossak found himself a smooth hollow in the stone close by—but far enough away from spouting water to be bone dry, and still retaining the sun's heat—and there curled up in his blanket. Hadj Dyzm retired yawning to an arbor in the willows, rustling about a bit amongst the branches until settled. Only then, before sleeping, was there more talk, and brief at that:

"When do you want my answer?" Tarra softly called in the night.

"Tomorrow at latest—else by noon I move on alone. But for goodwill, if that's what you seek, keep that saddle bag anyway—if only to remind you of a once-in-a-lifetime chance missed. You have a molehill; you could have a mountain."

And on that they settled down, except…neither one slept.

III

For Tarra it was like this: the old man had seemingly dealt with him fairly, and yet still something—many things, perhaps—bothered him. The yellowish texture of Dyzm's wrinkled skin, for instance; though why simple signs of age and infirmity should bother Tarra he couldn't imagine. And the old boy's voice, croaking like Khrissan crotala. A disease, maybe? His name, too: for "Hadj Dyzm" as name were more likely found attached to a man of cold Khrissa or Eyphra, and men of those parts rarely stray. They are rigidly cold, such men, brittle as the ice which winters down on them from the Great Ice Barrier and across the Chill Sea. And merchants they scarcely ever are, who by their natures are self-sufficient. And yet this one, at his time of life, alleged a longing for Klühn, city of sophisticates, warm in the winter and the temperate currents of the Eastern Ocean even as Khrissa in mid-summer. Or perhaps, weary of ice and frozen wastes, Dyzm would simply see out his life there, dotage-indulgent of luxuries and soft sea strands?

But what of the two who'd fled beleaguered caravan with him? Old Dyzm had mentioned precious little of them, and had seemed to regret even that! Anyway, if he were so enamoured of Klühn (via

Chlangi) why come this way—around the southern tip of Lohmi's mountains, in precisely the wrong direction—in the first place?

Lastly, why show Tarra *any* of his treasure? Why not simply make him a decent offer for his assistance in crossing unscathed the badlands twixt here and Chlangi, and thence to Klühn? Surely that were wisest...

These were the thoughts which kept Tarra awake, but Hadj Dyzm's were something else. For where the Hrossak's were vague, curious, inquiring things, Dyzm's were cunning-sharp and dire indeed. At any rate, he had not long settled before stirring, however furtively, and rising up in the night like a hunched blot on rocks white in the moonlight. Then, pausing only to listen to Tarra's deep breathing and so ensure he slept, (which still he did not, and which Dyzm knew well enough) the old man made his way up the terraces and quickly became one with the shadows.

Tarra watched him go through slitted eyes, then replaced his sword-stump in its scabbard, rose up and followed silently behind. And no hesitation this time, no feeling of guilt or question of "trust" to bother his mind. No, for his thoughts on Hadj Dyzm had commenced to come together, and the puzzle was beginning to take on form. How the last pieces of that puzzle would fall into place, Tarra could not yet say, but he had an idea that his immediate future—perhaps his entire future—might well depend upon it.

Straight to the waterfall went Hadj Dyzm's shadow in the night, with that of Hrossak fleeting not too far behind; so that this time Tarra saw the old man pass *behind* that shining spout of water, his back to the cliff, feet shuffling along a projecting ledge, and so out of sight. Tarra waited for long moments, but no sign of the oldster emerging from the other side. The Hrossak scratched impatiently at an itch on his shoulder, scuffed his feet and adjusted the scabbard across his back. Still no sign of Hadj.

Taking jewelled hilt of sword with its precious inches of steel in hand, finally Tarra ventured on to the ledge and behind the fall—and saw at once whereto the wily old tomb-looter had disappeared. Behind the fall, hollowed by water's rush through untold centuries, a moist cavern reached back into forbidding gloom. But deep within was light, where a flickering torch sputtered in a bracket fixed to the wall. Tarra went to the torch and found others prepared where they lay in a dry niche. Taking one up and holding it to the flame until it caught sputtering life of its own, he followed a trail of footprints in the dust of the floor, moving ever deeper into the heart of the cliff. And always ahead a coil of blue smoke hanging in the musty air, by which he was doubly sure that Dyzm had passed this way.

Now the passage grew narrow, then wider; here it was high-ceilinged, there low; but as the light of the flambeau behind him grew fainter and fainter with distance, until a bend shut it off entirely, and as Tarra burrowed deeper and deeper, so he became aware of more than the work of nature here, where ever increasingly the walls were carved with gods and demons, with stalactites cut in the likenesses of kings and queens seated upon dripstone thrones. A gallery of the gods, this place—of an entire mythology long-forgotten, or almost forgotten—and of them that worshipped, or used to worship, the Beings of that paleogaean pantheon.

Tarra gave an involuntary shudder as he crept silently twixt grinning gargoyles and doomful demons, past looming, tentacled krakens and pschent-crowned, widemouthed *things* not so much men as long-headed lizards; and it was here, coming round a second bend in the passage and suddenly into a great terminal chamber, that he reached the very heart of this secret, once-sacred place.

Or was it the heart?

For here—where the ceiling reached up beyond the limits of torchlight, from which unsighted dome massy, morbidly carven daggers of rock depended, and where the stalagmites formed flattened pedestals now for teratological grotesques beyond the Hrossak's staggered imagination—here the footprints in the dust led directly to a central area where blazed another faggot, this one thrust callously into talon of a staring stone man-lizard. And at this idol's clawed feet more bound bundles of dry wood, their knobs all pitched over.

Tarra lit a second torch and followed Dyzm's trail a few paces more, to the exact centre of the chamber. Which was where the trail ended—or rather, descended!

Between twin stalagmite thrones of winged, tentacled krakens, (images of loathly Lord Cthulhu, Tarra knew from olden legends of his homeland) steps cut from the very rock commenced what seemed a dizzy spiral dive into unknown bowels of earth. And up from that yawning pit came the reek of Dyzm's torch, and from vaults unguessed came clatter of pebbles inadvertently dislodged.

Now Tarra knew at this stage that he had come far enough. He felt it in his water: commonsense advising that he now retrace his steps. But to what end? No use now to plead ignorance of the oldster's secret, for certainly Dyzm would note the absence or use of two of his tarry torches. And anyway, 'twas curiosity had led the Hrossak on, not greed for more than he'd been offered. In no way did he wish any harm upon the other, (not at this stage of the adventure, anyway) but by the same token he saw no good reason why he should remain, as it were, in the dark in respect of the subterranean treasure vaults. Also he desired to know why, in the dead of night, any man should require to venture down into this place. What was it that lured the oldster? More treasure? But surely there would be time enough for that later? Alas, Tarra failed to take into account the greed of some men, which is limitless. To them those fabulous regions "Beyond the Dreams of Avarice" do not exist!

And so he set foot upon the first step, then the second, and by yellow light of flaring brand descended—but not very far. At the end of a single steep twist the corkscrew ended in a smaller chamber, where once again two stony sons of Cthulhu sat facing each other—this time across a circular shaft whose sides fell smooth and sheer into darkness. And here, too, some curious machinery: a drum of rope with pulleys, a winding handle and large copper bucket, all made fast to the weighty pedestal of one of the Cthulhu images. And tied to the other pedestal, a rope ladder whose rungs went down into gloom. Tarra peered over the rim and saw down there at some indeterminate depth the flickering light of Hadj Dyzm's torch.

Now the Hrossak examined the rope ladder more carefully, and satisfied himself that it was made of pretty stout stuff. Seating himself on the rim of the shaft, he leaned his weight on the ladder's rungs—and they supported him effortlessly. He began to lower himself—and paused.

Again that niggling mini-Tarra, the one that dwelled in the back of his mind, was whispering cautionary things to him. But cautioning of what? If an old man dared venture here at this hour, surely there could be little of any real danger? Tarra silenced the frantic whisperer in his head and peered about.

Seated there at pit's rim, he aimed his torch in all directions. There were unexplored niches and recesses in the walls here, true, and also he had this sensation of hooded eyes, of someone watching. But how possibly? By whom, watched? These stony idols, perhaps! And Tarra snorted his abrupt dismissal of the idea. At any rate, Hadj Dyzm was below, as witness the flare of his torch. Ah, well, only one thing for it—

And clenching the thin end of the faggot between his teeth, he once more set feet to rope rungs and began to descend. Up until which time, Tarra had not erred...

The flue swiftly widened out, like the neck of a jar, and at a count of only thirty rungs Tarra touched floor. There was the torch he had seen from above, guttering now on this cavern's floor, but of Hadj Dyzm—

The Hrossak stood with one hand on the ladder and turned in a slow circle, holding high his torch. Over there...more statues of Cthulhu and others of his pantheon. And over here...an open box carved from solid rock, its heaped contents spilling over on to the floor. But *such* contents!

Tarra stepped as in a dream toward that fabulous hoard, and reaching it heard Dyzm's hoarse, echoing chuckle—*from above*!

He fell into a crouch, spun on his heel, leaped back toward the ladder—in time to see it whisked up, out of sight. And more important far, out of reach. So that now Tarra knew how sorely he'd been fooled, and how surely he was trapped.

"Hrossak?" came Dyzm's guttural query from overhead. "You, Tarra Khash—do you hear me?"

"Loud and clear, trustworthy one!" Tarra almost choked on the words.

"Then hearken a while," the other chortled, "and I'll tell you *all* the tale, for I've seen what a curious lad you are and I'm sure you'll be enthralled."

"By all means," Tarra growled. "Why, you might say I'm a captive audience!" And he too laughed, but a trifle bitterly.

"In all truth," said Dyzm, "I really did come out of Eyphra with a caravan—but of sheerest necessity, I assure you. Mayhap you've heard of the sulphur pits twixt Eyphra and Chill Sea?"

Tarra had: effluvium of extinct blowholes, the pits were worked by a penal colony under the watchful, cruel eyes of guards little better than criminals themselves. It was said that men aged ten years for every one spent in those hellholes, and that their skins rapidly grew withered and yellow from…the…work!

Withered and yellow, aye. Which was a fair description of the way Tarra's brain felt right now.

He sighed, shook his head in dismay, sat down in the dust. He looked up. "You escaped, hey?"

"Not so fast, Hrossak! Oh, you're right, I was there, indeed I was—for three long years! And all that time spent planning my escape, which is all anyone does in that place, until finally it became imperative. You see, there was a ragged bone of a man in that place with me, and before he died he spoke to me of this place. His directions couldn't be simpler: come around the southern tip of the Mountains of Lohmi until you find a waterfall and pool, and so on. He had been here, you see, coming upon this place (quite genuinely) by accident. Later, weighed down with treasure, he'd fallen into the hands of mountain men. They were so awed by what he had with him that they let him live, even let him keep a bauble or two before cuffing him about a bit and pointing him in the direction of Eyphra. Aye, and weeks later he'd stumbled into that suspicious city a ragged starveling, filthy and verminous, so that when the people saw his few paltry nuggets and gems… Why! What else could he be but a thief? And so they'd taken away the last of his trove and sent him to dig in the sulphur pits, which was where I met him when they sent me there for murder. Ah!—but he'd already been there for four years, and it was something of a legend how long Death had fruitlessly stalked him. However that may be, all men must die in the end. And he was no exception…

"Now then: oft and again he'd told me the tale of these treasure vaults, but never how to get here until the very end, with the last gasp of his dying. And by then I knew he told the truth, for dying, what use would he have for lies? He knew he was finished, you see, and so had nothing to lose.

"For that matter, neither had I much to lose; which was why, at first opportunity, I ran off. No easy task, Tarra Khash, flight from the sulphur pits. I left three guards dead in my wake, and a fourth crippled, but at last I was free and running. Aye, and now I had somewhere to run.

"Bits of jewelry I'd taken from the dead guards bought me third-class passage on a caravan I met with where it entered the pass through Lohmi's peaks, following which I spent a deal of my time with a pair of guides, converting them from their loyalty to the caravan's master to my own cause. Ah!—but it's a powerful lure, treasure, as you've discovered."

Here Tarra gruffly interrupted. "What? *Hah!* You can have all your much-vaunted tomb-loot, Hadj Dyzm. Keep it and good luck to you. Nothing more than cursed curiosity caused me to follow you, and more fool me for that!"

Again Dyzm's chuckle, but darker now. "Well, and doubtless you've heard what curiosity did for the cat?"

Tarra nodded, almost groaning in his frustration. But then he took a deep breath, clenched his fists until the muscles of his arms bulged, and said: "But I've also heard how cats have nine lives. Be sure, Hadj Dyzm, that in one of them, this mouser will catch up with a certain rat!"

"Come now, Hrossak!" gurgled the other. "What's this I detect in your tone? Do you dare, in your unenviable position, to threaten? It bodes not well for our future dealings, I think! Be careful what you say. Better let me finish before you drop yourself even deeper in the mire. You see, I'm not an unreasonable man, and for all your treachery, I—"

"*My* treachery!" Tarra once more cut in, unable to believe his ears.

"Certainly. Didn't you follow me when I tended my camels in the dusk, spying on me all the way? I had thought you might discover the cave behind the falls there and then. But no, you needed more encouragement. And so I gave you it—tonight! Aye, and haven't you admitted following me here, as I'd known you would? Curiosity, you say. But should I believe that? Am I as great a fool as you, then?"

"Amazing!" Tarra gasped. "And I'm talking to a self-confessed murderer!"

"Several times over!" Dyzm emphatically agreed. "And they need-ed killing all—but in any case, that's quite another matter, part of an entirely separate set of circumstances. Now hear me out:

"Where was I? Ah, yes—

"—So, there I was journeying with the caravan, putting a deal of distance twixt myself and sulphur pits, and along the way recruiting for my treasure hunt. And half-way down Lohmi's eastern flank, lo! the mountain men struck. In great numbers, too. Now, perhaps on another occasion my converted guides might have stayed and fought and died for their rightful master, but now they had a new master and he had promised them riches. Once more the old principle surfaces, Tarra Khash. Namely: a poor man will risk his all for very little gain, but a rich man's lust for life is that much stronger. Hasn't he more to live for? So it was with the guides: my whispers had set deepest desires in motion, creating a conflict of loyalties. The choice was this: stay and remain poor and perhaps die—or flee and live and grow fat and rich. Need I say more? I doubt it..."

"You lured the traitors here," Tarra nodded, "leaving caravan and all to tender mercy of mountain-bred barbarians. Very well, and where are your disciples now?"

"Alas, I know not," said Dyzm, and the Hrossak sensed his shrug. "Except that you are closer to them than I am."

"What?" Tarra gave a start, peering all about at the flickering shadows cast by his dying torch. (Hadj's upon the floor, had long since expired.) "Are you saying that they're down here?"

"Aye, somewhere. More than that I can't say; I've not seen them for a bit..." And this time Dyzm's chuckle was deep and doomful indeed.

"You mean some harm's befallen them, and you've made no effort to find and save them?"

"What? Lower myself down there?" the other feigned shock at the very suggestion. "Haven't I explained? You speak to a man who toiled three long years in the sulphur pits, remember? And you think I would willingly incarcerate myself in another of Earth's dark holes? For be sure such would be prison to me and surely drive me mad! No, not I, Tarra Khash."

And now the Hrossak, for all that he was a hard man, felt genuinely sickened to his stomach. "You let them starve down here!" he accused, spitting out the sour bile of his mouth into the dust.

"I did not!" Dyzm denied. "Indeed I would have fed them well. Meat and fishes aplenty—water, too, if they'd needed it. My promise was this: a meal each time they half-filled this bucket here with gold and jewels. Any more than that and the rope might break, d'you see? And given a stouter rope they'd doubtless swarm up it. Anyway, starve they did not and my promise was, after all, redundant..."

"And that was their only incentive, that so long as they worked you would feed them?" Tarra shook his head in disgust. "'Young bucks,' you called them. Frightened pups, it seems to me!"

"Ah, no," answered Dyzm. "More than hunger goaded them, that has to be admitted."

His words—the way he spoke them, low and phlegmy, almost lingeringly—set Tarra's skin to tingling. After a while, in as steady a voice as he could muster, he said: "Well, then, say on old fox: what other incentives goaded them? Or better still get straight to the point and tell me how they died."

"Two things I'll tell you—" Dyzm's voice was light again, however throaty, "—about incentives. And one other thing about my age, for this fox is in no way old. 'Aged' I am, aye—by dint of sulphur steam in my throat and lungs, and my skin all yellowed from its sting—but not aged, if you see the distinction. And my belly puffed and misshapen from years of hunger, and likewise my limbs gnarly from hard labour. But my true years can't number a great many more than your own, Tarra Khash, and that's a bitter fact."

"I'd marked all that for myself," said Tarra, "but—"

"But let me speak!" Dyzm's turn to interrupt. And: "Incentives, you wanted. Very well. One: I would take four half-buckets of treasure— only four—and then lower the ladder and let them up, and all three of us would get our share. Two: the quicker they got to work and began filling the bucket, the better for them, for their time would likely be...limited."

Limited? Tarra liked not the word. "By the amount of food you could provide?"

"No, game is plentiful in and around the lake, as you've seen. Guess again."

"By the number of torches you could readily prepare, whose light the two would need in order to do your bidding?"

"No, the preparation of torches proved in no way inconvenient."

Tarra frowned. "Then in what way limited?"

He heard Dyzm's gurgly, self-satisfied sigh. "I cannot be sure," he finally said. "It was only…something that my friend in the sulphur pits warned me about."

"Oh?"

"Aye, for I also had it from him—in his dying breath, mind you, which was a deep one—that the ancient race of kings whose tombs and treasures these were, had set certain guardians over their sepulchres and sarcophagi, and that even now the protective spells of long-dead wizards were morbidly extant and active. Which is to say that the place is cursed, Tarra Khash, and that the longer you stay down there—in what you will shortly discover to be a veritable labyrinth of tombs—the more immediate the horror!"

IV

Horror? And the Hrossak cared for *that* word not at all! Nor on this occasion did he doubt the veracity of what Dyzm had said: it would explain why the pool and country around had not been settled. Nomads and hill men alike were wary of such places, as well they might be. Finally he found voice: "And the nature of this doom?"

"Who can say," Dyzm replied. "Not I, for the two who went before you did not live to tell me. But they did tell me this: that in a certain tomb are twin statues of solid gold, fashioned in the likeness of winged krakens not unlike the dripstone idols of these cavern antechambers. And having loaded three half-buckets of treasure for me, they went off together to fetch me one of these statues; their last trip, as would have been. Alas, they returned not… But you need a fresh torch, Hrossak, for that one dies." He let fall a fat faggot and Tarra quickly fired it.

"Now then," Dyzm continued in a little while, "this is what I propose. Find for me that tomb and fetch me a kraken of gold, and that will suffice."

"Suffice?"

"I shall then be satisfied that you are a sincere man and worthy to be my partner in future ventures. And when I have the statue, then shall I lower the ladder and we'll be off to Chlangi together, and so on to Klühn."

Tarra could not keep from laughing, albeit a mite hysterically. "Am I to believe this? Fool I am, Hadj Dyzm—great fool, as you've well proved—but *such* a fool?"

"Hmm!" Dyzm gruffly mused. He dropped more torches. "Well, think it over. I can wait a while. How long the demon guardians will wait is a different matter. Meanwhile: 'ware below!—I lower the bucket." And down came the bucket on the end of its rope.

Tarra at once tugged at the rope, testing it, and as the bucket came to rest upon the floor he swung himself aloft, climbing by strength of his arms alone. Man-high he got—and not an inch higher. With soft, twangy report rope parted, and down crashed Hrossak atop bucket and all. "*Ow!*" he complained, getting up on his feet.

Above, Dyzm chuckled. "Ow, is it?" he said. "Worse than that, Tarra Khash, if the rope had held! Did you think I'd sit here and do nothing until you popped up out of the hole? I've a knife here you could shave with, to cut you, or rope, or both. Oh, I know, 'twas desperation made you try it. Well, you've tried and failed, so an end to tomfooleries, eh? Now I'll lower the rope some and you can make a knot; after which you can get off and find me my kraken statue. But a warning: any more heroics and I'll make you fetch both!"

"Very well," Tarra answered, breathing heavily, "but first tell me something. Right here, a pace or two away, lies a great stone box of treasure. Doubtless your two dragged it here for you. Now tell me: why were its contents never hauled aloft?"

"Ah!" said Dyzm. "That would be their fourth haul, when they told me about the statues. I had forgotten."

"So," said the Hrossak, nodding, "returning with this box— their *fourth* haul and not the third, as you first alleged—these idiots told you about the golden, winged kraken idols, so that you spurned this latest haul in favour of the greater marvel they described. Is that it?"

"Something like that, aye. I'm glad you reminded me. Perhaps before you get off searching you'd like to—"

"I would *not* like to!" answered Hrossak hotly. "It's either contents of this box *or* one of these damned idols—if I can find 'em—but not both. Which, I rather fancy, is what they told you, too."

Hadj Dyzm was peeved. "Hmm!" he grumbled. "Perhaps you're not so daft after all, Hrossak. But…I've set my heart on an idol, and so you'd better be off, find and fetch it."

"Not so fast," said Tarra. "Your word before I go: you *will* fetch me up, when I return with statue?" (Even though he knew very well that Hadj Dyzm would not.)

"My word," said the other, very gravely.

"So be it," said the Hrossak. "Now, which way do I go?"

"I was right after all," said Dyzm, sighing. "You are daft—and deaf to boot! How should I know which way you must go? I would suggest you follow prints on dusty floor, as so recently you followed mine…"

V

A little while later Tarra knew exactly what the fox had meant by a labyrinth. Following sandal prints in the dust, he moved from cavern to cavern, and all of them alike as cells in a comb of honey. A veritable necropolis, this place, where bones were piled about the walls in terrible profusion, and skulls heaped high as a man's waist. Not all dead kings, these ossified remains; no, for most wore fetters about their ankles, or heaps of rust where ages had eaten the metal away. And about their shoulders small wooden yokes turned almost to stone; and each skeleton's right hand with its little finger missing, to mark him (or her) as property of the king.

Tarra wrinkled his nose. They had been savages in those days, he thought, for all their trappings of civilization, their carving and metal-moulding, their love of jewelry, their long-forgotten death-rituals, of which these bones formed the merest crumbling relics. Still, no time to ponder the ways of men whose race was old when the desert was young; there was much to be done, and not all of Hrossak's searching concerned with golden idols, either!

Tarra Khash remembered all too clearly the years he'd spent trapped in Nud Annoxin's well-cell in Thinhla. Hah!—he'd never thought to be in just such predicament again. And yet now…? Well, life is short enough; it was not Tarra's intention to spend the rest of his down here. Ideas were slowly dawning, taking shape in his brain like wraiths of mist over fertile soil as he pondered the problem.

Shuddering a little (from the cold of the place, he told himself, for he had not brought his blanket with him) he passed through more of the domed caves, always following the print tracks where they were most dense—but to one side of them, so that his own trail would be clear and fresh—and knowing that these ways had been explored before. At least he had something of an advantage in that; but they, his predecessors, had had each other's company. Company?—in this place of death Tarra would be satisfied right now by sight of rat, let alone fellow man!

His predecessors... He wondered what fate had overtaken them. Aye, and perhaps he'd soon enough find that out, too.

But for now—if he could only find something to use as grapple. And something else as rope. For the fox couldn't sit up there for ever. He too must eat and drink. Grapple and rope, aye—but what to use? A long golden chain, perhaps? No, too soft and much too heavy, and all other metal doubtless rotten or rusted utterly away. And Tarra aware with every passing moment, as ideas were first considered, then discarded, that the "guardians" of this place—*if* they weren't merely frighteners conjured out of Hadj Dyzm's own imagination—might even now be waking!

Such were his thoughts as he came by light of flaring faggot into a central chamber large by comparison as that of a queen at the centre of her hive. A queen, or a king, or many such. For here the walls had been cut into deep niches, and each niche containing massy sarcophagus carved from solid rock, and all about these centuried coffins the floor strewn with wealth untold!

But in the middle of this circular, high-domed cavern, there reposed the mightiest tomb of all: a veritable mausoleum, with high marble ceiling of its own held up by fluted marble columns, and an entrance guarded by—

Guarded? The word was too close to "guardian" to do a lot for Tarra's nerves. But like it or not the tomb *was* guarded—by a pair of golden krakens, wings and all, seated atop onyx pedestals, one on each side of the leering portal. Somewhat awed (for this must surely be the last resting place of the greatest of all these ancient monarchs) the Hrossak moved forward and stuck his torch in the rib-cage of a skeleton where it lay at the foot of the pedestal on the left...stuck it there and slowly straightened up, felt gooseflesh crawl on naked arms and thighs and back—and leapt backward as if fanged by viper!

Long moments Tarra stood there then, in torchlight flickering, with heart pounding, longing to flee full tilt but nailed to the spot as if his feet had taken root in solid rock. And all the while his gaze rapt upon that cadaver whose ribs supported hissing brand, *that skeleton which even now wore ragged robe, upon whose bony feet were leather sandals of the sort had made those recent prints in dust of ages!*

The Hrossak took a breath—and another—and forced his hammering heart to a slower pace and the trembling of his limbs to marble stillness. And breathing deeply a third time, he slowly crouched and leaned forward, studying morbid remains more closely. The bones were burned as from some mordant acid. In places their pitted surfaces were sticky and shiny-black with tarry traces, possibly burnt and liquefied marrow. Tatters of skin still attached, but so sere and withered as to be parchment patches, and the skull...that was worst of all.

Yawning jaws gaped impossibly wide in frozen scream, and torch-flung shadows shifted in empty sockets like frightened ghosts of eyes. Still crouching, shuddering, Tarra took up his torch and held it out at arm's length toward the other pedestal. As he had suspected (without, as yet, knowing *why* he suspected) a second skeleton, in much the same condition, sprawled beneath the other kraken. And again the word "guardians" seemed to echo in Hrossak's head.

But the images were only of gold, not loathsome flesh and alien ichor, and even were they alive—if they were, indeed, *the* guardians—their size would hardly make them a threat. Why, they were little more than octopuses, for all the goldsmith's loathsome skill!

Tarra gazed into sightless golden eyes, glanced at wings folded back, laid his hands upon tentacles half-lifted, apparently in groping query. Cold gold, in no wise threatening. And yet it seemed to the Hrossak there was a film of moisture, of some nameless tomb-slime, on the surface of the metal, making it almost slippery to the touch. That wouldn't be much help when it came to carrying the thing. And if he could not find means to manufacture grapnel and rope, then for certain he must put his faith in Hadj Dyzm—initially, anyway.

He moved round behind the pedestal, closed his arms about the belly of the idol until his hands clasped his elbows, lifted. Heavy, aye, but he thought it would fit into the bucket. Only...would the rope be strong enough?

Rope! And again a picture of rope and grapple burned on the surface of his mind's eye. Tarra eased the idol back on to its pedestal, bent down and tore at the tatters which clothed the mysteriously slain cadaver. At his touch they crumbled away. Whatever it was seared the bones—seared the flesh *from* those bones—it had also worked on the coarse cloth. No, he could hardly make a rope out of this rotten stuff; but now he had a better idea. Dyzm himself would furnish the rope!

First, however—

He checked his torch, which was beginning to burn a trifle low, then turned toward the open door of the sepulchre. This was sheer curiosity, he knew—and he minded what Hadj Dyzm had said of curiosity—but still he had to know what sort of king it was whose incarceration in some dim bygone age had warranted mass slaughter in and about these tomb-caves.

Pausing before the high, dark portal, he thrust out torch before him and saw within—

No carven coffin here but a massive throne, and seated thereon a shrivelled mummy all of shiny bone and leather, upright and proud and fused to marble seat by nameless ages. Indeed, the very fossil of a thing. A *thing*, aye, for the huge creature was not and had never been human...

Entering, Tarra approached a throne whose platform was knee-high, staring up at what in its day must have been a fearsome sight. Even now the thing was terrifying. But...it was dead, and dead things can hurt no one. Can they?

He held his torch high.

The mummy was that of a lizard-man, tall, thin and long-headed; with fangs curving down from fleshless jaws, and leathery chin still sprouting a goatlike beard of coarse hair; and upon its head a jewelled pschent, and in its talon of a hand a sceptre or knobby wand of ebony set with precious stones.

So this had been the living creature whose likeness Tarra had seen carved from the dripstone of the upper caves. Also, it had been a king of kings, and crueller far than any merely human king. He looked again at the wand. A fascinating thing, the Hrossak reached up his hand to jewelled, ebony rod, giving it a tug. But it was now one with dry claw, welded there by time. He tugged harder—and heard from behind him a low rumble!

In the next split second several things. First: Tarra remembered again his dream of a great slab door slamming shut. Then: he saw that in fact the wand was not held fast in claw but attached by golden link to a lever in the arm of the throne. Finally: even thinking these thoughts he was hurling himself backward, diving, slithering out of tomb on his belly as the door, falling in an arc from the inner ceiling, came thundering down. Then Tarra feeling that monstrous counterbalanced slab brushing his heels, and its gongy reverberations exactly as he had dreamed them!

His torch had gone flying, skittering across the floor in a straight line; but now, its impetus spent, it rolled a little in the dust. This had the effect of damping the flame. Still rolling, it flickered lower, came to rest smoking hugely from a dull red knob. The darkness at once crept in...

Ignoring his fear (snarling like a great hound at his back) Hrossak leapt to the near-extinguished brand, gathered it up, spun with it in a rushing, dizzy circle. This had the double effect of creating a protective ring about himself in the sudden, gibbering darkness, and of aerating the hot heart of the faggot, which answered by bursting into bright light. The shadows slunk back, defeated.

Panting, fighting to control mind and flesh alike, for this last close call had near unmanned him, the Hrossak suddenly found himself angry. Now berserker he was not—not in the way of the blood-crazy Northmen of the fjords—but when Tarra Khash was roused he really *was* roused. Right now he was mad at himself for ignoring his own instincts in the first place, mad at whichever ancient architect had designed this place as death-trap, mad at his predicament (which might yet prove permanent,) but most of all mad at the miserable and much loathed Hadj Dyzm, who must now be made to pay for all. Nor was Hrossak temper improved much by the fact that the skin of his hands, arms and chest had now commenced to itch and burn terribly, an affliction for which he could find no good cause or reason unless—

—Unless nothing!—for these were precisely the areas of his person which he had pressed against the golden kraken idol!

Was that vile metallic sweat he had noticed upon the thing some sort of stinging acid, then? Some poison? If so, patently the centuries had detracted from its potency. Before striding from the main chamber and following his own trail back toward the entrance shaft, Tarra stooped, scooped up dust, layered it upon the stinging areas. Also, he glanced once more at the golden idols.

They crouched, gleaming, upon their pedestals exactly as before... and yet somehow—different? Were they not, perhaps, more upright? Did their eyes not seem about to pop open? Had their tentacles not stretched outward fractionally, perhaps threateningly, and was not the sheen of slime upon their metal surfaces that much thicker and slimier?

The Hrossak snorted. So much for a wild imagination! But enough of that, now he must put his plan into action without delay. This place was dangerous; something hideous had happened to the men who came here before him; time was wasting and there could well be other horrors down here which as yet Tarra knew nothing about. He returned quickly to where the bucket lay upon the floor at the end of its rope.

"Ho!" came Hadj Dyzm's harsh greeting as Tarra fired a fresh torch. "And where's my idol, Hrossak?"

Tarra looked up. Dyzm's evil face peered down from ceiling hole, but anxiously, Tarra thought. "Oh, I've found your damned idols, foxy one," he called up, "and nearly came to grief doing it! This place is booby-trapped, and I was very nearly the booby!"

"But the idol," Dyzm pressed. "Where is it?"

Tarra thought fast. "Three things," he said. "First: the kraken idols lie on a lower level. Not deep, but impossible to scale carrying idol. Second: I have a solution for first. Third: as you've seen, I had to return for fresh torch."

"Clown!" snapped Dyzm. "Waster of time! Why did you not take spare faggot with you?"

"An oversight," Tarra agreed. "Do you want to hear my solution?"

"Get on with it."

"I need hauling gear—namely, a rope."

"What's this?" Dyzm was suspicious.

"To hoist idol up from below," Tarra lied again. "Also, 'twere a good test: a chance to see if the rope is strong enough."

"Explain."

"Easy: if the rope breaks from weight of kraken alone, certainly it will break with bucket and idol both."

"Ah!" Dyzm's suspicion seemed confirmed. "You want me to toss down the bucket rope in order to make yourself a grappling hook."

Tarra feigned exasperation. "What? Have I not already tried to climb, and did not the rope break? The idol, however, is fairly small, not quite the weight of a man."

"Hmm! How much rope do you need?"

Enough to hang you! Tarra thought, but out loud he said: "Oh, about ten man-lengths."

"What?" Dyzm spluttered. "You're surely mad, Hrossak! Am I then to give you a length *twice* as long as distance between us? Now surely you plan to make a grapnel!"

"Of what?" Tarra sighed. "Crumbling bones for hook, or soft gold, perhaps? Now who's wasting time? Even if it were possible, how could I climb with you up there to cut me or rope or both with your sharp knife? 'Twas you pointed that out in the first place, remember? And anyway, I have your promise to let down the ladder—or had you forgotten that too?"

"Now, now, lad—don't go jumping to hasty conclusions." Tarra could hear him shuffling about a little; a thin trickle of dust drifted down from above; finally:

"Very well, assume I give you the length of rope you say you need. What then?"

"First I fetch the idol. Then you lower what rope you have left, and I tie mine to it. Ah!—and to be certain it won't break, we use a double length. You then haul up idol in bucket. And if you're worried about me swarming up the rope, well, you still have your knife, right? *Then*—you toss down rope ladder for me. And the last quickly, for already I've had enough of this place!"

Dyzm considered it again, said: "Done!"

A moment later and the rope began coiling in bottom of bucket, and as it coiled so Tarra gazed avidly at the heavy *handle* of that container, which he knew he could bend into a perfect hook for hurling! Finally Dyzm cut the rope, let its end fall.

"There!" he called down. "Ten man-lengths."

Tarra loosened the rope from bucket handle, coiled it in loops over one shoulder. He must now play out the game to its full. Obviously he could neither make nor use grapple with Dyzm still up there, and so must first ensure his departure.

"Incidentally," he said, in manner casual. "Those booby-traps I mentioned. It wasn't one such which killed your last two partners."

And, "Eh?" from above, in voice startled. "How do you mean? Did you find them?"

"Aye, what's left of them. Obviously the work of your unknown 'guardians,' Hadj. But these caves are extensive, possibly reaching out for many miles under the desert. The guardians—whatever they are—must be elsewhere. If they were here...then were we both dead in a trice!"

"Then were *you* dead in a trice, you mean," the other corrected.

But Tarra only shook his head. "Both of us," he insisted. "I found one of your lads on a high, narrow ledge near-inaccessible. He was all broken in parts and the flesh slurped off him. The other, in like condition, lay in narrow niche no more than a crack in the wall—but the horrors had found him there, for sure. And would the funnel of this well stop them? I doubt it."

The other was silent.

Tarra started away, keeping his head down and grinning grimly to himself; but Dyzm at once called him to a halt. "Hrossak—do you have any idea of the true nature of these guardians?"

"Who can say?" Tarra was mysterious. "Perhaps they slither, or flop. Likely, they fly! One thing for sure: they suck flesh from bones easy as leeches draw blood!" And off he went.

Now this was the Hrossak's plan: that he wait a while, then cause a loud commotion of screaming and such, and shrieking, "The guardians! The guardians!" and gurgling most horribly until Hadj Dyzm must surely believe him dead. All of which to be performed, of course, right out of sight of him above. Then utter silence (in which Tarra hoped to detect sounds of fox's frenzied flight), and back to break handle from bucket, form grapnel, attach double length of rope, and so escape. Then to track villain down and break his scrawny neck!

That had been his first plan...

But now, considering it again, Tarra had second thoughts. Since he must wait down here for at least a little while, why not turn the interval to his own advantage? For even now, if things went wrong—if for instance, the real guardians came on the scene—he might still have to rely on Hadj Dyzm to get him out of here quickly. His chance of the latter happening, especially now, after putting the fears up the fox, were slim, he knew; but any port in a storm. Better slim chance than no chance at all. And so it were best if he *appeared* to be following Hadj's instructions right up to the very end. Anyway, the thought of stealing one of the idols was somehow appealing.

With these thoughts on his mind, he rapidly retraced his steps to the cave of the golden krakens where they waited on their pedestals before the tomb of the lizard-king, and—

By light of flaring torch the Hrossak gaped at transformation taken place in the idols. For they did *not* wait atop their pedestal—not exactly. And now, truth slowly dawning, Tarra began to discern the real nature of the curse attaching to these subterranean tombs. Doubtless the alien monarchs of this long-extinct race had been great wizards, whose spells and maledictions had reached down through dim and terrible centuries. But in the end even the most powerful spells lose their potency, including this one. What must in its primordial origin have been a swift metamorphosis indeed were turned now to tortuously slow thing—but deadly thing for all that, as witness the pair of charred cadavers.

With creep impossibly slow—so slow the eye could scarce note it—the kraken idols were moving. And doubtless the process was gradually speeding up even as the spell persisted. For they had commenced to slither down the length of their pedestals, sucker arms clinging to the tops as they imperceptibly lowered themselves. Their eyes were half-open now, and gemstone orbs gleamed blackly and evilly beneath lids of beaten gold. Moreover, the acid ooze which their bodies seemed to exude had thickened visibly, smoking a little where it contacted the onyx of the pedestals.

Tarra's first thought was of flight, but where to flee? Go back and tell Hadj Dyzm and the fiend would doubtless leave him here till krakens were fully transformed. And would there be sufficient time remaining to make and use grapnel? Doubtful...

Doom descended on the Hrossak's shoulders like an icy cloak; he felt weighed down by it. Was this to be the end then? Must he, too, succumb to kraken kiss, be turned to bag of scorched and tarry bones?

Aye, possibly—but not alone!

Filled now with dreams of red revenge, which stengthened him, Tarra ran forward and fastened a double loop of rope about the belly of the kraken on the left, yanking until its tentacle tips slipped free from rim of pedestal. And back through shadow-flickered caves he dragged the morbid, scarcely mobile thing, while acrid smoke curled up from rope, where an as yet sluggish acid ate into it. But the rope held and at last sweaty Hrossak emerged beneath the spot where Hadj Dyzm waited.

"Have you got it?" the fox eagerly, breathlessly called down.

"Aye," panted Tarra, "at the end of my rope. Now send down your end and prepare to wind away." And he rolled the bucket out of sight, as if in preparation.

Down came Hadj's rope without delay, and Tarra knotting it to the middle of *his* length, and Hadj taking up the slack. Then the Hrossak hauled kraken into view, and fox's gasp from above. "Beautiful!" he croaked, for he saw only the gold and not the monstrous mutation, the constantly accelerating mobility of the thing.

The rope where it coiled kraken's belly was near burned through now, so Tarra made fresh loops under reaching tentacles and back of wings. Once he inadvertently touched golden flesh of monster—and had to bite his lip to keep from shouting his agony, as the skin of his knuckles blackened and cracked!

But at last, "Haul away!" he cried; and chortling greatly the fox took the strain and commenced turning the handle of his gear. And such was his greed that the bucket was now forgotten. But Tarra had not forgotten it.

And so, as mass of transmuting gold-flesh slowly ascended in short jerks, turning like a plumb bob on its line, Hrossak stepped into shadow and tore handle from bucket, quickly bending it into a hook. Stepping back, he thrust hook through loop of rope before it was drawn up too high, and standing beneath suspended idol cried: "Now let down the ladder, Hadj Dyzm, as agreed, lest I impede your progress with my own weight. For it's a fact you can't lift idol and me both!"

"One thing at a time," the other answered. "First the idol."

"Damn you, Hadj!" cried Tarra, hanging something of his weight on the hook to let the other see he was in earnest—only to have the hook straighten out at once and slip from loop, leaving Tarra to fall to his knees. And by the time he was back on his feet, rope and idol and all had been dragged up well beyond his reach, and Hadj's chuckle echoing horribly from on high—for a little while.

Then, while Hrossak stood clenching and unclenching his fists and scowling, Hadj's voice in something of a query: "Hrossak—what's this nasty reek I smell?" (And idol slowly turning on its line, disappearing up the flue.)

"The reek of my sweat," answered Tarra, "mingled with smoke of torch's dying—aye, and in all likelihood my dying, too!" He stepped out of harm's way as droplets hissed down from above, smoking where they struck the floor. And now the idol almost as high as the rim, and droplets of acid slime falling faster in a hissing rain.

Tarra kept well back, listening to fox's grunting as he worked the gear—his grunting, then his squawk of surprise, and at last his shriek of sheerest horror!

In his mind's eye Tarra could picture it all in great detail:

The gear turning, winding up the rope, a ratchet holding it while Hadj Dyzm rested his muscles before making the next turn. And the kraken coming into view, a thing of massy, gleamy gold. Another turn, and eyes no longer glazed glaring into Hadj's—and tentacles no longer leaden reaching—and acid no longer dilute squirting and hissing!

Then—

Still screaming to burst his heart—fat bundle of rags entwined in golden nightmare of living, lethal tentacles—Hadj and kraken and all came plummeting down the shaft. Even the rope ladder, though that fell only part way, hanging there tantalizingly beyond Hrossak's reach.

And Hadj's body broken but not yet dead, flopping on the floor in terrible grip, his flesh melting and steaming away, as Tarra bent the bucket's handle back into a hook and snatched up a length of good rope. And horror of horrors, now the *other* kraken slithering into view from out the dark, reaching to aid its evil twin!

Now the Hrossak cast for dear life; cast his hook up to where the lower rungs of the ladder dangled. Missed!—and another cast.

Hideous, hissing tentacles reaching for his ankles, vile vapour boiling up from no longer screaming fox; the entire chamber filled with loathsome reek—and the hook catching at last, dragging ladder with it to slime-puddled floor.

Then Tarra was aloft, and later he would not remember his hands on rungs at all. Only the blind panic and shrieking terror that seemed to hurl him up and out of the hole—and up the spiral steps—and down the long tunnel of carven stalactites to the waterfall—and so out into the night. And no pause even to negotiate the ledge behind the fall, but a mighty dive which took him through that curtain of falling water, out and down under the stars to strike the lake with hardly a splash; and then the exhausted swim back to shore against the whirlpool's pull, to where a fire's embers smouldered and guttered still.

After that—

Morning found a rich, rich man following the foothills east with his camels. And never a backward glance from Tarra Khash...

KISS OF THE LAMIA

Bully boys out of Chlangi they were, desperadoes riding forth
from that shunned city of yeggs and sharpers, on the lookout for
quick profits in the narrow strip twixt Lohmi's peaks and the Desert
of Sheb. And the lone Hrossak with his team of camels easy meat
where they caught him in ambush, by the light of blind old Gleeth,
god of the moon. Or at least, he *should* have been easy meat.

But the master and sole member of that tiniest of caravans was
Tarra Khash, and meat were rarely so tough. For all his prowess, however (which one day would be legended in all of Theem'hdra), the
brawny bronze steppeman was, on this occasion, caught short. With
only the stump of a jewelled, ceremonial scimitar to defend himself,
and nodding in the saddle as he let his mount pick out the way through
badland rockpiles and gulleys, Tarra was hardly prepared for the three
where they saw him coming and set their snare for him.

Indeed the first he knew of it was when a sighing arrow plunked
through the polished leather of the scabbard across his back, sank an
inch into his shoulder and near knocked him out of his saddle. Then,
as a second feathered shaft whistled by his ear, he was off the camel
and tumbling in dust and grit, his hand automatically grasping the
jewelled hilt of his useless sword. In the darkness all was a chaos of
shock and spurting blood and adrenalin; where wide awake now Tarra

heard the terrified snorting and coughing of his beasts, huddled to avoid their kicking hooves as they ran off; where the moonlight silvered the stony bones of some ruined, long-deserted pile, and where the dust of Hrossak's fall was still settling as stealthy shadows crept in upon him.

Out of the leering dark they came, eyes greenly ablaze in greed and blood-lust, darting in the shadows, and fleet as the moonbeams themselves where the way was lit by Gleeth's cold light and by the blue sheen of far stars. Men of the night they were, as all such are, as one with the darkness and silhouetted dunes.

Tarra lay still, his head down, eyes slitted and peering; and in a little while a booted foot appeared silently before his face, and he heard a hoarse voice calling: "Ho! He's finished—feathered, too! 'Twas my arrow nailed him! Come on, you two!"

Your arrow, hey, dog? Tarra silently snarled, coming from huddle to crouch, straightening and striking all in the same movement. The stump of his not-so-useless sword was a silver blur where it arced under a bearded jackal's chin, tearing out his taut throat even as he screamed: "He's al—*ach-ach-ach!*"

Close behind the Hrossak, someone cursed and gripped the arrow in his back, twisting it sharply. He cried out his agony—cut off as a mountain crashed down on the back of his skull—and without further protest crumpled to the earth.

Tarra was not dead, not even unconscious, though very nearly so. Stunned he lay there, aware only of motion about him in the night, and of voices gruff as grit, coming it seemed from far, far away:

"Gumbat Chud was ever a great fool. 'My arrow!' he yells, 'my arrow!' And this fellow meanwhile slitting his throat nice as that!"

And a different voice: "Is he dead?"

"Gumbat? Aye. See, he now has two mouths—and one of 'em scarlet!"

"Not him, no—the stranger."

"Him too, I fancy, I gave him such a clout. I think it almost a shame, since he's done us such a favour. Why, with Gumbat gone there's just the two of us now to share the spoils! So waste no time on this one. If arrow and clout both haven't done for him, the badlands surely will. Come on, let's get after his beasts and see what goods he hauled."

The other voice was harder, colder: "Best finish him, Hylar. Why spoil a good night's work by leaving this one, perchance to tell the tale?"

"To whom? But...I suppose you're right, Thull. We have had a good night, haven't we? First that girl, alone in the desert, wandering under the stars. Can you believe it?"

A coarse chuckle. "Oh, I believe it, all right. I was first with her, remember?"

"You were last with her, too—pig!" spat the first voice. And: "Well, get on with it, then. If you want this fellow dead, get it done. We've beasts to chase and miles to cover back to Chlangi. Pull out the arrow, that'll do for him. His life—if any's left—will leak out red as wine!"

Thull did as Hylar suggested, and shuddering as fresh waves of agony dragged him under, the Hrossak's mind shrank down into pits of the very blackest jet...

Tarra Khash the Hrossak, inveterate wanderer and adventurer, had a lust for life which drove him ever on where other men would fail. And it was that bright spark, that tenacious insistence upon life, which now roused him up before he could bleed to death. That and the wet, frothy ministrations of his camel, kneeling beside him in starlit ruins, where it washed his face and grunted its camel queries. This was the animal Tarra had used as mount, which, over the two hundred miles now lying in their wake, had grown inordinately fond of him. Eluding its pursuers, it had returned to its master much as a dog might do, and for the past half-hour had licked his face, kneed him in the ribs, and generally done whatever a camel might for a man.

Finally coming awake, Tarra gave its nose an admonitory slap and propped himself up into a seated position. He was cold but his back felt warm, stiff and sticky; aye, and he could feel a trickle of fresh blood where his movements had cracked open a half-formed scab. In the dirt close at hand lay the man he'd killed, Gumbat Chud, and between them a bloody arrow where it had been wrenched from his back and thrown down. Tarra's scabbard lay within reach, empty of its broken sword. They'd taken it for its jewels, of course.

Staring at the arrow, his blood dry on its point, Tarra remembered the conversation he'd heard before he blacked out. He especially remembered the names of the two who had stood over him: Hylar and Thull, Gumbat Chud's bandit brothers. Rogues out of Chlangi, aye— and dead ones when he caught up with them!

But for now...the Hrossak was fortunate and he knew it. Only a most unlikely set of circumstances had spared him. The ambushers might easily have slit his throat, but they hadn't wanted to waste time. Indeed, Chud's arrow might have missed the scabbard and hit his heart, which would have ended things at once! Also, the reavers could have caught instead his camel—this one, which carried food, water, blankets, all those things necessary for the maintenance of life—and probably had caught the three pack animals, which were far more heavily laden.

Heavily laden indeed!

Tarra thought about all the gold and jewels those animals carried: twelve full saddle bags! And wouldn't those badland marauders lose their eyeballs when they turned them on that lot! What a haul! Tarra almost wished he was one of his ambushers—except that wasn't his line of work. Ah, well: easy come, easy go—for now. Until he caught up with those two. Anyway, it was his own fault. Only a damn fool would have tried to take a king's ransom through a den of thieves and out the other side. And he'd known well enough Chlangi's reputation.

Tomb-loot—*hah*! Ill-gotten gains. And hadn't his father always warned him that anything you didn't work hard for wasn't worth having? Trouble was, he'd never heeded his father anyway. Also, he *had* worked hard for it. Damned hard! He thought of the subterranean sarcophagi of ancient, alien kings whose tombs were source of loot— and of his narrow escape from that place—and shuddered. And again: tomb-loot, *hah*!

Tarra's head argued with his back as to which of them hurt worst. Climbing groggily to his feet, he gently shrugged his blanket robe from his shoulders, wincing a little where it had adhered to drying scab of blood, then washed the wound as best he could with clean water from a skin in the camel's packs. The arrow had not gone deep; his broken sword's leather scabbard had saved him. Now he wrapped that scabbard in a soft cloth and re-strapped it tight in former position across his back, thus staunching the flow of blood. Then...a kerchief

soaked in water round his head, and a bite of dried meat and gulp of
sour wine, and Tarra was ready to take up the chase. It wasn't a wise
pursuit, he knew—indeed it might well be the last thing he ever did—
but that's the way it was with Tarra Khash. Hylar and Thull, whoever
they were, had hurt him deliberately and for no good reason, and now
he would hurt them. Or die trying...

The night was still young, not long past the midnight hour, when
he struggled up into his mount's ridgy saddle and goaded the beast
once more in the direction of Chlangi, cursing low under his breath
as each smallest jolt set his head to ringing and his back to dull, angry
throbbing. And so, at a pace only a little faster than walking, Tarra
Khash the Hrossak journeyed again under moon and stars.

He went wary now, his eyes tuned to the night, but for a mile or
two there was nothing. Then—

Tarra was not aware what it was *exactly* which drew his eyes to the
cross lying silvered on the side of a dune; in other circumstances (were
his senses not so alert for strange smells, sights or sounds) then he
might have passed it by. It could have been a figure of white stone, or
a scattering of bones, or simply the bleached roots of an olive or carob
tree long drowned in the desert's ergs and sandpapered to a reflective
whiteness; but whichever, he turned his camel's head that way.

And as he drew closer...what he saw then brought him down from
the back of his beast in a blur of painful motion, tossing his blanket
over the naked, ravaged figure of a girl pegged down on the gentle slope of the dune. A moment more and he pressed water-soaked
kerchief to cracked, puffed lips, then breathed a sigh of relief as the
girl's throat convulsed in a choke, and breathed more deeply as she
first shook her head and finally sucked at the cloth where he held it
to her mouth. Then she gazed at Tarra through eyes bruised as fallen
fruit and dusted with fine sand, wriggled a little way back from him,
affrightedly, and tried to ask:

"Who—?"

But he cut her off with, "*Shh!* Be still. I'll not harm you."

Even as she continued to cringe from him, he tore up the long
pegs and ties which bound her to the earth and broke them, then
wiped her fevered face with damp rag and wrapped her in the blanket. A moment later and she lay across the camel's saddle, face down,

while he swiftly led the beast from this brutal place in search of some rude shelter.

In a little while he found low, broken walls with sand drifted against them, and to one of these pegged a sheet of tentage to form a refuge. Therein he lay the unprotesting girl and propped up her head so that she could watch him while he built a fire in the lee of the wall just outside the tent. Over the fire he boiled up soup from a pouch of herbs and dried vegetables, and likewise fried several near-rancid strips of bacon in their own fat on a flat stone until they were crisp and sweet. These he offered to the girl, but having merely tasted the soup and sniffed at the bacon she then refused both, offering a little shake of her head.

"Well, I'm sorry, lass," Tarra told her, squatting down and satisfying his own hunger, "but this is the best I can do. If you're used to finer fare I'm sure I don't know where I'll find it for you in these parts!" He went to the camel and brought her the last of his wine, and this she accepted, draining the skin to the last drop. Then, while Tarra finished his food she watched him closely, so that he was ever aware of her eyes upon him. For his own part, however obliquely, he watched her, too.

He little doubted that this was the girl those curs out of Chlangi had laughed about, which in itself would form a bond between them, who had both suffered at the hands of those dogs; but just as the bandits had done before him, he too marvelled at the mystery of it: a girl like this, wandering alone beneath the stars in so desolate a place. She seemed to read his thoughts, said:

"I make...a pilgrimage. It is a requirement of my...order, that once in a five-year I go to a secret place in the Nameless Desert, there to renew my...vows."

Tarra nodded. "Who is your god?" he asked, thinking: *for he's let you down sorely this night, and no mistake!*

"His name is...secret," she answered in a moment. "I may not divulge it."

"Myself," said Tarra, "I'm partial to Old Gleeth, blind god of the moon. He's out tonight in all his glory—do you see?" And he lifted up the skirt of the tent, so that moonbeams fell within. The girl shrank back into shadow.

"The light," she said. "So silvery...bright."

Tarra let fall the flap, sat staring at her through eyes narrowed just a fraction. "Also," he said, "I'll not have anything said against Ahorra Izz, god of—"

"—Scarlet scorpions," she finished it for him, the hint of a hiss in her voice.

Slowly Tarra nodded. "He's a rare one," he said, "Ahorra Izz. I wouldn't have thought many would know of him. Least of all a young sister of—"

"In my studies," she whispered, cutting him off, "I have concerned myself with all the gods, ancient and modern, of all the peoples of Theem'hdra. A god is a god, black or white—or scarlet. For how may one conceive of Good if one has no knowledge of Evil?"

And vice versa, thought Tarra, but he answered: "How indeed? Truth to tell, I didn't find Ahorra Izz at all evil. In fact I'm in his debt!"

Before he could say more or frame another question, she asked: "Who are you?"

"Tarra Khash," he answered at once, in manner typically open. "A Hrossak. I was set upon by the same pack of hairies who...happened your way. They robbed me. Aye, and they put an arrow in my back, too. Hence my stiffness. I was tracking them back to Chlangi when I found you. Which makes for a complication. Now I have your skin to consider as well as my own. Mine's not worth a lot to anyone, but yours...?" He shrugged.

She sat up, more stiffly than Tarra, and the blanket fell away from her. Under the bruises she was incredibly lovely. Her beauty was... unearthly. "Come," she held out a marble arm. "Let me see your back."

"What can you do?" he asked. "It's a hole, that's all." But he went to her anyway. On hands and knees he looked at her, close up, then turned his back and sat down. He unfastened the straps holding his empty scabbard in place, and her hands were so gentle he didn't even feel her take the scabbard away.

And anyway—what *could* she do? She had no unguents or salves, not even a vinegar-soaked pad.

And yet...Tarra relaxed, sighed, felt the pain going out of his shoulder as easy as the air went out of his lungs. Well, now he knew what she could do. Ointments, balms?—*hah*! She had fingers, didn't she? And now Tarra believed he knew her order: she was a healer, a very special sort of physician, a layer on of hands. He'd heard of such but never seen one at work, never really believed. But seeing—or rather, feeling—was believing!

"A pity you can't do this for yourself," he told her.

"Oh, I shall heal, Tarra Khash," she answered, her voice sibilant. "Out there in the desert, under the full moon, I was helpless, taken by surprise no less than you. Now I grow stronger. Your strength has become mine. For this I thank you."

Tarra's voice was gruff now. "Huh! If you'd take some food you'd grow stronger faster!"

"There is food and food, Tarra Khash," she answered, her voice hypnotic in its caress. "For all you have offered, I am grateful."

Tarra's senses were suddenly awash in warm, languid currents. Her hands had moved from his shoulder to his neck, where now they drew out every last trace of tension. Her head on his shoulder, she cradled his back with her naked breasts. He slumped—and at once jerked his head erect, or tried to. What had she been saying? Grateful for what he'd offered? "You're welcome to whatever I have," he mumbled, scarcely aware of her sharp intake of breath. "Not that there's much..."

"Oh, but there is! There is!" she whispered. "Much more than I need, and though I'm hungry I shall take very little. Sleep now, sleep little mortal, and when you wake seek out those men and take your vengeance—while yet you may. For if I find them first there'll be precious little left for you!"

Sweet sister of mercy? A healer? Layer on of hands? Nay, none of these. Even sinking into uneasy slumbers, Tarra tried to turn his drowsy head and look at her, and failed. But he did force out one final question: *"Who...are you?"*

She lifted her mouth from his neck and his blood was fresh on her pale lips. "My name is Orbiquita!" she said—which was the last thing he heard before the darkness rolled over him. The last thing he *felt* was her hot, salty kiss...

"Lamia!" snapped Arenith Han, seer and runecaster to the robber-king Fregg, of doomed Chlangi. "She was a lamia, a man-lusting demon of the desert. You two are lucky to be alive!"

It was Fregg's dawn court, held in the open courtyard of his "palace," once a splendid place but now a sagging pile in keeping with most of Chlangi's buildings. Only the massive outer walls of the city itself were undecayed, for Fregg insisted that they at least be kept in good order. To this end he used "felons" from his court sessions, on those rare occasions when such escaped his "justice" with their lives intact.

Chlangi's monarch was one Fregg Unst, a failed con man long, long ago hounded out of Klühn on the coast for his frauds and fakeries. His subjects—in no wise nicer persons than Fregg himself—were a rabble of yeggs, sharpers, scabby whores and their pimps, unscrupulous taverners and other degenerates and riff-raff blown here on the winds of chance, or else fled from justice to Chlangi's doubtful refuge. And doubtful it was.

Chlangi the Doomed—or the Shunned City, as it is elsewhere known—well deserved these doleful titles. For of all places of ill-repute, this were perhaps the most notorious in all the Primal Land. And yet it had not always been this way.

In its heyday the city had been opulent, its streets and markets bustling with merchants, its honest taverners selling vintages renowned throughout the land for their clean sweetness. With lofty domes and spires all gilded over, walls high and white, and roofs red with tiles baked in the ovens of Chlangi's busy builders, the city had been the veriest jewel of Theem'hdra's cities. Aye, and its magistrates had had little time for members of the limited criminal element.

Now...all good and honest men shunned the place, had done so since first the lamia Orbiquita built her castle in the Desert of Sheb. Now the gold had been stripped from all the rich roofs, the grapevines had returned to the wild, producing only small, sour grapes and flattening their rotten trellises, arches and walls had toppled into disrepair, and the scummy water of a many-fractured aqueduct was suspect indeed. Only the rabble horde and their robber-king now lived here, and outside the walls a handful of hungry, outcast beggars.

Now, too, Fregg kept the land around well scouted, where day and night men of his were out patrolling in the badlands and along the fringe of the desert, intent upon thievery and murder. Occasionally there were caravans out of Eyphra or Klühn; or more rarely parties of prospectors out of Klühn headed for the Mountains of Lohmi, or returning therefrom; and exceeding rare indeed lone wanderers and adventurers who had simply strayed this way. Which must surely elevate the occurrences of last night almost to the fabulous. Fabulous in Fregg's eyes, anyway, which was one of the reasons he had brought his scouts of yestereve to morning court.

Their tale had been so full of fantastic incident that Fregg could only consider it a fabrication, and the tale wasn't all he found suspect…

Now the court was packed; battle-scarred brigands rubbed shoulders with nimble thieves and cutthroats, and Fregg's own lieutenants formed a surly jury whose only concern was to "get the thing over, the accused hanged, and on with the day's gaming, scheming and back-stabbing." Which did not bode well for transgressors against Fregg's laws!

Actually, those laws were simple in the extreme:

Monies and goods within the city would circulate according to barter and business, with each man taking his risks and living, subsisting or existing in accordance with his acumen. Monies and etc. from without would be divided half to Fregg and his heirs, one third to the reaver or reavers clever enough to capture and bring it in, and the remaining one sixth part to the city in general, to circulate as it might. More a code than a written law proper. There was only one real law and it was this: Fregg's subjects could rob, cheat, even kill each other; they could sell their swords, souls or bodies; they could bully, booze and brawl all they liked and then some…*except* where it would be to annoy, inconvenience, preempt or otherwise interfere with, or displease, Fregg. Simple…

Which meant that on this occasion, in some way as yet unexplained, last night's far-scavenging scouts had indeed displeased Fregg; a very strange circumstance, considering the fantastic haul they'd brought back for him!

Now they were here, dragged before Fregg's "courtiers" and "council" and "jury" for whatever form of inquisition he had in mind, and

Arenith Han—a half-breed wizard of doubtful dexterity, one time necromancer and failed alchemist in black Yhem, now Fregg's right-hand man—had opened the proceedings with his startling revelation.

"What say you?" Burly, bearded Fregg turned a little on his wooden stool of office behind a squat wooden table, to peer at his wizard with raised eyebrows. "Lamia? This girl they ravaged was a lamia? Where's your evidence?"

Central in the courtyard, where they were obliged to stand facing into a sun not long risen, Hylar Arf and Thull Drinnis shuffled and grimaced, surly at Fregg's treatment of them. But no use to protest, not at this stage; they were here and so must face up to whatever charge Fregg brought against them. The fallen wizard's examination of their spoils, and his deductions concerning the same and the nature of at least one of their previous owners, that was simply for openers, all part of the game.

Sharing space in the central area were two camels, a pair of white yaks and, upon the ground, blankets bearing various items. Upon one: tatters of sorely dishevelled female apparel; upon the other, eight saddle bags, their contents emptied out in a pile of gleam and glitter and golden, glancing fire. Treasure enough to satisfy even the most avaricious heart—almost. Probably. Possibly.

"Observe!" Arenith Han, a spidery, shrivelled person in a worn, rune-embellished cloak scuttled about, prodding the yaks and examining their gear. "Observe the rig of these beasts—especially this one. Have you ever seen the like? A houdah fixed upon the back of a yak? A *houdah*? Now, some tiny princess of sophisticate kingdom might well ride such gentle, canopied beast through the gardens of her father's palace—for her pleasure, under close scrutiny of eunuchs and guards—and the tasselled shade to protect her precious skin from sun's bright ray. But here, in the desert, the badlands, the merest trajectory of a good hard spit away from Chlangi's walls? Unlikely! And yet so it would appear to be…"

He turned and squinted at the uncomfortable ruffians. "Just such a princess, our friends here avow, was out riding in the desert last night. She rode upon this yak, beneath this shade, while the other beast carried her toiletries and trinkets, her prettiest things, which is in the nature of princesses when they go abroad: frivolously to take small items of comfort with them. Ah!—but I have *examined* the beasts' packs. Behold!"

He scattered what was contained in the packs on to the dust and cracked flags of the courtyard—contents proving to be, with one exception, ample handfuls of loamy soil—stooped to pick up the single extraneous item, and held it up. "A book," he said. "A leather-bound runebook. A book of spells!"

Oohs! and *Aahs!* went up from the assemblage, but Han held up a finger for silence. "And *such* spells!" he continued. "They are runes of transformation, whose purpose I recognize e'en though I cannot read the glyphs in which they're couched—for of course they're writ in the lamia tongue! As to their function: they permit the user to alter her form at will, becoming a bat, a dragon, a serpent, a hag, a wolf, a toad—even a beautiful girl!"

Hylar Arf, a hulking Northman with mane of blue-black hair bristling the length of his spine, had heard enough. Usually jovial—especially when in a killing mood—his laughter now welled up in a great booming eruption of sound. One-handed, he picked the skinny sorcerer up by the neck and dangled him before the court. "This old twig's a charlatan!" he derided. "Can't you all see that? Why!—here's Thull Drinnis and me alive and kicking, no harm befallen us—and this fool says the girl was lamia? *Bah!* We took her yaks and we took *her*, too—all three of us, before Gumbat Chud, great fool, got himself slain—and you can believe me when I tell you it was *girl*-flesh we had, sweet and juicy. Indeed, because he's a pig, Thull here had her twice! He was both first and last with her; and does he look any the worse for wear?"

"We're not pleased!" Fregg came to his feet, huge and round as a boulder. "Put down our trusted sorcerer at once!" Hylar Arf spat in the dust but did as Fregg commanded, setting Arenith Han upon his feet to stagger to and fro, clutching at his throat.

"Continue," Fregg nodded his approval.

The wizard got well away from the two accused and found the fluted stone stump of an old column to sit on. Still massaging his throat, he once more took up the thread—or attempted to:

"About…lamias," he choked. And: "Wine, wine!" A court attendant took him a skin, from which he drank deeply. And in a little while, but hurriedly now and eager to be done with it:

"About lamias. They are desert demons, female, daughters of the pit. Spawned of unnatural union betwixt, *ahem*, say a sorcerer and a succubus—or perhaps a witch and incubus—the lamia is half-caste. Well, I myself am a 'breed' and see little harm in that; but in the case of a lamia things are very much different. The woman in her lusts after men for satisfaction, the demon part for other reasons. Men who have bedded lamias and survived are singularly rare—but *not* fabulous, not unheard of! Mylakhrion himself is said to have had several."

Fregg was fascinated. Having seated himself again following Hylar Arf's outburst, he now leaned forward. "All very interesting," he said. "We would know more. We would know, for example, just exactly *how* these two escaped with their lives from lamia's clutches. For whereas the near-immortal Mylakhrion was—some might say 'is'—a legended magician, these men are merely—" (he sniffed) "—*men*. And pretty scabby specimens of men at that!"

"Majesty," said Arenith Han, "I am in complete agreement with your assessment of this pair. Aye, and Gumbat Chud was cut, I fear, of much the same cloth. But first let me say a little more on the nature of lamias, when all should become quite clear."

"Say on," Fregg nodded.

"Very well." Han stood up from column seat, commenced to pace, kept well away from the hulking barbarian and his thin, grim-faced colleague. "Even lamias, monstrous creatures that they are, have their weaknesses; one of which, as stated, is that they lust after men. Another is this: that once in a five-year their powers wane, when they must needs take them off to a secret place deep in the desert, *genius loci* of lamias, and there perform rites of renewal. During such periods, being *un*-natural creatures, all things of nature are a bane, a veritable poison to them. At the very best of times they cannot abide the sun's clean light—in which abhorrence they are akin to ghouls and vampires—but at the height of the five-year cycle the sun is not merely loathed but lethal in the extreme! Hence they must needs travel by night. And because the moon is also a thing of nature, Old Gleeth in his full is likewise a torment to them, whose cold silvery light will scorch and blister them even as the sun burns men!"

"Ah!" Fregg came once more erect in his seat. He leaned forward, great knuckles supporting him where he planted them firmly on the table before him. "The houdah on the yak!" And he nodded, "Yes, yes—I see!"

"Certainly," Arenith Han smiled. "It is a shade against the moon—which was full last night, as you know well enow."

Fregg sat down with a thump, banged upon the table with heavy hand, said: "Good, Han, good! And what else do you divine?"

"Two more things, Majesty," answered the mage, his voice low now. "First, observe the contents of her saddle bags: largely soil! And does not the lamia, like the vampire, carry her native earth with her for bed? Aye, for she likes to lie down in the same charnel earth which her own vileness has cursed…"

"And finally?" Fregg grunted.

"Finally—observe the *motif* graven in the leather of the saddle bags, and embroidered into the canopy of yon houdah, and blazoned upon binding of runebook. *And*—" Han narrowed his eyes, "—carved in the jade inset which Thull Drinnis even now wears in the ring of gold on the smallest finger of his left hand! *Is it not indeed the skull and serpent crest of the Lamia Orbiquita herself?*"

Thull Drinnis, a weaselish ex-Klühnite, at once thrust his left hand deep into the pocket of his baggy breeks, but not before everyone had seen the ring of which the wizard made mention. In the stony silence which ensued, Drinnis realized his error—his admittance of guilt of sorts—and knew that was not the way to go. So now he drew his hand into view and held it up so that the sun flashed from burnished gold.

"A trinket!" he cried. "I took it from her and I claim it as a portion of my share. What's wrong with that? Now enough of this folly. Why are we here, Hylar and me? Last night we brought more wealth into this place than was ever dreamed of. Chlangi's share alone will make each man and dog of you rich!"

"He's right!" Hylar Arf took up the cry. "All of you rich—or else—" he turned accusingly to Fregg, "—or else our noble king would take it all for himself!"

And again the stony silence, but this time directed at Fregg where he sat upon his stool of office at his table of judgement. But Fregg was wily, more than a match for two such as Arf and Drinnis, and he was playing this game with loaded dice. Now he decided the time was ripe to let those dice roll. He once again came to his feet.

"People of Chlangi," he said. "Loyal subjects. It appears to me that there are three things here to be taken into consideration. Three, er—shall we say 'discrepancies?'—upon which, when they are resolved, Hylar and Thull's guilt or innocence shall be seen to hang. Now, since my own interest in these matters has been brought into question, I shall merely present the facts as we know them, and you—*all* of you—shall decide the outcome. A strange day indeed, but nevertheless I now put aside my jury, my wizard, even my own perhaps self-serving opinions in this matter, and let *you* make the decision." He paused.

"Very well, these are the facts:

"For long and long the laws of Chlangi have stood, and they have served us moderately well. One of these laws states that all—I repeat *all*—goods of value stolen without and fetched within these walls are to be divided in predetermined fashion: half to me, Chlangi's rightful king, one third to them responsible for the catch, the remainder to the city. And so to the first discrepancy. Thull Drinnis here has seen fit to apportion himself a little more than his proper share, namely the ring upon his finger."

"A trinket, as he himself pointed out!" someone at the back of the crowd cried.

"But a trinket of value," answered Fregg, "whose worth would feed a man for a six-month! Let me say on:

"The second 'discrepancy'—and one upon which the livelihoods and likely the very lives of each and every one of us depends—is this: that if what we have heard is true, good Hylar and clever Thull here have rid these parts forever of a terrible bane, namely the Lamia Orbiquita."

"Well done, lads!" the cry went up. And: "What's that for a discrepancy?" While someone else shouted, "The monster's dead at last!"

"*Hold!*" Fregg bellowed. "We do not know that she is dead—and it were better for all if she is not! Wizard," he turned to Arenith Han, "what say you? They beat her, ravished her, pegged her out under the moon. Would she survive all that?"

"The beating and raping, aye," answered Han. "Very likely she would. The staking out 'neath a full bright Gleeth: that would be sore painful, would surely weaken her nigh unto death. And by now—" he squinted at the sun riding up out of the east. "Now in the searing rays of the sun—now she is surely dead!"

"Hoorah!" several in the crowd shouted.

When there was silence Fregg stared all around. And sadly he shook his head. "Hoorah, is it? And how long before word of this reaches the outside world, eh? How long before the tale finds its way to Klühn and Eyphra, Yhem and Khrissa and all the villages and settlements between? Have you forgotten? Chlangi the Shunned—this very Chlangi the Doomed—was once Chlangi the bright, Chlangi the beautiful! Oh, all very well to let a handful of outcast criminals run the place now, where no right-minded decent citizen would be found dead; but with Orbiquita gone, her sphere of evil ensorcelment removed forever, how long before some great monarch and his generals decide it were time to bring back Chlangi within the fold, to make her an honest city again? Not long, you may rely upon it! And what of *your* livelihoods then? And what of *your* lives? Why, there's a price on the head of every last one of you!"

No cries of "bravo" now from the spectators but only the hushed whispers of dawning realization, and at last a sullen silence which acknowledged the ring of truth in Fregg's words.

And in the midst of this silence:

"We killed a lamia!" Hylar Arf blustered. "Why, all of Theem'hdra stands in our debt!"

"Theem'hdra, aye," answered Fregg, his voice doomful. "But not Chlangi, and certainly not her present citizens."

"But—" Thull Drinnis would have taken up the argument.

"—But we come now to the third and perhaps greatest discrepancy," Fregg cut him off. "Good Thull and Hylar returned last night with vast treasure, all loaded on these camels here and now displayed upon the blanket for all to see. And then they took themselves off to Dilquay Noth's brothel and drank and whored the night away, and talked of how, with their share, they'd get off to Thandopolis and set up in legitimate business, and live out their lives in luxury undreamed…

"But being a suspicious man, and having had news of this fine scheme of theirs brought back to me, I thought: "What? And are they so displeased with Chlangi, then, that they must be off at once and gone from us? Or is there something I do not yet know? And I sent out trackers into the badlands to find what they could find."

(Thull and Hylar, until this moment showing only a little dis-
quietude, now became greatly agitated, fingering their swords and
peering this way and that. Fregg saw this and smiled, however grimly,
before continuing.)

"And lo!—at a small oasis known only to a few of us, what should
my trackers find there but a *third* beast, the very brother of these two
here—and four more saddle bags packed with choicest items!" He
clapped his great hands and the crowd gave way to let through a pair
of dusty mountain men, leading into view the beast in question.

"We are all rich, all of us!" cried Fregg over the crowd's rising
hum of excitement and outrage. "Aye, and after the share has been
made, now we can *all* leave Chlangi for lands of our choice. That is to
say, all save these two…"

Thull Drinnis and Hylar Arf waited no longer. The game was up.
They were done for. They knew it.

As a man, they went for Fregg, swords singing from scabbards,
lips drawn back in snarls from clenched teeth. And up on to his
table they leaped, their blades raised on high—but before they could
strike there came a great sighing of arrows which stopped them
dead in their tracks. From above and behind Fregg on the courtyard
walls, a party of crossbowmen had opened up, and their massed
bolts not only transfixed the cheating pair but knocked them down
from the table like swatted flies. They were dead before they hit
the ground.

And again there was silence, broken at last by Fregg's voice shouting: "So let all treacherous dogs die; so let them all pay the price!"

And someone in the crowd: "The fools! Why did they come back
at all?"

"Good question!" answered Fregg. "But they had to come back.
They knew that I am a caring king, and that if they failed to return
I would worry about them and send out others to discover their fate.
And they knew also that with beasts so loaded down with gold and
gems, their pace would be slow and my riders would surely catch
them. Moreover, they would need provisions for their long trek over-
land, and extra beasts, and how to purchase such without displaying
at least a portion of their loot? And finally they knew that my intelligence is good, that I am rarely lacking in advance knowledge in

respect of travellers and caravans in these parts. What if I *expected* them to return with loot galore? And so they brought two-thirds of it back, and left the rest in the desert, to be collected later on their way to Thandopolis..."

As he fell smugly silent a new voice arose, a voice hitherto unknown in Chlangi, which said: "Bravo, lord Fregg! Bravo! An object lesson in deduction. How well you understand the criminal mind, sir."

All eyes turned to Tarra Khash where he now threw off his blanket robe and draped it over the back of the camel he led; to him, and to the beast itself, which trotted straight to other three and greeted them with great affection. Plainly the four were or had been a team; and since this burly bronze clout-clad Hrossak was their master...what did that make him but previous owner of treasure and all? Possibly.

Tarra was flanked by a pair of hulking thugs from the guardroom in the west gate, who seemed uncertain exactly what to do with him. Fregg could have told them; but now that he'd met the Hrossak, so to speak, he found himself somewhat curious. "You're a bold one," he told Tarra, coming forward to look him up and down.

"Bold as brass!" one of the guards ventured. "He came right up to the gate and hailed us, and said he sought audience with the king or chief or whoever was boss here."

"I'm boss here," said Fregg, thumbing his chest. "King Fregg Unst the First—and likely the last. Who are you?"

"Tarra Khash," said Tarra. "Adventurer by profession, wanderer by inclination..." And he paused to look at the dead men where their bodies lay sprawled in the dust of the courtyard. "Excuse me, but would these two be called, er, Hylar and Thull?"

"Those were their names, aye," Fregg nodded. "Did you have business with them?"

"Some," said Tarra, "but it appears I'm too late."

The session was breaking up now and the crowd thinning as people went off about their business. A half-dozen of Fregg's men, his personal bodyguards, stayed back, keeping a sharp eye on Tarra Khash. Others began to bundle up the treasure in the blankets.

"Walk with me a little way," said Fregg, "and tell me more. I like your cut, Tarra Khash. We seldom have visitors here; at least, not of their own free will!" He chuckled, paused, turned and said to his men:

"That ring on Drinnis' finger—I want it. Make sure it's with the rest of the stuff and bring it to me in the tower."

"Hold!" said Tarra. "A moment, King Fregg." He stepped to blanket and stooped, came erect holding the jewelled hilt of his scimitar. "I've a special affection for this piece," he said. "It belongs in the scabbard across my back. I hope you don't mind."

Fregg gently took it from him. "But I *do* mind, Tarra Khash!"

"But—"

"Wait, lad, hear me out. See, I've nothing against you, but you simply don't understand our laws. You see, upon the instant loot is brought into the city, said loot belongs to me, its finders, and to the city itself. And no law at all, I'm afraid, to cover its retrieval by rightful owner. Not even the smallest part of it. Also, I perceive these stones set in the hilt to be valuable, a small treasure in themselves." He shrugged almost apologetically, adding: "No, I'm sorry, lad, but at least three men—and likely a good many more—have died for this little lot. And so—" And he tossed the jewelled hilt back with the other gems.

"Actually," Tarra chewed his lip, eyed the swords and crossbows of Fregg's bodyguards, "actually it's the hilt I treasure more than the stones. Before it was broken there were times that sword saved my miserable life!"

"Ah!" said Fregg. "It has sentimental value, has it? Why didn't you say so? You shall have it back, of course! Only come to me tonight, in my counting room atop the tower, and after I've prised out the stones, then the broken blade is yours. It seems the least I can do. And my thanks, for in your way you've already answered a riddle I'd have asked of you."

"Oh?" Tarra raised an eyebrow.

"Indeed. For if you were rightful owner of this hoard in the first place, why surely you'd agonize more over the bulk of the stuff than the mere stump of a sword, not so?"

Tarra shrugged, grinned, winked, and tapped the side of his nose with forefinger. "No wonder you're king here, Fregg. Aye, and again you've gauged your man aright, I fear."

Fregg roared with laughter. "Good, good!" he chortled. "Very good. So you're a reaver, too, eh? Well, and what's a reaver if not an adventurer, which is what you said you were? You took this lot from a caravan, I suppose? No mean feat for a lone wanderer, even a brave and brawny Hrossak."

"You flatter me," Tarra protested, and lied: "No, there were ten of us. The men of the caravan fought hard and died well, and I was left with treasure."

"Well then," said Fregg. "In that case you'll not take it so badly. It seems you're better off to the extent of one camel. As for the treasure: it was someone else's, became yours, and now has become mine—er, Chlangi's."

Tarra sucked his teeth. "So it would seem," he said.

"Aye," Fregg nodded. "So count your blessings and go on your way. Chlangi welcomes you if you choose to stay, will not detain you should you decide to move on. The choice is yours."

"Your hospitality overwhelms me," said Tarra. "If I had the change I'd celebrate our meeting with a meal and a drink."

"Pauper, are you?" said Fregg, seeming surprised. And: "What, penniless, an enterprising lad like you? Anyway, I'd warn you off Chlangi's taverns. Me, I kill my own meat and brew my own wine! But if you're desperately short you can always sell your blanket. Your camel will keep you warm nights..." And off he strode, laughing.

Which seemed to be an end to that.

Almost...

―――――――

Tarra was one of the last to pass out through the courtyard's gates, which were closed at once on his heels. On his way he'd given the place a narrow-eyed once-over, especially the tumbledown main building and its central tower. So that standing there outside the iron-banded gates, staring up thoughtfully at the high walls, he was startled when a voice barked in his ear:

"Hrossak, I overheard your conversation with Fregg. Quickly now, tell me, d'you want a meal and a wineskin? And then maybe a safe place to rest your head until tonight? For if you're thinking of leaving, it would be sheerest folly to try it in broad daylight, despite what Fregg says!"

The speaker was a tiny man, old and gnarly, with an eye-patch over his left eye and a stump for right hand. The latter told a tale in itself: he was a failed thief, probably turned con man. But...Tarra shrugged. "Any port in a storm," he said. "Lead on."

And when they were away from Fregg's sorry palace and into the old streets of the city proper: "Now what's all this about not leaving in daylight? I came in daylight, after all."

"I'm Stumpy Adz," the old-timer told him. "And if it's to be known, Stumpy knows it. Odds are you're watched even now. You're a defenceless stranger and you own blanket, saddle, camel and gear, and leather scabbard. That's quite a bit of property for a lad with no friends here, save me."

"I wear loincloth and sandals, too," Tarra pointed out. "Are they also lusted after?"

"Likely," Stumpy Adz nodded. "This is Chlangi, lad, not Klühn. Anyway, I've pillow for your head, cabbage tops and shade for the beast, food and drink for your belly. Deal?"

"What'll I pay?"

"Blanket'll do. It's cold here nights. And as Fregg pointed out: you've your camel to keep you warm."

Tarra sighed but nodded. "Deal. Anyway, I wasn't planning on leaving till tonight. Fregg's invited me to call on him in his tower counting house. I have to get my sword back—what's left of it."

"Heard that, too," said Stumpy. *"Huh!"*

He led the way into a shady alley and from there through a heavy oak door into a tiny high-walled yard, planked over for roof with a vine bearing grapes and casting cool shade. "Tether your beast there," said Stumpy. "Will he do his business?"

"Likely," said Tarra. "He doesn't much care where he does it."

"Good! A treat for the grapevine..."

Tarra looked about. Half-way up one wall was a wooden platform, doubtless Stumpy's bed (Tarra's for the rest of the day), and behind the yard a low, tiled hovel built between the walls as if on afterthought. It might one time have been a smithy; cooking smells now drifted out of open door.

"Gulla," Stumpy called. "A meal for two—and a skin, if you please. Quick, lass, we've a visitor."

Tarra's ears pricked up. "Lass?" If not the old lad's wife, then surely his daughter. The latter proved to be the case, but Tarra's interest rapidly waned. Gulla Adz was comely enough about the face but built like a fortress. Tarra could feel his ribs creaking just looking at her. Looking at *him*, as she dished out steamy stew in cracked plates atop a tiny table, she made eyes and licked her lips in a manner that made him glad his bed was high off the ground.

Stumpy chased her off, however, and as they ate Tarra asked:

"Why the '*huh!*,' eh? Don't you think Fregg'll give me back my sword, then?"

"His own, more likely—between your ribs! No, lad, when Fregg takes something it stays took. Also, I fancy he makes his own plans for leaving, and sooner rather than later. I'd make book we're kingless within a week. And there'll be no share out, that's for sure! No, this is just what Fregg's been waiting for. Him and his bullies'll take the lot—and then he'll find a way to ditch them, too."

"Why should he want to leave?" asked Tarra Khash, innocently. "It seems to me he's well set up here."

"He was, he was," said Stumpy. "But—" and he told Tarra about the Lamia Orbiquita and her assumed demise. Hearing all, Tarra said nothing—but he fingered twin sores on his neck, like the tiny weeping craters of mosquito bites. Aye, and if what this old lad said about lamias were true, then he must consider himself one very fortunate Hrossak. Fortunate indeed!

"That treasure," he said when Stumpy was done, "was mine. I'll not leave without a handful at least. And I want that sword-hilt, with or without its jewels! Can I buy your help, Stumpy, for a nugget of gold? Or perhaps a ruby big enough to fit the socket behind your eye-patch?"

"Depends what you want," said Stumpy carefully.

"Not much," Tarra answered. "A good thin rope and grapple, knowledge of the weakest part of the city's wall, details of Fregg's palace guards—how many of them, and so forth—and a plan of quickest route from palace, through city, to outer wall. Well?"

"Sounds reasonable," the oldster nodded, his good eye twinkling.

"Lastly," said Tarra, "I'll want a sharp knife, six-inch blade and well balanced."

"Ah! That'll cost you an extra nugget."

"Done!—if I make it. If not...you can keep the camel." They shook on it left-handed, and each felt he'd met a man to be trusted—within limits.

Following which the Hrossak climbed rickety ladder to shady platform, tossed awhile making his plans, and finally fell asleep...

———

Tarra slept until dusk, during which time Stumpy Adz was busy. When the Hrossak awoke Stumpy gave him a throwing knife and sat down with him, by light of oil lamp and floating wick, to study several parchment sketches. There was meat sizzling over charcoal, too, and a little weak wine in a stone jar beaded with cold moisture. Stumpy lived pretty well, Tarra decided.

As for the Hrossak: he was clear-headed; the stiffness was still in his shoulder but fading fast; the two-pronged bite on his neck had scabbed over and lost its sting. What had been taken out of him was replacing itself, and all seemed in working order.

He took leave of Stumpy's place at the hour when all cats turn grey and headed for the south gate. At about which time, some three hundred and more miles away in the heart of the Nameless Desert...

Deep, deep below the furnace sands, cooling now that the sun was caught once more in Cthon's net and drawn down, and while the last kites of evening fanned the air on high—in a crimson cavern with a lava lake, where red imps danced nimbly from island to island in the reek and splash of molten rock—there the Lamia Orbiquita came awake at last and stretched her leathery wings and breathed gratefully of the hot brimstone atmosphere.

She lay cradled in smoking ashes in the middle of a smouldering island which itself lay central in the lava lake; and over her warty, leathery, loathsome form hunched a mighty black lava lump glowing with a red internal life of its own and moulded in perfect likeness of—what else but another lamia? And seeing that infernally fossilized thing crouching over her she knew where she was and remembered how she got here.

The whole thing had been a folly, a farce. First: that she failed to make adequate preparation for her journey when she knew full well that the five-year cycle was nearing its peak, when her powers would wane even as the hated moon waxed. Next: that having allowed the time to creep too close, and most of her powers fled, still she had not

333

used the last of them to call up those serfs of the desert, the djinn, to transport her here; for she scorned all imps—even bottle imps, and even the biggest of them—and hated the thought of being in their debt. Finally: that as her choice of guise under which to travel she had chosen that of beautiful human female, for once the change was made she'd been stuck with that shape and all the hazards that went with it. The choice, however, had not been completely arbitrary; she could take comfort in that, at least. The human female form was small and less cumbersome than that of a dragon; and where girls sometimes got molested and raped, dragons were usually slain! She could have been a lizard, but lizards making a beeline across the desert are easy prey for hawks and such, and anyway she hated crawling on her belly. Flying creature such as harpy or bat were out of the question; since they must needs flit, they could not shade themselves against sun and moon. Her true lamia form was likewise problematic: impossible to shade in flight and cumbersome afoot. And so she had chosen the shape of a beautiful human girl. Anyway, it was her favourite and had served her well for more than a century. The victims she had lured with it were without number. Moreover, yaks and camels did not shy from it.

Ah, well, a lesson learned—but learned so expensively. A veritable string of errors never to be repeated. The ravishment had been bad enough and the beating worse, but the loss of her runebook and ring were disasters of the first magnitude. Orbiquita's memory was not the best and the runes of metamorphosis were anything but easy. As for the ring: that had been gifted to her by her father, Mylakhrion of Tharamoon. She could not bear to be without it. Indeed, of the entire episode the one thing she did not regret was the Hrossak. Odd, that…

Stretching again and yawning hideously, she might perhaps have lingered longer over thoughts of Tarra Khash, but that was a luxury not to be permitted. No, for she was in serious trouble and she knew it, and now must prepare whatever excuses she could for her lateness and unseemly mode of arrival here in this unholy place.

Aye, for the eyes in the lava lamia's head had cracked open and now glared sulphurously, and from the smoking jaws came voice of inquisitor, demanding to be told all and truthfully:

"What have you to say for yourself, Orbiquita, borne here by djinn and weary nigh unto death, and late by a day so that all your sisters have come and gone, all making sport over the idleness or foolhardiness of the hated Orbiquita? You know, of course, the penalty?"

"I hate my sisters equally well!" answered Orbiquita unabashed. "Let them take solace from that. As to your charges, I cannot deny them. Idle and foolhardy I have been. And aye, I know well enow the price to pay." Then she told the whole, miserable tale.

When she reached the part concerning Tarra Khash, however, the lava lamia stopped her in something approaching astonishment: "What? And you took not this Hrossak's life? But this is without precedence!"

"I had my reasons!" Orbiquita protested.

"Then out with them at once," ordered the lava lamia, "or sit here in stony silence for five long years—which is, in any case, your fate. Of what 'reasons' do you speak?"

"One," said Orbiquita, "he saved me from Gleeth's scorching beams."

"What is that? He is a man!"

"My father was a man, and likely yours too."

"*Hah!* Do not remind me! Say on, Orbiquita."

"Two, though I suspect he guessed my nature—or at least that I was more than I appeared—still he offered no offence, no harm, but would have fed and protected me."

"Greater fool he!" the lava lamia answered.

"And three," (Orbiquita would not be browbeaten) "I sensed, by precognition, that in fact I would meet this one again, and that he would be of further service to me."

And, *"Hah!"* said lava lamia more vehemently yet. "Be sure it will not happen for a five-year at least, Orbiquita! 'Precognition,' indeed! You should have gorged on him, and wrapped yourself in his skin to protect your own from the moon, and so proceeded here without let and indebted to no one. Instead you chose merely to sip, summoning only sufficient strength to call up detested desert djinn to your aid. All in all, most foolish. And are you ready now to take my place, waiting out your five years until some equally silly sister's deed release you?"

"No," said Orbiquita.

"It is the law!" the other howled. "Apart from which, I'm impatient of this place."

"And the law shall be obeyed—and you released, as is only right—eventually... But first a boon."

"What? You presume to—"

"Mylakhrion's ring!" cried Orbiquita. "Stolen from me. My rune-book, too. Would you deny me time to right this great wrong? Must I wait a five-year to wipe clean this smear on *all* lamias? Would you suffer the scorn of *all* your sisters—and not least mine—for the sake of a few hours, you who have centuries before you?"

After long moments, calmer now but yet bubbling lava from every pore, the keeper of this place asked, "What is it you wish?"

"My powers returned to me—fully!" said Orbiquita at once. "And I'll laugh in Gleeth's face and fly to Chlangi, and find Mylakhrion's ring and take back my runebook. Following which—"

"You'll return here?"

"Or be outcast forever from the sisterhood, aye," Orbiquita bowed her warty head. "And is it likely I'll renege, to live only five more years instead of five thousand?"

"So be it," said the lava lamia, her voice a hiss of escaping steam. "You are renewed, Orbiquita. Now get you hence and remember your vow, and return to me here before Cthon releases the sun to rise again over Theem'hdra. On behalf of all lamias, I have spoken."

The sulphur pits which were her eyes lidded themselves with lava crusts, but Orbiquita did not see. She was no longer there...

Tarra Khash left Chlangi by the south gate two hours after the sun's setting. By then, dull lights glowed in the city's streets in spasmodic pattern, flickering smokily in the taverns, brothels, and a few of the larger houses and dens—and (importantly) in Fregg's palace, particularly his apartments in the tower. It was a good time to be away, before night's thieves and cutthroats crawled out of their holes and began to work up an interest in a man.

Out of the gate the Hrossak turned east for Klühn, heading for the pass through the Great Eastern Peaks more than two hundred miles away. Beyond the pass and fording the Lohr, he would cross a hundred more miles of grassland before the spires and turrets of coastal Klühn came into view. Except that first, of course, he'd be returning—however briefly, and hopefully painlessly—to Chlangi.

Jogging comfortably east for a mile or more, the Hrossak never once looked back—despite the fact that he knew he was followed. Two of them, on ponies (rare beasts in Theem'hdra), and keeping their distance for the nonce. Tarra could well imagine what was on their minds: they wondered about the contents of his saddle bags, and of course the camel itself was not without value. Also they knew—or thought they knew—that he was without weapon. Well, as long as he kept more than arrow or bolt's flight distance between he was safe, but it made his back itch for all that.

Then he spied ahead the tumbled ruins of some ghost town or other on the plain, and urged his mount to a trot. It was quite dark now, for Gleeth sailed low as yet, so it might be some little time before his pursuers twigged that he'd quickened his pace. That was all to the good. He passed along the ghost town's single skeletal street, dismounted and tethered his beast by a heap of stones, then fleet-footed it back to the other end and flattened himself to the treacherous bricks of an arch where it spanned the narrow street. And waited.

And waited...

Could they have guessed his next move? Did they suspect his ambush? The plan had been simple: hurl knife into the back of one as they passed beneath, and leap on the back of the other; but what now?

Ah!—no sooner the question than an answer. Faint sounds in the night growing louder. Noise of their coming at last. But hoofbeats, a beast at gallop? What was this? No muffled, furtive approach this but frenzied flight! A pony, snorting its fear, fleeing riderless across the plain; and over there, silhouetted against crest of low hill, another. Now what in—?

Tarra slid down from the arch, held his breath, stared back hard the way he had come, toward Chlangi, and listened. But nothing, only the fading sounds of drumming hooves and a faint whinny in the dark.

Now instinct told the Hrossak he should count his blessings, forget whatever had happened here, return at once to his camel and so back to Chlangi by circuitous route as previously planned; but his personal demon, named Curiosity, deemed it otherwise. On foot, moving like a shadow among shadows, his bronze skin aiding him considerably in the dark, he loped easily back along his own route until—

It was the smell stopped him, a smell he knew at once from its too familiar reek. Fresh blood!

More cautiously now, nerves taut as a bowstring, almost in a crouch, Tarra moved forward again; and his grip on the haft of his knife never so tight, and his eyes never so large where they strained to penetrate night's canopy of dark. Then he was almost stumbling over them, and just as smartly drawing back, his breath hissing out through clenched teeth.

Dead, and not merely dead but gutted! Chlangi riff-raff by their looks, unpretty as the end they'd met. Aye, and a butcher couldn't have done a better job. Their entrails still steamed in the cool night air.

The biters bit: Tarra's trackers snared in advance of his own planned ambush; and what of the unseen, unheard killers themselves? Once more the Hrossak melted into shadow, froze, listened, stared. Perhaps they had gone in pursuit of the ponies. Well, Tarra wouldn't wait to find out. But as he turned to speed back to his camel—

Another smell in the night air? A sulphur reek, strangely laced with cloying musk? And where had he smelled that dubious perfume before? A nerve jumped in his neck, and twin scabs throbbed dully as if in mute answer.

To hell with it! They were all questions that could wait...

Half a mile from Chlangi Tarra dismounted and tethered his camel out of sight in a shallow gulley, then proceeded on foot and as fast as he could go to where the east wall was cracked as by some mighty tremor of the earth. Here boulders and stones had been tumbled uncemented into the gap, so that where the rest of the wall was smooth, offering little of handholds and making for a difficult climb, here it was rough and easily scaleable. Fregg knew this too, of course, for which reason there was normally a guard positioned atop the wall somewhere in this area. Since Chlangi was hardly a place people would want to break *into*, however, chances were the guard would have his belly wrapped around the contents of a wineskin by now, snoring in some secret niche.

The wall was high at this point, maybe ten man-lengths, but Old Gleeth was kind enough to cast his rays from a different angle, leaving the east wall in shadow. All should be well. Nevertheless—

Before commencing his climb Tarra peered right and left, stared long and hard back into the night toward the east, listened carefully to see if he could detect the slightest sound. But…nothing. There were bats about tonight, though—and big ones, whole roosts of them— judging from the frequent flappings he'd heard overhead.

Satisfied at last that there were no prying eyes, finally the Hrossak set fingers and toes to wall and scaled it like a lizard, speeding his ascent where the crack widened and the boulders were less tightly packed. Two-thirds of the way up he rested briefly, where a boulder had long since settled and left a man sized gap, taking time to get his breath and peer out and down all along the wall and over the scraggy plain, and generally checking that all was well.

And again the stirring of unseen wings and a whipping of the air as something passed briefly across the starry vault. Bats, yes, but a veritable cloud of them! Tarra shivered his disgust: he had little time for night creatures of any sort. He levered himself out of his hole, began to climb again—and paused.

A sound from on high, atop the wall? The scrape of heel against stone? The snuffle of bored or disconsolate feet? It came again, this time accompanied by wheezy grunt!

Tarra flattened himself to wall, clung tight, was suddenly aware of his vulnerability. At which precise moment he felt the coil of rope over his shoulder slip a little and heard his hook clang against the wall down by his waist. Quickly he trapped the thing, froze once more. Had it been heard?

"Huh?" came gruff inquiry from above. And: *"Huh?"* Then, in the next moment, a cough, a whirring sound diminishing, a gurgle—and at last silence once more.

For five long minutes Tarra waited, his nerves jumping and the feeling going out of his fingers and toes, before he dared continue his upward creep. By then he believed he had it figured out—or hoped so, anyway. The guard was, as he had suspected might be the case, asleep. The grapple's clang had merely caused him to start and snort into the night, before settling himself down again more comfortably.

And perhaps the incident had been for the best at that; at least Tarra knew now that he was there.

With infinite care the Hrossak proceeded, and at last his fingertips went up over the sill of an embrasure. Now, more slow and silent yet, he drew up his body until—

Seated in the deep embrasure with his back to one wall and his knees against the other, a bearded guardsman grinned down on Tarra's upturned face and aimed a crossbow direct into the astonished "O" of his gaping mouth!

Tarra might simply have recoiled, released his grip upon the rim and fallen. He might have (as some men doubtless would) fainted. He might have closed his eyes tight shut and pleaded loud and desperate, promising anything. He did none of these but gulped, grinned and said:

"Ho! No fool you, friend! Fregg chooses his guards well. He sent me here to catch you asleep—to test the city's security, d'you see?—but here you are wide awake and watchful, obviously a man who knows his duty. So be it; help me up from here and I'll go straight to our good king and make report how all's...well?"

For now the Hrossak saw that all was indeed well—for him if not for the guard. That smell was back, of fresh blood, and a dark pool of it was forming and sliming the stone where Tarra's fingers clung. It dripped from beneath the guard's chin—where his throat was slit from ear to ear!

Aye, for the gleam in his eyes was merely glaze, and his fixed grin was a rictus of horror! Also, the crossbow's groove was empty, its bolt shot; and now Tarra remembered the whirring sound, the cough, the gurgle...

Adrenalin flooded the Hrossak's veins as a flash flood fills dry river beds. He was up and into the embrasure and across the sprawling corpse in a trice, his flesh ice as he stared all about, panting in the darkness. He had a friend here for sure, but who or what he dared not think. And now, coming to him across the reek of spilled blood...*again* that sulphurous musk, that fascinating yet strangely fearful perfume.

Then, from the deeper shadows of a shattered turret:

"Have you forgotten me then, Tarra Khash, whose life you saved in the badlands? And is not the debt I owed you repaid?"

And oh the Hrossak knew that sibilant, whispering voice, knew only too well whose hand—or claw—had kept him safe this night. Aye, and he further knew now that Chlangi's bats were no bigger than the bats of any other city; knew *exactly* why those ponies had fled like the wind across the plain; knew, shockingly, how close he must have come last night to death's sharp edge! The wonder was that he was still alive to know these things, and now he must ensure no rapid deterioration of that happy circumstance.

"I've not forgotten," he forced the words from throat dry as the desert itself. "Your perfume gives you away, Orbiquita—and your kiss shall burn on my neck and in my memory forever!" He took a step toward the turret.

"Hold!" she hissed from the shadows, where now a greater darkness moved uncertainly, its agitation accompanied by scraping as of many knives on stone. "Come no closer, Hrossak. It's no clean-limbed, soft-breasted girl stands here now."

"I know that well enow," Tarra croaked. "What do you want with me?"

"With you—nothing. But with that pair who put me to such trial in the desert—"

"They are dead," Tarra stopped her.

"What?" (Again the clashing of knives.) "Dead? That were a pleasure I had promised myself!"

"Then blame your disappointment on some other, Orbiquita," Tarra spoke into darkness. "Though certainly I would have killed them, if Fregg hadn't beaten me to it."

"Fregg, is it?" she hissed. "Scum murders scum. Well, King Fregg has robbed me, it seems."

"Both of us," Tarra told her. "You of your revenge, me of more worldly pleasures—a good many of them. Right now I'm on my way to take a few back."

The blackness in the turret stirred, moved closer to the door. Her voice was harsher now, the words coming more quickly, causing Tarra to draw back from brimstone breath. "What of my runebook?"

"Arenith Han, Fregg's sorcerer, will have that," the Hrossak answered.

"And where is he?"

"He lives in Fregg's palace, beneath his master's tower."

"Good! Show me this place." She inched forward again and for a moment the moonlight gleamed on something unbearable. Gasping, Tarra averted his eyes, pointed a trembling hand out over the city.

"There," he said, his voice breaking a little. "That high tower there with the light. That's where Fregg and his mage dwell, well guarded and central within the palace walls."

"What are guards and walls to me?" she said, and he heard the scrape of her clawed feet and felt the heat of her breath on the back of his neck. "What say you we visit this pair together?"

Rooted to the spot, not daring to look back, Tarra answered: "I'm all for companionship, Orbiquita, but—"

"So be it!" she was closer still. "And since you can't bear to look at me, close your eyes. Also, put away that knife—it would not scratch my scales."

Gritting his teeth, Tarra did both things—and at once felt himself grasped, lifted up, crushed to hot, stinking, scaly body. Wings of leather creaked open in the night; wind rushed all about; all was dizzy, soaring, whirling motion. Then—

Tarra felt his feet touch down and was released. He staggered, sprawled, opened his eyes and sprang erect. Again he stood upon a parapet; on one hand a low balcony wall, overlooking the city, and on the other an arabesqued archway issuing warm, yellow light. Behind him, stone steps winding down, where even now something dark descended on scythe feet! Orbiquita, going in search of her runebook.

"Who's there?" came sharp voice of inquiry from beyond the arched entrance. "Is that you, Arenith? And didn't I say not to disturb me at my sorting and counting?"

It was Fregg—Fregg all alone, with no bully boys to protect him now—which would make for a meeting much more to Tarra's liking. And after all, he'd been invited, hadn't he?

Invited or not, the shock on Fregg's face as Tarra entered showed all too clearly how the robber-king had thought never to see him again. Indeed, it was as if Fregg gazed upon a ghost, which might say something about the errand of the two who'd followed Tarra across the plain; an errand unfulfilled, as Fregg now saw. He half came to his feet, then slumped down again with hands atop the huge oak table that stood between.

"Good evening, Majesty," said Tarra Khash, no hint of malice in his voice. "I've come for my broken sword, remember?" He looked all about the circular, dome-ceilinged room, where lamps on shelves gave plenty of light. And now the Hrossak saw what a magpie this jowly bandit really was. Why, 'twere a wonder the many shelves had room for Fregg's lamps at all—for they were each and every one stacked high with stolen valuables of every sort and description! Here were jade idols and goblets, and more jade in chunks unworked. Here were silver statuettes, plates, chains and trinkets galore. Here were sacklets of very precious gems, and larger sacks of semi-precious stones. Here was gold and scrolls of gold-leaf, bangles of the stuff hanging from nails like so many hoops on pegs, and brooches, and medallions on golden chains, and trays of rings all burning yellow. But inches deep on the great table, and as yet unsorted, there lay Fregg's greatest treasure— which oh so recently had belonged to Tarra Khash.

"Your sword?" Fregg forced a smile more a grimace on to his face, fingered his beard, continued to stare at his visitor as if hypnotized. But at last animation: he stood up, slapped his thigh, roared with laughter and said, "Why of course, your broken sword!" Then he sobered. "It's here somewhere, I'm sure. But alas, I've not yet had time to remove the gems." His eyes rapidly swept the table, narrowing as they more slowly returned to the Hrossak's face.

Tarra came closer, watching the other as a cat watches a mouse, attuned to every breath, to each slightest movement. "Nor will there be time, I fancy," he said.

"Eh?" said Fregg; and then, in imitation of Tarra's doomful tone: "Is that to be the way of it? Well, before we decide upon all that—first tell me, Hrossak, how it is you've managed to come here, to this one place in all Chlangi which I had thought impregnable?"

Before Tarra could answer there came from below a shrill, wavering cry borne first of shock, then disbelief, finally terror—cut off most definitely at zenith. Skin prickling, knowing that indeed Orbiquita had found Arenith Han, Tarra commenced an involuntary turn—and knew his mistake on the instant. Already he had noted, upon a shelf close to where Fregg sat a small silver crossbow, with silver bolt loaded in groove and string ready-nocked. Turning back to robber-king he fell to one knee, his right hand and arm a blur of motion. Tarra's knife thrummed like a harp where its blade was fixed inches deep in shelf's soft wood, pinning Fregg's fat hand there even as it reached for weapon. And upon that pinned hand, glinting on the smallest finger, a ring of gold inset with jade cut in a skull and serpent crest.

Blood spurted and Fregg slumped against the shelves—but not so heavily that his weight put stress on the knife. "M-mercy!" he croaked, but saw little of mercy in the hulking steppeman's eyes. Gasping his pain, he reached trembling free hand toward the knife transfixing the other.

In a scattering of gems and baubles Tarra vaulted the table, his heels slamming into Fregg's face. The bandit was hurled aside, his hand split neatly between second and third fingers by the keen blade! Screaming Fregg fell, all thought of fighting back relinquished now to agony most intense from riven paw. Gibbering he sprawled upon the floor amidst scattering gems and nuggets, while Tarra stood spread-legged and filled the scabbard at his back, then topped his loot with hilt of shattered sword.

Until, "Enough!" he said. "I've got what I came for."

"But *I* have not!" came Orbiquita's monstrous hiss from the archway.

Tarra turned, saw her, went weak at the knees. Now he looked full upon a lamia, and knew all the horror of countless others gone before him. And yet he found the strength to answer her as were she his sister: "You did not find your runebook?"

"The book, aye," her breath was sulphur. "Mylakhrion's ring, no. Have you seen it, Tarra Khash? A ring of gold with skull and serpent crest?"

Edging past her, Tarra gulped and nodded in Fregg's direction where he sat, eyes bugging, his quivering back to laden shelves. "Of that matter, best speak to miserable monarch there," he told her.

Orbiquita's claws flexed and sank deep into the stone floor as she hunched toward the now drooling, keening robber-king.

"Farewell," said Tarra, leaping out under the archway and to the parapet wall, and fixing his grapnel there.

From below came hoarse shouts, cries of outrage, the clatter of many feet ascending the tower's corkscrew stairs. "Farewell," came

Orbiquita's hiss as Tarra swung himself out and down into the night. "Go swiftly, Hrossak, and fear no hand at your back. I shall attend to that."

After that—

All was a chaos of flight, of hideous screams fading into distance behind, of climbing, falling, of running and riding, until Chlangi was a blot, then less than a blot, then vanished altogether into distance behind him. Somewhere along the way Stumpy Adz dragged him to a gasping, breathless halt, however brief, gawped at a handful of gems, disappeared dancing into shadows; and somewhere else Tarra cracked a head when unknown assailant leaped on him from hiding; other than which he remembered very little.

And through all of that wild panic flight, only once did Tarra Khash look back—of which he wished he likewise had no recall.

For then...he had thought to see against the face of the moon a dark shape flying, whose outlines he knew well. And dangling beneath, a fat flopping shape whose silhouette seemed likewise familiar. And he thought the dangling thing screamed faintly in the thin, chill air of higher space, and he thought he saw its fitful kicking. Which made him pray it was only his imagination, or a dark cloud fleeing west.

And after that he put it firmly out of his mind.

As for Orbiquita:

She hated being in anyone's debt. This should square the matter. Fregg would make hearty breakfast for a hungry sister waking up from five long years of stony vigil...

In the Temple of Terror

I

Den of Thieves

Weird energies formed flickering green and blue traceries in the black clouds boiling over Klühn, patterned like webs of giant, lightning-spawned spiders, with central strands going down in a coil and lending the dome of a certain temple a cold and eerie foxfire all its own.

This was the first of three nights at the full of the moon, and the alien aurora was a thing familiar now to the inhabitants of Klühn where the city stood, a jewel of civilization and sophistication, at the mouth of the Lohr on the shore of the Eastern Ocean. Each month, when the moon was full, for three nights the sky would boil, while filaments of fire wove sentient skeins all funnelled down to the Temple of Secret Gods. And the aurora was the reason why Klühn's peoples—those of less adventurous or fool-hardy inclinations, at least; those unwilling to tempt whatever supernatural forces were at work here—were now abed, shivering in their sheets, leaving the streets to the handful of yeggs and sharpers and vagabonds who wandered there, whose souls were already sold.

Less than novel in the eyes of common residents (the aerial phe-nomenon had first occurred a year ago, and every month since), the manifestation was a thing of wonder to Tarra Khash; a wonder and a pestilence, for it threatened to ruin his sleep. Sleep was unsatisfactory at best of times—on bed of hard planks with one tattered blanket, and every smallest wind a freezing hurricane howling in through the iron bars of his cage, or causing it to sway at the end of its chain, suspended from the high, overhanging parapet wall of the Square of Justice—but with the night flickering green and blue like this it were impossible! And so, sitting there in the fabulous dark (or what should be dark), his blanket wrapped tight about him like the feathers of some strange, gaunt bird, Tarra stared and wondered, and pondered the wretchedness of his position and the path of fate which had led him to it...

Two weeks gone, having forded the Lohr some miles west of the fork, the Hrossak had entered Klühn through the West Gate; in dusk of evening had headed straight for the market area, sold his camel, bought clothes more fitting to city life and discarded his much-worn and now highly disreputable loin-cloth. Then, fitted out in silken shirt (with sleeves rolled up to show the width of his forearms), bell-bottomed, piratical trousers of a coarse weave, and leather calf-boots folded down near the top—with his scabbard slung across his back, jewelled hilt of ceremonial scimitar protruding, but iron-pinned to thwart would-be thieves—he had swaggered forth to find himself lodge down by the wharves. After hiring a luxurious turret room overlooking the bay on the one hand and Lohr's wide mouth on the other, and having bathed and filled his belly with meat and wine, and further having slept for an hour or two, then he had been ready for come-what-may.

Now, Hrossaks are a breed who believe in living, and Tarra was no exception. He could take it hard without complaint when neces-sary, but liked it soft on occasion, certainly. Recently, indeed for quite some little while, it had been the former, and in Tarra's eyes latter were long overdue. Which was why he had decided to let his hair down. The plan was simple: find an eatery and put away something rare and spicy—to supplement the not insubstantial meal already consumed, but not enjoyed in haste of chomping—drink a bottle or two of the rarest wine, then hie him to a bawdy-house and bed some luscious whore. Morning would be soon enough to worry about his wealth: what to do with it, how to spend it (for what was money for if not the spending?) and how best the fortune might be employed in furtherance of his future and pursuance of his career. Ah!—but there had lain the rub, there the roots of his dilemma...

For Tarra Khash was a wanderer, an adventurer, and wealth tends to moor a man much as an anchor holds fast the fleetest ship. He could buy himself a property, he supposed, high-walled and secluded, to serve as his base; but then he must look for a caretaker, too, servants to tend the place when he was away. All very difficult. But...such are the problems of rich men. Anyway, tomorrow would be time enough for all that; doubtless there'd be businessmen in the city to advise him this way or that—for a fee, of course.

These had been his thoughts on his first night in Klühn...

And on the second—

—The third, and etc.

Then, a week ago, he had stumbled somewhat intoxicated upon Ellern Thark's gambling den, and as easily as that his problems had all been solved.

Gambling hadn't been new to the Hrossak: he'd seen dice and cards of various sorts used in Hrossa for the amusement of steppemen, had even gamed himself on rare occasion; but there on the steppes the stakes had been so small as to be insignificant, while in Ellern Thark's place they were...something else! Why, a man could lose an entire fortune here in less than a week—or three days, if he tried hard enough and if crafty proprietor kept him topped up with booze!

That's all it had taken, three days; with Tarra staggering back to his turret room before dawn, sleeping it off, then back to Thark's place to send good money chasing after bad, and not once catch it; and Tarra never quite sober enough to realize that the dice were loaded and the cards marked, and always sufficiently optimistic to believe he'd get his money back. It had all become hazy in his head: a continuous clatter of dice, a dizzy blur of brightly daubed cards, an unending gurgle of fiery liqueurs and anaesthetic ales. Until finally—

Broke!

Neither nugget nor gemstone, jade- nor silver-piece, bauble nor button. Only the bejewelled hilt of his ceremonial sword, and a pinch or two of gold dust shaken out of now utterly vacant scabbard to satisfy his landlord's needs. Then and only then had the Hrossak started to put two and two together, and the sum always coming out five; and only *then* recalling certain things hitherto meaningless, which now took on aspect of vast import.

Clinching it, finally he overheard from where he sat, head in hands in a secluded tavern booth, how "that big dumb Hrossak" had been robbed of king's ransom at Ellern Thark's, and that had set a pot boiling in his belly whose steam could only find release in volcanic violence. While the pot boiled, however, building up pressure, Tarra had fuelled its fire with thoughts of all he'd gone through to win his fortune in the first place:

He'd thought of the desert-hidden treasure vaults of alien kings he'd robbed—or been sent to rob—and of the vengeance of the golden guardians of those subterrene sepulchres, which he'd only just escaped with skin intact; of his subsequent flight to Chlangi the Doomed, where lamia's kiss had seared his neck and possibly his soul, and where he'd had to steal back a portion of his tomb-loot from robber-king Fregg, now a pile of bones somewhere in Nameless Desert's heart. He'd thought of arduous camel-trek to Klühn, weighed down by scabbard full of gold and gems strapped firmly to his back, and of all he'd dreamed to do with that hard-earned fortune, dreams now turned to dust—by Ellern Thark, a sharper lower than a lizard's gut, boss of a fleapit den of thieves.

And then other vague memories had come, rapidly growing clearer, finally overlapping the mindless kaleidoscope of cards and dice and drink. Tarra had remembered how, on occasion, he'd seen Thark watching while he gamed, and how that fjord-born snake had winked at his dealers at certain times, or introduced fresh, cool dice into the game. Aye, too cool by far!

Hah! Tarra's luck had always seemed to run low where Northmen were concerned—at cards or at anything else, whether the dice were loaded or not—and now it seemed the pattern continued to run true. Well, he couldn't prove a thing and he knew it, but it wasn't only his pocket that was hurting and he must do something. Mayhem seemed the only answer, and yet—

Perhaps there was another way...

He still had the jewelled hilt of his sword, after all—for the moment, anyway—and that was surely worth a small fortune in itself.

Why not roll the dice one last time at Ellern's place? One last shot—for all or nothing!

And so that night Tarra had ventured yet again to the gambling den, and a sorry, sodden sight he must have been on arrival. The wonder was he was let in at all, but when he showed the thugs on the door the gems where they gleamed in the hilt of his shattered sword...

Inside it had been business as usual. The sigh and flutter of cards and the skittering of ivory and jade dice; the *oobs!* and *aahs!* of spectators; curses or guffaws of gamers; the lamps suspended from high-beamed ceiling, lending the scene glints of a coppery colour; and the half-clad Yhemni slave-girls, moving sinuously among patrons with trays of spicy sweetmeats and clinking goblets of wine, their dusky skins agleam with oils and their filed teeth flashing white in dark faces.

But in the crush of bodies about the tables, Tarra had spotted Ellern Thark at once—and Thark had spotted him.

The proprietor of the den was as big a northern barbarian as any Tarra had ever come across in all his wanderings, and big in *all* directions. Not yet thirty, Thark's aspect was truly awesome. A young, full-blooded Northman, his mane of hair was blue-black to match his eyes; and they in turn were set in the face of a hawk, scarred from knife and fist fights and weathered by northern winters. His arms and legs were trunks of muscle, likewise scarred in places, and his chest and back formed a wedge of meat rising up from a waist narrow as Tarra's own. Strong as an ox, devious and deadly formidable; that was Ellern Thark. The soft silks of his clothing couldn't hide it, and the wicked gleam in his slitted eyes where they gazed on Tarra Khash made no slightest attempt.

A moment earlier Thark had been deep in heated conversation with a yellow-robed, bald-pated priest of the Temple of Secret Gods, and Tarra had remembered how he had seen such in here on several previous occasions. This had caused him to revisit what little he had learned of their obscure and cryptic sect:

The first disciples of the order (he had been given to understand in casual conversation) had appeared in the city some five years earlier, arriving from Thinhla, Eyphra, even from as far away as Thandopolis, bringing with them the entirely conjectural ikons and instruments of their faith. Not far from Klühn's central plazas, they had procured land and commenced construction of their mighty ziggurat temple with its lesser outer domes and massive central dome of hammered copper, a project which had paid most of the city's builders and craftsmen well indeed and had kept them in work for all of four years—which had been good not only for them but Klühn in general. For Klühn was a commercial city and lived by its commercialism. Also, the peoples of Klühn were not opposed to a multitude of gods, even secretive ones, if such brought them wealth. And however cryptogenic the gods of these yellow-robed priests, they did not appear inimical; indeed the sect members kept well to themselves and bothered no one. At least, not at first. Later things had been different...

Now Klühn had various playboy princelings of mixed origins—socialites who dwelled here for the climate and good living in the main, rather than by laying claim to the lands around—but no real king, else the doings of the Secret Gods Sect came perhaps under closer scrutiny. But...after the temple was builded and its high outer walls erected fortress-like, then the changes had gradually come about and things were finally seen to be more complicated—and perhaps more sinister—than had at first seemed likely.

Even then the ordinary, normally industrious citizenry was not affected, not at first; only dealers in land, property, jewelry, gold and silver merchants, whoremasters, vice-lords and such felt the sting; and felt it where it most hurt: in their pockets. For it now appeared that the priests of the sect held within their temple an oracle of great power, all-knowing, all-seeing, and that the special function of this oracle was to advise the priests of any and all shady transactions taking place in the arenas of those aforementioned businesses and concerns, so that soon Klühn's over- and under-world barons alike found themselves in the grip of temple-spawned blackmail! And in a trice the priests had their fingers in every pie, and all concerned paid tribute to the Temple of Secret Gods, lest *their* most precious secrets be shouted abroad.

Then it had been the turn of Klühn's simpler folk, when they too had started to feel the pinch. For now they found themselves levied of a tax, which they must pay in respect of the protection they received from the yellow-robed priests. But protection from what? The answer to that was simple: against dark forces which even now strove to destroy Klühn and her citizens, whose periodic attacks only the presence of the temple itself staved off! (The temple, its oracle, and its priests, of course.)

The monthly manifestations of weird energies, aye! The boiling clouds and strange lightnings, the doomful darkness and flickering corpse-fires swirling over the city, whose forces seemed drained by temple's copper dome, and doubtless by efforts of droning priests and sphinxy oracle within! And what to do but pay, or else go unprotected from all this strangeness? For Klühn in her opulence and arrogance had sinned, and now sinners and innocents alike were taken to task, and the Secret Gods' Sect had come in their mercy to pave the city's way back to righteousness and sanctity in the eyes of their unknown gods.

So that the question now asked was this: had those strange and furtive priests really come to stave off a doom, or had the doom simply followed them here? And if so, what to do about it?

The answer to which was this: nothing!

For the original handful of yellow-robes was now an hundred, and the sellswords they'd hired an hundred more, so that only a fool or madman would say or go against them. And him who did—why, he simply vanished, or was ruined!—object lesson to more cautious men.

And Klühn, which had no king and hence no army, must suffer in silence.

It was just such a yellow-robe Tarra Khash had seen in heated conversation with Ellern Thark that night he had chosen to take his revenge, and he remembered now how both had seemed to glare at him across that thronging den of thieves and fools. Or maybe they glared because of their argument, which had perhaps spared Tarra from closer scrutiny. Aye, and just as well, that.

Anyway, Thark's acknowledgement of his presence had been merely cursory; what else should it be, in light of the fact that the Hrossak was obviously drunk and had doubtless rolled in the gutter on his way here? Well, his visit wouldn't last long. What little he'd brought with him could be robbed in a trice, just as his vaster fortune had been robbed. The man deserved no better; obviously he was even greater clown than Thark had first taken him for!

But as Thark's interest in him had waned, so Tarra had wormed his way closer to barbarian and yellow-robe, so that soon he was able to overhear something of their conversation. Ostensibly they watched a dice game while they talked, but that was just for show. In fact, it seemed the priest was giving Ellern Thark a hard time, at least from the harsh tone of Thark's agitated voice as Tarra heard him answer:

"Yes, yes, I've agreed all that—though all the gods know 'twere near impossible! Doesn't Gorgos know he's bleeding us dry? Why, if not for the fact that I've had a good week I'd not be *able* to pay! Easy as that. Unwilling is one thing—indeed something to be expected—but unable something else again. Blackmail all you will, you so-called 'priests,' but what weight will your threats carry when there's nothing left, eh? You'll bring the entire city down on your heads if you're not careful; aye, and your soldiers will surely be called upon to earn their keep then, by Yibb!"

"Calm yourself!" the other had answered sharply. "And waste not your ire on me, Ellern Thark. I am merely Gorgos' messenger. He tends the oracle, and he determines the toll. You *have* done well this week, beyond a doubt, else were your dues lighter. You have not always paid so high."

"High?" Thark burst out, his voice louder now than harsh whisper. "High? I call it *extortion!*"

"'Ware, Northman!" the yellow-robe's hiss was ice. "You live well here, would you jeopardize your position?"

At which junction there had come a roar of rage from the gaming table close at hand, where a burly merchant with fat hands dripping rings had grabbed the table's dice-caster by his skinny neck and was now shaking him like a rat. "Cheat!" the merchant roared, shaking away. "I can lose as fast as any man without help from you!" Finally he hurled the dealer to the floor—which was where Ellern Thark stepped in.

"Sir," he pushed through the crush, "that man's in my employ. If he's a cheat I'll break all his fingers and toss him in the street—refund your losses, too—but if he's innocent you've a problem on your hands. I'll not have my house impugned without chance to answer back. Neither beggar nor rich man calls Ellern Thark a cheat!"

"You?" the merchant had turned to him red-faced, taken in his massive size and the angry glint in his blue-black barbarian eyes. "*Huh!* I don't know about you," he said, "but this one—" he pointed at the choking, coughing dealer where he clawed at the floorboards, "—this one's a thief! Him and his dice both!" And he slammed down a pair of dice on the table. Thark, nimble-fingered, snatched them up at once.

"Are these the dice?" he snapped. "Did he cheat you with these?" He held the dice out—but Tarra saw his other hand now placed jauntily on hip, close to a silken pocket.

"Aye, with them," said the merchant. "Toss 'em and see for yourself. Sixes every time. They're weighted, obviously."

Thark grinned—but it was the grin of a crocodile. "These arc house dice," he said, "and innocent of trickery. As am I, and as is he whose throat you've sorely crushed. Lady Luck's the villain, sir—or villainess if you like. And no wonder, for I've heard she only runs with gentlemen..."

"*What?*" the other had been furious. He snatched back the dice (the ones Thark offered him), shook them, let them roll. A one and a three. Purple with rage, he stared, then turned on Thark. "You must've swapped 'em!" he roared. "Why you're a bigger—"

The Northman hit him once, stiff-fingered, his hand vanishing in the other's gut up to his wrist, propelling him off his feet and through the crush of people, all air expelled in one gigantic *whoosh* of breath, and accusation gone with it. "*Out!*" Thark bellowed, pointing, his men closing in on the merchant even as he caromed from a support pillar and fell. "Into the gutter with him—and don't let me see him in here again. What? Is this a brothel and are we whores, we should suffer insults from such as him? What were his losses, that so enraged him? Two small pieces of silver, I'll wager!"

"A little more than that, Ellern Thark," said damaged dealer's assistant, a dark Yhemni maid with gleaming breasts, standing by the table. "I hold the stakes." She tipped them on to the table: two small pouches of gold dust, a chunk of raw silver big as a man's thumb, two large rings aglitter with precious stones.

"A pittance!" cried Thark. "And would I give my house a bad name for this? Why, I'd gamble it myself on a single throw, high score wins!"

"Done!" Tarra Khash had then drunkenly rumbled, stumbling forward to clasp Thark's hand where it had strayed back toward his silk pocket. "Shake on it. And here—you shoot first." He picked up the dice, passed them to Thark.

Thark glowered at the dice in the palm of his great hand; his dark glance went to the stakes. "Where's your money, Hrossak? Haven't you lost enough yet?" His voice was cold as the Chill Sea.

Never taking his eyes from Thark's huge yet overly agile hands, Tarra fished out a huge ruby freshly gouged from the hilt of his sword. It joined the other items in keeping of the Yhemni wench, putting the rest of the purse in the shade. "Well?"

"So be it," Thark grunted, his lips curling back in half-grin, half-snarl. He blew on the dice, tossed them…a three and a four.

"Seven!" cried Tarra. "My throw!" He took up the dice, gave them a shake, let them roll. Two fives. "Good!" said Tarra, reaching for his winnings.

As the crowd pushed closer Thark wiped the snarl from his face, said: "There! That's the sort of game I like: quick and clean." He made as if to pocket the dice, appeared to change his mind. "Since your luck's in, Hrossak, mayhap you'd care to try it again?"

"Aye, why not?" Tarra gestured expansively, reeling just a little and thinking: *and here's where I close you down, dog!* "What stakes, Ellern Thark?"

"Why, what you see," said the other, the smallest niggle of a doubt beginning to form at the back of his mind. The Hrossak seemed drunk, and yet—

"A pittance!" Tarra had cut Thark's thoughts short. "You said it yourself—and my ruby the choicest morsel!"

"Very well," Thark answered, his face darkening again. "Beat me one more time—fairly mind!—and I'll pay four times the odds. Nay, for you, who've suffered such grievous losses here, I'll even make it fives! Now who could say fairer than that?"

Tarra had expected no less; he knew that Thark believed he couldn't lose. "Your word on it?" he said. "A fair game and no grudge held—and you'll bet odds of five to one I can't beat you again?"

"My word on it," Thark answered, growing uncomfortable under the gaze of so many eyes.

"And you'll cover anything I put up?"

"Should I have a scribe carve it in runes, Tarra Khash?" Thark shouted. "Now what's the delay?"

"No delay," said Tarra. "Only cover this!" And he'd produced and slammed down on the table the gem-crusted hilt of his sword, which amounted to everything he owned in the entire world of Theem'hdra.

At that a concerted gasp had gone up—and none louder than the hissing sigh of yellow-robed priest—while the crush of bodies had tightened as patrons vied for better vantage points. And no more pretended drunkenness on Hrossak's part, whose eyes now glinted keen as barbarian's own; but perhaps the sudden blossoming of respect and maybe even a little fear in Thark's northern breast, where his heart began to beat a little faster as he made a sign across the room to his cashiers in cage of iron bars.

Then from the strongroom was brought all the Hrossak's previous wealth, his ingots, jewels, nuggets of gold. And, "Satisfied now, Hrossak?" rasped Ellern Thark. "Is this what you wanted to see?"

"I think that'll do," Tarra had answered.

While all of this was in action, the yellow-robe had ogled and twitched, his gaze seeming riveted to Tarra's broken blade. Then, as Thark had blown on the dice in his fashion and prepared to throw them down, Tarra had thought to hear, however indistinctly, the said priest's excited whisper:

"Win, Thark! Win me that broken sword and consider all your dues paid for a year—aye, and Gorgos and all the priests of the temple in *your* debt for a change!"

Then the dice were rattling on the table, bouncing, skittering to a halt. Sixes, both!

And the massive Northman laughing, his hand moving toward the dice, doubtless to catch them up in triumph. But Tarra Khash moving first, snatching up the hilt of his sundered sword and smashing it down shatteringly on one of the dice—which had at once broken into pieces, displaying a base filled with lead! Thark's laughter dying on his lips...

...And in the ensuing silence, Hrossak's voice like knell of doom, saying: "It seems you lose, Ellern Thark—unless these loaded dice are your idea of fair?"

Then—

Thark's hand blurring toward hilt of wicked knife in his belt—a mistake, for Tarra's weapon was already in his hand. And while its blade was a mere stump, a six-inch shard, no more, still its edge was razor sharp. And in under Thark's ribs that shattered blade had driven, and across in a tearing of silk, and down to make a door in fleshy wall. And then through that door Thark's guts pouring, while his hands shot into the air, knife flying uselessly from shuddering fingers to lodge thrumming in ceiling joist. And still the stunned silence, until with a final tremor the barbarian's body had crashed like felled oak, life all spilled out and wet upon the shaken boards.

Then a motion to Tarra's rear—and swirly flash of yellow glimpsed out the corner of his eye—followed by sharp report like *snap* of great whip...shattering concussion...more flashes, all brightly hued, all rapidly turning dark...spiralling down into whirlpools of blackest jet...

II

Last of the Suhm-yi

The rest of it was very clear in the Hrossak's memory.

He had regained consciousness in a cell; the morning had seen him in a city court charged with Ellern Thark's sudden demise; chief witness for the prosecution was the yellow-robe of the previous night, his bald pate full of lies and treachery. Tarra had been framed neat as an eye in its orbit; it appeared that after the priest crowned him, two pairs of loaded dice had been "discovered" in his pockets. A would-be cheat turned murderer, the verdict had not been difficult to gauge in advance:

Ten days in a cage—time enough to repent his wicked ways and make his peace with the world, while the good folk of Klühn could come in hours of daylight and *tut-tut* and ogle at him where he dangled high overhead—and on the eleventh day the cage hauled up to its highest point, and securing pin knocked neatly out from the chain's last link. Then downward rush, and cage and bed and Hrossak and all dashed to pieces on the flags 'neath the frowning walls of the Square of Justice. And Tarra now suspended here, with only seven days left to him in all the world, pondering on all the fables he'd heard which had it that the justice of Klühn and the kindness of her citizens were finest and fairest in Theem'hdra. Well, perhaps, in days gone by—but hardly relevant now, and no comfort at all to Tarra Khash…

The clouds over Klühn were breaking up now, their boiling less frenzied, traceries of weird energy thinning out and growing fainter. In a little while it would all be over; the skies would grow clear again, Old Gleeth the god of the moon would blaze like a silver skull over the far horizon. A skull, aye, for Tarra's mood was grown very morbid; he could find nothing wholesome in anything he saw or thought of. His position seemed entirely hopeless. But—

"Not quite, Tarra Khash," said a voice quite close. "Not *entirely* hopeless."

Tarra started, causing his cage to rock a little, and sat up straighter on his plank bed. What? And had he been doing his thinking out loud, then? And skulking night-watch come to chuckle at him out of the shadow of the wall? He turned his sour gaze that way.

Inside the Square's massy walls ramps had been built and machines for the hauling of cages, and openings like arched windows had been cut through the walls themselves from which food could be passed on long poles to prisoners in their cages. During the day the Square was open to visitors, when citizens with grievances—relatives of murdered persons, perhaps, or victims of vile assaults, frauds and such, even simple curiosity seekers—could climb the inner ramps at will, pass through the walls and hurl rotten fruit, bad eggs and worse language at the criminals suspended there. Now, in one such arched niche, the one closest to Tarra, a shadow stirred half in feeble moonlight. Tarra stared hard, wondering who this could be, at this time of night, come to torment him.

"Who indeed?" came soft, silvery query out of darkness. "Who reads the misery of your thoughts in the night, Tarra Khash, and comes to discover you here, caged like a strange wild bird? Don't you know me? Have you so soon forgotten the Inner Isles, the isles of the Suhm-yi?"

"*Suhm-yi!*" Tarra's answer came out a gasp. "Forgotten? Of course not. Oh, I know you now, Amyr Arn, last of your race! But what do you here, so far from crater sea?"

"You've answered that already, Tarra," came answer like silver bells in the night. "Last of my race, you said—and once I thought so, too. But now—now I'm not so sure."

You mean there's another, like you? Here in Klühn?"

"Another, *un*like me. A female, aye—a Suhm-yi maid!"

Tarra jumped up, pressed his body to the bars, spread his legs to brace himself against the cage's sway. He had so many questions in him that they all vied to be out together, so that for long moments nothing was said at all. And then, just when he might have spoken, his words were anticipated.

"I'll tell you all," said Amyr Arn, "—but after I've got you down from here."

"Got me down? *Hah!*" Tarra laughed, however bitterly. "A job on your hands there, my friend. And how about the night-watch? Six of 'em, at least, in their guardroom at the base of the stone tower at the corner of the wall. Don't you think they'll have something to say about it?"

"Very little," Amyr answered, his voice a-tinkle. "I sent them up a flagon of wine all of an hour ago, when the sky was dancing with alien fires. A very special wine, it was—all laced with a rare, rare drug. By now they're snoring their heads off!"

"Oh?" Tarra gawped, then laughed and slapped his thigh. "And tomorrow, if I'm found absent, they'll likely wish they *had* snored them off! At least that's a peaceful way to lose 'em! But tell me, how'll you get me down?"

"*Shh!*" Amyr had cautioned. "Be quiet now. You'll see soon enough. Have patience—I'll be but a little while gone…" Tarra saw twin flashes of gold; then, where a shadow had stirred, the niche in the wall was empty of all but moonbeams and a swirl of fine dust…

For the next few minutes Tarra let his mind wander back a six-month to his adventures in the Inner Isles, that volcanic tumble of jewel islands lying central in the crater sea. He had gone there hot on the trail of a gang of murderous Northmen, Kon Athar and his bully-boys, after they'd butchered two prospector pals of his near the source of the River Thand high in the Great Circle Mountains. The barbarians had quested for treasure, and they'd crossed mountains seeking the legended Inner Isles where dwelled a half-fabulous (and only half-human, or perhaps totally *un*-human) race of manlike beings known only as the Suhm-yi, the "Seldom Seen."

Sailing the great crater sea on raft of logs, all the barbarian reavers found was this: isles of the Suhm-yi all layered in a thick red dust, and the Suhm-yi themselves—four-fingered, four-toed, silvery-skinned and golden-eyed—but every one of them dead. Dead of the poison in the dust, which had been blown there from some far volcanic disaster, and rained from the skies to kill them all off. All except two. Amyr Arn had been one, his mate, Lula, the other.

Amyr had been fishing when the Northmen came, far out on placid crater sea when they found his tiny jewel island. Aye, and they'd found his lovely Lula, too…

When Tarra Khash had followed their tracks to her body it was much too late, and then only the strict Suhm-yi code—which did not permit of vengeance—kept him safe from Amyr's wrath, his grief, his passion. Afterwards—

—They had buried her, and next day in Amyr's canoe Tarra had once more taken up the chase, and finally Kon Athar and his bullies were tracked down and slain. Tarra did this on his own, for again Suhm-yi vows would not permit Amyr to go with him. But at the end—strangely, for Amyr was not there—still the Hrossak had sensed the last of the Suhm-yi's intervention in the final vengeance, his hand in the thing; and since it doubtless saved his life, he'd welcomed that weird diversion. For it was not Tarra who struck Kon Athar down in the final fight but an arrow, speeding seemingly from out the very moon—a Suhm-yi arrow, Amyr's own—and Amyr nowhere in sight, but miles away upon another isle!

That was the fight where Tarra had lost his sword, or rather where he'd been left with only stump of curving scimitar blade; and it was also the last time he'd seen the Inner Isles, like ingots of silver gleaming under Gleeth's bright ray…

Tarra's cage gave a sharp downward lurch, jerking him where he sat on the edge of his plank platform. He turned his eyes upward but could see little, only the wall on one side like canyon of stone, and above, the gibbet arm from which his cage was suspended. Then came the creak of a pulley, the rattle of a chain (cut short in a moment) and again his cage fell an inch or two before jigging a little on the air. The Hrossak gulped, hoping his strange friend knew what he was about!

Evidently Amyr did for, having got the hang of it, now without a sound the cage descended smoothly a good man-length, coming to a gentle halt. Then a period when nothing seemed to be happening, except Tarra Khash listening to the thudding of his own heart, until once again the shadows stirred in the niche and golden eyes looked out and down a little on Tarra in the cage.

"Your turn now, bronze one," came Amyr's silvery whisper. "I only pray you're as strong as you look!"

"What must I do?" Tarra whispered back, senses all alert.

By now the last of the alien, webby spiderfires had flickered out in the sky overhead and the clouds were drifting west. Stars were gleaming through, and from the far horizon Gleeth's light slanted full on the face of the wall. Klühn's citizens were all abed, true, but still the air seemed suddenly fraught with urgency, both Hrossak and Suhm-yi knowing there was little time to waste.

"I've a grapple here," Amyr called across. "Catch and fix it firmly to base of cage. I'll attend to this end."

Tarra saw his plan, said: "The bars are strong, and there's a lock on the door. Even if I can haul cage and all to your niche, what then?" But even speaking he caught and fixed the three-pronged hook.

"I've a way with locks," Amyr answered, "—if you can hold cage steady while I work. There, my end of the line is fixed. Now, I shall pull from my end, and wind the line as we go, and you must haul from your end—except you cannot rest or loose the rope."

"Fear not," Tarra gruffly answered. "It means my life!" And now arm over arm he commenced to haul on the rope, the cage shifting from the perpendicular and towards Amyr in his arched-over niche. Swiftly the Hrossak worked, knowing he could not rest till it was done; Amyr, too, hauling and winding, until the cage dangled but an arm's length away from the window in the wall.

"Now hold fast!" warned Amyr, and leaning out he swiftly fixed another grapple. "There!—now take your ease, Hrossak."

Tarra rested—and felt the sudden agony in his muscles! All had been swiftly accomplished, aye, but with such an effort he'd scarce realized; and now his arms like leaden lumps, but silently screaming as blood once more thundered through burning sinew. Groaning softly, he watched Amyr's four-fingered hands working at the lock on the door, saw it spring open. After that—

The work of a moment to swing the door wide, take Amyr's glittering arm and step from cage to niche—and lean there in shadow against the wall, limbs atremble in sudden reaction. But in another moment:

"What now, Amyr Arn?" asked Tarra. "Where does your plan take us from here?"

"To my lodgings," the other answered, "where we can talk. Here, put this on." And for the first time, as he leaned out of the shadows, Tarra saw how he was dressed: in the yellow robe of a priest of the Temple of Secret Gods! Not only that, but the hooded robe he handed Tarra was yellow, too!

"Now what in all the—?" Tarra hissed, only to be cut off short with:

"No, no—don't go jumping to conclusions, my friend. It's no easy thing for a silver, comb-headed man to make his way in pink- and brown- and black-skinned city. Believe me, it were far easier to become a nameless, cowled priest than stay Amyr Arn of the Suhm-yi—however temporary the change! Aye, and you'll be safer swathed in yellow, too."

Donning the cassock, Tarra couldn't resist a chuckle; then Amyr was leading the way through the wall, down the ramps, past the silent guardroom in base of corner tower and so out into the night. And all unchallenged the pair strode through Klühn's dark streets to the poorer side of town, where with wooden latchkey Amyr let them into a cobbled courtyard, and in the inky darkness led Tarra up steep exterior steps to a high attic aerie.

"Nice," grunted the Hrossak, admiring the hideaway when lamp was lit, "but not much good for a fast getaway, if such were needed."

Amyr at once showed him a window in a gable where it overhung a back-street; showed him also a coil of rope, its end made fast to a stout roof timber. "There's your bolthole, Hrossak," he said, repeating the other's: "'if such were needed.'"

Tarra chuckled. "It seems you've learned a lot since leaving your Inner Isles and becoming a yellow-robed priest!" he joked. "And what would your Suhm-yi gods think of that, I wonder? Or do you perhaps worship the same Secret Gods?"

"'Ware!" said Amyr, his voice more lead than silver now. "That were true blasphemy, Tarra Khash. Secret Gods, did you say?" He tossed back his hood, shook his combed head in denial. "Demons, my friend, drawn down from nameless places far out beyond the farthest stars! But come, let's doff these robes and eat a bite together, and I'll tell you all I've done and learned since that time we said farewell."

They seated themselves side by side on a low bench, and from a table scarce higher than the floor ate a meal of fish soup and hard bread washed down with a little sour wine. Not much of a repast, but gourmet's delight to Tarra Khash, after three days of slops and crusts eaten in a swaying cage. And seeing his hunger, Amyr let him take the greater part; so that while the Hrossak munched, the silver-scaled Suhm-yi commenced his tale.

"After you had gone from the Inner Isles, Tarra Khash, for long and long I prayed to the gods of the Suhm-yi, especially Gleeth, who sits at the head of their table. And I asked Gleeth should I stay here now, in crater sea, friendless and forlorn, amidst the dust and bones and ghosts of the Suhm-yi, or should I climb the high peak named Na-dom, fling myself down on the rocks, and so put an end to it?

"Now Gleeth's a cold one and seldom answers, but perhaps he took pity on one who thought himself last of the Suhm-yi. One evening when the moon hung full and low, great golden orb in the eastern sky—even over Klühn as I judged it—it seemed to me the moonbeams formed a stream, all shining down on that distant city of men; and I found great portent in the slant and fall of Gleeth's rays that night. I knew the locations of all the cities of Theem'hdra from the maps of my fathers, do you see? Oh, they had been called 'the Seldom Seen,' my people of the Inner Isles, aye, but they themselves were far-seeing indeed! And it seemed I'd inherited the vision of my fathers. Anyway, that night I dreamed...

"I dreamed of my Lula, lost to me and gone forever from the world, and gone with her all the dreams of Suhm-yi who might have been— except this one dream, my dream. And then I saw that it was not my

Lula but some other. Suhm-yi, certainly, but a stranger. And it seemed she called to me from afar, crying in her loneliness even as I cried in mine, and I felt her pain deep in my heart like a blunt blade turning there.

That morning, starting up from my bed, I remembered my dream—but more than that I remembered a tale from my childhood. At first the memory was weak, but the harder I willed it to return the stronger it grew, until finally I remembered all.

"I had been a child when it happened: a visitation from the outside world, the arrival of a sorcerer from the lands of men beyond the crater sea, beyond the Great Circle Mountains, beyond the coastal forests of the east. Aye, for he hailed from Shadarabar, jungled isle of mystery beyond the Straits of Yhem, and his skin was as black as the magicks he practised on the tiny island he made his home, there in the Inner Isles of the crater sea. His name was Gorgos!"

Here Tarra Khash started, but remained silent.

Amyr paused and nodded his combed head. "The same, I'm sure. But he was old even then, and like many old men he feared Death's stealthy encroachment. As is the way with wizards, Gorgos sought immortality. He had studied all Mylakhrion's works in that vein—those which were available to him—and the runebooks and librams and tablets of many another mage gone that same way before. And his thaumaturgies were terrible on the island he made his lair; so that soon no blade of grass would grow there, no bird nest in withered tree, no lizard scuttle on the bare stone. Even the sea around that rock was barren of fish, for Gorgos worked his morbid magicks there.

"Now you may well wonder why, since Gorgos was but one man and the Suhm-yi were many, his presence was suffered at all in the Inner Isles. But remember, he had worked no evil among us, asked nothing of us, kept well to himself and went not abroad from his dark rock. And the Suhm-yi were not the enemies of men; we preferred our solitude, naturally, but Gorgos did nothing to interfere with that. Moreover, it was known he was a fugitive, that certain Yhemni kings wanted him dead, not to mention many fellow wizards; so that it were most unlikely he would shout his whereabouts abroad, the fact that he had come to the Inner Isles and found the legended Suhm-yi there. And so Gorgos was left to his own devices, and he left the Suhm-yi to theirs—for a little while!

"But just as there are magicians among men, so in olden times were there sorcerers among the Suhm-yi; and because our races are different, their studies were likewise diverse. Gorgos, making no progress toward immortality through endeavours of merely human research, eventually turned his inquiries toward the now extinct, esoteric explorations of the ancient Suhm-yi. To do this, he must study the librams of Na-dom, holy of holies of all the isles of the Suhm-yi, and to this end he came to our elders to ask permission to visit Na-dom—which permission was, of course, refused. Only the High Priests of our race had ever set foot on Na-dom, and then rarely, for the Isle of the Sacred Spire held not only the relics of olden Suhm-yi civilization but also its treasures. Moreover, Na-dom was favoured of the gods, who were known on occasion to rest from their labours upon the high and windswept peak.

"When Gorgos was told these things he appeared to understand, made apology for his lapse of etiquette—for his request had bordered upon insult—and took his departure back to bleak, forbidding isle of magick. But all a sham, a show, a ploy; for in the course of time he turned his dark eyes once more upon Na-dom, and this time went there without recourse to the elders, and studied there the librams of the ancients.

"Now, upon Na-dom, as I have said, were all the olden treasures of the Suhm-yi, long ago put aside as worthless relics of barbaric ages. What is gold, after all, but a bright, heavy clod of earth; and pearls but the cancer of seashells; and what are jewels but glittery pebbles of the earth? And how may they compare with the sparkling air, the deep pure sea, the rich living soil of the earth itself? But amongst these centuried remains of times immemorial were three curved swords, like as peas in a pod, which had been the property of the greatest of all Suhm-yi sorcerers. And Gorgos read in the olden runebooks how, by use of these strange swords, a learned mage might call down from beyond the stars powers more potent than any mundane magicks! And this he determined to do, in his search for immortality.

"The rest of the tale tells itself: Gorgos stole the runebooks and Swords of Power and made off with them. Fleeing the Inner Isles he took hostage a young girl-child and killed her parents, then set off in a ship of black sails across the crater sea and disappeared. From which day until now his whereabouts has remained secret in all the lands of

'Iheem'hidra, for if he had reappeared surely the elders of the Suhm-yi would know it, and perhaps even the code of all life itself could not have stayed their hands then.

"Aye, and now I find myself given to wonder: was the red dust of disaster which killed my people truly a thing of nature, unconscious of its scourge, or was it perchance sent by black-skinned, black-hearted, blackest of all black magicians, in order to forestall Suhm-yi vengeance? If so, then surely I know why I alone, of all the Suhm-yi, was spared.

"There, Tarra Khash. That is my tale—what do you make of it?"

Tarra sat for long moments without speaking, chewing over the story and the last morsels of food both. Finally:

"It seems to me," he said, "those streaming rays you saw at the full of the moon—that strange aurora over Klühn—was nothing but the same monthly manifestation self-evident in the clouds this very night, which would be there whether you'd prayed to your gods or not. That is not, of course, to belittle your gods, but—"

"I too have thought it," Amyr cut him short. "But who may fathom the designs of gods? I asked for guidance and received it; should we ponder the origin of a miracle or its result?"

Tarra nodded: "I take your meaning. However, it likewise seems to me that your feet are set upon a forked path. On the one hand you seek a mate, long stolen from the Inner Isles, and on the other you seek vengeance for your entire race. Now, this side of you is new and puzzling to me. One: would you now forsake the ways of your fathers, as you seem to have forsaken crater sea? And two, tell me this: how may a silver-skinned Suhm-yi female, full-grown by now, remain hidden in a city of dull-fleshed men? You said it yourself: no easy thing."

"Tarra," Amyr answered, "*you* said it seemed I'd learned a lot since leaving crater sea and venturing into the world of men. Well, never a truer word spoken. I have looked at men and learned to live like them—when it is at all bearable. I have even learned to kill like them, in protection of my own life. That which would have been unthinkable a year ago is now possible, tomorrow probable, the day after likely. We live and we learn. The ways of my fathers?—they were the ways of a race. And where is that race now? I am no longer naive, Tarra Khash; my quest has not been blind; I've more yet to tell you. But first your questions. You know of course the Suhm-yi talent of mind-reading? Certainly, for you remarked upon it at our first meeting. Well, and has not this Gorgos got himself an oracle in his Temple of Secret Gods?"

Tarra's jaw fell open. "Ah!" he gawped. "Your Suhm-yi she! A mentalist, of course!"

Amyr's smile was grim, golden-slitted. "And Gorgos uses her to blackmail Klühn's shady dealers. She picks their innermost secrets right out of their skulls; Gorgos threatens them with exposure; they pay and he uses ill-gotten gains to fund his sect of black magicians!"

"You're sure of all this?"

"I cannot be wrong," answered Amyr, but without pride. "I, too, am a mentalist, remember? And what thoughts would I read better than those of one of my own kind?"

The Hrossak slowly nodded. "Go on," he said. "Tell me what else you know. But first...tell me more about these three Swords of Power. For there's something strange here, I think—a peculiar coincidence, perhaps too peculiar—though as yet I'm not sure how it all comes together."

Now Amyr's smile was wide and open as he answered: "Ah! But I had hoped *you* could tell *me* something of that, bronze one... However, let me say a little more.

"Now when Gorgos fled the Inner Isles, taking with him the girl, runebooks, swords and all, the High Priests of the Suhm-yi worked a curse—a very ancient, very powerful curse—to follow after him. And because the Suhm-yi had lost things they treasured, the girl and relics both, the curse they invoked was this: that so long as the Suhm-yi dwelled in their secret place, on greeny-blue expanse of crater sea, Gorgos would never be able to keep unto himself anything he held dear. His most treasured possessions would be lost or stolen, his truest servants would sicken and die; worms would infest the very apples of his life, turning them bitter. And all of this for as long as a single Suhm-yi priest remained to renew the curse at its time of waning. And this, too, leads me to wonder about the red dust. For certainly...it were no simple Earth magic which came out of the sky to destroy an entire people! Aye, and that is why, before setting out upon my quest, I went to Na-dom and prayed to all the gods for the renewal of the curse. I am no priest, no, but I am the son of the highest of them all; and perhaps the gods have hearkened to me, and perhaps the curse is potent still. I hope so..."

Again Tarra nodded. "Let me take up the tale," he said. "Having left the Inner Isles, while making for parts unknown, Gorgos felt the first sting of your Suhm-yi curse: he lost the Swords of Power. And yes, I see by your expression I'm right!"

"Conjecture, Tarra, guesswork," answered Amyr. "But good guesswork. I've made discreet inquiry; it seems that for many a year Gorgos' hirelings have wandered abroad, seeking just such swords. What else have you deduced?"

"*Huh!*" the steppeman growled. "Why, 'tis plain that my sword— my broken scimitar, its hilt all set with jewels—was one of the very three! Which is why that lying yellow-robe made me out a cheat and murderer, when all I was guilty of in killing Ellern Thark was of doing Klühn a mighty favour!"

Amyr Arn seconded that with a sharp nod of his combed head. "I've heard of it, and I know you killed the Northman fairly—or at least as fairly as you could. All Klühn knows it—but only we two know why you took the blame."

"To give back to Gorgos one of his runic swords, eh?"

"To give him back the *third* sword!" said Amyr. "And so complete the set. Listen:

"One sword was rescued from the gut of a whale killed by whalers out of Khrissa. The ice-priests of that city would have kept it, but Gorgos went there and traded a few paltry spells for it. If they had not parted with it," Amyr shrugged in a very human way, "then perhaps had Gorgos offered more powerful magicks—but not by way of trade! At any rate, the ice-priests knew and feared him, and so he got the sword.

"The second scimitar was brought to Klühn by a madman who said he'd found it on a peak called the Mount of the Ancients. That's debatable, for it's said he came into the city naked, raving and filthy, and slew a dozen before the blade was wrested from him and he himself killed. A princeling bought the sword in auction and the money was spread between the kin of madman's victims. Shortly after that, members of the Sect of Secret Gods began drifting in, the princeling's apartments were ransacked and he disappeared without trace; likewise the sword from the Mount of the Ancients.

"As for your shattered sword—entire when last I saw it in the Inner Isles—this is what I have learned:

"That once upon a time in Thinhla there dwelled a fat and offensive jeweller—"

"Wait!" Tarra held up a hand. "Wait, Amyr, and hear the true story from me." He frowned a dark frown, sent his memory winging back. "Aye, a fat and offensive jeweller indeed. Nud Annoxin was his name, and when a certain Hrossak staggered out of steaming coastal jungles more dead than alive, what did Nud do but hurl him into dungeon cell! And who'd tell of it better than me, for I'm the Hrossak who rotted down there for four long years!"

Amyr drew breath sharply. "A lifetime!" he hissed. "What had you done to deserve such?"

"Oh?" said Tarra, raising an eyebrow. "And must it be that I'd 'done' something? I'll tell you: I had found the jungle-cursed catacombs of Ahorra Izz, god of scarlet scorpions. Aye, and I'd come out of that place with my pockets full of rubies. That was what I had 'done'—and Nud Annoxin a thief and torturer of no mean prowess, I can tell you. He starved and tormented me for what I knew of the scorpion temple, till at the end he knew it all—or most of it. But it earned him nothing—except perhaps the ire of the biggest, reddest, awfullest arachnid you could ever imagine, Amyr Arn! Ire and sting both, the hellish sting of Ahorra Izz!" Tarra gave a shudder.

"You did not kill Nud?"

Tarra shook his tousled head. "No, though it's true he died the night I made my escape. Oh, I *would* have killed him—indeed I stole a ceremonial sword from his wall so to do—but the scorpion-god beat me to it."

Amyr nodded. "And it seems you beat Gorgos' seekers to the sword; since when they've searched far afield, and never a word of it—until you were spied with shattered hilt in Ellern Thark's place. Queer twists of fate, eh?"

"Queer indeed! But say, what good's to them that busted blade, with razor curve all gone and many a jewel prised from hilt? Gorgos'll work no magick with that shattered stump, that's for sure."

"Oh?" said Amyr. "Try telling that to the swordsmith who the yellow-robes have picked up from his shop these last three nights, returning him each morning weary unto death after a night's work In the temple. Tell it to the jeweller similarly suborned."

Tarra's brows knitted darkly. "So, they make it whole again. What evil does this Gorgos work, Amyr?"

"Any evil," the other answered. "All evils, if they'll help achieve his one great ambition. He desires immortality, Tarra, as he has desired and searched for it for all of an hundred years! And if it means death and destruction for any—for many, for all—what is that to Gorgos? Which is why, tomorrow night, I go to kill him."

Tarra had expected something of the sort. "Also to write *finis* on Suhm-yi vengeance," he said.

Amyr nodded.

"Also to win yourself a bride, and so prolong your devastated race."

Again the nod.

"*Hmm!* Well, I wish you luck in all your endeavours. But tomorrow night? I shall probably be miles away by then."

"Go safely," said Amyr at once. "And always remember me."

"You do not seek my aid in this mad venture? To enter Gorgos' temple, his very lair, slay him, steal his silver-scaled oracle—get out with skin intact? It's instant death if you're caught—especially you, last of the Suhm-yi."

"I have not asked for your help. As for my life: what good is it, one alone against the world? If the gods would spare me, then am I already spared, but if my life is to be spent, what better cause, eh? As for *your* life, that is something else entirely."

"Is that why you saved it this night?"

"I rescued you because you are my one friend in all the lands of Theem'hdra. Also, you were innocent."

Tarra shuffled about on the bench. "And what are friends for if not to help their friends, eh?" He was growing exasperated; he stood in Amyr's debt and knew it. He *would* help if Amyr asked, certainly, but it came hard to actually volunteer his neck!

Amyr read his mind. "I owed you from that former time in the Inner Isles," he said. "Now all is square."

"Were all Suhm-yi so prideful?" Tarra rasped.

"All."

The Hrossak gritted his teeth, puffed himself up—then seemed to collapse into himself. He gave a great sigh. "Please," he said then, "my dear friend Amyr Arn—please allow me to assist you in your great act of revenge, in the killing of this evil Gorgos and the freeing of his oracle, the Suhm-yi maid you'd take back to crater sea. I would deem myself honoured."

At last Amyr smiled. "Very well," he said. "I will be glad of your help."

"Good." Tarra sat back—sat up straighter—smiled broadly for a while, then frowned. At last he said: "Anyway, I've my own reason for wanting to get into the Temple of Secret Gods."

"Oh?" said Amyr. "Can I guess it?"

"*Hah!*" Tarra answered, and: "Listen to him! You already know it, stealer of thoughts! I want my sword back, aye..." He slapped his thigh, grinned, gazed deep into the other's golden eyes. "Well, come on, out with it—what's the plan...?"

III

In the Temple of Terror

Ulli Eys of the Suhm-yi was beautiful. In Suhm-yi eyes (had there been such to see her) and by their standards—in human eyes—she would be beautiful in the eyes of *any* warm-blooded creature. Alas, Gorgos' blood was cold as ice, cold as his schemes of deathlessness, which alone concerned him.

Ulli's form was a woman's form, full and round and wondrous; her skin was silvery, with shimmering highlights; her eyes were liquid gold, her lashes silver-silk shutters. Her beauty was innocent and it was utter—and yet she was not aware of it. Indeed she believed—or had believed until recently—that she was ugly, an alien, unnatural, awful creature created of a sorcerer's spells. That was what Gorgos had told her, and over the years flown since her childhood in the Inner Isles, she had almost come to believe it.

Then, a year ago, out of the strange psychic mists of her dreams had come hope in the form of a voice calling to her in the night—to remind her of deep, warm oceans and jewel islands, and of her Suhm-yi heritage—telling her that she was not alone. Moreover, the voice had promised her freedom! It had promised a return to Inner Isles, a love to fill her life, a destiny great beyond measure. She would be the mother of a race, whose children would one day people the jewel isles just as she remembered them from her childhood. And no more wandering the parched deserts and strange cities of men, and no more stealing men's dark thoughts and secrets for her master, Gorgos. For he was *not* her master but a great thief, and Ulli herself the most precious thing he had ever stolen.

When first these night visions had come to her, in her innocence Ulli had spoken of them to Gorgos, who always set great store by everything she told him of her dreams and fancies. Indeed that was her purpose—the reason he kept and fed her, hiding her ugliness and strangeness from the prying eyes of other men—to perform her auguries and mind-readings for him who alone cared for her, however coldly, in all the world.

But when she had seen how her dreams affected him, the rages he would fly into at mention of this like mind which spoke to Ulli out of nowhere, then she grew more cautious. And later, when Gorgos pressed her with regard to suspected fresh incursions or mental revelations, she would simply shake her head and say no, the voice no longer came in the night to disturb her sleep. But in fact it did, ever stronger, making her nights happy and filling her days with longing.

And lately, for a three-month, why!—the dreams had been stronger far than ever before, until Ulli could no longer doubt but that they were real. Somewhere, somehow, *he* was. *He* existed despite all Gorgos' denials to the contrary, that in fact she was not unique of her kind. Amyr, his name, a good name—Amyr, last male of the olden Suhm-yi—and Ulli, the last female. And now he was coming, coming here, coming to steal her away!

And oh, how she longed to be stolen!

But such dangers here: Gorgos and his disciples, the temple's labyrinthine ways, the yellow-robes and their mad dedication to an obsessed, power-crazed master. And Ulli, because she remained innocent, half-feeling she betrayed the ancient black magician. And

Gorgos on the very verge of fulfilling his life's ambition, in which she had played so important a—

"Are you listening to me, Ulli?" Gorgos' voice, harsh as a file on glass, grated in her ears, shattering her chaotic thoughts and daydreams, drawing her back to cruel reality. "I'll swear you haven't heard a word! Where were you just then? What thoughts were you thinking, Ulli?"

His eyes were on her, cold, black, unblinking; his mouth was a black, fanged slit in skin wrinkled as an ebon walnut. She gasped; her hand flew to her mouth, she cowered back from him on silken cushions.

"What? *What?*" Gorgos pressed. "What thoughts *were* you thinking, my precious oracle, my silver-skinned pet—and were they really yours at all or the thoughts of some other?"

And now Ulli must lie:

"No thoughts at all, Gorgos my master. I am tired, no more than that. It wearies me, searching in the minds of Klühn's men and merchants and elite. Their secrets are often ugly, as you well know, and they leave a taste in my mind like slow poisons. Would that I need no longer search them out in their iniquities."

Gorgos' eyes slitted a little and stayed that way for a while, but at last he seemed satisfied with her answer. "Well, and perhaps you've done your last of that," he finally said. "For tonight—this very night— I'll finally call down to my command all the power I need. Then, if all goes according to plan, I shall be immortal, all-powerful, indestructible! Except—why!—what use shall I find for you then, my little Ulli?" His eyes were shiny black marbles where they fixed upon her, and his voice turned sibilant as he continued: "It's long been a scheme of mine to breed me some familiar creatures. You yourself could be said to be a familiar of sorts, I suppose; but what would be the result, I wonder, if I mated you with ghoul or night-gaunt?"

She knew better than to shrink back again, for Gorgos fed on fear. His vampire soul battened upon it. Instead she looked him straight in the eye, gold against jet, and said, "I have served you well master. Have you not said so yourself—that without me your temple were never builded, your servitors and soldiers never hired into your service?"

"True," he answered, his whisper the scrape of a claw on rusted iron, "all true. Aye, but perhaps you've been a two-edged sword for all that, Ulli Eys."

"A sword, master?" she answered. "With two edges? Why, whatever do you mean? Nay, I am but flesh and blood, and your poor servant."

Dark beneath his cowl, Gorgos' black eyes were shiny peering into hers. "Those golden orbs you wear for eyes," he said. "Sometimes I think me: what goes on behind them? And I answer: perhaps too much. You've been my oracle, true, and successful to be sure—but could you not be better? It's a custom in Khrissa to pierce the eyes of the snow larks to make them sing the sweeter. Now there's a thought, Ulli, there's a thought..."

Still she did not shrink, but perhaps she trembled a little. "And I have heard it said," she answered in a little while, "that while their songs are sweeter, it is always the same song. For the joy is gone out of them, and the sweetness is tinged with sadness, and whoever hears the blind snow larks singing is brought to tears." And again she reminded him: "I am your poor servant, O Gorgos."

He turned away, perhaps disappointed. "Aye, my servant—my secret oracle—but daughter of the Inner Isles for all that." And nodding knowingly, Gorgos strode out on to her balcony, his yellow, rune-inscribed robe belling behind him.

Ulli's rooms were in one of the outer domes. She had a small pool, blue-tiled, for bathing; soft white carpets of snow leopard pelts, and drapes of woven down; onyx shelves for her small collection of poems and books of songs and childish bric-a-brac, mainly beautiful and intricately coiled cowries from the shores of the crater sea. Curving windows of translucent shell opened on to a high, walled balcony, which perched at a height level with the great temple's outer wall. Central in the main room, a circular divan which also served as bed was heaped with silk cushions where it lay beneath the uppermost panel of the dome's curve, a thick circular window which magnified all the stars of night.

From her divan, Ulli watched Gorgos where he paused with his back to her at the balcony wall, his long curved fingernails tapping inquiringly upon the coping stones while his eyes gazed west. He was looking at the full moon, she knew, whose light must even now pour down on crater sea and Inner Isles. What went on in his mind, she wondered, just as he had wondered of hers? She could look, of course, but dared not. Gorgos was a magician of no small prowess and could sense such intrusions. Ulli shuddered. Indeed, his senses and thoughts were too keen far for her liking—and blacker than the pit itself!

And as well she didn't look into Gorgos' mind, for this time she would have shrunk from his thoughts, most assuredly. He was thinking: *she is Suhm-yi, she is the plague-carrier. A two-edged sword indeed! While she lives, I suffer—just as I have suffered ever since that day I stole her from the jewel isles. My plans have been thwarted, my greatest treasures lost or stolen. And yet through her I have regained all. Ah!—but when will the sword turn again, perhaps to strike with its perverse edge? Dare I wait to find out? Even I, Gorgos—whose breath shall be a gale, whose merest thought a command irresistible—dare I wait? No, for a curse is a curse; and this Suhm-yi curse remains potent, I feel it in my bones. So be it: tonight the Great Calling—the Unification of All the Dark Forces—and tomorrow...? Tomorrow I shall revel! After that, then time enough to be rid of her. First a trial mating or two, for the breeding of familiar creatures; and perhaps a blinding, to see if she will indeed sing the sweeter; but after that death by fire! Only the searing flame may still such a curse, and only when it is stilled will I, Gorgos, finally fear nothing in all the worlds of space and time! So be it, so—*

"—be it!" The last two words he spoke out loud.

"Master?"

Gorgos turned from the balcony, strode back into the room. "I have great works to perform, Ulli, thaumaturgies vast. Tonight is my night! The sword is forged, renewed, and the forces unite. The clouds are gathering over Klühn and the sorceries of far stars are seeded in the skies. Tonight you will not leave these apartments but stay here with all doors locked. For when I call the very Elementals of Evil out from the spaces between the stars, then nothing will be certain, nothing guaranteed, nothing entirely safe. The temple shall tremble tonight, Ulli, with all the applause of the Inhabitants of the Dark Worlds where they reel beyond the rim!"

In Gorgos' madness a white foam flecked the corners of his wide slit mouth, gaping in the shadow of his cowl; the yellow cowl which he now threw back to reveal his monstrous, bloated black head like a gargoyle's misshapen skull. And opening wide his great jaws he bayed with mad laughter for a little while, before striding from the room to a sudden peal of thunder and a pattering of large, unseasonal raindrops where they fell on the balcony's marble flags.

Back over his shoulder as he went, baying still, he cast, "As for you, Ulli Eys—well, we shall see. We shall see…"

———————

Tarra and Amyr had slept 'til noon, following which they had eaten a light meal in Amyr's garret hideaway and gone over again in what detail they could the elements of his plan. And the very barest elements they were, for Amyr believed that the simplest way was always the best, that any great and complicated scheme could only tangle them in its intricacies like flies in a web.

Of the Temple of Secret Gods, Amyr had learned a little from the mind of Ulli Eys. Labyrinthine the temple's ways, aye, but all halls and passageways following the same general pattern, so that Amyr believed he could confidently negotiate its corridors, stairways and chambers— *if* he and Tarra could get into the place. For gaining access might well prove the hardest part; if not, making an exit certainly would!

Amyr's intelligence, gathered from several sources in the city— namely, a handful of furtive informers he'd paid to keep their eyes and ears open—had alerted him that Gorgos and his priests would be busy this night, all of them engaged in secret rituals on the temple's fifth and topmost level, whose ceiling was the great copper dome itself. Because of this Gorgos' grey-clad soldiers would be much in evidence in the gardens and on the paths between the walls and the temple's outer domes, and atop the walls themselves and in the watchtowers and stone gatehouse-cum-guardroom. Unlike the Square of Justice, this Temple of Secret Gods would in no wise prove an easy nut to crack. (So Tarra had thought.) But crack it they must.

"How crack it?" he'd asked. "Shall we climb the walls, or don our yellow robes and simply walk in? Me, I'm a fair clamberer as Hrossaks go, but still I'd vote for walking. Those temple walls are high as the city's own, where a fall is certain death!"

"You shall walk in," Amyr had answered, "but I must climb."

"Why?" Tarra had wanted to know. "Why can't we go together, by whichever route?"

"The yellow-robes always go singly, that's why. It's the rule of the temple, for Gorgos fears conspiracy. He fears many things, not least of which the Suhm-yi curse. But two of us walking into that place together is plainly out of the question. And since I am demonstrably the better climber—"

"What?" Tarra cut him short. "How's that? I didn't say I *couldn't* climb! And what makes you so good at it? Climbing's for strong arms, Amyr, not spindly things like yours. Also, it requires fingers that grip and toes to match—aye, and preferably five to a member, not just four like you've got!"

At which Amyr had smiled, showing teeth like mother of pearl. And taking Tarra's hand in one of his, he'd said: "Shake me off, bronze one. Go on, show me how weak is my grip."

Tarra had tried, but to no avail; Amyr's hand struck fast to his as a fly to the seeping resin of mountain pines. Then the Suhm-yi had shown him his fingers: spatulate as a tree frog's and, when required, just as adhesive! "No, Tarra, I'll not fall but go up that wall sure as a lizard."

"Huh! So it appears." But now the Hrossak became concerned for himself. "And as for me, *I'm* to walk in bold as brass, eh? Simple as that!" And he gave his fingers a testy snap.

Amyr sighed. "Tarra, you're contrary. Isn't it what you said you wanted?"

"Wanted? I'm not sure now I wanted any of it! It's just the thought of me going afoot while you're lizarding it up the wall, that's all. And anyway, what do I do when I get in through the gate?"

"You go straight through the gardens to the temple, enter—all unchallenged, hopefully—then to innermost chamber, where finally you climb all the stairs to the topmost level. There you'll find me waiting, again hopefully, and there too we'll find Gorgos and slay him. Chaos will ensue. The yellow-robes will be in disarray. Many will flee, terrified that their master is dead; others will see an opportunity to loot; some may seek to kill us. There we have the advantage; we shall be armed, of course, but they bear no arms. Gorgos will not have them in the temple in case someone makes an attempt upon his life. Lastly we flee, collecting Ulli the oracle along the way. I shall know where to find her."

"Huh!" Tarra grunted again. "A good many of those false priests may very well be cowards and thieves just as you say, but I'm sure there'll be fighters among 'em, too. Very well, I'll face ten if I've a knife and they've none—but what of the soldiers? Are we to flee the temple pursued by howling pack of yellow-robes and hampered by girl, and rush straight into the arms of a small army?"

"Tarra," Amyr had answered, "I guarantee that if we get back to the gatehouse, then that the soldiers will not stop us." He grinned secretively.

"Are you going to let me in on it?" Tarra was suspicious.

"I'll only say this," said Amyr, "that the soldiers would as soon stop Gorgos himself as try to detain us! If all goes according to plan, of course..."

It fast approached the midnight hour as Tarra Khash hugged his yellow cassock about him, drew his head back into the heavy cowl and shufflingly approached the main gate in the great wall of the Temple of Secret Gods. At the same time and less than fifty yards away, where the wall stood in its own shadow, Amyr climbed with the speed and agility of a spider. He climbed...but at the same time kept his mind in contact with Tarra's. This was something of an effort—concentrating in two directions at one and the same time—and fine droplets of silvery-grey sweat beaded Amyr's face where they came through carefully applied blacking.

Close to the top of the wall he heard something, grew rigid, drew back his mental probe from Tarra's mind and sent all his senses ahead of him. Two soldiers, atop the wall, talking... They were nervous, and rightly so; the sky directly overhead was livid with weirdly silent, flickering lightnings, where black clouds boiled *locally* in a sky otherwise clear and bright with stars.

"This must be the worst I've yet seen it," one soldier whispered to his companion. "It's almost alive, that sky! What goes on tonight in the temple, I wonder?"

"No clean or entirely sane thing!" answered the other. "Bet your soul on that—if it's not already sold. Tomorrow when I collect my pay, that's the last this lot will see of me. He calls down demons from the stars, this Gorgos. At least, that's what I've heard. Now what sort of priestly activity is that, I ask? No, rumour has it that in fact he's a black magician, and his oracle's a female creature, silver as the belly of a fish! Ugh!"

"Aye," the voice of the first was hushed, "I've heard the same. And I think I'll join you tomorrow, when you quit. I'll become an assassin again, or go pirating in the Straits of Yhem. Either one'll be cleaner work than this. Better paid, too…"

While taking all of this in, Amyr had been on the move, ascending at an angle and coming up over the parapet some little distance away. Not for nothing had his race been named the Suhm-yi—the "seldom seen"—and now he became one with the shadows of the fortifications as he shrugged a bundle from his back, fixed belt and sword at his waist, draped himself in yellow robe. And silent as a breath of night air, he approached the two where they stood close together at the parapet in the glow of strange aerial energies.

"And I'll shun Klühn evermore," one was now saying, "even though I was born here." There was a shiver in his voice as he continued: "Or at least I'll stay clear as long as this nest of false priests worship their alien demon-gods here!"

"The both of us," said the other, nodding. "Aye, we're surely of a mind on that." He glanced nervously about, at the sky, at the drawn features of his companion. "The yellow-robes are all dupes, and Gorgos is a madman!"

Something moved close by, something sensed before it was seen. Then a stir of yellow, the swish of a cassock…and a third figure stood with the two. Beneath the cowl all was dark—except a pair of golden eyes, ferally ablaze. "What?" said Amyr Arn, his voice a venomous hiss. "Do my ears deceive me? Conspiracy, treason!"

And who could this be but Gorgos himself, flown here on the wings of magick, grown out of the very night to confront the two in their treachery. "Master, we—" they began to babble as one, then fell to their knees at his feet. As he instinctively stepped back, one of them clutched at the hem of his cassock. The robe came open, displayed his silvery body in the blue-green light of the eerie aurora. It further displayed the slender sword gripped in four-fingered hand.

Gasping their double-dose of shock, coming to their feet, snatching at their own weapons, the two were given no time to cry out. Amyr had not wanted to kill them; he had simply thought to test out his disguise. Well, the latter had seemed to work well enough— barring the accident of the trapped cassock—and as for the former:

Even as they sprang erect his rapier sliced the air between—sliced air and throats both, so that cries unvoiced became bloody gurgles as their swords, half-drawn, made twin thumps falling back into their scabbards. Then the two were toppling, and Amyr catching one and doing his best to muffle the fall of the other. And finally the night still again, with only the hideously seething sky for witness...

And dumping the bodies over the wall, Amyr sent his mind out again to discover Tarra Khash—

—Which was just as well.

Tarra stood between a pair of grey-clad soldiers just inside the gate. He deliberately kept himself in shadow, his cowl drawn well forward to hide his face. The soldiers held his arms, their sword points at his middle. "For the last time, priest," said one, "tell us the answer to the challenge. Say it now, or be taken before the Sergeant of the Guard."

"But haven't I already told you, my son," mumbled Tarra, "that I've forgotten the damned—er, I mean daft—thing? It's slipped my mind, that's all. Give me a clue."

"A clue?" the second soldier's voice showed his disgust. "I never heard anything like it! Fifty of your lot in and out of here today, and all of them knew the password."

"What's more," the first was becoming suspicious, "I never before heard a priest of *this* temple call any man his 'son!' You're for the Sergeant of the Guard, my friend. Or should I call you 'father?'" They began to haul him toward the light from the guardroom.

"No, wait!" cried Tarra, and beneath his cassock his hand caressed the sword Amyr had given him. "Once more, I beg you—try me with the password one more time."

Now their suspicions really were aroused. "What's this?" said one. "Frightened of the Sergeant of the Guard, is it? But all he'll do is verify your—"

"Please, *please*!" said Tarra, gritting his teeth, his grip tightening on hilt of hidden sword. "I'm in a hurry. There's this special ceremony tonight, you see, and—"

"All right, all right!" snapped the second soldier. "One last time. "I say 'night,' and you say—?"

"Gaunt!" said Tarra, the word popping into his mouth from nowhere. It was Amyr, stealing the password from the minds of the guards, filling Tarra's mind with it and leaving no room for anything else. "Gaunt," Tarra said again, as the soldiers loosened their grip on his arms and stood back. And yet again: "Gaunt!" he cried as they put away their weapons. "Yes, yes—that's it. Night and gaunt, of course!"

"Of course," the disgusted one snorted. "Very well, in you go— 'father.'"

"Thank you, my son," said Tarra, stepping between them and into the shadows of the courtyard beyond. "Have a good night..."

Not far away, the merest shadow seemed to flow silently down an inner wall and melt into the gardens toward the domed central buildings. Silent that is except for a single snort or barely suppressed chuckle. Though Amyr's ancestors would doubtless disagree, it seemed to him that there were men the Suhm-yi could befriend and learn to live with. Likeable, even worthy men. Aye, and Tarra Khash must surely be the very best example.

Part of the night, Amyr came along a path to one of the outer domes. Here he paused, crouching down in darkness. There wasn't much of the latter now; the aurora was building to a fiery crescendo and the undersides of the boiling clouds were ablaze. He gazed upward at the curve of the building. Down here, well-lit passageways and corridors; up there, dark balconies at every level. Darkness suited Amyr: "seldom seen" in daylight, in darkness he simply disappeared.

He began to climb the wall, casting his mental probe before him into the mazy hive of evil within...

***

Ulli Eys knew Amyr's mind immediately.

Alone and shuddering in her apartments—terrified by the bilious flow and flux of green and blue light beyond her windows, and by the incessant, pregnant heaving of the vilely illumined clouds where they tossed beyond the enlarging lens directly over her bed—she grasped at that mind as a frightened child fastens to its father. There was comfort in it, and there was something new, which had never been before: nearness!

"You!" she half-whispered, half-thought the word. "Here?"

Never before had Ulli sensed the presence—the close proximity— of one of her own; unless it were as a child in the Inner Isles and now forgotten. If she closed her eyes she was sure she might even reach out and touch him. But knowing he was here—actually *here*, somewhere in Gorgos' blasphemous temple—now she grew more frightened for him than she was for herself. "But you'll be caught!" she gasped, again half out loud.

"Ware, Ulli!" came Amyr's answer. *"Speak with your mind, girl. Merely think it, and I shall hear you. But do not speak with your tongue, lest someone see you and inquire to whom you address yourself."*

His voice was so warm in her mind, so resolute, self-assured, that she took courage from it. Her hands fluttering a little, nervously, she began to pace the floor of her room; and when next she spoke, it was with her mind alone:

"What do you here? Can I make you understand that of all nights, this is possibly the most dangerous? Tonight Gorgos attains power inconceivable, and possibly immortality!"

"Tonight Gorgos dies!" came back the answer. *"And his death were not merely your saving, Ulli Eys, but the saving of a world, I fancy."*

Again she was afraid. *"But how will you kill him? He is a mighty magician whose—"*

"Die he must," Amyr's mind-voice interrupted, *"however mighty his magick. A curse is on him, the curse of the Suhm-yi, and I am its instrument. Now I must be about my business. Fear not, Ulli, but keep your mind fixed fast upon me. Then, when it's over, I'll find you as surely as a north-stone points out the polar constellations. Prepare yourself, gather up what small things you would take with you, for tonight you go free at last!"*

"Wait!" she cried after him, but too late. Only a dim trace, an echo of his mind, remained. Amyr Arn was intent upon other things.

The mind of Tarra Khash was likewise intent—intent upon his body and on keeping it intact!

In the lower corridors, working toward the central area and the spiralling stairs he'd find there to take him up under the dome, Tarra was in something of a panic. The temple's maze was a veritable echo chamber, where every slightest sound from regions however far found its way to the Hrossak as he prowled along, senses alert. And such was the complexity of the way, where every hall and passage and arch-way of the labyrinth looked exactly like the one last negotiated, that despite the directions Amyr had earlier given—which had seemed simple enough at the time—now Tarra feared he was not only losing the way but also himself! Indeed, he could well picture himself lost down here forever—or until Gorgos and his priests found him. But however terrible that last thought, it was not the source of his grow-ing panic. That sprang from his awareness of the sure passage of time, that time was of the essence, and that even now Amyr Arn probably approached the rendezvous. Tarra must hie him there at once! But... which way to hie?

For now, pausing at the junction of five passages all exactly alike, Tarra turned his head this way and that, tossing a mental coin to decide which way to go. It seemed to him that the droning cacophony of a hundred yellow-robes all chanting their entirely incomprehensi-ble incantations came from...*that* way—straight ahead! But how to be certain in such a cauldron of sound?

On the other hand, because of the weird acoustics of the place—the dinning effect of its magnifying small sounds from afar—one tended to overlook sounds or events of a closer proximity. Such as fast-padding footfalls from behind! Tarra turned, agile as a cat, his sword drawn beneath his yellow robe of priesthood.

"What?" cried the priest bearing down upon him, who appeared in something of a hurry. "I thought I was alone in my tardiness. Well, small odds—there are more than sufficient voices raised in invocation 'neath the great dome this night. Myself, I attend out of curiosity; I wish to see the forms of these fabulous forces Gorgos calls down from the stars—and their effect upon him! Aye, for he's promised us a new god tonight. Will you join me, brother?"

The yellow-robe was upon him, catching his elbow, solving his problem of a moment earlier by leading him down a passage which angled slightly to the left—but at the same time presenting another problem of similar proportions. For in that final moment of confron-tation and contact the two had dimly recognized each other, and in the space of only two or three paces both had remembered!

Now, gasping, they whirled face to face once more, the priest knowing Tarra for a near-barbarian, a Hrossak, and Tarra knowing him as the bald-pate who'd coshed him at Ellern Thark's and later blackguarded him in the city court. *"You!"* they hissed as a man.

Then the priest's hand was at Tarra's throat, his other hand raised high. Upon his wrist he wore a wide, heavy strap of leather, all dully aglint with metal studs. And right now it was swinging for Tarra's head.

"So that's what you bonked me with that night," he rasped, ducking and thrusting all in one movement. His sword point pushed out his cassock a little way, slipped through, entered the priest's body under his ribs and sliced into his heart. His hand flew away from Tarra's throat; he strained up and back, as if to extricate himself from skewer's point, his jaws snapped shut in a snarling grimace, flew open again at once in a scarlet cough. And he fell.

Tarra let his sword slide free, stooped, wiped his blade red against yellow, quickly tossed back his robe and sheathed the bright metal. He dragged the body into the shadow of an arched doorway, out of the light of flickering flambeaux, returned to the passageway.

The chanting had risen to a fever pitch now, and surely something gathered itself all unseen, bunching its alien muscles in preparation—for what?

His skin atingle in nameless anticipation, in something closely approaching dread, still Tarra commenced to lope along the corridor toward the swelling sound; but before he could gather full momentum he emerged into a great hall where massive columns held aloft a titan, circular ceiling. The base of the central dome, it could only be, and about its perimeter stone steps winding upward...

IV

Spawn of the Star-Spaces!

The great circular room beneath the central dome was all of twenty man-lengths in diameter. From its fantastically rune-inscribed mosaic floor to the curving beams which held aloft the hammered copper plates of the dome itself, the vertical height was perhaps eight or nine man-lengths. Half-way up the inward curving walls, a narrow balcony circled the chamber, with four equidistant flights of stairs leading down to the cryptically inscribed floor. Back of the balcony, large oval windows looked out over the lesser domes, which clustered towards and seemed fused with the central body; like copper breasts growing from a larger breast, their nipples formed of the sky-scanning apex windows evident in all the lesser bubbles. The great chamber itself was lit by seven huge brass lamps suspended from ceiling beams, lending the place a brazen glow.

Tarra, coming headlong up the winding stairs between the lower walls of the central structure, slowed his speed barely in time as he emerged on to the narrow inner balcony through a demon-carved archway; and then it was all he could do to still a loud gasp of awe and astonishment at the tableau now spread before him. Slowing his hammering heart and bringing his breathing back under control, he took a careful pace forward and let his eyes absorb all.

Central on the floor of the chamber, some four man-lengths below the balcony, a raised marble altar-stone supported the spreadeagled, yellow-robed form of Gorgos. He lay on his back, arms and legs spread wide beneath his rune-embellished robe, his black eyes bulging in his black face, which was tilted back to gaze upon the circular window in the curving copper ceiling. Forming a broken circle about his upper torso, three curving ceremonial scimitars lay sinistrally arranged, hilts to points. The one on his left curved upwards from his ribs toward his outstretched left hand; above his head the second curved between his hands; the third arced down from his right hand toward his right side. Tarra knew immediately that one of these swords was his own familiar blade restored: even at a distance the jewelled hilts were unmistakeable. Which one was a different matter.

His gaze couldn't linger long there, however, for there was more to be taken in. The hundred priests of the temple, for instance (ninety-nine of them, anyway) where they formed a rhythmically swaying, frenziedly chanting circle right round the balcony, their arms held low, hands touching, all eyes upon Gorgos stretched upon his altar dais. Some of the yellow-robes were Yhemnis, Tarra saw, black-skinned and pouty-lipped. Aye, and there might even be a Hrossak or two among 'em, too. He stepped forward, broke the ring, thrust his hands down until they contacted others on both sides.

There: now he was just another priest—for the moment, anyway. Possibly Amyr was also here; certainly he was supposed to be.

"Oh, I'm here all right, bronze one," came a voice soft in his mind, and the "Yhemni" on his immediate left gave his smallest finger an even smaller tweak. Tarra's involuntary start went unnoticed in the clamour of chanting and swaying of cassocked bodies, but before he could do anything to betray himself:

"Don't speak!" Amyr's mental warning was sharp as a knife. *"Say nothing—don't even peep at me out the corner of your eye."*

The Hrossak's thoughts whirled chaotically—but only for a moment or two. Then: "What now?" he thought back.

"I haven't had time to think yet," came Amyr's answer. *"But we have to do something, anything, to stop what's happening here. Have you looked at the sky?"*

The urgency in the Suhm-yi's mind-voice got through to Tarra, making his hair tingle at its roots. And again that sensation of elemental muscles bunching to spring, of alien intelligences rushing invisibly to and fro, so that one could almost feel the wind from their membrane wings. The priests felt it, too, sensed the gibbering approach of...*something*—for their monotonously repetetive chanting now lost entirely what little coherency it had had, changing its pitch, rising even higher, becoming a raucous blare that set the jaws to aching even worse than rotten teeth. It made it hard to even think...

"The sky!" Amyr insisted. *"Look at it!"*

Tarra slowly cranked his head back until he looked up at a steep angle at the circular window on the heavens. He looked—stared—stood transfixed!

Beyond that window—more properly a portal, designed in five sectors which even now began to retract, drawn back by unseen machinery—the clouds were roiling and throbbing like a canopy of blue volcanic mud, alive with weird energies that scorched and sizzled soundlessly, focusing upon the dome. The window was fully open now, and in through the opening crept green and blue tendrils of hissing, crackling fire, at first exploratory, then insistent, finally pulsing in through the portal in a twisting, writhing column of cold luminosity that reached down to and fully enveloped Gorgos on his dais.

Simultaneous with the influx of these seemingly sentient energies, the priests commenced to circle widdershins, single-file, about the narrow balcony, their shrieking ceasing abruptly and replaced by deep, bass, mass explosions of a repeated *sound* or *word*, recognition of which brought a frantic mental response from Amyr Arn.

"Tarra, listen to that! Do you know what it is?"

"No," the Hrossak thought back. "But whatever it is, I don't like it!"

And, "Thromb...*Thromb*...THROMB!" sang the priests, their skipping paces growing shorter but gaining speed as they continued their mad, well-practised wheeling dance about the balcony.

"But I do know what it is!" said Amyr. *"The Thromb are the veriest demons of the deep dark spaces between the stars. They are part of Suhm-yi legend, most evil of all evil elementals, spawn of all the darkness and misery and horror of the blind, reeling worlds beyond the rim!"* ·

"Thanks," Tarra thought back, trying to shout with his mind over the throbbing din, for he couldn't understand how that was not necessary, "I'm glad you brought me! But if what you say is true, then Gorgos is done for. Surely he can't live in that torrent of twisting fires? It'll shrivel him like a moth in a candle's flame!"

"Shrivel him? Man, it's feeding him! The Suhm-yi had long suspected that Gorgos was not of this world—and now that suspicion is fact. He, too, is of the Thromb—doubtless called down by some crazed, long dead sorcerer. Aye, and now in his turn he opens the gates to all the Thromb. But before he can do that, first he must grow strong. Look, see how he feeds! See the sorcery of the dark stars!"

The form of Gorgos was bloating upon the marble dais. Seen almost as if through a jet of shining, snaking water, his outline shimmered, blurred—enlarged! And now, too, another manifestation of the spawn from the star-spaces; or perhaps the final phase of this, Gorgos' most terrible thaumaturgy.

For even as Tarra stared, his eyes jouncing in his head as he was whirled in the mad circling rush of the yellow-robes, the three scimitars enclosing Gorgos' upper half rose up from the dais and in their turn commenced to spin in mid-air, also widdershins, chasing each other in an ever-widening circle of flashing steel and glittering gems as they climbed slowly along the length of the column of living energy from the stars.

Beneath the circling swords, down on the dais where Gorgos' body throbbed and convulsed in the blue-green tube of eerie lightnings, a monstrous transformation was taking place. The magician's rune-covered robe bulged, splitting under the pressure from within, flying into tatters; beneath it he was huge, black, bloating larger still, but worst of all—

—Amyr had been right: Gorgos was never born of good clean earth—nor of any sane world or place or time! His voluminous yellow robe had hidden well the many groping tentacles and *appendages* and pustules with which, from neck to loins, his nightmare body was covered like a living mat!

Tarra dragged his eyes away, returned them to the circling swords. The glimmering of an idea was shaping itself in his mind.

Now the flying scimitars had wound themselves up halfway to the level of the balcony, and now too Amyr's mental cry was a sharp bark of frustration, rage and hatred in the Hrossak's mind:

"Tarra, we must act now—though I fear we're already too late. But at least we must try. Perhaps if we break this circle it will help. Come on, let's see if these crazy men can dance and chant their way through cold steel!"

In the next moment the two threw off their cassocks, turned back to back and commenced their gory work. Such was the tension in Tarra that the orgy of death which followed was almost a relief, though he was not, and never had been, a killer born. They slew, and as they slew continued to move to the left, Amyr pursuing and cutting down them that danced away from him, Tarra meeting his prey head-on and piling them up in a mound.

Such slaughter could not go long unnoticed or unanswered. The yellow-robes directly across the sweep of the balcony saw all at once, came to a disbelieving halt, began pointing, mouths agape. Others, piling into Tarra's kill, were tripped or skidded in blood and were brought down, creating even more of a blockage. Now outraged priests came clambering, screaming at the Hrossak across the mound of their slain colleagues; and others made a concerted rush on Amyr, however hampered by the narrowness of the way, which would only permit of two abreast.

Dispatching one screaming yellow-robe and toppling him over the balcony's low wall, Tarra found himself confronted by two more, flying at him in unison. He rammed home his rapier in one, but the other—quick-thinking if totally uncaring—immediately slammed both his covered forearms down on the flat of the thin blade where it skewered his staggering colleague. The blade broke, leaving Tarra with only the useless hilt.

"A curse on all puny swords!" roared the Hrossak. "Come on then, you bald-pates—come taste the iron in a steppeman's knuckles!"

A snarling pack of them perched on and behind the mound of their dead, tensed to spring. Amyr backed up to Tarra, his face and hands black, body and limbs a liquid red on silver. The yellow-robes crept inward, closing in on the pair like a pincer. And—

"Hold!" came a great, rumbling bass command from the centre of the chamber, a magnified blast of sound which drowned all else in its sheer volume and shuddering intensity. "Back from them, back! They are mine—especially the silver one. Hail, Suhm-yi! I had expected you—but not in the very hour of my triumph, to make it so much sweeter. Hail, creature of the Inner Isles—hail and farewell!"

Gorgos' hideous eyes, huge, black as night and bulging, had not once shifted from their vertical staring; but while his nightmare body continued to pulsate and expand, entirely covering the dais now, a yet more fearful metamorphosis commenced. Seeing it, Tarra no longer felt entirely in command of his own senses. The thing was so utterly—

"Is that...that...is it real?" he gasped.

"Oh, yes," Amyr answered out loud. "It's real, and I fear it's the end of us. The end of everything!" His voice was full of despair, full of horror.

Growing out of Gorgos' side, a black, hairy stalk had stretched itself out, snaking across the mosaic floor. As it approached the wall directly beneath the balcony where they stood, frozen in their dread, so the end bloated out like some loathsome fungus, forming the spindly-legged likeness of an enormous spider. And anchored to Gorgos by hairy stalk, up the wall the red-eyed nightmare crept, until the tips of its forelegs appeared, chitin-tipped and tapping on the top of the balcony wall.

Now Gorgos' head turned stiffly on its neck and his black eyes glared at the pair. And matching that glare, his slit of a mouth curved upward in monstrous smile. "The forces are unified!" his booming bass voice declared. "I am Gorgos—soon to be immortal—*soon to be Lord of all the Thromb!*"

It was now or never: Tarra's idea crystallized.

The swords where they flew: one of them flew out of true! Its jewelled hilt tilted a little and its blade vibrated as from some strange imbalance. Oh, the swordsmith's work was good, the jeweller's, too, and both had served their purposes; but they were only human and the original blade had been forged out beyond the stars.

"So be it!" Tarra shouted. "But if I'm to die it's with my once-true sword in my hand. And it's with fire, not fear, in my heart. So to hell with you, Gorgos!"

Amyr read it in Tarra's mind, came to his aid.

As Tarra leaped up on to the balcony wall and teetered there for a moment, getting his balance, so the Suhm-yi sliced at the Gorgos-spider-appendage as it hauled itself into sight. This served to distract its attention from the Hrossak, and in the next moment—

Tarra leaped, head-first, arms stretching before him.

His flight was meant to intercept that of the circling swords—one of them, anyway—but later he would give the success of that wild leap greater consideration, and wonder perhaps if he were not somehow assisted. Certainly the way his fingers met, firmly clamped upon and dragged the scimitar from orbit might hint of some divine aid or interference. But anyway, the connection *was* made; the familiar, brightly-jewelled hilt *was* grasped, the scimitar *was* snatched, however reluctantly, from its weird sorcerous circling. But having snatched it, instead of rushing down through four man-lengths of thin air to the marble floor, Tarra clung to the sword and almost felt himself lowered, as if some power futilely sought to hold that unruly blade in orbit; so that he came down feet-first and with scarce a jolt. And no sooner his feet upon the floor—lo!—the sword was his, all flightiness going out of it at once, its metal weighing heavy and deadly in his hand.

"Mine!" he snarled his satisfaction—and without pause brought the fresh-forged blade slicing down to sever Gorgos' hairy spider-stalk.

Such a howling and a gibbering then! Purplish pus spurted, and the bloated monstrosity on the dais writhed and bayed its torment in a bass, disbelieving, utterly astonished tone, different again from previous voice of ultimate triumph: "No, *no*! The forces must remain unified! I must let them in…I have promised…they will exact payment!"

The place was full of an awful stench now, and Tarra heard from behind him an abominable *squelching* and clashing. He turned, saw Amyr lizarding down the wall from the balcony—saw also the pseudo-spider where it had fallen to the floor and now collapsed in upon itself, visibly rotting, its legs clattering a terrible staccato rhythm of death upon the runic floor.

Overhead, the two remaining scimitars had gone into mad orbits all their own; they banged against the high beams, clanged on the copper of the dome, scythed among the dumbfounded, now terrified yellow-robes where they gawped and gasped all about the balcony. Also, there was anger in the unseen, alien energies now; their manifestation of flickering fire, forming the writhing column of blue-green light 'twixt ceiling-portal and dais, began to sway and bend and vibrate like small tornado, losing its coherency. It seemed the very air shrieked, whipping in small panic-ridden gusts all about.

Amyr bounded to Tarra's side. "I think we've won. Rather, I think *you've* won!"

Gorgos heard, or somehow knew what he had said. "Not yet!" came his bass croak like belch of thunder. Pseudopods sprouted, became hooks of chitin, bony claws and pincers, all lashing toward the two where they stood frozen in horror. But this time Amyr was quickest off the mark. *"You've done your bit, Hrossak,"* he said in Tarra's mind as he made a dive under the flailing, deadly barrier and on to the dais. *"Now it's my turn!"*

Then he was on his feet within the tossing, clashing wall of murderous armour, where now he seemed caught up in Gorgos' loathsome body tentacles. For a moment Tarra thought the horror had him—but then there came bright flash of rapier's razor edge and Gorgos's head leapt free, spurting, bounding from the dais to roll free on mosaic floor.

Tarra turned his face away then in disgust at the incredibly swift *katabolism* which took place atop the dais, and the indescribable stench that rose up—which must surely be poisonous—as Gorgos' pseudo-tissues turned to steaming slime and slopped over the altar-stone's rim. And, "There!" cried Amyr Arn. "Suhm-yi curse fulfilled, Gorgos. And how will you unify the forces now, eh?"

After which...madness!

All hell seemed let loose beneath the great dome. The small, sentient winds gathered into one howling gust which roared out through the ceiling portal, extinguishing the fires in the hanging lamps as it went; the spiralling column of blue-green radiation whirled faster yet, swaying erratically as it commenced a withdrawal; the yellow-robed priests moaned and screamed their terror, divesting themselves of their cassocks as they fled from the chamber en masse, their crush entirely blocking the exit, so that their milling bodies came pouring over the balcony in a churning flood of terrified humanity.

Tarra and Amyr sprang away from the dais, and yet at the same time felt pulled by some awful suction toward it. Overhead the portal was closing, and still the frenziedly whirling blue-green tongue of flickering energies withdrew. Its tip cleared the portal as the edges of glass approached a closure; and down through the final gap lashed sudden lightning in a prolonged burst, splitting the dais asunder and sending chunks of marble flying. Gorgos' body—what was left of it—seemed snatched up in lightning fork, dragged aloft, elongating and separating into vile lumps as it went. These...*portions*...of the magician, crashing against the sharp sectors of the closing window, burst portal and frame outwards into the night. Tarra and Amyr felt themselves lifted as by a great hand, dragged toward the gaping, broken portal. Up to the level of the balcony they were lifted, weightless as thistledown, and for one mind-searing moment it seemed they too must be drawn out into the spaces between the stars. But then—

—It was as if the chamber breathed in a great breath of air—a sort of cleansing psychic implosion—before expelling it in a mighty shout of denial. Gorgos should never have been, he was no more, the sane world was determined to be rid of him and every last trace of his works. And the same great hand which had picked Tarra and Amyr up, now hurled them sideways across the curving balcony, out through a shattering oval window and down toward Death in a shower of coarse glass fragments. Except Death was not expecting them, had made no arrangements to greet them, indeed did not yet want them.

Instead they whirled down, hugging together, through another window—this one thicker, circular, and laying along a horizontal plane—and finally plunged down upon a great round bed piled high with softest silk cushions. And there they lay, bruised and scratched and winded, but entirely intact, getting their breath as the world stopped whirling.

Amyr was first up, then Tarra, snatching up his jewelled sword from the tumbled bed. And when the Hrossak turned to stare about this lesser chamber beneath this lesser dome of copper—

What should he see but Amyr Arn, clasping to his bosom a sobbing creature, infinitely lovely and all of a silver sheen, even as he himself. Ulli Eys, certainly, oracle no more but glad prisoner now of a greater power far than any alien magick.

Then, all three, they fled the place—down into its mazy lower levels, through the empty, groaning corridors and halls, and out into the teeth of a suddenly raging storm—while behind them the temple tottered and was broken, and all the domes fell in upon the place, and the Temple of Secret Gods went the way of its monstrous master and became less than nothing.

And not a yellow-robe in sight, for all who lived had fled, the soldiers with them, so that all that remained of Gorgos' dream was an empty, high-walled square of ruins where not even the weeds would grow, and which from that day forward was shunned...

Within the hour the storm had blown itself out, the clouds had all raced madly away, clearing the sky, and the people of Klühn had come out to light their lamps and candles and dance in the streets. And all through the night they danced and feasted, and all the shops in the bazaars were thrown open, and everything was free to them who knew how precious was life and liberty. And all and all they had forgotten how sweet and clean the breeze off the sea could be, but would not forget again.

As for Tarra and Amyr and Ulli: they, too, would have stayed and revelled, but they had other things to do. All three, they travelled under the moon and stars, male and female Suhm-yi, commencing their long trek back to crater sea, and Tarra Khash the Hrossak—

Ah! But that's another story...

SORCERY in SHAD

FOR ANYONE WHO EVER WISHED HE OR SHE HAD
A FLYING CARPET, AND ALSO FOR THE HECK OF IT!

Contents

PROLOGUE

Absent from his place in Klühn for five long years, at last Teh Atht had come home. But he'd returned empty-handed, his quest cut short by word of a strange curse befallen his beloved sophisticate city on Theem'hdra's eastern strand. And he'd returned angry in the knowledge of five years utterly wasted, which had been better spent in more pleasurable or at least profitable pursuits.

In many guises and by mazy, tortuous route, Teh Atht had crossed and recrossed Theem'hdra from the Paps of Mam to Tharamoon, from the Teeth of Yibb to Grypha on its swampy promontory overlooking the Bay of Monsters. He had wandered in the Nameless Desert, abided awhile upon a jewelled isle in the mighty Crater Sea, sojourned and studied with sorcerous colleagues throughout all the length and breadth of the Primal Land, but to no avail. That which he sought ever eluded his grasp, which for all his magicks large and small came no closer to solution.

In cold and lonely Tharamoon, bleak in the Chill Sea 'twixt Frostlands and the nameless Northern Peaks, he'd dwelled a year in the crumbling manse of that once mightiest of mages Mylakhrion, searching in the rubble and ruin of centuries for a clue and discovering naught; and in the Desert of Sheb he'd likewise lingered in lamia's castle, hoping to discover in Orbiquita's absence some small pointer to that which he pursued—in vain.

The demons and djinn of the deserts could not or would not assist; dryads and naiads alike deemed it unwise to dabble; even the weed-crowned Krakens called up from deeps of ocean turned away and submerged themselves when confronted with Teh Atht's quest and query. They said they did not know, and perhaps they spoke the truth, and anyway the wizard was loath to use threats and thaumaturgies upon them. For Teh Atht deemed himself a white as opposed to black magician, and his reputation was a kindly one.

Then, in the tropical forests of the coast east of Thinhla—beneath the vine-entwined ruins of some city unremembered of man, where Ahorra Izz, the scarlet scorpion-god, guarded his toppled temple, in conversation with that most ireful arachnid—there Teh Atht first heard of the encroaching DOOM which even now threatened Klühn and its people, and the home he had builded there on a bluff above the bay. And this information was delivered, in doleful clacking voice, by none other than Ahorra Izz himself, who said:

"Have you done with picking my brains, wizard? For if so there's that which you should know, concerning that hive of prideful men which is your home, that city on Theem'hdra's eastern strand called Klühn."

"Klühn?" Teh Atht at once looked up from where he sat, trickling a world's ransom in rubies (all worthless to him) through his fingers upon a roseate floor. He frowned. "And what of Klühn, pray? And if indeed there's aught of which I should be appraised, tell me also how come you're so farsighted, and all shut in down here beneath the sunless jungle floor?"

Ahorra Izz chuckled, a hideous rasping sound in Teh Atht's mind, but stirred not at all before his visitor. Indeed, how could he? For he was a statue of polished stone half as tall again as a man, all seemingly carved from a single block, like some great gleamy fossil! And his eyes were rubies big as fists; and his scythe-like stinger, poised on high, was sheathed in some silver metal whose fashioning was a secret lost in time and space. But by virtue of Teh Atht's magick he spoke, albeit in the mage's mind alone. And this is what he said:

"'What' can wait, 'how' comes now. Myriad minion members have I; they scurry in the forests, thrive in the deserts and on the steppes, stay moist beneath the rim of rock and hunt under the moon. Now what say you, Teh Atht? How do you answer my riddle?"

The wizard uncrossed his legs, stood up and stretched. "Scorpions, of course. The green jungle scorpion, the rock scorpion of the uplands, the black desert scorpion and its grey cousin of Hrossa's steppes—but especially the scarlet scorpion of legend. And all make report to you, eh, here in immemorial vault?" But for all his yawn and careless shrug, still Teh Atht marvelled. With familiars far-flung and numerous as these, was any secret safe in all the Primal Land? Would that such an army worked for him! "And what have they told you, the scorpions of Klühn's alleys and secret temples?" he pressed.

"They have told me how in your long absence a strange sect is come into Klühn," Ahorra Izz answered, "and whisper of yellow-robed priests in a temple of terror! Their leader is one Gorgos—perhaps a man—but the 'gods' he worships are not of this world. Indeed, they are not gods! Demons of the star-spaces, the Thromb wait on Gorgos to open up the gates for them!"

Gorgos! And now Teh Atht gasped aloud—even Teh Atht, descendant of Mylakhrion! He had heard of that most monstrous necromancer, of course, and had thought him long dead. But alive? In Klühn? Calling down the Thromb from the spaces between the stars? Life itself—*all* life—were forfeit, come to a terrible termination, should he succeed. Panic struck at Teh Atht's heart, but only for a moment. Then a thought occurred. He stood stock still, stared up at scorpion statue, peered into its scintillant ruby eyes.

"Could it be you've tired of my presence here and grown weary of my questions? This disclosure of yours could well be a clever ruse, by means of which you're rid of me; for of course you know that I must now hie me to my manse in Klühn, and there weave works against this Gorgos."

"Go in peace, Teh Atht," the horror clacked. "And by all means return one day...if any days are left! I have enjoyed your visit."

And then the wizard felt that indeed the cancer in Klühn was no mere figment of fancy, and he felt the bitter winds of space blowing on his soul. "I get me gone at once," he muttered, and made to climb stone stairs.

"Wait!" cried Ahorra Izz. "A further tidbit you should know. There are three who work against this High Priest, this Gorgos who some say *is* a man. And one of this brave trio *is* a man! What's more,

I like him!" He chuckled in his weird way. "How's *that* for a riddle, O wizard?"

Teh Atht gathered up his rune-inscribed cloak, paused briefly at the foot of the stairs. "I'll answer it when next I visit," he said.

Ahorra Izz uttered his doleful chuckle. "Ah, ever the optimist!" he said. "So be it." But Teh Atht was no longer there to hear him...

In his one hundredth and forty-third year, but sprightly for all that, Teh Atht climbed the subterranean temple's stairs of stone toward jungle's floor. Weighed down by dreads half-formed and preoccupied with hasty planning, he forged willy-nilly through curtains and ropes of smoking cobwebs and stirred up dust of centuries unnumbered in his hurried ascent. Across great landings where stood lesser likenesses of Ahorra Izz, under vaulted ceilings all palpitant with myriad massed forms of the green-eyed pyramid bat, ever toward the tumbled ruins above he strove, and one thought uppermost in his mind: that even now in Klühn a foulness named Gorgos sought to rain Madness and Death upon an unsuspecting Primal Land.

Finally he reached the surface, came out from the arched entrance of a slumped ziggurat into bowels of foliage rampant. And dizzy from his climb and fetor of the vaults both, he paused awhile to breathe deep and blink in the emerald light, what little of it filtered down through the high canopy of vine and creeper and leprous orchid cluster. And he gazed all about upon the jungle-hid ruins and considered his position: literally, his *location*, all these twenty hundreds of miles from his beloved Klühn.

East of Thinhla, this place, tropical forest on the coast situated between unknown river morasses a-teem with leeches, crocodiles and cannibal fishes; where even the vegetation—some of it, anyway—was lethal, bearing spines and suckers all charged with potent poisons. Barriers entirely natural and wholly unnatural stood between Teh Atht and civilized sophisticate city; and yet, where other men might at once give up the ghost, lie down and die, the wizard merely considered his options. And they were several.

He could set out at once, in the way of more nearly normal men, and simply trek the jungle—and die, most assuredly, in the space of one hundred yards. Hardly a feasible option, that! He could abide here until darkness descend, then call down a grim of night-gaunts to fly him home; except he'd never much trusted gaunts, which were known to have a certain affinity with Yibb-Tstll, a dark god of monstrous appetites.

If he'd brought his carpet of levitation with him, then that would bear him home; but jungle-spawned rots were ruinous to fabrics delicate as that, and so he'd left his flying carpet home. On solid ground, he might simply infuse his boots with powers of league-long striding; but alas the morass was treacherous, and sad thing to step down from stride of several leagues into gluey, bottomless bog! No, more subtle magicks were required here.

He reverted to that spell beloved of Sheb's desert djinn, by means of which he'd landed himself here in the first place; a magick requiring four entire days and a deal of concentration in its construction. And thus, last rune uttered and final pass performed—transforming himself to single tuft of thistledown, and simultaneously conjuring out of the clouds a dust-devil to bend down among the treetops—he contrived to have himself picked up and whirled in a trice back home to Klühn.

Journey of months and years accomplished in minutes, before he spiralled down and expanded once more into a man on the topmost balcony of his tower overlooking the Bay of Klühn, and there he reeled awhile under the first stars of night as nodding dust-devil raced away toward windy wastes of desert.

And so Teh Atht returned home.

Staggering there atop that high place, still dizzy from his flight, he leaned upon parapet wall and gazed toward Klühn—and immediately grew still, shocked rigid by what he saw. Which was this:

That all the people were at play in the streets where multi-hued lanterns bobbed, and apparently no DOOM befallen, and indeed an air of great merry-making and rejoicing abundantly displayed! What? And had that double-damned deity of an arachnid tricked him after all? If the only curse visited upon Klühn were merriment, then what the loss?

Raging, he swept inside, sought out his familiars three to question them—and only then remembered how, five years ago before taking his departure, because he could not trust them, he'd immobilized all three with the curse of Curious Concretion. In stony state, they'd know nothing of matters transpired in Klühn; but finding them in their places, certainly no worse for wear however dusty, he immediately unspelled them anyway. There was one who hopped, one who flitted, and one that flowed like a pool of oil and served mainly to lubricate the works of Teh Atht's astrologarium, wherein swam miniature stars and worlds and moons important in the wizard's forecasting.

"You, and you," said Teh Atht, wagging a finger at the former pair, hopper and flitter, "to work! What? Do spiders dwell here now? Has someone bequeathed me a desert in my absence, and delivered it to boot? Make all tidy, at once! And you!" he dabbled a finger in the liquid one. "Go oil something…no, wait! Float me my shewstone down to the kitchen, where doubtless affairs are likewise disordered!"

Grumbling in their way, the three set to work while Teh Atht stomped to kitchen and revitalized ancient foods, and fried up a pan of cheese and onions. And while he ate ravenously, so his crystal ball came drifting on a pool of sentient oil; and now past the food in his mouth the wizard mumbled a rune of recounting. Up the leg of his table crept viscous retainer, balancing the shewstone on tip of sticky pseudopod and finally slumping to rest beyond Teh Atht's plate, where he could observe and eat at one and the same time. The milky sphere had slowly cleared, and now Teh Atht commanded: "Tell me about Gorgos. Was he here; if so when, and why? Show me all, without delay!"

And bending to his will as always, the shewstone obeyed…

Pictures appeared in the clear crystal—sharp and real as life but fast-fleeting, so that they showed much in a short space of time—according to Teh Atht's instructions.

It had started five years ago, shortly after he set out upon his fruitless quest, when the first yellow-robed members of Gorgos' priesthood had commenced to arrive in Klühn from far-flung parts. From Thinhla, Eyphra, Thandopolis they had come, bearing the strange ikons and instruments of their faith. Close to Klühn's heart they'd bought land, built a temple of hemispheres with one massive central dome of copper, a task which had kept the city's artisans in work for all of four years. Ah, but long before the work was finished, then, too, had Gorgos installed himself within his Temple of Secret Gods. And rumour had it he'd brought a female creature with him: a girl-thing of rare beauty, however alien, comb-headed and with shimmery silver skin. But only rumour, for she was never seen.

By means of an alleged "oracle," then the necromancer began to work blackmail upon the city's businessmen, its taverners, jewellers, merchants, using such ill-gotten gains to buy his priests, workmen, and finally soldiers! So that soon the entire city was in his grip, where none could escape the oracle's probing, the narrowed, penetrating eyes of the yellow-robes, the glaring and swaggering of armoured fighting men. But as if blackmail and other threats weren't enough, the master of that dire sect had a second trump card which no one could deny: magick, and a black and ominous magick at that!

For now the people found themselves levied of a tax, which they must pay in respect of the "protection" they received from Gorgos and his priesthood against...against what? Against dark forces which even now threatened to devour Klühn utterly, given shape and form in monthly manifestations of weird energies in the sky! Boiling clouds and strange lightnings, aye, and doomful luminous hell-webs on high, whose forces seemed mercifully (?) bled off by temple's copper dome, or deflected by the devotions of droning priests. For Klühn had sinned, apparently, and was now taken to task, which was why this Temple of Secret Gods had been builded here: to hold at bay a scourge and keep the city safe.

So said the priests; but common people wondered: what sin had they committed? And were the priests here to combat evil, or had it merely followed them, as fleas follow a dog?

"Hold!" cried Teh Atht, done with his food and impatient now. "I know most of this, and also that Gorgos would call down the Thromb, which were the end of everything! But quite obviously he was stopped. I know something of that, too. Three creatures put paid to his scheme for immortality as Lord of the Thromb, one of which was a man. Very well, now show me these three, for they interest me..."

And again the shewstone obeyed:

First there was the silver-skinned lass Gorgos brought with him to the temple in Klühn: his oracle, a Suhm-yi female gifted as all her race had been with the power of reading minds. Thus had Gorgos blackmailed Klühn. Stolen by the monster as a child and spirited away from her home in the jewelled isles of the Crater Sea, she had helped (however unwillingly) in the elevation of her master to great power. Ah, and also in his downfall! Teh Atht saw it all in his shewstone.

For now, come out of those same jewelled isles, a *male* Suhm-yi in search of a mate. Amyr Arn, his name, the last of his race other than Gorgos' she-creature—and his strange heart bent on vengeance! Not only would he take back Ulli Eys to where they both belonged, but if he could he'd put down her cruel master, too, and thus end forever the threat of the Thromb.

Recruiting to his cause a man—a common man, and yet extraordinary, too, in his way—the last Suhm-yi male had entered Gorgos' temple of terror to sabotage his plans. And none too soon! Just five nights ago, this had been, when the heavens were ablaze with eerie Thromb coruscations, and the temple's central dome gleamed orange and gold and colours all unknown in supernatural light from cauldron sky. Dressed in stolen or counterfeit robes of yellow, impersonating the temple's priests, Suhm-yi and colleague had smuggled themselves within, and—

But here the shewstone faltered; its picture faded and merged into mist, and the very crystal seemed suddenly filled with a roiling motion. A thaumaturgical turbulence, of course! Such had been the forces at work that night in and around Gorgos' temple that lesser magicks simply could not function.

"Peace!" said the wizard, fearing his shewstone might shatter. "Enough—for now. Well done!" And the whirlpool mists grew calm and quickly congealed, and the crystal sat there in its pool of living oil like some great luminous pearl.

Teh Atht scratched his narrow chin. "Just three of them," he mused. "Suhm-yi man and maid, and a roughneck off the streets. Against Gorgos, priests, soldiers and Thromb energies? Remarkable! Indeed, incredible!" And out loud to the shewstone: "What remained when all was done? Show me that, if you can—but not if it's discomforting."

The crystal cleared, a picture appeared, and Teh Atht gazed upon a familiar scene. Klühn near its centre, where Gorgos' Temple of Secret Gods had reared its copper domes and received its dark tribute from beyond the stars: now a high-walled square of gaunt ruins, shunned, where not even the weeds would grow!

The wizard tapped his fingernail on table-top and the scene slowly faded. "Suhm-yi man, maid, and one other…" He frowned. "Where are the silver-skins now?"

The crystal showed him: they trekked the plains west in the dusk, heading for their homeland in the isles of the Crater Sea. And there was a joy in them where he led, and she sat upon their yak with her hand on his upon the beast's neck. Teh Atht felt glad and nodded.

"And one other," he mused again. "Is he in the city still, this other? If so, show him to me." He waited, but no picture formed. "Gone then, but gone where? I have to know, for there's more to this one than meets the eye—even the all-seeing eye of a shewstone!"

And so Teh Atht uttered the rune of Sustained Scrying, propping his pointed chin in cupped hands the better to see what he might see. And indeed he saw a great deal…

I

CHANCE ENCOUNTER

Y our gold or your gizzard!" hoarse, desperate voice called out
through sooty twilight, from bushes at the foot of the bottleneck
up ahead, where the pass cut through a stony cleft. "I can slit either
your purse or your throat, so take your pick—only quick now, 'cos my
finger's itchy on the trigger of this crossbow!"

"Hold!" the lone camel rider sent back a shout, reined in his jittery
beast. "Now hold there, friend!" He made a dusky silhouette against
the indigo sky with its first fistful of stars. And he'd have made a fine
target, too, *if* his ambusher had a crossbow! That wasn't the case, but
no way the rider could know it.

"Put up your hands," the would-be thief now commanded, "so's I
can see there's no weapon in 'em."

"What?" his intended victim replied. "And would you really take
a man's life for nothing? Highwayman, you've picked a wrong 'un
tonight, I'm afraid—where loot's concerned, anyway. Man, I'm broke!
So stay your hand on that weapon. I've a loaf we can share, if you like,
and a skin of passable wine. But that's all…"

The ambusher's ears pricked up: he was *starving*! And there was
something in this lone wayfarer's voice, too. Memories stirred, of a

time not too far past in Chlangi the Doomed… "Who are ye, sitting there so nice in my sights?" he hoarsely inquired.

Astride his camel, the Hrossak tried to locate the other; no good, he was a shadow in the darker shadows of the bushes. But where- and who-ever he was, his voice had seemed strangely familiar. He could be any one of a dozen brigands the rider had tangled with along his mazy way.

The steppeman had put his hands up on the other's barked instruc-tions; but behind the right one, hanging down along his wrist from a point trapped between index and next finger, a balanced knife poised for swift release. Only let him get a precise fix on his ambusher's whereabouts, and—

"What's your name, I said?" the furtive owner of the gruff voice once more demanded.

"I'm a Hrossak," the rider replied, shifting a little in his saddle. Was that a movement there in the bushes, by the bole of that gnarly tree? Aye, it was that—the outline of a crouching man! "Khash, by name, after my father, naturally," he continued, letting his throwing arm drift back a little, "—though the gods alone know why, for he never had any either!"

A gasp from the gloom. "Tarra Khash!"

Tarra threw himself forward and out of the saddle, threw his knife, too. Only at the last, hearing that gasp and the other speaking his name, had he managed to deflect knife's flight—else the lurker in the bushes were a goner. Then he was rolling in dust, hurling himself headlong into the blackest shadows, snarling his rage in the dark-ness even as he snaked the curved ceremonial sword from its scabbard strapped to his back.

In another moment he crashed through brittle bushes, found a boulder and slid himself over to its safe side, there came to a crouch-ing halt… Close at hand, a wheezy, frightened panting. The Hrossak listened, grinned a humourless wolf's grin, called out: "And now it's your turn, friend. Seems you know me, which might or might not be a good thing. So in the dozen or so heartbeats you've left to live, best tell me who you are. That way I'll be able to say a few words over you, to let the gods know who I'm passing their way."

"Stumpy," the unseen other gasped at once. "Stumpy Adz, great lump! So called for a missing right hand—aye, and very nearly an ear, too! Come free me, quick! I daren't move my head for fear I slice my neck!"

Tarra took his first real breath in what felt like hours, lofted his scimitar and sheathed it unerringly in its scabbard, so that its jewelled hilt stood up behind his left shoulder where it curved into his neck. He put a hand on the boulder and vaulted it, glided soundlessly into the bushes and up to the twisted bole of the gnarly tree. And sure enough there stood Stumpy Adz, his head immobilized between a rough branch and the long, thin, razor-edged blade of Tarra's knife where it pinned his tatty collar to the bole.

"Old fool!" growled Tarra, snatching his knife free—but minding it didn't cut Stumpy's leathery flesh. "Some desperado you—*hah*! And what if it hadn't been me at all but some nighthawk, eh? And what if *he* really did have a crossbow? Indeed, a miracle of coincidence that it *is* me! Now what's this all about? What, you, a highwayman? At your age? And why the hell anyway? The last time I saw you, in Chlangi, I gave you gems to last a lifetime..." Eyes growing accustomed to the dusk, he glowered at the other, noticed his scrawny, down-at-heel condition. Stumpy was thin and bent as old Gleeth the crescent moon where he rode above the ridge.

"First you'd try to skewer me," the old man grumbled, gingerly fingering his unmarked neck, then sighing his relief when his fingers came away clean, "and now you'd have me talk myself to death—if you don't beat me to it! Well, I'll cut it short, Tarra Khash: hard times, my friend, hard times—which called for harsh measures. I knew I took a chance, but better dead than marooned out here, miles from anywhere, and slowly shrivelling to bones!"

Tarra noticed Stumpy's leanness, couldn't mistake his trembling, which wasn't alone reaction to his narrow escape. He whistled for his beast, which came at the trot. "Are you hungry, Stumpy Adz?"

The other groaned. "Hungry? I could eat the saddle right off your mount's back! Or you can keep the saddle and I'll wrap my gums round the camel instead!"

Over his own shock now, Tarra grinned. "Well, you fed and sheltered me once when I was in need." He grasped the other's frail shoulder. "So I suppose it's only fair I return the favour. Where can we make camp?"

Stumpy wearily led him to the face of the cliff, showed him a shallow cave—more a scoop out of the rock—where a great boulder had rolled free in ages past. Indeed the very boulder lay shattered now, a broken wall of jagged rock fronting the cave, which should shelter their fire and hide its light. "I was going to sleep the night here," said Stumpy. "With a little luck I'd wake with the morning, and with a great deal of luck I wouldn't!"

Tarra tethered his camel, started to gather up dry sticks and dead branches. But:

"Who needs a fire?" Stumpy muttered. "I've got my own, burning through the wall of my stomach! Stop torturing me and give me some food."

"Don't you want to see what you're eating?" Tarra frowned at him, struck hot sparks from his flint. The tinder caught at once.

"Just lead me to it and let me touch it," Stumpy grunted. "If it's edible I'll know it—and then stand well back!"

Yellow firelight flared as Tarra took down a saddle-bag. He opened it, produced apples, dried meat, a little cheese. Stumpy, hands shaking with hunger, seated himself upon a flat rock and fell to it. There were tears in his one good eye (the right one) as he got his few remaining teeth working on a piece of meat.

Tarra squatted down by the fire, warmed his hands, bit into an apple. He'd eaten earlier—a rabbit, taken on the plain with a well-aimed stone—and wasn't so hungry. But to watch Stumpy Adz going at it…

"How long?" Tarra asked.

"Four days," the grizzled oldster mumbled around mouthfuls, "maybe five. I've dreamed of this for so long, it's—*umf!*—hard to say if I was awake or—*umf!*—sleeping. Tarra, but this is *good*! Er, didn't you mention wine or some such?"

The Hrossak put on a surprised expression, shook his head. "No."

"Yes you—*umf!*—did!" Stumpy was indignant. "When you thought I had you in my sights, you offered me—*umf!*—half a loaf and some passable wine."

"But you didn't have a crossbow," said Tarra.

"What difference does that make?" Stumpy scowled.

Tarra shrugged. "Well, neither did I have the wine!"

But as Stumpy groaned his disappointment, so the Hrossak relented. He took out a small wineskin from the saddle-bag, uncorked it and took a swig, passed it over. Stumpy held up the skin, expertly squirted a quenching stream into his gaping maw. *"Ahhh!"* he said. And, *"Ahhh!"* again. Tarra reached out, neatly separated him from supply.

Now the Hrossak tossed his apple in the direction of the tethered beast, ate just a bite of cheese, took another pull at the skin's tube before plugging it. "Eat first," he told Stumpy, "and then I'll let you wash it down. But don't make such a pig of yourself that you get the cramps. There's water in the other pack for later." Then he said no more but let the old man get on with it.

While Stumpy wolfed his food, so he looked Tarra up and down. What he saw was this:

A big-hearted man, open as a book; an inveterate wanderer, with feet which wouldn't stop itching while yet there remained a hill unclimbed, or view unviewed; a great adventurer—the latter not so much by inclination as by accident. For troubles, trials and terrors, in forms numerous as the fingers on his hard hands, had seemed to dog the Hrossak's heels since the day he'd left his steppes. With one adventure leading into the next, sometimes it had seemed he'd been born under a cursed star. Or perhaps a lucky one? For here he was hale and hearty, come through it all with scarce a scratch.

Tarra Khash was young, maybe twenty-five or -six, and bronzed as the great idols of jungled Shad. They weren't much known for their guile, these steppemen, which meant he'd most likely be trustworthy; indeed in Chlangi, Stumpy had discovered that to be a fact. And it was of old repute that once a Hrossak befriends a man, then that he's his friend for life. But on the other hand, best not to cross one; their memories were long and they didn't much care for scores unsettled.

As for the physical man himself: he was a tall one, this Tarra, and for all that he was lean and narrow in the hip, still his muscles rippled under the clinging silk of a dark shirt and the coarse weave of his tight, calf-length trousers. Hair a dusty, tousled brown, and eyes of a brown so deep they verged on black; long in the limbs, with shoulders broad as a gate; strong white teeth in a mouth never far from a grin... aye, he was a likely lad, the steppeman. But in no wise a fool, and ever growing wiser in the ways of the world.

Tough? Oh, he was that all right! That curved wand of death he wore across his back, for example: the merest silly sliver of a sword when Stumpy saw it last. For all the hilt's pretty jewels, it hadn't been much to mention as a weapon. Ah! But didn't it hold fond fighting memories for the Hrossak? It must, for he'd risked his life for it! King Fregg Unst the 1st of Chlangi had stolen that from him in Shunned City; and Tarra, against all odds, had taken it back! And what of Fregg now? Best not ask…

No rings adorned Tarra's fingers, nor the lobes of his ears. There were thieves in Theem'hdra who'd take a man's entire arm just for a gemstone in a ring on his smallest finger! Stumpy's eyes went lower, to Tarra's soft leather boots where they came up almost to his knees— and the sheath stitched into the outside of the right-hand boot, which housed his throwing knife. Aye, and with that he'd be *deadly* accurate! *Too true*, thought Stumpy, fingering his neck again.

For his part, Tarra had likewise been looking Stumpy over. The old lad was a failed thief, as witness his stump for right hand. They were hard on light-fingered types in certain parts, and even harder in others. This had probably happened in Klühn, fairly sophisticate city. In Thinhla they'd have hanged him, and in Khrissa pegged him out on the frozen mud-flats at the mouth of the Marl with the tide rising.

Stumpy was tiny, old, gnarly as the tree Tarra's knife had pinned him to; but he'd been a fighter, too, in his time. Now he wore a patch over his left eye; or rather, he wore it over the empty socket. Grizzled and brown from all weathers, white-whiskered and with a couple of snaggy yellow fangs for teeth, he looked like some sort of dwarfy pirate! But Tarra knew that despite his telltale stump, eye-patch and all, still the oldster had a good heart. And a far too-healthy appetite!

"What are you gawping at?" Stumpy growled now, wincing a little and holding his belly.

"Cramps?" Tarra inquired.

"Likely," Stumpy grimaced again. "I suppose I ate too fast."

"Warned you," the Hrossak nodded. "All right, sit still and I'll see what I can do." He brought a blanket from his beast's back, spread it over Stumpy and tucked him to his chin, then picked him up gentle as a child and put him in a spot close to the fire, with his back to a warm sloping rock. Then he brought him a sip of water.

"But no more wine," he said, "for that'll only make it worse. It's your guts complaining about neglect and ill-treatment, that's all. So just rest easy for now and tomorrow you'll be all right."

It was night now and the sky aglow with stars, and old Gleeth riding high like the blade of a silver scythe. Tarra sipped wine, chewed on a morsel of meat, waited until the fire's warmth worked through to Stumpy's bones and softened them up a little. Finally the old lad stopped grimacing and groaning, vented a ringing fart and a somewhat gentler sigh, and:

"I suppose you'll want to know how come I'm here, penniless and all, after you left me rich just a four-month gone in Chlangi?"

"In your own time, Stumpy," said Tarra. "Tomorrow will do, if you're not up to it now."

"Oh, I'm up to it," the other growled. And in a moment: "Well, it was mainly the fault of that lass Gulla!"

Gulla was Stumpy's daughter, whom Tarra had met in Chlangi— but only "met" there, and that was all. He remembered her now and winced a little, but not so much that Stumpy would notice. She'd been a big girl, right enough: comely about the face but built like a fortress. It had bruised Tarra's ribs just looking at her! He'd considered himself lucky to escape unscathed.

"So," Stumpy continued, "she reckoned it was coming up to her marrying time, and she didn't much fancy the local stuff. Couldn't blame her, really. Pickings weren't much in Chlangi, unless she'd settle for a pockmarked pirate or warty son of mountain scum out of Lohmi; Fregg's lot were a right old riff-raff, as you'll doubtless recall. Anyway, I'd waited around until then—you know?—to let it be seen that I was still just poor old Stumpy, who never had two buttons to rub together. For if that gang of yeggs and sharpers had suspected for one minute that I'd been with you against Fregg that night—that I'd helped you, and been well paid for it—well..." He shrugged and let it tail off.

"Oh, they wouldn't give a toss for Fregg, but gemstones are something else again! And me with a king's ransom buried under my dirt floor, eh?" He chuckled, then asked: "Incidentally, what *did* happen to Fregg? They never found him—not that anyone looked too far! But unlike him to run off and leave his long-accumulated treasure-trove bursting at the seams like that, all for the taking. And his old rune-caster, too, Arenith Han: they reckon *he* was less than mincemeat!"

Tarra nodded. "Lamia got 'em," he said, but very quietly, and glanced narrow-eyed all about in the shadows beyond the fire's light. "Orbiquita! She had a grudge against both. Settled it there and then. But for Orbiquita, I'd likely be there now—broken bones in a shallow grave..."

"She took scum like them and not you?" Stumpy wriggled bushy white eyebrows in undisguised inquiry. "Funny! I thought she was supposed to lust after hot young bloods like you?" He shrugged again. "Anyway, I'd heard as much: that it was Orbiquita got 'em. And she didn't just take them two, neither. The way I heard it she killed a dozen that night, tore 'em to bits with her bare hands!"

"Not bare." Tarra shook his head, shuddered. "Scythes! Hands like scythes, and feet to match. Don't ask about her teeth..."

"Seems you've your own tale to tell," said Stumpy, wide-eyed now and mouth agape.

"Some other time," Tarra answered, "but not tonight. Night's the wrong time to be talking of lamias and such. And anyway, I'm more interested in what you've got to say."

"Well, then—" Stumpy continued, "—so there I was with a lass who wanted a man, and only a handful of cut-throats to choose from. So I bided my time until the whole town was drunk one night, then stole a camel and got while the getting was good. It wouldn't have done to buy a beast, for then they'd wonder where I got the money and come after me. But we were clean away, and we headed for the pass through the Great Eastern Peaks."

"On your way to Klühn," Tarra nodded.

Stumpy shook his grizzled head. "On the *route* to Klühn," he said, "but I've something of a rep there," (he waved his stump) "so that wasn't our destination. I'd set my heart on a little house in one of those white-walled villages at the foot of the Eastern Range, where sweet water comes down off the mountains and there are lots of green things to grow. That was all I wanted: peace and quiet, a house and garden, and a place to watch my grandchildren grow up fat and happy."

Tarra picked a scrap of meat from between his strong teeth. "Sounds about right," he opinioned. "So what went wrong?"

"Nothing, not right then. Got through the pass and cut south, eventually found us a village halfway down the Eastern Range, snuggled between twin spurs a mile across. A place with a stream and good, loamy soil in its gardens. An old boy had recently died there, and so we bought his home where it sat right at the edge of the water. I could fish right out of the window, if I wanted to! Women were scarce there and Gulla got courted for the first time in her life—by three of 'em! After a week she knew which one she wanted: the only one of 'em who was bigger than she was!" He grinned a gummy grin, Tarra smiling with him.

"So the both of you were well fixed up," the Hrossak nodded. "Now tell me the worst."

Stumpy's grin turned sour. "It was a queer thing, that," he said. "So queer I'm still not sure about it! But this is the way I remember it:

"Gulla and Robos—her lad—had gone off on touch-and-taunt. That's the local term for it, anyway: when just before marriage a young couple try it out, as it were, to see if all will fit properly and who's to wear the apron, etcetera. A week spent high up in the hills with only the goats and the clouds for company, where they'd build a shelter for two and do all their fingering and fighting, their *ooh*ing! and *aah*ing! and...you know? All of that stuff.

"They'd been gone, oh, a day or two. I woke up early one fine morning and thought: 'fish!' It was the sort of morning when you can feel 'em rising—the fish, I mean. So I took line and hooks, a blanket to stretch out on, a slice of stale bread to chew and roll into little balls for bait, and headed upstream. I climbed through the foothills and time lost all meaning to me, climbed till I found a pool in a rocky basin, with the water filling it and trickling over the rim. Perfect! I took a dozen small fish inside an hour, determined to have three for lunch turned on a spit, the rest to take home and smoke for later.

"Now, in that high place I could see for miles. Oh, I've only one eye, but it's a sharp 'un! And the air so clear and all.

"I fancied I could even see the Eastern Ocean, more than two hundred miles away, but that was probably just the flat, shiny horizon, or maybe a mirage. But I *was* sure I could see the ruins of old Humquass on the plain, which was once a vast fortress city so big its walls had roads built on top of 'em! Now the ruins lie to the south-east, and as I'm looking at 'em—at that far smudge of ancient jumble—I notice a cloud of drifting dust. Coming from that general direction but much closer. I watch and wait, and I keep fishing; though in all truth I've started to lose interest in the fish, for this new thing has trapped my attention. Dust, aye, rising up from a long straggly line that inches its way like a troop of ants along the eastern borders of Hrossa."

"A caravan?" said Tarra. "From Hrossa? Unlikely! Not much on commerce, my lot, and when they do trade it's usually by sea. No, they keep to themselves, mainly—er, with the odd exception, of course."

Stumpy raised an eyebrow, glanced at the other with old-fashioned expression on his leathery face. "The *very* odd exception, aye..."

And at last he continued. "Anyway, from Grypha or Yhemnis I can't say, but caravan certainly. At first sight, anyway. I fix a fire, cook my fish and maintain a watch. As I eat, the dust cloud gets bigger and closer all the time; and now, because the wind's in my direction, I can even hear the distant tinkling of bells, the snorting of beasts, the creaking of leather and clatter of wooden wheels striking pebbles. And I think: why, they're heading straight for Haven's Hollow!—that being the name of the village.

"And me perched half-a-mile up, so to speak, I get a bird's-eye view of it: I can even make out the beasts and their several burdens, and something of the masters who prod 'em along. Ah, but damned strange caravan this, Tarra Khash! Decked out to look like one, aye—but a ship under false colours for all that, be certain! Indeed, a pirate!"

"Not a caravan?" Tarra gawped. "Then what?"

"Raiders!" Stumpy spat the word out. "Slavers!"

Tarra felt the hairs come erect back of his neck. "Blacks?" he growled. "From Yhemni jungles, or Shad across the straits, d'you think? Scourge of Grypha and the southern coast all the way to Thinhla, those lads—but busy with their miserable, bloody work so far north? Unheard of!"

"Blacks there were." Stumpy nodded curtly. "And their leader a curlyhead, too—but others among 'em more bronze than black..." He looked accusingly at Tarra.

"Well *I* wasn't there!" the Hrossak protested. "I was in Klühn, and beset by problems of my own, believe me!"

"Oh, I do," said Stumpy. "No, not you, Tarra, but Hrossaks certain for I saw them with my own eye."

Steppemen, slavers? It was hard to swallow. But no reason why Stumpy should lie, so Tarra would have to accept it. And anyway, he'd met outcast Hrossaks before, however small a handful: outlaws, banished for their evil ways.

"Get on with it," he growled, somewhat surly now.

"It was their wagons and beasts that sent me scrambling back down the rocks and scree slides," said Stumpy. "They were no more than a mile or two away by then, and suddenly I was sore afraid—not for myself, but for all the new friends I'd made in that pretty little village down there. Friends and neighbours, farmers most of 'em, whose only iron implements were scythes and ploughshares. And hope against hope, even as I clambered down that too long way, still I prayed I was wrong."

"Something about their wagons, their beasts? Make sense!" said Tarra, but he felt something of the sick terror glimpsed in the old lad's fire-dappled mien.

Finally Stumpy blinked, scowled and got on with it:

"Well, they had a few ponies, rare enough in these parts," he said, "and a string of camels and yaks—but their real beasts of burden were great lizards! Hrossak lizards, Tarra Khash, which only steppemen have ever been able to control or master. But even so, the lizards and the camels weren't the only poor beasts toiling in that caravan. For chained to the long—the *too* long—wagons were slaves galore, taken, I imagine, from all the villages farther down the foot of the range. I could hear their moaning and crying now, and the clanking of their chains.

"I was halfway down from the pool by then, and that was when it happened." He paused, perhaps for breath.

"Well?" said Tarra, impatient now.

Stumpy hung his head. "Lad, it was a horrible sight. And nothing I could do about it. The raiders had come in sight of the village, and no longer any need for subterfuge. Now they could stop being a caravan. Slow-moving to this point, as soon as they saw the village and smelled blood the mask fell away. And then they were like hounds unleashed!

"The long wagons—five of 'em, the longest things on four pairs of wheels each I've ever seen—were left behind with a handful of overseers, who worked on the chained slaves with whips to keep 'em quiet. The ponies set off at a gallop, kicking up the dust, throwing a wide half-circle around the village. Camels took on two armed raiders apiece, went trotting into town where their riders quickly dismounted. This much I'll say: there were no Hrossaks in on the raping and blood-letting. No, for they'd mainly stayed behind to tend the big hauling lizards. But the blacks and a handful of coarse-maned Northmen..." He broke off, shook his head.

"Northern barbarians, too?" Tarra could see it all in his mind's eye, and he knew from personal experience that the reputation of the Northman wasn't just idle gossip.

Stumpy nodded. "Blacks and Northmen, aye," he answered grimly. "There were maybe two dozen families in that village. Lots of burly lads, all completely untried in combat, and a few pretty wives and daughters. But mainly the women were old—thank all that's good! As for heads of families: farmers and greypates, like myself.

"Now I'm three-quarters down from the heights and shouting myself hoarse, and people out in the fields looking up to see what all the commotion's about. The ponies and riders tightening their net and closing in on the village, and in the main street itself—butchery!"

"But why?" Tarra was aghast at visions conjured. "I thought you said slavers? What good are dead slaves?"

"Young 'uns, they wanted," Stumpy told him with a groan. "Young lads and only the prettiest maids—and of the last there were only two or three in Haven's Hollow, be sure. As for the rest: death for the aged of both sexes, rape and yet more rape for the girls, until the dogs had had their fill and put an end to it with their swords. Aye, damned few lasses and young wives, Tarra, and two dozen or more blacks and maned barbarians. I'll not draw you any pictures..."

The Hrossak ground his teeth, drove a balled fist into the palm of his hand. "Slave-taking's bad enough," he finally growled, "but what you describe is—"

"Devil's work!" Stumpy cut him off. "And that's what they were, those butchers: spawn of the pit!" And after a moment: "Do you want to know the rest?"

Tarra shook his head at first, then nodded, however reluctantly. "Aye, best tell me all and get it out of your system."

"My house was burning when I got down," said Stumpy. "The whole village was burning, and blood everywhere! The blacks and barbarians were in the alehouse, smashing barrels and pouring it down. I saw it all: the bodies in the fields, the naked, raped, gutted lasses, the lads bludgeoned senseless and shackled, and the blood and the fire—and I think I went a little daft. I came across a Northman in the shadow of a burning house, still having his way with some poor girl. She was dead—of terror, I suppose, with her eyes all starting out of her head—but he didn't seem to mind that. I minded it. I picked up his great sword and sliced the dog right down his sweaty, hairy spine!

"And that was it, what I needed! Killing him had given me pleasure, an amazing relief! I was transformed—into a berserker! Me, old Stumpy Adz, roaring in a blood frenzy! I rushed into the alehouse with my bloody sword, and cursed them all in their own heathen tongue—then skewered a frizzy through his gizzard. They'd laughed at me at first, but that stopped 'em. Then someone got up behind me and clonked me hard on the head. For me, that was the end of it. Everything went black and I knew I was going to die, and it didn't bother me much..."

"And yet they didn't kill you!" Tarra shook his head.

"Oh, they did," said Stumpy, "but only on the inside. Why didn't they kill me? But I was mad, wasn't I? A crazy man! The Yhemnis have a thing about madmen: they won't kill a loony, for if they do they have to care for his needs and carry him on their back for eternity in the afterlife. That's their belief. No, safer far to maroon him somewhere to die all on his own—which is what they did to me."

Tarra marvelled at the old lad's hardiness. "So they dumped you here, where for four or five days you've just wandered, eh?"

Stumpy shrugged. "I found a few berries, the wrong sort, and they made me sick. I got a little water from a spiky cactus, and that made me sick, too! Until at last I was sick of everything, not least life. Then I heard your beast coming clip-clop up the pass, and I thought: Stumpy, one way or the other, this misery ends right here."

Tarra nodded. "Fortunate for you it wasn't the other!" he said. He moved about in the glow of dying embers, found more branches and tossed them on the fire. And finally, turning again to Stumpy, he said: "Aren't you tired yet?"

For answer Stumpy buzzed like a nest of wasps. Tarra saw that his chin was on his chest, noted the steady rise and fall of the blanket. Out like a candle snuffed! That was good…

Or was it? The night had come in chilly and Stumpy had Tarra's blanket. He sighed, went to where his beast had gone to its knees, lay down along its flank. And using saddle-bags for a pillow, he quickly fell asleep—

II
BLACK CARAVAN, WHITE GOLD!

And as quickly came awake!
Much too quickly, so that his mind was almost left behind as his body sat itself up.

"On your feet, great lump!" Stumpy shouted again. "Come on, man, get a move on!"

Stumpy? A move on?

What the hell...?

Tarra brushed sleep from his eyes, remembered where he was and who with, and Stumpy's story of—how many hours past? Quite a few, for Gleeth was gone from the sky, and the stars fast-fading—and he scrambled stiffly, stumblingly to his feet even as his beast snorted and spat and reared aloft on spindly legs.

"Here, my hand," yelled Stumpy from camel's back, his voice shrill with urgency. "Quick man, take hold!"

"Take hold?" Tarra stumbled this way and that. Yesterday he'd come many, many miles, and he'd been very deep asleep. And now all of this motion and commotion; shadows moving in the dusk of pre-dawn; camel hissing and rearing, and the old idiot on its back screaming and beckoning. A nightmare, maybe?

No maybe about it! A crossbow bolt zipped past Tarra's ear, sliced a groove in beast's rump. Now the Hrossak was wide awake, and now, too, he leaped for Stumpy's outstretched hand—too late!

The camel was off like a shot from a sling, impelled by the pain in its rear. It toppled Tarra aside in its panic flight, threw him down in dead embers from last night's fire. Then camel and Stumpy, too, a single wild silhouette against the grey of dawn, sinking out of sight over the brow of the hill.

Spitting curses and ashes both, Tarra came upright—and a pony ploughed right into him. But he saw its rider, a Northman wild and woolly, and he felt a hand grip the hilt of the sword on his back even as he fell. With a whisper of steel the weapon was taken from him, and now all he had was his knife. He crashed through brittle bushes, rolled in dust, yanked out the knife from its sheath on his calf—and froze right there.

A frizzy stood over him, loaded crossbow pointed straight at his heart. *Goodbye, everything*, thought Tarra. Then—

"Don't kill him!" a low voice growled. "He's a live one, this buck steppeman, and a good thing for all of us if he stays that way. Aye, for Yoppaloth will be pleased to have him in his arena of death. What? Just look at those eyes: black as night and no flicker of fear in 'em, just fury. I'd say he's probably the meanest buck we've taken!"

Close by, a pony whinnied and there came sounds of a rider dismounting. Then a snorting and clattering of camels, and their humped outlines and smoulder-eyed riders hemming the grounded Hrossak in. Finally that low voice of authority again, but closer, saying: "You, Gys Ankh, outcast of your race no less than this one, get after that old madman. It was you urged me to let you kill him, so there'd be no witnesses. Well, now he's riding like the wind! So get after him and finish it. But by your hand, not mine. I'm not having that old bag of bones riding my back in the afterlife!"

There came a curse and the sound of hooves drumming, and the fading, "Yee, yee, *yee*-hiii!" of a Hrossak hot in pursuit. Hrossak, aye: Stumpy Adz hadn't been mistaken about the make-up of these polyglot raiders. And at last the owner of that doomful voice stepped into view: a tall, wiry Yhemni in rich red robe, his skull-like head topped with cockscomb of stiff-lacquered hair, painted red along its crest. Of mixed blood, Tarra could see, he was thin-lipped, slant-eyed, gaunt and hollow-faced. And black as any black man Tarra had ever seen. The Hrossak guessed it wasn't just the colour of his skin but also that of his life.

Away in the east the rim of the world grew milky with soft light as the sun escaped Cthon's nets and strove to rise again for the new day. Misty light glinted on Tarra's knife; and still the black underling stood over him, his deadly weapon steady on his heart.

"Well?" said the tall Yhemni chief of these cut-throats. "If you're going to throw that knife, throw it. Likely you'll nick Um-bunda, there, and maybe even kill him—but even dying he'll be sure to put his bolt in you."

Tarra found his voice. "So maybe I should toss the knife your way instead?" he growled.

Before he could redirect his aim, the spindly half-breed stepped quickly back into shadows. And now his voice came brittle as thin ice. "I'll count just five, Hrossak," he said, "and that's your—"

"Save your numbers," said Tarra, letting the knife fall with a clatter. "I can't beat all of you. One at a time, maybe, but not in a bunch."

With that he would have climbed to his feet, but half-a-dozen blacks fell on him at once, binding him securely. While this was happening their leader came close again and stood watching, his skull-face split in a grin. "So you're a fighter, eh? Well, you'll get your share of that, steppeman—in Shad!"

Fighting…in Shad…in a certain "arena of death"? And now Tarra had just about all of it. As his captors bundled him down to the stalled "caravan" (best think of it as a caravan, he supposed) so he cast his mind back on tidbits of information gleaned here and there in his wanderings. About certain wizards, for instance, with names like Mylakhrion—and Black Yoppaloth!

Aye, and it was rumoured that Shad had seen a long line of Yoppaloths. The current sorcerer bearing that name would be the ninth. Black Yoppaloth the 9th, of the Yhemnis. *Huh!* But Tarra supposed it had a certain ring to it. Blacker rumours still had it that in fact this was that same foul necromancer who'd lived in Mylakhrion's time more than a thousand years ago, though it was past Tarra's fathoming how that could possibly be. As for Shad across the Straits of Yhem: that might well be caravan's destination, but a certain grim-faced Hrossak wouldn't be with it when it got there, be certain! Shad...

Now what, if anything, did Tarra know about Shad? Nothing for sure, except that it was the twin of Yhemnis, which it faced squarely across seventy-five miles of windy straits. As for rumour: Shad was legended to be splendidly barbaric—a city of gold, bronze, ivory, iron-wood—jungle-girt hive of pirates and slavers. But merely legend? No longer; it seemed the latter was now indisputable fact! And yet many a year, indeed more than a century, since last Shad raided against whites and so far from jungled coast. Normally the blacks took other blacks, Yhemnis like themselves, from the coastal villages north and south of Yhemnis the city on the mainland's steamy coast. And vice versa, when mainland blacks would raid on Shadarabar. So what was different now? Had the two sides got together at last? Unlikely, for their rivalry was historic.

Dragged unceremoniously down to the winding, narrow trail through the pass, Tarra was manacled to the side of one of Stumpy's "too long wagons," where a dozen desperate youths and young men hung in their chains and their rags in various stages of exhaustion. A like number was chained on the other side. Then he was left alone, and as dawn turned to day along came a bronzed, greasy, scar-faced man on a lathered pony, jerking his mount viciously to a halt alongside Tarra. He took a cruel whip from his belt and shook down its coils to the earth, looked down at Tarra from under bushy black eyebrows, Hrossak on Hrossak. "That old fool who was with you," he grunted. "It seems he's got away."

Tarra shrugged. "Just an old loony," he said. "But not so daft he didn't know a good camel when he stole one!"

"Oh?" the other pulled in his chin, cocked his head a little on one side, seemed surprised by Tarra's answer. "Chatty, are we? Aren't you sort of overlooking the fact that you're now a slave?"

"It was you who spoke to me, friend," Tarra quietly reminded him, "and I supposed you required an answer. Also, we're two of a sort, and it seems to me both a bit out of place here. Me, I was on my way back to the steppes, when—"

The slaver's whip sang, and Tarra gasped his pain and shock and turned his face away. And again the angry snapping of the whip—

428

again, and again—as his silky shirt was reduced to ribbons on his back. Aye, and his back a little, too. When it was over, he also hung in his chains. But he'd not once cried out. And:

"There!" said his tormentor with something of satisfaction, coiling up his whip again.

Tarra found voice. "Seems I—*uh!*—must have angered you somehow…"

"No," the other shook his matted head of hair and grinned down at him—a sneering grin Tarra would never forget. He spat into the dust at Tarra's feet. "You didn't anger me, and not much likely to. That beating was for nothing, 'friend,' so mind you don't go doing something, right?" And he spurred his pony away, kicking up dust to sting Tarra's raw red stripes.

The chained steppeman gazed after him and thought dark red thoughts; and with much creaking, shuddering and jolting, finally the big lizards began to haul and wheels to turn, and the caravan got under way again…

By noon they were down out of the pass and heading south for ancient, ruined Humquass. The way was dry, dusty, a near-desert. With the sun at its zenith, the horizon shimmered white, and slavers and captives alike were feeling the heat. But at least the prisoners, trudging along in their chains, could stick to the shade of the big wagons.

If at first Tarra had wondered what they hauled, wondered about the cargo of those strange, long vehicles, he wondered no longer. At first opportunity, unobserved, he'd lifted up a flap of canvas and gazed beneath. Boats, great Yhemni canoes, but massive-built! And there'd be one to each of the five long wagons. They had sails, too, all folded down now, and chains that ran along the gunnels, and manacles on the oars. No need to wonder how these slavers would return to Shad: they'd go home in triumph, with their captives sculling them speedy across the straits. Why, there'd be room in vessels big as these even for the monster lizards!

Humquass was just in sight—a rim of jagged black edges on the scrubland's horizon, like low broken hills—when they came on an oasis. The great lizards smelled water and sent up a hissing like a vast pit of snakes, and their Hrossak riders let them build up to something of a lumbering trot as blue waters opened under spindly green palms. The long wagons were drawn in a circle round the oasis; huge wooden buckets of water were fetched for the beasts; the overseer blacks prowled up and down and inspected their captives, ensuring that all was well with them. Little need to worry about that, for they were burly lads all: white gold in Shad's slave-markets, or gladiators in a wizard's necromantic arena.

Tarra frowned and wondered: burly *lads*, aye, but hadn't Stumpy Adz also said something about lasses? He had indeed! The canvas on the first wagon was thrown back; blacks jumped up onto its platform, gestured with whips and gave guttural commands; frightened female faces appeared, and a dozen gorgeous girls were made to climb down. They paraded there by the wheels of the long wagon, chained together, trying their best to cover their modesty with what scraps of clothing had been left to them.

By now all of the beasts had been watered, the slavers had filled skins from the oasis, last ripples were dying on the surface of the blue pool under the palms. Along came red-robed frizzy boss on a pony, idling his mount where he gazed down on his lovely captives. Only a wagon away, Tarra could hear his raised voice:

"Go, bathe yourselves, wash off grime and grit. Swim, if you will, and take your ease for an hour. But hurry, before I change my mind!" And off they went, stumbling a little, soft-skinned under a harsh sun, to bathe themselves at pool's margin. And:

Oh–ho! But you're asking for trouble now, my gleamy black slavemaster friend! thought Tarra Khash. What? And hadn't he seen half-a-dozen Northmen during course of trek so far? And was it likely that those coarse-maned barbarians of northern fjords and mammoth plains would endure this flagrant flaunting of delicate female flesh? Tarra doubted it.

He was chained to that side of the wagon facing the pool. The others strung there with him hauled themselves wearily up onto platform, sat legs adangle, leaned back against giant canoe's curving strakes and in its shade. They hung their heads, slumped there and groaned of their aching bones; but Tarra merely stood watching the

girls where they bathed themselves not one hundred feet away. A slaver passed down the line with chunks of bread, ladling water from a
bucket. Tarra took a crust, sipped a little water, and the black passed
on. Tarra munched on dry, tasteless bread, stopped munching, felt
the corner of his mouth begin to twitch in warning spasm. It was too
quiet; a certain tension was in the air; it was going to happen now!

Three huge Northmen tethered their ponies to a palm farthest
from the pool, wiped sweaty palms down their leather-clad legs and
grinned at each other, and as on some silent command began to sham-
ble toward the pool in the tracks left by the girls. Involuntarily, Tarra
strained in his chains, glared at the huge single iron staple hammered
home in hardwood, which held him there immobile. A shadow fell
on him.

He looked up, eyes half-shuttered against the glare of sun. It was
the caravan's master, still astride his pony; and now Tarra recognized
the weapon in its scabbard at his hip. There could be no mistaking
that jewelled hilt or the curve of the blade's sheath. The gangly black
slaver had taken Tarra's sword for his own.

"They call me Cush Gemal," the Yhemni half-breed made belated
introduction. "And you?"

"Tarra Khash, a Hrossak," said Tarra. No need to name his race,
but he did so for pride's sake. Gemal saw that his eyes had gone back
to the Northmen, halfway now to the pool. One of them was peeling
off his shirt, displaying the bristly mane that ran down his back to
base of spine. Another's belt hung loose, swaying with his lurching
gait. The caravan's master followed Tarra's nervous gaze.

"No Hrossak females there," he said, curiously. "And yet you fear
for them."

"You'd do well to follow my example," said Tarra, "if you'd carry
them back to Shad intact!"

"Oh?" the slaver seemed half-amused.

In his agony of apprehension, Tarra had grown unmindful of his
tongue. "You've obviously little knowledge of Northmen," he groaned,
licking his suddenly dry lips. "No Hrossak women, you say? Man, you
couldn't trust those hairies with your pony!"

The other gave a guttural chuckle. "Ah, but I *do* know Northmen,
Tarra Khash! And I agree with you entirely. But the leader of that

trio has crossed me once too often, and this is my way of drawing him out."

"You'll do that right enough," Tarra gave a jerky nod, strained again at his chain, "with periodic parade of female flesh before the eyes of scum like that. But it won't do the girls much good…"

"I believe you'd actually interfere!" Cush Gemal marvelled. "Even though they'd kill you for it."

"Just let me out of these chains and I'll show you how right you are," Tarra grated.

The Northmen were at pool's rim, and as they came through the palms and rushes the girls saw them, saw their intention. They quickly crushed themselves together in a knot, used their hands to cover their nakedness. The barbarians stood ankle deep in the water and leered at them.

Gemal touched the hilt of Tarra's ex-sword. "Is it a good weapon?" he murmured.

"Depends who's using it," Tarra growled through clenched teeth. He couldn't turn his eyes from the frozen tableau at the pool, which wouldn't stay frozen much longer, he knew.

"Then let's see how well it does in the hands of Cush Gemal!" the other snapped, and suddenly animated, he spurred his pony toward the pool. As he rode he called ahead:

"*Hold!* You there, Gorlis Thad. What's this? Don't you know those girls are virgins? Indeed you do! Also why they were taken and who they belong to. Only bruise one of those fruits and Black Yoppaloth will flay you alive. Break one and he'll make drums of your hide and a fine fly-switch of your sweaty mane!"

Gorlis Thad! Top dog of northern pack a Thad, eh? Tarra had heard of this barbarous family, so huge it was almost a tribe in itself. Indeed he'd killed one, during a brief and vengeful visit to the isles of the Crater Sea. Thad: the name itself made his nostrils wrinkle, as if it carried a stench. The most ingrown, degenerate, murderous Northmen of them all, the Thads, and never a one born that a man— or any woman—could trust.

Gorlis must be the one who'd taken off his shirt, who'd waded into pool and was even now dragging a girl out by her hair. All chained together, where she went the rest must follow; and so they trooped along behind, all moaning and covering themselves with soaking rags, the water streaming from their lovely bodies.

At the edge of the pool Gorlis turned, saw the rider Cush Gemal bearing down on him. He'd heard his shouting, scowled at his threats. "What?" he shouted at the man on the pony where he reined to a halt close by. "You're worried about that stinking shaman six hundred miles away in Shad? Well, it's my skin, Gemal, so let me do the worrying, right?"

"Fool!" Gemal hissed. "Dolt! He could be watching you right now, at this very moment. Shaman? Aye, he is that, and his eyes are everywhere!"

Gorlis' sidekicks had also laid hands on a pair of girls, but at first mention of magick they turned them loose, stumbled up out of the water, stood glaring at their ringleader. Like most Northmen, they were cowed by merest mention of wizardry or witchcraft. But not, apparently, the Thad himself.

He scowled his scorn at them, looked up at Cush Gemal. "I've promised this fine pair of lads a bit of sweet meat," he said. "They're not much for going without—not while it's standing around just waiting to be taken—no, and neither am I. So I say unchain just three of 'em, for half an hour, and no harm done. I'll promise you that much: no harm done, not permanent anyway. We'll use one of the boats, so's not to get the other bucks worked up. Out of sight, out of *mind*, eh?" And now he grinned through his beard at the caravan's master.

Gemal sneered cynically, nodded his red-crested comb of hair. "Out of sight, out of mind? I'll say you are, Gorlis Thad!" The half-breed slaver slitted his eyes, swung easily down from his mount. "Why, Black Yoppaloth would know if you'd even breathed on one of his brides! What? You risk your eyes just *looking* at them! So I'll say it one more time, Gorlis Thad: let go that girl's hair and get back to your place, or there's trouble here and now..."

"Then let it be trouble!" Thad's hand snaked toward the throwing knife in his belt.

Watching all of this, Tarra Khash winced, or blinked, it makes no difference; but in any case he shuttered his eyes for a moment, the merest moment, before opening them on unbelievable scene. Prior to that, however, during the course of conversation between black slavemaster and northern barbarian, he had taken the opportunity to glance all about. Apart from the three Northmen central to this affair, at least five others looked on from where they sat or stood by the wagons. All were armed to the teeth, where with sidelong glances they measured up Gemal's superior numbers. In a fight it would be a close thing, for the four or five rogue steppemen would probably join with the Northmen against the blacks; even in steppes outcasts such as these, instinct to side with the underdog would be a powerful force. Outnumbered more than two to one, still they'd make a damn good go of it, Tarra knew. The Yhemnis must know it, too, and yet a curious thing: not a man of the frizzies seemed remotely concerned! They merely looked on, as if the outcome were already decided. Which perhaps it was.

But in any case Tarra had winced, or blinked, and now unblinked— then gaped at what he saw!

Gorlis Thad's knife was airborne, a silver streak speeding close to gleaming black breast—but Tarra's jewelled scimitar had some- how managed to sprout from Gemal's hand! Drawn from scabbard? What? In the blink of an eye? Even in two blinks? And yet there it was, deflecting hurtling knife like tossed apple; and Gemal thin-faced, nostrils flaring where he advanced on the stunned Northman. Fascinated, Tarra continued to watch.

Even in the water, one of Gorlis' colleagues had retained a great broadsword; now in a squeal of steel he unsheathed it, tossed it down on the sand at Gorlis' feet. One crashing blow of that great sword, and the slender scimitar would shiver to shards. And now the barbarian knew that he had Gemal's measure. He bent to retrieve the broad-sword—and Gemal leaped forward, edge of scimitar resting lightly on Gorlis' neck. The Northman froze, drew back his hand from hilt of broadsword where it lay.

His eyes went this way and that, and colour drained from his face. "And how's this for a fair fight?" he suddenly shouted.

Gemal, too, raised his voice: "*Now* he wants a fair fight, who without warning hurled his knife! What say you—do I give him one?"

The entire caravan, barring only slaves themselves, answered with one voice: "*Aye!*" And Tarra noted that the Yhemnis shouted loudest of all. He wondered: is Gemal *that* good? And got his answer in the space of a double heartbeat.

As Gorlis Thad straightened up, tall as Cush Gemal himself but blocky as a bull, so his half-breed opponent tossed down his scimitar alongside broadsword. "Now we're equal—" he started to say, but already the treacherous barbarian had uttered a *whoop* of savage glee, gone to one knee, grasped his weapon's hilt—which was exactly what Gemal had known he would do.

As Northman's hand closed on weapon's hilt, Gemal slammed his sandalled foot down on the other's wrist, stooped and retrieved the scimitar. It came alive in his hand as he straightened, slicing Gorlis through his trousers from groin to rib-cage.

Blood drenched the sand as Gemal lithely turned to face Gorlis' henchmen. "You?" he offered. "Or you?" They skulked away. And still Gorlis kneeling in the sand, holding in his unfettered guts. Then he looked up, through eyes already glazing over, to where Gemal sheathed his weapon and mounted his pony; and finally he fell face-down, mouth gaping, on the sand.

"Make ready!" cried Gemal, guiding his mount back toward Tarra Khash where the Hrossak openly admired him. "Load up! Tonight we make camp in yonder ruins." And not a man of the barbarians offering the slightest resistance, but all averting their eyes and carrying on with their duties as if nothing whatever had occurred. Which was perhaps to say a lot for commonsense, and an equal amount for Gorlis Thad's popularity.

Gemal rode close to chained Hrossak, briefly reined in. "It's a good weapon right enough, Tarra Khash," he said. "I thank you for gifting it to me."

As he spurred away Tarra looked after him and nodded. But to himself: "Best consider it a loan," he said, "for which repayment later…"

"Peace!" said Teh Atht, holding up long-fingered hand to stay his crystal's activity. "Let it be for now—but continue to watch and remember all. I shall doubtless desire to scry it later…"

His bones creaked as he stood up from his viewing, and as the shewstone reverted once more to opaque and milky sphere he groaned and stretched his cramped limbs a little. Since the Hrossak's moonlight meeting with Stumpy Adz in the pass, the wizard had slept when they slept, observed when they were up and about, and apart from that he'd done precious little else. There was much to fascinate him here, and also several mysteries to unravel.

Tarra Khash, for instance: he was a strange one, this Hrossak. Not often that a common man comes to the attention of lofty mage, whose thoughts and schemes would normally dwell on higher plane; and yet Teh Atht was interested—intensely so. Aye, for this wasn't the first time he'd heard of this brawny Hrossak, nor merely through any mundane or common gossip.

A certain lamia in her sulphurous lair knew of him, thinking strange, fond thoughts for a lamia! (This was Orbiquita, Teh Atht's "cousin," with whom by virtue of their blood bond he had the power to converse over vast distances. For Mylakhrion, that most fecund of all wizards, had been her progenitor, too; indeed, and according to legend, he was both "father" and "brother" to the entire sisterhood!) While Teh Atht had sojourned in her castle in Sheb, he'd tried to contact Orbiquita in the great subterranean cavern beneath the Nameless Desert where she slumped asleep, cocooned in lava, serving a sentence of five years solitude for some sin against lamia laws. He had *tried* to contact her, but all he got were dreams and fancies: dreams of Tarra Khash, in fact, whom she seemed to fancy more than somewhat!

Now, it were certainly not strange for lamias to lust after iron-thewed, handsome steppemen; but to *long* for a man? And with such affection? At the time Teh Atht had merely thought it odd, no more than that: it was her dream, after all, and dreams are curious things at best, which do not always tell the truth. And so, being no voyeur (shew-stone to the contrary), he'd not lingered but left her to her dreaming.

That had been the first instance. But then:

Ahorra Izz, scarlet scorpion god in his jungle temple, had also known of Tarra Khash; or if not his name, certainly he'd known of the man. "Three who work against Gorgos," he'd riddled, "and one of them a man!" A man called Tarra Khash, aye. Moreover, that singular arachnid deity had owned to "liking" him! First most loathsome lamia, and now ireful insect intelligence? Oh, he was a charmer for sure, this Hrossak, and perhaps much more than that. Worthy of further investigation, anyway.

Teh Atht's fruitless five year quest had left him weary, and he'd vowed that when he got home he would take his ease; yet now, sensing that his and a certain Hrossak's destinies were fast intertwined, he felt full of a strange urgency. It were imprudent (indeed, nigh impossible) to go direct to Tarra Khash and make his interest known: interest in the Hrossak himself, in his curved sword with its curiously fashioned and gem-studded hilt—ah, and *great* interest in Black Yoppaloth's current slavemaster, the cryptogenic Cush Gemal! For the steppe-man hadn't yet settled to captivity and would be doubly nervy; he might well react to magick in much the same way as a superstitious Northman, who would avoid it if he could, or fight it to the death if he couldn't! And so Teh Atht's eventual approach would need to be well considered and crafty in its execution. Wherefore, better to leave it until later, when the Hrossak had lost something of hope and might be ready to grasp at straws. Or whatever else the wizard had to offer.

And meanwhile?

Teh Atht sighed. One quest ended, however disappointingly, and another about to begin. Genuine, healing rest, of the sort he'd looked forward to—with his slippers, books, and perhaps a succubus or two to keep him warm nights—were now out of the question. A wizard's work was never done. He'd know no peace of mind until certain rid-dles were resolved. And who could say, perhaps it might mean the resolution of that earlier quest, too.

Where to start was easy, but first—

He went to his bedchamber, stretched himself out and uttered the rune of Rapid Repose, at once began to snore. Ten dreamless hours sped by in a like number of seconds, and refreshed Teh Atht sprang up. It wasn't as good as the real thing, of course, but better than nothing.

Now he must hie him to Nameless Desert, find a blowhole and descend to planet's fiery bowels, there seek audience with Orbiquita. Only this time in person, and not just mind to mind. Aye, he'd wake her up from sulphurous slumbers, and at last attempt to fathom her fondness for this mere man, this Tarra Khash. And *that*, too, would be a neat trick, if he could turn it. For a mortal, even a wizard, to commune face to fearsome visage with a lamia were nothing less than fraught!

But alas, no way round it. Not that he could see...

III
A MAGE IMMORTAL!

Tarra Khash lay under the moon and stars, a coarse blanket for his cover, with his stomach growling and his thighs on fire from forced march to ruined Humquass. He'd trekked a fair bit in his time, however, and knew that pain alone wouldn't kill him; not the natural pain of tired muscles, anyway.

Chains had been lengthened, allowing for a little mobility, but only one blanket to each pair of captives, so that he must needs share it with one other: a blond-haired, blue-eyed youth of some fifteen summers. A farm lad, Tarra guessed—with muscles a-plenty but little fortitude of mind—who'd snivelled a bit and then gone to sleep; but the Hrossak remained wide awake, only biding his time.

The moon had put on a little weight since last night, but not much; three weeks yet before it would swell into an orb; and where would a steppeman find himself then, and what would he be doing there? Fighting in some nightmare arena of magick? Best not to seek to know, he supposed.

Tarra turned carefully in the shallow, sandy depression he'd dug for himself and gazed all about. Outwards: Humquass' once-massive, now broken walls formed a black, fanged horizon, with the stars floating on jet above its rim. Inwards: the wagons were ranged in a wide circle around central fires already burning low, where a few black slavers squatted and conversed in lowered tones, while a handful of barbarians and Hrossaks gambled with dice. And close to the lead wagon with its precious cargo of pure maidens, there stood a silken tent, black, with black tassels at the four corners of its scalloped canopy. Cush Gemal's tent, where doubtless he slept on plump cushions even now.

The Hrossak's glittery eyes swept the area of the central fires. Many Yhemnis were bedded down there, wrapped in their blankets. The last three or four gamblers finished gaming, cursed their luck or collected up their winnings, slowly ambled off into the shadows. Two drunken Northmen remained, guzzling a wineskin dry, then leaning together and burping into firelight's glow. Tarra watched them, waiting until they, too, took their staggering departure.

There would be a watch out, of course—frizzies doing three-hour shifts through the night, perched high up in the broken walls—but they'd be looking outwards, watching for wandering nomads or possible pursuers. They'd not be much interested in what went on down here. Not that a lot would be going on, for Tarra was still chained. This was the problem to which he'd now apply himself.

He'd already studied his chains well enough: scrutinized each link, run them through his hard but sensitive fingers, looked for rust and signs of wear—all to no avail. Well forged, those chains—damn their makers to every hell! As for the manacles (manacles in name only, for they left one hand free): they were short, single sleeves of iron "worn" on a captive's right wrist, where they fitted too snug to be slid down over crafty fingers. Tarra's manacle, like those of all the rest, had two large rings or staples in its flange, through which the chain passed before returning to the wagon, where it further passed through a single large staple whose prongs were driven deep in ironwood frame. Then the chain passed down the flank of the wagon a double pace, to another staple which anchored the next captive, and so on. Even if a slave were strong enough to tear iron from ironwood, he'd still remain manacled between two more slaves. No, *all* of the staples would need to be wrenched out together, and even so the slave band would remain chained in a bunch.

Slaves, aye, and Tarra Khash starting to get used to the word. And him one of 'em...

He began to feel a mite sorry for himself, checked the feeling at once. What? Why, he'd be grovelling next, or whining in his sleep like this farmer's pup at his side! He gave the lad a gentle pat on his back anyway, then slipped out from under the blanket and crawled into the shadow of the wagon. It wouldn't hurt to have another feel at those staples; the more you study a problem, the surer its resolution—usually. Coming upright beside the long wagon, he held his chains taut so they wouldn't jangle against his wrist manacle.

Manacle...*hmmm*! And again he considered the iron sleeve on his wrist. They were locked with curious keys, these vile bracelets—or one curious key, at least. Tarra had only seen the one, when it had been used to shackle him; and of course he'd consigned to memory the face of the Yhemni who'd used and then pocketed it. All possibilities must be considered, including that there *might* come a moment of confusion, when it *might* be possible to clout a certain frizzy on the head and go through his pockets.

But now he put that thought aside for the moment; it would be a desperate measure at best, only to be considered if things got totally out of hand. Now he found his staple and tugged at it, then gritted his teeth and tugged harder, finally scowled and punched at it with his fist, which only served to bruise his knuckles. Solid as a rock, that iron loop, with just enough clearance for the chains to slide. A man would need to be superhuman to break these chains or wrench these staples loose!

Beginning to feel frustrated, Tarra turned to the nearest wagon wheel and fingered its wide rim. Ironwood, yes, but still only wood: even rolling over rock it wouldn't cut iron or snap chains, merely crush the rock!

There came a *hiss* and a *honk* from close by and Tarra started, then glanced quickly all about. The great lizard that hauled the wagon had sensed him standing there and queried his presence, but no one seemed to have noticed. The lizards were known to voice complaints like this periodically, usually warning of nothing whatsoever.

"*Tss! Tss!*" Tarra hissed low, in the way of Hrossaks cautioning their beasts. He stepped light round the front of the wagon and stroked the clammy hindquarters of the huge creature squatting there between massive shafts. The lizard turned its long neck and gloomed on him slit-eyed. "Quiet, old scaly," he husked, "or you'll wake the whole camp!"

Not very likely, for most would be well asleep by now, but still it were time Tarra returned to his own gritty bed. He turned from where he gazed at lizard's ridgy rump, went to all fours in the dark and crept back round to the side of the long wagon—then jerked to a halt where his chains were caught on something. Or where they were trapped *under* something.

...Like booted feet, for instance! Tarra stared at leather-clad feet where they stood square on his chains, then slowly lifted his gaze to see who it was who'd caught him creeping around. His heart sank. It was Gys Ankh, who'd chased and lost Stumpy Adz in the foothills, then taken his spite out on Tarra's back. Outcast Hrossak, no doubt for damned good reasons.

"Going somewhere, 'friend'?" Ankh made quiet inquiry, his scar a band of livid white over his right eyebrow and square down his face to his chin. "But I distinctly remember telling you to be good..." The coils of his whip snaked down onto the sand. Tarra's thoughts ran wild, in every direction, but all came back bloodied. He'd suffered once at the hands of this bully, and this time it was bound to be worse.

"Well?" Gys Ankh stood over him.

Tarra slowly came to his feet, wiped his hands down his pants as Ankh backed off to striking distance. The crack of the whip would be heard, of course, but what odds? What, someone chastising a stubborn slave in the night? Little cause for concern there. "I...I was restless," said Tarra lamely, with a shrug.

"Much more so in a moment," Ankh grinned lopsidedly. "Aye, damned restless! And how'll you sleep with sand in your grooves, 'friend'? Face-down, maybe? Not much good, that, for it's my intention to cut you there, too! Restless? I'll say you'll be." He drew back his arm sharply and the coils straightened out, slithering along the sand to his rear.

Things twanged in Tarra's head, then snapped: twin threads of hope and patience. He'd just run out of both. He fell to a crouch, leaned with a silent snarl toward his tormentor. Gys Ankh chuckled, backed off a pace. "Aye, come and get it, 'friend,'" he said. "Discover for yourself why they kicked me out of Hrossa!"

Tarra needed no more urging: he leaped, and Ankh snapped his whip—or tried to and almost jerked himself from his feet! He turned, saw the youth under the blanket where he'd taken firm hold on the end of his whip, went to kick him in the face. But silently raging Hrossak was on him, dropping chains over his head in a loop, shutting off air and sudden shriek of terror both. They crashed down together on the sand, Ankh groping for his knife, Tarra butting him, kneeing him in the groin, choking his life out, generally allowing him no space for thought or movement; and the youth holding the blanket over both struggling forms until the scarface stopped moving. Ankh managed to choke out one last word—a curse, Tarra suspected—twitched several times and went slack as a eunuch's foreskin. But for several moments longer, just to be absolutely sure, Tarra drew the chains even tighter about the bully's throat.

Now came lad's whisper, by no means cowed, even jubilant: "Is he—?"

Tarra nodded. "Stone dead, aye," he whispered, "or I'm not Tarra Khash. But quiet now, or you'll soon be able to ask him man to man!" They stuck their heads out from under the blanket, listened for long moments, breathed deep and grinned at each other in the dark.

"What?" said Tarra then, his voice low. "No tears? But I had you figured for a mother's boy. Whimpering and whining one minute, and helping me kill a man the next! So what's your story, eh?"

The lad hung his head. "Did you hear me crying?"

"Aye, though I suspect you were asleep."

"I wasn't sleeping," the other denied. "I think I've forgotten how to sleep! But I swear my tears were for someone else, not me." He ground his teeth in suppressed fury.

"For who then?"

The lad looked at Tarra, his young face white as chalk in the thin moonlight. "My sister. She's only a year older than me—but she sleeps with the other girls in that lead wagon!"

Tarra drew a sharp breath. This explained a great deal. He nodded. "Well, I can understand your misery," he said, "but not your interference on my behalf. You risked your neck to help me. Indeed, it's still very much at risk!"

The youth's turn to nod. "This dog Gys Ankh whipped me, too, when I was taken. If I was going to die a slave in Shad, knowing my sister for a naked whore in some black wizard's palace…" He shrugged. "I might as well die here and now, helping you to kill Ankh. At least I'd have my pride."

"Keeping your pride's one thing," Tarra grunted, "and keeping your head is another. Now we've to deal with this one before he stiffens up on us." The dead rogue Hrossak lay between them, his body still warm.

The youth shuddered. "Can't we dump him in the boat on the wagon there?"

"We could," said Tarra, "except it might be a noisy bit of work. So far we've not woken anyone up—and lucky for us these lads are knackered from walking all day and many a day. They're captives like us, I know, but by now some of 'em'll be desperate. They'd likely turn us in hoping to save their own skins. Anyway, wagon's the first place they'll look for him, just wait and see. Come morning, Gys Ankh gone and his mount still here? Sleeping off a skin too many in a nice warm wagon, obviously. Then they'd find him, and you and me closest to him. Hot irons applied in the right places, and be sure we'd talk…"

"So what do we do with him?"

"What's your name?" Tarra briefly changed the subject.

"Loomar," said the other. "Loomar Nindiss. My father took Jezza and me out of Grypha two years ago when our mother died. We built a little farm down south on the Eastern Range, close to Hrossa's borders—but not too close. There was the makings of a village there. Then, maybe three weeks ago—" Again he ground his teeth, hung his head.

"That's a familiar story," Tarra growled. "Can you dig, Loomar?"

"Dig?" Loomar looked up.

Tarra nodded. "Right here, right now. With your hands. Like this."

He started to scoop out sand, shoving it with his forearm out under the edge of the blanket. They took sand from under Gys Ankh's body, which slowly settled into the hole. An hour later it was done: a shallow grave, true, but no trace of the bully remaining on the surface.

Then Loomar showed Tarra the dead man's knife, nine inches of sudden death, its blade gleaming in starlight. "I took it from him when you were choking him," he explained, "else he might have stabbed you. I'm going to keep it."

"The hell you are!" said Tarra. "If they find that on you, they'll use it to skin you alive!"

"It's my skin," Loomar protested. "And anyway, why should they search me?"

"Because we're together," said Tarra, "and they'll most certainly search me! So you see, it's my skin, too. Now be reasonable." He gently took the knife, worked it point first, deep down out of sight into the sand. "And now—goodnight."

Loomar couldn't believe it. "You...you're going to sleep? On top of..."

Tarra cut him short. "Tomorrow's another day, son," he said. "A hard day, which can bring almost anything. We're not in the clear yet. Me, if I'm riding the rapids to hell, I want good strong arms for my paddle! So sleep. Believe me, you'll feel better for it. How'll you be any good to your sister, skinny as a runt and weary to death from lack of sleep?"

That last did the trick. Loomar rolled over, curled himself up. Tarra felt something of the tension go out of his body.

He gave Loomar's back a gentle punch, settled himself down, and in his usual way made overture to Shoosh, goddess of the still slumbers. *Lady, if you're out there, come and get me. I'm all yours.*

And eventually she came.

Morning was a confusion, until Tarra remembered where and what. During the night a wind had raced around the ruins, piling up the sand a bit on his side. When he yawned and opened his eyes, what breeze remained blew dust in his face and brought him spitting awake. It was just past dawn, last star a fading gleam, sun free of Cthon's nets and already pushing up his rim over the edge of the world.

The wind had made a good job of removing all traces of last night's digging; the sand had been greatly levelled out, except where it lay banked against obstacles—like Tarra's face and form. Big lizards coughed and honked to greet the dawn; camels snorted and spat; there was movement round the extinct fires and among the wagons.

A Yhemni slaver came striding, his baggy silken breeches flattening to the fronts of his muscular thighs.

Tarra expelled dry crusts from his nostrils, poked his tongue about carefully in a mouth that tasted like a Northman's sandal, blinked his eyes as the black slaver grabbed blanket, yanked it from his and Loomar's huddled forms. "Up!" the black grunted. "Dig holes, take bread, water. Then we go."

Tarra squinted after him as he moved among the rest of the slaves. He glanced at Loomar. "Dig holes?"

"To answer nature's calls," the youth replied, spitting out sand. "Or maybe Hrossak's don't?"

For answer Tarra carefully scraped a small hole where he'd slept, dropped his trousers and squatted. "Oh, we do," he said. "And what's more, I know just the right place for it!"

Loomar sprang to his feet and moved away; but he'd seen Tarra's meaning at once, nodded his admiration of the Hrossak's scheme. Now he waited for him to get done and tidy up the job with scuffed sand, then went and finished it off in like manner.

They weren't given water for washing and so made do with the clean white sand, which sandpapered grime from flesh clean as a whistle. Then chains shortened to draw slaves in close to the wagons, a ladle of water to sip from (all too briefly, before passing on down the line) and a crust of bread each. Tarra managed to snatch a big lump, which this time he wolfed without pause. Lots of activity now: loading completed and frizzies starting to mount up on their camels, Northmen clambering bareback aboard tough, shaggy, half-wild ponies, and Hrossak wagoners sitting bronze in the broad wooden saddles of their mighty lizard beasts—all except one. Five beastmasters yesterday, and this morning only four…

The last lizard in the circle sprawled all unconcerned between its shafts, honking disdainfully at its leathery brothers where they tried to call it up onto vast, waddling legs. Heads began to turn; slavers scratched their necks impatiently; Cush Gemal appeared on a pony near the lead wagon, pointed, waved, shouted, gave orders. Tarra Khash, trying to look puzzled, stood tethered to the side of his wagon, raised an eyebrow at Loomar Nindiss. Give the lad his due, he managed to look gauntly innocent.

Blacks began clambering over wagons, under canvas, into and out of boats; but no sign of Gys Ankh, and puzzlement rapidly turning to rage. A frizzy came down the line, clouting slaves about their heads, shouting: "Gys Ankh? Hrossak? You see? Where Gys Ankh?" He reached Loomar, who cowered back, then stepped past him and collared Tarra by the ear. "Gys Ankh? You see?"

"*Ow!*" said Tarra. And: "What did you say?"

"Hrossak!" the other shouted at him. "Where Hrossak?"

Tarra looked nervously all about, licked his lips, shrugged. "Er, I'm a Hrossak," he said, ingenuously.

"Not you!" the frizzy shouted, drawing back his fist. Tarra's left hand was free. He knew that if the black hit him he probably wouldn't be able to control that hand. It would simply lift the other's knife from his belt and plunge it up under his chin. Which in turn would write *finis* on all this.

Cush Gemal's voice intervened at the last moment, and all black heads turned in his direction. From close to the lead wagon, Gemal shouted: "Ankh's pony is here, and certain of his belongings. But if *he's* here it can only be under the sand! We can't linger over it, for a rider was seen last night circling the ruins. He was just a lone rider, and he kept a safe distance, but he could be the first of many. We're not the only raiders in the Primal Land, and not too far from Hrossa, either. Anyway, if there are pursuers they'll be fast and we're slow. So time's not for wasting. Therefore, make a quick search—then we go."

Tarra's frizzy turned from him, narrowed his eyes against the sun's glare where it struck on white sand. He spied the dappled, scuffed area where Tarra and Loomar had lain, the ridge of sand where it had banked against the sleeping Hrossak. He glanced sideways at the pair. "You, and you—you sleep?" He pointed at the patch of suspect sand.

"Er, yes, but—" said Tarra.

The black stepped half-a-dozen paces, probed with the toe of his sandal. His foot came out wet and stinking. "What? *What?!*" He turned on the pair in a fury.

"Me!" Loomar called out, shaking like a leaf in a gale. "I...I dig hole there..."

"Why—you—not—*say?*" the frizzy came stamping, his fists knots at his sides. And finally Tarra recognized him: the slaver with the key! He reached for Loomar, and Tarra reached for him—and Cush Gemal's voice reached all three. He leaned from his pony, snapped:

"Leave them be!" The black slaver scowled at them, nodded respectfully at Gemal, made off dragging his tainted foot in the sand to cleanse it.

"Tarra Khash," said Gemal. "You're a Hrossak. What do you know about these hauling lizards?"

Tarra looked up at him. "I know there's nothing I *don't* know about them!" he said. Gemal nodded, called stink-foot back, ordered Tarra's release.

"Hrossak," said Gemal, "you can walk or ride, it's your choice. Riding you'll save your feet and perhaps earn yourself a semi-permanent employment, maybe even a reward. From slave to beast-master by stroke of fate, or slave until death from some other sort of stroke. Make up your mind..."

Tarra looked at his freed right hand, clenched it tight, then looked again at Cush Gemal. "Seems the decision's made," he said.

Gemal nodded his crest of lacquered hair. "We'll see how trust-worthy you are—if at all! Except we'll not trust you too much, not just yet. There'll be a man behind you in the wagon, with a bolt aimed at your back. So just do what's expected of you and...I'll talk to you again, when we break at noon."

That was that. Tarra was led to Gys Ankh's beast where he used its knee as a step up to its broad back, and so into his saddle. A good many years since he'd last driven a big hauler like this one, but he didn't think he'd forgotten how. And anyway he'd soon find out. He looked about.

At the back of the saddle was a basket of greenstuff, tidbits for well-behaved beast; and hanging by the saddle a coiled whip, long and thin. This was also for the lizard, if he should turn awkward. Tarra could use the whip expertly—once upon a time, anyway. Back on the steppes, he'd often used the whip as a threat, never as an actual weapon. Kindness would normally get the job done far quicker. But of course this lizard was new to him, and Tarra himself strange to the lizard. That was something else he'd soon be finding out about.

"*Tsss! Tsss!*" he hissed. "Up, old scaly, and all's well." The great beast turned back its head, blinked slitted eyes, honked a disinterested inquiry.

"*Tsss!*" Tarra repeated, with some urgency now, aware of his back where it made a target broad as a tavern door. "Up, my leathery lad, or Tarra's in trouble!"

Out of the corner of his eye he saw Cush Gemal, standing in his pony's saddle and watching all. Tarra gulped, shook down the whip. The lizard's slitted green eyes turned a little red and his scales came down flat upon his hide. Then Tarra reached behind and took a fistful of greenstuff, wrapped it round with the tip of the whip and made a small knot. Without pause he flicked his arm and sent bundle of cabbage leaves snaking forward. Into one side of crusty mouth flew that morsel, and drawn back out in a flash without touching tender flesh. But greenstuff gone and lizard chomping happily! Of course, for Gys Ankh hadn't been here to feed him this morning.

"Double rations at noon, old scaly," Tarra urged. "Only let's be up now and moving, eh?" And again: "*Tsss! Tsss!*"

And at last response. Up came the rear legs, tilting Tarra forward, and up at the front one at a time, tilting him sideways and then straightening him out. He cracked his whip over the beast's snout, but well clear of delicate nostrils and horn-hooded eyes; and with a single snort the creature got going. The wheels of the wagon behind creaked as they started turning, and the slaves ranked on both sides began their accustomed shuffle. And now they were mobile.

"Good!" cried Cush Gemal from the side. "Take meat with me at noon, Tarra Khash, for there are things I'd like to know about you..." He cantered forward to the head of the caravan, which now wound out of ruined Humquass and headed just south of east.

The feeling's entirely mutual, thought Tarra, his bronze body swaying easily to the gait of his strange and massive mount. *There are things I'd like to know about you, too...*

In immemorially ordained cycles of an hundred years duration, the wizards of Theem'hdra were wont to pursue with increased vitality and inspiration their search for immortality. All save one, for apparently Black Yoppaloth of the Yhemnis had already found it. Or perhaps not. Mylakhrion, in his day, had seemed similarly interminable—and what was he now but dust and bones?

Now, there are men and there are men, and there are wizards and wizards. There *were* ways by which a man might aspire to aeons of existence; but black, inimical magick had never been Teh Atht's chosen route. White magick, or at worst grey, had always sufficed; though truth to tell, at various desperate times he'd been tempted. But to his knowledge black sorcery benefited no one, and least of all its users. Not in the long run.

Mylakhrion, perhaps the mightiest mage ever, had called on Great Cthulhu for means of infinitely elongating life, only to discover it shortened to nothing. Loxzor of the Hrossaks—a steppes-bred singularity among sorcerers, powerful necromancer in his life but dead now some six or seven hundred years—had likewise sought to control the uncontrollable...and for all his foul formulae had been eaten by a slime. Exior K'mool, Mylakhrion's one-time apprentice...well, his termination remained conjectural. Several times, tracing Exior's pattern in the spheres of his astrologarium, Teh Atht had discovered no sure surceasement; it could be that Exior had achieved that longed-for longevity, but not in this world. Essence-sniffing spells had failed to detect tiniest trace...

Ardatha Ell, who had wandered the worlds and universes and studied the secrets of spheres within spheres, was said to sojourn in Elysia; but since he was not of this world in the first place, his case should hardly be counted. And of other wizards, black and white, who had searched for life everlasting, only to discover that the search outlasted the life: their names were legion.

Azatta Leet had died in Chlangi early in his twelfth decade, ten of which had been spent deciphering a certain Rune of Revitalization. In the hour of his triumph, upon speaking the words of power, he had become a mindless prehistoric liquid which evaporated in a stray beam of sunlight, from which it had not the sense to crawl! "Revitalized," aye, but too far: for instead of returning to his youth he had become as his most remote ancestor, a denizen of oceans primal even to Primal Theem'hdra, and mortal to a fault.

Phaithor Ulm, doubtless hot on the trail of personal perpetuity, had necromantically examined exanimate intelligences which, disgruntled, had given him false information— by use of which he'd rendered himself as a handful of green dust. The pitfalls were many.

And yet at its peak the cycle sent sorcerers of all persuasions into frenzies of heightened activity, invariably reducing their numbers and rewarding none at all. As to the why of it: wizards are generally a prideful lot, and to achieve immortality would be to assume the most coveted mantle of all, the fame of Mylakhrion himself. Indeed it would be to surpass him, and in so doing become Wizard of Wizards! What? Why, lesser mages would crawl to the feet of one so mighty, imploring his very tutelage!

Hatr-ad of Thinhla (suspect sorcerer at best) might assume the duties of Teh Atht's hall porter; Khrissa's All-High Ice-Priest would be his potwatcher; Moormish of the Wastes would find employment translating tedious and meaningless glyphs...and so on. Sweet dreams! But if some other should stumble on the secret first: then picture Teh Atht as decoder, or porter, or potwatcher, and so on. Tasteless inversion at best.

Five years ago he'd sensed the onset of the cycle, set out upon his quest, only to have it end in the Temple of the Scarlet Scorpion, with a warning of DOOM about to befall all Theem'hdra, whose heart was his own beloved Klühn. Since then he'd returned home, discovered said DOOM diminished to extinction, and observed the antics of a man—a mere man—in his crystal shewstone. Ah, but perhaps not a "mere" man, and certainly a most interesting one.

And now Tarra Khash seemed bound for Shad in Shadarabar across the Straits of Yhem, to be used in certain ceremonies of Black Yoppaloth's devise. Him and likewise the many slaves and maidens taken there with him. And an entire century fled since last the Yhemnis of Shadarabar raided on mainland whites, and the cycle of immortality-lust fast approaching its peak among Theem'hdra's thaumaturges. Oh, a very definite connection here, aye, and a state of affairs in which Teh Atht perceived a rare opportunity.

Now, it is seen how the Primal Land's wizards were rivals all; none more aware of that fact than Teh Atht himself, who knew well enow the difficulties to be encountered in attempting to breach any fellow wizard's protections—the spells each sorcerer employed to maintain and ensure absolute privacy—*especially* at the onset of the looming hour of propitiation. To dare even the most covert surveillance of Black Yoppaloth's machinations at this time would result in dire rebuke, be sure! If indeed this were that same Yoppaloth of histories a thousand years old, retribution were surely swift and most certainly mordant!

Teh Atht had read somewhere how, as a result of just such imprudent prying, Exior K'mool of Humquass had invoked a certain Yoppaloth's wrath: the Yhemni mage had conjured against him a squad of onyx automatons, with quicksilver blood and unbreakable crystal scythes for arms. Not even the curse of Curious Concretion would work on them, because they were stone already! And how might one freeze or poison quicksilver blood? Only by extreme good fortune, and at the very last moment, had Exior recalled a laconic Rune of Liquescence (with which in less perilous times he'd reshaped poorly constructed shewstones), melted the scythe arms of the robots and so rendered them comparatively harmless. But still and all they'd clumped around Humquass for a week before the last of them stamped himself to cryptocrystalline shards.

Dangerous then to send any familiar creature spying on him, lest Yoppaloth discover it and send back something much worse; but what if Yoppaloth *himself* took to his own bosom just such a spy? Aha! Different story then, for sure—especially if that spy should be kept in ignorance of his role!

And wherefore Teh Atht's desire to spy on the Yhemni mage in the first place? Simply to discover if indeed he *was* that same Yoppaloth come down the centuries—and if so, how! Perhaps there was that in his methods which Klühn's resident sorcerer could use to his own ends. He doubted it, for the Yoppaloth of legend wasn't much known for white or even grey magicks, but it were surely worth the shot.

All of these thoughts had been in Teh Atht's mind while he drifted high over Theem'hdra to Nameless Desert. It was a journey he might have accomplished in minutes, but that would mean suffering the debilitating nausea of great speed; and also, he'd desired to spend time merely thinking things out. And so he'd flown a circuitous route and slowly, which were just as well; for as evening came down so he'd found himself nodding where he sat cross-legged, in contemplative attitude, in the softly indented centre of his levitator. Already the false vitality gained from magickally accelerated sleep was wearing off, his mind succumbing to weariness and dull sloth; and in any case it were never a good idea to go lamia-visiting by night.

Even now he spied a red-glowing blowhole reeking of sulphur and setting the sands a-shimmer with its heat, and knew that down there somewhere in a lava cavern where red imps leaped and cavorted, "cousin" Orbiquita kept her stony vigil, all cased in a sort of Curious Concretion of her own. He suspected she'd know very little of Black Yoppaloth, but probably a good deal about a certain Hrossak.

Still and all, however much or little she knew, it would all keep until morning. And so Teh Atht formed a Warm Web about himself and flying carpet both, and lay him down to sleep a genuine sleep. And his carpet circling safely on high, through all the long night...

IV
ORBIQUITA—CUSH GEMAL—
WEIRD MAGICK!

Orbiquita slept and nightmared. Nothing strange in a human being tossing in the throes of fever-dreams, conjuring monsters from subconscious mind—but weird indeed for a monster to conjure human beings! She dreamed of Tarra Khash (as she'd been wont to do a great deal recently), a Hrossak in trouble. And now he was brought back fresh to mind by Teh Atht's urgent, whispered inquiry:

"Orbiquita, are you awake? Wake up, cousin, for I wish to speak with you about a man called Tarra Khash."

The wizard had slept late, almost till noon. Then, starting awake, he'd remembered his reason for being here and mouthed a simple spell of Self-Contained Coolness. And all enveloped in a bubble of sweet air, he'd flown his carpet almost vertically into volcanic vent and descended to lamia lair.

"Oh, Tarra, Tarra!" Orbiquita moaned her brimstone passion. And she writhed somewhat in her cocoon of lava.

Teh Atht drew back a little, looked nervously all about. This was after all a forbidden place, and he risked much in coming here. He had his spells, his various protections, of course; but so did lamias, along with awesome armaments, and few as powerful as the Lamia Orbiquita. Forbidden and forbidding, this lava cavern, aye, for it was the inner sanctum of the entire Sisterhood: their secret Place of Places, their "holy" place, if that word had meaning at all to such as them. Teh Atht's eyes scanned what to him was a veritable scene from hell:

The great cave, one of many in a cavern honeycomb, was red with heat; from its bubbling lake of lava, grotesquely carved "islands" stuck up here and there like fungi of some alien moon. Keeping their distance, red imps like great glowing insects danced nimbly from island to island; they somehow managed to avoid the reek and splash of liquid rock, while glowering at Teh Atht most menacingly. Then one of them tossed a mass of burning sulphur (which bounced of course from the surface of his cool, encompassing, invisible sphere) and made vilely threatening gestures.

Annoyed, the wizard scowled and began to draw a pattern in the air with his forefinger, but when the thing was only half-shaped the imps took fright and raced off to safety, leaving him to his own devices. He grinned then, for his "spell" had been a bluff, an intricate nonsense, by no means inimical. No, for he needed all of his sorcerous strength and most of his concentration just to maintain a cool, clean biosphere in this furnace place.

And aware that his time was limited, again he turned to Orbiquita.

Her island stood central and smouldering in the oozy, gurgling, flowing red rock of the place, and upon it she sat all hunched up, cradled or enthroned in ash of tephra, like a stalagmite of lava aglow with its own fiery internal light. Externally she was layered with rock-splash, which had hardened on her warty, leathery hide, so that an ignorant person might mistake her for the veriest fossil; but her blowhole nostrils smoked and her loathsome bosom rose and fell in ponderous measure, and when her hands twitched in her dreaming, then scythe-like fingers clashed and grated together.

She was here as a penance, and here would stay for a five-year spell, at which time some similarly foolhardy sister would take her place. Thus the Sisterhood chose its guardians of this lair; but since there was little likelihood of anyone finding his way here—or even caring to—the Lamia in Residence usually weathered out her stay in stony slumbers.

"Tarra Khash," Teh Atht repeated. "I must speak with you, Orbiquita! If you know this man, which I verily believe you do—if you *have* known him—now wake you up and tell me about him. It's likely to his benefit as well as mine, I assure you..." And he drifted closer, carpet and life-sustaining bubble and all. Perhaps she heard his voice, or felt the cold like a draft upon her, or merely sensed the presence of an outsider; whichever, now she came awake.

Her face twitched, eyes cracked open and blinked, then glared sulphurously; great jaws gaped and lava layers scaled off in clattering scabs of stone; and finally, from a sudden eruption of steam and tainted reek came her rumbling, doomful voice:

"Who is it disturbs my sleep? Who *dares* come here to seek me out? Who speaks to me of...of Tarra Khash?" And here a strange, strange thing: for on speaking his name her voice broke and became more nearly human, more surely female, and now at last Teh Atht began to understand. He'd scarce deemed it possible before, but now he guessed the truth: Orbiquita, devourer of men, had finally found one to love!

Now she stood up and stretched, bloating to the full form and monstrous mass of true lamia. As the smoke cleared, so Teh Atht floated face to face with his "cousin," and wondered as he'd oft wondered aforetime how even the mighty Mylakhrion had cohabited with such as this. She sensed the thought, knew its author at once. And she nodded what were possibly a greeting, at least a sign of her recognition.

"Teh Atht," she said then, her voice descending to sibilant, perhaps sarcastic whisper. "Most wondrous mage of Klühn, come a-visiting his cousin in her shame." More fully awake now, she shook her head in a seeming puzzlement, so that lava shards splintered and went clattering. "And did I hear you mention a certain name? And if so what is it to you? Or is it that you're here simply to insult me?"

"Insult?" He peaked his thin grey eyebrows in a frown. "I uttered no—"

"Uttered, no—" she cut him off, "—but you *thought* an insult!" And she stretched back her leathery wings, leaned forward, hunched to the rim of her island. Her scythe feet gouged the rock as lesser knives gouge clay, and her breath was a sulphurous musk. "How could Mylakhrion bring himself to mate with lamias, indeed!"

"Ah!" Teh Atht held up a finger, backed off a little. "But I meant no offence, Orbiquita. One might similarly ponder the fact that lamias *consented* to such immemorial, er, unions! And then there's the sheer how of it, which were—"

"Paint me no pictures, wizard!" again she cut him off, her voice hissing like steam. Then she cocked her head on one side a little. "Oh, and are you so naive? Do you imagine he took my mother's mothers to bed clad in their true forms? Never! As women, he took them, and under some foul spell so that they could not revert and devour him! And who are you that you should find this so unnatural?" Here she smiled slyly, or at least did that with her face which Teh Atht supposed was a smile. "Why, haven't I heard it rumoured that you yourself bed succubi?"

Teh Atht grew warm despite his unbreakable bubble of cool, sweet air. "It is the *nature* of the succubus to come to men in the night!" he quickly protested.

"Huh!" she snorted from flaring nostrils. "And is it also the nature of men to *call* them to their beds? Make no denials, cousin, for I have read it in your mind. Mylakhrion's blood runs in your veins. He was an artful necromancer, aye, but he was also a lustful man—and all the men in his line after him…"

Teh Atht must break the deadlock, and would definitely prefer to change the subject. "You're in argumentative mood, Orbiquita," he said, "and time's a-wasting. I've so much air in here, and then no more. And so I say again: I meant no insult or injury. And I implore you: what can you tell me of a certain Hrossak, a man called Tarra Khash?"

Her turn to draw back, as if suddenly splashed in her eyes with acid. "I…I had forgotten," she said then, "how you have the power to read my mind as easily as I read yours. And so you're a peeping Tom, too, eh, Teh Atht? How much have you read?"

He shook his head and waved his arm placatingly. "Only that you've known him. And that by accident. I stayed a while in your castle and would have spoken to you from there, but you were dreaming. And your dreams were filled with this Tarra Khash…" And more hastily: "But I wasn't prying, as you see for yourself. Oh, I *might* have stolen your dreams, Orbiquita, but instead I came to you openly. Of course I did, for as you yourself have pointed out, we're of one blood."

She dwelled on that a moment. "And you want to know about… about Tarra Khash?" Abruptly she turned away. "Then I can't help you. I know nothing of him, except that he's a man. In every sense, a man…"

Teh Atht said nothing but waited, and eventually she turned his way again. "Well?"

He shrugged, casually played his ace: "Then he's likely done for, and my quest for immortality gone with him."

"Done for?" she hissed, alarm plain in the rippling of her warty flesh. "I had dreamed he was in danger, and are you saying it were no dream but reality?"

The wizard nodded. "Your lamia precognition, Orbiquita. There's a bond between you and him, no matter how you may deny it. And so, wherever he wanders, when he faces danger you'll sense it here in your lava cavern. Aye, and he faces it right now!"

She was all ears now, her breathing erratic, claws clashing willy-nilly. "How done for?" she demanded. "What, Tarra Khash, my Tarra, in danger most grave? You fear for his life? Even you, a mighty mage? Now tell me where he is, and the nature of this threat. Tell me at once, or flee this place while yet you may!" She went to probe his mind, on which Teh Atht at once drew shutters.

"We trade," he said. "A tale for a tale. You tell me what you know of him, and I'll return the favour—though little good it will do, with you pledged to guard this place for a five-year!"

She glared at him then and ground together teeth that could crunch granite. But eventually, and grudgingly, "So *be* it!" she said. "Now listen and I'll tell you all—or most…

"It was some months agone, the time of lamia renewal—of sisterhood vows and powers both. I was on my way here, to the Great Meeting of all my sisters, but I'd left it late and my magick had waned somewhat. Also, the moon approached its full, and as you're doubtless aware, lamias are not at their best in Gleeth's full glare. For my own reasons I travelled in human guise, a young girl mounted on a white yak, with a parasol to keep the moon from burning me. Then—skirting the Mountains of Lohmi *en route* for Nameless Desert—trouble!

"Villains out of Chlangi ambushed me, made off with my beasts, my book of runes, a ring come down to me from our ancestor Mylakhrion. Aye, and they took much more than that. They…they made vile sport with me under the leering moon, of a sort I'll not describe. Then they pegged me out naked in Gleeth's glare and rode off laughing.

"Tarra Khash found me, else I were not telling you this now. Injured, he was, for the same bunch of bandits had fallen on him, too. He'd taken an arrow in his back and seemed near all in. But I didn't know that when first I saw him. He was just another man come to molest me; what with moon's deadly ray and his ravishing, I'd surely be a goner come morning.

"But I was wrong. When by right he should be caring for himself, instead he cared for me. I fancy he even suspected my true nature, but still he cared for me.

"He cut me loose, covered me, put me on his camel and hurried me to a safe place. He sheltered me from the moon, built a fire, offered me food and drink. Indeed, he offered me whatever I needed for my comfort, all of what little he had. But that was how *he* viewed himself, not as *I* viewed him. Indeed, he had *much* to offer a moon-weakened, sorely depleted lamia. And so trusting was he that he put himself at my mercy, completely in my power.

"I could have taken all, slaked my thirst in a moment, but...I chose merely to sip. I kissed his neck," (Teh Atht shuddered), "tasted his blood—only a taste, no more. And good blood it was: rich and strong, a trifle wild, even heady! 'Twere a battle with myself not to gorge on him there and then and be done with it. Aye, and better for me if I had.

"But instead I balmed his wound, left him sleeping, used the strength he had given me to call up desert djinni who bore me here. I was late, without excuse, and so bound to do my stint in this brimstony place. Ah, but first I asked a boon of previous lava lamia: that she give me only sufficient time in which to avenge myself, regain my ring and runebook! To which she agreed.

"My powers were returned to me in full and I sped me to Chlangi the Doomed, where once again Tarra Khash was of service. He knew the where of my ring and book; what's more, he planned his own retribution on a certain Fregg, so-called 'king' of that city of dogs and thieves. Fregg had stolen his sword—the merest stump of a blade, however ornate and scintillant its hilt—but no man steals from Tarra

Khash. Not with impunity. Against all odds he'd take it back, and with my assist he did! And I got my revenge, my ring, my book. More than this, lava lamia got her breakfast, grilled alive on these searing rocks. And so Fregg's no more…"

Again the wizard shuddered. "And is that all?"

She glared at him. "No, not the half of it!" She glared again, then sighed, and her voice became a groan, almost a whimper. "For since then…he's in my mind, in my dreams, in the very air I breathe. Even in this place, over sulphur reek and roar of vented steam, I smell his breath, hear his voice. I care for nothing save memories, all too brief, of him." She looked at Teh Atht almost in desperation. "The iron has gone out of me, my will deserted me. What say you, has he spelled me, cousin?"

He nodded. "So it would seem, Orbiquita, aye. And a spell rarely broken, called the Lethargy of Love. More, I'd say the dosage were lethal!"

His words sank home and she started up. "Love? *Love?* You are mad! I am a lamia, and Tarra Khash a man. Does a spider love a fly? Does a browsing beast in a field love the grass? Does a roaring fire love a log? Only to consume it!"

"The symptoms of what ails you don't lie, Orbiquita," he answered. "You were in the guise of a woman when you met him, and women have their weaknesses. Ten thousand other men might have found you that night, and done what Tarra Khash did, and died for their pains. But they didn't find you, he did—and something stirred in your blood. The world itself is a cauldron, the mighty vat of some sorcerer god, and we are all ingredient to his works. That is all it was with you and Tarra Khash, that was all it took: chemistry!"

"Begone!" she groaned. "Go now, Teh Atht. Leave me to my thoughts, my miseries. For I think you may be right, and so I've a deal to ponder."

But as he caused his carpet to retreat from her and made to turn away: "No, wait!" she cried. "First tell me where he is and the nature of his plight. We made a pact, remember?"

Teh Atht turned back, told her all he knew as quickly as possible, for the air in his bubble was almost expended. "And now I must go," he breathlessly concluded, "or else stay here for good!"

"Will you not help him?" she cried as he turned away and made for furnace flue to the surface.

"Methinks it may be in my interest so to do," he answered over a distance, ascending through smoke, steam and bellows' belch. "But alas, it's hard to find the means. A hazardous business, Orbiquita, interference in the schemes of a fellow sorcerer. This much I'll promise you: I'll follow his course as best I can. And if aught of evil befalls him, at least I'll make report of it."

And bursting from the blowhole, dissolving his bubble and breathing clean air again, he heard in his mind her furious threat: "You'll make report? Of harm befalling Tarra Khash? To me? Think well before you do, Teh Atht. For if he dies you'll not need return here. I'll hound you to hell, 'cousin,' and gnaw on your ribs there!"

And, because lamias aren't much for idle threats, for a third time Teh Atht shuddered...

Tarra's backside and hips were bruised black and blue from his jolting ride; but they'd quickly harden to it, he knew. He was well out of practice, that was all; and anyway, better a few bruises than the torment of the slaves, now that they rested and their trembly limbs began protesting. Still and all, noon had come soon enough, when the slaver caravan groaned to a halt in its accustomed defensive circle. Then Tarra had climbed stiffly down, fed his beast the promised double ration, watered it, too, all the while casting cautiously about to see what he might see. Like perhaps a pony going spare, with saddle-bags, water and what all. But no such luck.

What he did see was the sly grin on a certain frizzy's face, and the way he kept his crossbow nocked and ever pointed just a little too close to Tarra Khash. Then came his summons to attend Cush Gemal in hastily erected, tasselled tent.

He went, with his Yhemni guard close behind, and found a fire already prepared, meat steaming on a spit, and Gemal inside on heaped cushions, taking his ease with a weird wooden smoke-pipe and a silver jug of wine. "Come in out of the sun," said Gemal. "Sit down, take wine, and in a little while eat. And meanwhile tell me your thoughts."

The half-breed slaver's voice was not unpleasant, Tarra decided. It was low, dark, should be warm but came out cold as snow on a mountain's peak. And strange for a Yhemni (or at least for a man of Shad and the jungles around), it was not without culture; with echoes doubtless of Gemal's mixed ancestry, and a hint of study and learning far above the accustomed level of lands beyond the Straits of Yhem. All of this from a few spoken words? Not entirely. Gemal's bearing and the respect he mustered in the other blacks, aye, and the light in his black eyes, all of these things were contributory to Tarra's analysis.

His ancestry... The steppeman wondered about that. Black as ebony, Cush Gemal, and yet thin-lipped, slant-eyed like certain tribes of Northmen, tall and cold as a Khrissan, ornately crested as any sophisticate of Klühn or Thandopolis. Of polyglot parts, this slaver, but in no way mongrel; exuding power, it was almost as if he came from a tribe or even a land apart, from worlds unknown. Either that, or there were elements of all the Primal Land in him, with jungle predominant.

Tarra looked at him again, openly, even admiringly; he hadn't forgotten how swift had come Gorlis Thad's uppance. Why, that burly bellowing Northman hadn't stood snowflake in hell's chance against this cold, black, hollow-cheeked, close to cadaverous chieftain! Now *there* was a thought! A tribal chieftain! Even a Chief of Chiefs—and why not? For certainly the way he commanded respect, not only from his own people but also Hrossaks and Northmen alike, would seem to place him in some such station.

All of this but a moment's thought, and Gemal's eyes dark on Tarra where the steppeman sat cross-legged on a large green cushion, with a small silver jug cool in his hand. And the sweet smoke of Gemal's pipe circulating in tent and Hrossak lungs both; and his low, knowing voice offering no threat but yet quietly urging as he now repeated: "Your thoughts, Tarra?"

The Hrossak's thoughts, especially in respect of someone who could have his head in a moment, would normally be private, unspoken. And yet now: "I'm thinking you're a strange one," said Tarra Khash, his tongue astonishing him with its frankness.

Gemal hardly seemed offended. He gave a laugh. "My thoughts about you are much the same!" he said. "I captured you, may kill you even now, and yet you don't hold me in awe. You spoke of *my* strangeness, not of your own fear."

"I hold you in something of wonder, perhaps, and a deal of curiosity. But awe?" Tarra shook his head. "I *know* you're not ordinary, not in any way—that's obvious to me as water's wet! But I'm not awed by your power over me; for here and now that power's a fact, and I can't change it—not here and now. If you do kill me, *then* I'll likely be awed, but only in the last second. Or perhaps in the second after that?"

Gemal puffed more smoke in Tarra's direction, smiled in his skull-like fashion, said: "More of your thoughts, Hrossak, for they're refreshing and they interest me greatly."

Tarra paused a moment before answering, sniffed the smoke and thought: *That's Zha-weed he's puffing on, which wizards use in their magicks, and less able addicts to lighten their burdens. It brings pleasing illusions and loosens the tongue...* And he also thought: *Perhaps I'll feed my big lizard a little of your Zha-weed, Cush Gemal, then set him free to create a diversion, and finally—*

"Well?" Gemal frowned, however slightly. His eyes had fastened on Tarra, and now their concentration grew intense.

"I intend—" Tarra began, automatically and out loud this time—at which moment the tent's flap was drawn back, pungent smoke blown aside and fresh air wafted in. It brought mouth-watering smells with it, and the Hrossak's mind cleared in a moment. "—to enjoy this good food you've offered me, Cush Gemal!"

Gemal scowled at the black who stood there with silver platter, sizzling meat, razor sharp carver, and scowled not a little at Tarra, too; but then, in another moment, he laughed out loud. The frizzy departed and for a little while they ate in silence. Then Gemal said:

"And have you no questions for me? Don't you even care about your fate? Surely you're curious about your destination, and what's to become of you there?"

Tarra shrugged. "I've always been a wanderer," he said, "an adventurer—though as you see for yourself, not so much from choice as by accident. Indeed in this respect it seems I'm accident prone! But it has to be said that this is something of an adventure, and entirely in keeping, even if it's not in accordance with my plans. What's more I'm on the move again, albeit in a direction which could be improved upon!

So all in all, p'raps I'm not so badly off." He shrugged again. "As for my fate: the fates of all men are wont to change from day to day. I was a slave; now I drive a lizard and eat with a Chief of Chiefs; who can say what's waiting for me tomorrow? You mentioned our destination, which I believe to be Shad. Ah, but Shad's still a long way off…"

"What?" Cush Gemal raised thin, slanting eyebrows. He smiled, but warningly. "That sounds close to a threat, Tarra Khash, however veiled! Should I put you in chains again, or do you choose to serve me well and faithfully for another day or two—and then go free?"

"My freedom?" Tarra stopped eating. "That's tempting. And all I must do is drive the big lizard?"

Gemal watched his face. The steppeman's eyes flickered briefly—perhaps longingly?—over the glittering, serrated edge of the carver where it lay on the silver platter between him and his host. Try as Tarra might, he couldn't keep from glancing at it. Gemal noticed but made no comment. Instead he answered the other's question:

"We're heading for the shallow salt lochs where they wash in from the Eastern Ocean. We came in by that route and it's how we'll go out. Another day and a half, two days at worst speed, and we'll be there. But it's important that there's no delay. These are momentous, world shattering times. Soon, in Shad…" He paused abruptly, blinked, flared his nostrils. And Tarra thought:

'Ware, Cush Gemal! It's the Zha-weed, my friend!

"Let it suffice to say," Gemal continued, "that I can brook no delay—and that the loss of a good Hrossak drover would inconvenience me. Of course, I could simply abandon one wagon and boat. But that would also mean abandoning a fifth of the slaves I've taken. Indeed it would mean slaughtering them! Black Yoppaloth has no plans at present for war with the mainland, and so there can be no survivors from this little trek, no wagging tongues carrying tales to mainland cities. We want no armadas sailing out of Klühn and Thandopolis on missions of red revenge against Shad!

"So you see I've a neat and tidy mind, Tarra Khash, the very opposite of yours in that I demand that things go *exactly* according to plan! I planned to take a certain number of male slaves and female beauties back across the water to Shad, and I'll do my utmost to make that plan work. Also, I planned to ship at least four Hrossak lizards, which are unknown in Shad and will make for magnificent parades in the arena. And so, if you'll continue as you've started and drive your beast to the water—and give me no problems along the way—there I'll pay you off and let you and beast both go free. That will leave me with a vessel to carry myself and Black Yoppaloth's brides, and four more for slaves and lizards."

"Why turn me loose?" asked Tarra, ingenuously. "That hardly seems the way of a slaver to me. Why take only four lizards when you could take five? Why attempt to strike a bargain with me when I'm in your power? And as for *paying* me…! Why even bother to explain anything to me when there's nothing I can do to change a thing, what- and whichever you decide?"

Gemal looked at him, nodded, smiled a wry smile. "You called me a Chief of Chiefs," he said. "But even a Chief of Chiefs can be lonely; aye, and especially he can grow sick of power. With these men you see around you: my every word is their command—which bores me utterly! It *pleases* me to have someone I can bargain with! Do you see? These men look on me as their master, and others see me as a monster, but I'm rarely seen simply as another man. You look on me with some curiosity, but with little or nothing of fear. However different you sense me to be, however strange, you *know* I am just another man. And I suspect you acknowledge no mere man as your master. But at the same time, I don't think you're incapable of humility. Perhaps in this we have something in common, perhaps not…

"Anyway, I like you for what I've seen in you—so much indeed that I might easily have taken you back to Shad simply to keep you with me, eventually to become my companion and friend. Aye, and I might still do it, so don't force my hand! Accept what I offer and leave it at that."

Tarra glanced at the knife again, then let his eyes linger there and deliberately drew Gemal's eyes to that same spot. The slavemaster looked at the shining blade, looked at Tarra, raised an inquiring eyebrow and waited.

"Why have you tempted me, Cush Gemal?" said Tarra. "Oh, only a fool would attempt to kill you here, I know…but still I *might* have tried. Or was this a test of some sort?"

Gemal smiled a thin, knowing smile and returned his gaze once more to the razor-honed carver. "Not so much a test as a trial," he eventually answered. "Or perhaps a lesson?—but only *if* you had taken the bait. If you had…then I would know we could never be friends, and by now you'd be dead." It wasn't a threat but a statement of fact, as Cush Gemal saw it.

"A trial? A lesson?" Tarra looked bemused. "What sort of lesson?"

"A lesson in trust. I was showing you how much I'd be willing to trust you. Or maybe I wasn't."

"I don't understand," Tarra shook his head.

"Reach for the knife, Tarra Khash," Gemal invited. "Do it swiftly. Take it up as if…as if to kill me!"

"What?"

"Do it!" the slaver insisted.

"But I have no desire to—"

"I know that, now," said Gemal, "but do it anyway. Go on! Test your mettle against mine—if you dare."

Tarra's father had used to say: "Never dare a madman or a fool, and never accept one from either!" His hand blurred into action, came to rest atop Cush Gemal's where it was there first!

"Yibb!" said Tarra, merely breathing the word. "And I thought *I* was fast!"

"You are," said the other, "and if your joints weren't quite so stiff you'd be faster still." He turned his hand on its back to clasp Tarra's in strong, slender fingers. "So now you see there's no subterfuge. I'd merely caution you against making trouble for yourself. For if you do I'll be obliged to chain you again, and kill you where the land meets the water. Or take you to Shad as a slave, which I've no wish to do. I'd have you as a friend, Tarra Khash, but never as a slave; for as a slave I'd need four others just to watch you! And anyway, I've read it in your eyes that Shad's not the way you wish to go, not in any event."

He stood up, drew the steppeman up with him. "So be it," he nodded. "When we reach the water I'll give you gold, enough to repay your costs, and turn you loose. For I have to agree: Shad's not the place for you. It's in my bones that there'd be trouble for you in Shad, perhaps for both of us."

They stepped from the tent. Outside, across a sky so blue it seared the eyes, faint wisps of cloud were drifting from the east. In that same direction but as yet far away, the sky was patterned like the scales of a fish; also, at the very edge of vision, it seemed that nodding dust-devils cavorted and careened, astir on the horizon's rim.

"Bad weather ahead," Tarra pulled a wry face. "It'll make the big lizards unruly."

Gemal nodded. "The season of storms approaches," he replied, frowning. "All the more reason to make haste." Suddenly he staggered, drew a sharp breath, grasped Tarra's shoulder with shaking claw, purely to steady himself. All his limbs were at once atremble. Close by, a pair of blacks saw, took fright and would have hurried away. Tarra wondered at their terror; but Gemal saw them, beckoned them to attend him. Trembling more than he, they crept close.

"Go," Gemal croaked in Tarra's ear as the frizzies took hold and gave him their support. "Get away from me. Back to your lizard and safety."

Safety? thought Tarra. *From what?*

The two shivering Yhemnis, eyes bugging and obviously mortally afraid, helped Gemal back to his tent. He went like an old man, seeming strangely shrivelled and drawn down into himself. But at the flap of the tent he caught his blacks by their wrists and drew them in after him.

Tarra wondered: *A contagious fever? Is that what's wrong with him?...* Or was it something else? "Cush Gemal!" he called out. "I'll drive the big lizard to the ocean lochs, never fear."

"I know it well enow, Tarra," came back the answer from inside the black tent. But it was a harsh, gasping croak, in no wise Gemal's previous voice, and there was more of pain than strength in it...

By the time Tarra got back to his monstrous beast and drew its hoods up over ridgy eyes, a wind had sprung up that drove the sand with stinging force. It would be a short blow, Tarra guessed, but a bitter one. The clouds were scudding now and beginning to pile one into the next; behind them, the sun a fading orange blob, growing ever more dim.

Tarra spoke words of reason to his beast and it huddled down. Then he crept under the big wagon, found Loomar Nindiss cowering with the rest of the slaves. The sand flurries weren't so bad under here.

He called the lad to him and Loomar came crawling and clanking, shouted: "What's up?"

"Eh?" said Tarra. "The storm, d'you mean?"

Loomar shook his head. "I saw you go to Gemal's tent. Is all well?"

"Maybe better than that," said Tarra. And he began to relate all that had happened. But—

"Ahhh!" a concerted sigh went up from all the slaves crouched under the wagon. They all stared wide-eyed and slack-jawed toward Cush Gemal's black tent. Tarra and Loomar peeped out from under wagon's rim, followed the massed gaze of the others.

A dust-devil—but a giant, almost a tornado—picked its way through a gap between two wagons and closed with Cush Gemal's tent. For a moment the tent belled out a little like an inflated lung, then fell slack as the wall of the twister enveloped it; but the tent was not drawn aloft, nor even caused to strain at its guys. And where the wind gusted all about, and smaller dust-devils raced here and there, in and about the ring of wagons—and where canvasses flapped in the spiteful wind, and beasts and men cowered from the sting of whirling sand—Gemal's tent stood as before, unflustered, becalmed, black tassels hanging slack! The tent was in no wise affected, for indeed it stood central in the silent "eye" of the twister! And there the great funnel of whirling sand remained, with Gemal's tent untroubled at its centre, while all about was a chaos of wind and rushing, circling sand.

But the frenzied rush of sand-laden air had seemed to create electrical energies, trapping them in the core of the twister; for while Gemal's tent remained untroubled, it was not unaffected. No, for ephemeral green fires shivered and danced in its silken, scalloped eaves and dripped like phosphorescent rain from its tassels—but only for a little while longer. Then—

In a matter of moments the uproar lessened and the swaying column that reached from dunes to sky broke up, hurling its tons of sand afar to fall like stinging rain; the clouds began to break up and beams of sunlight blazed through; lesser dust-devils dwindled and departed, racing off to extinction somewhere across the desert. Finally, blacks, Hrossaks, Northmen began to move again, emerging from various boltholes, mostly under canvas. But all eyes remained glued to Gemal's tent, from which the dancing green fires had now departed, where at last the flap was thrown back and tall, crested slavemaster emerged, began shouting orders. All appeared to be back to normal.

Tarra Khash marvelled. Five minutes ago the half-caste had seemed all in, gripped in the spasms of some mortal illness. Now he looked and sounded stronger than ever! What's more, he even seemed less emaciated, if that were at all possible.

The drive resumed almost at once, with Cush Gemal riding beside the lead wagon, but this time his tent was left standing till last. Tarra made a great show of removing sand from his lizard's eyes and nostrils, sat upon the beast's feet and cleaned its claws, generally made hard work of getting under way; and thus he contrived to be at the very end of the line when the caravan stretched itself out toward the east. And in this way, too, he could look back a little way to where shuddering frizzies decamped Gemal's tent and packed it away on a camel.

Then they scooped a shallow hole in the sand, in which they dumped a couple of former colleagues, covering them quickly before mounting up. This could only be the pair Gemal had drawn into the tent with him. So Tarra surmised. Difficult to say for sure, for from the one or two glimpses he'd managed to get they now seemed little more than bags of bones, shrivelled and sere as mummies.

And Tarra Khash knew he'd made a queer, queer friend indeed...

V

A Wizard's Quest— In Gemal's Camp

In one corner of the Primal Land, Cush Gemal's caravan of slaves lumbering for the salt water lochs now only forty miles away; and in another…

Teh Atht arrived at Orbiquita's castle in the mainly shunned Desert of Sheb and flew in through a high window. His flying carpet bore him down a vast, winding stone stairwell which opened into a great hall on the ground floor; and here he stepped down into dust and cobwebs, small drifts of sand blown in through various cracks, and the long accumulated litter of myriad mice and bats. He sighed and wrinkled his nose, carefully lifted the hem of his rune-embellished robe, looked all about in the gloom.

He sighed again. Lamias were less than fastidious, he knew, but Orbiquita must be slattern of all slatterns. Aye, and the slovenly creature his cousin, at that! But this wouldn't do; he could hardly entertain guests with the place in this condition.

"Go," he told the carpet in a tongue only it understood. "Fly fast to Klühn, return at once with the one who hops and the one who flits—but leave the one who seeps there, for he'll only slow you down."

The carpet rippled itself gracefully in acknowledgement of its master's command, backed swiftly away, spiralled up the corkscrew stairwell and disappeared.

And now the great white mage of Klühn thought back a little on how he came to be here…

Leaving Orbiquita in her lava lair, he'd first thought to pay a visit to the Suhm-yi man and maid who'd known Tarra Khash in Klühn and with him destroyed Gorgos' temple there. But that were easier thought than acted upon. Suhm-yi means "rarely seen," and if Amyr Arn and his love did not desire to be found, then it would prove singularly difficult so to do.

When last seen, Amyr and his Ulli were heading west toward the Desert of Sheb, first leg of their long trek home to Inner Isles. Very well, and Teh Atht had set off in that same direction. But as time crept on and the tired sun began to sink toward ever watchful Cthon beyond the rim of the world, where he waits out the day with his nets, so the wizard had wearied of hit-and-miss aerial surveillance. Then, too, in a small oasis far below, at the edge of Sheb's rolling dune expanse, he'd spied the tiny camp of some lone traveller.

Descending in a tight circle, Teh Atht had then made out a five-pointed Star of Power footprinted into the sand, with shimmery pool and shady palms nestled at its centre; at which he'd wagered with himself who this must be. None other but Moormish of the Wastes, whose simple protective device had backfired on him. At ground level it would scarce be noticed, but from up here it was a dead giveaway!

At first delighted, now Teh Atht soured a little as he circled lower. His mood was governed by what he knew of the man in the flat, nomad-styled tent below.

There were two such hermit sorcerers among Theem'hdra's fraternity (?) of wizards: Moormish was one and Tarth Soquallin the other, but the latter was off somewhere far to the west and hadn't been heard of for many a year. So this must be Moormish of the Wastes, who'd been named after his predilection for forlorn and perilous wastelands. It *could* be a common man, of course, but that seemed unlikely. First there was the protective star tramped meticulously in the sand, and second the location of the camp itself. Common men weren't much given to wandering here, where lamias were wont to dwell, and Chlangi the Doomed swollen like a ripe boil scant fifteen miles away, full of the scum of the land.

Naturally (for reasons which will be seen), if Teh Atht had a choice, it would have been Tarth Soquallin he'd choose to find here; old hermit Tarth had always been his close friend and confidant, ever since the time they'd served together under tutelage of Imhlat the Teacher. Moormish, on the other hand, was sour as a green lemon and much given to grumbling; he'd hardly welcome the unannounced arrival of *any* wizard here in his private place, not even one white as Teh Atht. But…beggars can't be choosers; a wizard is a wizard, even if he's a notorious grouch; and right now Teh Atht was sore in need of a reliable shewstone. Moormish, habitual wanderer that he was, would doubtless have his with him.

"Hail, Moormish!" cried Teh Atht, settling his carpet to the sand and stepping down before the gaping flap of the squat, dun coloured tent.

"Begone!" came back harsh cry from within. "Hop back on your carpet and scarper. You're an intruder here, Klühnite, whose presence will muddle my meditations!"

Ah, well, thought Teh Atht, *so much for a welcome! And no use beating about the bush here!* "Permit me a glimpse—the merest peep—into your shewstone, Moormish," he called out loud, "and I'll bother you no more but be off at once."

Moormish appeared shufflingly from the gloom within. Thin as mountain air, dry as a husk, tattered and grimy, he scowled blackly through deep-sunken eyes and prodded Teh Atht's chest with a knobbed walking stick. "Do you know why I live out here in the wilderness?" he snapped. "No, obviously you don't or you'd know better than to come. It's to avoid the 'company'—the peeping, prying, overbearing presence—of people like you. And not only people like you, but people like anybody! It's called the freedom of solitary existence, privacy, a lone retirement. I have *chosen* to seclude myself. And you have chosen to disturb me. Worse, you'd casually probe about amongst my most precious possessions: a 'peep' into my shewstone, a 'bite' of my bread, a 'sip' of my water. And all of these things left tainted by your touch!"

Now Teh Atht was offended. He'd asked for neither food nor drink and certainly had no intention of tainting Moormish's supplies. And as for spending a few moments in private with the old claustrophobe's crystal: be sure Moormish would deny him *that* privilege to the bitter end! Except Teh Atht had no time to spare, and so was driven to extremes.

The shrivelled sorcerer's stick was still touching his chest, fending him off. *Good!* And he sent a dose of Undiluted Deafness down it on the spot, which all unseen, unfelt, and especially unheard, at once blocked Moormish's eardrums.

"You're a crazed old recluse!" Teh Atht shouted then, at the same time smiling and nodding agreeably, testing his spell's efficacy.

"Eh?" said Moormish, squinting curiously. He put a finger in his ear and wiggled it violently.

Excellent! thought Teh Atht with a grin; and without further ado he uttered the curse of Curious Concretion, so that in a moment Moormish was marbled. Then, leaving the fossilized mage with finger in ear and stick jabbing at nothing—as grotesque a pose as one could wish—he moved past him into the gloomy, smelly tent and sought out Moormish's crystal.

The shewstone stood alone upon a low, circular wooden table, with several ancient, well-patched cushions piled close by. Teh Atht preferred to remain standing, straightway made himself known. The sphere answered in a simple code which the wizard at once deciphered, making it out to say: "Ah, Teh Atht! I've heard of you. And is old Moormish dead, then? He must be, or else you've stolen me!"

"No, not dead," Teh Atht chuckled. "Merely dumbfounded. Or perhaps deaf-founded? Or maybe even stone deaf-founded!" And he told the shewstone all.

"He'll be mad as hell!" the agitated sphere groaned, its milky screen all astir. "And he'll doubtless take it out on me."

Teh Atht shook his head. "He won't know," he said, "unless you yourself tell him. I certainly won't, not if we can come to some—arrangement?"

"Scry all you will," said the sphere at once. "I'm at your mercy."

After that it was the simplest thing to find Amyr Arn and Ulli Eys, and pinpoint their precise location and direction of travel. And so convenient their bearing and rate of travel that Teh Atht was given to utter a small cry of delight. Perhaps things were falling in order at last.

He thanked Moormish's crystal and began to turn away...then checked himself to ask: "Incidentally, does your master use you as an oracle, too? As diary, calendar, *aide-memoire*, and so on?"

"Aye, and other things to boot," the shewstone waxed bitter. "For when things go amiss with him, it's me who takes the blame. Only peruse my several bruises!"

Teh Atht had already noted the battered condition of the crystal, the dents and gouges where its picture was wont to blur and go out of focus. He offered his commiserations, said: "But of course he's sworn you to secrecy—that is, in respect of his most private and personal pursuits?"

"Vows I may not break," the shewstone replied, "on penalty of being myself broken!"

"A pity," said Teh Atht. "I had wondered if perhaps Moormish sought immortality, and if so how close he'd come to finding it..."

"But don't you all seek it?" the crystal seemed surprised. "Small secret that, Teh Atht! And how close are you?"

For answer the wizard merely sighed.

"Then go in peace, happy at least in the knowledge that Moormish is no closer. More I dare not say."

Teh Atht went. Outside the tent, shadows leaned more slantingly and the air was cool. A kite sat upon Moormish's shoulder, observing him curiously, perhaps hungrily. It pecked at his ear and squawked abrupt complaint, then soared aloft in search of softer fare.

Eradicating his footprints in the sand where they led from mortified magician in and out of tent, Teh Atht placed himself before Moormish and reversed the runic restrictions. Moormish blinked, withdrew his finger from his ear, said, "That's better!... Or is it?" He blinked again, gazed all about, suddenly staggered and let fall his stick where Teh Atht leaned his weight against it. He frantically rubbed at his eyes.

"What's this?" said Teh Atht in feigned concern. "Are you ill?" He took a pace forward but Moormish backed hurriedly away.

"My ears," said the other. "And then my eyes. You seemed to flicker just then, and suddenly it's grown quite dim!" He shivered.

"Dim?" said Teh Atht. "It's merely the sun slipped behind a cloud there in the west." He tut-tutted. "But don't your symptoms bother you, my friend?"

"Symptoms? What symptoms?" snapped the other. "And don't call me your friend. As for my shewstone: I'll show you the knob of my stick!" He stooped to snatch it up. "Now begone!"

Teh Atht shrugged. "So be it," he said, moving his mouth with vigour but merely whispering the words. And returning to his carpet he added, again in a whisper: "But if I were you I'd have it seen to."

"Eh?"

"There you go again!" Teh Atht now shouted. "Deaf as a post, eyesight playing tricks with you, and shivering as in some alien ague! Aye, and apparently loss of orientation, too. It's all this sand and solitude, Moormish. You need the company of men—a closer proximity of persons, anyway—and you could do with seeing a physician. I'd head for Klühn if I were you. And now, while you still may." He tut-tutted again, bade his carpet rise and proceed north by north-west.

Below and behind him, Moormish of the Wastes cocked his head on one side and glowered this way and that, rubbed his eyes again, finally stumbled uncertainly back inside his tent and lowered its flap. He might guess the truth eventually, but little he'd be able to do about it. It was sad, but Moormish really was failing, and his magick with him. The wizard when he flew away considered that in the circumstances he'd given the hermit best possible advice.

After that...

...There had been other matters Teh Atht must attend to—the first of which being to place himself in the path of silver-skinned man and maid. No great difficulty there, for he'd known the region through which they travelled well enough. Aye, and he'd also known that Orbiquita's castle lay directly in their way!

Evening was settling when the five long wagons formed their accustomed circle in the timeless sand. Tarra fed his beast; he played "work and reward" games with the huge creature, using greenstuff tidbits as prizes when the lizard "understood" his gestures and whistles and answered promptly to his instructions; he finally climbed up on its head and oiled behind the eye-flaps and the delicate scales which protected vestigial gills. The monster accepted him now as its master, possibly even as a friend, and made no complaint when he stood upon its lower lip to knock crusts of sand from the rims of its blowhole nostrils. The other Hrossak drivers made much the same ado of their own huge mounts, but Tarra's care was that much more special. He didn't merely desire a beast who'd work for him, but one who'd die for him if necessary. For it might just possibly come to that.

Meanwhile the slaves were fed, and Tarra noticed that their portions were bigger tonight and their water measures more nearly adequate; what's more, there were even small, sweet apples on the menu! He scratched his chin and nodded to himself: the trek was coming to its close, and supplies being balanced accordingly. Things must have worked out well, that food was still so much in evidence.

As the frizzy with the basket of bread and fruit finished distributing to the slaves of Tarra's wagon, so the Hrossak approached him for his share; but the slaver shoved him away, grunted something unintelligible, pointed to where fires were being lit and spits set up in the centre of the circle. Tarra got the message at once; after all, it seemed hardly right that a man who had broken bread with Cush Gemal should continue to eat with slaves...

He wandered to the rim of the inner circle of fires and stood looking on, his mouth fairly watering. Then a young Hrossak driver spied him standing apart, called out for him to come and join the mongrel crew gathered there. Apparently he'd been accepted. He went, watched small joints of meat go onto the spits and start sizzling, noticed out the corner of his eye a pair of Northmen riding in from the east leading a spare pony all laden down with baskets. He'd seen them ride on ahead some hours earlier, at which time the baskets had been empty. Now they were full, and the pony who carried them feeling the strain a bit; and as the dusty, bearded, broadly grinning pair reined in by the fires, so Tarra guessed what was the beast's load. Fruits of the sea, yes!—that great Eastern Ocean whose salt tang he now realized he'd been smelling all day long, which suddenly was quite unmistakeable—the baskets were full of large gleamy fish!

Expert fishermen, the Northmen hardly needed to brag how they'd netted this lot in a single cast: by simply walking into the loch, spreading a long net between them, and then walking out again! But they did anyway. True or false, Tarra cared not at all. Not while he knew he'd have a fine bit of fish for his supper tonight.

Then the wineskins came out, sour stuff but palatable enough after the first swig, and the joking, tall storytelling and gambling commenced. Tarra staying just a little apart and speaking when spoken to, and Hrossaks and Northmen alike all seeming in much lighter mood tonight, though for a fact the frizzies were as doleful and "black in the face" (Tarra kept both thought and word to himself) as ever. Ah, yes: trek's end in sight, and this lot plainly glad of it.

Tarra found himself a stone to sit on, listened to various tall tales from the Northmen, whose range and wit were astonishing. In gay mood they made for sparkling companions, these bristle-manes. A pity they were so untrustworthy, so volatile and, when roused, so notoriously bloodthirsty. Hrossaks, too, a humorous bunch, if a little dry and thoughtful about it. The steppemen were ever careful not to insult, because they themselves rarely forgave the insults of others.

Eventually the last rays of a setting sun stuck up like the spokes of a golden fan in the west; indigo spread across the sky from the east, darkening a blue in which the stars gleamed so much brighter; and Gleeth, the old moon-god, probed with his waxing horns from behind the far distant silhouette of the Eastern Range. A gentle evening breeze sprang up, not so much a trouble as a relief, and settled westward toward the lochs and the sea; and at last the meat was ready. Tarra settled for fish, lobbed a beauty expertly from spit onto his stone, stood fanning his hot fingers and listening to his belly rumble while it cooled a little. Then, with a warm place to sit, he broke open the crisped scaly skin to let out the fish's steam in splendid gusts. And as the slave-takers ate and relaxed from the day's drive, so silence descended. This was partly because mouths now found work chomping, mainly because Cush Gemal had put in an appearance, tall, spindly and gleamy red and black in the firelight.

Most of Gemal's Yhemnis kept to a fire of their own some little distance away; those who deigned to eat with the white- (and bronze-)

skins stood up to show Gemal their respect—their fear? Hrossaks and, reluctantly, barbarians followed suit.

"Sit," said Cush Gemal with a wave of his hand. "You've done well, all of you, so be at your ease. The salt lochs are only hours away—an early start tomorrow and we'll be there 'twixt dawn and noon, and well under sail by the time the sun slips from zenith. See how the breeze favours us? It's off the land, blows for the Eastern Ocean. Only let it keep this up and we'll sail all the way to Shad, and never an oar dipped! Now I'll walk alone with my thoughts awhile."

He strode away, then paused and turned. "Watchkeepers, don't drink too much. I fancy we're followed, however discreetly. So far our mission's a success—let's keep it that way. We want no problems so close to ocean's margin." Finally he glanced at Tarra. "Hrossak, someone should find you a jacket, to keep the sand out of your cuts. Aye, and there'll be flies to lay their eggs in you, by the time we reach the ocean's rim."

Tarra shrugged. "I'm quick to heal," he said, "but for a fact it does grow chilly nights."

Gemal nodded and walked away.

The young Hrossak who'd called Tarra over to the fire came and sat beside him. "Oho!" he said. "And it seems you've made yourself a fine friend! Aye, and chatting with him like a brother! There aren't many men that skinny black cockscomb will pass the time of day with—or night, as 'twere. I'm Narqui Ghenz. You're a Khash, aren't you? A name to be reckoned with on the steppes, once upon a time."

"Tarra," said that worthy, nodding. "I'm a wanderer. By now I'd have wandered home if I hadn't bumped into this little packet. What's your excuse?" And he continued to eat his fish.

"*Huh!*" said Ghenz. "You're fortunate in that you can still go home. Me, I took a wife too many. It's my head—or a couple of even worse bits—if I go back! Depends how you look at it, and who gets to me first. Me? I think I'd rather they took my head..."

Tarra stared at him. "You hardly seem old enough to have taken one wife, let alone two! A bit daft, wasn't it?"

"It was." The other grinned. "But not in the way you're thinking. They were other men's wives I took, not mine!"

For the first time in days, Tarra laughed. "Say no more," he said, "for I've been a bit of a ladies' man myself in my time." Then his grin turned to a frown. Yes he had, but that was before a certain female kissed his neck one night in the badlands near Chlangi the Doomed. A rare and fearsome female, that one, called Orbiquita; and yet... Tarra hadn't given much thought to women since then. A man seared by the sun doesn't stand greatly in awe of a hearth-fire. He fingered twin blemishes on his neck, white specks against the bronze, and his blood tingled in a strange, even a morbid fever. Then he saw Ghenz watching him wonderingly and came back down to earth.

"That explains why you're not in Hrossa," he said, "but not why you're here with this lot."

Ghenz shrugged. "Have you ever been to Grypha?"

"In my time," said Tarra, nodding. "When I was maybe your age. A Hrossak youth runs away from home, he heads for Grypha. A man gets himself banished, and his first stop's Grypha. It's been a refuge, of sorts, for exiled steppemen ever since they built it there. Grypha the Fortress, it was once called, for its peoples warred a lot with us Hrossaks in those days. Also, it had something of strategic value: it stands on the Luhr and so guards the west, and looks across the Bay of Monsters on Yhemni jungles and Shadarabar. Many of its olden fortifications are still standing, however battered; ah, but not so much warriors as wharf rats have inherited it now! A cesspool built on a swamp, whose stink is washed by the Luhr out into the Southern Sea. But even a river can't clear it all away. What, Grypha? Why, it's a byword for shady deals and shadier dealers—like some kind of steaming, sophisticated Chlangi, but not all *that* sophisticated!"

"That's what I meant," said Narqui Ghenz. "Chased out, I headed for Grypha—and discovered it to be the sinkhole of Theem'hdra, with villains black, white, brown and bronze all intermingled there like...like lumpy soup! Oh, there's money to be made there, for those who don't much care, but I'm a Hrossak and I like clean air. Except...where to go next? I'd thought of Thinhla, or Thandopolis way across the world, but they were such a long way off. It costs money to join a caravan west, and even more to take a ship. Work my passage? Out of Grypha? Likely I'd end up chained to an oar forever, or until I could no longer row—and then marooned on a rock somewhere to live out my life on crabs and seaweeds. So there I was in a bit of a quandary.

"Then, when I was all spent up, I heard of a fellow Hrossak recruiting lizard-handlers for some sort of trek. That was Gys Ankh, by the way—though devil only knows what's become of him! He *seemed* a decent sort at first, turned out to be a black-hearted bully. I'm glad he's gone.

"Anyway, there was to be a small down-payment—for services to be rendered, you know?—and a big lump of cash when the job was done. But all hush-hush and no questions asked. So I signed up. By the time I found out something of what it was all about we were meeting Cush Gemal and his Yhemnis at the inlet of a salt loch north of the Straits of Yhem, fifty miles or so south of where we are right now. Gemal and his blacks had brought their long wagons with them, in pieces in the boats, which all of us joined in to put together again. We Hrossaks had taken our lizards with us (Ankh had somehow stolen them out of Hrossa), they were soon hitched up, and then we headed for the villages along the east-facing side of the Great Eastern Peaks. Then, too, we discovered for sure what we'd become—slavers!"

"And that offended you?" Tarra stared straight into the other's eyes.

"Some," said Ghenz, uncomfortably.

"But not so much you'd risk running off and trying your luck on your lonesome, eh?"

"*How* run off?" Ghenz suddenly snapped. "What, and end up with a Yhemni bolt in my back? You've seen how Cush Gemal deals with troublemakers! But I'll tell you something: me and the other three Hrossaks, we've tended our lizards and that's it. No murder, no rape, no brutality of any sort toward the slaves or the girls. Gys Ankh was the only really rotten apple, and he's gone now. Anyway, what makes *you* so holy?"

"Calm down," said Tarra evenly. He looked casually all about, made sure no one would overhear their conversation. "How'm I to know these things until someone tells me, eh? So where do the Northmen come into all of this?"

"They were recruited in Grypha, too," Ghenz replied, "—for their riding skills. With those ponies of theirs they could ride down runaways, act as scouts, form a fast-moving rearguard if necessary. Aye, and they were paid well for their labours, half in advance—enough to ensure they'd stay on right to the end, anyway. Moreover, they were promised equal shares of all plunder taken, like the rest of us, and women galore along the way. Any woman they wanted—*except* Black Yoppaloth's brides. Those were to be the pick of the crop, taboo, strictly untouchable. As Gorlis Thad discovered the hard way!"

Tarra was silent for a while, then: "Did you understand when you started out how you'd be finishing up in Shad?"

"No," Ghenz shook his head, "nor will we. We see the big lizards safely across the water to Shad, get paid off there, and Gemal lends us a crew of blacks and one ship to sail us back to the mainland. That's Hrossaks and barbarians alike."

Tarra slowly nodded, picked a while on the bones of his fish. And quietly he said: "And you believe he'll do that, do you?"

"Eh?" Ghenz raised his eyebrows. "But that's our agreement! I mean, what else would he do with us?"

"Oh, nothing much," Tarra shrugged. "Except maybe butcher you, take back whatever he's given and whatever else you've got—including the gold out of your teeth—and feed your carcasses to certain little jungle-bred friends of his! Did you know there are supposed to be cannibals in Shadarabar's jungles?"

Ghenz went a little white. "You mean you think he'll pay us off with black treachery?" he hissed.

"It was just a thought, that's all," said Tarra, standing up and stretching his joints. "Me, I'm not much bothered, since I get off at ocean's rim." He made to walk away but Ghenz followed, caught at his arm.

"Listen," he said, "I've a jacket for you. Since Gemal seems to think highly of you, that might stand me in his favour."

"That's kind of you," said Tarra. "But best to take all I've said with a pinch of salt. I was just thinking out loud, that's all." He walked with Ghenz to the youth's wagon, accepted a warm, fur-lined jacket and tried it on. It was a good fit. Ghenz was meanwhile silent, his brows black where they formed a scowl in the middle. Finally he asked:

"How can we be sure he'll not deal with us badly?"

"Dunno," said Tarra. "But if I were you I'd first observe how he deals with me."

"Eh? How do you mean?"

"Well, he's promised to make good my losses and my time, let me keep my big honker and turn us both loose when we reach the loch. I figure if he sticks to that, then that he'll probably play fair by you lads, too. We can only wait and see. But as you've seen for yourself, life's pretty much easy-come, easy-go to him. I'm talking about the butchery in the villages, to which he must have agreed; about Gorlis Thad, who he cut down like a blade of grass, without a backward glance; and about these blacks of his, who fear him mightily—and who I've noticed are wont to shrivel and drop dead if they spend too much time in his company..." And Tarra watched the youth's reaction to that last.

He wasn't quite sure just what he expected, but he was sure that what he got wasn't it. "Disease," said Narqui Ghenz, shrugging. And his expression didn't change at all.

"Eh?" Tarra's jaw fell open. "What's that you say? Disease?"

"Why, yes," Ghenz added matter-of-factly. "What else? It's something out of the jungles, which only takes the blacks. They collapse, dry up, die very quickly and without pain. When did you see it?"

"Back at our last stop," said Tarra. "In the storm? And as for that storm—did you ever see weather like *that* before? That weird green glow round Gemal's tent? Two frizzies went in there with him, just before that 'storm' broke. Gemal himself went in looking fit to die, and came out full of fight! But when we moved out of there I was last in line, and I saw the other two. They weren't fit for anything but a shallow grave."

Still Ghenz was unconvinced. "That makes eight of 'em, then," he said. "Two where we met their ships out of Shad, at the salt loch; two more on the fourth night, after we'd done our first village; another two on the seventh night, just before we picked you up; and now—"

"—They're falling faster, then?" Tarra cut him off.

"Eh?"

"This 'disease' is gaining ground, picking up speed, burning through 'em ever faster. And always taking them in pairs..."

Ghenz thought about it. "So it seems. But why concern yourself, since it's only the blacks?"

Tarra almost answered: *And what happens when Gemal runs out of blacks?*—but he thought better of it. What he did say was: "Me, I took one look at that freakish storm, that cold green fire in the heart of the twister around Gemal's tent, and I thought: magick! And when I saw those corpses, well, that sort of confirmed it."

Ghenz laughed. "Then you'd be better off speaking to the Northmen," he said. "They're the ones for the spook stories!"

Tarra partly understood the other's point of view. Ghenz was a young man, open as a book and straight off the steppes (where wizards were given short shrift, and had been ever since the days of ill-legended Loxzar of the Hrossaks) and he wouldn't have come across much in the way of the Dark Arts. Not yet, anyway. But Tarra's own far-flung adventures had bent his beliefs to the contrary—very much so. And as for that peculiar storm and the green fires accompanying it…well, Tarra had been witness to much the same sort of thing once before. And not so very long ago.

That had been in Klühn, at Gorgos' Temple of Secret·Gods, and it had heralded the very Blackest Magick imaginable! Tarra remembered it well, would never forget it: those weird energies building over Klühn, patterned like the webs of giant, lightning-spawned spiders, with strands of fire spun down like alien silk to the dome of that temple of horror. Thromb energies, they'd been, which opened gates in space and time to let in Forces from beyond the stars—or would have, if Tarra Khash and Amyr Arn hadn't cut them off at source. That source had been Gorgos, gone now back where he belonged—or what remained of him, anyway.

"Are you all right?" Ghenz had taken his arm. "Staring at the stars like that, with your eyes all vacant…"

"Was I?" said Tarra. He sniffed the air, said: "I was gauging the weather, that's all."

"Oh?" Ghenz was interested, doubtless in respect of forthcoming voyage to Shad. "Well, what's it to be? Fair or foul?"

"A bit of both, I think," said Tarra. And to himself: *changeable, at best*. Then he excused himself and headed back to the fires.

"Fancy a game, Hrossak?" called out one of three Northmen where they tossed coins in the firelight.

"Gambling's for them who can afford it," Tarra ruefully replied. "Me, I've only the jacket I wear on my back, and that's where it's going to stay. But I'll watch awhile, if it doesn't bother you." It didn't, and Tarra stood watching. In just a few more minutes one of the three pulled a wry face and turned out his pockets, signifying that for him the game was over. Never good losers, Northmen, he stooped and snatched up the square Khrissan gaming coins, bent them one at a time between thumb and fingers and tossed them down. Undaunted, the two remaining players took out new coins and began a two-sided game of pitch-and-toss all over again. One of the two would end up lucky, or unlucky depending how the other took it. Meanwhile Tarra and the sulking, hulking loser went off to sit together and stare into a fire.

"Gambling's a damned fool's game," growled the Northman in a little while. "And I'm a fool born!"

Tarra nodded his agreement. "I've lost my shirt on occasion, too," he admitted.

"Oh?" the barbarian hardly seemed interested. "And what's your poison?"

"Dice," said Tarra.

"*Hah!* Not likely!" The other was vehement. "What, dice? Too easily loaded, for my liking."

"As I discovered," said Tarra, scowling into the dying embers.

"But what the hell," said the Northman, shrugging. "All life's a gamble."

"True, very true." Tarra nodded again. "And Yibb only knows that the stakes are high enough, this time around."

"Eh?"

"This trek, I mean," said wily Hrossak. "What? And here's you and your lot—aye, and my lot, too—all sailing off to Shad with Cush Gemal, and not a lad of you knowing a single thought that's in his head. And how's that for playing with loaded dice?"

"Eh?" said the other again, frowning.

"I mean," Tarra was patient, "what if he's playing you false? D'you think you can bend him like a thin Khrissan gaming piece? Not on your life! And once you're in Shad, why, then you're at his mercy."

The Northman scowled in his beard, slitted his eyes and stared hard at Tarra, finally shook his head. "I don't follow you," he said, and Tarra could see that he really didn't. And for the first time he began to understand something of Cush Gemal's power.

"You're not worried," he said, but more slowly and carefully, "that you might end up marooned, or worse, in Shad?"

"You know," the other replied, "Gorlis Thad used to sound much the same as you; used to say much the same sort of things. Likewise Gys Ankh. Trouble-makers, both of 'em. Well, you saw what happened to the Thad, and as for Ankh—who knows? But when that bronze bastard went missing, you didn't see Cush Gemal making much of a fuss over it, did you? 'Ware, steppeman! That tongue of yours could do for you."

"Do you take his word, then," Tarra pressed, "that he'll see you safe home again once he's shipped you to Shad?"

The other thought about it, finally nodded. "Aye," he said, simply as that. "Oh, he's a queer 'un, be sure: black as squid-slop and cold as ice on the moon. And yet somehow warm, too, at times. But...I think I trust him. Indeed, I think we *all* trust him; and it seems there's a sticky end for them that don't. So if I were you I'd give it a little time, steppeman, and see how he grows on you."

"I think I know what you mean," said Tarra, slapping his knees and driving himself to his feet. "He *is* growing on me!"—*like a wart, and you know how hard they are to get rid of.*

Moving back toward his big lizard and its wagon, where already the slaves were bedded down, he almost stumbled over a heap of cooked fish, untouched, still smoking in the night. He took up an armful, some meat, too, and distributed the food to the chained unfortunates. Then he sat beside Loomar Nindiss and watched that ever-hungry lad wolf his portion. Done at last, Loomar asked him:

"Well, what have you found out?"

"Nothing much," Tarra shrugged. "Except that tomorrow you sail for Shadarabar over the Straits of Yhem. I've tried to sway this lot against it, but—" And he shrugged again.

"And you?" Loomar's eyes shone soft in moon- and starlight.

"Not me," Tarra shook his head. "Cush Gemal's warned me against it. And when someone like that utters a warning, I reckon men should heed him..."

VI

AMYR AND ULLI

Amyr Arn and Ulli Eys were Suhm-yi (indeed, they were the last members of that never numerous, especially insular race) and therefore mentalists; they had their own tongue and were natural linguists, but they were equally at home with telepathy. The latter mode required a certain familiarity; it improved with use and proximity; in the old days, it had never been used without mutual consent. It need hardly be said that in two such as Amyr and Ulli, all codes and conditions were well satisfied.

Now, travelling by the light of the stars in the Desert of Sheb—where only the wind gave voice, and then low and moaning—the Suhm-yi man and maid found themselves unwilling to break the silence, and so conversed by mind alone and sparingly.

"A light ahead," said Amyr voicelessly, "in that jut of deeper darkness there."

From the back of their single beast, where Ulli had the better view: "I had noted it, husband," she likewise replied.

"These are strange lands," he said, "and often threatening. We'd best be prepared for whatever lies in wait."

Ulli smiled down on him where he loped ahead, leading their plodding yak, and he felt her smile on the back of his neck, which gleamed something less than its customary silver under the stars. "I know you will be prepared, Amyr," she answered. "And while I am with you, I know no harm will befall. Or if it should, then that it will be a greater thing than our two hearts together, which is a size beyond my imagining."

"Ulli," he said, "I have forgotten the old ways. No, I have forsaken them. For survival. Peace was ever the way of the Suhm-yi, peace at all cost: a code of conduct I left behind in the Inner Isles when I came to seek you out. I came, found and freed you; but if I'd walked in the old ways, it were a short walk, be sure! You speak of our hearts: mine is full of you, and also full of sin. I desired and took revenge. And I have taken the lives of men. In this Primal Land, I have learned dishonourable ways, at times reverting to a primal savagery. Aye, and truth to tell, it did not disgust me..."

She smiled again, but sadly. "Husband, I was stolen from the Inner Isles as a child. I never knew the old laws, the old ways. But I've known the wiles of Gorgos, and I've read in the minds of men all of their black secrets. Oh, there *are* good men, but others are putrid in their cores; and it was my lot to discover them for my morbid master." She had stopped smiling and even shuddered a little. "Dishonour? I hardly think you know the meaning of the word, not even now. And as for evil, you are an innocent!"

"Still, there *is* evil in Theem'hdra," he insisted. "And so I must warn you: I'll not be still if we're threatened. And if it should ever come to that, I beg you look away. I'd not have you look upon me with blood on my hands."

"You forget," she said, "how I've already seen you smeared in blood of men, *and* slime of Gorgos! You and Tarra Khash both— and I was not disgusted. I felt only relief: that I was free of fear and foulness, and that a mate had come to find me when I had thought all hope fled. We've both suffered taints, Amyr, but that's behind us now. In the jewel isles we'll build anew, and temper the laws we pass down to our children with knowledge of the world outside the Crater Sea. That way they'll be ready, if men should come again defiling and destroying..."

"So be it," he said, and without looking back gave the merest nod of his comb-crested head.

Now, approaching more closely the dark silhouette lit in one window with a warm, welcoming glow, Amyr saw that the place was a castle or fortress—a manse, anyway, but large, sprawling and high-walled. Well provisioned refuge, doubtless, for whoever dwelled within; and Amyr began to feel the weight and responsibility of his and Ulli's journey pressing down on him.

Coming from Inner Isles to Klühn, he'd travelled alone and fast, unhindered and driven on by the urgency of his mission. But now he had a future, where before there'd been none; and now, too, he had Ulli to consider, and he knew that the perils of the Primal Land were many. Three-quarters of the return trek still lying ahead, much of it through badlands—and Ulli Eys more precious to Amyr than life itself, to be guarded and guided each step of the way.

For that reason he'd chosen the route which would seem least populated: out of Klühn and across the rugged Great Eastern Peaks, through the southern bulge of Sheb's Desert and over the Mountains of Lohmi, then follow the fringe of Ell's wasteland to the Great Circle Range, beyond which lay the Crater Sea and jewelled Inner Isles. Least populated, perhaps, but for what reason? And where populated, by what?

Lamias, allegedly, in Sheb, where one such was said to have her castle—perhaps that very lair which loomed ahead! Thieves and vagabonds, too, in ruined Chlangi the shunned city, some sixty or seventy miles south. And this only the beginning! The Mountains of Lohmi were home to small but fierce tribes of degenerate, barbarous mountainmen; and in the Desert of Ell, where lay a forbidden city of antique mystery, there dwelled demons and ill-natured djinn.

Aye, numberless miles and dangers ahead, and already Amyr feeling his strength waning, sapped by furnace sun and drawn from his muscles by sands that sank underfoot, making every step an effort of will. And only a quarter of the way covered, with the worst of it still to come.

The night's chill had freshened Amyr's Suhm-yi awareness; suddenly he felt his silvery skin prickling, a weird sensation of eyes watching, perhaps as a spider watches the fly fresh trapped in its web. "Ulli," he said, without speaking. And:

"I know," she likewise answered.

Between the castle and the travellers a jumble of weathered rock protruded slanting from the sands. Amyr led his beast with its precious burden into the heart of the outcrop's shadow...

In Orbiquita's castle, Teh Atht sat in his cousin's Room of Runes and gazed into her shewstone, which must surely be unique in that it was the petrified eye of a Roc! The stone had no voice, and its view was quite vertiginous—bird's-eye, no less!—but the pictures had startling clarity and depth. Ideal for Orbiquita who, in winged guise, was well acquainted with views from aerial angle; less so for Teh Atht, who'd prefer a picture scried at sea-level. Still and all, he supposed he must count himself lucky that he'd found this most secret chamber (hidden as it had been behind a pivoting slab of stone), let alone the lamia-ensorcelled orb of some sadly defunct aviasaur.

Of course, he could go out onto the tiny balcony and spy out the land from there, but it was a spooky light in the desert at night and not to be trusted; likewise the wizard's eyes weren't what they used to be. By now the Suhm-yi couple had doubtless seen Teh Atht's lantern blazing forth from the window of a room on this same floor, and he must hope they'd be attracted to it. One small lamp in habitation huge as this must signal a single habitant; and this Suhm-yi male, who'd helped slay Gorgos and bring down his temple, would hardly be the sort to turn aside or flee from one lone dweller.

Indeed, the friendly light should lure these weary travellers, and they'd find Teh Atht the perfect host when they came knocking on his door. So thought the wizard; and but for the fact that he *was* a wizard (with all the habits of that species, including scrying), so it might have worked out. But—

—Teh Atht frowned and peered closer at the shewstone, and wondered what was wrong here. Male, female and beast, all three had passed into the shadow of that fang of rock there, and by now should have reappeared on the other side. So what was holding them up? Could it be they were making camp there, with the castle a mere stone's throw away, and welcoming lantern blazing for all to see?

He drew the picture closer; which is to say, he soared down upon the crag from on high, fighting back the vertigo he felt welling inside as the scene in the stone rushed up to meet his gaze. Now he was in the shadow of the slanting rock, poised directly over the girl-creature where she sat silent and tranquil and waiting upon the back of her yak. But waiting for what? Then, scanning the shadowed area all about, Teh Atht gave an odd little twitch when he saw that Ulli Eys was quite alone!

He caused his view to retreat from her, gazed down on the desert between fang of rock and castle, saw—nothing! And where was the Suhm-yi male now? And what was he up to?

At that precise moment Amyr Arn's spatulate four-fingered hands came up one at a time over the carved parapet wall, where like a great slender gecko he clung to the vertical stonework. His crested head followed, a silver shimmer against the dark of the night, and his golden eyes took in at a glance the scene in the secret room: a candle's glow silhouetting the seated form of a rune-cloaked wizard where he hunched over his shewstone, his back to the intruder. Then, silent as a shadow, Amyr was up onto the balcony, inside the room, closing the distance between himself and his target. And in his hand a gleam of silver brighter far than the shimmer of his own un-human flesh.

"Where *is* he?" Teh Atht mutteringly demanded of Orbiquita's crystal. "Show him to me at once!"

"Why scry?" whispered Amyr from behind, in Teh Atht's very ear. "Save your eyesight, wizard. Spy on me no more from afar, but only turn your head!"

Teh Atht gave a gasp, began to do just that—and froze! Cold steel touched the soft umber leather of his throat, and a four-fingered hand of iron gripped his shoulder. "I..." He gulped, aware that death stood only a breath away. And again: "I..."

"Utter no runes, wizard," warned Amyr Arn, "no crafty spells. Ah, for your first sorcerous syllable will likewise be your last!"

The biter bit! thought Teh Atht. *And how's this for wizardry!* But out loud and hurriedly, he husked: "I know this looks bad, my young friend, but believe me I acted in all innocence. Old habits die hard, that's all, and the shewstone is merely a tool of my trade."

"Clever words won't sway me," said Amyr, "nor lies deceive. Your hourglass is tipped and the sands are running. Speak swift, 'ere they run out."

Teh Atht at once commenced to babble, each word coming fast on the heels of the last. As he spoke Amyr looked behind the words, used the mentalist art of the Suhm-yi to penetrate the wizard's mind and read what was written there. In the old times that were unthinkable, but the old mores no longer applied. He saw the wizard's quest clearly delineated—his search for immortality—and read names a-plenty in connection with that quest. Among those names were his own, his darling Ulli's, that of Tarra Khash, and—and also the name of the mercifully exanimate Gorgos!

"Hold!" said Amyr then. "What? And is that what you are? Blood of Gorgos, his sorcerous kin, corrupted by him? You know of him, for I've read it in your mind. Aye, and you know something of a certain Hrossak, too, who has been my one friend among men. Now cease your babbling and answer only my specific questions.

"First, why have you lain in wait for us here? What was your plan for us?"

"I can show you much better than tell you," said Teh Atht. He carefully stood up; and Amyr's knife slipping easily from his throat to his breast, where it poised just under his heart, so light it might not be there at all.

"Lead on," said Amyr.

They went to the room where the lantern hung on a hook under the arch of a wide balcony, sending its rays out into the still desert. Here a table was set for three, all laden with meats and fruits, water and wines, cheeses and honey. Of hopper and flitter no sign, for Teh Atht had sent them below stairs to find a place of their own.

"This was my plan for you," said the wizard with a wave of his arm. "To welcome you here in the castle of my cousin Orbiquita—herself absent, I'm happy to relate—and to satisfy your needs. Here you can eat, drink, bathe, rest your weary bodies from the rigours of the sands, and all in safety absolute. And for payment, why I'd merely follow the customs of civilized folk in this Primal Land and beg of you...a story?"

"A story?" Amyr lowered silver shutters on his eyes, until they were golden slits. "What sort of story?"

'Teh Atht shrugged innocently. "Perhaps the story of your wanderings," he said, feigning only a polite and routine interest, as required by etiquette. "Or maybe a tale of Tarra Khash the Hrossak: how you met him and became his friend, and how with his help you brought down Gorgos' Temple of Secret Gods in Klühn. Or perhaps something of his past, if you know it—for example: how and where he came by that fancy jewelled scimitar of his?"

Now Amyr's knife tickled a little where suddenly, however gently, its point pressed through the silk of the wizard's cloak and rested on his pale flesh. And now: "You're either very brave or very foolish," said Amyr, the chimes of his voice more lead than silver. "I told you Tarra Khash is my friend. And should I betray him?"

Teh Atht smiled and shook his head. "I'm neither brave nor foolish," he said. "And you are not a killer; not natural born, anyway. Oh, I know you've looked at me with your mentalist's eyes, and I know you've found no harm in me. But I've looked at you, too, through the eyes of a wizard. Your caution isn't so much for yourself as for your lady, which I can understand well enow. But betray Tarra Khash? To me? In what way? I merely seek to save his life, and thought you'd like to help me. Indeed, I *know* you will! So put away the knife."

For a moment their eyes met: the wizard's faded and almost colourless, Amyr's golden as burnished coins. Then the Suhm-yi male nodded, sheathed his knife in the scabbard at his belt, said: "But don't think you can lie to me, Teh Atht. I can read right through your words to the very thoughts that form them. There's more to this than the saving of Tarra's life. You seek immortality, and he's the key. Now tell me: what is it threatens him?"

"First your lady," said the wizard. "Bring her in from the desert. There's food here and wine; I take it you eat like ordinary men? And I need no spells to tell me how weary you are. Now let's start again, on friendlier footing—the way I planned it in the first place, however badly it were fumbled. Agreed?"

Amyr nodded again, if a trifle slowly, and called out to Ulli in his mind, *Wife, come to the castle. You'll find us waiting below. I think all's well, but be alert for danger.*

Then he followed Teh Atht downstairs to the huge hall, all tidied now and seeming more gaunt and vast than ever, where the wizard called upon hopper and flitter to show themselves. They came and were introduced. "My familiars," said Teh Atht. "Incapable of harm, however ugly. You may hear them at their work, but they'll stay out of sight so as not to alarm your lady. There, and now I have no more secrets."

Out into the courtyard they went, and the wizard opened the great outer door on Ulli where she waited. Without pause she urged her yak inside, where Amyr helped her dismount and presented her to Teh Atht. "Delighted," said the wizard, truly awed by Ulli's alien beauty. "But let's go indoors at once; the air grows chill out here, and there's all you'll need of comforts laid out within..."

They entered, climbed to the prepared room, dined well on the food Teh Atht's familiars had set out for them. And as they ate so the wizard told Amyr all he had learned of the travails of Tarra Khash. Then at last the travellers were done with eating and their host with talking, and now it was Amyr's turn. He stood up, paced a while, said:

"Teh Atht, you came here on a flying carpet. So you said."

"The very carpet where now you stand." The wizard nodded. "A little worn, but airworthy still."

Amyr paused and looked down at the carpet—a fairly unremarkable rug, uniformly fawn except in its corners where four black, oddly curving esoteric symbols were woven into the material—then continued pacing. And in a little while:

"Teh Atht, when first I...I *came upon* you," Amyr went on, attempting something of diplomacy, "you were scrying our slow progress in a crystal ball—doubtless ensuring that no harm befell us along the way. I assume that crystal to be Orbiquita's shewstone?"

"Of course, for this is her castle." Teh Atht shrugged. He looked back and forth, between Suhm-yi man and maid, then sighed. "Have I not made myself understood? Scrying is the *way* of wizards!"

Amyr nodded thoughtfully, continued pacing. "Flying carpets, shewstones—black magick! The ways of wizards.' *Hmmm!*" he mused. "And Tarra Khash, our one friend among men, captive of the slave-taker of just such a foul sorcerer, eh?"

Fearing himself ranked alongside Black Yoppaloth of the Yhemnis, now Teh Atht waxed a little indignant. "I thought I'd already made myself perfectly clear," he said. "We're not *all* cut of the same cloth!"

"Oh?" Amyr turned and stared hard at the wizard through penetrating golden eyes. "No, perhaps you're not," he finally allowed, "but whichever, I suspect you're all of a very intricate and mazy weave." He nodded again, but more sharply, decisively. "Very well, I would see Tarra's predicament for myself—in the shewstone!"

They all three went to Orbiquita's secret chamber behind the pivoting slab which was its door, and there the wizard activated the petrified Roc's eye. Knowing almost exactly where to look, it took only seconds for Teh Atht to locate his target; and then, all three heads together—the wizard's and those of his silvery, un-human guests alike—their rapt eyes saw...

...**Tarra Khash lay** sleeping under the moon and stars. He was curled in the leathery elbow of his big hauler, snoring gently into the corrugations of that hugely folded reptilian limb. His bed, while somewhat musky and subject to sudden, shuddery convulsions, was at least middling warm. Blood did course in those great veins, however sluggishly; and that was important, for this close to the Eastern Ocean the night breezes tended to blow cold. Tarra's new jacket had kept him warm for a while, but then the big lizard had scratched himself with a blunt claw, and the jacket, caught on a scale, had been snatched away. Now the Hrossak lay exposed to starlight and breezes both, silken shirt ragged on his back, shivering a little as the temperature fell. The cold might wake him up, but unlikely; today had been a hard one for all concerned, and Tarra no exception. He was weary in every limb and would probably sleep through a volcanic eruption.

Standing close by, just now returned from his solitary stroll in the dunes, Cush Gemal looked down on him and his black eyes shone in the darkness. Behind him, keeping a respectful distance, a pair of Yhemni watchmen waited on their master's command. Nor was it long in coming:

"Fetch a blanket," Gemal ordered, but quietly for all the depths of his tone. "Drape it over him—but don't waken him. He needs his sleep as much as any man. And so do I..." He turned away, but over his shoulder reminded: "Keep well your watch this night." Then he strode away toward his black tent—and paused.

He looked up, jerking his head sharply, and his black eyes grew huge. "What?" he said, almost in a whisper. And again, sharp as ice now: *"What!"*

"Master, what is it?" his blacks ran toward him, their hands fluttering in sudden alarm...

———

...**In Orbiquita's secret** chamber, Teh Atht knew only too well what "it" was. He commanded the shewstone, "Be still!" And throwing up his hands he turned his face away. At the same time he lurched against his guests, buffeting them aside. And as the picture in the shewstone dwindled and faded into mist, so he sighed long and loud. A close thing, that. Another moment and the eyes of Cush Gemal might well have seen right through the space between, out of eye of Roc and *into* those of the three who had watched! To Amyr and Ulli, by way of explanation and apology both, he said: "He sensed us!"

"What?" Amyr was astonished. "Is it possible?"

"For a great wizard, aye," Teh Atht nodded, his face chalk now in place of its usual faded umber.

"But he's only a slaver, in Black Yoppaloth's employ!" Amyr was plainly puzzled.

Teh Atht nodded slowly, gave the matter some consideration. "That he is," he finally muttered, "and under his protection, too. It becomes obvious: Yoppaloth has spelled him, given him a guardian aura. Only penetrate it—which with our combined and concentrated gazing we did—and Gemal knows it! Ah, but his master, Shad's sorcerer, is cautious to a fault! He would keep *all* of his works secret, even the business of his hirelings; and the closer we draw to the appointed hour, the more effective his protections become."

"The appointed hour?" This time it was Ulli's tinkling voice that questioned.

"The hour of his renewal, when like the phoenix he'll rise up again restored! That's what this is all about: somewhere in this mystery lies the secret of Yoppaloth's immortality..."

They went back to the room where they had dined, found the table standing empty of every last trace of their meal, and Teh Atht bade his guests be comfortable on a low, cushioned couch. Amyr declined, but paced the floor as before. "Now here's the thing," he said in a while. "I do believe you will help Tarra Khash if and when you can, and *if* he needs it, if only to appease your dreadful cousin. But as for saving his life—why, it hardly seems threatened! Indeed, this curious slaver Cush Gemal appears to have taken to him. So what is it you're really up to, Teh Atht? Is it perhaps that you've caught a whiff of Yoppaloth's immortality, and that now you fear to lose it?"

Teh Atht appeared hurt. Then: "Very shrewd," he said, unsmiling. "But why ask, when you can read it all in my mind?"

"That is not our way," said Ulli at once. "Before, Amyr read your thoughts to protect me. Now that you've proclaimed yourself a friend, he may no longer intrude. We are all private people, Teh Atht, and our minds inviolate."

Amyr frowned. Ulli had it right, of course, but on this occasion he wished that she had not.

"Madam," said the wizard, "your candour in this matter fills me with a great relief." He gravely nodded his approval. "But still I fear your husband distrusts me."

Amyr's golden eyes narrowed a little. "Is that so strange?" he said. "After all, we already know of this lusting of yours after immortality, which seems to me unnatural. It is nature's way that things are born to die; without death there can be no purpose in living; what man would grasp at each new day, if days were interminable? And yet you insist upon this immortality."

"Am I lectured?" Teh Atht cried, apparently amazed. "I am what I am, and I cannot change it, I'm a wizard, and the world full of wonders which I can never hope to grasp. Not in one short span. Can't you see? I have runes to unriddle, mysteries to plumb, all the secrets of space and time to unravel—and neither time nor space to even begin! I'm a quester—no, a *hunter*—after knowledge, Amyr Arn; but as any hunter will tell you, it's the chase that counts, not the kill! This thing is a puzzle of a thousand pieces, and one by one I track them down and fit them in until the picture is complete."

"I see," said Amyr, nodding. "So one by one you're gradually fitting together all the pieces of this great puzzle, are you? And who can say but that as I tell you my pieces, they, too, will fit in place, so that the puzzle more rapidly nears completion."

"But that's it exactly!" cried Teh Atht. "And Tarra Khash would seem to be a key piece, as you correctly deduced from just one small peep into my mind. Which is, of course—entirely in keeping with my altruistic nature, and not to mention Orbiquita's vile threats—the reason I'll keep Tarra Khash from harm. If I can."

Amyr stopped pacing, faced the wizard squarely. "And if the puzzle completes itself *before* Tarra is safe…what then? Immortality is immortality: an infinite extension of life. What weight would a lamia's threats carry then, Teh Atht, to one who cannot die? And of what value the life of a mere man to a mage immortal, eh?"

"Eh?" Teh Atht repeated him, blinking rapidly. "What are you saying?"

"Who will there be," Amyr pressed home his point, "in the hour of your triumph, to ensure you don't desert the Hrossak's cause and leave him to whichever fate awaits him?"

Teh Atht puffed himself up. "A wizard's word is his word!" he said.

"And do you give me your word? That if I tell you what I know of him, and of his sword, you'll see him master once more of his own destiny?"

"I'll do my best," said Teh Atht.

"That isn't good enough," Amyr shook his head. "On those terms I'll tell you nothing."

"But what do you expect me to do?" the other potested. "Fly in there on my carpet, physically snatch him away?"

"Why not?" Amyr stared hard at him. "Indeed, that seems to me the most direct and logical course. Then, out of gratitude, he'd probably answer all of your questions himself."

"Logic?" Teh Atht's brow took on a darker shade. "I'll have you know, Amyr Arn, that the blood of Mylakhrion himself flows in these veins—and you talk to me of logic? You've seen how this Cush Gemal is protected by Black Yoppaloth's magick. What? He even knows when he is spied upon! And yet you'd have me swoop down in broad daylight—"

"At night," Amyr corrected him.

"—swoop down anyway, and steal the Hrossak away? What is that for logic? Madness! Black Yoppaloth would work vile magicks against me, and against you, too—as he worked them upon a time on the person of Exior K'mool. Last of the Suhm-yi, are you? Let me tell you that when the Mage of Shadarabar was done with you, there'd *be* no more Suhm-yi! None at all!"

"Very well," said Amyr, "if you fear this Yoppaloth so, then show me how to fly your carpet and I'll bring Tarra out of there."

"What?" The wizard seemed aghast. "Are you mad? You, control my carpet? Impossible! Long ago I laid upon its weave irreversible runes so that it might never be stolen. It would fly you into the sun, or maroon you on the moon, or drown you in ocean deeps; aye, and then fly home to me. And even if such a plan were feasible—which it is not—still the necromancer Yoppaloth would trace the source of this…this *invasion*, back to me. No, there is honour among wizards, Amyr Arn. Codes of conduct exist for us, too, just as they do for the Suhm-yi. I may not be seen to interfere with the legitimate works of another."

Amyr nodded. "You may spy upon him—so long as he remains in ignorance of it—but you may not openly work against him." His silvery tone was scathing. "And did you say 'legitimate'?" Now he raised scaled, glinting eyebrows in caustic inquiry. "The legitimate works of another?"

"All works of wizardry may be termed legitimate," Teh Atht blurted, "except where they work against another wizard."

Amyr snorted and cried: "Enough! Your words have the shape of a maze: we might tramp for hours and get nowhere. Do what you will, but expect no help from me. We thank you for your hospitality, and now we'll be on our way." He took Ulli's hand and she stood up.

Flabbergasted, Teh Atht could say nothing. He considered various runes, then un-considered them. None of them seemed of much use here. Curious Concretion wouldn't solve the problem but only stiffen Amyr's tongue to stone; his brain, too, so that its secrets could not be stolen. Hypnotism? What? Against a quicksilver mind like this? And as for any sort of threatening move in the female's direction…

"Wait!" Ulli Eys held up her tapering, delicately spatulate hands. And to Amyr: "Husband, if you refuse Teh Atht your assistance, then it seems to me that Tarra Khash likewise goes without. Is there no middle road?"

Amyr looked at Teh Atht; the wizard in turn gazed at him; Ulli looked from one to the other and back. And after a while Amyr nodded his crested head. "Fly us to Inner Isles—now, tonight—and on the way I'll tell you all I know of Tarra Khash and his jewelled scimitar, which be sure amounts to a great deal."

"Done!" cried Teh Atht at once. "But, why didn't you say so before? Why, that were the simplest of all solutions! Safety for yourself and the lady, and missing pieces of puzzle for me: who can say fairer than that?"

"Hold!" said Amyr. "Hear me out, for I'm not finished. Then, when my wife is safe, fly me to the Eastern Ocean's strand, there to wait on Tarra's arrival with the slaver caravan."

"But—" Teh Atht began to protest, for he knew there was scarcely time for all of this flying in a single night, and that in any case it went against his plans. But then he saw the stubborn set of Suhm-yi jaw, the glint that brooked no denial in alien, golden eyes. And he shrugged. "Very well," he said, "but at ocean's rim, there I leave you to your own devices."

"Good enough," Amyr replied. "And if worst comes to worst, be certain your name shall not be mentioned."

"So be it," said Teh Atht. "And likewise, if I can later be of assistance…"

As for Ulli: she cried a little inside, but her husband was Suhm-yi and his was a debt of honour. He owed Tarra Khash, and this would be payment in full.

Then, without more ado, the white wizard of Klühn ushered his passengers aboard the carpet and bade them sit together toward the rear, and he took up a position in front and crossed his arms on his chest. He uttered a rune and the burdened carpet rose up, indented a little where they sat; and windows crashed open at the levitator's approach; and out into the night they drifted, their destination the dreaming jewel isles of the Suhm-yi…

Away across deserts and plains and peaks, almost as far east as south, Tarra Khash lay snug in the crook of a saurian elbow, with a blanket draped over him to keep out the chill. Overhead, the stars turned slowly in their titan wheel, Gleeth the moon god waxed a little more full, and clouds were haloed silver where they drifted inland from the sea. At least, most of the clouds were silver.

But one of them was black and seemed to pulse and throb like some strange angry squid! Aye, and it had positioned itself in the sky so as to shut out the moon's gleamy glare from Cush Gemal's tent. Loomar Nindiss, unable to sleep for thoughts of his sister lying chained in the hull of the boat on the platform of the lead wagon, had watched this strange black cloud swell and pulsate as it sped in from the east—and he'd also seen it slow down until it stood on high, stationary over Gemal's tent.

Then, only moments ago, the chief of the slavers had thrust aside the flap at tent's door, stuck out his lacquered topknot and ebony head and beckoned to his black night watch where that pair prowled the outer perimeter. They had flown to him at once, their robes turning them to fluttering rags of movement in moon and starlight; but as they'd approached Gemal more closely, so they had slowed until they barely crept forward. At the last, edging fearfully into the shade of the tent, then they had seemed simply to disappear, jerked inside and out of sight.

After that...

...The black cloud turned green at its rim, sent down emerald coruscations like curtains of shimmering rain to engulf Gemal's travelling pavilion. Then a wind sprang up, at first low and moaning, which gathered up sand-devils and sent them nodding and cavorting, to and fro in the central space. Grit was blown in Loomar's eyes and he blinked them, and after dabbing away cleansing tears looked again. Ghost-fires danced in the scalloped eaves of Gemal's tent, which glowed green in its heart like some poisonous gem on night's dark cushion.

Then on high, having seemingly emptied itself of morbid energies, the black cloud shrank and quit its peculiar pulsing, turned more nearly yellow and drifted off westward with its commoner cousins. The witch-lights about Gemal's tent paled to eerie lambencies that finally flickered out; the fretful wind fell to a bluster, then to a gentler, steady breeze. And the night was back to normal.

Normal?

Two less frizzies to worry about, come morning, thought Loomar. *Little wonder Gemal brought so many of them with him! And if that's the lot of Gemal's own people, what of us slaves? And in particular, what's in store for Jezza?*

It was thoughts such as these which denied him his rest...

VII
TEH ATHT'S...TREACHERY?—
ORBIQUITA'S DEFIANCE

E ncased in his invisible Climatic Capsule, Teh Atht's gravity-
defying carpet sped high over the foothills of the Mountains
of Lohmi; spied below, there flickered the fires of certain fierce
tribesmen who'd inhabited that range since times immemorial. The
carpet's master paid the guttering campfires scant heed, however,
for Amyr Arn had commenced his story, which held far more
of fascination.

"And so this gang of cut-throat barbarians were come into the
Crater Sea," Amyr continued, "and landed their raft on the beach of
the tiny jewel island which Lula and I had made our home.

"Lula was alone when they found her...to this day I cannot speak
of what they did. Northern barbarians are...*barbaric*! At that time
we had considered ourselves last of the Suhm-yi; after the Northmen
were done, I *was* the last. It was not until later that I learned of the
cruel fate of Ulli Eys, and set off to rescue her from Gorgos.

"Anyway, then there was Tarra Khash the Hrossak. He pursued
this evil gang for his own reasons. And when he found my Lula, dead,

he was…kind to her. He couldn't know that I watched—or how close he came to death!

"For a while I was insane, but what was done was done. Eventually Suhm-yi teaching and training took over; my anger subsided and I reverted to type; I could no more pursue and punish the evildoers than blaspheme against my gods. Indeed, to take revenge would *be* to blaspheme against those gods! So I had been instructed. But Tarra Khash was not Suhm-yi, and against him, too, had these barbarians wronged greatly. He pursued them across the Crater Sea, while I remained behind and prayed for him. In those days, you see, I had standards and a code to live up to. Ah, but I have learned much since then.

"At that time, however, I could only pray. Old Gleeth, so-called 'blind' god of the moon, answered those prayers of mine. He took his time about it, as gods are wont to do, but indeed he answered them. By then, Tarra had killed five out of six bullies in a fair fight; but the last, Kon Athar, the massive leader of that band, had broken the Hrossak's scimitar with his great broadsword. Tarra was in trouble. Wounded, trapped on a beach, he could fight no more. Only magick could save him. But where magick is concerned, old Gleeth is a powerful god indeed!

"I was far, far away from Tarra, upon the Rock of Na-dom where it rises lonely from the sea. Na-dom is a holy place, the *only* place where Suhm-yi priests might ever commune with the gods. But Gleeth sees far, gazing down 'blindly' upon the whole world, on all of Theem'hdra. He hearkened to me and saw me there upon the rock of Na-dom; ah, but at the same time he saw the sore plight of Tarra Khash.

"'Take up your bow,' he commanded me, 'and shoot an arrow into my eye.' Madness? Perhaps. But I did as Gleeth commanded. And the eye of the moon-god blinked, swallowing up my arrow. Later I was to learn that Tarra saw that same blink of the moon's eye, which for him was salvation!

"For now Gleeth spat out the arrow, which bedded itself in Kon Athar's back even in that instant when he would deliver his final killing blow. And of course, that blow never fell. The barbarian was dead, and Tarra saved…"

"And so you became friends," Teh Atht spoke up without looking back, "and eventually the Hrossak told you the secret of his sword?"

"Secret? Has it a secret, then?" Amyr answered, devious as the wizard himself. "I don't know about that; only that it has a history, which were almost but not quite forgotten. If forgotten things are secrets, then perhaps you are correct. In any case, Tarra could not tell me anything for he did not know. His curved sword had come into his hands almost by accident. Or maybe not. The ways of the gods are strange and mazy. I shall get to the scimitar's 'secret,' never fear, but first let me tell you more of Tarra Khash.

"From the night of my prayers to Gleeth, the shooting of my arrow into his blinking eye, and the subsequent death of Kon Athar, I saw Tarra no more until that recent time in Klühn. Between times I had learned that I was not last of the Suhm-yi, but that Ulli Eys was captive of Gorgos in his Temple of Secret Gods. I was the last *male*, and Ulli the last female, of our people. I vowed to bring her back to Inner Isles or die in the attempt. For without her, what use to live? And so I journeyed to Klühn.

"In so-called 'sophisticate city,' there I found the Hrossak falsely accused and sentenced to death on some trumped-up charge of temple priests. I freed him, which was not difficult, but for which he considered himself in my debt. Once you have won Tarra's friendship, then it's yours for life—or for death, as the case might well have been! But prior to freeing Tarra, I had taken the trouble to learn a lot more of this Gorgos: that were necessary, if I was to enter his temple and steal Suhm-yi maid away from him.

"What I had learned was this:

"That Gorgos was in league with the blackest, most monstrous Forces of Evil, and that he would open gates out beyond the nethermost spheres to let in—"

"The Thromb!" Teh Atht finished it for him, nodding. "Yes, that much I've already learned. And yet even so—even knowing that he stood against the very gates of hell itself—still he entered with you into Gorgos' temple?"

"Who, Tarra?" Amyr's silvery voice was grave. "Aye, be sure he did. What's more, it were no longer sufficient simply to rescue Ulli, but now we must also destroy Gorgos, destroy him utterly!"

"And you succeeded," Teh Atht breathed. "Flesh and blood against...against *that*! And still you succeeded..." And then, turning his head just a little: "But surely that must have been the point where his jewelled sword entered the story, eh?"

Amyr nodded. "Aye, and now I shall tell you about that sword— for that was the other reason Tarra must enter Gorgos' temple. The priests of that place had taken his shattered stump of a sword and made it whole again. That was the reason he'd been falsely accused in the first place: so that they might steal his sword, which one of them had recognized! Ah, but pity the man, or creature, who'd steal from Tarra Khash!"

"Recognized it, you say?" Now Teh Atht turned his head fully to look back at Amyr where he sat upon the carpet, one arm holding safe his Ulli.

"Indeed," Amyr nodded. "Even as you yourself would seem to have recognized it…" And he watched Teh Atht's reaction.

The wizard frowned. "Have I?" he said. "I think not. Oh, faint memories stir, but—" Then his eyes went wide, and suddenly he snapped his fingers. "Here I sit in conversation with a man of the Inner Isles, of the very Suhm-yi, and my mind so mazed in the puzzle that I can't see the twists for the turns! A sword, aye! A great curved scimitar, with jewelled hilt, ceremonial until the day a certain Hrossak gave it life by taking it in his calloused hand! Ah, but what *sort* of cer- emonies had it known before that, eh? Strange ceremonies indeed! And did not the Suhm-yi in their heyday boast the finest white— or silver—wizards of all? That they did. I've read of it in runebooks older than my ancestor Mylakhrion himself!" He slapped his thigh. "A sword, aye! Why, *it's one of the three Suhm-yi Swords of Power!*"

"And there you have it," Amyr Arn slowly nodded.

"What?" Teh Atht half-turned his body, the better to see who he was talking to, and the carpet at once began to fly in a vast circle. Its flight-path was controlled by the directional attitude of its master. "But I disagree, for there I *don't* have it! I know that the Hrossak's sword is one of the three legended Suhm-yi Swords of Power, but not how it was lost from Inner Isles, or how it came into his posses- sion. I know that it's now the property of one Cush Gemal, slaver in the employ of Black Yoppaloth, but not how—" He sat himself bolt upright and his jaw fell open.

"Not how?" Amyr prompted him.

"Not how it will benefit Black Yoppaloth!" Teh Atht blurted out. "What? That mighty necromancer of jungled Shadarabar? Why, he'll know the sword in a trice, the moment he claps eyes on it! And with its mystical, magickal properties, it will make him master of all Theem'hdra!"

"Good!" said Amyr vigorously.

"Good? But then you *are* mad!" Teh Atht cried. "How, good?"

"Because now you have a real reason to see Tarra set free," Amyr answered, smiling. "One thing for Black Yoppaloth to be immortal, but another entirely that he's also omnipotent! And what of all you lesser wizards then, eh? Would he even tolerate your petty squabbles and runecastings? I doubt it."

There was no answer to that, and so Teh Atht simply groaned and said, in lowered tone: "Come, tell me the rest of it, for the more I know the more clearly I might see how to deal with this problem. *If I can deal with it at all!*"

And in a little while, when the carpet flew straight once more and passed over the yellow fringe of the Desert of Ell, so Amyr continued:

"It was Gorgos stole the swords, at the same time as he stole away the maiden Ulli Eys. She would guarantee his escape, for no Suhm-yi would interfere while there was slightest danger to Ulli. Later, he used her as a mentalist, to steal the secrets of his rivals and opponents. And all against her will, she was his 'oracle' in the Temple of Secret Gods. He stole all three swords from the place of treasures on Na-dom.

"But the priests of my people cursed him: that so long as a single member of our race survived in the jewel isles of the Crater Sea, he would know no peace. His truest servants would sicken and die, his most treasured possessions would be lost or stolen. It was a very powerful curse, of course, and the first things he lost were the Swords of Power. For years he searched for them, to make them his again, but to no avail; and always the Suhm-yi curse worked against him. In the end he must have divined that he was cursed, and then it would have been a simple matter to discover the source of his torment. His answer was...devastation! He sent a poisoned cloud from volcano's vent to choke all Suhm-yi to death! All were killed, except myself and my young wife. Following which...but the rest of it you know."

"But Gorgos' troubles weren't over yet." Teh Atht nodded. "For you were left alive. Aye, and Suhm-yi curse fully realized in the end. Now tell me: what of the swords, after he had lost them?"

"When Gorgos had made himself something of a force to be reckoned with in Theem'hdra," Amyr answered, "then he sent out false priests into the land. They, too, searched for the swords. One of them was eventually found in the gut of a whale, harpooned by a whaler out of Khrissa. Gorgos acquired it for a song. A princeling of Klühn bought the second sword in auction to hang on the wall of his apartments. Later, when Gorgos was established there in his temple, the princeling disappeared without trace. Likewise his gem-studded scimitar.

"As for the third sword, that had fallen into the hands of a very fat, very offensive jeweller in Thinhla. His name was Nud Annoxin, and he dealt with Tarra Khash very badly indeed. Alas for him, he likewise sinned against Ahorra Izz—"

"Another of the steppeman's weird friends!" said Teh Atht.

"—Arachnid lord of scarlet scorpions," Amyr went on. "Tarra would have killed Nud Annoxin for what he did to him, but scorpion-god got there first. And so Nud's ceremonial scimitar became the sword of the Hrossak."

"All fits," said Teh Atht, "except for one oddly shaped piece. What use to Gorgos a broken sword?"

"None at all," replied Amyr, "not until he had it repaired! Then: it was very nearly a perfect job, but not quite. There was a certain slight imbalance. That was how Tarra knew which of the three swords was his, enabling him to snatch it back again. Which was what in the end put paid to Gorgos' evil schemes—and to Gorgos himself."

After a while the wizard asked: "How does the sword aid Tarra Khash?"

"That I've seen, not at all." Amyr shrugged. "He's no wizard, like you, Teh Atht. But he *is* a wizard swordsman! A fighter born, the Hrossak. He's probably better with it than any other man—but using it as a sword, not as a wand."

"*Hmm!*" said the other, and there followed a long silence.

Now they were flying over the Black Isle, that enigmatic rock to the east of the Crater Sea proper, then skimming the peaks of the Great Circle Range, and moments later dropping down over the moon-mirroring Crater Sea. Ahead, the scattered jewel isles of the Suhm-yi.

"Observe," said Teh Atht. "We climbed to a considerable height in order to clear the mountains back there. This was not without effort both on my part and the carpet's. Now, however, we can soar! Journey to Inner Isles is close to an end."

He leaned forward and the carpet likewise tilted. Now it seemed to poise in mid-air, then dipped forward and gathered speed, and in a great sweeping glide went whistling down to level out just above the still waters of the Crater Sea. Islands reared their low hills and night-dark foliage on every hand.

"Which will you make your home?" the wizard inquired.

"Any will do," Amyr answered. "I'll build a boat and we can decide later. But for now, one of the smaller islands, I think. Like that one there." And he pointed.

Teh Atht flew the carpet close to the shore of the indicated islet. "Well, here's hoping all goes well with you," he said. "And who knows, we may even meet again."

"Now hold!" cried Amyr, warning chimes sounding in his head. "The deal was we'd put down Ulli safe and sound, then that you'd fly me—"

But Teh Atht wasn't listening.

He clung fast to the carpet's fringe, uttered a breathless rune of Instant Inversion. All within the Climatic Capsule was immediately upended—with the exception of gravity itself! Amyr and Ulli fell like stones—all of six or seven feet into tranquil, temperate waters. And overhead, repeating his rune and correcting carpet's orientation, Teh Atht squinted anxiously down to ensure his passengers had come to no harm. Like all island peoples, the pair could swim like fishes, and the wizard saw that already they stood upright in the shallows watching him.

"And how's *this* for a wizard's word?!" Amyr choked back his fury.

Teh Atht hovered out of reach, sadly shook his head.

"Do you think I enjoy this?" he said. "It isn't for me but for you! Last of the Suhm-yi, Amyr Arn, you and your Ulli both. An entire race of beings in your bodies, but no use one without the other. Fearless you are—but where a certain Hrossak's concerned, foolish too. Oh, I know well enow how you'd rush off to his rescue, and perhaps to your death—but what of Ulli then?"

"All of that is our concern!" Amyr cried.

"No," Teh Atht denied. "It's mine. And I'll not see myself damned to all eternity for what might well amount to genocide! So you stay here in your jewel isles, and I'll do what I can for Tarra Khash."

"Cheat!" Amyr shook a clenched fist. "Be sure your treachery will find you out. You'll do what you can for Tarra? Am I supposed to believe that? You're in this for yourself!"

Teh Atht gazed gravely down, finally nodded his agreement. "True enough," he said, "and useless to deny it. Certainly I've my own interests to look after; aye, and it's a sad fact that you'd likely get in my way. Which can't be allowed. But always remember this, Amyr Arn: I'm a white wizard, not a black magician—and there's a big difference, my friend..." With which, and without further ado, he bade his carpet rise up and bear him home.

...Home to Klühn.

Returning along almost the same aerial route, though naturally in the opposite direction, Teh Atht reflected on all he'd learned.

He now felt that he knew Tarra Khash personally; certainly he believed he recognized the Hrossak's persuasive power over people—not to mention creatures and even deities! Time alone would tell if he was right. But if he was...well, there was a certain magick in it, albeit of a sort beyond the range of "mundane" magicians. As for the steppeman's sword: that, too, was *very* special! Veritably a Sword of Power. One thing for sure: it must not be allowed to fall into Black Yoppaloth's hands in Shad.

Which in turn meant Teh Atht would likely have his work cut out for him. For how to stop Cush Gemal taking the sword with him across the Straits of Yhem?

With matters such as these to distract him, the wonder is that Teh Atht spied, far below, emerging from a pass on the Klühn side of the Great Eastern Range, a pair of creatures whose freakish forms he knew at once. They were keeping up a fair pace (considering the ground they'd covered, which had taken them more than halfway home) but both were wearying now, and their flits and hops were less vigorous. Teh Atht swooped down, called them aboard the carpet.

For once they were glad to see him. Flitter clung with his claws to the tail end of the carpet, folding his wings back like a dart and gliding, while hopper simply flopped down centrally, causing something of a sag. And shortly thereafter all three of them were back in Teh Atht's apartments overlooking the Bay of Klühn.

Worn out, the wizard's familiars went to their private places and at once fell asleep; Teh Atht saw the sense in that, snatched a ten-second "night" in a state of Rapid Repose. After that, with dawn showing faintly pink on the eastern horizon, it was time for breakfast. Following which...business as usual.

Time now to discover what the shewstone had recorded, and to see how things stood at present. Ah, but all very softly-softly! In no wise a clever thing to scry on Cush Gemal too intently, or for too prolonged a period. No, in no wise wise at all...

Tarra came awake with the strange, nagging sensation of being scrutinized both from afar and close at hand. There was a pink flush on the eastern horizon; smallest stars were fast fading; a hooded figure, furtive however familiar, leaned over him.

Someone leaning over him?

The Hrossak whipped his blanket aside and continued the motion to snatch for hilt of scimitar—where it no longer protruded above his shoulder! A hand hard as old leather clamped itself to his face and mouth, and well known voice hissed in his ear: "Be still! It's me, Stumpy!"

Tarra relaxed in the lizard's elbow and Stumpy withdrew his hand. But in another moment: "Stumpy Adz?" Tarra hoarsely whispered. "What the hell—!"

"*Shh!*" Stumpy cautioned, desperately squinting all about.

"Shh?" said Tarra. "Are you totally daft? If they catch you, they'll have your ribs for tent pegs!" He sat up, gazed all about in the deceptive false-dawn light. "How'd you get past the watch?"

"What watch?" Stumpy answered with a question of his own. "Nothing stirs round here, believe me. Now let's cut the blather and get out of here!"

Tarra slid down from his honker's elbow, but carefully, so as not to disturb the slumbering giant. "Where's your—" he checked himself, "—no, *my* camel?"

"Behind the dune over there," Stumpy was fairly dancing with anxiety. "Come on, man, let's scarper!"

Tarra shook his head, hung back, tried to get his brain going. He should hurry along with Stumpy, of course; the camel was a good big 'un and could easily carry two; and the slavers, so close to the end of their murderous trip, weren't much likely to come in pursuit. This was Tarra's big chance, probably the only chance he'd get.

But—

"Listen," he said. "Here's what I want you to do."

"What?" Stumpy couldn't believe his ears. What did the great ox think he was doing, wasting time like this? *"What?"* he said again, hopping to and fro between one foot and the other. "What I want *you* to do is come with me, now, before the camp wakes up and—"

Tarra's turn to stifle. He grabbed Stumpy's neck in one hand, clapped the other over his mouth, shook him like a rag doll. "Listen, old friend, and listen good," he grated from between clenched teeth. "I knew it was you following us, and I hoped and prayed they wouldn't get you. Well, wily old devil, they didn't. And I appreciate you coming for me like this, which is something no man in his right mind would have tried. But...but I *can't* come with you!"

Stumpy's one good eye popped wide open. Tarra waited until his wriggling subsided, released him. "Why not?" Stumpy breathlessly demanded then. "Why damn it to hell *not*!?"

"Because—" (Tarra wasn't quite sure himself) "—because there's a young lad here who needs a friend. Aye, and his sister, too. Innocents, both of 'em, Stumpy. Also, the frizzy boss has my sword, and I'm not going anywhere without it. And finally..."

Stumpy's shoulders slumped. "Finally, you've never been to Shad before, eh?" he said.

Still gritting his teeth, on impulse, Tarra hugged him, released him, said: "Now you get back across that dune, aboard that camel, and ride the hell for Hrossa! Tell 'em right across the steppes all you know—especially that there's Hrossaks been taken into slavery by Shad, which is a lie, I know, but tell 'em anyway—and ask to be taken down into Grypha. Tell the Gryphans, too, and then board a ship for Klühn. Before you know it, all this corner of Theem'hdra will be up in arms against Shad and Shadarabar. *That's* the best thing you can do! Maybe we'll meet again if I come out of this in one piece, and if I don't—"

"*You there!*" came shout in throaty Yhemni tones. A frizzy stood centrally in the circle, close to where last night's fires had burned. He'd bedded down there with several others, who now were stirring and tossing aside their blankets. "What do?" His jaw had fallen open.

"Run!" Tarra hissed.

Stumpy ran.

The black slaver came stumbling, tripped on a companion and went to his knees. When he came erect again, Tarra saw he'd picked up a crossbow. Other Yhemnis were climbing to their feet; slaves groaned and stirred under their wagons; a big lizard grumbled and honked disdainfully.

Tarra took a deep breath, held it, stared after Stumpy. The old lad was halfway up a steep dune, wallowing like a stranded whale. The black with the crossbow came running, skidded to a halt beside Tarra. He stared hard at him, then lifted his weapon and aimed it at Stumpy's back where his scarecrow figure was limned against the dawn at the crest of the dune. Tarra stood with his back to his lizard where it had just this moment started awake. Its great eyes rolled to gaze at the black leaning across its foreleg, aiming his weapon.

Tarra slid two fingers under a limp scale, nipped the tender follicle there. Old Scaly reared up, sent the Yhemni marksman flying. His bolt zipped skyward, going nowhere in particular. The black got up. "Stupid…*lizard!*" he spat, aiming a kick at the great beast. Tarra got between, shoved him onto his rump again.

"None of that!" he growled. "What? Injure this valuable beast? Land one kick on that scaly hide and I'll have him bite you in halves!"

Stumpy was almost forgotten; the thudding of a hard-ridden camel's hooves came faintly from far away, fading; the furious black got up and yanked out his knife, and for a moment Tarra thought the man would go for him. Then:

"What's all this?" Cush Gemal came jerkily striding, reminding Tarra of nothing so much as a spindly, two-legged black spider. "What's it mean?" Gemal demanded.

The raging black controlled himself, put away his knife, backed off. Tarra turned to the slaver chief. "We had a visitor," he said. "Some wasteland scavenger, a lone thief. I woke up, saw him sniffing about, crept up on him. Then this idiot," he jerked his thumb at the cowering black, "came shouting and shooting, scared him off! It was probably the one who's been trailing us. No harm done, though, that I can see."

Gemal flared his nostrils, narrowed his eyes at the thoroughly cowed Yhemni. He stepped closer, appraised the Hrossak keenly through eyes gleamy as wet pebbles. Tarra gazed back, apparently undismayed. Gemal couldn't know how he held his breath. Then the caravan's master turned to a pair of Northmen where they'd mounted-up on ponies. "Get after him!" he cried. "Catch him and kill him, whoever he is if you can. And if you can't...then meet us at the ocean loch."

As they goaded their mounts to a gallop he turned back to Tarra, and in softer tone: "Was it the way you reported it, Hrossak?"

Tarra shrugged. "Why don't you question your night watch?" he said. "They'd be the ones with the answers. And if they haven't any, then I'd want to know what they've been doing all night!"

Gemal's gaze was so penetrating, Tarra believed he might be looking right into his soul. But then those eyes blinked and the scowl lifted from the slaver's face. Finally, raising his voice, Gemal addressed the entire camp:

"Make ready at once!" he shouted. "I'll brook no more delay. We ate well last night; this morning we breakfast at ocean's rim, before making sail. And now make haste, for the sun's almost up."

With that it seemed the incident was over, and Tarra could start breathing normally again. Watching Gemal stride away in the direction of his tent, he heard—"Pst! *Pst!*" He looked, saw Loomar Nindiss' eyes staring at him from the shadows under the wagon.

"What is it?" Tarra whispered, pretending to check various chains and fastenings on the great shafts.

"That was no raider," Loomar whispered back. "You knew him." It was no way an accusation, just a statement of fact.

"Keep your voice down, lad," Tarra told him. And in another moment: "So I knew him. So what?"

"You could have run off."

"Should have," Tarra answered. "Were you the only one awake?"

"I think so. I've been awake most of the night. But listen: Cush Gemal won't be talking to the night watch, as you suggested."

"Oh?"

"No, for last night there came a black cloud that let down green fires round Gemal's tent. And I saw him call the night watch inside with him. They didn't come out again."

Tarra thought about it, offered a slight nod of his head, said, "Thanks for the information. But Loomar, let's try to be more discreet in future, eh? There are people here—and one in particular—who'd consider that you see, hear, speak and think entirely too much! You'd lose your eyes, ears, tongue, and very likely several other bits if they overheard what you just said. Aye, and so would I!"

Following which he strode away, and went to see to Old Scaly...

All of which, in his apartments in Klühn, Teh Atht the white wizard saw and heard. What he did *not* see was this:

In the lava lair of lamia Sisterhood, the Council of Five sat in extraordinary session, of which fearsome gathering Orbiquita herself was the youngest and most junior member. Unthinkable that a lamia serving out her five-year term as Mistress of the Cavern should convene such a meeting in the first place, but Orbiquita had done just that, which was what made it extraordinary.

But Chairmistress she was not; no, for that honour went to Iniquiss, oldest and by far wisest of all that monstrous brood. The other three were Hissiliss, Suquester and Scuth. Having heard Orbiquita out, now Iniquiss barked:

"*What?* And have you called us down here from our various pleasures and pursuits to listen to drivel such as this? Methinks it's simply a scheme to cut short your irksome but well-earned detention here!"

Orbiquita, entirely unmindful of Iniquiss' magnitude, snapped, "Not the case! You know well enow that in that event—and if my deception were discovered—then that my term would be doubled. I know it, too, and I'm no such fool. No, the case I have made is reliable in every instance, and my plea stands: that I be allowed a period of time in which to pattern certain events in the outer world of men. That is all."

"All? That is all?" Hissiliss hissed, belching her astonishment in brimstone gusts. "But isn't this the same Orbiquita who already took time off to go canoodling with a man—an entirely *human* man, that is?"

"Juicy news travels fast," Orbiquita growled, venting steam. "Aye, one and the same, snakeface. There *is* only one Orbiquita! But no canoodling, I promise you. I owed him a debt and repaid it."

"But you *would* canoodle," Hissiliss sulphurously insisted, "if 'twere possible?"

Orbiquita made no comment, and: *"Hah!"* Hissiliss snorted.

"Is your current request centered in this same...man?" Iniquiss wrinkled her plated snout.

Orbiquita offered up a snort of her own. "How can you gnaw on their bones," she said, "and yet talk about them as if they were unclean? Men *sired* us! Some of us, anyway. Yibb-only-knows what sired you four..."

"Insults will get you nowhere!" Suquester and Scuth, who were true sisters, shouted together.

"I'm the one insulted!" Orbiquita gave back. "Are my rank and position in the Sisterhood entirely ignored? Am I not a member of the Council of Five?"

"A member currently undergoing corrective punishment," Iniquiss reminded. "Won't this...this *business* keep until your term is served?"

Orbiquita shook her head vehemently and sent lava crusts flying all about. "No, it won't. By then Tarra'll likely be dead, and—"

"Tarra! Tarra!" Suquester and Scuth chorussed.

"—and you four will be to blame," Orbiquita finished.

"To blame?" Hissiliss had a habit of repeating statements for emphasis. "For the death of a man? Orbiquita, I've been the death of countless men, we all have, and never before suffered 'blame'! Would you have us eat stones?"

"This man's a wizard, right?" Iniquiss did her best to understand. "He's put an unbreakable spell on you, for his own lustful or thaumaturgical purposes. Well, if that's the case, perhaps we can—"

"It's not the case," Orbiquita groaned, finally lowering her head. "Would that's all it were. But no, it's worse than that. Far worse..."

For long moments the four lamias where they floated on lesser crusts around Orbiquita's central island were awed, horrified, silent until Iniquiss inquired: "Do you...love him?"

Orbiquita could only nod, while steaming tears rolled down her warty cheeks. The four were stunned, but not for long.

"That settles it!" said Suquester and Scuth as one. "His life's in danger, is it? Good! Let him die." Hissiliss nodded her agreement, to which Iniquiss added:

"That were surely for the best, Orbiquita. You're poisoned, sister, plain to see. Or at least, the human female within you is poisoned. And this slow poison called love—love of and for a man—is the deadliest lamia poison of all! I've seen others taken by it in my time, and every one a hopeless case. But if this Tarra were dead—"

"Do you threaten him?" Orbiquita looked up, red-eyed, flexed her claws until they sank into and scarred deep her lava island. "Do you *dare* threaten him?" She looked as if she'd fly in their faces.

"No," said Iniquiss, "we do not. Neither do we offer him our assistance—nor yours! Your request is denied." She turned to the other three. "Sisters, we go."

The four spread their leathery wings, prepared for departure. But:

"Wait," said Orbiquita, and her doomful tone froze them fast. "There remains only one way in which this problem might find resolution."

"The 'problem,' as you call it, is already resolved, Orbiquita," said Iniquiss after a while. "In this matter we cannot be swayed. Only be thankful that for all your transgressions, still we allow you to keep your seat on this council! In this way your shame—which is ours—goes no further. What? And should we bring the entire Sisterhood into disrepute?"

"I would bring the Sisterhood to the very doors of *destruction*—" Orbiquita glowered...then trembled in her every fibre, "—to prevent harm coming to my Tarra!"

"Shamelessly ensorcelled!" cried Hissiliss.

"Maddened by a man!" sputtered Suquester and Scuth together. "Disgusting!"

"There is a way," Orbiquita insisted. "You know my meaning. Do you drive me to it?"

Iniquiss, for all that she was old and wise and felt something of pity for Orbiquita, gave a snort of derision. "What?" she said. "Renounce the Sisterhood, and trade five thousand years and more for the short span of a fragile human female? And what is that for a threat, sister? Why, you'd no more renounce the Sisterhood than—"

"Here and now," Orbiquita cut her off, her voice more doomful yet, "I renounce the Sisterhood!"

The four were shocked almost rigid. "Think what you're doing!" Iniquiss howled then. "You may say it only one more time with impunity, and if you utter those words a *third* time—"

"I renounce the Sisterhood!" Orbiquita shrank down into herself, shuddering in every limb as she calculated the consequences of what must be done.

For a moment, aghast, the four drew back; then Hissiliss cried: "She's bluffing! Only four foolish sisters in all lamia history have ever—"

"Damn you all!" Orbiquita whispered. "Only *look* at yourselves! You are loathsome; *I* am loathsome; five thousand years of this is no future. I have found a man like no other man. You shall not keep me from him. So hear me now, when one last time I say—"

"No!" they all cried out together. But too late.

Orbiquita drew herself up in all her horror, threw wide her wings and cried, quite irrevocably: *"I renounce the Sisterhood!"*

Following which, there was nothing anyone could do about it…

VIII
SHIPS OF SORCERY

The salt sea! Oh, this was only a loch, green where it met the shoreline and brackish, a long scummy finger of water pointing inland from the vast "hand" of the true ocean, but it was salty and tidal. Coming down from yellow dunes onto a shore whose salt-crystal pools sparkled white under a blazing sun, the "caravaneer" Cush Gemal saw it lying there and shielded his jet-black eyes against its incredible blaze of blue water, stretching eastwards away and away. And he led his wagons right down to water's rim.

The wagons were lined up where the beach sloped seaward, and stones were put under their wheels to keep them from rolling. Then the big steppes-lizards were unhitched, canvasses thrown back, tailboards let down. And now the five Yhemni boats stood at last all in open view, cradled on their shallow-draft wagons where the great wheels came three-quarters up their strakes. The slavers fed themselves and then the slaves, and the latter were loosened from the respective wagons but kept in batches, chained together. And now it was time for the launching of the first boat.

This was no big deal, indeed its mechanics were rudimentary. The stones were yanked away from the lead wagon's wheels and a gang of trotting, then galloping Yhemnis guided the shafts into the shallows, wagon rumbling along behind, until only wheels stuck up and flat-bottomed boat drifted free. Then an anchor tossed overboard and the boat lying waiting, with its former vehicle now forming a platform 'twixt sand and sea.

Five times this happened, and Tarra Khash watching all: seeing slaves driven aboard the boats and chained to their oars, masts hauled into position and sails readied, four big honkers herded protesting and with no small degree of Hrossak skill aboard their boats. Now the craft they'd hauled would carry them, right across the sea to Shad. Four of the five, anyway.

The fifth boat in the water, which had been aboard Tarra's wagon, was Cush Gemal's; now he came striding in his spindly way, with a handful of blacks behind him leading bevy of stolen virgins. "Well, Hrossak," said Gemal to Tarra where he stood patting the stumpy foreleg of Old Scaly, "and now it's farewell. A pity I couldn't have known you better, but perhaps for the best in the long run. Here, this is yours. It will more than repay anything I've taken from you." He thrust a leather pouch into Tarra's hand, stood waiting while the steppeman checked its contents.

Tarra weighed three small golden ingots in his hands, glanced admiringly at a large fistful of glowing, flawless gemstones. "Repayment?" he said. "Well, it seems I haven't much to complain about on that score. After all, what have you had of me? A few days of my freedom? Others before you took far more than that. My labours? But what are muscles for if not for working? As for my camel, lost when first we met: why, the tenth part of these gemstones could buy me a whole caravan!"

"You're well satisfied, then?" Gemal smiled in his skull-like fashion.

"But then there's my sword," said Tarra, almost as if Gemal hadn't spoken. He inclined his head toward that weapon where it swung at Gemal's hip. "And the fact is, I've become somewhat attached to that. It's stood me in good stead in many a fight, and I really feel naked without it."

The smile slipped from Gemal's face. "Haven't I paid you enough? Are you bargaining with me?"

"There was a time not long ago, in your tent, when you said you liked my company *because* I bargained with you," Tarra answered. "Have you changed your mind, then?" And before Gemal could answer, he gave him back the heavy sacklet. "Keep this, Cush Gemal, for I've no need of it. Oh, I know there's plenty more where this came from, but keep that, too. Keep all of it, for it's only stolen wealth anyway. What I'd really appreciate is that curved scimitar, which is rightly mine."

Gemal kept his rising anger under rein. "What I take stays taken," he finally answered. "No deal, Tarra Khash. And anyway, the sword pleases me. There's something about it..." Again he held out the pouch. "Now take what I'm offering and go."

Tarra sighed, shrugged. "The sword's yours then," he said. "So maybe I can bargain for something else?"

Gemal looked puzzled. "Such as?"

"There's a young slave I've grown fond of, name of Loomar Nindiss. If you could see your way to letting him go free with me..."

The slaver's frown lifted at once. "One slave? That were a simple matter." He looked toward the boats. "If you'll just tell me—"

"Two slaves," Tarra cut him short. "He has a sister, Jezza."

Gemal's head snapped round and his black eyes fastened on Tarra's. "What? One of Black Yoppaloth's brides?" He looked at the girls where they stood chained in their misery, waiting to board the boat. And: "Which one is Jezza?" he called out.

Jezza hung her head, stepped forward. She was a beautiful flower, scarce opened, not yet fully in bloom. Her hair was black silk flowing onto her shoulders, her eyes blue as the sky, skin delicate as milk. Gemal looked at her for long moments, finally turned back to Tarra. "It were your death if you so much as touched one of my master's brides," he growled. "Especially that one!" And before Tarra could make further comment: "Now listen. You've twice refused my money, and all you have left is your lizard and your life. Don't bargain yourself into an early grave, Hrossak. Go now, while still you may."

Again Tarra's shrug. "Well then, since I'm broke again and you're bent on taking my young friend and his sister with you to Shad—not to mention all the rest of the people on those boats—it seems there's only one thing for it. I'll just have to come with you!"

Gemal shook his head in astonishment, then tilted his lacquered cockscomb to peer at the steppeman slantwise. "I'll never fathom you, Hrossak," he said. "But haven't I told you that Shad's no place for the likes of you? Didn't I say I felt it in my bones we'd both be sorry if ever you came to Shad? I can't see any good coming out of it; I don't even like the feel of it! No, I'll not take you."

He turned to his blacks. "Get these girls aboard," he ordered. But when he turned back…still Tarra stood there, his expression unaltered. "What now?" The slaver's tone had risen a notch.

"Do you remember our contest in your tent?" Tarra gazed at him unflinching. "The knife, which you reached first?"

"What of it?" Gemal was curious in spite of himself.

"I've been practising," Tarra scratched his chin, tried to control a nervous tic tugging the flesh at the corner of his eye. "Now let me try to make one last bargain with you. Or if not a bargain, perhaps a small wager?"

By now all the boats bar Gemal's were fully loaded, waiting, sails slack where they were held side on to the breeze. Only Tarra himself, Gemal and two of his Yhemnis remained on the shore. And of course Old Scaly. "You've nothing to wager with," Gemal pointed out.

"Oh, but I have," said Tarra. "You said it yourself: my lizard and my life."

Gemal laughed, but a trifle shrilly, almost desperately. "And you'd really gamble the latter? Against what?"

"Against a trip to Shad, with you, in your boat there." And again Tarra's shrug. "I always was a wanderer, Cush Gemal."

"*Madman!*" Gemal hissed. "I think you're mocking me!" He stood erect, scowling, then quickly made up his mind. "Very well, what's the bet?"

Tarra took a step closer, lifted his hands chest high, thumbs pointing in toward his body. And Gemal knew what the bet was, for he saw the Hrossak's eyes where they peered at the jewelled hilt protruding from the scabbard at his hip. "I've been practising, like I said," Tarra repeated. "And now who's fastest, Cush Gemal? Shall we see?"

Gemal's black lieutenants also stepped closer. Tarra looked at them, then at their master. Gemal had likewise lifted his hands chest high. "My sword?" he said. "But you can't possibly win, Tarra." His voice was soft as the sand underfoot. "Why, I've only to let my hand fall, and—"

"Ready when you are," said Tarra. And in the selfsame split second Gemal made his move. His hand blurred down toward the jewelled hilt, came to rest on top of Tarra's, jerked back in shock and disbelief!

The eyes of Gemal's frizzies popped. They drew long, curved knives—but Tarra's was longer. It slithered from its scabbard in a whisper of steel, came to rest with its point tickling Gemal's windpipe. "And how's this for bargaining?" The Hrossak's turn to whisper.

Gemal's blacks backed off. The clatter from the ships had died down in a moment. All was silent, with only the slaps of sails, the occasional grunt of a honker and the *hush, hush* of wavelets on the strand to disturb the electric atmosphere.

"What do you want?" The knob of Gemal's throat bobbed only half an inch from needle tip of scimitar.

"At the moment, staying alive's my only concern," Tarra answered.

"No one will harm you, so long as I'm not harmed," Gemal husked.

Now would seem the best chance Tarra had had, possibly the best he'd get; there was nothing he couldn't demand and win. But how long would he keep it? And anyway, that hadn't been his deal. Whatever Cush Gemal had or had not done, so far he'd played fair with the Hrossak. And what if Tarra did demand Jezza and Loomar's release, and a trio of ponies to carry them out of here? By the time all was arranged and the ponies off the boats, someone would have put a bolt in him, be sure. Even now he could hear small splashes as frizzies, coming out of their stupefaction, slipped overboard of the boats to swim ashore. All of these thoughts taking but a moment to pass through Tarra's mind. Then—

He let fall the tip of the scimitar, direct into the mouth of its scabbard, then tilted the hilt and slid the weapon rattling home. Gemal's jaw fell open and his eyes disbelievingly followed the length of the curved blade as it went home in leather; then those same astonished orbs turned themselves on Tarra. "Totally insane!" he declared.

"What?" said Tarra, his face open and completely innocent. "But it was only a game, sort of. Or maybe a lesson. A lesson in trust, in faith." Gemal's very words, as he'd spoken them in his tent that time.

"You mock me!" The slaver's black eyes were round as saucers. "Do you think you can teach me anything?"

"Not you, no," Tarra told him, shaking his head. "But it might teach those men you travel with a thing or two. Take me with you to Shad and they'll see you're a man of your word, a man of honour. They'll have faith in you. But only have me killed…their trust dies with me. A very bad move, for a man whom so many various people seem to trust beyond all normal bounds."

For a moment the tableau held: the two staring at each other on that narrow strand, Gemal's men starting to creep forward again, and the ships on the loch silently waiting. And then the slaver chief threw back his head and laughed. And mercifully, there wasn't an ounce of malice in all his gales of laughter.

"Tarra Khash," said Gemal when at last he could, "truly I believe you're the first man—the first true *man*, mind and muscle—I've met in too many years! Very well, then, Shad it is. Aye, and we'll make room for your big lizard, too. Except—" and his eyes narrowed and grew sterner, "—don't ever tell me I didn't warn you…"

All of this, through the eye of his marvellous shewstone, Teh Atht observed in private in his apartments overlooking the Bay of Klühn. And he marvelled at Tarra Khash's audacity and skill in side-stepping (what were for any other man) certain death, and he wondered at the Hrossak's penchant for flirting with that Ultimate Opponent Invincible. Invincible, to anyone not already immortal.

As for Tarra's perversity—and how else might one describe his apparent determination to crawl into the jaws of hell?—the wizard was torn two ways. On the one hand he feared for Tarra's life…but on the other he was mindful of his own prime objective, to discover Black Yoppaloth's most secret secret. For if indeed the steppeman should reach and penetrate jungled Shad's barbaric splendours, be sure Teh Atht would be right there with him—in mind at least, if not in the flesh.

And so the wizard sat in the room of his astrologarium, with his back to the whorl and reel and interminable turmoil of fortune's myriad stars, planets and moons, and watched (but carefully, so as not to become himself subject of some other's scrutiny) the events aboard

Cush Gemal's five boats, where now they bore out through the mouth of the loch and into the Eastern Ocean, bearing very nearly south for Shad.

He saw the land recede in the wake of the boats where they ploughed the waves abreast, and the darkening of the sky as storm-winds drove clouds from the east. Ah, but these were strange clouds, bred of forces outside of Nature!

Until now the boats had gone but slowly, with only sufficient of wind to propel them as made rowing unnecessary; but as the sky darkened so the wind freshened, and it was a wind that blew against the ships, which reared up the waves and made the going rough and roaring. Then—a wonder! Even in Teh Atht's eyes—an astonishing sight!

Far overhead the storm clouds fetched a halt, colliding a while in a mighty confusion before turning and racing in a new direction—*in the direction of Shad itself*! And now, still amazed, the white mage of Klühn turned his wary gaze on the black tent of Cush Gemal where that smallest of pavilions had been erected and made fast in the very prow of his boat. And he saw the scintillant green fires which fell from the sky to flicker in its scalloped eaves and along its ridges, and drip like flaming incense from its tassels.

He glimpsed, too, the shrivelled-seeming slaver who leaned a little from his tent's door to beckon to a pair of his faithful, fearful black retainers; and how though they shivered as from some burning fever of the soul, still they could not refuse but went in unto him. Ah, and how the great winds steadied themselves and blew true on the ships of Shad from that time onward! And Teh Atht knew he was seeing magick at work here as mighty as any he could produce, and blacker than any he'd ever dare to conjure.

It was, could only be, Black Yoppaloth working through the medium of his slaver-in-chief, hastening his vessels home to him; and for what foul purpose? Had he already seen Gemal's new sword, Teh Atht wondered? Had he recognized it as a Sword of Power? For of course Yoppaloth was capable of scrying on these distant events, even as Teh Atht himself. What? He was capable of raising a *storm* in those foreign waters, to blow his ships home! And with these slaves and innocent girls, used in some unhallowed rite, and with that sword... would there be any limit to the undying monster's power then?

Suddenly Teh Atht knew what he must do.

He did not relish it, but he had felt the bitter winds of the outer immensities blowing on his soul, had seen his heart—perhaps the heart of Theem'hdra itself—gripped in a mighty black fist and crushed until it dripped blood. Only a vision, one of many possible futures, true, but one which could not be suffered to become reality.

A shipwreck might be the answer: send Cush Gemal and his recently won scimitar to the bottom of the Eastern Ocean! And Tarra Khash? And those strong young slaves? And all twelve of those lovely, innocent lasses? But what would their fate be, anyway, in dark and jungled Shad? Better far the salty kiss of ocean than the mouldering lips of liches, and weedy rather than weird graves. And Orbiquita, when she discovered how her Tarra had drowned? All hell to pay there, but it would pass. Aye, and feelings of guilt would pass, too, balanced against the continuing certainty and comparative serenity of Theem'hdra's future.

So be it, a wreck!

There were islands about, and more ahead: tiny, weathered crests of rock upthrusting from ocean floor, last vestiges of land-bridges which once joined Shadarabar to the mainland. Unmarked on any map, these islands, reefs and sandbars were a menace best avoided. To that end the magick winds blew Cush Gemal's five boats well to the east of the first group of islands, so that only their rocky spires were glimpsed through the spray, and the breakers crashing on their reefs. Aye, one such group safely navigated, but more coming up fast ahead.

And now Teh Atht considered a magick of his own making. For having had some little time to think about it, he believed he could emulate Black Yoppaloth's seemingly gigantic effort, however reduced in scale. Indeed it should be a fairly simple thing, though for a fact it would leave Teh Atht very much open to discovery. Still and all, however great the risk, it was more than balanced by the dire threat poised even now over the entire Primal Land.

Sympathetic magick was the answer. Primitive witchcraft. But coupled with the complexities of Teh Atht's more esoteric thaumaturgies, it should work! Quickly he stood up, strode to the weirdly mobile globe of alien plasma which was his astrologarium, rapidly calculated the co-ordinates of Cush Gemal's planet. It was, he saw, that same sphere (subject of many a previous calculation) which influenced Black Yoppaloth's affairs: a small dark moon on the rim, which even now swam into view around the bulk of a vast and cratered parent world. So Yoppaloth and his strangeling slavemaster shared similar origins and destinies, did they? All to the good: let *both* be blind a while!

Now the white wizard took from his pocket a black silk handkerchief, the while calling to his third familiar that he show himself. Out from the very plasma the liquid one appeared, spurting like a squid in miniature star-spaces. Teh Atht held out his square of silk, saying: "Take it, quickly now, and drape it over yonder moonlet."

In a moment the thing was done, and now the moon reeled blindly in a darkness other than that of its parent's shadow. "There!" said Teh Atht, satisfied. "And now perhaps they'll not sense me while I work against them." Then, uttering a brief malediction against the moon and all in its sway, he returned to his shewstone. It were time now to make a test.

Taking a bowl of water in which he'd recently freshened his face, the wizard stirred its contents to motion and set it down beside the shewstone. He took up an old quill and broke it into five small pieces, dropping them into the bowl. Five ships of Shad, all bobbing on the water in line abreast. Then, half-shuttering his eyes, Teh Atht began to breathe slow and deeply, and was soon in self-induced trance.

His eyes narrowed to slits, filmed over as if varnished, while his breathing became so slow as to almost falter. And as the scene in the shewstone expanded in the eye of his mind, until he could almost fancy himself there aboard Cush Gemal's boat, so he commenced to blow gently on the five quill ships. Now, with skilful puffs, he separated Gemal's vessel from the others, and concentrating on that one alone drove it sideways toward the rim of the bowl—except that to Teh Atht the bowl was now grown to an ocean, and its rim a treacherous sandbar jutting out from craggy islet...

Tarra Khash saw the other four ships forging away, felt a strange sideways current drawing Cush Gemal's vessel westward. Ahead a tiny island, where a long low line of waves showed breaking over a reef or sandbar. The Hrossak made rapid calculations, saw that at this rate of veer the ship would soon run aground!

He clambered round the bulk of Old Scaly where he crouched amidships and honked his distress, made his way back to the Yhemni steersman at the long-handled tiller.

"Man, your rudder's broken!" he bellowed. "We're heading straight for that hazard!"

"Not broken," the black yelled back, fighting with the tiller. "Something bad wrong!"

"Bad wrong?" Tarra lent his own strength to the unequal struggle. "You're damned right there is!" He looked ahead through wind and spray, saw that in another minute they'd hit. The slaves had seen the danger, too, and were tearing at the chains that bound them to useless oars. Tarra turned back to the steersman. "Who has the key to those chains?" he demanded.

"I have it, in belt," the frizzy shouted back, scowled at Tarra and narrowed his dark eyes. "And I keep!"

"We have to release them," the Hrossak allowed himself to stumble against the man. "Else when the boat hits, they're goners!"

"No do," the black shook his head. "Only if master say so…"

"Can't wait for that," Tarra yelled. He grabbed the other's belt, tore loose the large iron key which he found there, tossed it to one of the slaves where the end of the chain was padlocked to his oar. Even as he did so the boat gave a lurch; the steersman had released the tiller to snatch out a knife. A second black, knife drawn, likewise came scrambling, converging on Tarra, and others cracked whips with less than their accustomed accuracy in a vain attempt to quell the panic of the slaves.

Now terror held full sway: chains were rattling through their staples; blacks stumbled here and there, at a loss what to do next; in the front of the boat, close behind Gemal's tent, screams rang out from the helpless knot of girls as their doom roared ever closer. And suddenly—

"*Blind! Blind!*" A mad cry rose above wind and water and all the rest. "Who has done this? What curse is on me now?" Cush Gemal was there in the prow of the boat, just now emerged from his tent, one hand clapped to his eyes and the other outstretched and groping wildly in the air. He reeled to the shuddering of the sideways drifting vessel, swayed to and fro to the tune of its lurching.

Tarra Khash had his own problems. As the former steersman made a wild stab at his throat, he ducked sideways and felt the keen edge of the man's knife slice the lobe of his ear. Then he kicked his attacker in the groin and knuckled him under the nose, caving in his upper lip. The second black came from the rear, of which Tarra wasn't aware until he heard his gurgling scream. He turned, saw the frizzy go down, one hand bent behind him where he vainly strove to grasp the knife in his spine.

Tarra would know that knife anywhere: he'd once buried it in the sand beside the body of a previous owner. And there on a starboard bench, no longer chained—one arm clinging to a shipped oar for balance and the other outstretched in a life-saving, death-dealing throw—who else but Loomar Nindiss!

And then the boat hit!

"Hit" (if the word conveys a shattering and flying apart) is probably the wrong word. "Reared upon" might be better; for indeed the flat-bottomed boat reared upon the sandbar. Driven at a furious pace, it slid home on the wide reach of submerged sand and pebbles, reared on its prow like a bucking pony, teetered there for a moment before falling back with a colossal *slap* in the water. But in that moment of slithering collision and slingshot rearing—

Cush Gemal, girls, slaves, slavers and all were hurled high in an arc of thrashing bodies, came down in a frenzy of flailing limbs into the sea beyond the sandbar—which was a great deal calmer and not nearly so deep as the thundering ocean proper. Indeed the sandbar had formed something of a lagoon or harbour, where now ejected crew and captives floundered in water only chest-deep.

As for Old Scaly: his great weight had saved the day, stopped the boat from capsizing into the lagoon. But at the moment of the collision he'd commenced sliding forward, levelled Gemal's now ragged tent, crashed through the shallow rail of the prow and plunged headlong into the sea close to the milling swimmers. Tarra Khash was miraculously fortunate: in the very rear of the boat, his trajectory had been higher, tossing him up into the sail. There he'd been cushioned in the slackening bell of canvas; had slid down the sail 'til his feet met the boom; finally, dizzily, had lowered himself to the deck.

Behind the Hrossak, roaring water and foaming spray; here beneath his unsteady feet the boat, now empty, firmly lodged in sucking sand; ahead the shallow, calm and lagoonlike waters, and jumbled rockpile of an island close at hand. Tarra's head stopped spinning and he looked at the swimmers where they were striving for the shore. He found his voice to yell: "The lizard! Cling to Old Scaly!" For the giant lizards of Hrossa were blundering good swimmers and buoyant as corks.

Then the steppeman's eyes searched out Cush Gemal—and found him lying prone on the bottom! Overboard went Tarra Khash in a shallow dive, which took him down to where Cush Gemal lay stiff as stone on a swirly bed of sand and gravel. Stiff as stone?—he *was* stone!—but pumice, not granite. And pumice floats!

As Tarra tugged, so the slaver boss came free and drifted to the surface; and the Hrossak, utterly astonished and feeling himself dreaming, propelling him ashore face-up, like some old figurehead carved of leaden driftwood.

Then gravel sucking soggily underfoot, and hands reaching to haul the steppeman up out of clinging water, and blacks gawping at their grey-carved master bobbing on his back in the shallows. But in the next moment Cush Gemal came back to life and his black eyes were flecked with a red fury.

He sprang up in the water, stepped to dry land. His bloodshot eyes scanned the sky and fixed on something no one else saw. He pointed, shouted:

"You—you dog—*you*!" And then, in an agony of frustration: "Ah!—too *late*! But *next* time, my veiled friend! Never fear, for *next* time I'll know you! Aye, and then we'll discover what magick may do, eh?" With that, green fire leaped unannounced from his pointing fingertips, hurled itself harmlessly into the sky and burst in an incendiary flash of emerald flares. Following which Cush Gemal seemed to shrivel down into himself, and without another word collapsed into the arms of Tarra Khash...

Out the corner of one half-shuttered eye, Teh Atht had seen a black silk square slide from a miniature moon and flutter into the path of a flaring star. Bursting into flame, the silken kerchief's yellow flash of fire had distracted him, and his long-distance spell of Curious Concretion was broken. Panic gripped him and he at once strove to come fully awake, out of his trance.

He succeeded only just in time; a moment longer and Cush Gemal would have penetrated the veil and found him out. And leaping from his seat and away from the shewstone, he only just managed to avoid a severe singeing as the surface of that sphere sent gobbets of green fire racing round the room of the astrologarium like tiny comets.

In that same instant, too, it had dawned on Teh Atht just who he was dealing with here. Cush Gemal? Ah, so he termed himself; but in fact this could only be one man. Little wonder he shared the same star as Black Yoppaloth; indeed, he *was* Black Yoppaloth! And Klühn's master mage shuddered as he realized how close he'd come to revealing himself to that immortal monster...

***

Tarra sat in morbid mood on the scaly flank of his dead honker and watched the work in progress. As the magickal storm had blown itself out, so the other four ships had returned and two of them had disgorged their slaves, who now worked to free Cush Gemal's stranded vessel from the quaggy grip of the sandbar. Labouring in six inches to a foot of choppy water, they dug away at the sand under the boat's flat bottom and slowly inched the craft off the bar into shallow water. Since the sandbar was not a true reef, the harbour it formed was not completely enclosed; open-ended, a ship might easily sail away from the rocky islet—that is if it could sail at all.

Amazingly, apart from the damage to the prow's rail and upper strakes where Old Scaly had crashed through them, Gemal's ship had suffered no real wreckage. Some of the starboard strakes were sprung, but the ship was so constructed that these could be tightened back into position by using a tourniquet system of knotted ropes. The flat bottom, of ironwood, was cracked in places but not split open, and already a lone frizzy was on board, caulking the cracks with a raw jungle resin which hardened to glass on contact with water.

The vessel would soon be seaworthy again, and apart from the loss of a couple of crewmen (whose bodies, mercifully, had not been washed up) little real harm had been done. Tarra's part in freeing the slaves had apparently gone unobserved, or those who'd observed it (said disappeared crewmen) were no longer around to make accusations. The only real loss by Hrossak's lights was that of his lizard. Tarra's honker had collapsed on lumbering ashore, and in a little while died, probably from an overdose of stress. Their great hearts could stand any amount of work, but they weren't much for suffering sudden or successive shocks. Or there again, perhaps something had got broken inside when the massive beast crashed through the boat's prow.

As for Cush Gemal: for a little while his life had been in real jeopardy—from the slaves if not from anything else. On this ocean-girt rock they far outnumbered their former masters, and none of them with an ounce of feeling (other than hatred) for the man who'd taken them into captivity. As the wind had abated more yet and it dawned on the young slaves that however cold and wet, at least they were alive and unfettered, so they'd begun to mutter darkly about Cush Gemal and his few remaining retainers. With only a handful of frizzies left to guard this lot, things might have got ugly right there and then—but that was when Tarra had spotted the four unscathed ships tacking with the wind as they returned to the isle of the wreck. Aye, and he'd spotted more than just that.

Across and above the island's central ridge of rock, whereto when last seen Gemal's limp form was being carried by a pair of his numbers-depleted blacks, now the sky was dark with a wheel of revolving spray and boiling cloud; and down from this aerial cauldron dangled the narrowing funnel of a twister, whose whorl held corkscrew streamers of green fire that gave the jutting ridge of rocks a weird coruscation and forbade intrusion.

"It's my guess," Tarra had told the gawping slaves and the small knot of shivering girls, "that when next you see Cush Gemal he'll no longer be vulnerable. And see those ships there? If you did somehow manage to kill him, what then? His lads would come ashore and slaughter you, violate the girls, finally sail off home to Shad no worse for wear. Or...they'd simply leave us marooned here, to die in our own good time. Wherefore I say: leave well enough alone. For now, anyway." And that had been that.

And sure enough, the swaying, nodding but apparently *tethered* tornado of green fire eventually collapsed in upon itself; and as the boats landed on the shore some little time later, so Gemal came striding like a spider across the ridge and commenced shouting orders in his accustomed fashion. But no sign of the pair of frizzies who'd crossed that ridge with him. At which Tarra Khash had narrowed his eyes and nodded, and said to himself: *Well, Cush Gemal, and now I believe I know you for sure.* For the Hrossak was no more a fool than was a certain white wizard of Klühn.

And anyone standing close to the steppeman might have seen him nod again, or even heard him mutter: "Oh, indeed I do! As I believe I've known you, in my way, right from the start..."

IX

POWERS OF LIGHT, POWERS OF DARKNESS!

Iniquiss and Hissiliss, most senior members of the lamia Council of Five, had returned at long last to the Sisterhood's inner sanctum. There upon her lava island crouched the lamia Orbiquita, impatiently awaiting her release from all vows, when finally she might go forth into the world as a woman. Born half-lamia, half-girl child, her form had been human; a foundling, she'd been adopted by wandering nomads, following which the monster in her had rapidly taken ascendency; until, expelled by her foster-parents, the Sisterhood had taken her in. This was usually the way of it. But the human woman in her had never been totally eradicated, so that she'd always felt herself waiting like some dull star for a glorious nova to release her long-suppressed beauty. Tarra Khash had been the catalyst, and soon the transformation would be complete.

Of the fact that she *was* beautiful in her female form, Orbiquita had little doubt; she'd often enough reverted to that delicious shape in the past, using it to seduce the foolish men (of course) who formed the Sisterhood's principle source of food. Oh, they could eat other meat readily enough, but the flesh of men had a strength and a flavour to it away and beyond that of simple beasts; a taste which from now on she'd necessarily relinquish—as must she relinquish all thoughts such as these! But old habits die hard, and Orbiquita could not help but feel a little afraid of her new and incredibly fragile life in the harsh dawn world which awaited her. Not that she intended that her lamia sisters should see that fear; be sure that she did not.

"The hour of reckoning, Orbiquita," said Iniquiss, folding back her wings to seat herself in a lava niche in the great cavern's splash-stone wall.

"When we must make it plain," Hissiliss added, finding herself a comfortable scab of tephrite lying sullen in the molten reek, "just what your renounciation means to you, delineate your many losses as set against no gains whatever!"

"No gains?" Orbiquita repeated her. "Except I'll be a woman. Gains enough there—so get on with it."

"Defiant to the bitter end," Iniquiss gloomed. "So be it." And in another moment, reading from a bone-leaved runebook: "Insomuch as you have renounced the Sisterhood, word of which we have right-fully relayed to all loyal sisters, these things which I shall now read are reckoned to be your lot. Now hear me:

"You, Orbiquita, who have known unbridled power, henceforth shall suffer total loss of strength."

"Not so," Orbiquita shook her head, "for I'll have a woman's strength, and they're not such weaklings as you'd make out. Strong men fall down before them, anyway."

"Loss of *lamia* strength, she meant," Hissiliss hissed. "Soft hands and feet, you'll have, with human fingers and toes. Not the great scythes you wear now, against which no creature in all the Primal Land may stand unscathed."

"Soft fingers, soft toes?" said Orbiquita. "Soft breasts, too, soft belly and thighs. Not your loathsome limbs and warty paps! Oh, I'll manage. Your sort of magick's not the only sort, snakeface."

"You shall have neither your own former strength," Iniquiss continued, while Hissiliss fumed and smouldered, "nor that of the Sisterhood and its individual members. You will be on your own, Orbiquita, for all future time—or for all the time the future allows you."

Again Orbiquita disagreed. "Three calls for aid I'm allowed!" she cried. "Don't rob me of my rights, Iniquiss. I've read the rules, too, you know. Three times I may call on the Sisterhood for its aid, or individual members thereof, and then no more. So it's written."

"She talks of her rights!" Hissiliss jumped up and set her cake of lava tilting. "Rights? When you've renounced the Sisterhood?"

Iniquiss merely shrugged. "It *is* her right, and so it *is* written—but it's also written that her sisters have the right to refuse such calls, if they see fit. You've not made many friends in the Sisterhood, Orbiquita."

"Name me one dear sister who has!" Their subject was unrepentant.

"Just so long as we understand one another," Iniquiss told her, turning a bone page. And finding her place:

"Your lamia powers—of metamorphosis, into dragon, lizard, harpy, bat, clinging gas and seeping moisture—are all foresaken, yours no longer. In the one shape you have chosen, that of a human female, you'll remain. Aye, and you'll live out only that number of years appropriate. The thousands you might have known are already flown forever!"

"I'll know the days of a woman," answered Orbiquita, but with something less of defiance, "and her nights." But then, brightening: "And in the arms of my chosen man, they'll be long nights and sweet. Not the noisome nights of the Sisterhood."

"Your 'chosen' man?" Hissiliss' sibilant whisper was amplified by cavern acoustics. "Have you paused to consider, he may not want you?"

In her vast armoured body, Orbiquita's heart quaked. Indeed she had considered it, and she knew that certain men were fickle. But if love is blind, hers for Tarra Khash was also deaf. Not dumb, however. "Snakeface," she said, "this I vow: that when I die they'll write on my stone, 'Here lies a woman who loved and was loved.' But what will they write on your monstrous menhir? I'll tell you:

> 'Here lies a beast with gorgon's crown—
> This stone was raised to keep her down!'

"Hissiliss!" Iniquiss' cutting voice terminated her sister's shriek of impotent rage. "You're no match for this one where sarcasm's concerned. Can you not console yourself that you'll soon be rid of her?"

"We'll *all* be rid of her!" Hissiliss cried.

"For myself, I think it a shame," said Iniquiss, which was as much of emotion as she cared to show. And to Orbiquita:

"You know of course that you must give up, along with all the powers and years you might have known, all personal possessions?"

"All save one," Orbiquita nodded. "I may keep one small thing, according to lamia law."

"Possessions!" Hissiliss seemed hardly surprised. "She has possessions, does she? Another human attribute, this garnering of goods. Obviously she was never a true lamia! What possessions does she have?"

"Several," Orbiquita answered for herself. "My castle in the Desert of Sheb, I leave to the winds and sands of times I'll not know. My Roc's eye shewstone, to whosoever finds it there. Then there's my runebook, which I bequeath to you, Iniquiss; perhaps there's that in it which might increase your knowledge, or at least amuse you. But the one thing which I shall keep is a ring, too small for lamia digits but perfect for the finger of a woman. It is of jade and gold and bears the skull and serpent crest of my ancestor Mylakhrion. This I shall keep, for it's all I have of family, of noble ancestry."

"Noble! Noble!" Hissiliss snorted.

"'Ware, sister!" Orbiquita warned, dangerously low-voiced. "I'm still lamia for the moment, and you still have eyes!"

"Now hear this, my final statement and decree," Iniquiss' voice of authority got between them. "Orbiquita, you have renounced the Sisterhood. So be it. There is no turning back. Here you stay for however long the final metamorphosis requires. At the end, the cavern imps shall warn of your imminent death, for a merely human female could never survive in this lava heat and reek and sulphurous cavern atmosphere. At that time you'll be borne to the surface, naked and shorn of all lamia trappings and skills. Do you understand?"

"I do," said Orbiquita.

"Your lamia memories will fade, though they may briefly recur from time to time. Likewise, it is possible that on occasion, in desperate times, the lamia which must now lie forever locked within you may briefly surface. This at your own peril, for humankind abhors us and they would rid themselves of us if they could. Is this clear?"

"It is clear."

"The Primal Land is harsh," Iniquiss continued. "What merely irritated you as a lamia may easily destroy you as a girl. Snake's bite and scorpion's sting will be fatal; knives, arrows, axes and swords likewise. And in lonesome places, men may molest you. Do you recognize these hazards all?"

"I recognize these hazards," Orbiquita repeated. "But I also know that I might bask in sunlight unharmed and unafraid, and walk with a lover under the full moon and never fear Gleeth's rays."

"Then it is done," said Iniquiss. "Orbiquita, you are—or very soon will be—lamia no more!"

She closed with finality her book of bone leaves, whose sound was that of some great sepulchral door slamming, or perhaps a gong heralding a new dawn...

***

Blind old Gleeth the moon-god (though why "blind" is hard to explain, for indeed when he wished to he could "see," or at least know intuitively, almost all the many, mazy doings of men) looked down blearily on the Primal Land and frowned; or perhaps it was just a cloud passing over his crescent face. Waxing steadily, his silver horns were filling out and his reflective plains and dry ocean beds were dazzling. A fairly "young" moon in that ancient time, his face was far less cratered than it would be in, say, another two hundred million years.

As for his frown: it might be caused by something he saw through sleepfilmed eyes, which displeased him; or it could be that he "heard" something drifting up to him from the surface of his parent planet, which made him irritable. Something, perhaps, like the distant, tinkling prayers of a silver-skinned priestling. What? Suhm-yi prayers? But how could that be, since the Suhm-yi were no more? Then Gleeth remembered that the Crater Sea's secret race was not extinct, not entirely, and he grudgingly roused himself up from rarely disturbed slumbers.

His crater-walled eyes sought out the Inner Isles where once the Suhm-yi dwelled, especially that rock called Na-dom, beloved of the gods. For indeed Na-dom was Holy of Holies, whose aspect alone would turn back the merely curious. No jewel isle this but a gaunt and solitary crag rearing like some sea-beast's talon from the Crater Sea, which beckoned not but merely forbade intrusion. Black as night, that needle rock, and standing well apart from more mundane islets, for which reason the gods were sometimes wont to visit there. Or at least give ear to the priests who hailed them therefrom. Even as Gleeth now gave ear. And in a little while, drifting up to him from Na-dom, this is what he heard:

"Gleeth! Old Gleeth!" cried Amyr Arn, who knew almost nothing of the priestly preparations and ceremonies requisite to reaching out and speaking to the gods. "Old god of the moon, hear me now, as once before you heard me."

And this will be Amyr Arn, said Gleeth, but to himself, so that Amyr did not hear him. *It can only be him, for he is the last. What can he want of me now?*

"Look down on me," Amyr cried, as if in answer, "and take pity."

Pity? Pity? Why should I pity you? You 're alive, young, strong. Pity? Or should I pity you because you are alone, last of the Suhm-yi? Is that your meaning? Very well, then I pity you. Now go away and leave me alone. And still Gleeth spoke only to himself, so that Amyr heard nothing.

"I ask this boon of you not for myself but for a man, whom once before you helped, in time of need."

A man? Gleeth wondered what was all of this. *An unbeliever? Suhm-yi prayers for help were one thing, but a man...?*

"This man *believes!*" cried Amyr Arn, for all the world as if he had heard, although he had not. "His name is Tarra Khash, who knows you for a kind, benevolent god. Gleeth, listen to me: I know you are old, and that they say you're deaf and blind, but I believe you see and hear well enow. You heard me before, when last I dared to call your name, and now I call it again."

Tarra Khash? Faint memories stir! But I'm tired and can do without all this. Weary of questions, of the very effort of thought itself, the old god of the moon began to drift back into sleep.

"I'll not give in, old moon-god," Amyr shouted his frustration from the roof of Na-dom. "I'll call upon you night after night, forever, if need be, until you answer me one way or the other."

Do you threaten, Amyr Arn? The moon sailed all serene and silent on high. *Tarra Khash? I know him, aye. A Hrossak. He sails in a boat en route for Shad. What of it?*

"Gleeth! Old Gleeth!" Amyr despaired.

Aye, you're right, Amyr Arn. Old and tired... A Hrossak...? He sails in a boat for Shad... Now go away, last son of all the Suhm-yi... Your people worshipped me once, but they are no more... So leave me in peace... A god's no good without his worshippers... Old and tired... Tarra Khash? I know him, aye...

And so the old god of the moon went back to his timeless dreaming, and in a little while Amyr Arn climbed wearily down from Na-dom and paddled his canoe back across the Crater Sea to his Ulli on the island they'd now make their home. But be sure he wasn't finished yet. No, for there'd be another night tomorrow, and when the moon rose into the sky again, Amyr would be back.

And so Gleeth slept, and the light of his silver crescent swept down and pointed a path right across the Primal Land. Five ships of Shad sailed that silvery swath on the Eastern Ocean, where now they crossed into the Straits of Yhem; and in the stern of the fifth, keeping the tiller, there sat Tarra Khash alone with his thoughts.

Drowsy in the night, where warm winds blew now from jungled Shadarabar, Tarra's thoughts weren't much to speak of: fleeting memories of his travels and travails, his adventures and near-disasters. He saw again a woman, or rather a girl, as he'd seen her once in the badlands under Lohmi. She never had told him her name, though he'd found it out soon enough, and then almost wished he hadn't. But she'd balmed his back where ambusher's arrow had nailed him, and her soft breasts had cradled him where he rested against her. Then— she'd kissed his neck with a kiss of fire!

She'd taken his blood while he slept—a little, a splash—and unbeknown even to herself had put something back in its place, like the fever-fly who sips and imparts poisons. Hers had not been poisons of the flesh but of the spirit, reacting only with blood which was ready for them. Nor were they true poisons, but rather passions. Tarra had known women, females, before. But none like this. And since that time—that kiss, which raised twin craters on his neck, small pinches that ached a little even now—he'd had no time for other loves. Or perhaps more important, no inclination.

Love? Was that it? He snorted in the night under the blind old moon and straightened the bar of his tiller. Then never a love more hopeless in all of time, in all the Primal Land. For later he had seen that female who kissed him, seen her in her true form, which was a shape out of nightmares and madness!

Some small irritation, on his leg where his pants were torn, distracted him. Something moved there. He went to swat, but paused when he saw what perched upon his knee. A small scorpion, greeny-grey: the sort which lives on the weeds and under the stones of certain tropical islands, whose venom is invariably fatal—or very nearly so. But Tarra Khash was immune, who'd been stung so often as a youth that the poisons no longer worked. Indeed, as a lad he'd been a legend on the steppes, renowned for the number of stings he'd taken, which should have killed but merely sickened and in the end had no effect at all.

Now, in the star- and moon-cast shadow of the sail, he peered at his small passenger and it peered back, with tiny faceted eyes yellow as flames. Doubtless he'd picked the creature up on the isle of the almost-shipwreck. Well, and he had nothing against scorpions, of whatever sort. He took it up between thumb and finger, stared at it where it made no effort to sting him, said: "Best go where you're safe, small friend. Find a niche for yourself between the strakes, where it's nice and damp." And so saying he put the scorpion down behind the box of the tiller. It quickly scuttled out of sight.

"*Hah!*" said a now familiar voice close by. "Is there nothing you're afraid of, Hrossak?" Cush Gemal (for the moment Tarra continued to think of him under that name) stood watching, though how he'd drawn so close, so quietly, were a mystery.

"I'm afraid of some things," Tarra answered. "Sorcery, maybe—and maybe people who appear in the night out of nowhere, all sudden-like and unannounced."

SORCERY IN SHAD — Powers of Light, Powers of Darkness!

They stared at each other for long moments, until Gemal sensed the Hrossak's new awareness and noticed a certain light in his eyes—the light of knowledge. He nodded then, and very quietly said: "I can see that you've learned something of the truth..." And then, after a moment's consideration: "Very well, you shall know all of it. Accompany me." He snapped skeletally thin fingers and one of his Yhemnis came running, took the tiller and left Tarra free to follow Gemal as he made off down the ship's wide central space, between the sleeping girls where they lay chained together under their blankets, toward his repaired tent standing as before in the prow...

———————

As they went, the small greeny-grey scorpion came out from behind the tiller frame, stared silently after them with tiny flame eyes from between the steersman's spread legs. And all it had seen with those faceted eyes, and all it had heard in its scorpion fashion, were seen and heard and known in certain other places: in the deep, all but forgotten fane of the Scarlet Scorpion himself, Ahorra Izz, and also in Shad, in a certain arena of death, where stood a likeness of that same arachnid deity.

Both facets in their separate places had received the selfsame message, which was this: that Tarra Khash was on his way to Shad. And from deep below the creeper-entwined crypt which was his fane, the true god Ahorra Izz now spoke across all the leagues between to lesser idol, who however awe-inspiring in his way, was nevertheless only a simulacrum of himself:

"*Have ye seen?*" he clacked his mentalist message. "*Tarra Khash, a Hrossak, is coming to Shad. Ye may come across him, or perhaps he shall stumble across ye. Now hear ye: this man may not be harmed by any scorpion, neither creature, graven image, nor even myself. I forbid it, for we stand in his debt.*"

"*Here in the arena of death,*" came back the answer on the winds of night, "*I hold small sway. There are many gods here, Ahorra Izz, where I am but a one. And I am but an image, with nothing of magick in me. Hewn in stone out of your likeness, I stand and stare with crystal eyes, impotent of all save the seeing of sights and the hearing of sounds.*"

"And yet I say to ye," Ahorra Izz insisted, *"that if ye hear him cry out for aid, or see him in dire peril, then shall ye give assist."* And he explained his meaning.

And deep down beneath Black Yoppaloth's ziggurat palace in Shad, around the rim of the subterranean arena of death, standing in a circle formed of other earth gods and many far more blasphemous effigies, a huge scorpion carved of chalcedony heard the words of its parent god and grimly acknowledged them...

Way across the Straits of Yhem low in the sky over Theem'hdra's farthest horizon, Gleeth the moon-god rode silent and serene, but not entirely deaf or blind. He had "seen" and "heard" many things this night, and not alone the pleading of Amyr Arn of the Suhm-yi. Of the latter: even now Amyr paddled a canoe across the deathly calm waters of the Crater Sea, and beached it on that tiny island where Ulli waited on the shore to melt into his arms. And this, too, was witnessed by old Gleeth, not yet quite asleep.

Not the last? the moon-god sighed his sleepy amaze, but kept it to himself. *What? And shall there be more Suhm-yi to worship me after all? They were ever my favourites among the world's races; but I had thought they were no more, and a god needs his subjects.*

His silver rays cut a swath across all the Primal Land—and across the Straits of Yhem, where five boats forged for Shad—even reaching Shadarabar itself. And now the old moon-god started more fully awake, for in Shad he spied that which caused him more than a little of alarm.

It was in the sky, which was his domain of immemorial right, and it was this:

A great black cloud which boiled where no cloud should be, not born of currents of upper air but rising like some diseased puffball of smoke from below, and forming a ring that spun and sucked up the mists of the jungle swamps into the night sky, compressing them there, swirling them as if spun from within, like some dark and evil whirlpool of the skies. Except it was nothing out of the heavens but some subterraneous hell. And even as Gleeth watched, so the flat plateau of the twister grew darker yet—black as the Stygian bowels at planet's core—and its rim began to glow with the green and writhing phosphorescence of things long rotted. It whirled its weird funnel over all the fabulous city of Shad, but its stalk remained constant, seeming rooted in a ziggurat palace at the wild jungle's fringe.

Then…out of the whirling mass were shot like stones from a giant's sling several smaller, even stranger masses, which hurtled meteoric across the skies and out over the Straits of Yhem—and there paused. And now these eerie imps of the underworld curved down and around, fashioning themselves into green-glowing winds which blew on the ships of Yoppaloth and hastened them home.

All of which the moon-god found exceedingly interesting. And he remembered Amyr Arn's pleading, and he wondered about the fate of a certain Hrossak. But…dawn would soon be here and the sun risen to outshine him, and there was always tomorrow night to consider these strange events and their stranger connections. Tomorrow night, aye, when he'd waxed a little more and grown stronger. It could all wait until then, he was sure…

Dawn.

Yes, it would soon be dawn, and still Teh Atht fretted as he paced to and fro and hither and thither through the halls and corridors of his manse in Klühn.

"How long, 'til dawn?" he asked himself for the tenth time. And answered: "An hour at least…" A whole hour, before he'd dare return to the room of the astrologarium, where he'd left his shewstone. Eleven hours sped by since his magick had gone so disastrously wrong and almost revealed him to Cush Gemal—or rather, to Black Yoppaloth. And in all that time no wink of sleep taken, no morsel of food passed his lips, but only this fretting and gnashing of teeth to occupy him, as he'd paced and prowled and considered his position—which was not an envious one.

Fantastic events were in the offing, and Teh Atht knew it. More, he could feel himself at the centre of whatever was coming, without yet knowing what it would be. The answer, if it could be fathomed, lay in the room of the astrologarium, in the rush and reel of all Man's astrological moons and planets and stars, but for now Teh Atht dare not return there. Worse, his shewstone remained in that same room, without which even the smallest scrying were out of the question.

But go back into that room? No, not possible, not until he could be sure that Black Yoppaloth had quit searching for him. For all he knew the shewstone remained lethally inverse, only waiting to be activated and thus reveal him to the enemy—who'd sworn to have him! Perhaps that most powerful necromancer waited even now for him, just beyond the crystal ball's opaque curtains—which he daren't under any circumstances throw open. And this was Teh Atht's predicament.

Hopper and flitter, sensing their master's distress, had spent the long, weary hours with him—the one invariably underfoot and the other always just overhead—but Teh Atht scarcely noticed them as he wandered his mazy manse, wringing his tapering hands and vainly seeking a solution to the problem. He had considered calling his third familiar, that entirely liquid one, out of the astrologarium; but what if something *else* was there in that magickally sealed room even now—something perhaps of Yoppaloth's sending—and what if that something should come out *with* the liquid one?

"Coward!" Teh Atht cried, causing hopper and flitter to start with his outburst. He threw wide his bell-cuffed arms in the corridor where he stalked, shook his fists at the stone walls. "Oh, *coward*, Teh Atht! What? And are you not a great wizard in your own right?"

Aye, but white! some inner voice whispered back. *My magicks are white, and his are black. I have scruples—some—and he has none. I tried to kill him, and if he discovers me, which he'll surely try to do, he can and will kill me!*

"Then act now!" he cried. Following which his voice at once fell to a whisper: "While yet there's time..."

But at night? When baneful spells were that much more likely to succeed?

Teh Atht rushed to a window facing east across the sea, gazed out. On the horizon, the first blush of dawn, or perhaps a false dawn. Day was coming, and the darkness soon to be banished. And he knew in his bones that time was narrowing down. Soon Black Yoppaloth's renewal would be at hand; soon Tarra Khash would be at greatest peril; and all *too* soon the lamia Orbiquita would require an explanation. The more he considered the intricacies, the more intricate they became.

"Hopper, flitter, to me!" he cried, turning from the window. "Enough is enough! I now return to the room of the astrologarium— and you go with me. Three brave hearts together!" Alarmed, they drew back at once, but he reached out with a simple bind-you-to-me and they were drawn close, flitter obliged to fasten to his high collar while hopper clung to his rune-inscribed robe. And so they proceeded to the room of the astrologarium.

Here it was that the white wizard had brought about the wrecking of Black Yoppaloth's boat, and his blindness; and here, too, while the astonished necromancer had been hurled into the sea, he'd cursed him with Curious Concretion to make sure he'd sink. Alas, by virtue of the fact that the last was a sending of some distance, and diluted through the medium of the shewstone, it had been weakened: instead of granite, Yoppaloth had become pumice, a softer stone by far. What's more, a man or creature fixed in a state of Curious Concretion does not breathe or even need to, and so Yoppaloth had not drowned. In a deeper ocean, as marble, say, he'd have gone to the bottom at once; and when the spell was broken, then he'd be flattened by pressure or drowned on the way back up. But that had not been the case.

The spell *had* been broken, when by chance Teh Atht had been distracted by the blazing kerchief, which same mishap had simultaneously returned Yoppaloth's sight. The attempt on the necromancer's life had not been blundered, not by any means, but was simply ill-starred. Perhaps Teh Atht should have used his astrologarium to choose a more opportune moment.

The entire episode must therefore be counted as a failed experiment, which in its failing had produced no small hazard of its own. This had been when Yoppaloth attempted to strike back, as Teh Atht had struck, through the very shewstone itself; and only the speed of the latter's retreat therefrom had saved him from a painful blistering, and probably from much worse than that.

After that, praying that in the moment of inversion the crystal ball had deactivated, Klühn's mage had quickly left the room of the astrologarium, locked and spelled shut the door; and now, nearly twelve hours later, he stood once more outside that room, key in hand

and chewing his lip. On his way here he'd reinforced by will and rune a handful of personal protections to ward off what might possibly lie in wait for him within; and finally, voice trembling just a little as he unspelled the door, he inserted his key in the lock and turned it, then pushed that portal open.

Inside…nothing was changed that he could see at a glance; driving hopper and flitter before him, he crossed the threshold; no dire apparition sprang out upon him. Teh Atht drew a deep breath, retracted his wand, shot further quick, cursory glances all about. Then he crossed the room and approached the shewstone—but cautiously, ever ready to jump back at first sight or intimation of unusual activity. Nothing…

He activated the crystal, which at once spat out several bright green sparks—residuum of that earlier, more deadly display—and fell quiescent. Startled by the sudden sputtering, hopper and flitter had taken their departure, but came creeping and winging back as Teh Atht lowered his shielding hands from before his eyes. And there the shewstone reposed as before, milky-deep and vaguely aswirl, and nothing noticeably amiss. That is, nothing amiss with the crystal sphere.

But—

The astrologarium itself was far from right! The infinitely accurate soar and swing of its multi-hued nebulae and simulated stars seemed strangely out of kilter.

Teh Atht remembered the green meteorites which, hurled at him by black Yoppaloth, had erupted from the shewstone to bound and rebound all about the room, and wondered if they could have affected the balance of this miniature, man-made universe. The astrologarium had used up years without number and magicks likewise innumerable in its construction and was his pride and joy. Half dreading to discover damage, he slitted his eyes to peer deep into its lucid plasma infinities.

And as he peered, so his third and uniquely liquid familiar came flowing from the spaces between pigmy planets, expanding from mere amoeba to blob of resin, finally into half a gallon of clear, glutinous jelly as "he" or it approached the rim. Teh Atht extended a hand, upon which with a *plop* the astrologarium ejected the weird, wobbling intelligence into his palm. There that freakish familiar quickly elongated himself slugwise along the wizard's arm, clinging there like a sheath of sentient slime.

Employed mainly in the maintenance and lubrication of the astrologarium, the liquid one felt and was disturbed by any serious fluctuations therein; and quite obviously (or obvious, at least, to Teh Atht's practiced eyes) the creature *was* agitated. Concerned, he comforted his familiar creature, let him seep into a voluminous pocket of his robe, then commenced to search the finite infinity of small worlds for the cause of such perturbation. And now indeed he saw the imbalance, portent of changes *vast* in the mundane world of men!

Strange dark stars stood in alien alignment; moons and planets were shadowed in eerie eclipses; the astrologarium itself seemed to hold its breath. "The stars are...wrong!" the wizard gasped aloud—and at once, with his own words still ringing in his ears, staggered back from the cosmic display. Staggered, aye; for depending on one's point of view, the stars weren't wrong at all; indeed, it could be said that they were very nearly *right*!

But for whom?

X

CUSH GEMAL'S STORY

Between times...Tarra Khash had proceeded with Cush Gemal to his black tent in the prow of a roughly repaired boat forging for Shad.

There he accepted a seat on cushions only just dry from their salt water dousing, gazed at his weird host by the light of a small green lantern.

And finally he ventured: "Perhaps I'm unwise to accept your hospitality like this. Some come in here who don't come out again. And others make small splashes in the night, when they go overboard..."

Cush Gemal smiled a strange sad smile, more properly a twisting of his bony features. "Would that it could be otherwise," he said. "But it cannot. I do what I must for survival. I am what I am."

"A sorcerer," said Tarra evenly, with a slow nod. "A necromancer. Indeed, Black Yoppaloth himself! You said you'd tell me all. Well, here I am, and all ears."

Black Yoppaloth nodded, drew himself up a little straighter where he sat. Then he reached across suddenly to touch Tarra's shoulder. The Hrossak felt the iciness of that touch, drew back. He shivered and said: "Cold as a fjord!"

"Colder than that," the other corrected him. "And growing colder all the time! My time approaches, do you see? You don't see? Then I'll explain. Except I would ask you, don't interrupt. Let me tell it all, and then you might understand. Agreed?"

"Some things I already understand," said Tarra. "Like how mistaken I've been to save your life: once when you lay on the bottom of the sea, where I should have left you, and once when the slaves might have killed you if I hadn't persuaded them otherwise. What I don't understand is why I did these things."

"Then hear me out and maybe you will," said the other. And this is the story he told:

"First let me tell you, I am not the original Black Yoppaloth. I am the second. Oh, I know there are certain legends which have it that there have been nine Yoppaloths, but that's a mere myth put about by Theem'hdra's lesser mages. Most of them desire to keep secret the fact of my immortality; a jealous lot, they prefer not to believe in a superior sorcerer. Rather, they do not wish to lessen their own estates in the eyes of ordinary men. But in their hearts they fear me as a mage without peer. Ah, if only they knew!

"But in fact there have been only two Yoppaloths: the first—who grew mighty toward the end of Mylakhrion's time, more than eleven hundred years ago—and the second, myself, lord and master of kingless Shadarabar for the past millennium.

"But how can this be? I am a man like other men, as you have seen. I have man's moods and passions, man's lusts—though burning less fiercely now—and all his normal appetites. In aspect I might appear less like a true wizard than even the lowliest rune-caster! Indeed, only my physical appearance—which sets me aside somewhat, but not I think too far—belies the fact that I am *entirely* ordinary. Where are my familiars, my cloak of sigils, wand of power and runebooks? What? A wizard? How so? Well, let me tell you that I am *not* a wizard—not in the common meaning of the word! And yet I am extraordinary. Would you believe it if I told you that I have been what I have been, that I am what I am, because there is no alternative?

"More than a thousand years ago, I was a blond-haired, green-eyed lad living in a village south of the Lohr River where it meets the Eastern Ocean. Ah? Astonishment in your face, Tarra Khash?

Say nothing, hear me out. A lad, aye, white-skinned—far paler than your bronze hide—and green-eyed, whose mother tended a vegetable patch while her husband fished. That was my family, and twenty more like it in that little village by the sea, at the mouth of the Lohr. But all of this a thousand years ago, Tarra Khash, and Klühn itself no bigger than a small town in those days.

"I was thirteen when Yoppaloth came up from Shadarabar along the coast with his ships out of Shad. All along the way he'd butchered and raped, looted, burned and taken slaves. His ships were crammed with slaves, and *his* ship carried a handful of virgins, which he guarded most jealously."

"I've heard this tale before." Tarra could not help but interrupt.

"Then hear it again!" cried the other. "Yoppaloth came to my village in the night from where he'd anchored his ships down the coast. My mother died that night, horribly! And my father—a bull of a man, for all that he was a fisherman—roared and raved and slew like a berserker, but in the end was taken. And Yoppaloth well-satisfied to have found a fighter like him for his arena of death. I was taken, too, for I was young, and blond and green-eyed; indeed I was a handsome lad... and Yoppaloth was a pederast!

"And so we were shipped to Shad. On the voyage Yoppaloth took me for himself, and because life was dear I made no real protest. While I pretended to love him, I loathed him. But I learned how to control myself and how not to cry out, how to show no fear and even how to feign enjoyment of his enormities; but inside I had set myself a goal, which was this: one day, by fair means or foul, I'd kill him!

"The ships arrived in Shad; slaves were put ashore, along with twelve wondrous virgins; all were herded through the gorgeous, sweltering city into Yoppaloth's palace at the edge of a mighty jungle. In a very little while the necromancer came to trust me. I was given free run of the palace; I could do whatever I wished, go where I pleased— except the slave-quarters, which were forbidden. And that was where I most wanted to go, for my father was there.

"Out of frustration, I wandered the length and breadth of that great palace: to the topmost roof of its five ziggurat tiers towering above the jungle, and down into the many mazy levels below. And I discovered great wonders and greater horrors! I found Yoppaloth's sunken arena, guarded by giant statues of all the dark gods and beings of an hundred alien pantheons, and I saw the work in progress there. The floor of that place was of sand turned red with the powdered blood of men; ah!—but now that floor was being freshened, replaced, made clean for—

"For what? I was soon to find out!

"Yoppaloth, that great black-skinned, black-hearted beast of a sorcerer, had made a pact with the dark god Yibb-Tstll. The pact was this: that Yoppaloth would worship Yibb and make sacrifice unto him all his days, for which the payment would be immortality! Well, and he *had* worshipped him, and payment was due now. And so that hell-god had instructed Yoppaloth in his dreams what he must do, and the preparations were these: that he must bring back an hundred slaves to Shad, and a dozen young virgins, all to be used up in the arena of death.

"Now, I will not describe the ceremonies attendant unto Yoppaloth's initiation, or the orgy of blood which preceded the hour of that vile rite, but I will say this: that Yibb-Tstll was to be paid *well* for Yoppaloth's eternal life, paid in the coin of life itself, and that Yibb-Tstll is an eater of souls!

"For an hundred years the necromancer had fed that god of outer spheres on the souls of his people—usually miscreants sentenced in his courts, where there *was* only one sentence: the arena of death—but on this special occasion, the occasion of Black Yoppaloth's ascendance to immortality, the dark god's orgy would be that much more prodigious! The way of it was this:

"The slaves would be set to fight for their lives, but not against other slaves—not even against men. They were to fight monsters out of the jungles and swamps, and others out of necromantic nether-pits, against which only the strongest would survive intact of mind and limb. And to ensure they fought well, they'd be promised that in the event of ultimate victory, then that they'd have their freedom. Ah, but victory would be hard in the winning; and in any case the promise was a lie, as will be seen. Aye, for no man ever escaped with his life from Black Yoppaloth's arena of death.

"And as each brave (or not so brave) fighter died in his turn, so the monstrous god Yibb-Tstll would wake from the stone of his idol and flow forth, and take his soul. So that even in death there was no surcease of agony, no freedom from horror.

"I have said that I will not describe that—*tournament*—in its entirety; nor shall I. But I will say this: that my father was the bravest, strongest champion of all. I know for I was witness to it all. I saw him go up against beasts from the deepest jungles of Shadarabar, and monsters from Yoppaloth's necromantic nether-caves, and rise bloody but victorious over all—until the final bout. For that last grim battle was against Black Yoppaloth himself!

"Black Yoppaloth, aye! That vile creature who'd steeped himself in all the sin of this Primal Land, where sin is usually the way of it, and all the horror of his own necromantic existence, until nothing more than putrescence of mind and spirit were left in him; and at his command all the spells of dark dimensions, which at will he could call to his aid. Against evil and *power* such as that, how might a simple fisherman win, eh?

"At one end of the arena stood a dais of blood-veined onyx, above which a chimney went up through all the levels of the ziggurat above, to the orchid-scented air of Shad. Ah, that such vileness should be so perfumed! And before the dais a pit whose rim was of green and red glass, fused from the sand of the arena; aye, a pit going down as if toward hell itself, and very likely passing *into* that or those hells! Up from that pit at the appointed time, up from mazy and menacing bowels of earth undreamed, Yibb-Tstll would call the awesome energies of the Great Old Ones themselves to batten upon Black Yoppaloth and bequeath unto him the final boon—immortality. But only after he himself had dispatched the final champion of champions, and when Yibb-Tstll had taken his soul.

"And so atop that dais—that great black and red sacrificial slab— the two fought, my father and the cheating, lying monster Black Yoppaloth. Aye, and my father might have won; for he remembered his wife and how she had died, and his strength was that of ten men, even though much of his iron blood had now leaked out of him. But the foul, puffed Yoppaloth, seeing the berserker he stood against and feeling the weight of his blows, became afraid and would not fight a clean fight. He used his magick to forge chains about my father, and only when he'd bound him securely moved in for the kill. And seeing that it would soon be finished, Yibb-Tstll called forth his instrument of transfiguration, by which Yoppaloth would be made immortal.

"Up from the slippery throat of the glass pit to hell, and from what caverns of immemorial night below, swept a black, boiling cloud which had its own coherency, its own body and being. Alive with the warp and crackle of green and putrescent fires it was; and it whirled there like a small tornado, nodding over the dais where my father stood in chains of magick, clutching his bloodied, battered sword, likewise impotent, while Yoppaloth advanced upon him with a devastating weapon of his own. It was a pole like a pike, that weapon, but it was not a pike. Driven home in flesh and when its handle was twisted, then its slender head would put out razor grapples and knives *inside* the victim, making a pulp of all his organs. Twisted the other way, the scythes would retract and the head could be withdrawn, leaving a man mangled on the inside, while outside he might appear only slightly mutilated. It was Yoppaloth's favourite instrument of torture, which appealed to his perverted brain.

"Above the arena were many tiers of seats going up like some mighty council chamber, in which were seated the puppet officials and 'important' persons of Shad, and many insignificant princelings and shamans of Shadarabar's jungle tribes. I was in the first tier, on a balcony looking down on the dais, and beside me stood a huge Yhemni guard with a long sword in his belt. As below Black Yoppaloth drove his awful pike into my father's body, so I knew I could restrain myself no longer.

"Not caring whether I lived or died, with my father's screams of torment in my ears, I drew the guard's sword and sprang up onto the balcony, and from there down upon the dais—upon the monster himself. But in the moment of time between my father's scream and the reaction it brought in me—things had happened.

"Yibb-Tstll's idol, stone no longer, had flowed forward to receive tribute of the toppling cadaver which had been my father; the swirling, whirlpool cloud of alien energies from the pit had spawned emerald lightnings which wove themselves into a mesh about the foul, fat form of Yoppaloth; the entire dais streamed with licking rivers of tomb-fire. You have seen such fires, Tarra Khash.

"But for all that had happened, that *was* happening, I knew only one thing: which was that Yoppaloth must die, here and now! What

I could not know was this: that in his dying, *another* Yoppaloth would be born.

"In my wild plunge from the balcony, I had driven my sword before me; and in the last instant before I struck, then Yoppaloth sensed all was not well and looked up. He was a sorcerer, yes, but even magick takes a little time in the weaving; and dazed by the green lightnings and astonished by the intrusion, the necromancer was at my mercy. Into his gaping mouth I drove my blade, and down that throbbing gullet, until the sword jammed within him! Then my hurtling weight was on it, and the keen edge cut him open like a gutted fish! He was sheared through lip and wobbling black chins, through throat, breast and gut, and fell with me to the dais' cold stone. Aye, and that stone *was* cold, preternaturally so! I ignored the alien rime which dusted its surface, leaped up and split Yoppaloth's head through his skull, shattering his mad and corrupt brain.

"And lo, where the green fires from some subterranean hell had fastened on him, *now they enveloped me!*"

Black Yoppaloth II's voice had fallen to the merest murmur, the veriest shiver of sound. Tarra leaned forward, ears straining, to miss no single word that was spoken. And so fascinated the Hrossak, that he ignored utterly his own possible danger in that tattered black tent on a ship speeding for Shad. "The immortality of the Great Old Ones was conferred upon you instead of him!" he finally gasped.

Yoppaloth, staring at him with eyes of doom, eventually nodded. "Indeed, for after what I'd done to the necromancer no power in all Theem'hdra—neither magick nor medicine—could ever have returned him to life. But the weird green lightning webs of the pit had to expend themselves somewhere. And they did...in me!"

Black Yoppaloth's glittery eyes were deep and cold as the black borehole of which he'd spoken, of which he now once more spoke:

"The cold blackened me," he said. "That coldness of the pit, evil exhalation of alien gods. It blackened my skin and my eyes and my soul, which may never more be purified. I *am* immortal! Unless by some unknown means a man or wizard slay me, or some accident unforeseen, I *shall* live forever. But no disease may ravage me, be sure, and time alone shall not prevail.

"In my first hundred years I aged to a man, since when I've stayed as you see me now; except I've suffered...certain alterations. But while cities of stone have crumbled and been rebuilded, and mummies withered in their sarcophagi, and men have come and gone in their many thousands, I have lived on, *must* live on—if Yibb-Tstll is not to walk free forever in the world of men!

"Did I say that the necromancer I destroyed was a cheat and a liar? And if *he* was these things, how then the immemorially evil Old Ones? How then Yibb-Tstll?

"Do you know the legend of the Old Ones, Tarra Khash? I shall tell it:

"Even before this Primal Land was born of a vast volcano—that mighty cone which houses the Inner Isles—and before ever men came to the world, there were Others here seeped down from worlds of antique horror. They came with the Cthulhu spawn, which built their cities in steaming fens before ever the first lungfish crawled out from the sea upon the land. Yibb-Tstll was one of them, Tsathoggua the toad-thing another, Yogg-Sothoth of the shimmering globes a third, and Ithaqua the Wind-Walker, who is worshipped in Yaht-Haal to this very day, a fourth. And yet these are only a handful. They were legion, these beings, a veritable army, and they fastened on the inchoate worlds of our sun, and on the worlds of other stars farther afield.

"Authors of incredible sin, they had come here to escape the wrath of others mightier still, who followed them and bound them with awesome magicks, and prisoned them in places beyond Man's five senses to perceive. Indeed, Man was merely one of nature's lesser visions, a faint possibility, when all these things transpired. But while the aeons wore on and men came to be, still the prisoned Old Ones waited out their time in dark forgotten corners, sunken sepulchres and alien spheres. The Hounds of Tindalos were trapped in time itself, and the Thromb throbbed in cauldrons of gravity in the hearts of collapsed stars. But down all the ages the Old Ones had retained their dark instinct for evil and certain immundane skills. One such skill which was theirs was mentalism, which now they turned upon the untutored, innocent, sleeping minds of men.

"Thus have the cults of Cthulhu and his minion creatures risen, and thus are they kept alive by his unspeakable dreaming! And always the Old Ones, who are themselves immortal, strive to return; which one day, when the stars are right, be sure they will. Even now Ithaqua strides in partial freedom, mercifully confined to those frozen lands north of the Great Ice Barrier, where men may not live, and to the routes of the winds that blow between the worlds; and Cthulhu lies in his sunken house, which went down in the year of the red moon under the sea. Ghatanothoa is worshipped still in Eyphra, and men have made unto themselves idols in the hideous shapes of Tsathoggua and Yibb-Tstll, one of which glooms even now in my arena of death in Shad. Mine now, aye, as is this undying nightmare which fools crave and call 'immortality'!

"Now how may men, even sorcerers supreme, have dealings with beings such as these and go unscathed? The answer is simple: they may not! Mylakhrion, that mightiest of mages, sought Cthulhu's secrets and perished. A race of lizard-kings dwelled upon a time in the land of Lohmi; they, too, worshipped the Great Kraken, and where are they now? Gone, extinct! And Yoppaloth? That first Yoppaloth, whom I slew, would he have fared any better? Could he have done any better than the second Yoppaloth, myself, in the thousand years gone by since that time I killed him? No, for he was a coward and mad, and I think he would have let the Old Ones in—while I have done all in my power to keep them out!

"Ah, I see in your eyes that I've lost you. What, and have I rambled so? But you are a man I can talk to, Tarra Khash; and talk I must, for these things have burdened my sorry soul long enough. Let me then say on:

"In the moment when I slew Yoppaloth—as the pit-spawned emerald fires withdrew from me and the cloud itself fled back down into the gibbering dark—then the dead sorcerer's people would have killed me. Oh, they were glad he was dead and no mistake, for now they saw that their own miserable existences were safe, as they'd never been when he lived; but now that he *was* dead it would be good to show how brave they were, grand sport to come down upon me in the arena and slay me. Indeed, they would have done it—if not for a weird intervention!

"The dark god Yibb-Tstll had spent an hundred years grooming Yoppaloth for the part he was to play in a great resurgence of Old

Ones' power. Most of a millennium yet to go before the necromancer would be—or would have been—ready. And should the god admit defeat and return once more to stone, and begin his search for dark receptacle again? And what of the alien infusions I had received from unthinkable pits of Cthonian horror at Earth's core? Should they, too, be wasted? I had destroyed Yoppaloth utterly, but in so doing had shown that my own instinct for destruction—even as a boy—was as great, greater than his.

"Moreover, within the limits I have mentioned, I was now immortal; unless I, too, was somehow slain or fall victim to some shattering cataclysm, I might live forever—or until They were ready!

"Yibb-Tstll 'saved' me—as I reckoned it then. Have you ever seen a likeness of him, Tarra Khash? Even an idol made in his image? Better for you if you never know that dubious privilege. And certainly the *real thing* is far worse! But he saved me and let it be known in several ways that he approved of me. First, when they shook their spears and knives at me, he came to me; and he opened his billowing cloak to let out his gaunts of night, which he set about me as my guardians, to let the men of Shad see that I was their new mage and master, not to be harmed, indeed inviolate. Then, even before those watching thousands, he hunched over the riven carcass of the dead Yoppaloth and took his soul—took it in that singular way of his, with terrible 'hands' more loathsome than any weapon of Yoppaloth's devise—and having done so tossed it, aye, and the corpse of my poor father, too, into that pit itself. And finally Yibb opened his cloak again to embrace me as his newly chosen one, following which I fell upon the dais altar as one seared and dead. But I was not dead, merely depleted. And after that they could not kill me, for he had declared me their master. Master of Shad and Shadarabar, aye, but prisoner, too. For no way I could escape from that jungled isle, where now I had become Yibb's instrument in the world of men.

"In days I was well again, and days became weeks, weeks months; so time passed…I found myself heir to Yoppaloth's palace, his slaves; heir to his power, within limits; heir, too, to much more than these things. A man may not be touched by the aura of the inner immensities and remain unchanged. I had been changed. Where were my green eyes, blond hair and pale skin now? Gone! I was black, and not merely in aspect. Evil was in me, and it was growing there.

"Yibb-Tstll—or his avatar, locked for the main in its stone idol in the arena of death, just as the god himself is locked in alien voids outside this universe—was wont to visit me in the night, in my deepest dreams, to remind me of my debt. For like it or not, I had also inherited the first Yoppaloth's pact: I had immortality, and Yibb-Tstll must have his worship, his sacrifices. Sacrifices, Tarra Khash—an annual offering of souls—and mine the hand of death which now must point out the victims. Ah, but I did that readily enough!

"They were the ones who'd stood up in their stone tier seats, in their pomp and barbaric splendour, to applaud Yoppaloth's terrible tournament; the ones who'd roared their heathen approval when he'd thrust that nightmarish pike of his into my father's side and twisted the handle. And I remembered each and every one of them—each tribal chief or piddling shaman, every personage of estate in Shad—the lot! And by twos and threes as the years slowly passed, so they met their fates in the arena of death. Not slaughter on such a scale as I'd seen that first time, no, but terrible for all that. To see a man taken *alive* by Yibb-Tstll, and have his soul torn out of him, is...terrible! It is still terrible even now, ten thousand souls later.

"And so I kept down any would-be rivals, enemies, by feeding their souls to Yibb; and so his evil grew in me, a cancer spreading through my entire being.

"I became a man with a man's needs, took wives and tired of them—or allowed them to grow too close to me—then offered them to my god. Of children there were none. If a woman carried my child, she went to Yibb. My cruelties, all inspired by the monster-god himself, became enormous. Now I could understand why the first Yoppaloth's acts and appetites had been so gross; for at day's end and before sleeping, I would lie awake and feel the same fate which took him reaching to engulf me. It was my imagination—or was it?

"Whichever, it could not be allowed: I was immortal and would not be slain, neither by any man, nor by magick or any unthinkable accident. And so I must protect myself... But how?

"I was no magician, no sorcerer or necromancer. I *had been* a mere youth when taken to Shad. I knew nothing save those vile things Yibb-Tstll had shown me and instilled in me. But the one thing I did have in abundance was time. And given time even an ignorant man may do—may learn—almost anything.

"Magick was the answer. I was already becoming legendary to the Yhemni, and the legend grew as they aged and died and I lived on. They saw me now as a great necromancer, but I was not! And so, since I had now resigned myself to Shad and Shadarabar (where else could I go in Theem'hdra and be accepted?) I determined to *become* that legend, to indulge myself in the first Yoppaloth's legacy and learn all the mazy alchemical and necromantic secrets he'd left behind him. And who could say, perhaps I'd also discover a way to break Yibb's hold on me, leave Shad forever and cleanse myself, and thus make at least partial return to the innocence of yore.

"Such were my thoughts during periods of high spirits, when on occasion I was given to believe I might rise above the pits I'd already fathomed and others which plunged deeper yet. But when my darker side held sway and I heard Yibb's call in the night, then I'd sneer at my own childish whimsies. Nevertheless, I set about to discover all I could of the former Yoppaloth's magicks and mysteries, the full extent of his esoteric and necromantic knowledge.

"In nether dungeons hewn from the bedrock beneath his palace, he had kept creatures of unbelievable hideousness, hybrid things spawned of madness, which he'd used in his annual tournaments. Since some of these—*anomalies*—were at least part-human and intelligent, I determined to question them as to their genesis: I determined to know how Yoppaloth had created them. The most advanced of these beings, able to converse, told me that the wizard had simply followed Yibb-Tstll's instructions in this regard, for he himself had not the magickal skills to produce such miscegenies.

"I found it passing suspicious to discover Yoppaloth lacking in such matters, but put this out of mind and proceeded next to explore his laboratory. Here another revelation: such devices as he'd owned were meagre things, in no way complicated but rather crude and unbecoming of a mage of alleged magnitude. Where were his shewstones, his dire familiars, his potions and poisons and other persuasions? Where were his books and, more essentially, his runebooks? No library at all that I had discovered; no tractates, codices, scrolls or inscribed tablets, nor any incunabula whatever! Nothing! A wizard? Even a middling magician? From where I stood, Black Yoppaloth the First had not even owned a wand!

"And so I arrived at an hitherto unthinkable conclusion: he'd been no mage at all but had relied entirely upon his mentor, Yibb-Tstll, for whatever he'd required in the way of morbid magicks. In this I was somewhat mistaken, but not utterly...

"Eventually I came across Yoppaloth's most secret place, a locked tower room, which I broke open to discover its purpose. And now at last I could see for myself how the monster god had used and misused—and planned to *further* misuse—his priestling. For *here* were his magicks— but all of them limited to a single purpose, all channelled along the same sad route. Yoppaloth's 'magick' was that of the ultimate coward: each charm, each rune, all powers and potencies, were without exception designed *for his own protection*!

"Here were deflective devices, to turn aside the perilous spells and caustic conjurations of others; and here likenesses of Yoppaloth in precious metals, upon which certain mordancies might spend themselves in place of their true target. Here were antidotes for every known and some unknown poisons, runes against the Red Rot and Purple Pestilence (which might easily fret to nothing even a man supposedly immortal!) and assorted activates to counter and work against the senders of other thaumaturgical terrors.

"And the fantastic truth which all of these things revealed to me was this: that Black Yoppaloth's every living moment had been one of abject fear, indeed a palsy of fright! So that all that remained was to discover *what* he had so feared, and *why*."

Tarra Khash could keep silent no longer. "And did you discover those things?"

"Aye," the other nodded, as the light from the green lantern burned lower, "I did. It was all written there in the pact itself! There in that secret room, kept locked an hundred years except when Yoppaloth cowered there. And this is what he'd set his seal upon:

"That he would serve Yibb-Tstll, and through him the Old Ones, until the time of their return, which was to be a period of one thousand years. In that time, for his pains, Black Yoppaloth would be Lord of Shad and Shadarabar and master over all therein, but afterwards he would become the undisputed Master of all Theem'hdra, mighty above all men. Indeed, all man's works would be his, everything, and none to stay his hand. All the wealth of the cities would be his, and even the cities themselves, and the entire world would belong to Yoppaloth—so long as he served the Old Ones, did their bidding and made sacrifices unto them.

"Until that time, he would feed Yibb-Tstll on the souls of many men and make him strong; periodically, he would make small sacrifices to the god, and annually would glut him with souls. And each hundred years he would prepare for Yibb and the Old Ones a special feast, preceded by an unthinkable orgy of blood spilled in detestable combat; and the games would be of his devising, cruel almost beyond imagination, for which the Old Ones, though they could not be there in the flesh, would bless him and look upon him as their one true priest in the world of men.

"And that was the pact against which Black Yoppaloth, great fat fool, had set his seal, to which he'd sworn, upon which oath he'd pledged his soul! And how could he lose? Cruel by nature, the pact guaranteed an excess of cruelty lasting a thousand years, and then lasting an eternity; greedy, an entire world had been promised him to rule, mighty above all men. And yet, even signing, even pledging his soul to this calamitous compact, Yoppaloth felt a tremor in his limbs, a sudden shaft in his heart. So that for the first time he felt—afraid! But that had been only the beginning of the fear.

"Now, in his dreams, he heard the booming laughter of the Old Ones and felt them near as never before; and so he determined to reassure himself, by calling up Yibb-Tstll to come to him and tell him how it would be when in fact the Old Ones came and made him Master of the World. And the monster-god had declared that it *would be* as promised, exactly so, and had shown him the future he'd set his seal to. The future, aye, but in no wise the future as Yoppaloth had pictured it! For this is what Yibb-Tstll showed him:

"A future world where men were no more—a world *cleared off* of the entire human race—where Man's cities lay crumbling in vast red blighted deserts. And rising in the distance, the twisted spires and turrets of cities vast and grey and terrible, mighty windowless mausoleums, and mad, cyclopean statuaries whose very angles defied Yoppaloth's eye to fathom their true shapes and perspectives. The cities of the Old Ones! And so he saw the world over which he'd one day rule, and finally he *understood* the words of the pact.

"'Mighty over all men'—because there would *be* no other men! 'Ruler of all Man's cities and works'—crumbling piles shattered by the Old Ones' coming, or simply fallen into the decay of ages, untended in a world without human tenants. But…if Yibb and the Old Ones would destroy the entire human race, then how might Yoppaloth make sacrifice unto them? Must he sacrifice the beasts of the fields? And was this how he'd spend his immortality, in the never-ending service of creatures from black pits of earth, far stars and darkling spheres?

"At which point Yoppaloth, who to this juncture had been half-mad, went completely insane! For he knew now that he was doomed. Beasts for sacrifice? But he had seen no beasts in that future world—there had been no beasts! *Nothing* had lived there, save the Old Ones themselves in their terrible cities, and puffed Shoggoths in foul black lakes. And if they had left nothing that he might sacrifice to them, then the pact would be broken and his own soul forfeit. Aye, and Yoppaloth had *seen* how Yibb-Tstll took the souls of men and knew only too well how monstrous would be his fate.

"His only hope was this: that if he served Them *exceedingly* well in the thousand years before their coming, then that they'd leave some small part of Theem'hdra for him, and stock it with men and beasts, so that he might continue to serve them. And so, Tarra Khash, this was Yoppaloth's lot up to the moment when I killed him…"

And now Black Yoppaloth II fell silent, and in the near-darkness as the lantern burned lower still, only the gleam of his black eyes and certain greenly illuminated highlights of his skeletal features could be seen…

Hypnotized by his ominous host's story, and by the circumstances of its telling, Tarra Khash was silent for long moments; then, with an effort of will, he dragged himself back to the here and now. "And so you inherited his curse," he finally said. "Which seems to me a very difficult thing to understand."

"How so?" The other glanced at him.

Tarra shrugged. "He'd spent the best part of an hundred years gathering protections for his life—indeed he *was* protected by Yibb and the Old Ones themselves—and yet you succeeded in killing him."

"Good!" said the other. "That was a mystery which puzzled me, too, when first I gave it thought. Especially having found the necromancer's secret tower room and read his story. But while I have *called* him a necromancer, wizard, mage and such, in truth he was none of these things. I reason it like this:

"That in the moment of supramundane influx—when that whirlwind from subterranean regions would have transferred to Yoppaloth strength to resist the ages, which I received in his stead—then that all his protective devices were cancelled. The magick of the Old Ones was greater than his and put all such petty spells and simples aside, which left him open not only to Their device but also to my sword."

Tarra nodded. "Since when you've accumulated magicks of your own, such as the powers you call on to give you strength, which you draw like a vampire from your victims. Also the bolt you hurled at some unseen foe, back there on the island where all very nearly came unstuck."

Yoppaloth shook his head, gave a wry laugh. "I am protected," he answered, "right enough—and certainly I've done what I can to protect myself—but as for any other form of magick...I have none! Do you not see? Even in a thousand years, I have learned nothing of the true thaumaturgies. The Old Ones, through Yibb-Tstll, have kept all such knowledge from me. What? And do you think they'd let me dabble, and perhaps discover a means to rid myself—and the world—of their curse?"

"But I have *seen* you hurl a bolt of green fire, which expended itself in the sky!" Tarra insisted.

"I was *warned* that someone spied upon me," the other patiently explained, "and was delivered of just enough power to deal with the incursion. I tell you, I have no magick—not of my own making! Even the winds which blow me home to Shad, they are not of my calling. They are *sent*, by powers whose sway over me is great and greater than any puppet-master's over his puppets..."

Tarra shook his head in wonder. "Then your fix is exactly the same as that of the first Yoppaloth," he said.

"No, it is worse than that of the first Yoppaloth," the other gloomed, "for he had worried over his fate for only one century, while I have worried over mine for ten. It drove him mad in a very little while, and as for me... Well, in any case, that fate is now upon me."

"Upon you?" Things were only just beginning to connect up in the Hrossak's mind. He frowned—then gasped: "A thousand years—the compact nears completion!"

Black Yoppaloth nodded. "Indeed," he said. "It matures tomorrow night, in Shad, in the arena of death!"

"Turn back the boats!" Tarra cried at once. "Flee! There's no alternative, for you've seen what the Old Ones intend for this world."

The other laughed a harsh, grinding laugh. "I've fled more times than I can number," he answered. "Always they bring me back."

"Then kill yourself!" The words slipped out before Tarra could stop them.

"Oh?" The other's gaze was bleak upon him. "And would you be so brave? Yes, I dare say you would. Well, I have tried—and failed—and then been punished. Do you forget? I'm immortal."

"Unless some man kill you!" Tarra barely breathed the words; but this time at least, he let them come out of his own will.

Their eyes met in the near-darkness. "But how?" Black Yoppaloth whispered. "It can't be done, until tomorrow night. And even then only at the exact moment, that single instant of time."

Tarra felt the muscles bunching of their own accord in his arms, felt his fingers crooking, his body trembling as he fought against its leaning towards his host. Immortal Black Yoppaloth might well be, but there were certain things a man must find out for himself. At which moment, the guttering lantern went out...

Tarra forced himself to relax, heard Black Yoppaloth's frosty voice in the sudden, smoky darkness:

"You see, Tarra Khash? Protected!" Then fingers of ice took Tarra's shoulder, drew him to his feet, thrust him from the tent. He stood blinded by moonlight, gazed back into utter darkness. "I knew you'd be tempted," came that cold, cold voice from within. "And didn't I tell you not to come to Shad? Didn't I warn you? Well, and now we're almost there, and so another warning:

"No man will harm you in Shad, Tarra, so long as you stay well clear of my palace. That's my word. Even if you come there, they'll not harm you—but be advised in this matter, do not come."

"Because in that case *you* would harm me?"

Silence answered the Hrossak's question.

"But what good will it do to stay away?" Tarra pressed. "The world is doomed anyway."

"So it would seem," the cold voice agreed, "but would you risk a thousand-year nightmare for yourself—or immediate physical destruction and eternal torment for your living soul—when it can all be ended for the world in a single moment?"

Tarra gritted his teeth, slowly turned away; but from behind:

"Tell me just one thing, Hrossak. That first time in my tent, the trial with the knife: did you let me win?"

"I don't know," Tarra answered truthfully. "Maybe I could have moved faster. But I knew that if I won I lost: if I tried to kill you, then that you or your Yhemnis would surely kill me."

"Hmm!" the other mused.

"And you?" Tarra's turn to question. "At ocean's rim, the trial with the sword? Oh, I know I moved faster that time than ever before in my entire life—but did you let *me* win?"

After a moment: "Perhaps," said Yoppaloth. "It was that or kill you, which I had no desire to do. And of course I knew that you couldn't kill me. So—maybe Shad was always your destiny after all. We can only wait and see."

Then there was nothing but silence and the soft slap of waves against the hull, and in a little while Tarra moved away...

XI
VARIOUS MAGICKS!

Anew dawn came to Theem'hdra, turned to a new day, which in time lengthened toward evening. Perhaps the last evening.

As the sun surrendered to Cthon's nets and dipped down under the rim of the world, so Orbiquita was borne safely to the surface of the desert. Changing even as her ex-sisters carried her up from the brimstone reek of their secret place, the excommunicated lamia lost all of her loathsomeness and metamorphosed into that delicious human female form she had always loved best; so that by the time the blow-hole opened to a smoking pit, her delicate lungs were burning and her eyes streaming from the sulphurous heat and stench. Lamia memory was fading, too, but not so much that she'd forgotten her rights.

"To Teh Atht," she gasped, choking out the words as they dumped her unceremoniously onto the side of a dune which was already cooling in its own shade. "Take me to my cousin, in his manse in Klühn."

Iniquiss was with them and listened awhile to their grumbling, but finally she gave the request her approval. "Aye, take her to that puny sorcerer relative of hers, if that's what she wants," she said. And to Orbiquita: "Two more requests, my girl, and then you're on your own."

As a cloud they flew her over the Mountains of Lohmi, the plains and scrublands, the Great Eastern Range and the River Lohr, then dipped down out of a sky already sprinkled with stars toward the softly litten aerie which was Teh Atht's manse. And all accomplished at a great, whirring speed, so that Orbiquita—a mere girl now—was breathless from the headlong rush of it and dizzy in the spiral of the final descent to her cousin's place, built on the craggy stub of a promontory in the rounded bite of the Bay of Klühn.

There, all day, the wizard had worriedly paced the crystal-paved flags of his rooms, finally going up to a tower workshop he no longer used and out onto its balcony. And there, too, he now saw against the stars and dark blue sky a darker knot of figures falling, and wondered at this weird aerial phenomenon. But not for long.

"Lamias!" he breathed as their shapes became more apparent, and he at once threw up a Keep-Ye-Out, which might have worked with one lamia but not with an entire flock. They dropped right through the spell, their wings beating their hot, foul stink into Teh Atht's face as they deposited Orbiquita upon his balcony.

"What?" he cried, falling back from them, toward the archway leading to the descending stone stairwell. "What? Lamias—with whom I've nothing of disagreement—invading my house and at such a time? Or is it merely portent of the hastening calamity? Are you, then, the chosen harbingers of a world's doom?"

"Our visit is portent of nothing, wizard," Iniquiss breathed brimstone upon him, pushed Orbiquita into the protection of his uplifted arms. "Except this poor creature desired to be brought here, to the manse of her cousin!"

"Her cous—?" Teh Atht began to repeat the Great Lamia's words, until his jaw fell open and stopped him. He looked at the lovely naked girl in his arms, then at her vile ex-sisters where they lifted off on leathery membrane wings. "Orbiquita?"

She by now was recovered from her momentary nausea, and she clutched at him in seeming desperation. "Does he live?" she begged, in an urgent but entirely human voice, indeed with the voice of a sweet girl. And then of course Teh Atht knew for a certainty that this was Orbiquita.

"Tarra Khash?" he said, quite needlessly.

"Of course, Tarra Khash," she answered, with that creeping into her voice to hint of what she'd recently been. "Only say that he lives, cousin, for if not I'll call down Iniquiss and her brood and beg of them my second boon, which will involve yourself most direly..."

By now the lamia flock was risen far up into the night, but still Teh Atht peered nervously after them and held the girl close. And when at last they were diminished to black specks against the stars, then he answered: "Aye, he lives, cousin—for now. We *all* live—for now! But what's this? Have you broken your vows, put the Sisterhood behind you? For a man? Incredible!"

She nodded, shivered, and he at once took her inside and down into warm apartments where he found clothes for her. Then he led her to the room of the astrologarium and showed her the flux and flow of its plasm, explaining to her the awesome meaning which he read in the doomful rush and reel of moons, planets, comets and stars. Following which, when his words had sunk in, he said:

"And so you see, Orbiquita, how all of your trials are come to naught. Your Tarra is doomed, as are we all—as is the world!"

She had been patient, but now demanded: "Show him to me."

"Have I not explained?" Teh Atht threw wide his hands. "I *dare not* use my shewstone! For all I know Black Yoppaloth is waiting for me even now on the other side of the scrying. And in any case, this is only a small—"

"But the merest glimpse!" she pleaded, cutting his protests short. "A glimpse—of Tarra alone and not this necromancer you so greatly fear."

Fear Shad's monstrous mage? Yes, Teh Atht had to admit that he did. But the contradiction was clear: what use to fear anyone or anything when the sands of time were running out for all Theem'hdra, a process due to terminate in ultimate chaos, death and destruction this very night? Teh Atht hesitated a moment longer, then strode to his shewstone.

Activating the orb, he commanded: "Seek out the Hrossak and let me see him—for an instant only!" Then he shielded his eyes and advised Orbiquita to do the same.

The crystal ball's screen opened, then closed at once. But not before the maiden and mage had seen Tarra seated by lantern's gleam on the flat, walled roof of a tavern, where an obese, worried-looking Yhemni proprietor served him booze before shuffling back to a low bar. Other than these two, however, tradesman and customer, the place had seemed very empty and lonely.

"There!" said Teh Atht, nodding. "In Shad, as I foretold. Alive and well, it would seem. Meanwhile the evening turns to night, and there are far more important things to—"

He paused and his eyes grew very round. And in that moment all became clear to him, the pieces of the puzzle falling into place and locking there, so that the white mage of Klühn could see all at a glance. Before...everything had seemed coincidental, but now at last the final connection was made.

The astrologarium had told him that the world was to end, that tonight the stars would stand in strange conjunction, when the Ultimate Forces of Evil would stride forth to claim their sovereignty. This much he had known, but not the mechanics of the thing. Now he knew all, knew *how* they would breach those dimensional gates which so long had held them at bay. Black Yoppaloth was in their service, and held the keys to their immemorial prisons. Tonight, in his arena of death, the necromancer was going to let them out, and let them *in* to the comparatively sane and ordered world of men! And nothing, no one, no man strong enough to stand in Yoppaloth's way. Unless...Tarra Khash?

Out of darkness, light at the end of a tunnel. But a very faint light, holding little of promise as yet. Still, a little hope is better than no hope at all.

Teh Atht turned from the contemplation of his now quiescent shewstone, said: "Orbiqu—?"

She was no longer there!

From above came a faint whirring of wings, the harsh tones of barely female voices in seeming argument, a hot waft of sulphur and hell's own vapours. Teh Atht, for all that he was old and tired, ran from the room of the astrologarium and took the stone stairs three at a time. Lurching out onto the topmost balcony, he saw that he was too late, saw the lamia flock distantly limned against the sky where the indigo horizon met the black of space.

Orbiquita's second boon had been granted: to be with the man she loved on this one last night of all nights! By the light of the stars, and of Gleeth, whose rim now showed rising over the mountains, the creatures she had called her sisters winged her south for Shadarabar!

On the roof of Na-dom, Amyr Arn turned the bleak bronze discs of his eyes toward Gleeth, whose rim was up over the edge of the world. Bronze those eyes of his, aye, where they should be golden, and bleak, too, his frame of mind. Suhm-yi senses, which numbered in excess of Man's usual five, had warned him that things were far from right in the Primal Land. And not alone for Tarra Khash, though certainly he were the focus.

The stars, reflected in the Crater Sea far below, seemed somehow to peep and leer in a manner strange and ominous, and an unseasonably chill wind had blown all day from the south-east, which by rights should have been a warm breeze. And these things, plus the leaden weight of his own heart within him, told the silver-skinned Suhm-yi male that much was amiss. Worse, instincts keen as a knife had connected these omens inextricably to the plight of Tarra Khash, whom Amyr Arn loved as a brother.

And so he'd come up again to Na-dom's peak, that jagged fang beloved of the gods, to call upon Gleeth for his aid and implore the benevolent old moon-god to do whatever was in his power to do for a Hrossak in peril far away in distant Shad. And now Gleeth was rising, fat-bodied and blunt-horned, and there was something of strength in him where he cleared the rim of the horizon and sailed for the sky. Now Amyr could make his obeisances, commence his prayers and beg of Gleeth his favours. But as to whether the moon-god (traditionally deaf and blind) would see or hear him, that was a different matter...

The same moon shone at a shallow slant down upon barbarically splendid Shad, where now the taverns and dwellings were beginning to empty as a silent populace made its teeming way through the streets toward Black Yoppaloth's palace at jungle's fringe. All of marble, copper, gold, ivory and iron-wood, Shad's domes and spires, roofs and façades caught and gave back the moon's glints; likewise the white, often sharply pointed teeth of Shad's people, and their golden bangles, earrings and other trinkets—and the sweat on their shiny-black trembling faces. Aye, for their terror was also reflected, and not alone by moon and starlight. No, for another source of illumination lit Shad this night, the alien aerial beacon which called the people to Black Yoppaloth's nightmare games.

Tarra Khash saw this malevolent manifestation from across the city—this weird wheeling of a corkscrew cloud, alive with coiling green serpents of fire, whose funnel stem went down to Yoppaloth's palace as if tethered there—and tossed back his fiery Yhemni drink at a single gulp. For the hellish twister over Shad seemed full of pent power, crouching on high like some silent beast, only waiting its chance to roar out loud and spring down upon the city. The clouds at its rim rolled and boiled and seethed with that now familiar phosphorescent emerald bile, and its corkscrew coil had origin in the palace whose ziggurat tiers rose square, dark and menacing across a night-gleaming panorama of vine-clad spires, domes and turrets.

The Hrossak had seen much the same sort of display before one time in Klühn, and knew that it was not of Nature's doing. Nothing of good clean earth, air, fire and water this, but born of magicks beyond the mundane mind of man to conceive; and Tarra could not help but shudder as he called for another drink.

That time in Klühn, not so very long ago: yes, it had been much like this, and yet different. Then he'd had Amyr Arn of the Suhm-yi at his side, and a positive mission in mind, with at least a chance of success. But now? What could one man, alone in a strange heathen land, hope to achieve against this? Attempting to brave the terrors of that palace would put him in jeopardy not only of his life but his immortal soul! *If* he could find his way to the arena of death, and *if* no one stopped him along the way—what then?

Tarra cursed a conscience which would not let him be to die in peace or pieces but kept prodding his all too vivid memory. The look on Loomar's face when the ships had docked in Shad's harbour this morning and the slaves—Loomar Nindiss included, and his sister, Jezza—were led away through the leering, jeering black throng. The astonishment of Northmen and rogue Hrossaks alike as they, too, had found themselves chained and dragged cursing from the dockside toward the ziggurat palace.

And what of those poor lads and lasses now?—the slaves at least, if not the betrayed mercenaries? But Tarra Khash, he'd been set free, to go his way and live whatever remained of his or anyone else's life this day. And now that day was evening, and soon it would be blackest night. The last night...

Galvanized, Tarra stood up so quickly he banged his knees, clouted the table with a fist hard as horn, gritted his teeth, scowled and sat down again. What? Challenge Yoppaloth on his own ground, in his own palace and on his terms—and hope to win? And *if* he won—why, even then he'd lose!—become heir to all the horror of a thousand-year nightmare, as the Old Ones fashioned *him* in his turn as their gateway to chaos and hell on earth! So perhaps Shad's necromantic master was right: sit back and do nothing, and let the world go to blazes in one last mad catastrophic awakening of ancient evil.

But...the madman Yoppaloth had taken his sword, and no man had ever stolen from Tarra Khash. Not and kept what he'd taken. And if this really was the last night, well wouldn't the risk be worth it? Wouldn't *anything* be worth it? Yes, it would—but first he'd put another drink away.

"Coward!" Teh Atht said it out loud for what must be the tenth time; said it to himself, for there was no one else to hear him. Even hopper and flitter, sensing the doom hanging in the air, had gone off on their own to hide. As for the wizard's third familiar, the entirely liquid one: he was in the astrologarium even now, blindly smoothing the way for the world's slippery slide to hell.

And again, for the last time: "Coward!" cried Teh Atht—but coward no longer—and he strode with great purpose and determination to the table where rested his shewstone. For he'd come to the same inescapable conclusion as Tarra Khash himself: since the end was nigh, what use to hide from it? Orbiquita, no longer lamia but soft and fragile human female, had gone in search of her Hrossak, had begged her sisters to fly her direct into the jaws of death; and Amyr

Arn, if he'd had his way, would have long since beaten her to it. So what was lacking in the white wizard of Klühn, who at the flick of a wrist could command more sheer power than both of these might muster in their entire lifetimes?

Nothing was lacking in him, except he'd been old and afraid. Well, he couldn't make himself young again, but fear was simply a state of mind, which the mind recognized in degrees. To have been afraid of what *might* happen to himself had been one thing, but his fear of what *would* happen if he took no action was far greater. With that resolution made, now he would see what could be done, would do what must be done.

"The Hrossak!" he cried, activating his shewstone. "Let me see him. Let me know his circumstances. Let me at least try to make amends for my failures, while still there's time."

The orb's opaque screen cleared: Tarra Khash sat as before at a wooden table on the flat, open roof of a tavern where it looked out across a square, out across Shad itself. Behind the Hrossak the sky was fantastically patterned, where green lightnings leaped and coruscated along the undersides of madly gyrating clouds. And seeing that vast aerial confusion of forces, Teh Atht knew he'd been right to seek Tarra out and attempt some sort of intervention. For certainly this was the portal which the Old Ones would use to gain entry into this sphere.

But first things first: now he must discover what Tarra had learned, if anything, of the man or monster he'd travelled with all these days and nights. Metempsychosis would be the answer, not a mode the wizard liked greatly (for fear of getting stuck in someone else's body) but he'd committed himself, and no turning back now. First he must take simple precautions—against the Yhemni taverner doing damage when he discovered himself transposed—and then he'd be on his way.

He clambered onto the table with the shewstone and spelled an Admirable Adhesion onto the floor all about, which at once turned soft and gummy. That should do the trick! Now for the transmigration, a more complicated magick far, which would take some little time in the fixing. Teh Atht concentrated, peered deep into the crystal ball, fixed the lumbering Yhemni with his eyes where he approached Tarra's table with another drink, and—

˙If **you want** more drink, order now." The fat black's guttural jungle tones startled Tarra back to reality, or maybe back from the alcoholic pit he'd been pursuing for much of the day. Indeed, he'd been drinking almost unabated since Black Yoppaloth had gone off with his captives and left him standing alone on the dockside; it had seemed a very logical thing to do.

Several things had seemed logical, on what was scheduled to be the world's last day. Bedding a woman or three, starting a fight, getting roaring drunk. But while Tarra made no racial discrimination, he'd known Shad's beauties wouldn't appeal to him; no woman did these days, not since he'd accepted the kiss of a certain lamia. As for brawling: Yoppaloth had decreed that no one harm him, but that didn't mean they couldn't throw him in chains! Which had left only getting drunk, something he was passably good at. But not this time; for, try as he might, and despite all the liquors which had scalded his throat and innards, he'd somehow stayed at least relatively sober.

"Order now?" he repeated the taverner. "Why, are you going somewhere?"

The other grinned a wobbly, sickly grin, showing teeth filed to fine points. "Yes I am," he nodded. "Into the jungle and find a place to hide! Until tomorrow. The jungle, aye, where there are only beasts to worry about, shelter for the thousands who have sense enough to stay away from the master's palace."

"What do you fear?" Tarra asked him.

"Death!" said the other at once. "The shrieking madness of Yoppaloth's arena! The corpses and hybrid monsters which he pits against his gladiators!"

Tarra scowled. "With your size and weight and—teeth! You, an eater of men, afraid?"

The other scowled back. "I'll eat men, when I can get 'em," he answered. "But Yoppaloth eats souls! And the slaves aren't the only ones who fight in his arena; if he runs out of captives, there's always plenty more meat amongst the onlookers."

"What's to stop me going into the palace?" Tarra questioned.

"Nothing," the Yhemni cannibal answered. "The more the better! Why, with luck you may even come out again!"

Tarra nodded. "Except he's forbidden me to go."

"He? Who? Black Yoppaloth?" The black's eyes stood out in his head. "Then you're mad to even think of it—and I'm mad to stand here talking to you!" He began to turn away. "I wish you luck, Hrossak, and—" And he paused, almost as if frozen there, half turned away.

Among all the strangeness, Tarra sensed a weird addition. Slowly the Yhemni turned back to face him; his fat black lips opened, spoke—and Tarra gasped! Gone now the man's untutored jungle slur and mode of expression, his gurgled formation of unfamiliar words. And in its place—the voice of a scholar! Oh, the *voice* was the same, but the way it was used, and what it said:

"Tarra Khash, you don't know me but I know you well enow." The huge man seated himself in a chair opposite, stared at Tarra through eyes which had lost all their sloth. "Now listen, you're a strong man and can stand any shocks I throw you, and so I'll name names and then you'll know I speak the truth. Do you understand? If so close your mouth and nod."

Tarra had been gaping. Hardly knowing why he obeyed, nevertheless he did. And the fat, black, strangely altered Yhemni taverner nodded in his turn and rapidly spoke these words:

"Stumpy Adz, Amyr Arn, Ahorra Izz, Orbiquita! There, and now you know that I know you. Now listen and I'll tell you a stranger thing: I am *not* the Yhemni taverner you take me for. Oh, I inhabit his body, for the moment, but my mind is the mind of another. Or rather, his is."

Tarra's jaw had fallen open again.

"You remember on that island where I wrecked your ship, and turned Yoppaloth to stone so that he'd sink?" The black's voice was urgent now. "Well, *do* you remember—when Cush Gemal, or more properly Black Yoppaloth, hurled a bolt of green fire into the sky? He hurled it at me! I was the wizard who scried on him that time, and did my best—or what I thought was my best—to destroy him. Close your mouth."

Tarra snapped his jaws shut again, shook his head to clear it—both of alcoholic fumes and of madly whirling thoughts. And at last he found words of his own to speak. "If you're not the man I see before me, then who are you?"

"Teh Atht," the other replied. "White wizard of Klühn. And right now *this* fellow's mind is in my body in my manse in that city. I swapped places with him, d'you see, in order to speak to you. Now listen, if we're to defeat Black Yoppaloth and keep them out who he'd let in, there are things I need to know. First off: I notice you're not wearing your sword. Does he still have it?"

Tarra nodded.

"That's bad. You know that blade's a Suhm-yi Sword of Power?"

Again Tarra's nod.

"But does Yoppaloth know it?"

"Not from my lips, no."

The black man sighed his relief. "Well, that's one point in your favour, anyway."

"In my favour?" Tarra frowned. "How do you mean?"

The other continued as if he hadn't heard him: "But it's strange that with magick such as his...I mean, I'd have sworn he'd immediately recognize such a sword."

"Magick?" The Hrossak was coming to grips with the situation. "Such as Yoppaloth's? *Huh!* He has no magick! Not of his own making. He's protected by the Old Ones, that's all." And again: "Huh!—that's *all*, indeed!—and by his own protections, which with their permission he's gathered over the years. But harmful magick to command? He has none. He can deflect, turn back another's spell upon the sender, use what powers the Old Ones may lend him—and that's all. They've taught him a little necromancy, too, and the making and mating of hybrid creatures for his arena, but that's the lot. And now? Why, now I fancy he's little more than a dangerous madman—a madman with the destiny of the whole world in his hands, yes—but no more a sorcerer than I am!"

Teh Atht's black host's turn to gape. And after a moment: "That might explain a great deal," he whispered. "For instance: I had expected him to seek me out when he discovered how I spied on him, but he did nothing except threaten."

"He wouldn't know where to begin," said Tarra.

"But he *did* hurl a bolt at me, which could have caused me great harm!"

"Power of the Old Ones," the Hrossak insisted. "The same green fires which twist and writhe in the maelstrom over the palace even now. Look, see for yourself." And he turned where he sat and pointed at the sky over Shad. "He uses that power occasionally, when he has to, but it depletes him mightily, and then like a vampire he draws on the strength of others to fill himself up again."

"But it's recorded that upon a time he sent onyx automatons against the wizard Exior K'mool!" Teh Atht protested.

"The Old Ones may well have," Tarra countered, "on his behalf, but not Yoppaloth himself. No, for if he has any magick at all, it's only—"

"Yes?"

"—It's only that people trust him. I mean, I know it sounds daft, but it's the truth. For all he's a crazy butcher, he commands respect, even loyalty. Damn me, *I* respect him!"

"*Ah!*" said the other, and sat back in his chair. Then he straightened up, looked directly into Tarra's eyes. "When you said he was no more a mage than you yourself, you came nearer to the truth than you knew. That magick you speak of is very special, Tarra Khash, a natural earth magick which men seldom aspire to. It explains your mutual attraction, yours and Yoppaloth's. And now I know why Ahorra Izz, Orbiquita, Amyr Arn and others I've seen or spoken to like and respect you so well. For it's a magick you share with him, do you see?"

"Me, magick?" Tarra could only snort, shake his head.

"Aye." The white wizard nodded his huge black curly head. "A magick which might yet save us all…"

The whirling cloud over Shad was slowly descending, lighting up the city's roofs and domes and minarets with a reflected green shimmer. Where before the city had been hushed, silent, now sounds came drifting on a wind stirred up by the lowering twister. The massed sighing of a great host of people! And then other sounds—screams! And finally the roar of a crowd's voice lifted in savage applause.

"The games in Yoppaloth's arena of death," Tarra gasped. "They've started!"

"How long will they go on, before—?" Teh Atht left the unspeakable unspoken.

"There are a lot of slaves to die first," Tarra answered.

"Then it's high time I was on my way back to my own body," said the other. "With luck I'll see you again, presently, in the arena of death."

"What?" Tarra felt the hairs rise up on the nape of his neck, but despite his dread, he understood well enough what Teh Atht meant.

The black man smiled a strange smile, and—*was changed in a moment*! Gone now Teh Atht, and the Yhemni taverner Moota Phunt returned to his rightful body. His eyes opened wide; he sprang up, fell down in a faint.

Tarra got to his feet, stood over the fallen man. He felt faint himself—both from excess of drink, and from the stink of DOOM which now hung almost tangible in the hot, jungle-perfumed air—but no time for fainting.

Time for only one thing now...

———

Teh Atht was back in his own body, on all fours on the gummy floor of the astrologarium, to which he adhered quite admirably. He cancelled the spell, stood up and dusted himself down, called hopper and flitter to attend him, and likewise the liquid one out of his astrological plasm. One glance at that miniature universe, where its wheeling spheres moved ever closer to completion of the pattern, told the white wizard that time had very nearly run out. In a matter of hours, the stars would be right. And before that he must be back in Shad.

Then, familiars three in attendance, he donned his Primary Robe of Runes and materialized his favourite wand; and moments later he and his troupe sped out from a high balcony, making all speed for Shad aboard his fantastic flying carpet. Faster than ever before, that wonderfully woven vehicle arced skyward and raced south, and Teh Atht in the prow pointing the way with his wand, never worrying that he might burn the carpet's power right out of it, but only that he get to Shad in time.

Except...in time for what?

———

At about the same time as Teh Atht crossed the Lohr, Orbiquita and her ex-sister escorts were descending toward jungled Shad. Black Yoppaloth's palace, by virtue of the many lights along its five tiers and the roar of the rabble echoing up from its vaults, was at once apparent; Orbiquita directed she be delivered there, where *exactly* being determined when she spied, on the roof of the third tier, a high-walled garden with many marble archways leading into the building at its back. For there beyond these ornate archways she'd spied rooms of fine furnishings and piled cushions, where languished a dozen gorgeous girls all scrubbed clean and clad only in silks and perfumed oils. Black Yoppaloth's harem, beyond a doubt.

The garden itself was deserted, however, for all twelve of the girls were huddled together within their quarters; and so unseen the lamia flock deposited Orbiquita there, before bidding her farewell and taking once more to the night sky. Following which she was quite alone, but resolute in her pledge that if her Tarra was in bondage to Yoppaloth, then that she'd find him here somewhere.

There in the garden she quickly shed her outer garments and hid them in a bush, and, attired as scantily as the rest, entered into the harem and found her way to huddling with the other girls. And all the while she was trying to think what best to do next. A problem which was taken out of her hands at once, for at that point precisely came an amazing diversion!

A white youth, little more than a stripling, arrived at the great latticed doors to the harem, beyond which stood a huge Yhemni eunuch. The guard started up and set about the stranger at once, to chase him away, but the boy had a knife. Before the black knew what was happening, Loomar Nindiss had slit his throat, taken the key to the harem and used it to slip inside. There he tremblingly approached the cowed girls and drew out his sister, Jezza, from their midst.

No longer chained to her companions, she left them easily enough (albeit reluctantly, for they'd all become familiar as sisters to her) and went with Loomar into the garden; the others followed after— Orbiquita likewise, to see what was happening—and began begging the youth to rescue them also. Loomar, beside himself with anxiety, frustration and regret, could only shake his tousled head; all their pleading must go for naught. His own and Jezza's escape would not be easy; any attempt to steal away the rest of the girls *en masse* would be madness!

Then he'd scaled the garden wall and, uncoiling a slender rope from his waist, had drawn up Jezza after him. A moment more and the pair had disappeared from view.

As Orbiquita and the other girls trooped back into the harem, several of them began arguing that they should raise the alarm. If not, when the dead eunuch was discovered, which must be shortly, then they'd all be implicated. And Black Yoppaloth's rage would be great. At this point Orbiquita spoke up, her voice softly sibilant as she said:

"No, we had nothing to do with it, and none can say we did." She closed the doors, reached a slender hand through their latticework and turned the key in the lock, then tossed it down alongside the dead guard. "There, and now when he's found we'll not be suspected—and those two will be away and running. For the guard and his key are out there, and we are all safe in here, and the door is locked. All is as it should be, with the exception that a eunuch is dead."

"That and the fact that we number only eleven!" one of them tearfully protested.

"Strange," said Orbiquita, very quietly, "for I make the count twelve!"

Sure enough, when they checked they found she was right, and only then did they notice the stranger in their midst. They drew back a little from her then, but Orbiquita merely put a finger to her lips, turned her head a little on one side and cautioned them. "Let it be," she warned, her eyes very bright and feral. "Or believe me, you'll have more to worry about this night than Black Yoppaloth's anger."

And then, because she looked so strange and seemed so certain, they said no more...

Atop Na-Dom's flat summit, a fretted needle spire of rock like a finger pointed skyward. And through the stem of this tallest crag, a hole like an oval eye, through which a man might gaze into the heavens on all the stars shining down on Theem'hdra. And the hole in the rock was the Eye of Gleeth, which Amyr Arn had used aforetime, and many a priest of the Suhm-yi before him.

The moon's orbit was taking him behind that lone spire even now, and soon his silver orb would fill the hole exactly like an eye, with the dark occluded section of its surface a huge eyeball gazing toward the east and somewhat south—gazing in fact upon far Shadarabar. Amyr Arn looked in that same direction, followed the silver swath of the moon across the Crater Sea, and saw auroral lights where never those lights should be. A green, crawling, sprawling aurora—a great emerald blotch disfiguring the horizon—weird and unhealthy there in the far south-east. And:

"Gleeth!" Amyr cried in his silvery voice. "There! Now you see it for yourself. Strange dark forces are at work in the Primal Land. Even in the sky, which is your domain, they manifest themselves. Now Tarra Khash is surely at the heart of this mystery, and I fear for his life. Indeed, I fear for all Theem'hdra! And so I beseech you, Gleeth, old god of the moon, look down in favour on the Hrossak this night, and aid him if you can."

A lone cloud drifted across Gleeth's face, when for long moments his rays were dimmed and their pathway across the Crater Sea faded to a thin gleaming. When at last the cloud passed, the moon had swung more surely into position behind the spire, so that indeed Amyr fancied he gazed upon some vast cycloptic eye set in a face of stone. But when he would have called again upon Gleeth for his assistance—

Hold! came the voice of the moon-god, in his ears or mind he knew not. *Say no more, Amyr Arn of the Suhm-yi. I have seen and understand all. They call me "blind" and "deaf," but I am neither one nor the other. I have made myself blind to many of Man's doings, true, for they were not fit to be seen; and certainly I have been deaf to many a man's exhortations, which were unworthy. But in you yourself I can find nothing ignoble, and in the Hrossak Tarra Khash only a very little. You are both singularly rare creatures. Which is as well, for these are singularly rare times.*

Now hear me: I feel in my orbit a tremor, the dreadful lure of stars and planets acting upon me in unison, and I know that calamity strides in the star spaces, bearing down upon this region of space and time. And you are right: Tarra Khash is the key, his is the single power by which a cosmic catastrophe may be avoided. I say "may," for events teeter upon a very narrow rim, be certain! The Hrossak cannot win on his own. Others know this, too, and rush to his side even now. And you? Would you also stand beside Tarra Khash on this night of nights?

"Would that I could," Amyr breathed, hardly daring to speak in case he broke the spell. "But how? His troubles lie in Shad, far away over mountains and rivers and plains. Grim peaks, great deeps, burning deserts separate us. There are days and weeks of travel lying between. Do you speak in riddles, old moon-god?"

Do you remember, Gleeth answered, *when you fired an arrow into my eye? And how I swallowed up that arrow and shot it out many miles away to kill the northern barbarian Kon Athar? This will be similar. Except it will require a deal more of faith. Faith in me, Amyr Arn. Your forefathers were the most faithful of creatures. And you?*

"Only tell me what I must do," Amyr replied.

Now quickly, said Gleeth. *You see the silver swath I cut across the Crater Sea? It leads to Shad. Only follow it.*

"But...how?" Amyr felt his silver skin grow cold.

Like the arrow. Run, dive, shoot yourself along my moonbeam path—to Shad!

"Hurl myself down?" Amyr's round eyes grew rounder still.

No, not down—along! And I'll set you down safe in Shad. But quickly, while yet I stand in the oval of the pierced spire.

Faith? And did Amyr have such faith? And if he had not, what then?

"Old Gleeth," he cried, "I put my faith in you!" And he ran to the rim of Na-dom and hurled himself headlong into the glare of the moon's silver path...

Two meetings occurred almost simultaneously: the first between Tarra Khash, Loomar Nindiss and his sister, and the second between Teh Atht and the lamia Sisterhood. The first was relatively down to earth:

Tarra Khash, loping through Shad's deserted streets toward the ziggurat palace, came round the corner of a building and almost collided with a pair of fleet shadows hurrying in the opposite direction.

He instinctively reached for a sword which was no longer there, then fell into a defensive crouch. And:

"Caught!" Jezza gasped. "Oh, Loomar, what now, my brother?"

Keen eyes pierced the green-glowing gloom. Came recognition!

Tarra took a deep breath. "Loomar Nindiss!" he sighed. "And Jezza. How'd you get her away?"

The youth fell into Tarra's arms, hugged him. "Tarra Khash!" he gasped, getting his wind. "I never thought I'd be so grateful to see a Hrossak!"

Tarra caught up Jezza and gave her a quick hug to reassure her, then shoved her into her brother's arms. "Quickly," he said, "tell me what's happening and how far it's gone. Also, how you got away."

"Yoppaloth set me free," said the youth. "Out of deference to you. He told me: 'Go, enjoy your freedom while you can. And thank Tarra Khash that he befriended you.' After that, I killed a harem guard, snatched Jezza, came here. But as for the rest: the tournament has begun, and men are dying in the sorcerer's arena of death. Now come with us, Tarra, and we'll flee this place. Maybe we can steal a boat, and—"

"No." Tarra shook his head. "All of this ends—tonight. Maybe for me—for you, too, and the whole world—and maybe, just maybe, not. I can't come with you. I've a date with Black Yoppaloth in his infernal arena."

"You go to the palace?" Loomar couldn't credit his own ears. "To kill Yoppaloth? Five thousand blood-crazed Yhemnis attend the games; you haven't a cat's chance in hell!"

"Cats have nine lives," said Tarra, simply. "Now go, hide yourselves in the city. If all comes to naught fleeing will do you no good anyway. If all turns out for the best—maybe I'll see you later."

"Very well," said Loomar, "but take this with you." He gave Tarra a knife, which the Hrossak at once recognized. He snorted, said:

"Just a lad, they never did search you."

Loomar nodded. "I *was* a lad," he said, "once…"

Then: Tarra wasted no more time or words but turned and loped into the shadows…

The second meeting, between Teh Atht and the lamia Sisterhood, happened like this:

As the white wizard followed Theem'hdra's eastern seaboard south and soared above the mouths of the salt lochs where they opened into the Eastern Ocean, so he spied Iniquiss and her brood coming in across the Straits of Yhem at a somewhat lower altitude. Knowing the lamias of old—and knowing also that they had taken Orbiquita to Tarra Khash, and that therefore they might have news of him—he turned westward, dipped down toward them and flew parallel for a while.

Iniquiss spotted him, scowled, flew closer; at which hopper, flitter and the entirely liquid one made themselves small as possible and crowded behind their master. "Ho, wizard!" she called out. "How now? And is this a chance meeting or what?"

Teh Atht inquired after Orbiquita, learned her whereabouts as last known, then quickly explained his mission. And he likewise hinted that the lamias might care to take a hand in whatever was to proceed, for *all* the world's creatures would be imperilled together if the Old Ones were allowed to return—lamias included.

Iniquiss gave what he said some little consideration; Orbiquita was owed one last request; perhaps it were not well to desert her at this eleventh (almost twelfth) hour. "Very well," she called out, above the cackle of her protesting lesser sisters, "we'll return to Shad at once. But don't let us detain you—go on ahead and save a little time."

Teh Atht required no more urging but turned his carpet south again, and in a little while crossed the Straits of Yhem...

Amyr Arn's flight on Gleeth's moonbeam carrier seemed languid as liquid silver, but in fact it was accomplished with speed and no small measure of discomfort, the latter coming at journey's end. From first leap into space from the flat summit of Na-dom, his silvery hide and its contents had been disassembled, had flowed into and along Gleeth's beam, had sped over the Primal Land like a fleeting moon-shadow, finally to be reassembled from dappled silvery light close to Yoppaloth's palace in Shad—over a moat of crocodiles where the ziggurat's lower east wall faced the jungle!

Splashing down and gathering to himself his wildly whirling senses, the last Suhm-yi male saw needle-toothed snouts ploughing the scummy water in his direction, made at once for the ziggurat's slimy, water-lapped wall. No entirely human creature could have hoped to scale that slippery surface of vertical marble blocks—not in the area where it met the water—but Amyr was not human.

His spatulate fingers (one less to each hand than in human beings) found crevices others would miss, and the suction of his fingertips never failed him but left astonished crocs chewing on weeds where a moment earlier his slender body had knifed through water, and Amyr already his own height up the wall, and going for all he was worth. Like a lizard he climbed, and into the first window he could find, and from there following the arena's swelling roar down dripping, disused, nitre-festooned stairwells and along winding corridors, until he'd passed through something of a maze to find himself in a dungeon of sorts, where an archway covered by a grid of iron bars at last blocked his way. But here the arena's noise was an uproar, and beyond the bars—

—Black Yoppaloth's arena of death! And even if there had been no bars, the sight Amyr saw then must certainly have stopped him dead in his tracks...

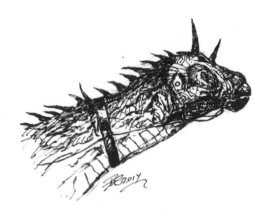

XII
To Win Is to Lose!

arra Khash looked down on that same mad scene of death and destruction; *down* on it, aye, for he'd entered the ziggurat palace at a higher level and come here by a different route. And never a man to challenge his presence in this place, for all of the palace guards—and the majority of Shad's citizens, too—were here to witness Yoppaloth's monstrous games. What Tarra (and Amyr, too) saw was this:

A circular arena, all ringed about by statues of a great many gods, their circle being broken in only one place where stood a square, blood-hued onyx dais. And in front of the dais, going down to depths beyond imagination, the glass-throated pit of which Yoppaloth II had spoken, out of which and up through the chimney above, passed the writhing tail of the greenly illumined twister.

Tarra's gaze took in the arena in its entirety: it must be forty-five to fifty paces across wall to wall, like a mighty pit itself within walls rising up maybe twelve to fifteen feet. Set in these walls, iron-barred archways led to nether vaults; above them an amphitheatre or stadium, with tiers of stone-hewed seats, going up and up, divided at intervals by aisles permitting access.

Odd, but I think I've seen all this before! Tarra told himself where he looked grimly down over the heads of the Yhemnis massed in front of him. *Last time it was in Klühn: Gorgos and his Temple of Secret Gods. And now it's here. Ah, but last time it worked out in my favour, while on this occasion...?*

He let dumbfounded, horrified eyes scan the arena, whose walls above the archways were adorned with jutting, red- and yellow-flaring flambeaux. In places there were still patches of yellow sand, but mainly the sand was red and slimed. Evidence of a great slaughter lay everywhere: torn bodies, and bodies without limbs, and other remains which weren't human at all. As for the remaining combatants: a tight knot of figures was fighting even now. Fighting? In the centre of the arena, a mighty melee!

There were Northmen in it, just two of them left—and it did Tarra's Hrossak heart a power of good to see a trio of steppemen there, too, one of them being Narqui Ghenz, with whom he was somewhat familiar—and also a hulking, towheaded youth who could only be the last survivor (along with Loomar and Jezza) of all the slaves Black Yoppaloth had shipped here. Six of them left, only six, of the hundred and odd they'd once numbered; and the bulk of them strewn in bits and pieces all around the arena. Gods, what a battle it must have been!

As for the cause of the mayhem: no need to look far for that— or those!

Back to back and side by side, Northmen, Hrossaks and bull-shouldered youth stood; their weapons were huge claws and mandible pieces torn from dead opponents; more of these hybrid monstrosities—things from Yoppaloth's subterranean vats and breeding dungeons—ringed them all about. And of the latter...they were things out of a madman's worst nightmares!

They had human parts, some of them, human legs and thighs and occasionally heads, but for the most part they were entirely alien. Squat, lobsterish, red-eyed and slavering and huge! Or spiderlike, with many human arms. And one was slender and shaped like a mantis, half as tall again as a man, with chitin-plated hooks at the ends of its forelegs; but its head was a man's, with tusks like a wild pig curving from its chomping mouth!

Nor were these hybrids the worst, for there were others which may or may not have been men entirely, but which *were* in any case quite dead—but active nevertheless! And these were all the proof Tarra needed to show that indeed Yoppaloth's masters had taught him something of necromancy, for they'd obviously been called up from the grave! And a full dozen of these monsters and corpses encircling the knot of survivors, while as many again stood back, only waiting to take their turn should one of their blasphemous brothers fall in the fray.

Even as Tarra watched, the mantis-creature fastened its hooked hands about the neck of one of the coarse-maned Northmen and yanked him bodily from the tight central knot. He was lifted up, hurled down in the gory sand well apart from the others. Badly wounded and clasping his torn neck, he lay there for a moment, then stumbled to his feet; and Tarra fully expected that the mantis-thing or some other monster would pounce upon him and make an end of it. But that wasn't the way these games were played. No, for the beast things of the arena merely singled out and weakened the prey, whose doom was to be sealed in an entirely different manner.

Black Yoppaloth cried, *"Hold!"* And the howling of the Yhemni mob in the amphitheatre seats and aisles faded to silence in a moment. His voice was not the voice Tarra had known; like the man himself, it was bloated now; its keen edge had gone, leaving it dull and booming, more like the croak of some vast, obscene and blear-eyed frog. And now he came, down the dais steps and striding almost drunkenly toward his victim, the crippled Northman, so that Tarra would not have known this were him if not for his height, his robes, and the crimson-lacquered crest of his head.

And in his hand…the Suhm-yi Sword of Power—Tarra's sword—against an unarmed, half-dead Northman! The Hrossak gulped back his rage, for rage was no good here—but he saved it for later. How could he ever have imagined there was anything of nobility in this monster? Yoppaloth's personal magick? So the wizard Teh Atht had avowed; but now, to Tarra Khash, the bestiality of this creature seemed obvious. And as for Tarra's sharing this power: it was the last thing he wanted. He'd be a man and live a life, not a lie! As for this "show" in the arena: why, there wasn't even a contest in it, and it had never been intended that there should be!

591

All activity in the arena of death had ceased; the encircled group of human combatants could only look on, like the now breathless, bloodthirsty spectators themselves. Tarra wondered if they'd be so bloodthirsty if they knew their own lives hung in the balance this night. He guessed not, but hated them all the same. And so Yoppaloth strode to the doomed man, came up to him and showed him the scimitar's keen, curved blade. "To make the end of it easier for both of us!" And he laughed with that monstrous voice of his.

Before the other could think or even move, Yoppaloth struck *upwards* with the sword, twice, slicing into the tendons under the barbarian's arms and in his armpits. And now he was truly crippled. He cried out his agony, crumpled into a seated position on the slimy sand. Tarra gaped, astonished both by Yoppaloth's cruelty, and by the sheer *speed* he'd displayed, which far surpassed anything the Hrossak had hitherto witnessed. Aye, and Yoppaloth's accuracy, too, which had been better than hairbreadth.

And the Hrossak was still gaping when the fiend tossed down his sword to the sand, leaned forward and grasped the barbarian's head between his powerful hands. In the next moment, then Tarra understood the bloated appearance of the necromancer, for now Yoppaloth began to draw off what was left of his victim's living strength!

This must be how it had been for the Yhemnis taken in Yoppaloth's black-tasselled tent. The Northman seemed to age visibly; his skin turned to leather in the time it takes to tell; he shrivelled down into himself, becoming an old, old man. Nor was his torment finished, for as his limbs began a spastic twitching and his flopping trunk toppled from Yoppaloth's grasp—even as he commenced his journey into death—so something stirred into *life* in that terrible arena.

A green shimmer had sprung up about a certain massive stone idol, one of the many dozens whose carved figures paraded in a grotesque circle around the arena. It was the image of Yibb-Tstll the Soul-Stealer, whose stony surface suddenly took on a molten emerald appearance. Tarra already knew something of Yibb-Tstll—mainly what Yoppaloth had told him, that the demon god took souls and was one of the Old Ones—but now he fixed his eyes more firmly on the idol and observed for himself. This was the first time he'd seen an actual likeness of that Dark Deity; but as his eyes widened, so he learned why Yoppaloth had warned him that to know Yibb-Tstll was a most dubious privilege.

The statue was all of nine feet tall; of more or less manlike proportions, it had a head of sorts—a polished black node atop unevenly sloping stone shoulders—with a pair of eyes which were frozen in odd-seeming positions. One was more or less naturally placed, if a little high, but the other was down where the corner of a mouth might be found in a more normal piece of sculpture.

The sloping shoulders were cloaked, as was the body beneath; but the cloak, carved of the same basaltic stone as the god, was open in front to reveal many polished black breasts. This seemed an anomaly in itself, since the figure was supposedly male! Beneath the petrified folds of the cloak and half obscured, a cluster of night-gaunts clung tightly, almost lovingly, to the barely glimpsed body of the god. In sum, the idol was a nightmare—and much more so when suddenly it came to life!

That was Tarra's first thought, that Yibb-Tstll lived and moved in the arena of death, but then he saw he was mistaken. In fact what he saw was only a simulacrum or spirit of the Dark Deity himself, a "ghost," which now flowed *out* from the stone and separated itself from it, and, completely detached, moved like a green-glowing wraith toward Yoppaloth and the stricken, dying Northman.

As it went, so the thing took on something of solidity, until with the exception of its colour it was the twin of the statue which housed it—but one which left no tracks in the gore-spattered sand! Then, with its cloak billowing in a sickly slow-motion, it closed with Yoppaloth and their mutual victim and paused while the necromancer drew back. The spectators, crowded in the amphitheatre, had been silent, awed up to this point; now they roared their applause:

Yes! Let it be now! *Take* his soul and send him to hell, damned forever!

Greenly illumined, the monster-god stood over the Northman's shrivelled, twitching form. The god's feet, or whatever propelled him, were hidden beneath his billowing cloak; his eyes, glowing like balefires, were full of a hideous mobility; they *slid* over the surface of his head and face with a swift and apparently aimless motion, like the meandering of slugs but vastly accelerated. Then—

The demon-god reached out from beneath his billowing cloak three grey- and black-mottled things which might be arms, each terminating in a nest of seven grey worms which must serve as fingers. Two of these arms grasped the pitiful husk of the Northman and drew him upright like an empty sack; the third loathsome member spread itself wide, like some weird, seven-armed squid, and the tips of its digits entered eyes, ears, nostrils, mouth! Then they slid home to fill those orifices entirely, and the barbarian's face and head were enveloped in the slime-filmed web of that awful "hand."

Yibb-Tstll took nothing physical (there was little left to take), but what he *did* take made all of the preceding torture merely a prelude. He took the very soul! The Northman's shell collapsed entirely, and as the Dark Deity withdrew his slimed "fingers" from his head, so there sounded a shriek whose origin could only be hell—the hell of the barbarian's knowing that he'd be tormented for all eternity!

In the next moment the horror of the vacillating eyes let what it held upright collapse, withdrew its ropy arms back inside the cloak, flowed back to its idol sanctuary and melted into the stone. The green glow remained, flickering over the basalt like liquid cancer...

And the "games" recommenced.

Again the defenders, only five of them now, found themselves under attack from their inhuman, hybrid, and corpse adversaries; and almost at once the young Hrossak Narqui Ghenz was taken. *"No!"* Tarra cried out, as a spiderlike monstrosity dragged Narqui screaming from the knot of survivors. Tarra's cry was lost in the renewed uproar of the crowd, and when he would start forward down the steps of an aisle he found his way blocked by their milling black bodies where they scrambled to seek better viewing positions. Ignoring him as he fought his way through their crush, they had eyes only for the scene in the arena.

The spider-thing had pierced Narqui's body with poisoned fangs; he stood, swaying, one hand to his bleeding wounds, mouth open half in shock, half paralysed by venom. And Yoppaloth bearing down on him, carrying a weapon as before. But this time he'd left the scimitar with the gem-studded hilt behind atop the onyx dais; the weapon he held was similar to a pike, but it was not a pike; Tarra Khash knew *exactly* what it was.

Reaching the low balcony wall which ringed the deep arena and contained the first tier of stone seats, Tarra was in time to witness Yoppaloth's thrust. Again he cried out: "No!" But too late. The slender head of that dreadful weapon drove home in Narqui's side. This time, however, Tarra's cry had been heard loud and clear, for the spectators had once more fallen silent. It was heard by all who watched, and also by Black Yoppaloth himself. All eyes turned to Tarra Khash. But his own fierce gaze burned only on the face of Yoppaloth.

Narqui Ghenz had fallen to his knees, his hands grasping the shaft of Yoppaloth's weapon where it pierced him. He turned his eyes pleadingly on his tormentor, but Yoppaloth was gazing up at Tarra Khash. "So," he said, "you've come. And didn't I warn you to stay away, Hrossak?"

As his words echoed in that unholy place, so swords shrilled as they flickered from scabbards, and a moment later guards came plunging from the rear of the amphitheatre, hurling Yhemni citizens aside where they blocked the aisles. The first of these overeager bullies reached Tarra, found himself kneed in the groin as the steppeman ducked under his arc of steel. A second later and Tarra had wrested the sword from him, used its hilt to club him unconscious. Child's play—but other guards were closing with him.

"*Stop!*" Yoppaloth commanded. And to Tarra: "Very well, Hrossak, since we both know why you're here—come, join us in the arena!"

Their eyes locked and Tarra knew he stared at a man bereft, a man bought and paid for in madness by the Old Ones! And yet he held the lunatic's gaze, until the necromancer found it a mighty effort of will to break the spell. And Tarra thought, *perhaps there's magick in me after all!*

But then Yoppaloth threw back his crimson-crested head and laughed, and he shouted: "Come on, what are you waiting for? What's another steppeman more or less?" And with that he twisted the metal hand grip of his terrible pike.

Tarra heard Narqui's shriek of unbearable agony and it was like a fire that burned him. Something snapped in his head and bled fury like acid into his brain. Yoppaloth laughed again and turned his back on the Hrossak where he reeled in horror and outrage on the high balcony; he withdrew his weapon from Narqui's body, grasped the mangled man's head and commenced to draw off his remaining strength; and Yibb-Tstll, too, once more came flowing from his idol to claim his tribute of a soul.

Up above the arena, someone tried to take Tarra's sword away from him. Almost without thinking, he butted the man in the face, jumped up onto the wall; and taking the sword in his teeth, he leaped down to the sandy floor. He landed, rolled, came upright with the sword in his hand. It was high time a Hrossak showed what he could do!

Meanwhile...

Amyr Arn had found and carefully released the catches which held the iron grille in place across the arched entrance to the arena; now, seeing Tarra leap down amongst the beast-creatures, he put his shoulder to the bars and shoved. The gate crashed down in the sand, and before the dust could settle Amyr had bounded into view.

The arena and amphitheatre were well lit by many dozens of flambeaux, but the light they cast, while ample, was ruddy and yellow, reflecting like molten gold from the silver sheen of Amyr's Suhm-yi skin. Naked except for a loin-cloth, he might well have been one of Yoppaloth's creatures, but the undisputed Lord of Shad and Shadarabar knew that he was not.

"What?" cried Yoppaloth where he'd returned to his dais. "And is Shad full of trespassers this night? Well, we'll not worry how this one got here; no, for it's a fact he'll not be leaving!"

Tarra had started after Yoppaloth, but a wall of hybrids and corpses had turned him aside, driving him toward the four original combatants. Not that he went unprotesting: a spider-thing with a man's face perished on the point of his sword, likewise a pair of corpses where he left them headless, twice-dead on the sand; but the rest of them were too many for him, and finally he joined the bloodied, weary knot of survivors. By then, too, he'd spotted Amyr Arn, and at first had been unable to accept the evidence of his own eyes. Then Amyr (a mentalist, and familiar with the Hrossak's mind) had sent:

Ask about it later, bronze one, if there's to be a later. Right now we've a fight on our hands! And he came weaving his way through the arena's many monstrosities, to join the beleaguered group in the centre.

Tarra had time only to give Amyr Loomar Nindiss' knife before the surrounding hybrids and tomb-spawn closed their ranks again. And then all was mayhem.

In the fighting, Tarra saw that Yibb-Tstll had taken Narqui's soul. He vowed revenge. He'd not rest until Yoppaloth and the monster-god who was his mentor and tormentor were stopped, or until he himself was dead—which at the moment looked like being his fate anyway. No way the six of them could hold out against odds such as these. Then:

"Wait!" cried Yoppaloth, and again the arena fell quiet as the vat-things drew back a little. From his dais, Yoppaloth called out: "The time draws nigh—my time, the world's time, the Hour of the Coming—and still the contest draws on. Events have been delayed. Ah, but I know a way to speed things up! Hrossak, do you remember how your pure heart quailed at the waterhole, when the Northmen would have taken my brides and used them? I couldn't allow it, you'll recall—for they weren't 'my' brides at all but Yibb's! Innocents, virgins in mind and body: such souls are the tenderest tidbits to one such as Yibb-Tstll."

He turned his bloated face up to the amphitheatre's crush. "Guards, now bring on the girls—and we'll witness how a heroic Hrossak reacts to that!"

At least Jezza's away, Tarra thought, though what good it would do her or her brother in the long run he couldn't say. But he saw the terrible logic of Yoppaloth's twisted mind: no way Tarra and his handful could hope to protect a bevy of helpless girls in this pit of monsters; all of their time was consumed in simply keeping themselves alive! On the other hand, Yoppaloth knew Tarra, and knew he'd be obliged to try.

The girls were quickly brought on stage, led from their "harem" quarters down into the bowels of the ziggurat and then deeper still, finally jostled into the arena through one of the barred, floor-level hatchways, and the grille fastened in place again behind them.

In the interim another Hrossak had been taken, nipped off at the knees by a lobsterish nightmare and dragged away screaming for Yibb and Yoppaloth's delight; and in that same interval of time the twirl of morbid green light rising into the arena from the throat of the

polished glass pit had contracted and drawn down its whirling mushroom head through the chimney, so that the brightness of the twister
had acquired something of density, spinning there like a great green
top or inverted cone of near-solid matter.

And this was the same phenomenon which thus far had deterred
Teh Atht from making a descent of the chimney aboard his flying
carpet; for try as he might, he could only get so close to that twisting
green flux of awesome energy before being shoved violently away. His
white magick and the unimaginably dark magick of the Great Old
Ones simply did not and would not mix! So that when Iniquiss and
her brood had come on the scene and spied him across some small
aerial distance, he'd still been aimlessly circling the emerald spiral of
alien energy, vacillatory to the last as he pondered what to do next. At
which time, obligingly, the twister's stalk had shortened, drawing its
flat cap down out of sight.

But meanwhile...

In the arena and the amphitheatre which overlooked it: several
entirely unscheduled occurrences, the first of which had devastating
effect upon the Yhemni onlookers.

Now, in certain of Theem'hdra's steamy jungles and hothouse
regions, in the walls of olden pyramids and crumbled ruins, there dwelled
a species of yellow scorpion; likewise in the massy walls and floors of
Black Yoppaloth's palace, where they'd bred mainly unsuspected for
a thousand years. Shy of men and of daylight, this especially *virulent*
scorpion was seldom observed, and when seen invariably avoided.

Picture then the hysteria which spread rapidly through the
amphitheatre when thousands of these deadly stingers were discovered acrawl about the feet of the spectators; and not only in the
amphitheatre, but also down in the pit of the arena itself, where the
arachnids converged in streams upon Yoppaloth's monstrosities—
but *not* upon the girls or the surviving men!

A second unforeseen event, one very likely connected with the
first, was this: that the great greenstone statue of Ahorra Izz, which
stood in the circle of gods close to where the virgins had been thrust
into the arena, was now a-shimmer in much the same way as Yibb's
with an eerie light—except that in the case of Ahorra Izz the glow
was red. And where Yibb-Tstll came greedily flowing from his statue,

cloak billowing and trio of tentacular arms reaching, now Ahorra Izz moved in that mechanical way of his species out from *his* likeness to block the way.

And so the two simulacra faced up to one another, neither one of them capable of harming the other, but nevertheless fixed in a weird stalemate; while behind Ahorra Izz, seeing how that arachnid intelligence protected them, the girls crowded in a close pack. All of them except one, who had gone to her knees in the sand as if in an attitude of prayer.

And this was the third event of moment, for indeed Orbiquita prayed—that she be granted the last of her three requests. "Iniquiss!" she cried. "Now hear me, if the distance between is not too great. This boon I beg of you is unheard of, I know, but still I most earnestly implore it. This one last time, for however brief a spell, give me back my lamia semblance and the lamia powers that went with it. For just a little while, pray let me be the creature I used to be!"

Following which she could only wait, to see what, if anything, transpired.

Amidst all the uproar—of Yhemni spectators where they leaped and careened, some of them even toppling into the arena after feeling the deadly stings of incensed scorpions; likewise of shrieking hybrids, by no means immune to those same stingers—hope welled up in Tarra's bronze breast. That special magick Teh Atht had told him about, *his* magick, was working for him at last. What?—and was there any other man in all the Primal Land could claim Ahorra Izz for a champion?

As the milling monstrosities in the arena fell back a little and tried to save themselves from their new, far smaller adversaries, so Tarra grasped his Suhm-yi friend's elbow and said: "Amyr, now take this sword and give me back that knife. I think the tide's turning our way. Now's my chance to come up against Yoppaloth."

"What, with only a knife?" Amyr was astonished. "And him able to strike like lightning, so swift the eyes can't follow?" He shook his head, kept on fighting. "I think not."

Tarra hadn't time for arguing. He threw down the Yhemni sword at Amyr's feet, said: "Use it or not, as you wish, but I've no need of it. My sword is on that dais, with Yoppaloth, and I've a feeling it's the one weapon in all the world that can save us."

Amyr stooped, picked up the sword, gave Tarra the knife. "I'm coming with you," he said.

"No." Tarra's answer was direct. "Stay here and help save these brave lads, if you can. They're just about all in. But what's between Yoppaloth and me requires only the two of us." And with that he was away, weaving through the beleaguered hybrids toward the onyx dais. A pair of corpses got in his way, which were fearful things to look upon but not much as fighters; he smashed them into many pieces and carried on.

And atop the huge onyx block which was Tarra's target, the first intimation of failure—or of victory?—had crossed Yoppaloth's unbalanced mind. Like a man in a dream he saw events coming to a head, and for once was powerless to stop them. In one small corner of his mind—a corner containing a last dim spark of sanity—Black Yoppaloth knew that his case was hopeless: even "winning" he would lose, for when the Old Ones came they'd have no use for him. But in the mad part of his brain, which was by far the greater part, still he thought he might hold them to their pact. Oh, he'd be a lonely immortal, for sure, in a world emptied of all earthly life; but at least he'd retain his soul. Wouldn't he?

He saw the steppeman coming at a run, saw some way behind the Hrossak a beautiful naked girl, also running, and behind her the flowing, green-glowing manifestation of Yibb-Tstll. If the monster-god couldn't get at the bulk of the girls where they sheltered behind Ahorra Izz, at least he could fasten upon this one who'd somehow become estranged from the group. But the fate of the girl was no concern of Yoppaloth's; her approach faded into insignificance compared with the approach of Tarra Khash, his face a mask of grim intent.

A pity it had come to this; there had been that about the Hrossak which appealed. Curious, but Yoppaloth had genuinely liked him! But...he *had* warned him not to come here. And in any case, what would be the loss of one perfectly ordinary man set against the destruction of a world full of men? Yoppaloth took up his hideous weapon, propped its handle against his sandalled right foot. And so he stood, like a guard at ease, calmly waiting for the steppeman to come to him. Which, obligingly, Tarra proceeded to do.

By now the diminished but brilliant tornado of green light flowing up from the pit's glassy throat seemed more solid than ever, striking emerald glints from Yoppaloth's black skin and lending its phosphorescent fire to his eyes. Also, a strange massed *sighing* had commenced, faint at first but rapidly increasing in volume; not the sound of human voices, no, but rather the rushing of the winds which blow in the lungs of the Earth itself, or those of the alien gods known to inhabit it.

"Almost time, Tarra Khash," said Yoppaloth as Tarra skirted the pit and skidded to a halt in the sand at the foot of the dais. "The time I've waited for and dreaded for almost a thousand years. You should have heeded my warning and stayed away; for you see, we're both in the same boat. To win we must lose! And yet—I knew you would come."

"Winning—losing—I only know you have to die!" Tarra answered. "And I only wish it wasn't so." He hurled his knife straight for the other's throat—and the necromancer stood stock still, not even attempting to move. The knife seemed to bend around him, a blur of steel which should never have missed its target, but which did by inches! And Yoppaloth laughed.

"Protected, Hrossak!" he cried. "Had you forgotten? Immortal, and protected by the magick of the Old Ones—especially now."

Tarra sprang up the steps of the dais and faced the madman only a pike's length away; and still Yoppaloth stood there, apparently unconcerned, even smiling his cold, cold smile. Cold, aye, and now Tarra could feel the bitter rime of nameless gulfs reaching up to him, working on his marrow. He had to bring this thing to a conclusion, and right now.

Yoppaloth saw his mental anguish, said: "Care to try again, steppeman? Perhaps with this?" He reached out a foot and kicked Tarra's scimitar unerringly to the other's feet. Instinctively, Tarra half-stooped for the sword, heard Yoppaloth's caution: "Except it's no game we're playing this time, Tarra Khash!" Then—

In a gleaming blur of motion, Yoppaloth hoisted his weapon, whirling it to point direct at Tarra's middle. Tarra saw the wicked knives and barbs of the thing, all lying flat and close to its pointed metal head. He knew what those terrible tools could do to his guts, grimaced at the thought—and continued the downward sweep of his arm toward

601

familiar gem-studded hilt! But his apparently foolhardy move was a feint; not once did he take his eyes from his opponent; he saw Yoppaloth take a forward pace almost as if he moved in slow motion.

The pike came lancing at him but Tarra twisted his crouching body, grabbed the staff of his opponent's ugly weapon and turned it aside, grasped and lifted his scimitar. And the Suhm-yi sword seemed almost to come to life in his hand! Yoppaloth was within range, vulnerable as never before. So Tarra thought. He struck for the other's neck…and the blade of the scimitar shivered to a halt only a skin's thickness from the veins that pulsed there. It *vibrated* in Tarra's iron grip as he strove to force its razor edge into flesh—but the protections of the Old Ones were too strong, or he was too weak.

The sighing of alien spheres had risen to a howl that drowned everything else out, and the whorl of green light from the pit was so dense, so *cold*, that time itself seemed frozen atop the dais. For Tarra, anyway, if not for Yoppaloth. "Protected!" the madman shrieked. "Until the very last instant, protected! If you'd waited but a moment longer…but now, farewell!" And he drew back his pike and drove it point-blank at Tarra's middle.

Tarra closed his eyes, if only to deny Yoppaloth the sight of the horror written in them, and waited for the torment to begin. Already he could smell hell's brimstone breath, and—

…Brimstone? And that gasp of utter astonishment—Yoppaloth's? As a vicious squealing of torn metal ensued, Tarra opened his eyes— upon a fantastic scene!

A moment before: there had been the impression of a gorgeous girl standing close by, and of the nightmare god Yibb-Tstll closing on her with ropy arms extended. All seen on the periphery of Tarra's awareness, blurred and out of focus in the tension of traded blows. But now…

The girl was gone, disappeared, and in her place—

Lamia!

And Tarra knew *which* lamia she was. Twin scars on his neck itched furiously—even at a time like this—and a strange, fascinating pungency was in the air.

Orbiquita stood beside the dais, Yoppaloth's pike trapped in a hand like a nest of scythes. She stripped away the brightly gleaming blades and grapples, twisted the lethal head of the pike until metal screamed, then nipped it off and hurled it down on the sand—and Yoppaloth was left with only a pikestaff.

Now! came Suhm-yi mind-voice in Tarra's reeling head. *Now or never, bronze one! I feel it—whatever it is—mounting to a crescendo!*

Alone Tarra could never have struck that final blow, for his entire body ached with the cold of dark dimensions, which was freezing him solid through and through. But he was not alone. The Suhm-yi Sword of Power was with him. It sliced toward Yoppaloth's neck, sliced *into* it and cut three-quarters through!

Then Orbiquita snatched Tarra from the dais.

Behind her, wildly threshing, the simulacrum of Yibb-Tstll flowed this way and that. Cloak billowing with loathsome motion and eyes sliding in crazed orbits all about his head, his confusion was obviously boundless. He had pursued a girl and now perceived a lamia! No easy victim this, but upon the onyx dais—

Yibb-Tstll flowed swiftly toward the onyx steps. Yoppaloth would be his victim. And why not, since the so-called sorcerer had failed to keep his compact with the Old Ones? Tarra Khash looked on, saw Yoppaloth's anguished eyes—his sane eyes—gazing into his own. *Finish it*, those living eyes begged him. *Don't let him have my soul!*

Yibb-Tstll was on the dais, leaning over Yoppaloth in the veritable flood of green energy from the glassy pit. Tarra ducked out of Orbiquita's protective grasp, aimed his stroke true. And with that simple, merciful act the Gate Between Spheres was closed; and in the next moment, several things happening simultaneously, defying human senses with their rapidity and shattering finality.

One: the ages caught up with Yoppaloth at once; as his head leapt free, so he crumbled into smoulder, was blown away in the blink of an eye. Not even bones remained, and Yibb-Tstll groped namelessly in dust! Two: the singing of the spheres went from a shriek to an equally deafening silence, was quite simply shut off—likewise the sentient, shining, pit-spawned twister—leaving Tarra and every other living creature in the arena staggering. Three: Yibb-Tstll's simulacrum froze, literally turned to ice-cold stone atop the dais, and the onyx sheen of his form became as one with the massive slab of onyx where he stood. Four: Orbiquita took Tarra into her arms again, except that now and for always they were the arms of a beautiful girl. Five: the Hrossak's bulging eyes took in at a sweep the area of the arena and amphitheatre, and refused to accept what they saw. Lamias flew like a flock of vile, gigantic birds, harrying the last of the Yhemnis where they fled through the exits in a mad rout; and in the central space, midway between sand and vaulted ceiling, a carpet floated on air, where with his incredible retainers sat a small man in runic robes, holding out a wand toward the dais and looking just as astonished as Tarra Khash himself.

The wizard flew his carpet close to Tarra and Orbiquita, said: "I'm Teh Atht, and I'm old and tired. But it seems the world is safe again, Hrossak, and unless I'm mistaken we're alive, you and I."

"Am I?" said Tarra.

"We're all in your debt, steppeman," the wizard told him.

"Are you?" Tarra's eyes finally focused. "You owe me favours, do you?"

"Indeed we do!"

Tarra's knees finally gave way and he sat down in the sand. "Then do you think you could possibly explain what has happened here?" he said. "But before that—is there any chance you could first get us the hell out of this place?"

EPILOGUE

Tarra Khash was not unmindful of his friends, even the fearsome ones. In Shad, later that night, after much had been explained and many tales told, he walked with Orbiquita through deserted streets (the Yhemnis would not come out of their jungles for long and long) and when they were alone under a clear, moonlit sky gave thanks to Gleeth for Amyr Arn's assistance. Likewise he praised Ahorra Izz for the part he and his minion scorpions had played in this thing; and finally he offered silent thanks to Iniquiss and the Sisterhood, who probably didn't hear him and wouldn't much care anyway, for they never had a lot to do with men—except when they were hungry.

He thanked Orbiquita, too, in a manner mutually agreeable, by means of which he discovered that his interest in women was not extinct after all, and she that her transition was going to be worth all its attendant trials. But that's not to be gone into here...

Now, as they made their way back to the encampment's fire, their arms wrapped about each other, meandering in their walk as lovers are wont to do, Tarra's mind unmazed itself a little and matters hastily discussed began to fall into place and make sense. "Curious Concretion!" he suddenly said.

"Your pardon?" Orbiquita's head was in the crook of his neck, her perfume in his nostrils. She, too, had been dreaming. "Did you say something?"

"Something your cousin, Teh Atht, said," Tarra answered. "About the end of it, back there in Yoppaloth's arena of death. In that final moment, when the Gateway was to have been forged through Yoppaloth—when I killed him before Yibb-Tstll could take his soul—the wizard put a certain spell of his, a thing called Curious Concretion, on the dais and on Yibb-Tstll's simulacrum. I'd seen it work before, this spell, but then it had been diluted by distance and other circumstances. In the arena, however, he gave it all he'd got, and he struck when I struck, which was *precisely* the right moment."

"The trouble with spells," said Orbiquita, who still retained a little lamia knowledge, though it was diminishing as she firmed more fully into her delicious human female form, "is that they eventually wear off."

Tarra shook his head. "Not this one," he said. "The Old Ones *would* have come into this world through Yoppaloth, except he was already dead. I *should* have taken his place, been obliged to complete the compact, except I was no longer on the dais. Result: Yibb-Tstll's simulacrum copped the lot. Curiously Concreted for all eternity, immortalized in onyx! Him and the dais both..."

They arrived back at the encampment in one of Shad's squares not far from the waterfront. Loomar Nindiss and Jezza were there, where the sole surviving Hrossak of Yoppaloth's mercenaries—a lean, handsome adventurer, much like Tarra himself—seemed to be paying the girl a deal of polite attention; also the last Northman, who just happened to be the one who'd lost his shirt that time, when Tarra had watched their gaming. Tek Mangr was his name, and he'd been busy (with the ages-accrued instinct of all Northmen) filling a sack with Yhemni loot; now he stood guard over spoils and encampment and virgin girls all. Then there was the towheaded youth, who also prowled to and fro around the campsite area with a great Yhemni sword in his hand; and also Amyr Arn, sitting silently on his own, doubtless dreaming of his Inner Isles and how he'd soon be home with Ulli Eys; and lastly Teh Atht. The wizard's familiars were also about somewhere, but he'd thought it best that they keep out of sight. In all, a pretty polyglot band.

Orbiquita spoke to Teh Atht: "Cousin, I've your promise that tomorrow you'll see these people safely back where they belong?"

Seated by the fire, he nodded. "It will keep me busy awhile; but after what all have been through—and the DOOM avoided—what's a little time? I can afford it, I think." And to Tarra: "Mind you, if I possessed that sword of yours, I'd likely end up with all the time in the world, eh?"

"What?" Tarra gave a snort of disbelief. "You know, for a wizard you're not too bright. Haven't you learned anything? The stars are immortal, maybe, and also space and time, which go inward and outward forever—but men come and go, they're born and they die, and that's the way it was meant. Would you live to see the mountains crumble, the oceans dry up, the sun itself expire? Not me."

Arm in arm, he and Orbiquita walked out of the firelight, made for the wharves. "Where are you off, Tarra?" the bearded Northman called after them.

"We'll find ourselves a boat for the night," Tarra answered. "If we're still here in the morning we'll see you then. But if the wind's favourable and the water calm...good luck, anyway, to all of you."

In Tarra's mind, Amyr's fond farewell: *Long life, bronze one. Come visit me some day, in the jewel isles of the Suhm-yi.*

I will, Tarra promised, also silently.

"Hrossak!" Teh Atht had got to his feet. "About that sword..."

"Forget it," Tarra told him, and he touched the gem-studded hilt where it protruded over his shoulder, just to be sure it was still there. "The sword's mine. Men have died for it, and probably will again." Then the city's shadows took him and Orbiquita into their embrace.

"Then if you'll not give it to me," it was the wizard's last throw, "perhaps I could borrow it for a while?"

But the steppeman and his love had already walked into the night, and into the dawn of a new life. The Primal Land was waiting, and for all that the world was old, still it was very young, too. The last Teh Atht saw of the pair was their single dark outline merging with the greater darkness, and then they were gone.

And never a backward glance from Tarra Khash...